THE PERSISTENT DESIRE

THE PERSISTENT DESIRE

A Femme-Butch Reader

Edited by Joan Nestle

Boston ♦ Alyson Publications, Inc.

Typeset and printed in the United States of America.

This is a paperback original from Alyson Publications, Inc.,
40 Plympton St., Boston, Mass. 02118.
Distributed in England by GMP Publishers,
P.O. Box 247, London N17 9QR England.

This book is printed on acid-free, recycled paper.

First edition, first printing: June 1992

1 2 3 4 5

ISBN 1-55583-190-7

Book design, copyediting, & production: Lynne Yamaguchi Fletcher
Proofreading: Tina Portillo

Library of Congress Cataloging-in-Publication Data

The Persistent desire : a femme-butch reader / edited by Joan Nestle.
— 1st ed.
    p. cm.
Includes bibliographical references.
ISBN 1-55583-190-7 (pbk.) : $14.95
    1. Lesbians—United States—Literary collections 2. Lesbians-
-United States—Sexual behavior. 3. Lesbians' writings, American.
    I. Nestle, Joan, 1940– .
PS509.L47P47 1992
810.8'035206643—dc20

92-6166
CIP

Contents

Acknowledgments

To Amber Hollibaugh and Esther Newton, who planned a book like this ten years ago; to Ruth Helmich, who spent unpaid hours transcribing tapes; to Manuela Soares for her editing and talks; to Morgan Gwenwald for her help with the photographs and her generosity of spirit; to Saskia, who never says no to my pleas for help; to the women of the Lesbian Herstory Archives, who are my family; to Naomi Replansky and Karyn London, who kept me going with their telephone calls; to Lynne Yamaguchi Fletcher, for patience and long hours of work; to all the women who sent in the stories of their desire and who took the risk of self-disclosure and the journeys back to painful places; and especially to Lee Hudson, who never gives up, thank you.

Dedicated to Jeanie Meurer (1931–1991),
whose femme self lit up the world, and
Deanna Alida (1948–1991),
whose butch self carried songs of love

Joyce Culver

Jeanie Meurer and Deborah Walsh, New York, 1986

Joan Nestle

Flamboyance and fortitude:
An introduction

This book is dedicated to Jeanie Meurer, a femme woman from the old days who died in 1991, surrounded by the women who loved her. On a warm May afternoon, we gathered to commemorate her life in a cavernous Greenwich Village church whose spaces Jeanie's flamboyant spirit nonetheless filled. One after another, her butch lovers rose to celebrate her gifts, to thank her for the zest and color, the delights and flavors, the abundance of enthusiasm she had brought into their lives. We saw Jeanie's home, filled with her collectibles, her wall of earrings, her puppets, her masks, her cooking pots; we saw Jeanie wave at us from mountaintops and camel backs; we heard her sing her favorite show tunes, and she flirted with us from behind huge blossoms and from rooftops. We heard a child tell how Aunt Jeanie had made it all right to walk barefoot in the rain and a very butch lover named Blue tell how Jeanie had insisted in the midfifties that she attend a parents' meeting in the school she taught at in her butchiest of selves. We heard a young woman thank Jeanie for giving her the courage to love and look the way she wanted to.

I had known of Jeanie from the Sea Colony (a working-class Greenwich Village bar that flourished in the late fifties and sixties); she was a famous femme when I was just starting out. We had reconnected in the eighties, when she was active in women's music groups, but she really came into focus one evening when I was talking about the Lesbian Herstory Archives at a fund-raiser. I was so used to being the only woman in a room who remembered the vice squad raids or who blushed at the mention of femme passion that I did not realize her presence until she said, "I know; I was there." And then I saw her — peroxide blonde, full breasted, marked by color — and I knew I had met a survivor. We connected afterward and promised to make an oral history tape together. The last time I spoke to Jeanie was on the train as she was on her way to work — she gave a theater workshop in a school for special children — and once again the promise was made.

As I sat in church that May, I realized that Jeanie and the femme women of her generation were a passing tradition, and I wanted other women to know what their glory had been. I realized that I had spent many long hours listening to butch women tell their stories, but I had put off listening to Jeanie. My own femme self-hatred had made me a careless listener. That afternoon, however, Jeanie gave me a final gift: as the butch women stood, a little uncomfortable, trying to find words for what Jeanie had given them, their fortitude shone through, as did their need of her flamboyance, her demanding of full life from them.

I imagined Jeanie unbuttoning their shirts, encouraging them to throw their voices to the farthest corners of the room. Later, as I was standing in the vestibule, waiting to go out into the waning day, the butch woman who had done most of the speaking said to me, "When Jeanie died, she knew what she needed to know: that she was loved." Flamboyance and fortitude, femme and butch — not poses, not stereotypes, but a dance between two different kinds of women, one beckoning the other into a full blaze of color, the other strengthening the fragility behind the exuberance. We who love this way are poetry and history, action and theory, flesh and spirit.

❖

For more than a hundred years now in America, the butch-femme couple has been the private and public face of lesbianism, and yet, we still understand little about this form of lesbian erotic identity. Everyone has taken a turn at denigrating the butch-femme couple — from the sexologist at the turn of the century who spoke about the predatory female masculine invert and the child woman who most easily fell her victim, to the early homophile activists of the fifties who pleaded with these "obvious" women to tone down their style of self-presentation, to the lesbian-feminists of the seventies who cried "traitor" into the faces of the few butch-femme couples who did cross over into the new world of cultural feminism — yet this form of self- — and communal — expression has persisted. In small towns and big cities, butch-femme couples created lives of minor miracles. Coping with daily ostracism, they took care of each other, and as the years passed, they spilled out of their homes into the bars and clubs that would herald the politicized lesbian world of the seventies. This anthology reveals the intimate exchange of pleasures, promises, and ordeals that femmes and butches transformed into history.

At the crux of the modern discussion about butch-femme identity is the question of its autonomy: does the longevity of butch-femme self-expression reflect the pernicious strength of heterosexual gender polarization — or is it, as I would argue, a lesbian-specific way of deconstructing gender that radically reclaims women's erotic energy? Are femmes and butches dupes of heterosexuality, or are they gender pioneers with a knack for alchemy?

14

Many of the women who speak in this book believe in the originality of their choices. Others report on what they have seen. What moved me the most as I read the poems, short stories, essays, and even the letters accompanying the submissions was the inherent eroticism of this subject. Never have I been so wooed, so played with, so enticed as I have been by the butch women who wrote to me. Even the discussions around editing the pieces were filled with erotic play; this playfulness became even more precious after reading what many of these women had to say about their struggle with gender rigidity and bigotry.

Some modern lesbian philosophers, such as Marilyn Frye, have lamented the lack of a lesbian sexual language and the paucity of lesbian sexual codes and rituals. I have always been struck by the ahistorical quality of this yearning for a public lesbian sexual self, since lesbian life in America from at least the thirties through the sixties was organized around a highly developed sense of sexual ceremony and dialogue. Indeed, because of the surrounding oppression, ritual and code were often all we had to make public erotic connections. Dress, stance, gestures, even jewelry and hairstyles had to carry the weight of sexual communications. The pinky ring flashing in a subway car, the DA haircut combed more severely in front of a mirror always made me catch my breath, symbolizing as they did a butch woman announcing her erotic competence. A language of courtship and seduction was carefully crafted to allow for expression of both lust and love in the face of severe social repression. The butch contributors to the anthology bring this world alive again while having the courage to show the wounds behind the stance.

Femme correspondents connected with me in a different way. Many were grateful for my past work and for the opportunity to announce their identities in their own voices. Their statements reflected one bitter irony: if, in the straight world, butches bear the brunt of the physical and verbal abuse for their difference, in the lesbian-feminist world, femmes have had to endure a deeper attack on their sense of self-worth. Leather and denim, flannels and vests — butch women could easily adapt these prevailing signs of feminist gender resistance into superficial passports to acceptance, but the femme woman, in her lace and silk, high heels, and lipstick, had no place to hide. Many learned to pass as a "dyke" in public while in their homes and in their beds, they flew their flags of color and sensuality.

The femme voice is underrepresented in historical records, though markings of her presence abound. Often, she is the security behind the butch display, the one who makes the public bravado possible. Lady Una Troubridge's words to Radclyffe Hall, while spoken by a white, upper-class, Christian woman, capture some of the enduring aspects of femme power: "I told her to write what was in her heart, that so far as any effect upon myself was concerned, I was sick to death of ambiguities..." Yet to others, the femme woman has been the most ambiguous figure in lesbian history; she is often described as the nonlesbian lesbian, the duped wife of the passing woman, the lesbian who marries. Because I am a femme myself, I know the complexity of our identity; I also know how important it is for all women to hear our voices. If the butch deconstructs gender, the femme constructs gender. She puts together her own special ingredients for what it is to be a "woman," an identity with which she can live and love.

Both butch women and femme women raise difficult issues that we as a community often avoid or deny. Many of the butch women in this collection write about their battle with gender, their feelings of discrepancy from their womanly appearance. These are not the voices of Havelock Ellis, Sigmund Freud, or Karen Horney; these are our *own* women expressing their need to create another category of women's gender to explain their view of their bodies and their way of loving, their search for erotic dignity and pleasure. In this collection, stone butches and passing women speak in their own voices in a public forum, allowing us to engage in a gender dialogue within our own gender. In their modern voices, they push the discussion further than I could have imagined ten years ago, when the Barnard conference on sexuality marked the formal beginning of what was to be known as the "sex wars." Here, butch women claim their "cocks" and their cunts.

The femme contributors challenge us with discussions of their womanness, some rejecting traditional femininity while celebrating their femme flamboyance. In addition, their narratives often show a different relation to sexuality, to their experience of lust and vulnerability. Some powerfully express their desire to be the slut, the whore, for their women, in practice and in self-image (not surprisingly many contemporary femmes are leaders in the prostitutes' rights movement). Some femmes, both historically and in the present, use the word *wife* to define themselves, exemplifying Jewelle Gomez's assertion that a "femme often inhabits a stereotypic place in a nonstereotypic way." The femme wife, like the stone butch, became a movement anathema in the seventies and eighties, and because these women were exiled so completely, we lost a chance to understand how complex gender subversion and erotic need are. But we lost something else as well, a chance to listen to and wonder at such stark examples of human courage. Now, with the language of deconstructionism hanging heavy in the air and a renewed appreciation for multigendered identities, these women can stand before us again. The 1990s femmes who speak here add another layer of complexity to the historical femme identity; femme tops, for example, speak of their desire to take an even firmer hand in assuring their sexual pleasures, vividly exemplifying that femme receptiveness is a high and very active art.

In addition to clearly expressing their "femme hunger," a term coined at the Sex and the State conference in Toronto in 1985, several of the femme contributors chose to give voice to a deep anger, an anger born out of long years of political and social containment and devaluing. In fact, many of the contributors, both butch and femme, document journeys of exile, particularly during the seventies, when the lesbian-feminist orthodoxy, though still young, was at its most restrictive. But anger at an ideology is not rejection of it. After twenty years of lesbian-feminism, we can now see what the trade-offs were and have a better insight into the dialectic of oppression and resistance. Authors like Lee Lynch and Lyndall Mac-Cowan suggest that butch-femme women put the concept of "queer" back into the lesbian-feminist discourse, a concept that I believe can only deepen our discussions of women, sex, and gender.

I have expanded the discussion of butch-femme life by including voices from other countries and other histories. Women from the Philippines, Australia, England, and Mexico tell us about their culture's version of this way of loving. In the Philippines, the word *tomboy* replaces *butch*, and this is not just a linguistic substitution but carries its own history. The discussion of erotic gender identity also extends to the struggle against colonization. Some have said that lesbianism is a Western illness, but here we see that liberation struggles are complex movements of complex people, who carry all their identities into the battle against their nation's degradation.

I am also pleased that several of the contributors have never published before. I wanted new speech from new speakers. I wanted disclosures and explorations of fragile things like need and discrepancy, stance and erotic self-creation. I chose not to edit wherever possible. Contradictions, differences, problems become very clear in the variety of voices and forms. For instance, in the essay by Rita Laporte, reprinted from *The Ladder*, she alludes to working-class butch-femme bars in an embarrassed manner, disowning the women who gathered there while giving support to butch-femme monogamous middle-class marriages. The issue of class and its unanswered challenges runs through many of the pieces presented here — but I am not satisfied. The connections between class and the swirl of debate around butch-femme women needs to be explored further.

I wanted this book to be an exploration, a celebration, a discussion, a revelation taking place among friends. So, I have not included essays by the critics of butch-femme. I will no longer entertain debate over my right to desire a butch woman. Those of us who love this way know the challenges we face and the problems we have wrestled with along the way, and we know that a way of loving is not a formula for a perfect life. Butches and femmes must struggle against all the elements that can tarnish any lesbian way of loving — jealousy, insecurity, chemical dependencies, and the erosive power of homophobia — but we also have our own special concerns: preserving femme sexual self-confidence in a world that sees her as unselected goods; preserving butch dignity in a world that sees her as a freak. Life in the fifties and sixties for working-class femmes and butches was not easy or safe, and so the narratives of this period are full of grit and pain, but they are also some of the finest lesbian writing I have read. This book reserves space for us to have a fuller conversation with ourselves, our history, and those who are interested in how women recast gender and desire.

The voices collected here span two hundred years of lesbian history, starting with William Cullen Bryant's respectful observations of a "married" lesbian couple in 1843 and ending in a femme's thank-you for the gift of touch, a piece originally written to be read and handed out in the Women's Prison in Kingston, Canada. I have arranged these pieces in two sections. The first follows a nearly chronological order so that the voices of each decade can be heard in their own social time; the second section presents contemporary views of femme and butch, constituting a dialogue on the present and future forms of this way of loving. But I hope that this movement through time and themes does not give an impression of a progressive evolution of butch-femme identity. The 1990s butch woman describing how she incorporates feminism into her once-stone-butch style is no more or less an authentic voice than the street lesbian of the 1950s who used her physical toughness to secure a public space. One voice is not a repudiation of the other. The courtly butch, the femme wife, the punk femme, the butch bottom, the femme slut, the street butch, the bulldagger and her lady, the lesbian-feminist femme, the movement butch, the tomboys are all here to reconnect us with our history and our creations.

I wanted to do this book because, as a lesbian, I never want to hear again in my lifetime the defensive disclaimers I grew up with: not all lesbians are truck drivers; not all lesbians dress like men; not all lesbians play at being husband and wife. I am tired of the cruelty of these disavowals. We, of all people, must be able to cherish the woman in the stereotype and the cunning in the transformation of gender restrictions into gender rebellion. Marriage is not what this society means by marriage when two women do it; passing women are not men, though their survival might depend on others thinking that they are; a woman poppa is a gender creation of her, of our, own.

And I wanted to edit this book because I am a femme woman, tired of devaluation by myself and others, tired of past and present attacks on the integrity of our desire, tired of the penalties we have had to pay because we look like "women" — from straight men, from so-called radical feminists, and from some lesbian separatists who, because of their anger at the social construction of femininity, cannot allow us to even exist. I understand the possibility for surface confusions, but we deserve more careful thinking and feeling. As feminists, we continue to fight back with a femme proclamation of independence. I subtitled this anthology "A Femme-Butch Reader" to herald this new voice in identity politics and break the traditional rhythms of the phrase and image. Femmes are the Lavender Lace Menace within our community. For my femme sisters — the queerest of the queer, as one contributor says — this book is only the beginning.

The sex wars and the raging debates that followed showed us what we as a movement had left undone, unexplored. We thought we had put gender in its place in the early 1970s by taking a political stance, but we were only postponing the lesbian-specific discussion we needed for a larger cause — changing women's history. But a women's history that has no place for femme-butch women will find itself impoverished. The stone butch and the femme wife are as much acts of the imagination as they are of the flesh. Contrary to what they seem, they are refusals to accept imposed boundaries. This book is not meant to convince any woman that femme-butch is the right way to love; neither is it an apology or an explanation of our desires. Most of the women who speak in these pages know that erotic desire and gender ambivalence are at the heart of their difference. They have been aching to tell how it was, how it is when the want is too large to stay in its place. They offer you their stories in the hope that some pains will never come again and that some joys will never be extinguished.

❖

I want to thank three women — first, Liz Kennedy and Madeline Davis, who have devoted at least the last ten years of their lives to documenting the working-class butch-femme community of Buffalo, New York. Every time I heard a chapter of their work, whether it was at the Berkeley Women's History Conference or in a small storefront in Buffalo or in a huge auditorium in Amsterdam, I came away healed and enlightened. They helped me cherish a way of loving by showing me its communal and thus historic face. And I have a special debt of gratitude to Bobbi Prebis, who wears her butch history so well that in her person she is a testimony to the generosity of the human spirit some of us have found in this way of loving.

❖

Over thirty years ago, in a dark room on the Lower East Side of New York, a passing woman named Esther whispered to me, "Darling, raise your hips," and as I did, she slipped a pillow under me so that her lips and tongue could give me and her the pleasure we both sought. In that moment, this book was born.

Postscript

In the final weeks of last year, I learned that Deanna Alida, a contributor to this book, had been killed in a traffic accident. One New York paper reporting the accident described the victim as an "unidentified man."

I first met Deanna in 1973 in the old firehouse home of the Gay Activist Alliance on Wooster Street in New York's Soho district when she was a cast member in Jonathan Katz's ground-breaking play *Coming Out.* I have a photograph of her from that play before me as I write. There she stands in a white shirt with suspenders to hold up her pants, her arm draped around a sister performer, looking squarely out at the audience. In 1990, we appeared on the same stage at New York's Lesbian and Gay Community Services Center to discuss and celebrate femme and butch identities. I told Deanna about this book, and she was excited to be part of it. Several weeks later, in a letter inviting Lee, my lover, and me to a party at the home of her lover, Avital, Deanna enclosed a photograph of herself sitting securely upon her beloved mare, Almaviva Morena. Deanna Alida, opera singer, performer, celebrant of beauty, butch lover of women, was one of the longest-standing members of the New York lesbian-feminist community. She was buried in her tuxedo, surrounded by friends who were grateful for all the gifts she so generously shared. I will always think of Deanna when I say we are not speaking of roles but of identities. Her butch self was not a masquerade or a gender cliché, but her final and fullest expression of herself.

1. The persistent...

A butch and femme of the 1930s

William Cullen Bryant

To the *Evening Post**

Keene, New Hampshire, July 13, 1843

I passed a few days in the valley of one of those streams of northern Vermont, which find their way into Champlain. If I were permitted to draw aside the veil of private life, I would briefly give you the singular and to me most interesting history of two maiden ladies who dwell in this valley. I would tell you how, in their youthful days, they took each other as companions for life, and how this union, no less sacred to them than the tie of marriage, has subsisted, in uninterrupted harmony, for forty years, during which they have shared each other's occupations and pleasures and works of charity while in health, and watched over each other tenderly in sickness; for sickness has made long and frequent visits to their dwelling. I could tell you how they slept on the same pillow and had a common purse, and adopted each other's relations, and how one of them, more enterprising and spirited in her temper than the other, might be said to represent the male head of the family, and took upon herself their transactions with the world without, until her health failed, and she was tended by her gentle companion, as a fond wife attends her invalid husband. I would tell you of their dwelling, encircled with roses, which now in the days of their broken health, bloom wild without their tendance, and I would speak of the friendly attentions which their neighbors, people of kind hearts and simple manners, seem to take pleasure in bestowing upon them, but I have already said more than I fear they will forgive me for, if this should ever meet their eyes, and I must leave the subject.

* From *The Letters of William Cullen Bryant*, edited by William C. Bryant II and T.G. Voss, vol. 2, 1836–1849 (New York: Fordham University Press, 1977), pp. 338–339.

Radclyffe Hall

Miss Ogilvy finds herself

About "Miss Ogilvy," Radclyffe Hall noted: "This story, in which I have permitted myself a brief excursion into the realms of the fantastic, was written in July 1926, shortly before I definitely decided to write my serious study of congenital sexual inversion, The Well of Loneliness.

"Although Miss Ogilvy is a very different person from Stephen Gordon, yet those who have read The Well of Loneliness *will find in the earlier part of this story the nucleus of those sections of my novel which deal with Stephen Gordon's childhood and girlhood, and with the noble and selfless work done by hundreds of sexually inverted women during the Great War: 1914–1918."*

1

Miss Ogilvy stood on the quay at Calais and surveyed the disbanding of her Unit, the Unit that together with the coming of war had completely altered the complexion of her life, at all events for three years.

Miss Ogilvy's thin, pale lips were set sternly and her forehead was puckered in an effort of attention, in an effort to memorize every small detail of every old war-weary battered motor on whose side still appeared the merciful emblem that had set Miss Ogilvy free.

Miss Ogilvy's mind was jerking a little, trying to regain its accustomed balance, trying to readjust itself quickly to this sudden and paralyzing change. Her tall, awkward body with its queer look of strength, its broad, flat bosom and thick legs and ankles, as though in response to her jerking mind, moved uneasily, rocking backwards and forwards. She had this trick of rocking on her feet in moments of controlled agitation. As usual, her hands were thrust deep into her pockets, they seldom seemed to come out of her pockets unless it were to light a cigarette, and as though she were still standing firm under fire while the wounded were placed in her ambulances, she suddenly straddled her legs very slightly and lifted her head and listened. She was standing firm under fire at that moment, the fire of a desperate regret.

Radclyffe Hall. "S.H." stands for "Same Here."

Some girls came towards her, young, tired-looking creatures whose eyes were too bright from long strain and excitement. They had all been members of that glorious Unit, and they still wore the queer little forage-caps and the short, clumsy tunics of the French Militaire. They still slouched in walking and smoked Caporals in emulation of the Poilus. Like their founder and leader these girls were all English, but like her they had chosen to serve England's ally, fearlessly thrusting right up to the trenches in search of the wounded and dying. They had seen some fine things in the course of three years, not the least fine of which was the cold, hard-faced woman who commanding, domineering, even hectoring at times, had yet been possessed of so dauntless a courage and of so insistent a vitality that it vitalized the whole Unit.

"It's rotten!" Miss Ogilvy heard someone saying. "It's rotten, this breaking up of our Unit!" And the high, rather childish voice of the speaker sounded perilously near to tears.

Miss Ogilvy looked at the girl almost gently, and it seemed, for a moment, as though some deep feeling were about to find expression in words. But Miss Ogilvy's feelings had been held in abeyance so long that they seldom dared become vocal, so she merely said, "Oh?" on a rising inflection — her method of checking emotion.

They were swinging the ambulance cars in mid-air, those of them that were destined to go back to England, swinging them up like sacks of potatoes, then lowering them with much clanging of chains to the deck of the waiting steamer. The porters were shoving and shouting and quarreling, pausing now and again to make meaningless gestures; while a pompous official was becoming quite angry as he pointed at Miss Ogilvy's own special car — it annoyed him, it was bulky and difficult to move.

"*Bon Dieu! Mais dépêchez-vous donc!*" he bawled, as though he were bullying the motor.

Then Miss Ogilvy's heart gave a sudden, thick thud to see this undignified, pitiful ending; and she turned and patted the gallant old car as though she were patting a well-beloved horse, as though she would say: "Yes, I know how it feels — never mind, we'll go down together."

2

Miss Ogilvy sat in the railway carriage on her way from Dover to London. The soft English landscape sped smoothly past: small homesteads, small churches, small pastures, small lanes, with small hedges; all small like England itself, all small like Miss Ogilvy's future. And sitting there still arrayed in her tunic, with her forage-cap resting on her knees, she was conscious of a sense of complete frustration; thinking less of those glorious years at the Front and of all that had gone to the making of her, than of all that had gone to the marring of her from the days of her earliest childhood.

She saw herself as a queer little girl, aggressive and awkward because of her shyness: a queer little girl who loathed sisters and dolls, preferring the stable-boys as companions, preferring to play with footballs and tops, and occasional catapults. She saw herself climbing the tallest beech trees, arrayed in old breeches illicitly come by. She remembered insisting with tears and some temper that her real name was William and not Wilhelmina. All these childish pretenses and illusions she remembered, and the bitterness that came after. For Miss Ogilvy had found as her life went on that in this world it is better to be one with the herd, that the world has no wish to understand those who cannot conform to its stereotyped pattern. True enough in her youth she had gloried in her strength, lifting weights, swinging clubs, and developing muscles, but presently this had grown irksome to her; it had seemed to lead nowhere, she being a woman, and then as her mother had often protested: muscles looked so appalling in evening dress — a young girl ought not to have muscles.

Miss Ogilvy's relation to the opposite sex was unusual and at that time added much to her worries, for no less than three men had wished to propose, to the genuine amazement of the world and her mother. Miss Ogilvy's instinct made her like and trust men for whom she had a pronounced fellow-feeling; she would always have chosen them as her friends and companions in preference to girls or women; she would dearly have loved to share in their sports, their business, their ideals, and their wide-flung interests. But men had not wanted her, except the three who had found in her strangeness a definite attraction, and those would-be suitors she had actually feared, regarding them with aversion. Towards young girls and women she was shy and respectful, apologetic and sometimes admiring. But their fads and their foibles, none of which she could share, while amusing her very often in secret, set her outside the sphere of their intimate lives, so that in the end she must blaze a lone trail through the difficulties of her nature.

"I can't understand you," her mother had said, "you're a very odd creature — now when I was your age..."

And her daughter had nodded, feeling sympathetic. There were two younger girls who also gave trouble, though in their case the trouble was fighting for husbands who were scarce enough even in those days. It was finally decided, at Miss Ogilvy's request, to allow her to leave the field clear for her sisters. She would remain in the country with her father when the others went up for the Season.

Followed long, uneventful years spent in sport, while Sarah and Fanny toiled, sweated, and gambled in the matrimonial market. Neither ever succeeded in netting a husband, and when the Squire died leaving very little money, Miss Ogilvy found to her great surprise that they looked upon her as a brother. They had so often jibed at her in the past that at first she could scarcely believe her senses, but before very long it became all too real: she it was who must straighten out endless muddles, who must make the dreary arrangements for the move, who must find a cheap but genteel house in London, and, once there, who must cope with the family accounts, which she only, it seemed, could balance.

It would be: "You might see to that, Wilhelmina; you write, you've got such a good head for business." Or: "I wish you'd go down and explain to that man that we really can't pay his account till next quarter." Or: "This money for the grocer is five shillings short. Do run over my sum, Wilhelmina."

Her mother, grown feeble, discovered in this daughter a staff upon which she could lean with safety. Miss Ogilvy genuinely loved her mother, and was therefore quite prepared to be leaned on; but when Sarah and Fanny began to lean too with the full weight of endless neurotic symptoms incubated in resentful virginity, Miss Ogilvy found herself staggering a little. For Sarah and Fanny were grown hard to bear, with their mania for telling their symptoms to doctors, with their unstable nerves and their acrid tongues and the secret dislike they now felt for their mother. Indeed, when old Mrs. Ogilvy died, she was unmourned except by her eldest daughter, who actually felt a void in her life — the unforeseen void that the ailing and weak will not infrequently leave behind them.

At about this time an aunt also died, bequeathing her fortune to her niece Wilhelmina, who, however, was too weary to gird up her loins and set forth in search of exciting adventure — all she did was to move her protesting sisters to a little estate she had purchased in Surrey. This experiment was only a partial success, for Miss Ogilvy failed to make friends of her neighbors; thus at fifty-five she had grown rather dour, as is often the way with shy, lonely people.

When the war came she had just begun settling down — people do settle down in their fifty-sixth year — she was feeling quite glad that her hair was gray, that the garden took up so much of her time, that, in fact, the beat of her blood was slowing. But all this was changed when war was declared; on that day Miss Ogilvy's pulses throbbed wildly.

"My God! If only I were a man!" she burst out, as she glared at Sarah and Fanny, "if only I had been born a man!" Something in her was feeling deeply defrauded.

Sarah and Fanny were soon knitting socks and mittens and mufflers and Jaeger trench-helmets. Other ladies were busily working at depots, making swabs at the Squire's, or splints at the Parson's; but Miss Ogilvy scowled and did none of these things — she was not at all like other ladies.

For nearly twelve months she worried officials with a view to getting a job out in France — not in their way but in hers, and that was the trouble. She wished to go up to the front-line trenches; she wished to be actually under fire, she informed the harassed officials.

To all her inquiries she received the same answer: "We regret that we cannot accept your offer." But once thoroughly roused she was hard to subdue, for her shyness had left her as though by magic.

Sarah and Fanny shrugged angular shoulders: "There's plenty of work here at home," they remarked, "though of course it's not quite so melodramatic!"

"Oh...?" queried their sister on a rising note of impatience — and she promptly cut off her hair: "That'll jar them!" she thought with satisfaction.

Then she went up to London, formed her admirable unit, and finally got it accepted by the French, despite renewed opposition.

In London she had found herself quite at her ease, for many another of her kind was in London doing excellent work for the nation. It was really surprising how many cropped heads had suddenly appeared as it were out of space; how many Miss Ogilvies, losing their shyness, had come forward asserting their right to serve, asserting their claim to attention.

There followed those turbulent years at the front, full of courage and hardship and high endeavor, and during those years Miss Ogilvy forgot the bad joke that Nature seemed to have played her. She was given the rank of a French lieutenant and she lived in a kind of blissful illusion; appalling reality lay on all sides and yet she managed to live in illusion. She was competent, fearless, devoted, and untiring. What then? Could any man hope to do better? She was nearly fifty-eight, yet she walked with a stride, and at times she even swaggered a little.

Poor Miss Ogilvy sitting so glumly in the train with her manly trench-boots and her forage-cap! Poor all the Miss Ogilvies back from the war with their tunics, their trench-boots, and their childish illusions! Wars come and wars go but the world does not change: it will always forget an indebtedness which it thinks it expedient not to remember.

3

When Miss Ogilvy returned to her home in Surrey it was only to find that her sisters were ailing from the usual imaginary causes, and this to a woman who had seen the real thing was intolerable, so that she looked with distaste at Sarah and then at Fanny. Fanny was certainly not prepossessing; she was suffering from a spurious attack of hay fever.

"Stop sneezing!" commanded Miss Ogilvy, in the voice that had so much impressed the Unit. But as Fanny was not in the least impressed, she naturally went on sneezing.

Miss Ogilvy's desk was piled mountain-high with endless tiresome letters and papers: circulars, bills, months-old correspondence, the gardener's accounts, an agent's report on some fields that required land-draining. She seated herself before this collection; then she sighed, it all seemed so absurdly trivial.

"Will you let your hair grow again?" Fanny inquired ... she and Sarah had followed her into the study. "I'm certain the Vicar would be glad if you did."

"Oh?" murmured Miss Ogilvy, rather too blandly.

"Wilhelmina!"

"Yes?"

"You will do it, won't you?"

"Do what?"

"Let your hair grow; we all wish you would."

"Why should I?"

"Oh, well, it will look less odd, especially now that the war is over — in a small place like this people notice such things."

"I entirely agree with Fanny," announced Sarah.

Sarah had become very self-assertive, no doubt through having mismanaged the estate during the years of her sister's absence. They had quite a heated dispute one morning over the south herbaceous border.

"Whose garden is this?" Miss Ogilvy asked sharply. "I insist on auricula-eyed sweet williams! I even took the trouble to write from France, but it seems that my letter has been ignored."

"Don't shout," rebuked Sarah, "you're not in France now!"

Miss Ogilvy could gladly have boxed her ears: "I only wish to God I were," she muttered.

Another dispute followed close on its heels, and this time it happened to be over the dinner. Sarah and Fanny were living on weeds — at least that was the way Miss Ogilvy put it.

"We've become vegetarians," Sarah said grandly.

"You've become two damn tiresome cranks!" snapped their sister.

Now it never had been Miss Ogilvy's way to indulge in acid recriminations, but somehow, these days, she forgot to say "Oh?" quite so often as expediency demanded. It may have been Fanny's perpetual sneezing that had got on her nerves; or it may have been Sarah, or the gardener, or the Vicar, or even the canary; though it really did not matter very much what it was just so long as she found a convenient peg upon which to hang her growing irritation.

"This won't do at all," Miss Ogilvy thought sternly, "life's not worth so much fuss, I must pull myself together." But it seemed this was easier said than done; not a day passed without her losing her temper and that over some trifle: "No, this won't do at all — it just mustn't be," she thought sternly.

Everyone pitied Sarah and Fanny: "Such a dreadful, violent old thing," said the neighbors.

But Sarah and Fanny had their revenge: "Poor darling, it's shell-shock, you know," they murmured.

Thus Miss Ogilvy's prowess was whittled away until she herself was beginning to doubt it. Had she ever been that courageous person who had faced death in France with such perfect composure? Had she ever stood tranquilly under fire, without turning a hair, while she issued her orders? Had she ever been treated with marked respect? She herself was beginning to doubt it.

Sometimes she would see an old member of the Unit, a girl who, more faithful to her than the others, would take the trouble to run down to Surrey. These visits, however, were seldom enlivening.

"Oh, well ... here we are..." Miss Ogilvy would mutter.

But one day the girl smiled and shook her blonde head: "I'm not — I'm going to be married."

Strange thoughts had come to Miss Ogilvy, unbidden, thoughts that had stayed for many an hour after the girl's departure. Alone in her study she had suddenly shivered, feeling a sense of complete desolation. With cold hands she had lighted a cigarette.

"I must be ill or something," she had mused, as she stared at her trembling fingers.

After this she would sometimes cry out in her sleep, living over in dreams God knows what emotions; returning, maybe, to the battlefields of France. Her hair turned snow white; it was not unbecoming yet she fretted about it.

"I'm growing very old," she would sigh as she brushed her thick mop before the glass; and then she would peer at her wrinkles.

For now that it had happened she hated being old; it no longer appeared such an easy solution of those difficulties that had always beset her. And this she resented most bitterly, so that she became the prey of self-pity, and of other undesirable states in which the body will torment the mind, and the mind, in its turn, the body. Then Miss Ogilvy straightened her aging back, in spite of the fact that of late it had ached with muscular rheumatism, and she faced herself squarely and came to a resolve.

"I'm off!" she announced abruptly one day; and that evening she packed her kit-bag.

4

Near the south coast of Devon there exists a small island that is still very little known to the world, but which, nevertheless, can boast an hotel: the only building upon it. Miss Ogilvy had chosen this place quite at random, it was marked on her map by scarcely more than a dot, but somehow she had liked the look of that dot and had set forth alone to explore it.

She found herself standing on the mainland one morning looking at a vague blur of green through the mist, a vague blur of green that rose out of the Channel like a tidal wave suddenly suspended. Miss Ogilvy was filled with a sense of adventure; she had not felt like this since the ending of the war.

"I was right to come here, very right indeed. I'm going to shake off all my troubles," she decided.

A fisherman's boat was parting the mist, and before it was properly beached, in she bundled.

"I hope they're expecting me?" she said gaily.

"They du be expecting you," the man answered.

The sea, which is generally rough off that coast, was indulging itself in an oily ground-swell; the broad, glossy swells struck the side of the boat, then broke and sprayed over Miss Ogilvy's ankles.

The fisherman grinned: "Feeling all right?" he queried. "It du be tiresome most times about these parts." But the mist had suddenly drifted away and Miss Ogilvy was staring wide-eyed at the island.

She saw a long shoal of jagged black rocks, and between them the curve of a small sloping beach, and above that again, blue heaven. Near the beach stood the little two-storied hotel, which was thatched, and built entirely of timber; for the rest she could make out no signs of life apart from a host of white seagulls.

Then Miss Ogilvy said a curious thing. She said: "On the southwest side of that place there was once a cave — a very large cave. I remember that it was some way from the sea."

"There du be a cave still," the fisherman told her, "but it's just above highwater level."

"A-ah," murmured Miss Ogilvy thoughtfully, as though to herself; then she looked embarrassed.

The little hotel proved both comfortable and clean, the hostess both pleasant and comely. Miss Ogilvy started unpacking her bag, changed her mind, and went for a stroll round the island. The island was covered with turf and thistles and traversed by narrow green paths thick with daisies. It had four rock-bound coves of which the southwestern was by far the most difficult of access. For just here the island descended abruptly as though it were hurtling down to the water; and just here the shale was most treacherous and the tide-swept rocks most aggressively pointed. Here it was that the seagulls, grown fearless of man by reason of his absurd limitations, built their nests on the ledges and reared countless young who multiplied, in their turn, every season. Yes, and here it was that Miss Ogilvy, greatly marveling, stood and stared across at a cave; much too near the crumbling edge for her safety, but by now completely indifferent to caution.

"I remember ... I remember..." she kept repeating. Then: "That's all very well, but what do I remember?"

She was conscious of somehow remembering all wrong, of her memory being distorted and colored — perhaps by the endless things she had seen since her eyes had last rested upon that cave. This worried her sorely, far more than the fact that she should be remembering the cave at all, she who had never set foot on the island before that actual morning. Indeed, except for the sense of wrongness when she struggled to piece her memories together, she was steeped in a very profound contentment which surged over her spirit, wave upon wave.

"It's extremely odd," pondered Miss Ogilvy. Then she laughed, so pleased did she feel with its oddness.

5

That night after supper she talked to her hostess, who was only too glad, it seemed, to be questioned. She owned the whole island and was proud of the fact, as she very well might be, decided her boarder. Some curious things had been found on the island, according to comely Mrs. Nanceskivel: bronze arrowheads, pieces of ancient stone celts; and once they had dug up a man's skull and thighbone — this had happened while they were sinking a well. Would Miss Ogilvy care to have a look at the bones? They were kept in a cupboard in the scullery.

Miss Ogilvy nodded.

"Then I'll fetch him this moment," said Mrs. Nanceskivel, briskly.

In less than two minutes she was back with the box that contained those poor remnants of a man, and Miss Ogilvy, who had risen from her chair, was gazing down at those remnants. As she did so her mouth was sternly compressed, but her face and her neck flushed darkly.

Mrs. Nanceskivel was pointing to the skull; "Look, miss, he was killed," she remarked rather proudly, "and they tell me that the axe that killed him was bronze. He's thousands and thousands of years old, they tell me. Our local doctor knows a lot about such things and he wants me to send these bones to an expert: they ought to belong to the Nation, he says. But I know what would happen, they'd come digging up my island, and I won't have people digging up my island, I've got enough worry with the rabbits as it is." But Miss Ogilvy could no longer hear the words for the pounding of the blood in her temples.

She was filled with a sudden, inexplicable fury against the innocent Mrs. Nanceskivel: "You ... *you...*" she began, then checked herself, fearful of what she might say to the woman.

For her sense of outrage was overwhelming as she stared at those bones that were kept in the scullery; moreover, she knew how such men had been buried, which made the outrage seem all the more shameful. They had buried such men in deep, well-dug pits surmounted by four stout stones at their corners — four stout stones there had been and a covering stone. And all this Miss Ogilvy knew as by instinct, having no concrete knowledge on which to draw. But she knew it right down in the depths of her soul, and she hated Mrs. Nanceskivel.

And now she was swept by another emotion that was even more strange and more devastating: such a grief as she had not conceived could exist; a terrible unassuageable grief, without hope, without respite, without palliation, so that with something akin to despair she touched the long gash in the skull. Then her eyes, that had never wept since her childhood, filled slowly with large, hot, difficult tears. She must blink very hard, then close her eyelids, turn away from the lamp, and say rather loudly:

"Thanks, Mrs. Nanceskivel. It's past eleven — I think I'll be going upstairs."

6

Miss Ogilvy closed the door of her bedroom, after which she stood quite still to consider: "Is it shell-shock?" she muttered incredulously. "I wonder, can it be shell-shock?"

She began to pace slowly about the room, smoking a Caporal. As usual her hands were deep in her pockets; she could feel small, familiar things in those pockets and she gripped them, glad of their presence. Then all of a sudden she was terribly tired, so tired that she flung herself down on the bed, unable to stand any longer.

She thought that she lay there struggling to reason, that her eyes were closed in the painful effort, and that as she closed them she continued to puff the inevitable cigarette. At least that was what she thought at one moment — the next, she was out in a sunset evening, and a large red sun was sinking slowly to the rim of a distant sea.

Miss Ogilvy knew that she was herself, that is to say she was conscious of her being, and yet she was not Miss Ogilvy at all, nor had she a memory of her. All that she now saw was very familiar, all that she now did was what she should do, and all that she now was seemed perfectly natural.

Indeed, she did not think of these things; there seemed no reason for thinking about them.

She was walking with bare feet on turf that felt springy and was greatly enjoying the sensation; she had always enjoyed it, ever since as an infant she had learned to crawl on this turf. On either hand stretched rolling green uplands, while at her back she knew that there were forests; but in front, far away, lay the gleam of the sea towards which the big sun was sinking. The air was cool and intensely still, with never so much as a ripple or bird-song. It was wonderfully pure — one might almost say young — but Miss Ogilvy thought of it merely as air. Having always breathed it she took it for granted, as she took the soft turf and the uplands.

She pictured herself as immensely tall; she was feeling immensely tall at that moment. As a matter of fact she was five feet eight, which, however, was quite a considerable height when compared to that of her fellow-tribesmen. She was wearing a single garment of pelts which came to her knees and left her arms sleeveless. Her arms and her legs, which were closely tattooed with blue zig-zag lines, were extremely hairy. From a leathern thong twisted about her waist there hung a clumsily made stone weapon, a celt, which in spite of its clumsiness was strongly hafted and useful for killing.

Miss Ogilvy wanted to shout aloud from a glorious sense of physical well-being, but instead she picked up a heavy, round stone which she hurled with great force at some distant rocks.

"Good! Strong!" she exclaimed. "See how far it goes!"

"Yes, strong. There is no one so strong as you. You are surely the strongest man in our tribe," replied her little companion.

Miss Ogilvy glanced at this little companion and rejoiced that they two were alone together. The girl at her side had a smooth brownish skin, oblique black eyes, and short, sturdy limbs. Miss Ogilvy marveled because of her beauty. She was also wearing a single garment of pelts, new pelts; she had made it that morning. She had stitched at it diligently for hours with short lengths of gut and her best bone needle. A strand of black hair hung over her bosom, and this she was constantly stroking and fondling; then she lifted the strand and examined her hair.

"Pretty," she remarked with childish complacence.

"Pretty," echoed the young man at her side.

"For you," she told him, "all of me is for you and none other. For you this body has ripened."

He shook back his own coarse hair from his eyes; he had sad brown eyes like those of a monkey. For the rest he was lean and steel-strong of loin, broad of chest, and with features not too uncomely. His prominent cheekbones were set rather high, his nose was blunt, his jaw somewhat bestial; but his mouth, though full-lipped, contradicted his jaw, being very gentle and sweet in expression. And now he smiled, showing big, square, white teeth.

"You ... woman," he murmured contentedly, and the sound seemed to come from the depths of his being.

His speech was slow and lacking in words when it came to expressing a vital emotion, so one word must suffice and this he now spoke, and the word that he spoke had a number of meanings. It meant: "Little spring of exceedingly pure water." It meant: "Hut of peace for a man after battle." It meant: "Ripe red berry sweet to the taste." It meant: "Happy small home of future generations." All these things he must try to express by a word, and because of their loving she understood him.

They paused, and lifting her up he kissed her. Then he rubbed his large shaggy head on her shoulder; and when he released her she knelt at his feet.

"My master; blood of my body," she whispered. For with her it was different, love had taught her love's speech, so that she might turn her heart into sounds that her primitive tongue could utter.

After she had pressed her lips to his hands, and her cheek to his hairy and powerful forearm, she stood up and they gazed at the setting sun, but with bowed heads, gazing under their lids, because this was very sacred.

A couple of mating bears padded towards them from a thicket, and the female rose to her haunches. But the man drew his celt and menaced the beast, so that she dropped down noiselessly and fled, and her mate also fled, for here was the power that few dared to withstand by day or by night, on the uplands or in the forests. And now from across to the left, where a river would presently lose itself in the marshes, came a rhythmical thudding, as a herd of red deer with wide nostrils and starting eyes thundered past, disturbed in their drinking by the bears.

After this the evening returned to its silence, and the spell of its silence descended on the lovers, so that each felt very much alone, yet withal more closely united to the other. But the man became restless under that spell, and he suddenly laughed; then grasping the woman he tossed her above his head and caught her. This he did many times for his own amusement and because he knew that his strength gave her joy. In this manner they played together for a while, he with his strength and she with her weakness. And they cried out, and made many guttural sounds which were meaningless save only to themselves. And the tunic of pelts slipped down from her breasts, and her two little breasts were pear-shaped.

Presently, he grew tired of their playing, and he pointed towards a cluster of huts and earthworks that lay to the eastward. The smoke from these huts rose in thick straight lines, bending neither to right nor left in its rising, and the thought of sweet burning rushes and brushwood touched his consciousness, making him feel sentimental.

"Smoke," he said.

And she answered: "Blue smoke."

He nodded: "Yes, blue smoke — home."

Then she said: "I have ground much corn since the full moon. My stones are too smooth. You make me new stones."

"All you have need of, I make," he told her.

She stole close to him, taking his hand: "My father is still a black cloud full of thunder. He thinks that you wish to be head of our tribe in his place, because he is now very old. He must not hear of these meetings of ours; if he did I think he would beat me!"

So he asked her: "Are you unhappy, small berry?"

But at this she smiled: "What is being unhappy? I do not know what that means anymore."

"I do not either," he answered.

Then as though some invisible force had drawn him, his body swung round and he stared at the forests where they lay and darkened, fold upon fold; and his eyes dilated with wonder and terror, and he moved his head quickly from side to side as a wild thing will do that is held between bars and whose mind is pitifully bewildered.

"Water!" he cried hoarsely, "great water — look, look! Over there. This land is surrounded by water!"

"What water?" she questioned.

He answered: "The sea." And he covered his face with his hands.

"Not so," she consoled, "big forests, good hunting. Big forests in which you hunt boar and aurochs. No sea over there but only the trees."

He took his trembling hands from his face: "You are right ... only trees," he said dully.

But now his face had grown heavy and brooding and he started to speak of a thing that oppressed him: "The Roundheaded-ones, they are devils," he growled, while his bushy black brows met over his eyes, and when this happened it changed his expression, which became a little subhuman.

"No matter," she protested, for she saw that he forgot her and she wished him to think and talk only of love. "No matter. My father laughs at your fears. Are we not friends with the Roundheaded-ones? We are friends, so why should we fear them?"

"Our forts, very old, very weak," he went on, "and the Roundheaded-ones have terrible weapons. Their weapons are not made of good stone like ours, but of some dark, devilish substance."

"What of that?" she said lightly. "They would fight on our side, so why need we trouble about their weapons?"

But he looked away, not appearing to hear her. "We must barter all, all for their celts and arrows and spears, and then we must learn their secret. They lust after our women, they lust after our lands. We must barter all, all for their sly brown celts."

"Me ... bartered?" she queried, very sure of his answer, otherwise she had not dared to say this.

"The Roundheaded-ones may destroy my tribe and yet I will not part with you," he told her. Then he spoke very gravely: "But I think they desire to slay us, and me they will try to slay first because they well know how much I mistrust them — they have seen my eyes fixed many times on their camps."

She cried: "I will bite out the throats of these people if they so much as scratch your skin!"

And at this his mood changed and he roared with amusement: "You ... woman!" he roared. "Little foolish white teeth. Your teeth were made for nibbling wild cherries, not for tearing the throats of the Roundheaded-ones!"

"Thoughts of war always make me afraid," she whimpered, still wishing him to talk about love.

He turned his sorrowful eyes upon her, the eyes that were sad even when he was merry, and although his mind was often obtuse, yet he clearly perceived how it was with her then. And his blood caught fire from the flame in her blood, so that he strained her against his body.

"You ... mine..." he stammered.

"Love," she said, trembling, "this is love."

And he answered: "Love."

Then their faces grew melancholy for a moment, because dimly, very dimly in their dawning souls, they were conscious of a longing for something more vast than this earthly passion could compass.

Presently, he lifted her like a child and carried her quickly southward and westward till they came to a place where a gentle descent led down to a marshy valley. Far away, at the line where the marshes ended, they discerned the misty line of the sea; but the sea and the marshes were become as one substance, merging, blending, folding together; and since they were lovers they also would be one, even as the sea and the marshes.

And now they had reached the mouth of a cave that was set in the quiet hillside. There was bright green verdure beside the cave, and a number of small, pink, thick-stemmed flowers that when they were crushed smelt of spices. And within the cave there was bracken newly gathered and heaped together for a bed; while beyond, from some rocks, came a low liquid sound as a spring dripped out through a crevice. Abruptly, he set the girl on her feet, and she knew that the days of her innocence were over. And she thought of the anxious virgin soil that was rent and sown to bring forth fruit in season, and she gave a quick little gasp of fear:

"No ... no..." she gasped. For, divining his need, she was weak with the longing to be possessed, yet the terror of love lay heavy upon her. "No ... no..." she gasped.

But he caught her wrist and she felt the great strength of his rough, gnarled fingers, the great strength of the urge that leapt in his loins, and again she must give that quick gasp of fear, the while she clung close to him lest he should spare her.

The twilight was engulfed and possessed by darkness, which in turn was transfigured by the moonrise, which in turn was fulfilled and consumed by dawn. A mighty eagle soared up from his eyrie, cleaving the air with his masterful wings, and beneath him from the rushes that harbored their nests, rose other great birds, crying loudly. Then the heavy-horned elks appeared on the uplands, bending their burdened heads to the sod; while beyond in the forests the fierce wild aurochs stamped as they bellowed their love songs.

But within the dim cave the lord of these creatures had put by his weapon and his instinct for slaying. And he lay there defenseless with tenderness, thinking no longer of death but of life as he murmured the word that had so many meanings. That meant: "Hut of peace for a man after battle." That meant: "Ripe red berry sweet to the taste." That meant: "Happy small home of future generations."

7

They found Miss Ogilvy the next morning; the fisherman saw her and climbed to the ledge. She was sitting at the mouth of the cave. She was dead, with her hands thrust deep into her pockets.

Femme voices from the literary world

This century has been marked by lesbian creative couples who lived in what appeared to be a married state or carried on tempestuous romances, chasing each other from continent to continent. Even being married to men did not deter some passionate femme women from fulfilling their longing for "mannish" women. Amy Lowell and Ada Russell, Radclyffe Hall and Lady Una Troubridge, Margaret Anderson and Jane Heap, Colette and Missy, Vita Sackville-West and several women, among them Virginia Woolf and Violet Trefusis, are just a few of the couples and couplings that are upper-class versions of butch-femme partnerships. Even in these widely known alliances, the femme women continue to be dismissed as the lesser woman although their diaries and letters leave records of constancy, flamboyance, erotic bravado, and wit.

Alice B. Toklas (1877–1966)[1]

1946* Oh Carlo could such perfection and happiness and such beauty have been and here and now be gone away?

1946 But now this new separation — this going away again is very hard and the old one still is like it was and always will be.

1947 I have the manuscript [*Q.E.D.*, Stein's first lesbian work]. It is a subject I haven't known how to handle ... It was something I knew I'd have to meet one day ... to cover my cowardice I kept saying, well when all else is accomplished.

1948 And now without Baby [Gertrude Stein] there is no direction to anything, it's just milling around in the dark — back to where one was before one was grown.

1949 Dead is dead but that is why memory is all and all the immortality there is.

---

* Gertrude Stein had died in Paris in 1946.

1957 If there were not still things to do for Gertrude, there would be no reason for one to go on.

1958 I am nothing but the memory of her.

1959 On Monday I get to work on the memoirs. The white ducks are bathing in the lake. The white cow and horse are being brought in and the mallard ducks are fighting — heaps of love.

1960 Have you read Mercedes de Acosta's book *Here Lies the Heart?* There is a classic description of Greta Garbo. A friend said to me one day — you can't dispose of Mercedes lightly — she has had the two most important women in the U.S. — Greta Garbo and Marlene Dietrich.

1966 Do come back I shan't last forever.

Margaret Anderson (1886–1973)[2]

I already knew that the great thing to learn about life is, first, not to do what you don't want to do, and, second, to do what you do want to do...

Jane [Heap] and I began talking. We talked for days, months, years...

Jane and I were as different as two people can be ... The result of our differences was — argument. At last I could argue as long as I wanted. Instead of discouraging Jane, this stimulated her. She was always saying that she never found enough resistance in life to make talking worth while — or anything else for that matter. And I had always been confronted with people who found my zest for argument disagreeable, who said they lost interest in any subject the moment it became controversial. My answer had been that argument wasn't necessarily controversy ... I had never been able to understand why people dislike to be challenged. For me, challenge has always been the great impulse, the only liberation.

Violet Trefusis (1894–1972)[3]

Mitya [Violet's term of endearment for Vita Sackville-West], you don't know to what a pitch I have brought my truthfulness with L. This is the sort of conversation that takes place constantly:

L: What are you thinking about?

Me: V [Vita].

L: Do you wish V. were here?

Me: Yes.

L: You don't care much about being with men, do you?

Me: No, I infinitely prefer women.

L: You are strange, aren't you?

Me: Stranger than you have any idea of.

Lady Una Troubridge (1887–1963)[4]

It was after the success of *Adam's Breed* that John [Radclyffe Hall] came to me one day with unusual gravity and asked for my decision in a serious matter: she had long wanted to write a book on sexual inversion ... It was her absolute conviction that such a book could only be written by a sexual invert ... to speak on behalf of a misunderstood and misjudged minority.

It was with this conviction that she came to me, telling me in her view the time was ripe, and that although the publication of such a book might mean the shipwreck of her whole career, she was fully prepared to make any sacrifice except the sacrifice of my peace of mind.

She pointed out that in view of our union and of all the years that we had shared a home, what affected her must also affect me and that I would be included in any condemnation. Therefore she placed the decision in my hands and would write or refrain as I should decide.

I am glad to remember that my reply was made without so much of an instant's hesitation; I told her to write what was in her heart, that so far as any effect upon myself was concerned, I was sick to death of ambiguities, and only wished to be known for what I was and dwell with her in the palace of truth.

Notes

1. From Edward Burns, ed., *Letters of Alice B. Toklas: Staying on Alone* (New York: Vintage Books, 1975).

2. From Margaret Anderson, *My Thirty Years' War: The Autobiography: Beginnings and Battles to 1930* (New York: Horizon Press, 1969), pp. 11, 107, 122–123.

3. From Philippe Julian and John Philips, *The Other Woman: A Life of Violet Trefusis* (Boston: Houghton Mifflin, 1976), letter no. 18.

4. From Una, Lady Troubridge, *The Life of Radclyffe Hall* (New York: Citadel Press, 1961).

Mabel Hampton at the Lesbian Herstory Archives,
New York, 1978

Lillian Foster, lifelong partner of Mabel Hampton, 1942

Mabel Hampton (1902–1989)

The following is excerpted from oral history tapes made at the Lesbian Herstory Archives, New York, 1981, with Mabel Hampton, an African-American lesbian woman who called herself "Poppa," among other things. From the LHA collection.

Mabel: Down here it was just like two couples,* Joan and Deborah and Mabel and Lillian; we got along lovely, and we played, we sang, ate, it was marvelous! I will never forget it. And Lillian, of course, Lillian was my wife.

I had Joan laughing, because I called Lillian "Little Bear." But when I first met her, in 1932, she was, to me ... a duchess — the grand duchess — and I can't remember what she called me now. But later in life, a number of years later, I named her. I got angry with her one day and I called her the "Little Bear" and she called me the "Big Bear," and of course, that hung on to me all through life. And now we're known to all our friends as the "Big Bear" and the "Little Bear."

Joan: Did you like to wear men's clothes?

M: Yes. I like to wear pants. Then I always dressed kind of tailored: skirt and blouse and things like that. But I like the pants and the cap. But I never considered myself being a man. Because I never liked the men that much. And anything I don't like, I don't take up. And I always took up being a woman because I liked the women and what they stood for.

J: What was the word you called yourself?

M: I had quite a lot of my friends that were known as studs, and the stud comes as part of the way they dressed, I think. You see, because they dressed nicely and had short hair and things like that. But I didn't care, I

---

* Mabel Hampton and Lillian Foster were staying with the editor and Deborah Edel after a fire had destroyed their South Bronx apartment.

kept my hair. I didn't bother with the hair. I just liked the suits and the pants and the pants and the shoes. I didn't want to be tied down to anything. I just wanted to be myself.

I never considered marrying. I had so much trouble when I was little, a little girl going to school, and my uncle tried to rape me, and then in every house, even people I went to work for, the men would try to touch me on my buttons — and I didn't like it. So, therefore, they meant nothing to me, because they were always doing something I didn't like. And if you do something I don't like, I don't bother with you. Good riddance to you.

From a very early age, I knew that I would never marry. I didn't see any sense in marrying something that I didn't like. And that meant I had to always work, and I've always worked. And right up until I pass away I will be working.

And I took care of my women. Lillian — from 1932 to 1978 we were together. We didn't part. We quarreled a little bit and maybe that's all; tongue and teeth falls out, but we just went on. I know she's happy now that I am just myself.

Lisa E. Davis

The butch as drag artiste: Greenwich Village in the Roaring Forties

For Eileen, who would've enjoyed this

About fifty years ago in Greenwich Village, nightclubs operating under the protection of the New York mob featured floor shows with dykes and gay boys (as they said back then) performing in drag. The girls (as they said back then) wore white tie and tails, a tux, or a costume with trousers. They were the butches. You might find some gorgeous femme working there, too, as a stripper, since LaGuardia had closed down the midtown burlesque houses a few years back. She gave the joint class, the bosses said, and she was the only girl in a skirt, when she was wearing it.

Male drag in those days was feathers, sequins, and showgirl glamour, and in their pictures, at least, the guys really looked like movie stars: Marlene Dietrich, Rita Hayworth.

The butches were even more gorgeous. Slender, wistful girls stared out of eight-by-ten-inch close-ups with curly hair or straight hair, blonde or dark, cut short like a boy's and slicked back with Vitalis or Vaseline Hair Tonic. They had beautiful, androgynous faces with smooth cheeks and sculpted jaws. One looked like Errol Flynn. They passed not only on stage, where everybody knew the score, but on the street, too. Most of them owned few or no female clothes, and on visits in drag to the Copacabana, for example, they used the men's facilities without incident to avoid confusion in the powder room.

The downtown shows opened with a chorus, and the finale brought everybody back on stage. In between, individual performers sang and danced to popular songs and show tunes. When the butch crooners sang, the fans swooned. They may have had good voices, but their real talent was for women: the ones who went to nightclubs in long dresses and mink stoles, like the heroines of a black-and-white movie.

45

Even those dames who were supposed to be straight found the butches irresistible. Their bravado and defiance of convention commanded respect, and nobody would have to worry about getting pregnant. But whatever the attraction, the women who tried it once generally liked it and stuck with it. As the saying went back then, "This year's trade is next year's femme."

Stagestruck female fans tipped their favorites exorbitantly and bought rounds of drinks for everyone. They hung around in mobs waiting for their butches to finish the show. The offers ranged from one-night stands to thirty-five-foot yachts. Sometimes a wealthy femme married her dyke in Mexico and endowed her with a small fortune. Rich and beautiful women seemed to be popping out of the woodwork.

Meanwhile, everybody in the show worked six nights a week, three shows a night — 10:30 p.m., 12:30 a.m., 2:30 a.m. — for a token salary of $10 to $25 a week. (Closing time was 4 a.m., when everybody went around to Reuben's, the people who invented the sandwich, on East 58th Street, just off Fifth, with the after-hours crowd, or up to Harlem.) The rest of the money the kids raked in, which was considerable, they made in big tips from customers, who had already paid high cover charges and minimums to be there.

The audience was generally straight, though gay people came to see their friends perform. Everybody found their way downtown sooner or later — socialites, uptown swells, show people, bankers, con artists, mobsters, Wall Street brokers, gigolos, lawyers, and hookers, plus out-of-towners and tourists from all over. People lined up outside the bigger clubs, hoping for a table for the next show. Most were just looking for thrills and a few laughs. A few were looking for more.

It's no secret that two women together is a favorite male fantasy, and for the kinky johns who frequented the clubs back then, dykes had a special allure. Offers to a butch chorine for a sexy threesome with a hooker — or from straight couples — weren't rare. You could always just say no, but the money was good.

Dykes weren't strangers to the business end of things. For instance, one of the biggest madams in the city was into girls ("Men are for business, but girls are for pleasure," she used to say), and some of the butches had lovers who were uptown hookers — women who were paid top dollar for their services. It was easy for the butches to slip into the same line of work, but the price was usually high — drugs, booze, oblivion. The scene lost its glamour pretty fast.

From the mid- to late forties, the most elegant and prestigious clubs with gay entertainers were the 181 Club, at 181 Second Avenue between Eleventh and Twelfth Streets in what is now the East Village (then still the Lower East Side), and the Moroccan Village, at 23 West Eighth Street, billed in the forties as "the Gayest Spot in the Village" but occupied for years now by a belly-dance emporium called the Darvish. The site of the

*"Blackie," a prominent New York male impersonator
of the 1930s and '40s*

181 Club, left to ruin for many years, was recently renovated and now houses the Village East Cinemas. The doors to the 181 (which bore that number until the renovation) are the last ones at the south end of the building.

A forerunner of both of these, but much less debonair, was the Howdy Club on Third Street in the Village, which dates from the late thirties. And the history of these clubs, as I know it, ends with the 82 Club, at 82 East Fourth Street, which replaced the 181 around 1953. Smaller and less plush than the 181 Club, the 82 lasted into the late fifties, to be phased out by television and the decline of mob influence. After long neglect, the space it once occupied has reopened as Woody's in the Village.

Nightclubs with gay floor shows were completely separate from the lesbian bars of the period, except that many of the dykes who worked in drag went to the bars. Also, tending bar or hanging out at the bars were ways of meeting people who could put you in touch with people who could get you into show biz. They didn't advertise. It was whom you knew, and whether or not you looked the part.

There were a number of lesbian bars around back then. From the late thirties, on Third Street or Bleeker, there was a place called Willie's and John's, in the shadow of the Sixth Avenue El. In the same neighborhood from the forties were El's, the Welcome Inn, MacDougal's Tavern, Tony Pastor's, the P[rovince]town Landing, and Ernie's. In fact, Third Street was *the* street of lesbian bars. The Welcome Inn and MacDougal's stood in the block presently occupied by the NYU Law School.

I've heard that femmes congregated in one bar while butches started out the night in another. That older women stuck pretty much to one bar and younger women to another. That you could check your coat in one place and go off down Third Street to another, then come back and pick it up later. They tell me that before women wore pants on the street, which wasn't until World War II, the dykes had three-piece suits made with a skirt and slacks to match the jacket. They'd wear the skirt on the street and change into the slacks when they got to the bar.

None of this has been written down anywhere, so you'll just have to trust me. It was all told to me by old friends. They were the butches in drag who worked the floor shows in those Village clubs.

They'd sit around on a Sunday afternoon and tell stories and pass around photo albums. Nobody thought of their lives as history, much less lesbian history. That didn't exist. As my friend Frankie said to me recently (somebody was looking for "older lesbians" to interview), "Older *lesbians*, for chris'sake! Do they have to use that word? Only the bastards on the street used that word! You know, 'Hey, lezzie, wanna suck my cock...'"

We're all history now. I'm pushing fifty and the dykes I'm talking about are pushing seventy. I've known some of them for upwards of twenty-five years, and they've known one another for fifty. Some couples have been together thirty years and more.

When I met them, in the sixties, they'd only been out of show business for a while and still loved to talk about it. I was in my twenties and very dumb. They were in their forties and had been there and back. They saved my life so many times it would bore you, and thought nothing of it. I was always going off with some drunk who finished up the evening by clobbering me over the head. Once, my lover moved with someone else into the house *we* were supposed to be buying together. Frankie called a lawyer while I cried. "You gotta cut your losses," she said.

Looking back on it, I think they were used to pulling one another out of scrapes (it came with the territory), and they didn't expect me to be perfect. I basked in this nonjudgmental atmosphere.

The experience of working in the clubs together had forged a great bond among them, forming something like a sorority for poor kids who had no college, but riskier. In the fifties, you could still get busted by the vice squad for being a transvestite ("masquerading" as a man) unless you wore three pieces of women's clothing.[1] So you can imagine the rigors of life for a butch who worked in drag in the forties. And they *did* wear men's underwear. The bosses of the clubs were always after them to clean up their acts, to avoid trouble with the cops. But repeated spot checks turned up a medley of BVDs and jockey shorts, and no ladies' underwear, on the butches.

All this sounded like great fun to me, and still does. So imagine my surprise when my friends didn't jump at the chance a couple of years back to go on tape and camera and tell their stories to the world. I told Frankie we could collaborate.

"This stuff is dynamite," I said. "Don't you think it's about time to come out of the closet with it?"

"All that was a hundred years ago," Frankie barked at me. "Nobody wants to hear about it."

"How do you know?" I said.

She shot me a look she'd perfected eons ago, when girls like me came and went in her life, like through a revolving door.

"You want somebody to know," she said, "you tell 'em."

"Maybe I will," I said.

Frankie folded up her albums and stuffed the eight-by-tens back in their boxes.

"You know the people who ran the clubs don't like publicity," she said after a long pause.

"But that was years ago, Frankie," I said. "All those people must be gaga or at the bottom of the river by now."

"Well, I'm still around," she said with a deadpan delivery. "And they don't forget."

"Don't get paranoid," I said. "They wouldn't care. They even make movies about them now."

"This wasn't a movie, sweetheart. This was the real thing." Frankie tossed the photos back into their suitcases and slammed down the lids.

From that I deduced she wasn't quite ready for her close-up. If Storme wanted to go on camera, that was her business.[2] But don't mention Frankie's name. Or anybody else's name. They might sue. And no pictures, please. The family might get hold of a copy. Her nephews and nieces. The shop where she still works part-time.

I understood all that, having lived a gay life only a few steps ahead of the police when I was young. So I've kept a low profile here while dropping a few hairpins. Frankie's name isn't Frankie, of course. I never knew a Frankie, though I know that there were some in the clubs. And our conversations are collages of many chats over the years.

What I know, thanks to "Frankie" and others, about butches working in the clubs of the forties has led me to look into related topics. To place my friends into some sort of framework, I've read everything from the history of vaudeville to *The Valachi Papers*. What I've learned has reinforced my convictions about the importance of this slice of oral history.

Women working as male impersonators began to appear on the English-speaking popular stage from the middle of the last century. They played saloons, variety shows, and music halls, most of them as "song-and-dance men."[3] In fact, male (and female) impersonators were standard vaudeville acts, and sexually mixed audiences didn't find their routines threatening.[4]

The greatest of them all, a paragon of Edwardian virtue, was an English music hall star who chose the unlikely stage name of Vesta Tilley. She was brought to America many times, the first in 1894, finally earning a salary of $2,500 a week, which made her one of the highest paid vaudevillians of her day.[5] On stage and off, Vesta appears to have been as straight as an arrow and married well.[6] But her greatest fans were always working women, and for them she became a sort of folk heroine of the music halls.

But other women doubtless went into the business because it suited them in more ways than one. Like the pioneering male impersonator Annie Hindle, who in 1886 in Grand Rapids, Michigan, married her female dresser after the show. Throughout her career, Hindle received numerous "masher notes" from fans in the audience, all women.[7]

This kind of adulation by women of women on stage dressed in butchy clothes is evident throughout this history. The sexual implications are impossible to measure, though there must have been some — even if pre–World War I audiences, as everyone insists, were as innocent as lambs.

But during the war and the Roaring Twenties, a lot of things came out of the closet. In 1921, a doctor at the New York City Women's House of Detention described in the *Medical Review of Reviews* "that class of female who ... gains sexual satisfaction from association with other females." Besides being "a common occurrence among prisoners," it was, he noted, "also quite common among actresses, more particularly of the chorus girl type ... They wear strictly tailor-made clothing, low shoes and they seldom wear corsets. The hair is usually bobbed."[8] Sounds like some of "Frankie's" old photos.

By the thirties, vaudeville was dead, nightclubs were in, and audiences had wised up. Male and female impersonators were no longer polite family entertainment but a sort of theatrical sideshow, perhaps already tarred by the brush of the crime syndicates (which had made a fortune under Prohibition) and the sex industry they managed.[9] Witnesses to that era would be approaching eighty and rare nowadays. But I know that a couple of women had been in the business for years and were still on the circuit when my friends entered the clubs. They were about ten years older and idolized by the younger performers.

A hostile source comes to the rescue with a few hints about the period. In a nasty little quasi guidebook called *New York Confidential*, published in 1948, Lee Mortimer, a reporter for Mr. Hearst's New York *Daily Mirror*, recalled that "until a decade ago" "floor shows in which most entertainers are fairies, men playing the female roles" had played "midtown night clubs" that "catered to the twisted trade." Apparently, a police crackdown in the late thirties had driven "the pouting queens and Lesbians" to Greenwich Village.[10]

Although Mortimer's short chapter on the Village in the forties — "Where Men Wear Lace Lingerie" — is a lexicon of period homophobia, it also contains some fairly reliable information. He knew about the "female homos' hangouts" on Third Street but said one was presided over by "an old and disgusting excuse for a woman" who induced thousands of innocent girls "to lead unnatural lives." And he may have exaggerated a little about the "congenital abnormals" — "male magdalens" and "female monstrosities" — who engaged in "unspeakable saturnalias" that tourists could view for a price. For Mortimer's money, the Village was a trap where "Nature's mishaps" preyed on the unsuspecting, where "fags" and "skirted women-hunters" were always on the prowl for victims.

He couldn't recommend the Village to tourists, but Mortimer thought segregating the "variants" into one section "where an eye can be kept on them" was a good idea. He regretted that one institution — "the most notorious Lesbian night club in New York," located "on Second Avenue, south of 14th Street, on the lower East Side" (p. 75) — had slipped through the net. That was the 181 Club, of course, where most of my friends worked at one time or another.

Despite hate-mongers like Mortimer, not to mention frequent police raids, people still wanted to see gay floor shows. The clubs thus became a lucrative underworld business that the mob kept afloat through favors and payoffs. The gay entertainers I knew saw mobsters as welcome allies in an endless struggle with the extortionate tactics of greedy cops. (Remember that the rioters at Stonewall pelted the detectives with *coins* — pennies and dimes, nickels and quarters.)

THE PERSISTENT DESIRE

A strange item in *The Valachi Papers* bears out this long-standing association and raises other questions. It was sensational news in 1952 when Anna Genovese sued her husband of many years, Don Vito, for a divorce. She talked a lot about the family's enterprises, but no move was made to shut her up. One of Don Vito's lieutenants, however, paid for his indiscretions with his life. He'd been "a partner first with Genovese in some of his nightclubs in the Greenwich Village area and then with Mrs. Genovese in running some others, catering to Lesbians, which were not, in her words, 'part of the Syndicate.'"[11]

Details of these transactions may remain forever murky. But didn't I hear that the manager of the 181 Club was a Pete Petillo? Was he a brother to Anna Genovese, née Petillo? And was the 181 one of the family businesses? Certainly, Don Vito himself had deep roots in the Village and numerous ties, including his legitimate cover operations on Thompson Street.[12]

People who live in glass houses don't throw stones, and I've never had any quarrel with the gay world's underworld connections. I believe the mob is no more crooked than the Democrats and Republicans, as Mario Puzo pointed out somewhere. To me it's all just another chapter of lesbian history.

But the people really prepared to write this chapter should consider doing it before too long. Our recent history is oral history, and it's important to capture the memories of those days while we still have women (and men) around who lived them. These testimonies can explain vital links in the chain of circumstances that led us out of the underworld, to Stonewall and beyond.

To all you gay entertainers from way back when: after you read this, if you read this, maybe some of you will reconsider speaking up, getting yourselves recorded and videotaped. I've done my best with the material I had, but I was hardly born back then. Only you know the million and one stories from those times and places, and you'll never have a bigger and better audience than you do right now.

In that spirit, I welcome complaints, corrections, and additions to this history. In fact, nothing would please me more than to hand over the mike and see all you kids back in the spotlight, where you belong.

Notes

1. Joan Nestle, *A Restricted Country* (Ithaca, N.Y.: Firebrand Books, 1987), p. 162.

2. Some of them have seen Michelle Parkerson's film *Storme: The Lady of the Jewel Box* but didn't know Storme when she was with the Jewel Box Review, 1955–1969. A lot of them were out of the business by then anyway. They knew guys from the Jewel Box, and remembered Tommy, the dyke who did the show before Storme.

3. Laurence Senelick, "The Evolution of the Male Impersonator on the Nineteenth-Century Popular Stage," *Essays in Theatre* 1, no. 1 (November 1982): 31–44.

4. Douglas Gilbert, *American Vaudeville: Its Life and Times* (New York: Dover, 1968). See pp. 395–410 for a list of "Fifty Years of Standard Acts, 1880–1930."

5. Charles W. Stein, ed., *American Vaudeville* (New York: Da Capo Press, 1984), p. 114. Tilley's contemporary and a female impersonator of equal prestige was Julian Eltinge, who, like Vesta, appeared in early films. See photographs of them both in Homer Dickens, *What a Drag: Men as Women and Women as Men in the Movies* (New York: Morrow, 1982).

6. Reading Sara Maitland's book *Vesta Tilley* (London: Virago, 1986) would make you think Vesta was the straightest woman who ever lived, an impression she definitely cultivated. Her husband was the son of a well-to-do Jewish music hall entrepreneur who was knighted in 1919, making her Lady de Frece. She also made films and played a Royal Command Variety Performance in 1912, but "when she appeared in her trousers Queen Mary turned to the other ladies of the Court and all of them buried their faces in their programmes, keeping themselves pure from the shocking sight of female legs" (p. 47). Bummer.

7. Senelick, "The Evolution of the Male Impersonator," pp. 36–37.

8. Jonathan Ned Katz, *Gay/Lesbian Almanac* (New York: Harper & Row, 1983), p. 402.

9. Female impersonation had been considered an acceptable fixture in vaudeville and Broadway follies, without any negative identification of the performers as homosexuals. A female impersonator from the old days testified in 1977 to that peculiar blind spot: "Until the nightclub came along in the '30s, 'homo' was not inevitably attached to female impersonation" (quoted in Kaier Curtin, *We Can Always Call Them Bulgarians* [Boston: Alyson, 1987], p. 18).

10. Chicago: Ziff Davis, 1948, pp. 74, 75. *Washington Confidential* (New York: Crown, 1951), authored by Lee Mortimer with Jack Lait, offers some insights into the early homosexual purges of the McCarthy era. *Chicago Confidential,* by the same authors, I haven't seen. According to *New York Confidential,* "it is a law violation for entertainers to appear in 'drag' (clothes of the opposite sex)" (p. 74). The police consistently busted men dressed as women for attempting to defraud the public. In their disguises, they might lure men, especially servicemen during the war, into hallways with the promise of a good time. These "Gay Deceivers" were collared by the cops and their images collected by the famous photographer Weegee (Arthur Fellig) in his historic collection *Naked City* (Cincinnati: Zebra Picture Books, 1945; see especially pp. 174–175). One of Weegee's photos — "Transvestite in a Police Van, 1941" — was sold as a postcard by the Museum of Modern Art (New York) in conjunction with its 1991 show "Art of the Forties."

11. Peter Maas, *The Valachi Papers* (New York: Simon & Schuster, 1986), p. 191.

12. Ibid., pp. 90–91, 117.

Cheryl Clarke

Of Althea and Flaxie

In 1943 Althea was a welder
very dark
very butch
and very proud
loved to cook, sew, and drive a car
and did not care who knew she kept company with a woman
who met her every day after work
in a tight dress and high heels
light-skinned and high-cheekboned
who loved to shoot, fish, play poker
and did not give a damn who knew her "man" was a woman.

Althea was gay and strong in 1945
and could sing a good song
from underneath her welder's mask
and did not care who heard her sing her song to a woman.

Flaxie was careful and faithful
mindful of her Southern upbringing
watchful of her tutored grace
Long as they treated her like a lady
she did not give a damn who called her a "bulldagger."

In 1950 Althea wore suits and ties
Flaxie's favorite colors were pink and blue
People openly challenged their flamboyance
but neither cared a fig who thought them "queer" or "funny."

When the girls bragged over break of their sundry loves,
Flaxie blithely told them her old lady Althea took her dancing
every weekend

and did not care who knew she loved the mind of a woman.

In 1955 when Flaxie got pregnant
and Althea lost her job
Flaxie got herself on relief
and did not care how many caseworkers
threatened midnight raids.

Althea was set up and went to jail
for writing numbers in 1958
Flaxie visited her every week with gifts
and hungered openly for her through the bars
and did not give a damn who knew she waited for a woman.

When her mother died in 1965 in New Orleans
Flaxie demanded that Althea walk beside her in the funeral procession
and did not care how many aunts and uncles knew she slept with a
    woman.

When she died in 1970
Flaxie fought Althea's proper family not to have her laid out in lace
and dressed the body herself
and did not care who knew she'd made her way with a woman.

Sandy Kern

The following is excerpted from an oral history tape made with Sandy Kern, a Jewish, working-class, butch lesbian, at the Lesbian Herstory Archives, New York, 1984. From the LHA collection.

Sandy: The year was 1945. It was during the war. I was about fifteen and we were having one of our blackouts, maneuvers — I forget what they were called, but we had these blackout practices, and we were sitting in the dark, me and my friend Minnie, who calls herself Mickey now.

We were sitting on the stoop in Brooklyn and I had my arms around her because it was dark. I wasn't scared; I was happy for the darkness, because I was able to put my arms around her and smell her. She had a very particular and beautiful smell. And so I was sitting like that with her, and she was embracing me too, when the lights went on, quite suddenly, or so it seemed, because I was oblivious to the time. And there was a woman who lived in the building that we were sitting in front of and she saw us holding each other that way. That was the first time I heard the word *lesbian*. She said in a very typical Jewish way, she said, "Look at this! A couple of lesbians." That was the first time that I heard that word.

The very next day I ran to the library, the Glenmore Street Library, and I looked up the word *lesbian* and I felt so proud of myself because it talked about the Isle of Lesbos and it mentioned something about Radclyffe Hall, who wrote something called *The Well of Loneliness*, which I took out that very same day and read and reread and reread.

So that was my first experience in hearing that I had a label: besides being a girl, beside being Jewish, I was a lesbian. Yippee!

Many years later, after I left home, I was with this woman who was several years older than I. I won't go into it now as to how I knew her, but we became lovers, and we had arranged to meet in Prospect Park in Brooklyn.

We met and we walked and suddenly we were pounced upon by this pack of young men. I mean, that was the first time that I was really frightened. I was carrying a book that they took and tore up, screaming, "Lesbians," and, "Weirdos." We ran. We ran out as fast as we could. She

I'm proud of my lesbianism, and I can swim too. Central Park, 1950s.

Missing my woman and feeling sad. On the roof of Amboy Street, Brooklyn, 1950s.

Snapshots from Sandy Kern's photo album

Above: Having fun and feeling good on the beach. Riis Park, Brooklyn, 1950s.

Right: Waiting for my ship to come in. The Battery, South Street Seaport, 1960s.

got into a cab, I got onto a bus, and one of them came onto the bus with me and I was really frightened. I felt like a hunted animal, because nobody came to my assistance. Everybody seemed hostile. I didn't know where to run. He finally got off — I guess he had his kicks by then.

Joan: Do you remember how you were dressed?

S: I was dressed the way I dressed for many, many years. It was sort of a uniform, I guess. I had sneakers on, dungarees — in those days, we used to roll them up — and a sweatshirt tucked into my pants. That's the way I was dressed. My hair was short, as it is now. I had no makeup on. But she was dressed as a woman; she wore a dress, a summer dress. She had long hair, which she braided and wore around her head. I have a picture of her somewhere I'll show you. She was German, American-German, but she looked like a real German *frau*. She was very robust. [*Cups her hands under her breasts*] She wasn't obvious by a long shot, but the two of us together — they knew right away that we were lesbians, and they hounded us through the park. I think that was the worst experience I ever had. There were other experiences, though.

When I lived in the Village [Greenwich Village, New York], I could not leave my home and go out into the street without hearing some kid calling, "Hey, lesbian," and they threw things. One kid, I remember, had a dog and he hit the dog with this chain. When he saw me, he threw the chain at me. "Lesbian." But I think he used another word. "Lezzie," that's it. "Hey, lezzie, look at the lezzie, queer, creep." I mean, out loud in the street. That only happened in the Village though. Because I lived there in the Village.

J: How did it make you feel, day after day, when you went out in the streets and heard those things? How did you keep a sense of yourself?

S: Well, I had to go to work and I had to compromise. I always wore skirts to work and I never had trouble when I wore a skirt and lipstick. That was a sort of shield. I remember wearing ... a Playtex rubber girdle for years. I remember coming home and just tearing out of my clothes and changing into my comfortable jeans and sneakers. I didn't let those creeps make my life miserable. I never did. I went out at all hours of the night. So they yelled at me. So what! I learned to lock them out of my head. I mean, it was only when they came after me physically that frightened me. But I didn't lose my identity. I knew who I was and I wasn't ashamed of what I was. Right from the beginning, as I said, I always felt proud and special.

I used to have this fantasy that there was a ray of light shining on me wherever I went. That's the way I really felt: special.

Ira Jeffries

My mother's daughter

I was fortunate to have had a mother who was a lesbian, and a father whose oldest sister and niece were involved with women. Unfortunately, my great-grandmother, Fannie Koontz, who raised my mother after my grandmother Odessa was killed in an auto accident, had no such inclination, and was so intolerant of such a lifestyle that Bonita, my mother, was not allowed to bring those "bulldagger women" into our home.

Fannie Koontz, who was illiterate, but only in the sense that she couldn't read or write, was sharp as a tack when it came to figures and money. In fact, she was a gambler and a card shark who played the numbers all of her life and hit frequently for big bucks. Granny always had a bosom full of money, the only place she kept her stash. She also was a great cook, and worked in "white folks' kitchens" until cataracts stole her sight and arthritic knees crippled her.

Bonita was almost a high school graduate and was a fantastic dancer with a flair for comedy. Ethel Waters, the actress, wanted to take my mother on the road with her, but my grandmother would not hear of it because of Ethel's reputation as a "bulldagger" — and then, of course, there was little ole me to raise. I'm sure that my mother resented Fannie Koontz for preventing her from becoming an entertainer and having as her mentor the great Ethel Waters. I remember the arguments when I was three, four, and five years old that only stopped when I screamed at the top of my little voice.

Over the years, people have asked me when I came out or when I realized that I was gay or a lesbian. After some thought, I came to the conclusion that I've always been gay, and I've always been out — it's just that I didn't know it at the time. I remember "fooling around" with other little girls at the very early age of five. I also remember taking a little girl behind a door in the hallway of my apartment building on West 119th Street one summer day, and asking her to take down her panties so that I could "see her down there." She was very cooperative. I was a precocious child. Aggressive too, and yet shy.

59

THE PERSISTENT DESIRE

I could say that officially I came out at the age of fourteen, in 1946, when my mother, who had been observing my behavior with my little girlfriends from the neighborhood, asked me point-blank if I liked girls. Luckily for me, Bonita and I had established the kind of relationship in which we could discuss anything, and so, after some initial hemming and hawing, some denial and hesitation, I reluctantly said yes, I did.

Then, as I kept my gaze glued to the floor, my mother proceeded to give me her consent and her blessings for my lesbian life. She also warned me about "the life" and society's condemnation of "funny women." At this time, I didn't know Bonita's sexual orientation, which is why I felt so awkward and embarrassed. I found out a year later, when a "friend" of Bonnie, as my mother was affectionately called in her circle, told me, adding that her mother and Bonnie were lovers.

My father, Eddie, on the other hand, resented the fact that I was gravitating toward a lesbian lifestyle, but he could do nothing about it because I lived with my mother. I am sure they had innumerable discussions about it, because I remember that whenever I used to visit my daddy, he would trash my mother and grandmother, blaming Fannie Koontz for their separation. But Daddy was twenty-two years older than my mother, Bonita was a handsome woman, and he had hit her once too often.

Daddy had hoped that someday I would marry so that he could gift me with a beautiful set of Greek china. Well, you know, I never saw that china. When I was around eighteen years old, I fell from my daddy's favor when I wrote him a hellified letter "reading him" for all those years of verbal abuse he had heaped on my mother. He never forgave me for that letter, he told me some ten years later. He also told me, when he realized that I was "out and never coming back," "I can outfuck you any day!" I was astonished at his language, because he never spoke like that to me. At that moment I felt sorry for my father, this man who felt it necessary to make such a sexist, macho statement to his daughter. Even so, I understood his hurt and disappointment regarding my sexual orientation and his realization that I would never marry.

Bonita, who passed on in 1981, was my best friend as well as my mother. I could discuss anything with her and she would advise me as best she could. Oh yes, she made mistakes, and some serious errors in judgment on my behalf, but considering the repressive, oppressive, and homophobic environment she was raised in and had to deal with every day of her life, I understand what influenced her decisions.

What sustained me through some very difficult times, and saved my life on many occasions, is the sense of dignity, pride, and self-worth Bonita taught me. She encouraged me in all my endeavors, and when I spoke to her of my "big dreams," which were rather unrealistic for a young black girl growing up in the 1940s, she never once said that it couldn't be done. She told me instead that I could do anything I wanted, and become whatever I wanted, if I wanted to badly enough, but that it was up to me.

*Ira Jeffries (far right), with her girlfriend, Snowbaby, and her mother,
Bonita (standing), celebrating Ira's sixteenth birthday in a Harlem club.
"I'm the butch but I'm not allowed to dress as I please yet."*

She never dictated the life path I should follow except to insist that I
get an education so that I would have more options than she and my
grandmother had had and wouldn't have to work in factories or become
anyone's maid. I think I've turned out pretty well, considering I've been
in hell's kitchen and back.

I have always considered myself butch identified. I have never felt
feminine. I wore dresses because my mother bought my clothes, but as
soon as I drew my first paycheck at age seventeen, I paid down on my first
suit. Over the years women have asked why I dress so mannish. My
response has been that I like wearing man-tailored clothing; it's the way I
choose to express myself. It is becoming more apparent every day that I
am exactly where I'm supposed to be, and I am doing exactly what I'm
supposed to be doing.

Elizabeth Lapovsky Kennedy &
Madeline Davis

"They was no one to mess with": The construction of the butch role in the lesbian community of the 1940s and 1950s

Our research on the history of the lesbian bar community of Buffalo, New York, during the 1940s and 1950s has been unique in showing the multifaceted meaning of butch-fem roles,[1] which constituted a symbolic pattern that pervaded all aspects of social and cultural life. Butch-fem roles were a deeply felt expression of individual identity and a personal code guiding appearance and sexual behavior; they were a system for organizing social relationships delineating which members of the community could have relationships with whom; furthermore, they were working-class lesbians' only means of expressing resistance to the heterosexual world in this prepolitical era of gay and lesbian history.

Scholars have not yet given this same kind of scrutiny to the uses of masculinity and femininity in the gay male community, nor have they attempted to deepen our understanding of gender by comparing lesbian and gay communities. On the surface, the butch and the gay fairy or queen seem to have had similar positions in the forties and fifties: they both used the inversion of gender roles to announce gayness. However, as we came to know the lesbian community of the past, the differences between the butch and the queen became apparent. After listening to hours of butch life stories, we realized that butches rarely used camp humor as a way of presenting their vision of the world;[2] rather, they surrounded themselves with an aura of solemnity. In this paper, we explore the position of the butch in lesbian culture in order to illuminate this puzzling lack of camp.[3] We first look at the use of masculinity in the construction of butch appearance in the 1940s and 1950s, exploring its meaning for the individual and the process of community resistance. We then look at the relationship between masculinity and butch sexuality and compare the role of the butch with that of the queen.[4]

This work derives from a nearly completed manuscript, *Boots of Leather, Slippers of Gold: The History of a Lesbian Community*. The research is based on oral histories collected from forty-five narrators, of whom thirty-three actually participated in some aspect of the Buffalo public lesbian community during the 1930s, 1940s, or 1950s. Of these, twenty-five are Euro-American, six African-American, and two Native American. Our method is ethnohistorical; that is, we use oral histories to construct a community history.[5] The working-class lesbian bar community of the forties was fairly homogeneous: mainly white with a few individual Native Americans and African-Americans. In the fifties, the community became class stratified and racially integrated. Although butch-fem culture existed in all subcommunities, the butch role was less "obvious" or "flamboyant" in the more upwardly mobile crowd, which is therefore not considered in this paper. A distinct African-American lesbian social group centered around open house parties existed in Buffalo from at least the 1950s, and most likely earlier. In the process of integration, the African-American community kept its distinct base but also interacted with the predominantly white bar community, and whites began to attend African-American parties. To the best of our knowledge, the differences in the butch role in the African-American and Euro-American subcommunities were not great; therefore, we do not treat them separately. We intend our generalizations to be true of both cultures, but to end the invisibility of African-Americans in history, we sometimes indicate the cultural or racial identity of the narrators.

Before exploring the specific uses of masculinity in the Buffalo lesbian community, we want to review why masculinity takes on such importance in the development of twentieth-century lesbian social life. Several scholars have addressed this question. Modern lesbian culture developed in the context of the late nineteenth and early twentieth centuries, when elaborate hierarchical distinctions were made between the sexes, and gender was a fundamental organizing principle of cultural life. In documenting the lives of passing women, Jonathan Katz argues that, in the context of this nineteenth-century polarization of masculinity and femininity, one of the few ways for women to achieve independence in work and travel and to escape passivity was by assuming the male role.[6] In a similar vein, Jeffrey Weeks holds that lesbians' adoption of male images at the turn of the century broke through women's and lesbians' invisibility, a necessity if lesbians were to become part of public life.[7] Expanding this approach, Esther Newton sets the adoption of male imagery in the context of the New Woman's search for an independent life, and delineates how male imagery helped to break through nineteenth-century assumptions about the sexless nature of women and introduce overt sexuality into women's relationships with one another.[8] Finally, George Chauncey has argued that during the early twentieth century there was no cultural concept of ungendered sexual relationships. For men to have sex with men, they needed to recreate masculine and feminine sexual identities, and we assume the same to be true for women.[9]

The key identifiers for butchness during the forties and fifties were image and sexuality. In the forties, in bars on the weekend, butches cut a masculine appearance. When we asked Reggie, a butch narrator, if she could tell that Ralph Martin's was a gay bar on her first visit by the way people touched, she replied, "No, you could tell by their dress ... the butches were very butchy, very, ties, shirts." These forties butches put a great deal of time and energy into their appearance. Arden remembers, "They would starch [their shirts] until they would break. If there was a wrinkle in them, they would put them back in the water." They wore cuff links, and those who could afford them wore jackets. Pants were just becoming acceptable for women during the war, and butches started wearing them when going out to the bars, though they had to have them custom tailored, since ladies' pants were not yet easily available. They wore flat shoes, the most masculine style they could find, and wore their hair cut short over their ears. In addition, they cultivated masculine mannerisms in the little details of self-presentation — manner of walking, sitting, and holding a drink, and tone of voice. The total image, although masculine, was not aggressive or rough. Our narrators describe their image as "severe," never tough. Reggie contrasts butches of the forties with the rowdy bar lesbians of the next decade: "Your butches were butchy, but they were kind, you know. Not saying that there's not any kind butches [later]; don't misunderstand. They weren't the macho type, and they didn't go out and want to fight right away."

The masculine image that butches projected was of necessity ambiguous — otherwise they would have been passing women, not butches. All the forties butches we spoke to knew women who passed as men, but saw themselves as different. Leslie comments philosophically on a passing woman of her acquaintance who wore a binder and looked like a man: "[Perhaps] this was the lesser of two evils, rather than be in the middle like us, not looking like men or women. But we weren't trying to fool the public." They saw the butch identity, the butch essence, as distinct from male, and when classifying themselves as other than butch, they used the term *homo*.

One aspect of butchness was personal identity, a lesbian's expressing what she felt about herself. But there was also a more social dimension, that of resistance to heterosexual norms. Appearing butch announced lesbians to the public. Somewhere in their life stories, most of our narrators explain that to appear butch meant that they were "not denying" who they were. The concept of "not denying" is at the core of the resistance of the forties and fifties. By displaying butchness, lesbians became visible to one another, thereby becoming a recognizable presence in a hostile world. During the forties, when lesbians were discreet about separating work and family from social life, appearing butch was particularly powerful. Those who did took tremendous risks. Our butch narrators vividly remember being recognized for who they were, whenever they went out, and contrast their situation to that of fems. Leslie observes:

> Fems didn't look like homos. When they were walking on the street they didn't get any harassment, so gay life was not that difficult for them. The only time they had any trouble was when they would go to the bar on Saturday night. There might be some straights making comments there. And afterwards, when you would go out to eat at a restaurant. That got so bad that I stopped doing it. It wasn't worth it to have to deal with all the men making comments and poking fun. The biggest problem is going out on the street, and who bothers a fem when she goes out alone? She doesn't have to face that kind of thing.

The butch role was so powerful in drawing attention to lesbians that it caused discomfort within the community. Some butches were thought to go too far and were derogatorily described as "being obvious about" or even "advertising" who they were. Many butches felt they needed to be more circumspect about their appearance to protect their own identity and avoid problems in relation to work, family, and the law. In addition, some lesbians felt that "being obvious" was not an effective strategy for change, because it aroused too much hostility. Dee, for instance, disliked obviousness:

> Well, some of the ones that went to extremes I thought [were] rather ridiculous. Again, I always found it repugnant to wear a sign on my forehead. 'Cause to me, we live in a straight society and we should have to conform. We can be gay when we're in our own crowd at a house party; when we're out in public we should sort of not flaunt gaiety. I never went for that idea.

Her objections to the obvious butch-fem image go beyond that of her personal discomfort. She did not and does not think that approaching the straight world in this manner was wise for lesbians. We questioned her about whether or not there was a positive side to the obviousness of the butch role, such as asserting that lesbians exist: "Not necessarily, not if they're being scornful. They could make their way as a lesbian without, shall I say, shocking the general public. I think there's other ways to attain that end of lesbianism."

The basic elements of butch appearance continued into the fifties but were transformed. The years of socializing together in the bars gave rise to a distinct culture and identity, as well as increasing pride. This manifested itself particularly in fifties lesbians' willingness to reach out to newcomers and to introduce people to lesbian life. This new lesbian consciousness, in combination with rebellion against the increased repression against gays and lesbians during the McCarthy era and the rigidification of sex roles during the early years of the cold war, created a bolder attitude toward the straight world. The most rebellious subgroup of this community, those who are often stereotyped as "bulldaggers" or "diesel dykes" and whom we call bar dykes, expressed their resistance primarily through the butch role.[10] The bar dyke was little inclined to accommodate the conventions of femininity and pushed to diminish the time she spent hiding and to eliminate the division between her public and private selves. She also added a new element of resistance: the willingness to stand up for and defend with physical force her fem's and her own right to be who she was.

Bar dykes, black, Indian, and white, cultivated an extremely masculine look, generally wearing more articles of male clothing than butches in the forties or than the more upwardly mobile crowd of the fifties. Since they went out to bars every night, not just on weekends, they had to have appropriate butch clothes for both casual wear and for dressing up. Regulars at Bingo's in the midfifties remember white butches wearing sport jackets, chino pants or sometimes men's dress pants, and men's shirts — button-downs, western shirts, or tuxedo shirts with ties on the weekend. When out during the week, they would dress more casually in shirts and chinos. Among younger white bar dykes in the late fifties, blue jeans and t-shirts became popular, particularly during the week. The late fifties image is captured by Ronni's description of herself: "I played a very dominant, possessive, butch, truck-driver role at that time. I wore a crew cut and shirts. I used to have my pants tapered at the bottom. I'd have my cuffs taken in, you know. I'd go have my hair cut at the barber." On weekends they would still dress up but strictly in men's clothes. Penny loafers and dress boots were common, often worn with argyle socks. White bar dykes wore their hair in greased-back DAs.[11] Black studs adopted a more formal look even on weeknights, wearing starched white shirts with formal collars and dark dress pants whenever they went out. Their shoes were men's Florsheim dress shoes worn with dark nylon socks. They had their hair processed and wore it combed back at the sides and cut square at the back. None of these butches, white or black, ever carried purses.

Certain items of male clothing acquired a special significance among bar dykes. The t-shirt symbolized the daring of lesbians wearing male clothing, as Sandy recalls with particular fondness:

> This is very funny but it's really the truth: if you think about it, butches, we've always worn t-shirts. That was our thing, right? And most of the time, why did we wear t-shirts? Because we didn't wear a bra. We came way before the ERA movement. When did they start this big thing, about fifteen years ago? We had thrown those away. We just threw them away and put on t-shirts. And boy, when you wore a t-shirt — *wow* — they didn't look to see where your tits were. Oh, you have a t-shirt! We were the Original.

A 1950s butch:
Lynne Berry in Worcester,
Massachusetts, 1955

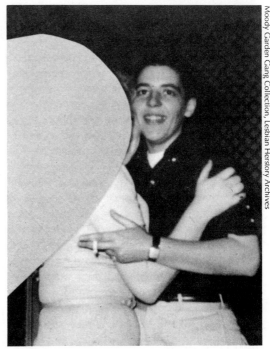

Sandy was small breasted; not all butches were. Little Gerry, a full-breasted butch, remembers fems of the time joking, "Butches have all the cleavage, and they don't even want it." Breasts unquestionably presented a problem for those cultivating a butch image. Fuller-breasted butches had to choose clothes that camouflaged their bosoms. They would often sew the cups of their bras so that their breasts wouldn't look so pointy. Butches might also wear binders, strips of cloth or Ace bandages wrapped around the chest. They were not tight, but gave the appearance of a smooth front so that men's shirts would fit better. Also, binders helped butches look ambiguous enough on the streets to avoid some male harassment.

The differences between the image of the bar dyke and that of the forties butch extended beyond clothing to their mannerisms. "Rough" and "tough" were commonly used to describe the bar dyke, adjectives that were never used for the forties butch.[12] Bar dykes' entire comportment reflected this image. D.J., who came out in the forties but was at home with the bar dyke crowd, identified willingness to fight as a distinctive mark of the butch: "It used to be strictly the appearance of the person, the way you handled yourself. In other words you had to knock about sixteen people around to let them know you were [butch]." This tough image prevailed not only in fighting, but in one's entire presentation of self. For instance, Little Gerry recalls learning: "If you were in a bar, and someone called your name, you never turned around smiling. I remember Sandy [a more experienced butch] objected to that kind of friendliness."

The attitude of bar dykes toward their clothing differed notably from that of butches of the forties or of the elite fifties crowd. Both butches and studs felt it important to appear masculine as much of the time as possible. Partly this was because they went out to bars during the week as well as on weekends. But more than this, butches and studs felt driven to dress like who they were and to rebel against the conventional standards of femininity. Sandy, a white leader, worked at an office job at the end of the decade and was required to wear feminine clothes to work. "I hated it," she remembers, and explains how, once she found the bars, she would not wear skirts anymore:

> I wasn't in the gay scene, so it didn't matter if someone saw me, 'cause they didn't know me anyhow. And then after I started going around — found the gay bars, the gay people — I just went the way I felt like going, and that was ... my butch way. And then after you meet different girls — well, you couldn't meet them after work. You'd have to go home and change, and then you couldn't leave the house. It was daylight and the neighbors would see you, so you couldn't go out until it was dark, and then sneak out. And then if you were working and went out for lunch or something, you wouldn't want anyone from the gay crowd that thought you were "wow" saying something, to see you prancing around in a little skirt — why that would just blow the whole shot. So that ended the job.

Butches and studs took other extreme measures to appear butch as much of the time as possible. Arlette, a black fem, remembers how studs who lived at home would change their clothes in the car so that they would not offend their parents but could look the way they wanted when they were out:

> I knew girls right here in Buffalo would go out, and they would have to change clothes in cars ... [This one girl] didn't want her parents to see her in these men's type of clothes, so she would change clothes in the car or in somebody's house. Then, before we could take her back home, she'd have to change clothes again, to get back to the girls' stuff, before she could go home.

Bar dykes had created a culture that valued asserting the truth of who they were. They looked down on those who couldn't take risks, particularly the more upwardly mobile lesbians. By the late fifties, they had become competitive about butchness and held that to be truly butch, the best butch, you had to look butch all the time.[13] Sandy articulates the importance of this image:

> The ones that were butch were butch. Now there might have been the butches that were still the sissies — they'd come and order a drink and

hide in the bathroom all night, stuff like that ... afraid someone would see them. And they couldn't have short hair like us, they couldn't wear clothes — if they didn't want to, I mean, that's a different story, but most of them wanted to, but they were afraid to. Candy asses, you know. And of course, the butches that were butches, like myself, the rest of us that were, we ruled them, because we didn't give a shit. But those candy asses — took their girl, shut up, you know. They had no say-so.

Not all the bar dykes managed to look butch all the time; many still modified their appearance as required by work, family, and partners. However, the respected leaders of the late fifties and early sixties rarely altered their appearance. They were butch all the time, and that was part of their charisma.

Society's reactions to butches and butch-fem couples were usually hostile, and often violent. Being noticed on the streets and harassed dominates the memories of our black and white narrators. Ronni's description is typical:

Oh, you were looked down upon socially. When I walked down the street, [people in] cars used to pull over and say, "Hey, faggot, hey, lezzie." They called you names with such varying ... such maliciousness. And they hated to see you when you were with a girl. I was the one that was mostly picked on, because I was identified. I was playing the male part in this relationship and most guys hated it. Women would look at me in kind of a confused looking [way], you know: straight women would look at me in kind of wonder.

Piri, a black stud, remembers how the police used to harass her for dressing like a man:

I've had the police walk up to me and say, "Get out of the car." I'm drivin'. They say, "Get out of the car," and I get out. And they say, "What kind of shoes you got on? You got on men's shoes?" And I say, "No, I got on women's shoes." I got on some basket-weave women's shoes. And he say, "Well, you damn lucky." 'Cause everything else I had on were men's — shirt, pants. At that time, when they pick you up, if you didn't have two garments that belong to a woman, you could go to jail ... and the same thing with a man ... They call it male impersonation or female impersonation and they'd take you downtown. It would really just be an inconvenience ... It would give them the opportunity to whack the shit out of you.

All our narrators mention this law — although some say it required three pieces of female clothing, not two, and we have been unable to confirm the existence of such a law — and were clever at getting around it while maintaining their masculine image. However, the police used such statutes to harass black lesbians more than whites.

Not surprisingly, with the severe harassment, the butch role in these communities during the fifties became identified with defending oneself and one's girl in the rough bars and on the streets. Sandy describes the connection between her appearance and her need to be an effective fighter. The cultivated masculine mannerisms were necessary on the street.

> Well, you had to be strong — roll with the punches, more or less — if some guy whacked you off [put you down], said, "Hey, babe," you know. Most of the time you got all your punches for the fem anyhow, you know. It was because they hated you... "How come this queer can have you and I can do this and that..." You didn't hardly have time to say anything, but all she would have to say [was] no, when he said, "Let's go, I'll get you away from this." And she would say no. He [would be] so rejected by this no that he would, boom, go to you. You would naturally get up and fight the guy — at least, I would. And we all did at that time, those that were out in their pants and t-shirts — that's what we did at that time. And we'd knock them on their ass, and if one couldn't do it, we'd all help. And that's how we kept our women. They cared for us, but you don't think for a minute they would have stayed with us too long or something if we stood there and just were silent ... Nine times out of ten, she'd be with you to help you with your black eye and your split lip. Or you kicked his ass and she bought you dinner then. But you never failed, or you tried not to ... You were there, you were gay, you were queer, and you were masculine.

The aggressive butch role was the most developed in the leaders of the late fifties. Their leadership was based on being able to defend themselves and their friends in a hostile environment, and they took this responsibility extremely seriously. According to Vic, "It was strictly, you go in the bar and whoever was the baddest butch ... survived, and if you didn't, you got your face broke and that was it. So you had to be there." Annie, a white fem, concurs that these leaders were strong and effective fighters: "You went like into a straight bar, especially with the butches, and they had strength; they was no one to mess with. Some guy would start a fight with them, or call them 'queer' or 'lezzie' or whatever, then they'd ... Too bad for the guy. He'd better be strong." The whole atmosphere generated fear, which further fostered the tough stand even in those, like Stormy, who were hesitant about fighting: "Lots of us had to look real tough, because underneath we weren't really secure about ourselves. We were scared."

The pressure on butches and studs to not deny who they were and to defend themselves generated an extraordinarily complex and confusing relationship to masculinity. These butches, particularly the leaders, were extremely masculine, and often thought of social dynamics in terms of male and female relationships. Yet at the same time they were not men; they were "queer." They did not refer to one another by masculine pronouns, and they adopted unisex rather than exclusively masculine names. Throughout their life stories, they emphasize acquiring masculine characteristics while not being male. The prominence of masculinity in their vision of themselves and in their understanding of the world is perhaps responsible for the 1980s confusion between these butches and passing women, and the assumption that these women were trying to be men. But to recognize their masculinity and not their "queerness" is a distortion of their culture and their consciousness.

Butch appearance reflected this ambiguous relationship between masculinity and "queerness." Although in most situations the severely masculine clothing of these butches identified them as queer, these same clothes could also serve as a cover. Butches frequently exploited the option of looking like men on the surface to draw less attention to themselves on the street. Stormy, one of the older bar dykes, explains why some women taped their chests to look flat: "It was easier to walk down the street if at first glance people thought you were a man." She also notes: "It was the local core butches who usually looked more butch. Sometimes it was a matter of what neighborhood you came from. You might feel safer if you went out dressed more like a guy so people wouldn't hassle you late at night." Although they cultivated that cover, they relied on it only to move through difficult situations.

Similarly, as macho as these butches were as fighters, they were always aware that they were not men. In tough situations they thought strategically and used all their resources, including their femaleness. In confrontations with the police, if they thought it would help them, they would bring up that they were women. They regularly appeared in court in feminine clothes to play on judges' prejudices about women's capabilities and receive a lenient judgment. Sandy's story is typical:

> I didn't have any [court clothes]; I borrowed them ... That was the one great advantage of being gay ... you beat the court. I beat 'em every charge ... Beat all of my cases ... [They were for] assault. One was on a police officer ... He could [identify me], but they didn't believe I did it to him. They didn't believe I could do it. He was in there, his head was all wrapped up; he had a concussion, broken nose, eyes — and [he was] about a six-footer. And there I am, looking as pathetic as I could. And I remember the judge, he says, "You did that? ... Why you couldn't weigh a hundred pounds soaking wet," he said to me. I says, "Ninety-eight." He says, "I don't believe you did this; no, I have to throw this out." Cop's name was Donovan. Dick Donovan ... He was a troublemaker. That happened in the Mardi Gras, that I got his ass ... 'Cause I always say, Swing, don't stop, because don't give them a chance. Don't give them a chance, they'll kick the shit out of you.

In their interactions with men in the bars, butches wanted to be respected as men but not treated as if they were men. Vic, who particularly objected to men's locker room talk about women, summarizes her philosophy on this subject:

As butch as I am, I demand respect from men, straight men, not from gay guys, but I demand it from straight men. You know, not to opening doors and giving me their bar stool. But there is a definite limit drawn to what they can say to me. Even though they talk to me as a butch or a man, however they relate to me, they will not talk to me the way they talk to their locker room buddies or something; I don't want to hear that. And I demand respect from them. Straight men, I mean. I have to. Can't talk and sit around, "Well, how are you doing with your old lady?" and this and that. They would never talk to me like that. I wouldn't allow it for a minute ... I don't expect them to do anything for me, but I demand that little bit of respect. I am a woman, and you're gonna treat me like one regardless of how I am dressed. Don't treat me like I'm a butch queer, 'cause I won't allow it. Then you're gonna have to hit me or I'm gonna hit you. Because I get very physical along those lines with [guys]. I'll have to go down [fight; go to the mat], you know, if it's over my woman or over myself. Or you, whoever I would be with, 'cause I can't allow that.

The absolute seriousness of these butches' relation to masculinity is striking. The only times this lesbian bar culture played with masculine and feminine identities (other than in the courts) were on rare occasions when butches would go out dressed in extremely feminine garb.[14] Such masquerading, however, did not throw the meaning of masculine identity for women into question but rather reinforced its "rightness"; the fun and humor came from the dissonance caused by known butches' taking on of a feminine appearance. Other gay and lesbian bar patrons treated them as if they were in drag.

The relationship between masculinity and butch sexuality is similarly complicated. Inherent to the butch-fem dyad was the presumption that the butch was the physically active partner and the leader in lovemaking. As D.J. explains, "I treat a woman as a woman, down to the basic fact [that] it'd have to be my side doin' most of the doin'." Insofar as the butch was the doer and the fem was the desired one, butch-fem roles did indeed parallel heterosexual male-female roles. Yet, in contrast to the dynamics of most heterosexual relationships, the butch's foremost objective was to give sexual pleasure to a fem; it was in satisfying her fem that the butch received fulfillment. As D.J. puts it, "If I could give her satisfaction to the highest, that's what gave me satisfaction." The ideal of the "stone," or untouchable, butch that prevailed during this period epitomizes this emotional and sexual dynamic. A stone butch does all the "doin'" and never allows her lover to reciprocate in kind. To be untouchable meant to gain pleasure from giving pleasure.

The key to understanding the butch-fem erotic system is to grasp that it both imitates and transforms heterosexuality. The obvious similarity between butch-fem and male-female eroticism is that they are both based on gender polarity: in lesbian culture, masculine and feminine appearance was central to erotic attraction. In addition, there are also more-subtle parallels. Even the butch's concern with pleasing her fem did not originate in lesbian culture. The middle-class marriage manuals of the thirties and forties emphasized the importance of husbands' pleasing their wives.[15] On the whole, these books treated women's sexuality as mystical and hidden, having to be awakened by a loving man. They urged husbands to satisfy their wives and extolled the joys of mutual orgasm. Although part of heterosexual culture, these ideas never fully challenged male sexual practice; most men still emphasized their own satisfaction and rarely expended the energy necessary to learn the complexities of the female body and regularly satisfy their wives. Furthermore, the ideal of the untouchable bears a striking resemblance to male sexuality's exclusive focus on the penis's power, ignoring the sensuality of the entire male body.[16]

Despite these similarities, several features of lesbian erotic culture distinguished it sharply from the heterosexual world. First, the butch-fem erotic system did not consistently follow the gender divisions of the dominant society. The active, or "masculine," partner was associated with the giving of sexual pleasure, a service usually assumed to be "feminine." In contrast, the fem, although the more reactive partner, demanded and received sexual pleasure and in this sense might be considered the more self-concerned or even more "selfish" partner. The polarity of active and passive does not adequately capture the butch-fem dyad. Although the butch was more aggressive, the fem was not passive. Her responsiveness showed that she actively wanted to be desired, and to offer her experience of pleasure to her butch.[17] Second, the butch's pleasure was always connected to the act of giving; her ability to pleasure her fem was the key to her own satisfaction. This was not true of men. Rather, the advice books and columns were aimed at "taming" the "true" male sexuality, usually felt to be brutish and uncontrolled, by emphasizing the woman's pleasure. The unique sexual desire of the butch opened the pathway for women to explore and enjoy their sexual potential. Third, and finally, butch-fem erotic culture contained few sanctions against women's expression of sexuality; sexual expression was associated primarily with pleasure. The dangers inherent in sex for heterosexual women in a male-supremacist society — loss of reputation, economic dependency, pregnancy, and disease — were absent in the lesbian community. Butches challenged rather than reinforced patriarchal rules about women's sexual expression.

In the forties, when sexuality was not commonly talked about, the community did not and could not enforce its own sexual norms; nevertheless, most of our butch narrators saw themselves as the leaders in lovemaking, and gained their satisfaction from giving their partners pleasure. Within this sexual framework, butch lesbians broke through the dominant society's norms about women's sexuality, and created active sexual lives pursuing casual as well as long-term serious relationships. In the 1950s, lesbian culture, and lesbians' resulting consciousness and sense of pride, had developed sufficiently to enable all of its members to leave their traditional women's upbringing and embrace new sexual attitudes and practices. Sex became a topic for public discussion in the lesbian community. In addition, most of our butch narrators who came out in the fifties recall having been teachers or students of sex. The changes in sexual mores had both a freeing and a repressive effect. Ideas about sexuality expanded and developed, and sexual feelings were validated. But at the same time, the changes led to standards being set for correct sexual behavior for members of the community. The stone butch ideal was publicly acknowledged and butches felt pressure to conform. Toward the end of the decade, the standard became so strong that many butches never experienced being made love to and those who had experienced it before entering the community no longer allowed it.

The community's increased interest in setting standards for butch eroticism in the late fifties was partly related to the growing cohesion of the community, and the discussion of sexuality as part of its culture. Butch-fem sexuality could not have been policed without a community to enforce norms through discussion and action. The social pressure for clearly defined roles also grew from the increased defiance of the community, which relied particularly on the butch role. This exaggerated the difference between butch and fem and demanded that butches perform well in defending their own and their fem's right to be part of the world. The tough butch who could take care of business became idealized. Untouchability expressed difference from the fem, control over one's life, and ambivalence about one's female body, all characteristics of the butch persona. This strong concern for role-appropriate eroticism developed in creative tension with the culture's validation of sexuality and emphasis on learning about and exploring new sexual practices. The butch was competent not only as a fighter but also as a lover. In reaction to the dominant idea that women needed men for sexual satisfaction, these women projected themselves as better than any man in bed. Sandy explains what it meant to be an untouchable butch: "I didn't want to be a man, but I wanted to be treated like one, put it that way ... Right. I wanted to satisfy [women] and I wanted to make love." The tension between the rigidification of roles and the openness about sexuality resulted in an erotic system predicated above all on the sexual satisfaction of women.

This discussion of the butch role provides a basis for exploring some of the similarities and differences between the butch and the fairy in pre–gay liberation lesbian and gay communities. In her recent article "Towards a Butch-Femme Aesthetic," Sue-Ellen Case, in the process of reclaiming the butch-fem lesbian heritage, assumes that butches and queens have been quite similar throughout this century and created parallel camp cultures.[18] Since the uncovering of lesbian history is a new endeavor, such a position is understandable but needs to be considered in the context of newly available information. The butch and the queen were similar in that both used gender-inverted appearance — dress and mannerisms — to convey their identity to other homosexuals and to the rest of the world. Appearance in both communities also conveyed erotic interest, and fostered a vision of sexuality based on difference. Within this general framework, there were some subtle distinctions. Fairies took on the feminine pronoun, for example, whereas butches rarely took on the masculine. Also, queens tended to take on feminine names, often the names of movie stars, whereas butches tended to use unisex names or keep their original names. A butch referred to as Clark Gable or Roy Rogers would be an anomaly, even though many had such fantasies about themselves.

The queen and the butch differed most strikingly, however, in that the lesbian community had no parallel to the camp culture that developed around queens in male homosexual communities, despite the fact that butch identity was constructed around being masculine but not male, and was therefore based on artifice.[19] Although all butches can be said to be in drag, few butches performed as male impersonators. Buffalo had one such performer; although many respected her, few aimed to imitate her. In addition, our narrators comment more on her talent as a singer than on her gift as a male impersonator. No cultural aesthetic seems to have developed around male impersonation.[20] Furthermore, camp humor and camp performers were not central to the lesbian community of this period. Judy Grahn captures this difference in recalling her first gay bars:

> The dikes [sic] and femmes of the bar provided a kind of low-key solid background of being; the queens (often with a sailor or two in tow) took the foreground, talking in loud voices, using flamboyant costumes and body language to create a starry effect. Sometimes they came in full drag, with wigs and makeup, and at other times just with a big fluffy sweater for a costume but always the particular broad gestures, lilting voice, and special queen talk. Or shrieking.[21]

Although the Buffalo bar dykes would have been considered "trouble" rather than a "a low-key solid background," their presence was not signaled verbally, and therefore Grahn's identification of the cultural contrast is nevertheless accurate.

From her study of female impersonators, Esther Newton identifies three elements that together constitute camp — incongruity, theatricality, and humor.[22] How these come together is nicely conveyed by a quote from one of the female impersonators she interviewed:

> Homosexuality is a way of life that is against all ways of life, including nature's. And no one is more aware of it than the homosexual. The camp accepts his role as a homosexual and flaunts his homosexuality. He makes the other homosexuals laugh; he makes life a little brighter for them. And

he builds a bridge to the straight people by getting them to laugh with him.[23]

If we assume that camp humor is based on juxtaposing incongruous extremes, it should flourish in the lesbian community as well as in the male homosexual community. But talking to these old-time butches, one is not struck by their campy sense of humor, as one is when listening to or reading about old-time queens. Rather it seems to us that butches were unquestionably smart and quick, but their strategy for survival was assertion, and sometimes aggression, whereas queens based their strategy on wit, verbal agility, and a sense of theater. Gay men took care of and healed people through their words. Judy Grahn remembers one evening in the late fifties when two policemen came over to the table where she was sitting with a friend. They shone a flashlight in their faces and required them to say their first and last names out loud.

> Sweat poured down my ribs as I obeyed. After they left, my friend and I sat with our heads lowered, too ashamed of our weakness to look around or even to look each other in the face. We had no internal defense from the self-loathing our helplessness inspired and no analysis that would help us perceive oppression as oppression and not as a personal taint of character. Only the queens with their raucous sly tongues helped us get over these kinds of incidents. They called the policemen "Alice Blue Gowns," insulting them behind their backs. "Alice Blue Gown tried to sit on *my* nightstick but I said No. You dirty boy! I know you're menthrating!" one plump faggot in a cashmere sweater would begin and soon we would be laughing and feeling strong again.[24]

This difference between the butch and the queen is rooted in the system of male supremacy. Gay male camp is based not simply on the incongruous juxtaposition of femininity and maleness, but also on the reordering of particular power relationships inherent in our society's version of masculinity and femininity. The most obvious cause for the minimum development of camp among lesbians was that masculinity was not and still isn't as incongruous as femininity in twentieth-century American culture and therefore not as easily used as a basis for humor. Concomitantly, although individual women might be able to sexually objectify a man, women as a group did not have the social power to objectify men in general. Therefore, such objectification could never be the basis for a genre of humor with wide appeal.

But why didn't camp develop and thrive within the lesbian community itself? Because the structures of oppression were such that lesbians never really escaped from male supremacy. In lesbians' actual struggles in the bars or on the streets, authority was always male. For queens to confront male authority was a confrontation between two men, on some level equals. The queen was playing with male privilege, which was his by birthright. For women to confront male authority is to break all traditional training and roles. Without a solid organization of all women, this requires taking on a male identity, beating men at their own game. Passive resistance or the fist is most appropriate for the situation, though not a very good basis for theater and humor.

Our analysis of the social meaning of the butch appearance and sexuality leads us to hypothesize that the extreme seriousness of masculinity for butches is based in their usurping of male privilege, their assertion of women's sexual autonomy, and their defending of a space in which women could love women. It was the rough, tough butches who found new bars and became the bartenders and bouncers, always prepared to fight to protect themselves and their community if necessary. They protected their fems from the advances of straight men. They also actively nourished and pursued their desire for women, despite having been raised in a world where women's sexuality was at best suspect. The only time that butches played with the incongruity of being masculine while being female was when harassed by the law. Every lesbian laughs and enjoys the dramatic moment when a butch charged with assault on an officer reveals her femaleness as a defense, emphasizing her frailty. But in most other contexts, there is nothing really humorous or theatrical about butch artifice. In this woman-hating society, and in the dangerous environment of the bars, the butch had to be able to assert and defend herself. Seeing the butch role develop in the actual context of the community clarifies that the butch role differed from that of a queen in that it carried the burden of twentieth-century women's struggle for the right to function independently in the public world.

Notes

1. We are using the spelling *fem* rather than *femme* on the advice of our narrators. They feel that *fem* is a more American spelling, and that *femme* has an academic connotation with which they are uncomfortable.

2. Camp in the lesbian community has been the subject of two recent and provocative papers in critical theory: Sue-Ellen Case, "Towards a Butch-Femme Aesthetic," *Discourse* 11 (Winter 1988–1989): 55–73; and Kate Davy, "Fe/male Impersonation: The Discourse of Camp," in *Critical Theory and Performance,* an unpublished manuscript edited by Joseph Roach and Janelle Reinelt. We found out about the latter too recently to digest it for this article.

3. By concentrating on the butch role alone rather than on the butch-fem dyad, we run the risk of distortion caused by separating out one of two integrated elements. Sue-Ellen Case provocatively suggests that they are an inseparable dyad that together compose the female subject. But space and time required us to focus on the butch alone. Our book *Boots of Leather, Slippers of Gold: The History*

of a Lesbian Community, to be published by Routledge in 1992, fully explores the interaction of butch and fem.

4. This paper was first presented at the Constructing Masculinities conference sponsored by the Rutgers Center for Historical Analysis, December 8–9, 1989, in a session organized by George Chauncey. We thank you, George, because the conception of the paper benefited greatly from our joint discussions. We would also like to thank Joan Nestle for her thoughtful feedback in the process of revising the paper for this book.

5. For more information on our method, see Madeline Davis and Elizabeth Lapovsky Kennedy, "Oral History and the Study of Sexuality in the Lesbian Community: Buffalo, New York, 1940–1960," *Feminist Studies* 12, no. 1 (Spring 1986): 7–27; and our forthcoming book *Boots of Leather, Slippers of Gold.*

6. Jonathan Katz, *Gay American History: Lesbian and Gay Men in the U.S.A.* (New York: Thomas Y. Crowell, 1976), pp. 209–211.

7. Jeffrey Weeks, *Coming Out: Homosexual Politics in Britain from the Nineteenth Century to the Present* (London: Quartet Books, 1977), pp. 115–117.

8. Esther Newton, "The Mythic Mannish Lesbian: Radclyffe Hall and the New Woman," *Signs* 9 (Summer 1986): 557–575.

9. George Chauncey, Jr., "The Sisters and Their Men: Male Homosexual Practices and Identities in Working-Class New York, 1890–1930, paper presented at the Rutgers Center for Historical Analysis, October 3, 1989.

10. *Bulldagger* was a term used more often in the black community, *diesel dyke* in the white community. Both communities used the term *butch,* although the black community frequently used the term *stud* as well.

11. The DA — the letters stand for duck's ass — was a popular hairdo for working-class men and butches during the 1950s. All side hair was combed back and joined the back hair in a manner resembling the layered feathers of a duck's tail, hence the name. Pomade was used to hold the hair in place and give a sleek appearance.

12. This development parallels an increased male concern with physical toughness in the society at large as documented in Donald J. Mrozek, "The Cult and Ritual of Toughness in Cold War America," in *Rituals and Ceremonies in Popular Culture,* edited by Ray B. Browne (Bowling Green, Ohio: Bowling Green University Press, 1980), pp. 178–191.

13. We are not sure whether or not this kind of competitiveness existed among black lesbians, because the evidence is not as full.

14. This freedom to play with the butch image does not appear to have existed in the forties. One narrator recalls that in the forties her reputation as a butch was shot when, after an office party, she went to the bar fashionably dressed as a woman.

15. John D'Emilio and Estelle Freedman, *Intimate Matters: A History of Sexuality in America* (New York: Harper & Row, 1988), pp. 265–274; Atina Grossman, "The

New Woman and the Rationalization of Sexuality in Weimar Germany," in *Powers of Desire: The Politics of Sexuality*, edited by Ann Snitow, Christine Stansell, and Sharon Thompson (New York: Monthly Review Press, 1983), pp. 153–171; and Margaret Jackson, "'Facts of Life' or the Eroticization of Women's Oppression? Sexology and the Social Construction of Heterosexuality," in *The Cultural Construction of Sexuality*, edited by Pat Caplan (London: Tavistock, 1987), pp. 52–81.

16. This idea comes from Peter Murphy, "Toward a Feminist Masculinity," *Feminist Studies* 14 (Summer 1989): 356, where he is discussing Emmanual Reynaud's *Holy Virility: The Social Construction of Masculinity*.

17. These attributes of butch-fem sexual identity remove sexuality from the realm of the "natural," challenging the notion that sexual performance is a function of biology and affirming the view that sexual desire and gratification are socially constructed.

18. Sue-Ellen Case, "Towards a Butch-Femme Aesthetic," *Discourse* 11 (Winter 1988–1989): 55–73.

19. For a full discussion of female impersonators and camp culture, see Esther Newton, *Mother Camp: Female Impersonators in America* (New Jersey: Prentice Hall, 1972).

20. This pattern of the unique male impersonator seems to be true nationally. Some women are well-known and singled out, such as Gladys Bentley, but nowhere is there mention of the male impersonator as central to lesbian bar culture. For a discussion of Gladys Bentley, see Eric Garber, "A Spectacle in Color: The Lesbian and Gay Subculture of Jazz Age Harlem," in *Hidden from History: Reclaiming the Gay and Lesbian Past*, edited by Martin Bauml Duberman, Martha Vicinus, and George Chauncey, Jr. (New York: New American Library, 1989), p. 324. [**Ed.'s note:** But see Lisa Davis's article "The Butch as Drag Artiste," earlier in this volume.]

21. Judy Grahn, *Another Mother Tongue: Gay Words, Gay Worlds* (Boston: Beacon, 1984), p. 32.

22. Newton, *Mother Camp*, pp. 104–111.

23. Ibid., p. 110.

24. Grahn, *Another Mother Tongue*, p. 32.

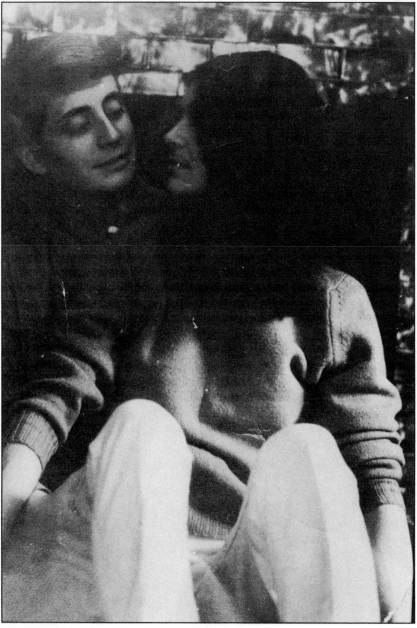

Lesbian Herstory Archives

Leslie Feinberg with lover, circa 1967

Leslie Feinberg

Butch to butch:
A love song

I watch myself in the bathroom mirror as I turn up the collar of my shirt, draping the tie over my shoulders. This is a ritual I enjoy — calling up my gender spirit.

I notice your reflection in the mirror. You're standing in the doorway, wearing that sweet black slip I love to see you in. You saunter over to me, wrapping your arms around me — one hand on my chest, another rubbing my belly, then slipping lower. I swallow hard. You smile at my reaction.

"This is why we're late," I remind you. This is the second time this evening we've gotten dressed to go out. The femme challenge: can you make us late one more time?

Verbally you agree to get dressed, but you continue to kiss my face and neck.

"I got lipstick on you," you say, carefully wiping it off.

You get as close to leaving as the door, then turn to watch me dress.

"Do you remember when you wore your first tie?" you ask me.

I hesitate. "Yes."

"When?"

"More than a quarter of a century ago," I answer laughing, but I'm shaken by my own words. "It's a long story," I add.

You look hurt. I promise to tell you someday when we have time.

You're in the bedroom dressing now as the memories overtake me.

❖

I was fourteen years old. I'd finally heard a co-worker at my after-school job talk about a gay bar her brother went to in nearby Niagara Falls. I memorized the name, "Tifka's," and called Information for the address.

Now I was standing in front of Tifka's, afraid, thinking, "This is the last place I could possibly fit. What if I don't?"

I wore a blue-and-red-striped dress shirt, navy blue jacket to hide my breasts, black pressed chinos, and sneakers, because I had no dress shoes.

I stepped inside the bar, and it was just a bar. The patrons turned to look at me: male and female "working girls," drag queens, a couple of fierce-looking butches, and some straight male drunks. There was no turning back.

And I didn't want to. These were my people. I just didn't know how to penetrate this society.

I bellied up to the bar and ordered a Jenny.

"How old are you?" the bartender asked.

"Old enough," I countered and put my money down on the bar.

A round of smirks rolled around the bar.

I sipped the beer and tried to act however fourteen-year-olds think is cool. An older drag queen studied me carefully. I picked up my beer and walked toward the back room. That's when I saw women dancing together, butch and femme. I almost started to cry, that's how much I wanted to believe that it could be possible, that it could happen to me.

"You ever been in a bar like this before?" the drag queen asked me.

"Sure, lots of times," I answered quickly. She smiled.

Then I wanted to ask her something so badly that I forgot to keep up my lie. "Can I really buy a woman a drink or ask her to dance?"

"Sure, honey," she said, "but only the femmes."

She laughed. She told me her name was Lola.

I focused through the dark and smoke of the back room on a woman sitting at a table alone. God, she was beautiful. The music was slow; I wanted to dance with her. I made a beeline for her before I lost my nerve.

"Would you dance with me?" I asked, and then the world turned upside down.

I felt my feet leave the floor. Lola and the bouncer had picked me up and hurled me backwards. They practically carried me into the front bar and set me on a bar stool.

Lola put her hand on my shoulder and looked me dead in the eyes. "Kid, there's a few things I should tell you. It's my fault. I told you it was okay to ask a woman to dance. But the first thing you should know is — don't ask Butch Al's woman!"

I was making a mental note of this when Butch Al's shadow fell across me. The bouncer stood between us, and the drag queens kind of shooed her into the back room. It happened in a flash, but a glimpse of this woman had floored me.

A glimpse of Butch Al was a glimpse of power, a memory I was afraid to hang onto, and afraid to let go of.

I sat trembling at the bar long after the momentary excitement had died down for everyone else.

I felt exiled to the front of the bar. I was more lonely than before I came in, because now I knew what I wasn't a part of.

Then suddenly a red light over the bar started flashing. Lola grabbed my hand and dragged me through the back room into the women's bathroom. She put the toilet seat down and told me to climb up on it. She closed the stall door partway and told me to stay there quietly. The cops were here.

So there I crouched. For a long time. It wasn't until I frightened a femme half to death as she opened the stall door that I discovered the police had left long ago with their payoff from the owner. Everyone just forgot the kid was hidden in the bathroom.

As I emerged from the john, everyone in the back room had a good laugh, at my expense. I retreated to the front bar again and nursed a beer.

Later, I felt a hand on my arm. It was that beautiful woman I had asked to dance. It was Butch Al's femme!

"C'mon, honey, come sit with us," she offered.

"No, I'm okay out here," I said as bravely as I could. But she put her arm around me gently and guided me off the bar stool.

"C'mon, join us. It's okay. Al won't hurt you," she reassured me. "Her bark is worse than her bite."

I doubted that. Especially when Butch Al stood up as I approached their table.

She was a big woman. I don't know how tall she really was; I was only a kid at the time. But she towered over me in height and stature.

I immediately loved the strength in her face. The way her jaw set. The anger in her eyes. The way she carried her body.

Her body both emerged from her sport coat and was hidden. Curves and creases. Broad back, wide neck. Large breasts bound tight. Folds of white shirt and tie and jacket. Hips concealed.

She looked me up and down. I widened my stance. She took that in. Her mouth refused to smile, but it seemed her eyes did.

She extended a beefy hand. I took it. The solidness of her handshake caught me by surprise. She strengthened her grip; I responded in kind. I was relieved I was not wearing a ring. Her clasp tightened, as did mine. Finally she smiled.

"There's hope for you," she said. I flushed at how gratefully I embraced her words.

I guess you could explain away that handshake as bravado. But it meant more than that to me then, and it still does.

It's more than a way of measuring strength. A handshake like that is a challenge. It seeks out power through incremental encouragement. At the point of maximum strength, once equity is established, then you have really met.

I had really met Butch Al. I was really glad. And scared. I needn't have been. No one was ever kinder to me.

She was gruff with me all right. But she peppered it with mussing my hair, hugging my shoulders, and giving my face something more than a pat and less than a slap. I liked it. I appreciated the affection in her voice when she called me "kid," which she did frequently.

She took me under her wing and taught me all the things she thought were most important for a baby butch like me to know before embarking on such a dangerous and painful journey. In her own way, she was very patient about it.

In those days the bars in the tenderloin district were gay by percentage. Tifka's was about 25 percent gay. That meant we had a quarter of the tables and dance floor. The other three-quarters were always squeezing us out. She taught me how we held our territory.

I learned to fear the cops as mortal enemies, and to hate the pimps who controlled the lives of so many of the women we loved.

And I learned to laugh. That summer, Friday and Saturday nights were full of laughter, and mostly gentle teasing.

The drag queens would sit on my lap and we'd pose for Polaroid pictures. We didn't find out till much later that the guy who took them for us was an undercover cop.

I was given room to explore my own butchness.

I could look at the old bulldaggers and know that was me; how they looked was how I felt inside. And I learned what it was I wanted from a woman by watching Butch Al and her lover, Jacqueline.

They let me hang with the two of them that summer. After the bar closed, we'd walk down the street, pretty tipsy, one of us on each of Jacqueline's arms. She'd throw her head up to the heavens and say, "Thank you, God, for these two good-looking butches," and Al and I'd lean forward and wink at each other and we'd laugh for the sheer joy of being who we were, and being it together.

They let me sleep over on the weekends on their soft old couch. Jacqueline cooked eggs at four a.m. while Al taught me. It was always the same lesson: toughen up.

Al never exactly said what was coming, never spelled it out. But I got the feeling it was scary. And I knew she was worried about me surviving it. I wondered if I was ready for it. Al's message was: you're not!

That was not encouraging. But I knew what gave Al's lessons such a sharp edge was the urgent need she felt to prepare me for a difficult life. She never meant to cut me. She nurtured my butch strength the best way she knew how. And, she reminded me frequently, no one had done that for her when she was a baby butch — and she survived. That was strangely reassuring. I had Butch Al for a mentor.

Al and Jackie groomed me, literally. Jacqueline gave me haircuts in their kitchen.

They took me to secondhand stores to get me my first sport coat and tie. Al combed the racks, pulling out sport coat after sport coat. I tried each one on. Jackie would tilt her head, then shake it, no.

Finally the perfect sport coat was selected. Jackie smoothed my lapels and nodded in approval. Al gave a low whistle of appreciation. I had died and gone to butch heaven!

Then came the tie. Al picked it out for me: a narrow black silk tie. "You can't go wrong with a black tie," she informed me solemnly. And, of course, she was right.

It was fun, all right. But sex was dawning on my horizon, and Al knew it.

One night, at the kitchen table, Al pulled out a cardboard box and handed it over to me to open. Inside was a rubber dildo. I was shocked.

"You know what that is?" she asked me.

"Sure," I said.

"You know what to do with it?"

"Sure," I said.

Jacqueline rattled the dishes. "Al, for chris'sake. Give the kid a break, will you?"

"A butch has gotta know these things," Al insisted.

Jackie threw down her dish towel and left the kitchen in exasperation. This was to be our butch "father-to-son" talk. Al talked. I listened.

"Do you understand?" she pressed.

"Sure," I said. "Sure."

Al was satisfied she had imparted enough information by the time Jackie returned to the kitchen.

"One more thing, kid," Al added. "Don't be like those bulldaggers who put this on and strut their stuff. Use a little decorum, you know what I mean?"

"Sure," I said. I didn't.

Al left the room to take a long shower before bed. Jacqueline continued to dry the dishes, at least long enough that the blush had drained from my face and my temples had stopped pounding.

She sat down on a kitchen chair near me.

"Did you understand what Al was telling you, honey?"

"Sure," I said, and vowed to never say that again.

"Is there anything you don't understand?"

"Sure," I thought to myself.

"Well," I started slowly, "it sounds like it takes a little practice, but I get the general idea. I mean that noon and midnight stuff sounds, well, like you got to practice it to get it right."

Jacqueline looked confused. Then she started to laugh, and she couldn't stop. "Honey," she'd start, but she was laughing too hard to continue.

"Honey. You can't learn to fuck from reading *Popular Mechanics*. That isn't what makes a butch a good lover."

This is what I needed to know!

"Well, what does make a butch a good lover?" I asked, trying to sound like the answer didn't mean all that much to me.

Her face softened. "That's kinda hard to explain. I guess being a good lover means respecting a femme. It means listening to her body. And, even if the sex gets a little rough or whatever, that inside you're coming from a gentle place. Does that make sense?"

It did not. It was less information than I wanted. It turned out, however, to be just the information I needed. It just took thinking about it for the rest of my life.

Jacqueline took the rubber cock from my hands. Had I been holding it all this time? She placed it carefully on my thigh. My body temperature rose. She began to touch it gently, like it was something beautiful.

"You know, you could make a woman feel real good with this thing. Maybe better than she's ever felt in her life." She stopped stroking the dildo. "Or you could really hurt her, and remind her of all the ways she's ever been hurt in her life. You got to think about that every time you strap this on. Then you'll be a good lover."

I made a mental note to think about that a great deal. I listened. I hoped there was more. There was not. Jackie puttered around in the kitchen and I went to bed.

I slept fitfully.

The weight of sex was pressing in on me from without and within, and everyone at the bar knew it.

So when Monique started playing with me, flirting with me, I had to put my cards on the table.

Monique used her sex like a weapon. She was scary. A number of butches we knew had burned themselves by getting too close to Monique's fire.

Did she really want me?

The butches said it was true. So it must be. And somehow everyone knew at once that next Friday I would lose my butch virginity with Monique.

On Friday night, the butches poked me, clapped me on the back, adjusted my tie, and sent me over to her table. As Monique and I left together, I noticed that none of the femmes were encouraging me. Why wouldn't Jacqueline look at me? She just tapped her long painted nails on that whiskey glass and stared at it like it was the only thing in the room.

Did she sense the impending tragedy before I did?

The next evening I came late to the bar, hoping Monique and her crowd would not be there waiting. They were.

I slunk over to our table and sat down. No one knew exactly what had or (most importantly) had not happened the night before. But everyone knew something was very wrong.

I sat in shame, rubbing my forehead with my hands, wondering how long this evening could possibly last. A long time. A very long time.

Monique whispered something to a butch sitting near her. The butch crossed the room and approached our table.

"Hey," she called to me. I didn't look. "Hey, femme, you wanna dance with a real butch?"

I twisted in my seat. Al said something to this butch so quietly I couldn't hear.

"Oh, I'm sorry, Al, I didn't know she was your femme."

Al stood up and hit the butch before any of us knew what had happened. Then Al looked at me expectantly.

"Well," she said. She was holding up the butch, who was doubled over.

Al wanted me to hit the woman, to defend my honor. I couldn't see anyone in the room I would want to hit, except maybe myself. I felt I had no honor to defend, and no energy.

The butches nearest Monique stood to cross the room. Al and the other butches in our crowd stood in front of the table to defend me.

Jacqueline put her hand on my thigh to reassure me that I didn't have to fight. She needn't have. Lola came up behind me and put her hands on my shoulders. The femmes were closing ranks with me too.

I just sat with my face in my hands, shaking my head, wanting it to all stop, but it wouldn't.

Monique's crowd did back down. But none of us could leave the bar until they did, otherwise we'd get jumped.

It was going to be a long night.

Al was furious with me.

"You gonna let that bulldagger talk to you that way?" she shouted at me, thumping the table for emphasis.

"Shut up, Al," Jacqueline said. It surprised me enough that I raised my face to look at her. She was glowering at Al.

"Just leave the kid alone, will ya please?"

Al stopped yelling at me, but she turned her back to me to watch the couples dancing. Her body language said she was still pretty disgusted with me.

Jacqueline just kept tapping her glass as she had the evening before. It took me a long time to learn femme Morse code.

After a while the bar crowd started thinning out.

Yvette came in. Jacqueline watched her with obvious concern.

"What's the matter?" I asked, roused from my own self-pity.

Jackie studied my face for a moment. "You tell me," she said.

I looked at Yvette. She was about Jackie's age, whatever that was. Like Jackie, she had worked the streets since she had been a teenager. Al made Jackie stop when they got together. Al could support them both on the money she earned at her job at the auto plant.

Yvette didn't have a butch who worked in the factories. Yvette didn't have anyone but the other working girls.

"She looks like she had a hard night," I offered.

Jacqueline nodded. "Those are mean streets. We get real hurt out there."

I marveled at the intimacy suggested in this information. Then she seemed to change the subject.

"What do you think she wants right now?" Jacqueline asked me.

"To be left alone," I said, thinking of my own need.

She smiled. "Yes and no."

Okay, I bit. "Yes and no?"

"Yeah, she wants to be left alone. She doesn't want one more person in this goddamn world to ask anything from her tonight. But she sure could use some comfort, you know what I mean?"

"Sure," I said, and then I thought about it. Maybe I really did understand.

"She might really like it if a butch like you went over and just asked her to dance, you know? Not hit on her."

I thought maybe I could do that. I started to jump up from my seat. Anything to take the heat off my own shame.

Jacqueline pulled my sleeve. "Do it gently, understand?"

I thought I did. I walked slowly across the room to Yvette. She had her head in her hands. I cleared my throat. She looked at me wearily and sipped from her drink.

"What do you want?" she asked me.

"Ah, I thought, would you dance with me?"

She shook her head. "Maybe later, baby, okay?"

Maybe it was the way I just stood there. There was no going back across the room in front of Monique's group or mine without having danced. I hadn't thought of that. Had Jackie?

Or maybe Jacqueline's eyes connected with Yvette's from across the room. But finally Yvette said, "Yeah, why not," and stood up to dance with me.

I waited for her in the middle of the dance floor. The music had already started, but I stood still, with her hand in mine, until she kind of relaxed and moved toward me.

Someone had put the butch-femme anthem on the jukebox: "Stand by Your Man." I found a step that was half as slow as I usually danced it. After we'd danced for a few moments, Yvette told me, "It's okay to breathe, you know."

Then we laughed, real hard together. It felt good, and it was private.

Then I felt her body move closer and we kind of melted together. I discovered all the sweet surprises a woman can give a butch: her hand on the back of my neck, down my back. Sometimes her hand was open on my shoulder, sometimes it was balled up like a fist.

The music stopped and she started to pull away. I let my hand fall from her back, but I held onto her other hand gently, until the next song began to play.

"Please," I said.

"Honey," she answered laughing, "you just said the magic word."

We danced a few slow songs in a row. Our bodies swung effortlessly in the centripetal force that unites two bodies in a circle of dance. The slightest shift in the pressure of my hand on her back changed her position and the intensity of the motion of her body.

I never ground my thigh into her pelvis. I knew as a woman she was wounded there. That was the place I protected myself, too, even as a young butch. My wound covered hers for protection. I felt her pain; she knew mine. I felt her desire; she aroused mine.

Finally the music stopped and I let her go. I kissed her on the cheek and thanked her. She returned to her seat, allowing a new comfort to settle into her pain.

I crossed the dance floor to return to my table. I was forever changed.

Jacqueline patted my thigh and flashed me a sweet smile. The other femmes — male and female — looked at me differently. As the world beat the stuffing out of us, they tried in every way to protect and nurture our tenderness. My capacity for tenderness was what they'd seen.

The other butches had to see me as sexual now, a competitor. Even Al looked at me differently.

As painful as this whole ritual had been, it was nothing less than a rite of passage.

I didn't feel cocky. If anything I had confirmed to myself that humility was exactly the correct emotion when seeking the power of a woman's passion.

Strong to my enemies, tender to those I loved — that's what I wanted to be like when I grew up. The following night, I would have to put these qualities to the test. But for tonight, I was happy.

The next evening was a boisterous Saturday night. We were all feeling our oats, laughing and dancing. Out of the corner of my eye I was kind of looking for Yvette. Jacqueline must have known it, because she explained to me that Yvette's pimp wouldn't let her have a steady butch. My stomach tightened in rage. I still kept an eye out for her. After all, a pimp can't know everything that's going on, right?

When the red light started flashing over the bar, I took myself to the women's bathroom and assumed my post on the toilet. A long time passed. I heard thumping and several shouts. Then it was quiet.

I peeked outside the bathroom. All the stone butches and drag queens were lined up facing the wall, hands cuffed behind their backs. Several of the femmes who the cops knew were prostitutes were getting roughed up and separated from the rest of us. I knew by now it would take at least a blow job to get them out of jail tonight.

One cop spotted me and grabbed me by the collar. He threw me across the room to be handcuffed. I tried to look for Al, but they had already started taking people to the police vans outside.

Jacqueline rushed up to me. "Take care of each other," she said, looking at the doorway. "Be careful, honey," she added.

I nodded. The handcuffs pinning my arms behind my back hurt. I was in a serious mood. I was scared too. I would be very careful. I hoped Al and I could take care of each other.

Al was in a different van than I was. By the time they nabbed me, the butch tank van was full and I rode with Lola and my other drag queen sisters. I was glad. Those whose hands were cuffed in front stroked my face and told me not to be afraid. They said I'd be all right. I hoped they were right. If that was true though, I wondered why they looked as scared as I did.

At the precinct I saw Yvette and Monique, already arrested on a street sweep. Yvette gave me a smile for courage. I gave her a wink. A cop shoved me from behind into the belly of the precinct. I was headed for the bull's tank.

They were taking Al out of the cell as they were bringing me in. I called her name. She didn't seem to hear me.

The cops locked me up. At least my wrists were free now from the handcuffs. I could smoke a cigarette.

What was going to happen now? Through a grated window I saw some "Saturday-night butches" getting booked. They had taken Butch Al in the opposite direction.

The drag queens were in the large cell next to ours. I saw Lola and we smiled. At that moment three cops ordered her out of the cell. Her body pulled back slightly. She had tears in her eyes. Then she walked forward with them, rather than be dragged out.

I waited. Butches and femmes were being taken in different directions. What was happening? When would I be booked?

The cops brought Lola back before Al. About an hour had passed. When I saw her, my heart broke. Two cops were dragging her. She could barely stand up.

Her hair was wet and in her face. Her makeup was smeared. Blood ran down the back of her seamless stockings.

They threw her into the cell. She stayed where she fell. I could hardly breathe. I waited. Finally, I spoke to her in a whisper, "Honey, you want a cigarette? Want to smoke? C'mere, over here by me."

She looked dazed, unwilling to move. Finally she slid over to the bars beside me, facing me.

I lit a cigarette for her and handed it to her. As she smoked, I slid my arm through the bars and touched her hair, then rested my hand on her shoulder. I spoke to her quietly. She didn't seem to hear me for a long time.

Finally, she leaned her forehead against the bars and I put both my arms around her.

"It changes you," she said.

I waited for her to continue.

"What they do to you in here, what you take every day on the streets, it changes you."

I listened.

"I can't remember if I was ever as sweet as you are when I was your age," she said smiling. Then she looked serious. "I don't want to see you change. I don't want to see you after you've hardened up."

I sort of understood. But I was really worried about Al and I didn't know what was going to happen to me. This other stuff sounded more philosophical. I didn't know if I was going to live to an age where experience would have changed me. I wanted to live through tonight. I wanted to know where Al was.

The cops announced that Lola was being bailed out.

"I must look a mess," she said.

"You look beautiful," I answered, and I meant it. I looked at her face for a last moment and wondered if the men who touched her really loved her as tenderly as we did.

"You really are a sweet butch," Lola said before she left.

That felt good.

The cops dragged in Al just after Lola left.

She was in pretty bad shape. Her shirt was partly open, and her pants zipper was down. Her binder was gone, leaving her large breasts free. Her hair was wet. There was blood on her mouth and nose. She looked dazed, like Lola.

The cops pushed her into the cell. Then they approached me. I backed up until I was up against the bars. They stopped and smiled. One cop rubbed his crotch. The other put his hands under my armpits and lifted me up three inches off the floor and slammed me against the bars. He put his thumbs deep into my breasts and his knee between my legs. Everywhere he found my young womanhood and hurt it.

"You should be this tall soon — tall enough that your feet would reach the ground. When they do, that's when we'll do to you what we did to your pussy friend Alison," he taunted me. Then they left.

Alison. That must be Butch Al's name. Alison. The contradiction meant something to me, but I couldn't explain it.

I grabbed my pack of cigarettes and lighter and went over to where Al was slumped on the floor. I sat down next to her slowly. I was shaking.

"Al," I said, extending the pack.

She didn't look up. I put my hand on her arm. She pushed it off.

Her head was down. I could just see the expanse of her wide back, the curves of her shoulders. I touched them, without thinking twice. She let me.

I lit a cigarette and smoked with one hand, and touched her back with the other. She began to tremble. I put my arms around her. Her body softened against me.

She was hurt. The parent had become the child. I felt strong. There was comfort to be found in my arms.

"Hey, look at this," one cop yelled to another. "Alison found herself a baby butch. They look like two faggots." The cops laughed.

My arms took more of her into my circle to protect her. It was as though I could ward off their jeers and keep her safe in my arms.

I had always marveled at her strength. Now I felt the muscles in her back and shoulders and arms. I experienced the power of this stone butch, even as she slumped wearily in my arms.

The cops announced to us that Jacqueline had posted our bail. We were taken out of the cell. The last words I heard from the cops were "You'll be back. Remember what we did to your friend."

What had they done? The questions came back again. Jacqueline looked from Al's face to mine asking the same. I had no answers. Al offered none.

In the car, Jacqueline held Al in a way that made it look at first glance like Al was comforting her. I sat quietly in the front seat needing comfort, too. I didn't know the gay man who drove us. "Are you okay?" he asked me.

"Sure," I answered.

We got to Al and Jackie's house. Al ate her eggs as if she didn't taste them. She didn't talk. Jacqueline looked nervously from Al to me and back again. I ate. I did the dishes.

Al went into the bathroom to clean up before bed.

"She'll be gone a long time," Jacqueline said.

How did she know? Had this happened many times before?

I dried the dishes. She turned to focus on me for the first time this evening. "Are you okay?" she asked.

"Yeah, I'm all right," I lied.

"Did they hurt you, baby?" she asked, coming closer to me.

"No," I lied.

I turned away from her to signal that I had something important to say. I recognized it even then as an adult move I would repeat many times in the future.

"Jacqueline," I said quietly. She looked surprised to hear her whole name spoken. "How do I know if I'm strong enough?"

She came up behind me and turned me around by the shoulder. She pulled my face against her cheek.

"Who is, honey? Nobody's strong enough to deal with this shit. You just get through it the best you can. Butches like Al and you don't have a choice. It's gonna happen to you. You just gotta try to live through it."

There was probably something very important in that answer, but I was already burning with another question.

"Al wants me to be tough; you and Lola and the other femmes are always telling me to stay sweet, stay tender. How can I be both?"

Jacqueline turned away to signal me that she had something important to say. I listened.

"Al's right, really. It's selfish of us girls, I guess. We want you to be strong enough to survive the shit you take. We love how strong you are. But butches get the shit kicked out of their hearts too. And, I guess, we just sometimes wish there were a way to protect your hearts and keep you all tender for us, you know?"

I didn't. I really didn't.

"Is Al tender?"

Jacqueline's face tightened. The question threatened to reveal something that could pierce Butch Al's armor. Then Jacqueline saw that I really needed the answer.

"She's been hurt real bad. It's hard for Al to say everything she feels. But, yeah. I don't think I could be with her if she weren't tender with me."

Al was moving around in the hallway. Jacqueline looked apologetic. I signaled that I understood. She left the kitchen. I was alone. I had a lot to think about.

I lay down on the couch. After a while Jackie brought the bedding in. She sat down beside me and stroked my face. It felt good.

She looked at me for a long time with a pained look. I didn't know why, but it scared me. I guess I figured she could see what was coming and I couldn't.

"Are you really okay, honey?" she asked.

I smiled. "Yeah."

"Do you need anything?"

Yeah. I needed a femme who loved me like she loved Al. I needed Al to tell me exactly what they were going to do to me next time and how to live through it. And I needed Jacqueline's breast.

Almost as soon as the thought crossed my mind, she put my hand on her breast.

She turned her head in the direction of the bedroom as though she was listening for Al.

"You sure you're okay?" she asked one last time.

"Yeah, I'm okay," I said.

She laughed quietly. Her face softened. She touched my cheek and pulled my hand away from her breast.

"You're a real butch," she said, shaking her head.

I felt proud when she said that. Real proud.

I couldn't understand all the sounds I heard coming from their bedroom that night. I had no information about anything I needed to know about. I fell asleep.

In the morning I woke up early and left quietly.

I never saw Butch Al again.

They weren't at the bar the next couple of weekends. I heard some stories about what had happened to Al. I didn't choose to believe any of them.

The summer passed. I quit school and got a job at a plant in my own hometown. I began looking for the bars where the factory butches hung out.

Summer turned into fall and I stopped going to Niagara Falls on the weekends.

Just before Christmas, I went back to Tifka's to see the old crowd. Yvette wasn't there. I heard she died alone in an alleyway, her throat slashed from ear to ear. Lola overdosed, purposely.

No, no one had seen Al. Jackie was working the streets again.

I walked against a bitter wind from bar to bar along the strip. I heard her laughter before I saw her. There was Jacqueline in the shadow of an alley, sharing an ironic laugh with some other working girls. She saw me a moment later.

She came over to me readily, smiling. I saw the glaze of heroin across her eyes. She was thin, very thin.

She faced me. She opened the collar of my overcoat to straighten my tie. She turned up my collar against the cold.

I stood with my hands buried deep in my pockets. I felt kind of like I had the night I danced with Yvette.

We were asking each other and answering a lot of questions with our eyes. It all happened real fast.

I saw the tears start to spill from her eyes. Then she turned to go. I finally found my voice to speak...

❖

Your presence in the bathroom doorway pulls me back to the present. I've been lost in memories. You've been standing in the doorway long enough that your look has turned to concern.

"Are you okay, honey?" you ask me.

"Sure," I answer, laughing at myself gently. We both realize that my answer is both not true and very true.

You put your arms across my chest again, looking at my face for answers. I have none. I do have a question though. And as soon as the question comes up in my heart I have to ask it. "Am I..."

"Are you what, honey?"

I hesitate. "Am I tender?"

You look like you're close to tears. "Yes," you answer firmly. "You are so tender. I don't think I could be with you if you weren't."

Now I feel close to tears.

"Do you still want to go out?" you ask.

I nod. "Give me a minute." You look worried, but leave me alone.

I look at my own reflection and it makes me smile. I see the child, cross-dressing in front of the mirror. I see the baby butch, the factory "he-she" who would later have to pass as a man to survive. I see the whole course of my life which has brought me to this moment. Never once did I betray who I was.

In many ways, Al, you gave me all the answers I needed with the gift of my first tie.

This tie is more than just a symbol. It is an acceptance of who we are. It is an affirmation of all the pride we can muster.

Thank you, Butch Al. I miss you so much. I wonder what happened to you. I wish I could tell you where this journey has taken me.

I loved you so. I love you still.

You'd be proud of me. I'm living it.

Judy Lederer

A letter

March 20, 1991

Dear Joan:
  The spirit moves:
  1950. For those who do not remember 1950, let me set the stage: television existed, and I had seen it on display in a store but didn't know anyone who owned one. Sex existed, but no one talked about it, except in euphemisms: she's "that way" or "you know" meant a woman was pregnant; she "does things" meant she had sex; she "does things to other girls" meant she was gay. The word *homosexual* was used only in newspapers in "were-arrested" stories, all of which referred to men.

  I was never called a lesbian. We were "queers" or "perverts" or the worst group-you-wouldn't-want-to-be-caught-dead-with: "dykes." And we were also arrested, but it never made the papers — I guess because it was so ordinary, not newsworthy.

  The word *butch* was used to describe mannish behavior. She walks butch, she thinks butch, she looks butch, but I do not recall she *is* a butch. A tough-acting woman in man's clothes was called a butch diesel. I desperately wanted to be a butch diesel.

  This would be a great accomplishment for a sixteen-year-old suburban kid, cruising weekends in the Village. I had been in "the life" on the streets — it wasn't enough. I wanted to go into the butch diesels' bars, to be accepted as one of them. They were tough, cocky, sure of themselves. They intimidated by their very existence. And they never ended up in a cage at the Country Club [the Women's House of Detention, located in the heart of the Village], never fell victim to street sweeps. They were cool!

  How to start...

  For openers, I took the bus to New York wearing a skirt and blouse and carrying a purse containing a hip flask of stale beer, a nice-fitting man's shirt, and a pair of men's slacks, liberated from my half brother. The bus station — then about half a block east of the south end of Times Square, before the Port Authority Terminal was built — was a stinking hole, but it did have rental lockers and an alley nearby.

I changed into the boy clothes in the alley, plastered my pageboy girl hair back into a decent DA (duck's ass, dear children: it came to a pointed line down the back of the head — very popular with greasers), and jammed the flask into one back pocket. No wallet; loose money went in the right front pocket. Then I put the girl clothes and purse in the locker and *voilà* — instant freedom to walk the streets literally unmolested.

Understand: boys and men could walk the streets — just walk, not solicit or what have you, just plain be on the streets at night — and no one would challenge them. But a girl or woman alone had to be a hooker or lost and in need of protection. This was handy if one was working the streets but of no use at all if one wanted to be accepted as a butch diesel and not just a street kid.

I had already found *the bar* to be entered. I had been shown it by a street friend who was highly amused that I did not at first believe that the "men" entering were really women. You couldn't tell unless you heard them talk, and even then sometimes I wasn't sure. I had finally accepted the truth and had watched them go in, alone or with snazzily dressed women. But I had never dared enter; it was out of my league. Well, no longer — I was ready!

So in I went. All conversation stopped, all eyes upon me. This was standard whenever any stranger entered a gay bar in those days. The darkness of the bars allowed those inside to see the person entering before his or her eyes adjusted to see them. If you passed muster, if the patrons concluded you were not a vice cop or a known troublemaker, conversation would start again.

Which is not to say you would be accepted. No, you would be ignored, watched, tentatively approached if ... But first, the pin-drop silence. Oh Lord, the agony of waiting to see if they would accept me! And then, finally, the silence was broken: "Oh my God, Millie," someone said, "it's Prince Valiant!"

And everyone roared with laughter, and I knew, I knew ... My hand reached up to find that my baby-fine hair had shed the beer glop and had drifted down and forward to hang limply about my ears. I reached for the flask, then realized it was too late. What would I do with it? Pour it on my head? I just held it on the table, too numb to move, too embarrassed to speak or even lift my head.

The eternity ended when the waitress asked if I wanted something to eat. Every gay bar I recall in those days was nominally a café, so they had to serve food (hamburgers, fries), and especially if you were not known, you had to order whatever overpriced, inedible food they offered. Then you would be asked if you wanted anything to drink with it. I knew about that game from other bars, but still speechless, I only nodded.

I would love to say, "And then everyone came over and said, 'Welcome,' and we all lived happily ever after." It didn't happen. I ate the burger, left the fries, and split. Then they spoke: "Good night, sweet prince..." "A valiant effort..."

I never went back. I don't recall the name of the place or where it was. It wasn't Fleur de Lys, Page Three, Swing Rendezvous, any place that I knew afterwards. It was much smaller, just a hole in the wall.

I never got to be a butch diesel, just butch, then a butch.

And good for a laugh, always...

Judy

From *Jet*, February 1954

Women who pass for men

For thirty years, a hefty Mississippi woman lived as a man, sternly bossing a ten-acre farm and caring for an attractive, cream-colored "wife" and her daughter by a previous marriage. When the "man" died two years ago, an amazed undertaker discovered that Pete Bell was really a woman.

At the wife's request, the masquerade was hushed and the burial certificate listed no sex. The widow explained that her husband was an unwanted child who adopted mannish poses and attitudes in order to please a father who wanted a male heir. Incredulous citizens in the small town pooh-poohed the report, claiming, "Old Pete just couldn't have fooled me."

The deception which characterized Pete Bell's life mirrors the problems of hundreds of women who are trapped in the half-shadow, no-man's-land of the man-woman. Despised by society, they travel an uncharted road which often leads to a jail cell.

Very often the masquerade is only uncovered by an accident or a necessary visit to a doctor. After an automobile accident, Cincinnati doctors discovered that "Charlie Harris" — who had posed as a man for forty-five years — was a woman. Harris's true sex was revealed to a woman who knew her as her stepfather. Mrs. Ida Belle Redd said Harris (who died recently in Cincinnati at the age of 107) married her mother in 1902.

At the other end of the spectrum are part-time men: women who for various reasons reject feminine roles and, while retaining female trappings, compete with men for jobs — and other women. These "sometimes women" feel contempt for girlish pursuits. Some are athletic women; others, intellectual or executive types.

One of these is a famous Harlem woman executive, attractive and youngish, who rejected femininity for a manlike existence. She attends stag parties, takes an active part in jokes aimed at "silly, gullible" women.

Her constant companion is an attractive secretary who shares her lavish, one-bedroom apartment.

Problems posed by manlike women are so deep that the public has hardly begun to understand them. Doctors and psychiatrists are coordinating their work in the light of new psychosexual findings. Their research indicates that operations and psychiatric treatment can free many women of maleness caused by an imbalance of female and male hormones.

Other cases may prove more difficult, although extended psychiatric treatment may cure those whose maladjustments started in childhood. Parents, fathers particularly, often drive girls to the brink of abnormality. Stuck with an unwanted daughter, they force the youngster to play rough and impress upon her mind a love for everything masculine. Later, these same parents are furious when the girl rejects masculine suitors. Without adequate guidance, the girl will become a jealous, possessive man-woman facing the frustration of living in a society which in most instances has not provided an answer to her problems.

This type of jealousy is often reflected in police records. In Detroit, Leatrice Calloway, twenty-one, was sentenced to ten to twenty years for the murder of her female "sweetheart," Marion Ware. Miss Calloway said she shot Miss Ware for dating a man. Ohio was shocked by a similar love slaying. Mrs. Evelyn Butler, 25-year-old mother of two children, was sentenced to the electric chair for strangling and drowning Mrs. Evelyn Clark. Testimony indicated that the two women had been lovers. Mrs. Clark has appealed the death verdict.

The lives of some strange women, however, have happy endings. Gladys Bentley, entertainer, says injections of female sex hormones three times a week hastened her return to womanhood.

Now writing a book on her experiences in the "twilight zone of sex," Mrs. Bentley — who is happily married to a West Coast cook — said, "I want the world to know that those of us who have taken the unusual paths to love are not hopeless."

Women who fall for lesbians

During the man-shortage years of World War II, a masculine-looking freshman coed who walked with a swaggering gait checked into the girls' dormitory of a well-known midwestern college and promptly struck up a more-than-casual friendship with another first-year coed. In a short while, the campus was buzzing with gossip of their hush-hush romance.

Soon thereafter, the offending student was expelled, and her impressionable young victim went on to become a writer for a national broadcasting firm.

Many such young women, however, are not so lucky as to escape the designs of female sex deviates. For according to Dr. Alfred Kinsey in his book *Sexual Behavior in the Human Female*, nearly one out of five American women experience homosexual relations of some type, either as a pursuer or pursued, and their ages range from early childhood to middle life.

Just why some women fall for lesbians is perhaps best summed up in an observation made by writer-researcher Arthur Guy Mathews, who stated recently in a health magazine: "The lesbian makes a point of seeking out widows, lonesome women, the victims of broken love affairs, and those who have suffered from nervous breakdowns and other mental ills." Additional victims come from the ranks of the sexually uninitiated, as was true in the case of the college coed. And, with one woman in four remaining unmarried in the U.S. today, spinsters more and more are becoming likely prey for lesbians.

One Missouri schoolteacher, for example, who found herself getting on in years without the comfort and companionship of a man, succumbed to the wily advances of a lesbian of similar age, and opened her home to her. They lived together in presumed "spinsterhood" the remaining days of their lives. When the lesbian finally died of a heart attack, the then-retired teacher, grief stricken, soon followed her in death.

Similarly, a romance between a New York woman doctor and her nurse has been winked at and accepted by Harlem society for years.

Many women who fall for lesbians possess all the physical attractiveness — including good looks and shapely figures — with which to attract desirable males. Nevertheless, they wander into the shadowed world of sex perversion on thrill-seeking jaunts, or out of boredom, as a result of neurotic tendencies. Usually such women, if they are of sound mind, tarry with their lady lovers only long enough to "see what it's like," then return to normal courtship with men.

The lesbian, like the male homosexual, who stalks a married home is to be considered a dangerous person. Dr. Mathews points out, "If she so much as gets one foot into a good woman's home with the intention of seducing her, she will leave no stone unturned to win the love of the person, and eventually destroy her life for good."

When the Negro wife of a traveling husband became lonely and depressed in a small Texas town, she fell into company with a lesbian and became so infatuated that she finally divorced her husband.

Because a heavy toll can be taken from the mentally maladjusted, hospitals and social agencies are sometimes loaded with lesbians who pose as befrienders of the weak.

A young colored war widow who cracked up under the shock of her husband's death was sent to a mental hospital, where a homosexual female took her under her wing. When the woman was well enough to leave the institution, the lesbian took her into her own home for the period of readjustment. There, in the quiet of a country cottage, the woman was seduced and told that she was intended for a new way of sex life. Six months later the widow suffered a second mental collapse and was back in the hospital. Again she was released in the care of her lady lover. Within another month the widow was once more a mental patient. The vicious cycle continued until a doctor discovered what was going on, then called in the lesbian and banished her under threat of imprisonment.

Yet, despite the lesbian's power of persuasion or slyness of approach, she stands a slim chance of debauching a normally sexed woman who is happily married or deeply in love with a man. Studies show that most women feel it is still much nicer to have a man around the house.

Leslie Feinberg

Letter to a fifties femme from a stone butch

I'm lying in my bed tonight missing you, my eyes all swollen, hot tears running down my face. I don't think I've ever felt so all alone. There's a fierce summer lightning storm raging outside.

Tonight I walked down streets looking for you in every woman's face, as I have each night of this lonely exile. I'm afraid I'll never see your laughing, teasing eyes again.

Earlier, I was walking in this big city with a woman. A mutual friend had fixed us up, sure we'd have a lot in common, since we're both into "politics."

Well, we sat in a coffee shop and she talked about Democratic politics and seminars and photography and problems with her co-op and how she's opposed to rent control. Small wonder. Daddy is a real estate developer.

I couldn't understand what she was talking about most of the time. I'm looking at her while she's talking, thinking to myself that I'm a stranger in this woman's eyes. She's looking at me, but she doesn't see me.

Then she finally says she hates this society for what it's done to "women like me" who hate themselves so much that they have to look and act like men.

I feel myself getting flushed and my face twitches a little and I start telling her all cool and calm about how women like me have existed since the dawn of time, before there was oppression, and how their societies respected them, and she's got her very interested expression on, and besides it's time to leave.

So we walk by a corner where these cops are laying into a homeless man and I stop and mouth off to the cops and they start coming at me with their clubs raised and she tugs my belt to pull me back. And I just look at her, and suddenly I'm feeling things well up in me that I thought I had buried. I'm standing there remembering you like I don't see the cops about to hit me, like I'm falling back into another world, a place I want to go to again.

And suddenly my heart hurts and I realize how long it's been since my heart has felt anything.

I need to go home to you tonight. I can't. So I'm writing you this letter.

I remember years ago, the day I started working at the plant and you had already been there a few months, and how your eyes caught mine and played with me before you set me free. I was supposed to be following the foreman to fill out some forms, but I was too busy wondering what color your hair was under that white paper net and how it would look and feel in my fingers, down loose and free. And I remember how you laughed gently when the foreman came back and said, "You comin' or not?"

All of us he-she's were mad as hell when we heard you got fired the next week because you wouldn't let the superintendent touch your breasts. I still unloaded on the docks for another couple of weeks, but I was mopey. It just wasn't the same when your light went out.

I couldn't believe it the night I went to that new club on the West Side (a new bar almost every other week). There you were, leaning up against the bar, your jeans too tight for words and your hair, your hair all loose and free.

And I remember that look in your eyes again. You didn't just know me; you liked what you saw. And this time, ooh, woman, we were on our own turf. I could move the way you wanted me to, and I was glad I'd gotten all dressed up.

Our own turf ... "Would you dance with me?"

You didn't say yes or no, just teased me with your eyes, straightened my tie and smoothed my collar, and took me by the hand.

You had my heart before you moved against me like you did. Tammy was singing "Stand by Your Man," and we were changing all the "he's" to "she's" inside our heads to make it fit right. After you moved that way, you had more than my heart. You made me ache and you liked that. So did I.

The older butches always warned me, if you want to keep your marriage, don't go to the bars. But I've always been a one-woman butch. Besides, this was our community, the only one we belonged to, so we went every weekend.

There were two kinds of fights in the bars. Most weekends had one kind or the other, some weekends both.

There were the fist fights between the butch women — full of booze, shame, jealous insecurity. Sometimes the fights were awful and spread like a web to trap everyone in the bar, like the night you-know-who lost her eye when she got hit upside the head with a bar stool.

I was real proud that in all those years I never hit another butch woman. See, I loved them too, and I understood their pain and their shame, because I was so much like them. I loved the lines etched in their faces and hands and the curves of their work-weary shoulders. Sometimes I looked in the mirror and wondered what I would look like when I was their age. Now I know!

In their own way, they loved me too. They protected me, because they knew I wasn't a "Saturday-night butch." (The weekend butches were scared of me, because I was a stone he-she. If only they had known how powerless I really felt inside!) But the older butches, they knew the whole road that lay ahead of me, and they wished I didn't have to go down it, because it hurt so much.

When I came into the bar in drag, kind of hunched over, they told me, "Be proud of what you are," and then they adjusted my tie sort of like you did.

I was like them. They knew I didn't have a choice. So I never fought them with my fists. We clapped one another on the back in the bars and watched one another's back at the factory.

But then there were the times that our real enemies came in the front door — drunken gangs of sailors, Klan-type thugs, psychopaths, cops. You always knew when they came in, because someone had the foresight to pull the plug on the jukebox. No matter how many times it happened, we all still went, "Aw..." when the music stopped, and then we got down to business.

When the bigots came in, it was time to fight, and fight we did. We fought hard, butch and femme, men and women together.

When the music stopped and it was the cops at the door, someone plugged the music back in and we switched dance partners. We in our suits and ties paired off with our drag queen sisters in their dresses and pumps. It's hard to remember that it was illegal then for two women or two men to sway to music together. When the music ended, the butches bowed, our femme partners curtsied, and we returned to our seats, our lovers, and our drinks to await our fates.

That's when I remember your hand on my belt, up under my suit jacket. That's where your hand stayed the whole time the cops were there. "Take it easy, honey. Stay with me, baby, cool off," you'd be cooing in my ear as if singing a lover's song sung to warriors who needed to pick and choose their battles to survive.

We learned fast that the cops always pulled the police van right up to the bar door and left snarling dogs inside so that we couldn't get out. We were trapped, all right.

Remember that night you stayed home with me after I got my hand caught in the machine at the factory? That was the night ... you remember. The cops picked out the most stone butch of them all to destroy with humiliation, a woman everyone said "wore a raincoat in the shower." We heard they stripped her, slow, in front of everyone in the bar, and laughed at her trying to cover up her nakedness. Later she went mad, they said. Later she hung herself.

What would I have done if I had been there that night?

I'm remembering the busts in the bars in Canada. Packed in the police vans, all the Saturday-night butches giggled and tried to fluff up their hair and switch clothing so that they could get thrown in the tank with the femme women — said it would be like "dyin' and goin' to heaven."

We never switched clothing. Neither did our drag queen sisters. We knew, and so did you, what was coming. We needed our sleeves rolled up, our hair slicked back, to live through it. Our hands were cuffed tight behind our backs. Yours were cuffed in front. You loosened my tie, unbuttoned my collar, and touched my face. I saw the pain and fear for me in your face, and I whispered it would be all right. We knew it wouldn't be.

I never told you what they did to us down there — queens in one tank, stone butches in the next — but you knew. One at a time they would drag our brothers out of the cells, slapping and punching them, locking the bars behind them fast in case we lost control and tried to stop them — as if we could.

They'd handcuff a brother's wrists to his ankles or chain him, face against the bars. They made us watch.

Sometimes we'd catch the eyes of the terrorized victim, or the soon-to-be, caught in the vise of torture, and we'd say gently, "I'm with you, honey, look at me, stay with me, we'll take you home."

We never cried in front of the cops. We knew we were next.

The next time the cell door opens it will be me they drag out and chain spread-eagled to the bars.

Did I survive? I guess I did. But only because I knew I might get home to you.

They let us out last, one at a time on Monday morning. No charges. Too late to call in sick to work, no money, hitchhiking, crossing the border on foot, in rumpled clothes, bloody, needing a shower, hurt, scared.

I knew you'd be home if I could get there.

You ran a bath for me with sweet-smelling bubbles. You always laid out a fresh pair of white BVDs and a t-shirt for me and left me alone to wash off the first layer of shame.

I remember, it was always the same. I would put on the briefs, and then I'd just get the t-shirt over my head and you would find some reason to come into the bathroom, to get something or put something away. In a glance you would memorize the wounds on my body like a road map — the gashes, bruises, cigarette burns.

Later, in bed, you held me gently, touching me everywhere, the tenderest touches reserved for the places I was hurt, knowing each and every sore place — inside and out.

You didn't flirt with me right away, knowing I wasn't feeling confident enough to be sexy. But later you coaxed my pride back out again, showing me how much you wanted me. You knew melting the stone again would take you weeks.

Lately I've read these stories by women who are angry with stone lovers, even mocking their passion when they finally give way to trusting, to being touched.

And I'm wondering: did it hurt you, the times I couldn't let you touch me? I hope it didn't. You never showed it if it did. You knew it wasn't you I was keeping myself safe from. You treated my stone self as a wound that needed loving healing. Thank you. No one's ever done that since. If you were here tonight — well, it's hypothetical, isn't it?

I never said these things to you.

Tonight I remember the night I got busted alone, on strange turf. You're probably wincing already, but I have to say this to you out loud.

That night, we drove ninety miles to a bar to meet friends who never showed up. (Later we found out they were at home drinking and fighting.)

That night, when the cops raided the club, I was the only he-she in the place, and that one cop with gold bars on his uniform came right over to me and told me to stand up.

He put his hands all over me, pulled up the band of my jockeys, and told his men to cuff me: I didn't have on three pieces of women's clothing. I wanted to fight right then and there because I knew that chance would be lost in a moment.

But I also knew that everyone would be beaten that night if I fought back, so I just stood there. I saw that they had pinned your arms behind your back and cuffed your hands. One cop had his arm across your throat. I remember the look in your eyes. It hurts me even now.

They cuffed my hands so tight behind my back that I almost cried out.

Then the cop unzipped his pants real slow with a smirk on his face and ordered me down on my knees.

At first I thought to myself, "I can't!" Then I said out loud to myself and to you and to him, "I won't!" I never told you this before, but something changed inside of me in that moment. I learned the difference between what I can't do and what I refuse to do.

I paid the price for that lesson. Do I have to tell you every detail? Thank you.

When I got out of the tank the next morning, you were there; you bailed me out. No charges — they just kept the money. You had waited all night long in that police station. Only I know how hard that was for you to withstand their leers, their taunts, their threats. I knew you cringed with every sound you strained to hear from back in the cells. You prayed you wouldn't hear me scream. I didn't.

When we got outside into the parking lot, you stopped and put your hands lightly on my shoulders and avoided my eyes. You gently rubbed the bloody places on my shirt and said, "I'll never get these stains out."

Damn anyone who thinks that means you were relegated in life to worrying about my ring-around-the-collar.

106

I knew exactly what you meant. It was such an oddly sweet way of saying, or not saying, what you were feeling. Sort of the way I shut down emotionally when I feel scared and hurt and helpless and say little funny things that seem so out of context.

You drove us home with my head in your lap all the way, caressing my face. You ran the bath. Set out my fresh underwear. Put me to bed. Stroked me carefully. Held me gently.

That night I woke up and found myself alone in bed. You were drinking alone at the kitchen table, head in your hands. You were sobbing.

I took you firmly in my arms and held you, and you struggled and beat against my chest with your fists, because the enemy wasn't there to hit. Moments later you recalled the bruises on my chest and cried even harder, sobbing, "It's my fault, I couldn't stop them."

I've always wanted to tell you this: in that one moment I knew you really did understand how I felt in life. Choking on anger, feeling so powerless, unable to protect myself or those I loved most, yet fighting back again and again, unwilling to give up. I didn't have the words to tell you this then. I just said, "It'll be okay, it'll be all right."

And then we smiled ironically at what I'd said, and I took you back to our bed and made the best love to you I could, considering the shape I was in. You knew not to try to touch me that night. You just stroked my hair and cried and cried.

When did we get separated in life, sweet warrior woman? We thought we'd won the war of liberation when we embraced the word *gay*. Then, suddenly, there were professors and doctors and lawyers coming out of the woodwork telling us that meetings should be run by Robert's Rules of Order. (Who died and left Robert god?)

We dressed up after work for the new meetings on campus, but they drove us out, made us feel ashamed of how we looked. They said we were male chauvinist pigs: the enemy. It was women's hearts they broke. We were not hard to send away. We went quietly.

The plants closed, something we never could have imagined.

That's when I was sent into exile and began passing as a man. Strange to be exiled from your own gender to borders that will never be home.

You were banished too, to another land, with your own gender, and yet forced apart from the women you loved as much as you tried to love yourself.

For more than twenty years I have lived on this lonely shore, wondering what became of you. Did you wash off your Saturday-night makeup in shame? Did you burn in anger when women said, "If I wanted a man, I'd be with a real one"?

Are you turning tricks today? Are you waiting tables or learning WordPerfect?

Are you in a lesbian bar looking out of the corner of your eye for the butchest woman in the room? Do the women there talk about Democratic politics and photography and co-ops? Are you with women who bleed only monthly on their cycles?

Or are you in another blue-collar town, lying with an unemployed auto worker who is much more like me than they are, listening for the even breathing of your sleeping children? Do you bind his emotional wounds the way you tried to heal mine?

Do you ever think of me in the cool night?

I've been writing this letter to you for hours. My ribs hurt bad from a beating two weeks ago. You know.

I never could have survived this long if I'd never known your love. Yet still I ache with missing you. I need you so.

Only you could melt this stone. Are you ever coming back?

The storm has passed now. There is a pink glow at the horizon outside my window. I am remembering the nights I fucked you deep and slow until the sky was just this color.

I can't think about you anymore; the pain is swallowing me up. I have to put your memory away, like a precious sepia photograph. There are still so many things I want to tell you, to share with you.

Since I can't mail you this letter, I'll send it to a place where they keep women's memories safe. Maybe someday, passing through this big city, you will stop and read it. Maybe you won't.

Good night, my love.

Bonni Barringer

When butches cry

When butches cry
no mountains quake
no islands form
only to slip into the sea

Nor do trees fall
nor lightning strike
nor any other god-done thing

When butches cry
they weep, they wail,
they gnash their teeth
and moan

Strong woman's pain
it's just the same
except it's mostly done
alone.

Elly Bulkin

An old dyke's tale:
An interview with
Doris Lunden

Born in New Orleans in 1936, Doris Lunden came out into the French Quarter in 1953. She left New Orleans in 1957, lived briefly in Corpus Christi, and moved to New York City in 1958. Following her recovery from alcoholism, she became an activist in the gay, lesbian, antinuclear, and peace movements. She changed her name to Blue just around the time she became a grandmother in 1980, after this interview was conducted. Since 1982, she has lived in a community of lesbians in the Florida Keys.*
Cathy Cockrell assisted in editing the interview excerpted here.

Elly Bulkin: I thought we could start with talking about your coming out and with your experiences of being a lesbian in the fifties.

Doris Lunden: I started coming out when I was thirteen, when I fell in love with Gloria, the girl down the block. I wasn't really conscious that this was a taboo until my aunt began to react to my being so open about my feelings. It was just after that time that I heard the word *lesbian* and I went to the library to do the research that I think has been done by so many lesbians throughout history. From that time I realized that I should be quiet about my feelings. It was just after that that I found *The Well of Loneliness* at the drugstore bookracks — of course, I went back to that bookrack, I haunted it, and I found other books, perhaps half a dozen. Before that time I had no inkling how many lesbians there might be. Then I did at least get the idea that there were probably some more in my city.

I was in reform school and I had a lover there. After I got out, my lover's father was in prison and when he got out of prison he used to be able to take her out on the last Sunday of the month and she'd want to come and

---

* See also Sky Vanderlinde's memoir "Loving Blue," in this volume.

see me. So he would take her to my house. He took us to a place called the Starlet Lounge once, which was a gay bar that I later came out into ... in the French Quarter in New Orleans. I realize now that he knew that we were lovers and was saying it was neat, which was really quite amazing. But then he went back to jail and that setup ended and I went back to reform school eventually.

EB: What were you in for?

DL: The first time I was running away all the time and they kept threatening me with the House of the Good Shepherd every time they retrieved me. The House of the Good Shepherd was like a convent operated by Catholic nuns, but it was funded by the city as a reformatory for girls. It occupied a whole block in New Orleans and had a big wall around it; all the windows had shutters and it was used to scare every little girl in New Orleans into conformity. I think that one of the greatest things I ever did was that I finally accepted that I did not want to remain where I was and that I was eventually going to go to this place and I went and put myself in. I went up and I rang the bell and I said, "I don't have any place else to go," and they took me in. I hoped that it would force my father into finding someplace to live where I could live with him, and it did.

EB: Were you living with your aunt?

DL: No, I was living with a woman that I called my aunt who'd been a friend of my mother. I lived with an awful lot of people after my mother died when I was about ten. I lived primarily with my godmother, a woman who had also been a friend of my mother. Traditionally in French families, godmothers really do take responsibility for the children if something happens to the mother. My godmother and I had an incredible struggle about power and control and independence and so on. So I would run away. And I used to run to my father when I was younger, but he'd always bring me back, so I saw that I had to get by on my own. I guess two weeks was the most that I managed to avoid the cops. They'd find me. But once you've been in reform school it's very easy to go back. Next time I got into trouble I was sent back to reform school. We were stealing license plates from wrecked cars and selling them. It was a little racket. But because I had already been there, I just got sent back. It was in reform school that I first heard about the Goldenrod, which was a lesbian bar; it was in a residential area out near the lakefront, in the suburbs.

EB: What year was that?

DL: Probably '52 or '53. I was about sixteen. (I was born in '36.) So I got up my courage and decided to go to this bar. It was just beautiful; it was full of women and they were friendly and they invited me to sit at their tables, introduced themselves, introduced me around. Then I met a woman there that I liked...

I guess it was a couple of weeks, it wasn't very long after, and I was there with a girl I had been in reform school with. I was sixteen, she was fifteen. All of a sudden all the lights went on, the jukebox stopped, and the police came in and said that it was a raid and everyone was under arrest. Poor Pat! She gave her real age and I never saw her again after that; I'm sure she was sent back to the House of the Good Shepherd. I didn't lie about my name; somehow I thought they'd know I was lying about my name, so I gave them my real name and I gave them my real address, but I lied about my age — I said I was eighteen. They took us all to the precinct and booked us and put us in a cell. Then later that night or early in the morning the owner got us out on bond and they set the court date for the next night. Some women were saying that there'd been reporters outside and they were really scared.

The next morning I went down to the drugstore (the same one where I had found *The Well of Loneliness*) to get a cup of coffee and bought the newspaper and started looking for the police reports, where most arrests were reported in the paper. My father religiously read the police reports, so I knew he was going to find out about it if it was in the police report. It wasn't there and I was so relieved. Then I turned back to see what the news of the day was and the headline said, "64 Women, 1 Man Arrested." There were all kinds of remarks about what kind of bar it was, about the sign saying "no males allowed."

That night we had to go to court and I discovered then that they had raided every gay bar in New Orleans. It was like a big cleanup. I had never seen so many gay people in my whole life; I had no idea that there were so many gay people. It was really exciting! I almost forgot to be scared about whether I would be convicted or not. My case was dismissed, but I think that that set me free in some way.

EB: Were the other cases dismissed?

DL: I think they were. There may have been instances where people were found guilty of something; usually the charges were things like "wearing the clothes of the opposite sex" for drag queens and for butch lesbians, or "no honest, visible means of support." It was true; most of us didn't have any honest, visible means of support. If you chose to dress in such a way that clearly identified you as gay, it was impossible to get any kind of straight job, assuming you would want one. Most often all of those charges were dismissed when you came before a judge; I don't know why particularly, except that I believe the arresting was intended as a kind of harassment — when it was intense enough it drove people away.

Some of us just didn't have any other place to go. We were just caught every time they happened to walk in when we were there. Whereas for other people, just being there in that bar was one of the riskiest things they'd ever done in their lives. If they even witnessed an arrest, even if they didn't get taken in, it was usually sufficient to scare them away for years to come. You see how this kind of stuff works to limit what kinds of risks people take. When I look back at that now, I am really amazed that people were persistent; I really wonder why I was unconscious that I was part of a resistance.

You can guess what happened to the lives of all those women as a result of that raid. Most of them were closeted, were from New Orleans, many of them living with their families and with jobs. I think they thought they were pretty safe there in that bar. It was probably shocking to them to get included in that sweep.

Back at home, I was just dismissing it by saying, "Well, I just went to see what kind of bar it was and it happened to be the night." My father didn't pursue it, but my brother, who was a year younger than I, was really freaked out by this. When I had gotten out of reform school, he had this girlfriend whom he was really crazy about and could hardly wait to have me meet her. I did meet her, and gradually she began to follow me around and to take my side in the arguments we had and stopped seeing him. What I discovered later was that everybody in the neighborhood was speculating that I was a lesbian and they literally did follow us around and peek in windows to see if we were kissing. I think he was angry about this kind of stuff when here I get arrested in this bar and it's real clear that I was a lesbian. He became hostile and we had a really bad fight in which I was hurt and that's when I left home.

I was hurt really bad and I called up this woman whom I had been seeing from the Goldenrod and told her what had happened and she said, "Take a cab and come over." I wound up living with her for a while. Actually I wound up living with her off and on for a year and a half.

But then I was free. The cat was out of the bag. I didn't have anybody that I had to worry about anymore and I could go ahead and explore whatever it was I wanted to do. I didn't have any idea what I was going to do to make a living; I didn't even think about it. I had lived in a family or in a number of families where nobody was really in a profession. I guess my godfather, who was a merchant seaman, was the most in a profession of anyone that I knew. The only person that I knew who went to college was my mother — somebody famous from her hometown had put her through college. So I didn't have too many notions about what I was going to do. I always knew I wasn't going to get married, but I didn't have any plans about what I was going to do to take care of myself.

Then I began dressing up and wearing these clothes that were taboo before. I had already had short hair, but now I really began to go at it, and I got a crew cut and blue suede shoes like Elvis Presley was singing about.

But I had an economic problem — I was totally dependent on this woman whom I was involved with. She was living with her husband and her four children. She had her room and he had his room and she had to visit him once a week. But she was otherwise free to pursue her own interests as long as she took care of the house, and he would go to work and bring the money in. When I lived with her I lived there in her room in his house. That was very weird, considering the head I was coming from, the kind of role I imagined myself playing. Sometime before the raid, I had read in *Sexology* magazine about Christine Jorgenson and sex-change operations. I really started thinking that that's what it was — my *feelings* are natural so it must be my *body* that's wrong, and it's too bad they don't have an operation for me. I think at that time, before I found a community, I would have been very willing to have an operation in order to set things right. I had an awful lot of the kind of values that I thought I should have if I was a boy, that I would want to get married and support my wife and all that. That was really at odds with what was going on, which was that I was living with this woman in her husband's house. I didn't even dare say anything; I had no economic power.

We were going to all these bars and I was observing, I was learning — it was like school for me. I saw that a lot of butches had "old ladies" who were prostitutes. Some of them had several "old ladies" and that was called "sister-in-lawing"; they actually lived together, two or three "old ladies" and a butch. That was *very* admired, that was a pimp par excellence. But I was coming from too square a place to relate to that at the time, so the only option for me was prostitution. I didn't even expect to get a job in a bar at that time; I wasn't even of age but nobody knew it.

So one night Virginia and I were at the bar and this guy propositioned me and I went with him. I'd never been in bed with a man in my life, so I thought I'd find out … God, it was really, really awful. But I got the twenty dollars and I came back and I tried to buy a drink for Virginia and she wouldn't let me; a lot of people were upset, because they knew I had never done anything like that before. And that was the end of it. Except that in a few months I realized that I was pregnant. Once I was pregnant I figured, "I can't get any more pregnant," and I needed money, so during that period, until I was too pregnant, I was a prostitute. I didn't do anything different — I didn't dress up or do anything like that — but there were plenty of people coming into those bars looking for sex and there were a lot of men who, I think, felt more like men if they could get a lesbian to go to bed with them.

EB: They thought they were going to change your life.

DL: It seemed really important to them that you said that you enjoyed it. So I just saw it as an acting job basically. Lila and I were buddies — she was a drag butch like I was. We used to do shows together and we thought this was hysterical, because we were both stone butches, so we would never have anything to do with each other sexually; but we would just put on these great shows that we'd make a lot of money for — and I can just remember laughing in her cunt while all these guys would think we were sexually excited.

Right: Doris "Big Daddy" King, Stacey "Stormy" Lawrence, and Doris Lunden (then Doris Dubois), who is pregnant in this photo. Early morning outside Sy's 435 Lounge on the Esplanade in the French Quarter, New Orleans, spring 1954.

Below: Doris and Sunny, New Orleans, 1956

115

Lila had been kicked out of college for being a lesbian. She came from a middle-class background. She, too, got pregnant. She went home to her family after the baby was born. Her parents were taking care of the baby and she came back and very shortly got pregnant again and then she went back and was finally going to get married.

Between living with Virginia and being on my own I spent the next four years in those bars. I went from being a prostitute to learning to be a pimp, although we didn't call them pimps. I had a lot of lovers who were strippers. Strippers make money not so much by dancing but by B-drinking. I did B-drinking too, looking to roll somebody if they were flashing a lot of money. After Linda was born, I was real careful; I didn't want to get pregnant again. But I did a lot of other stuff like sex shows. A lot of people did.

When I came out in the bars of the French Quarter, I was coming from a place of being mad as hell that I was a girl, because clearly it was a boy's world. Later on I was falling in love with other girls and thinking of myself as a man trapped in a woman's body — I think I bought that kind of an idea for quite a long time. And when I did hit the bars, I had the right kind of build; I could pass as a boy and that was valued. It was considered really good that I had such small breasts; I didn't even have to wear a breastband. Women used to wrap their breasts, strap them down so that they wouldn't show. I didn't have to do that in order to pass. So that gave me more mobility; I could go outside into the "American Zone" (outside the French Quarter). If you were an obvious lesbian in an area where you weren't known or you didn't have friends, you could get the hell beaten out of you.

What I discovered when I hit the bars was very extreme butch and femme and that seemed to fit with my notion of having boys' feelings and so on. I was a no-touch butch. If you didn't pick a role — butch or femme — and stick with that, people thought you were mixed up and you didn't know who you were and you were laughed at and called "ki-ki" — a sort of queer of the gay world.

Butches were also vulnerable in that if you slept with a woman and let that woman touch you, she could turn around and brag about that to everybody and ridicule you publicly. This was called "flipping a butch." It was a really long time before I realized that there might have been another reason why I chose my role and that had to do with wanting to be in control. As the butch, I felt I was in control; if I wasn't letting anybody touch me sexually, I would be in control. The fear of being passive was something I never really had to confront until the women's movement. I *did* confront it from time to time, because my emotions would sometimes be in conflict with what I thought was in my best interests. With a lover who wanted to make love to me too, I would feel excited, but I also felt that there were very good reasons why I shouldn't allow that to happen, because of how it might affect my privileges, how it might affect my standing in the community.

EB: Did you find that there was more flexibility when you were involved in more serious or long-term relationships?

DL: My feeling now is that most lesbians into roles cheated a whole lot more than I did. I really took all that more seriously than they did and I believe that part of the reason for that was that this other personal thing was going on — that I was really afraid of my feelings and afraid of not being in control. I never had to look at that as a personal problem to deal with until I got involved in the women's movement.

After I left home my brother found out that I hung out in the Starlet Lounge and he and his friends used to come and taunt us. There was nothing that could be done about that, because that's what the bars were, that's where they made their money — with the tourists coming to look at the queers. We were only a small part of the population of the bar actually — we were the sideshow. No wonder we did all the drugs and stuff. I didn't acknowledge to myself that I was part of a sideshow and that I was on display, but that was exactly what it was.

The bars weren't integrated at all. I remember one time we went to an all-black bar. Somebody knew somebody there. It was literally illegal for white people to go to an all-black place or vice versa.

EB: Was it a gay bar?

DL: It was a huge place where some gay people went, the Penguin Club.

EB: Did you have problems when you went?

DL: No, but it was a really amazing experience for me, because I grew up in New Orleans during segregation — I never went to school with any black children. I lived in poor neighborhoods, so there were black people in the neighborhoods. But it was as if there was some kind of invisible wall — we didn't even go to the same movie theater. That's part of how you would develop some kind of social contact between groups of people. We didn't drink out of the same water fountain, which created certain fantasies or larger-than-life feelings or ideas — I'm sure much the way that a lot of people feel about *lesbians* — that *black* people were completely different. I remember when I was little I was told that black people had blue blood — and I believed it until I saw a black man come staggering out of a bar having been stabbed in the abdomen and bleeding.

To go into this Penguin Club it was as if I were doing the *most taboo* thing to be there. They said that if the police come in, to tell them that you know the owner, and that would make it okay, if you were a personal friend of the owner. I don't know what the hell we'd have been charged with. I danced with this black woman there and I remember feeling as if I were doing this really exciting, daring thing. The feeling, I think, both ways, was a lot of curiosity and amusement — it was friendly, like we came from different planets and had an encounter somewhere. That's what it felt like.

Later, when I was about four months pregnant, I went to Chicago for about a month and I was just amazed that the bars were integrated and there were black bus drivers. It amazed me how this just happened and it didn't disrupt anything at all. I was coming from a city where the buses had a divider that said "for colored only" and whites could move the divider back and forth and all of the black people had to sit in back of it. I had never thought to question that black people had to sit in the back of the bus or that there were different drinking fountains. I was plenty curious about what the water tasted like in the "colored only" drinking fountain. But I never had any friends who were black — not until New York, not until the early sixties. Eventually I was driven out of New Orleans by the police.

EB: How did they do that?

DL: The charges began to get more serious and they began to do things like break the door down and tear the whole apartment apart looking for drugs. And I was using some drugs and the chances were that sooner or later they would catch me — I wasn't any big drug dealer and I wasn't a junkie, but everybody fooled around with some drugs in that kind of situation at that time. They arrested my lover for prostitution and she was convicted and given a suspended sentence, probably because she was white and had no record. They picked her up at our house, where she had brought a john. They offered to make a deal that if we'd pay them $250 they wouldn't show up at court to testify and we paid them and they showed up to testify. We knew that it was going to be really bad from there on out.

We had a chance to get out so we did. We were in Corpus Christi, Texas, for a year and a half before coming to New York.

When I came to New York in the late fifties my brother had come out and he was living there with a drag queen who was working at a club on Second Avenue called the Ace of Clubs. Anyhow, his lover got me a job working there — it was all female impersonators in the show and all lesbians wearing tuxedos or black suits and ties waiting tables. My lover, Sunny, stayed in Texas to find a home for the animals and then she came up. I didn't like that job at that Ace of Clubs.

I had a lot of attitudes after we got out of New Orleans about what I had been involved in and a lot of sense of shame about it. I kind of wanted to "go straight," morally speaking. That was fed into me by Sunny. It took me a long time to realize that she really thought that she was better than me — she had had a couple of years of college before she ran away, and her family had money and she'd lived in Hawaii for a while. I've had this experience a lot with middle-class lovers — I've had this sort of fatal attraction for girls from the other side of the tracks — I guess there's something fascinating about women whose lives have been different. And some pretty self-oppressive attitudes of thinking that they *were* made of finer stuff. I call this the "diamond in the rough" syndrome. Many of my lovers have seen me as a diamond in the rough and they were going to polish me up — and to some extent they have.

So Sunny met this gay man in a donut shop who was an aspiring dancer and through him we met some other people. They were all sort of intellectual; I was kind of attracted by all this but I wasn't well received by them. They loved Sunny, but they couldn't get past the way I dressed. I was dying to go to the opera and see *Carmen* and I thought I'd just wear my suit and go to the opera. But they just freaked! Someone loaned me a dress and I went to the opera and I began to accept that part of going straight. By this time I had a job in a factory and I had to wear a skirt to work. Nobody said I had to wear a skirt; in fact I think I probably looked weirder in a skirt, because no matter how I dressed I would *not* give up my hair. I wore a lot of hair oil in my hair and it was a slicked-back Tony Curtis–type hairstyle. No matter how I modified my clothes, my hair stayed the same. Even when I thought I looked passable — everyone knows I'm a woman, they won't mistake me for a man — that was when I looked the most bizarre.

I was involved in a group that read plays. I was reading everything, I was consuming, I was soaking up culture, I was feeling excited by all this. I was in this group that read plays so I could get rid of my southern accent; I believed, and nobody disputed, that it sounded uneducated, ignorant. I made some efforts at modifying how I dressed to try to fit in with a group of people whom I wanted some kind of intellectual stimulation from. Their attitude toward me was always that I was very bright (diamond in the rough) and that nobody would ever be able to tell that I didn't have a couple of years of college. I felt *incredibly* inadequate about my ninth-grade education. They used to say that if I was going to try to get a job I should just lie and claim I'd had a couple of years of college. I couldn't do it; I felt the gaps; no matter how much I read and how much I knew, I could never be sure that there weren't these *big* gaps that were perfectly obvious.

About that time Sunny and I broke up and I began to get involved with Jeanie, who lived on the top floor and up till then had been straight. All of our friends were gay or knew lots of gay people but were freaked out about *us*. She was also very reluctant to get involved with me, because she didn't want to be a lesbian. In the midst of all this I got word about my daughter. I had given her up for adoption when she was a year old, although I had a lot of guilt about it. There was an agreement that I would be able to see her and when she was older she would know that I was her mother. Instead, they just disappeared after the papers were signed.

EB: You knew the people who adopted her?

DL: Yes, a guy who was the manager of one of the bars that I hung out in and his wife. In fact, she took off with Linda and left him. This was some three years later. My godmother was calling to say that she was going to adopt my daughter, that the woman was no longer able to take care of her. By this time my life had changed enough that I felt I could take care of Linda. *Everybody* got involved. We got money together and I flew down there to get to her. There was this big scene and I got her. Nobody wanted to give her to me, because I was a lesbian; I went down there pretending that I wasn't a lesbian anymore and was on the verge of getting married.

EB: So she had been legally adopted.

DL: Yes, she had. I never did get her back legally. But I got her up here and once I did I changed addresses and disappeared. She was four and a half then.

Jeanie and I moved in together and we became like this little family. I would never have made it without Jeanie. We were very isolated, because none of our friends could accept that we were lovers; it made them all uncomfortable, perhaps because we were in such obvious roles.

EB: Did you know any other lesbians who had kids?

DL: No. I was very careful to keep Linda separated from my social life, so we would only invite over trusted friends when Linda was at home. When we had a party, I would arrange for Linda to spend the night with my brother. If anybody ever made remarks about how she was really a cute kid, she'd make a nice little lesbian when she got older, I was just really upset. I guess I was pretty self-hating.

EB: Did she ask questions at all about it, when she got a little older?

DL: Not really, but she used to make remarks that would flip me out. I remember one night Jeanie and I were getting dressed to go out to a dance and she came over and said, "Gee, Mommy, you look so handsome," and then she said to Jeanie something about how she "looked beautiful." I remember being amused on the one hand and a little unnerved on the other. I'd go to PTA meetings and make efforts to look as straight as possible. I always felt guilty, because I didn't encourage her to bring friends home, but encouraging her to bring friends home meant such a trip for myself in order to play the role that I thought a mother was supposed to play. Because I didn't have any friends who had children, she didn't really have many kids to play with.

I guess I came out to her when she was ten or eleven. In fact, I just checked it out with her — we were talking about prejudice and I talked about prejudice against lesbians and I said, "You know, Aunt Jeanie and I were more than just friends." (By this time, Jeanie and I had split up.) She said, "Yeah, I knew that." She used to have this timing, of finding a way to quietly walk into the bedroom when we were necking or something like that. That was really difficult, because I thought we shouldn't show any affection in front of her.

120

During that time we made friends with a black woman named Norma Dee, who lived in our neighborhood. She and her daughter Snooky were involved with a black lesbian social club. This club used to give these *big* dances up at the Hunts Point Ballroom, so we went up to one of those dances and we made a lot of friends. There were some interracial lesbian couples that we were friends with. I guess all the civil rights stuff was going on in the midst of this but I didn't know shit about any of that; I wasn't political. But that was the most satisfying social life I ever had. One thing I see that's happened in my life, probably because of the erratic kind of childhood I had, was that I had no skills in how to maintain friendships. I sort of bounce along and if people don't continue connections, I lose them. Jeanie played that role.

EB: Making the contacts.

DL: Right. I guess partly that's why I didn't learn how to do it too. I guess that's one of the other injuries of roles. Years later when the white lesbian community got organized and Lesbian Lifespace decided to have the "first ever" lesbian boatride, it just was a laugh to me, because I had been on a lesbian boatride organized by black lesbians *many* years before.

Norma Dee did parties too — it was how you paid the rent if you were short of money; she did sewing and that was sort of erratic. At a pay party you would pay fifty cents to get in, and there might be a coat check for a quarter, and then there'd be fried chicken dinners, salad, greens, and all that for a dollar, and then the drinks were fifty cents. I was frequently the bartender at these affairs. Norma Dee and Snooky and Jeanie and I started a social club — we had one big event at our house, but it never got off the ground. At these big dances, there weren't all lesbians that came — a lot of family members came. My impression was that the attitude of the black community toward lesbians was not the hostile thing that I observe now. These were the only women I knew who were out to their families.

EB: And seemed accepted?

DL: Yeah. So the dances consisted of a certain percentage of men, some of them gay and some of them members of the family. There was a great variety of ages — young teenage dykes all decked out in the finest threads and fifty-year-old dykes who didn't come out too often but would come out for some big thing. Black lesbians had a whole network of things that would go on.

I continued to be friends with Norma Dee, but I don't know what happened to the rest of it — I lost contact. There might have been some other things going on that I wasn't thinking about too consciously, but I know that there was a young white lesbian from the bars who had been up to Harlem who got beaten up and stabbed. Also, I played on a softball team called the Amerks that was mostly black women, and we practiced on Randall's Island and then we used to come over to a bar on 125th

Street to get beers after practice; they would not leave me there; they would want to wait until I was ready to leave and see that I got on a train. They were concerned about my physical safety as a white person in Harlem. So those things may, without my being conscious of it, have had their effects. It became easier to go in places where there were mostly white people.

EB: This was the middle or late sixties?

DL: I'm sure that this was when the black movement began to be militant. But I wasn't on to any of those things.

EB: The movement from a civil rights to a Black Power focus?

DL: That's probably what was going on. That just fascinates me — how our choices and what we do is not so clear to us, that we're pushed and channeled in this direction and that without knowing why...

EB: ...and looking back and seeing it in some clearer historical context. When did you start being aware that there was a women's movement?

DL: I didn't discover the women's movement until after I discovered the gay movement. I attended some of the Gay Liberation Front dances and I went to DOB dances and meetings, although I was too drunk most of the time to understand the ideas being discussed. I marched in the second annual gay pride march in 1971, and was so drunk I could hardly stand up. I was in the last years of a twenty-year bout with alcoholism.

In early 1972, after a hospitalization and several months of sobriety, I went one Sunday to the GAA Firehouse. I had one or two friends on the Lesbian Liberation Committee of GAA whom I had known premovement, so I had some sense that I was connected. When I got involved in the movement I was real afraid that I would be attacked by lesbian-feminists for my past role-playing. That was a hard time, because I was going through a lot of that alone and in silence. My first thoughts about roles were to recognize that they were exploitative of other women and I should be ashamed of that — and I *was* properly ashamed of that. It was a lot longer before I realized the ways those roles had been oppressive to me. I did very slowly go through a whole process of change. Being around a community of women who felt really good about themselves showed me for the first time that there were all kinds of reasons why I would want to be a woman. These young amazons came along and said, "We're powerful and strong, independent," and all the things I knew I had to be but didn't think I could be as a woman. To some extent, some of the changes in the ways I behaved at first were conforming rather than actual change — conforming so as not to be rejected. One thing that's really amazing to me was to note how very little my clothing habits have changed over all these years and what an education it's been to see that the change has been other people's heads and the way they perceive me, because *I* have not changed that much but *they* have changed incredibly and I feel that about lesbian-feminists as well as everybody else.

I wonder about the changes; as much as they *seem* so profound, I wonder whether they are. I come in contact with a lot of young lesbian-feminists who are college students or college graduates. But if you go where you find women who don't relate to the movement, things aren't all that different than they used to be. That makes sense. If role-playing, heterosexual role-playing, is taught through propaganda and especially through the family, then the way your family plays its role can have a lot of effect on how you see yourself, how you behave in your relationships. In my instance, if I had two people to choose to identify with and I wanted to be a survivor, then I would have chosen my father — to survive. I think I must have done that, and I'll spend the rest of my life finding all of that and doing something about it where it's not in my interests or where it's exploitative of somebody else.

From the diary of Marge McDonald (1931–1986)

Born in the small Appalachian mining town of Nelsonville, Ohio, Marge McDonald moved to Syracuse, New York, in the late fifties so that she could live a lesbian life. A poet, writer, and collector of lesbiana, Marge willed her writings and books to the Lesbian Herstory Archives. Right before she died, Marge had returned to Nelsonville for one final attempt at reconciliation with her family. Unfortunately, she did not live to see this achieved. Her writings had to be rescued from a family intent on their suppression. The following excerpt, carefully typed and dated, captures the moment a 23-year-old Margie entered the butch-femme community of Columbus, Ohio, in 1955.

March 31, 1955, Thursday

Well, it happened today, after months of driving around every night until morning, restless, always hunting. I found it!

Betty, my neighbor, just got in from Massachusetts. She came over to see me and was telling me about a bar she had visited there. She and her girlfriend had dropped into a bar to get a drink and there were nothing but women there. When the waitress started flirting with her, they left. We both laughed about it. I said, "I wish I knew a bar like that in Columbus so that Ted (imaginary boyfriend) and I could go — just for kicks."

"We passed a place like that the other night when we were taking Shirley home. Bob said it was a place where queers hang out, but I can't remember where it is."

"Can you find out?"

"Wanda will remember. When she gets off from work at seven, we can pick her up and find out where it is."

So we picked up Wanda. After a while, I brought up the subject of the queer bar and asked where it was, being careful to mention that I wanted to go there with Ted. She showed me where it was. I was numb inside with anticipation, fear, excitement, everything. Sis, the girl sitting beside me, said she thought it might be fun to see such a place. We dropped the other kids off, then decided to investigate the place. I was hoping Sis would go with me, because I didn't want to go in there by myself. I needed someone to bolster my courage. As we walked in the door, I was so excited I could hardly walk!

There was a long bar running down the left side of the room, a jukebox at the back, and shuffleboard up front, and on the right side of a partition, there were booths, tables, and a piano. Near the door, men were sitting at the bar — but at the back, women in slacks and shirts were sitting, talking, drinking.

Sis and I sat down in a booth on the other side. A heavyset woman with shoulder-length, brown, wavy hair took our order. Sis and I eagerly drank in the fact that she was in slacks and a t-shirt. We sat there laughing and looking around, but we couldn't see too much, because the partition blocked our view of the women at the end of the bar.

After a while, we left — but Saturday evening at about eight o'clock (April 2, 1955), we went back and this time we sat at the bar among the women. We had decided that we couldn't see enough sitting in the booth. Sis whispered to me that some women on the other side of her had said, "Here's two new customers." We laughed and after a while, Sis said, "Let's go. I don't like this place very well." I replied, "Oh, I don't know, I sort of like it here." But we left and went down to Casey's, another bar, and had a beer. I feigned sickness and got rid of her and ten o'clock found me driving around the block near the Town Grill [the name of the bar], trying to summon up enough nerve to go in by myself.

Finally, having whipped up my courage, I walked in and took a seat among the girls at the bar. I was a wreck. My elbows were shaking even though I had them propped up on the bar. I was too frightened to look at anybody. I stared straight in front of me. A cute girl with brown hair and warm eyes came up and took my order for a beer after I proved I was twenty-one (I was twenty-three at the time).

I had sat there for a while when the girl on my left turned and said something about the weather. I mumbled some stupid reply about being so nervous I could hardly talk. I mentally kicked myself for not having started a conversation. I had sat there for what seemed like an hour but probably wasn't, when a pretty blonde walked up to me and said in a warm friendly voice, "I hope you don't think I am being fresh, but I have noticed that you are new here and that no one has been talking to you. They think you are a policewoman. I'm JoAnne and I want you to feel free to walk up and say 'Hi' to me anytime you see me." I managed a weak smile and said I would. I sat there, my brain jumping from one thought to another so fast my head was swimming. But through it all came the hope that they would accept me and like me and the fear that they wouldn't. I sat there looking at a boyish-looking girl behind the bar in slacks and a man's shirt. She had short dark brown hair and wore no lipstick. She attracted me that first night more than anyone. After 11:30, the crowd started thinning out and soon there were only a few left at the bar.

The woman on my left finally started a conversation and we talked about everything — books, music. After talking awhile, she had managed to draw out the pertinent facts that I was a homosexual but that I had never been around my own kind before.

❖

Her name was Lynn and we sat and talked until closing, twelve a.m. on Saturday. They locked the door and still we sat there. She kept playing "Ebbtide" on the jukebox and talking about her life in the navy. She said that if she had known what she was in the navy, she would have been court-martialed.

At about 12:45, we left. I insisted on giving her a lift home. She lived in the North End in a trailer, and on the way, I learned a lot of things that left me very surprised. I had supposed that you just met a girl and fell in love. I found out that the more masculine girls were called "butch" and the feminine girls were "femme." A "homosexual" was a "gay" person. A so-called normal person was a "straight" person. Well, I thought, Margie, you are in the "gay" life now!

Lynn warned me that it was no bed of roses and I agreed to that. I could realize that society would condemn me, people would shrink from me as if I were a leper, but I also realized that there would be the happiness of being around my own kind to make up for it. I decided that the happiness would outweigh the sorrow and that the "gay" life was for me.

When we arrived at the trailer, she invited me in for coffee. I accepted eagerly, glad of the chance to talk and be alone with a gay person. Lynn was obviously butch. She wore men's jeans, a t-shirt, and she walked like a boy. I asked how you could tell the difference between a femme and a butch and was told that a butch is the aggressor when making love. I decided I was butch, but she said she thought I was a femme. She soon drew my story out of me.

I found myself telling her of my father, who had died when I was five. I had a wonderful aunt, Dora, who because she could not have children sort of adopted me ... She centered her world around me, but because she was very religious, I ... hurt her deeply. I like to smoke, wear slacks, drink, and had my hair cut very short. She was brokenhearted about it.

I told Lynn how on New Year's Eve of 1949, I married a boy I had known for seven months. I thought I loved him; I didn't like it at home. I guess I thought being loved by him was better than not being loved at all. I had had crushes on girls when I was in my early teens. I thought it was just a stage I was going through and that I had outgrown it, until I developed a crush on a girl at work while my husband was in Las Vegas in the air force.

I spent the next six months going to a psychiatrist. He told me that when you put a person who is a child emotionally into a world full of adults and expect this person to act like an adult, it is too much for them and they retreat into a world of their own. He thought he had cured me of being a homosexual. I had an affair with a man just to prove to myself it was over.

On Thanksgiving, 1954, I went up to my husband's sister's house for dinner. Their mother and I were very good friends and when we were alone, she told me about her girlfriend and how beautiful their love had been. She told me that she had loved *me* for a long time. She said all of this without knowing I was a lesbian, just because I was easy to talk to. I was very surprised and began thinking about loving women again. Her daughter was in New York and I went up every night to keep her from becoming too lonely.

After a few weeks, I admitted that I had always been attracted to women. I decided then that I might as well stop fighting my true feelings and be happy. I stopped dating men and began the search for my own kind. I would drive around the city, feeling so lonely, thinking of all the people like me in this city, yet I couldn't find them. I knew the Blue Feather was for men and that it was listed in the white pages of the telephone book but not in the yellow pages, so I started going through the white pages, writing down the names of every bar that wasn't listed in the yellow pages and investigating them. I was only through the B's when I found the Townie.

Five o'clock found us sitting side by side on the couch still talking. We thought we should get some sleep, so Lynn decided to be my pillow. She held me in her arms. My face was against her breast. I wasn't sleepy though, so we continued to talk all the while. I was so happy to be so close to a woman. I lifted my face and she kissed me. My first kiss from a woman! I could never describe my feelings, so I won't even try.

It is sufficient to say that as long as I live, I shall never forget that moment — or the kiss.

Mabel Hampton Special Collection, Lesbian Herstory Archives

Mary Jane Butler, "running buddy" of Mabel Hampton, 1930

Audre Lorde

From "Tar Beach"

Gerri was young and black and lived in Queens and had a powder blue Ford that she nicknamed Bluefish. With her carefully waved hair, buttoned-down shirts, and gray flannel slacks she seemed just this side of square without being square at all once you got to know her. Through her Marion and I met other black lesbians who didn't come to Laurel's — the gay-girls' bar we frequented on weekends. By Gerri's invitation, and frequently by her wheels, we started going to parties on weekends in Brooklyn and Queens at different women's houses.

As a couple Marion and I were out of it a lot, since much of the role-playing that went on was beyond us. It seemed to both of us that butch and femme role-playing was the very opposite of what we felt being gay was all about — the love of women. As we saw it, only women who did not really love other women or themselves could possibly want to imitate the oppressive and stereotyped behavior so often associated with being men or acting like men. Of course, this was not a popular view. There were butches and there were femmes, but *lesbian*, like *black*, was still a fighting word.

Yet, Gerri's friends never put us down completely. Yes, we were peculiar, Marion and I, from our different colors right down to our raggedy-ass clothes. We had no regular jobs and queer heads — inside and out. The Afro hadn't been named yet, much less become popular, and Marion's shaggy-bowl haircut was definitely not considered dyke-chic.

But we were also very young at nineteen and twenty-one, and there was a kind of protectiveness extended to us for that reason from the other women that was largely unspoken. Someone always checked to see if we had a ride back to the city, or somewhere to stay over for the night. There was also some feeling that as self-professed poets we could be a little extra peculiar if we needed to be.

One of the women I met at one of these parties was Kitty.

When I saw Kitty again one night years later in the Swing Rendezvous or the Pony Stable or the Page Three — that tour of second-string gay-girl bars that I had taken to making alone that sad, lonely spring of 1957 — it was easy to recall the St. Albans smell of green Queens summer nights and plastic couch covers and liquor and hair oil and women's bodies at the party where we first had met.

In that brick-faced frame house in Queens the downstairs pine-paneled recreation room was alive and pulsing with loud music, good food, and beautiful black women in all different combinations of dress and semi-dress.

There were whipcord summer suits with starch-shiny shirt collars open at the neck as a concession to the high summer heat, and white gabardine slacks with pleated fronts or slim Ivy League styling for the very slender. There were wheat-colored Cowden jeans (the fashion favorite that summer) with knife-edge creases, and even then one or two back-buckled gray pants over well-chalked buckskin shoes. There were garrison belts galore — broad black leather belts with shiny thin buckles that originated in army-navy surplus stores — and oxford-styled shirts of the new, iron-free Dacron with its stiff, see-through crispness. These shirts, short-sleeved and man-tailored, were tucked neatly into belted pants or tight, skinny, straight skirts. Only the one or two jersey-knit shirts were allowed to fall freely outside.

Bermuda shorts and their shorter cousins — Jamaica shorts — were already making their appearance on the dyke-chic scene, the rules of which were every bit as cutthroat as the tyrannies of Seventh Avenue or Paris. These shorts were worn by butch and femme alike and for this reason were slow to be incorporated into many fashionable gay-girl wardrobes. Clothes were often the most important or only way of broadcasting one's chosen sexual role.

Here and there throughout the room the flash of brightly colored below-the-knee full skirts over low-necked tight bodices could be seen, along with tight sheath dresses and the shine of thin high heels next to bucks and sneakers and loafers.

Femmes wore their hair in tightly curled pageboy bobs, piled high on their heads in sculptured bunches of curls, or in feather cuts framing their faces. That sweetly clean fragrance of beauty parlor that hung over all black women's gatherings in the fifties was present here also, adding its identifiable smell of hot comb and hair pomade to the other aromas in the room.

Butches wore their hair cut shorter: in a DA shaped to a point in back, a short pageboy, or sometimes in a tightly curled poodle that predated the natural Afro. But this was a rarity, and I can only remember one other black woman at that party besides me whose hair was not straightened — an acquaintance of ours from the Lower East Side named Ida.

On a table behind the built-in bar stood opened bottles of gin, bourbon, scotch, soda, and other various mixers. The bar itself was covered with little delicacies of all descriptions: chips, dips, and little crackers and squares of bread laced with the usual dabs of egg salad and sardine paste. There was a platter of delicious fried chicken wings and a pan of potato-and-egg salad dressed with vinegar. Bowls of olives and pickles surrounded the main dishes, along with trays of red crabapples and little sweet onions on toothpicks.

But the centerpiece of the whole table was a huge platter of succulent and thinly sliced roast beef set into an underpan of cracked ice. Upon the beige platter each slice of rare meat had been lovingly laid out and individually folded up into a vulval pattern with a tiny dab of mayonnaise at the crucial apex. The pink-brown folded meat around the pale cream-yellow dot formed suggestive sculptures that made a great hit with all the women present. Petey — at whose house the party was being given and the creator of the meat sculptures — smilingly acknowledged the many compliments on her platter with a long-necked graceful nod of her elegant dancer's head.

The room's particular mix of heat-smells, music, and Marion's introduction, half fading as she drifted off with her cocked cigarette and inevitable bottle of beer, gives way in my mind to the high-cheeked, dark young woman with the silk-deep voice and appraising eyes.

Perched on the edge of the low bench where I was sitting she absently wiped specks of lipstick from both corners of her mouth with the downward flick of a delicate forefinger.

"Audre ... that's a nice name. What's it short for?"

My damp arm hairs bristled in the Ruth Brown music and the heat. I could not stand anybody messing around with my name, not even with nicknames.

"Nothing. It's just Audre. What's Kitty short for?"

"Afrekete," she said, snapping her fingers in time to the rhythm of it and giving a long laugh. "That's me. The black pussycat." She laughed again. "I like your hairdo. Are you a singer?"

"No."

She continued to stare at me with her large direct eyes.

I was suddenly too embarrassed at not knowing what else to say to meet her calmly erotic gaze, so I stood up abruptly and said in my best Laurel-terse tone, "Let's dance."

Her face was broad and smooth under too-light makeup, but as we danced a foxtrot she started to sweat and her skin took on a deep shiny richness. Kitty closed her eyes partway when she danced, and her one gold-rimmed front tooth flashed as she smiled and occasionally caught her lower lip in time to the music.

Her yellow poplin shirt — cut in the style of an Eisenhower jacket — had a zipper that was half open in the summer heat, showing collarbones that stood out like brown wings from her long neck. Garments with zippers were highly prized among the more liberal set of gay girls, because these also could be worn by butch or femme alike on certain occasions without causing any adverse or troublesome comments. Her narrow, well-pressed khaki skirt was topped by a black belt that matched my own except in its newness. Her natty trimness made me feel almost shabby in my well-worn riding pants, my usual uniform for parties.

I thought she was very pretty and I wished I could dance with as much ease as she did, or as effortlessly. Her hair, dressed in the popular style of short feathery curls around her head, had been straightened; but in that room of well-set marcels and DAs and pageboys, it was the closest cut to my own.

Kitty smelled of soap and Jean Naté, and I kept thinking she was bigger than she actually was, because there was a comfortable smell about her that I always associated with large women. There was another spicy herblike odor that I later identified as a combination of coconut oil and Yardley's Lavender Hair Pomade. Her mouth was full and her lipstick was dark and shiny — a new Max Factor shade called "Warpaint."

The next dance was a slow "fish" that suited me fine. I never knew whether to lead or to follow in most other dances, and even the effort to decide which was which was as difficult for me as having to decide all the time the difference between left and right. Somehow that simple distinction had never become automatic for me and all that deciding usually left me very little energy with which to enjoy the movement and the music.

But "fishing" was different. A forerunner of the later one-step, it was in reality your basic slow bump and grind. The low red lamp and the crowded St. Albans parlor floor left us just enough room to hold each other frankly, arms around neck and waist, and the slow intimate music moved our bodies much more than our feet.

Merril Mushroom

How the butch does it: 1959

1. The butch combs her hair

The butch combs her hair. She combs it at home in private. This is the functional combing. She stands in front of the mirror. Holding the comb between her thumb and first two fingers, she slaps the flat of it against her other palm, then places the comb down on the edge of the sink.

She leans forward and peers at her reflection, flicks her first three fingers though the front of her hair, pulls a curl down over her forehead. She tilts her head sideways and looks at her reflection from beneath lowered eyelids. The butch is sultry. The butch is arrogant. The butch is tough. She picks up the bottle of Vitalis and pours a generous amount into her palm, rubs her hands together, and strokes the lotion through her hair, rubbing carefully to be sure that each strand is well coated, yet not greasy. Then she turns on the water and wets her hair with her hands. Now she is ready to begin.

The butch lifts the comb from the side of the sink. She stretches both her arms forward, then bends her elbows. Now! One-two-three-four, she strokes the comb carefully through one side of her hair, following the path of the teeth with the flat fingers of her other hand, barely touching herself as she smooths. The pattern of hair wings back above her ears, back, back, all the way to the middle of her head. Then, five-six, the sides are lifted on the comb to fall in a wave over the top.

Okay, one-two-three-four, comb the other side in the same manner, five-six, over the top. Now back to the first side again, going straight up to the top this time, seven-eight-nine-ten, then the other side in the same pattern. The butch pats her hair as she combs it, pressing it gently into place. She admires her reflection, tilting her head this way and that. Then she lifts the comb to vertical, places the edge of the teeth carefully at the top of the middle of the back of her head, and draws it precisely down the center, pushing the ends of her hair into the furrow, creating a longitudinal cleft above her neck — a perfect duck's ass.

Now the butch concentrates on the top of her hair. She uses the comb expertly to settle the waves into a pompadour. When she is finally satisfied with the effect, she pulls the teeth of the comb carefully down through the center and over her forehead, then uses her fingers to push, pull, and tease the front into one very casual-looking lock that curls over her brow.

The butch makes eyes at her reflection. She is ready to go out. She is satisfied with her appearance.

2. The butch combs her hair

The butch combs her hair. She combs it in public. This is the "show" combing, done primarily for effect. The butch shows off. She draws the comb from her pocket smoothly, holding it between the thumb and index finger of the dominant hand. She stretches both arms out forward, then crooks her elbows, ready to begin.

The butch spreads her legs, balancing her weight on the balls of her feet. She holds the comb ready to her hair, the fingers of her other hand extended, ready to smooth stray ends if necessary. She leans over to the side, bending away from the side she will be combing, tilting her head toward the comb. Her elbows jut until they are almost horizontal. She squints, concentrates, and then she lowers the comb. She will not comb her hair just yet — there is something more she wishes to do to show off:

With the first two fingers of the hand that does not hold the comb, the butch pulls a cigarette out of the pack that is either in her breast pocket or rolled up into the sleeve of her t-shirt. She places the white cylinder between her teeth, closes her lips around it, and rolls her head back just a little. She pulls out her Zippo, flicks the flame on and ready to the end of the cigarette in one expert motion, inhales deeply, then snaps the Zippo closed with her thumb, palms the lighter, and curls the index finger of that same hand around the cigarette, withdrawing it from her mouth. Still holding the cigarette, she slips the lighter into her hip pocket, pushing it down with her thumb, then grasps the cigarette firmly between the tips of her thumb and index finger. She places it back between her lips, then swiftly combs her hair, four strokes on each side, then two, then the top. Skillfully, seemingly carelessly, the butch fingers her pompadour and casual curl into place. Then, with a flourish, using her comb followed by the fingertips of her other hand, she creases the duck's ass down the middle of the back.

All this time, smoke from the cigarette in her mouth has been curling up into her face. Although she squinted her eyes, she did so only in concentration on her task. At no time did she close her eyes against the smoke, nor did she cough or gasp for breath. The butch is tough, stoic. Only at the completion of the combing does she remove the cigarette from between her lips, and she does not draw in a deep breath immediately thereafter.

Merril Mushroom in the1950s

Now the butch returns her comb to its pocket. She does not reach up to check on her hair, to make sure that all is as it should be. She trusts that she looks wonderful, that her hair is impeccably in place, perfectly styled. She is satisfied with her performance.

3. The butch plays pool

The butch selects her cue. She eyes the sticks that line the wall, looking every one over from end to tip. The four fingers of each hand are thrust into her hip pockets, thumbs resting outside the fabric beneath the swell of her belly, causing her elbows to jut out from her sides. She tosses her head and throws her shoulders back, nods once, then pulls one hand from her pocket to take the stick of her choice from the wall. Now her other hand comes up to stroke the length of the wood. She feels the weight of the stick, tests its balance. As she sights down it, she strokes it along her cheek. She smiles, moving her tongue slowly back and forth behind her slightly parted lips.

Now the butch sets the butt of the stick against the floor and straightens out the elbow of the hand she holds it with, turning her arm slightly so that her triceps bulge and ripple. Then, giving the stick a little toss into the air, she catches it neatly at the middle and strides over to the pool table, where she picks up the little cube of blue chalk. She blows across the top

135

of it, looking around the bar, lips pursed into a kiss for the one whose eye she catches. She lowers the chalk deliberately, grinds it suddenly and hard across the end of the cue stick, rubs it around until tiny blue grains shower from it. Gently, she blows away the excess, then leans the stick up against the side of the table.

Now the butch reaches into her breast pocket and pulls out a half-full soft pack of Camels. She gives it a sharp flick of the wrist, and two cigarettes shoot out of the pack a half inch and a quarter inch respectively. Raising the pack slowly to her mouth, the butch takes the end of the longer cigarette between her lips and pulls it free. She tucks the pack back into her breast pocket, then pulls her Zippo from her hip pocket. She crooks her elbow, raising the lighter. Slowly, deliberately, she flicks open the lid so that it rings, thumbs the wheel smartly, and dips the end of her Camel into the flame. Inhaling deeply, loudly, she snaps the Zippo shut and returns it to her hip pocket. She grips the cigarette between her thumb and first two fingers and takes several more deep drags, blowing smoke out sharply. Then she places the cigarette on the edge of the pool table.

The butch bends and lifts the wooden rack from beneath the table. She runs her fingers suggestively around the lower point of the triangle, grins, raises one eyebrow. Suddenly she flips the rack into the air, catches it, raps it against the palm of her other hand, and sets it down smartly in its proper place with the top point just touching the silver mark. She picks up her cigarette again, smokes some more, then drops the butt to the floor and grinds it out with the toe of her boot. She places her middle finger on the quarter that her challenger has placed on the edge of the pool table, hesitates for just one moment, then slides the quarter off the edge of the table, snaps it up against her thumb, and spins it smoothly into the slot.

The balls crash down. The butch pulls them from the tray quickly, four at a time, two in each hand, banging them onto the tabletop inside the rack. She plucks a few of the balls out with her fingertips, swiftly, snapping them down, expertly rearranging them so that they alternate striped and solid with the eight ball in the center. That done, she grips the rack, pauses for a moment, then snaps the balls into place with a sharp crack and smoothly lifts the rack up and away, leaving the balls in a perfect triangle on the surface of the table.

Flaunting etiquette, the butch picks up the cue ball and carries it to the other end of the table. She spins about, bending backwards slightly and leading with her shoulder. She sets the white sphere down with a flourish, holds her stick out at arm's length for a moment, then takes her stance. Turning sideways toward the table, she spreads her legs, bends her knees, and finds her balance. She raises her stick, sights along it, then lowers it. She rearranges the cue ball, then rearranges her stance, aware of the many eyes on her. Aware of the women who are watching her every move, she poses, then turns back to the table, and quickly, gracefully, projecting all strength and energy, she places her left hand on the tabletop, bends at the hips, rests the cue stick in the crease between her thumb and forefinger, and wallops the cue ball with the end of the stick. The cue ball hurtles across the table and smashes into the side of the triangle of balls just next to the upper point. With a crash, pool balls scatter across the table, and two solid-colored balls with low numbers roll into the corner pockets.

The butch looks over at her opponent, her face expressionless except for one slightly lifted eyebrow. She casually picks up the chalk and rubs it over the end of her cue stick. She does not smile, but she is very pleased with her performance. She nods magnanimously to her opponent, then turns back to the table to take her next shot.

But, first, she lights another Camel.

Joan Nestle

The femme question

For many years now, I have been trying to figure out how to explain the special nature of butch-femme relationships to feminists and lesbian-feminists who consider butch-femme a reproduction of heterosexual models, and therefore dismiss lesbian communities both of the past and of the present that assert this style. Before I continue, my editor wants me to define the term *butch-femme,* and I am overwhelmed at the complexity of the task. Living a butch-femme life was not an intellectual exercise; it was not a set of theories. Deep in my gut I know what being a femme has meant to me, but it is very hard to articulate this identity in a way that does justice to its fullest nature and yet answers the questions of a curious reader. In the most basic terms, butch-femme means a way of looking, loving, and living that can be expressed by individuals, couples, or a community. In the past, the butch has been labeled too simplistically the masculine partner and the femme her feminine counterpart. This labeling forgets two women who have developed their styles for specific erotic, emotional, and social reasons. Butch-femme relationships, as I experienced them, were complex erotic and social statements, not phony heterosexual replicas. They were filled with a deeply lesbian language of stance, dress, gesture, love, courage, and autonomy. In the 1950s particularly, butch-femme couples were the front-line warriors against sexual bigotry. Because they were so visible, they suffered the brunt of street violence. The irony of social change has made a radical, sexual, political statement of the 1950s appear today a reactionary, nonfeminist experience. My own roots lie deep in the earth of this lesbian custom and what follows is one lesbian's understanding of her own experience.

I am a femme and have been for over twenty-five years. I know the reaction this statement gets now: many lesbians dismiss me as a victim, a woman who could do nothing else because she didn't know any better, but the truth of my life tells a different story. We femmes helped hold our lesbian world together in an unsafe time. We poured out more love and wetness on our bar stools and in our homes than women were supposed to have. I have no theories to explain how the love came, why the crushes on the lean dark women exploded in my guts, made me so shy that all I could do was look so hard that they had to move away. But I wasn't a piece of fluff and neither were the other femmes I knew. We knew what we wanted, and that was no mean feat for young women of the 1950s, a time when the need for conformity, marriage, and babies was being trumpeted at us by the government's policymakers. Oh, we had our styles — our outfits, our perfumes, our performances — and we could lose ourselves under the chins of our dancing partners, who held us close enough to make the world safe; but we walked the night streets to get to our bars, and we came out bleary-eyed into the deserted early morning, facing a long week of dreary passing at the office or the beauty parlor or the telephone company. I always knew our lives were a bewildering combination of romance and realism. I could tell you stories...

About the twenty-year-old femme who carried her favorite dildo in a pink satin purse to the bar every Saturday night so that her partner for the evening would understand exactly what she wanted...

Or how at seventeen I hung out at Pam Pam's on Sixth Avenue and Eighth Street in Greenwich Village with all the other femmes who were too young to get into the bars and too inexperienced to know how to forge an ID. We used this bare, tired coffee shop as a training ground, a meeting place to plan the night's forays. Not just femmes — young butches were there too, from all the boroughs, taking time to comb their hair just the right way in the mirror beside the doorway...

Or how I finally entered my world, a bar on Abingdon Square, where I learned that women had been finding one another for years, and how as young femmes we took on the vice squad, the plainclothes policewomen, the bathroom line with its allotted amount of toilet paper, the johns trying to hustle a woman for the night, and the staring straights who saw us as entertaining freaks. My passion had taken me home, and not all the hating voices of the McCarthy 1950s could keep me away from my community.

❖

Every time I speak at a lesbian-feminist gathering, I introduce myself as a femme who came out in the 1950s. I do this because it is the truth and it allows me to pay historical homage to my lesbian time and place, to the women who have slipped away, yet whose voices I still hear and whose V-necked sweaters and shiny loafers I still see. I do it to call up the women I would see shopping with their lovers in the Lower East Side supermarkets, the femme partners of the butch women who worked as waiters in the Club 82. I remember how unflinchingly the femme absorbed the stares of the other customers as she gently held onto the arm of her partner. Butches were known by their appearance, femmes by their choices. I do it in the name of the wives of passing women whose faces look up at me from old newspaper clippings, the women whom reporters described as the deceived ones and yet whose histories suggest much more complicated choices. And if femmes seemed to be "wives" of passing women, the feminine protectors of the couple's propriety, it was so easy to lose curiosity about what made them sexual heretics, because they looked like women. Thus femmes became the victims of a double dismissal: in the past they did not appear culturally different enough from heterosexual women to be seen as breaking gender taboos, and today they do not appear feminist enough, even in their historical context, to merit attention or respect for being ground-breaking women.

❖

If we are to piece together a profound feminist and lesbian history, we must begin asking questions about the lives of these women that we have not asked before, and to do this we will have to elevate curiosity to a much more exalted position than concepts of politically correct sexuality would ever allow us to do.[1] Politically correct sexuality is a paradoxical concept. One of the most deeply held opinions in feminism is that women should be autonomous and self-directed in defining their sexual desire, yet when a woman says, "This is my desire," feminists rush in to say, "No, no, it is the prick in your head; women should not desire that act." But we do not yet know enough at all about what women — any women — desire. The real problem here is that we stopped asking questions too early in the lesbian and feminist movement, and rushed to erect what appeared to be answers into the formidable and rigid edifice that we have now. Our contemporary lack of curiosity also affects our view of the past. We don't ask butch-femme women who they are; we tell them. We don't explore the social life of working-class lesbian bars in the 1940s and 1950s; we simply assert that all those women were victims.[2] Our supposed answers closed our ears and stopped our analysis. Questions and answers about lesbian lives that deviate from the feminist model of the 1970s strike like a shock wave against the movement's foundation, yet this new wave of questioning is an authentic one, coming from women who have helped create the feminist and lesbian movement that they are now challenging into new growth. If we close down exploration, we will be forcing some women once again to live their sexual lives in a land of shame and guilt; only this time they will be haunted by the realization that it was not the patriarchal code they have failed but the creed of their own sisters who said they came in love. Curiosity builds bridges between women and between the present and the past; judgment builds the power of some over others. Curiosity is not trivial; it is the respect one life pays to another. It is a largeness of mind and heart that refuses to be bounded by decorum or by desperation. It is hardest to keep alive in the times it is most needed, the times of hatred, of instability, of attack. Surely these are such times.

When I stand before a new generation of lesbians and use this word *femme*, I sometimes feel very old, like a relic from a long-buried past that has burst through the earth, shaken the dust off its mouth, and started to speak. The first reaction is usually shock and then laughter and then confusion, as my audience must confront their stereotyped understanding of this word and yet face the fact that I am a powerful woman who has done some good in this brave new world of lesbian-feminism. But the audience members are not the only ones going through waves of reactions. I too wonder how I will be perceived through these layers of history. A 1980s lesbian activist who defines herself as a femme poses the problem of our plight as an oppressed people in a most vivid way.

Colonization and the battle against it always pose a contradiction between appearances and deeper survivals.[3] There is a need to reflect the colonizer's image back at him yet at the same time to keep alive what is a deep part of one's culture, even if it can be misunderstood by the oppressor, who omnipotently thinks he knows what he is seeing. Butch-femme carries all this cultural warfare with it. It appears to incorporate elements of the heterosexual culture in power; it is disowned by some who want to make a statement against the pervasiveness of this power; yet it is a valid style, matured in years of struggle and harboring some of our bravest women. The colonizer's power enforces not only a daily cultural devaluing but also sets up a memory trap, forcing us to devalue what was resistance in the past in a desperate battle to be different from what they say we are.[4]

Both butches and femmes have a history of ingenuity in the creation of personal style,[5] but since the elements of this style — the clothing, the stance — come from the heterosexually defined culture, it is easy to confuse an innovative or resisting style with a mere replica of the prevailing custom. But a butch lesbian wearing men's clothes in the 1950s was not a man wearing men's clothes; she was a woman who created an original style to signal to other women what she was capable of doing — taking erotic responsibility. In the feminist decades, the femme is the lesbian who poses this problem of misinterpreted choice in the deepest way. If we dress to please ourselves and the other women to whom we want to announce our desire, we are called traitors by many of our own community, because we seem to be wearing the clothes of the enemy. Makeup, high heels, skirts, revealing clothes, even certain ways of holding the body are read as capitulation to patriarchal control of women's bodies. An accurate critique, if a woman feels uncomfortable or is forced to present herself this way, but this is not what I am doing when I feel sexually powerful and want to share it with other women. Femmes are women who have made choices, but we need to be able to read between the cultural lines to appreciate their strength. Lesbians should be mistresses of discrepancies, knowing that resistance lies in the change of context.

The message to femmes throughout the 1970s was that we were the Uncle Toms of the movement. If I wore the acceptable movement clothes of sturdy shoes, dungarees, work shirt, and backpack, then I was to be

141

trusted, but that is not always how I feel strongest. If I wear these clothes because I am afraid of the judgment of my own people, then I am a different kind of traitor, this time to my own femme sense of personal style, since this style represents what I have chosen to do with my womanness. I cannot hide it or exchange it without losing my passion or my strength. The saddest irony of all behind this misjudgment of femmes is that for many of us it has been a lifelong journey to take pleasure in our bodies. Butch lovers, reassuring and kind, passionate and taking, were for many of us a bridge back to acceptance of what the society around us told us to scorn: big-hipped, wide-assed women's bodies. My idiosyncratic sexual history leads me to express my feminist victories in my own way; other women, straight or gay, carry these victories of personal style within, hesitant to publicly display them, because they fear the judgment of the women's community. Our understanding of resistance is thus deeply diminished.

In the 1970s and 1980s, the femme is also charged with the crime of passing, of trying to disassociate herself from the androgynous lesbian. In earlier decades, many femmes used their appearance to secure jobs that would allow their butch lovers to dress and live the way they both wanted her to. Her femme appearance allowed her to cross over into enemy territory to make economic survival possible. But when butches and femmes of this style went out together, no one could accuse the femme of passing. In fact, the more extremely femme she was, the more obvious was their lesbianism and the more street danger they faced. Now lesbian style occurs in the context of a more and more androgynous-appearing society, and femme dress becomes even more problematic. A femme is often seen as a lesbian acting like a straight woman who is not a feminist — a terrible misreading of self-presentation that turns a language of liberated desire into the silence of collaboration. An erotic conversation between two women is completely unheard, not by men this time but by other women, many in the name of lesbian-feminism.

When one carries the femme identity into the arena of political activism, the layers of confusion grow. In the spring of 1982, Deborah, my lover, and I did a Lesbian Herstory Archives slide show at the Stony Brook campus of SUNY. We were speaking to fifty women health workers, four of whom identified themselves as lesbians. I wore a long lavender dress that made my body feel good and high, black boots that made me feel powerful. Deb was dressed in pants, shirt, vest, and leather jacket. I led a two-hour discussion working with the women's honest expressions of homophobia, their fears of seeing their own bodies sexually, and the different forms of tyranny they faced as women. Finally, one of the straight women said how much easier it was to talk to me rather than to Deb, who was sitting at the side of the room. "I look more like you," she said, pointing to me. She too was wearing a long dress and boots. Here, my appearance, which was really an erotic conversation between Deb and myself, was transformed into a boundary line between us. I walked over to Deb, put my arm around her, and drew her head into my breasts. "Yes," I said, "but it is the two of us together that makes everything perfectly clear." Then I returned to the center of the room and lied. "I wore this dress so you would listen to me but our real freedom is the day when I can wear a three-piece suit and tie and you will still hear my words." I found myself faced with the paradox of having to fight for one freedom at the price of another. The audience felt more comfortable with me because I could pass, yet their misunderstanding of my femmeness was betraying its deepest meaning.

Because I am on the defensive many times in raising these issues, it is tempting to gloss over the difficulties that did exist in the past and do now. Being a femme was never a simple experience, not in the old lesbian bars of the 1950s and not now. Femmes were deeply cherished and yet devalued as well. There were always femme put-down jokes going around the bar, while at the same time tremendous energy and caring was spent courting the femme women. We were not always trusted and often seen as the more flighty members of the lesbian world, a contradiction to our actual lives, where we all knew femmes who had stood by their butch lovers through years of struggle. We were mysterious and practical, made homes and broke them up, were glamorous and boring all at the same time. Butches and femmes had an internal dialogue to work out, but when the police invaded our bars, when we were threatened with physical violence, when taunts and jeers followed us down the streets, this more subtle discussion was transformed into a monolithic front where both butch and femme struggled fiercely to protect each other against the attackers. Feminists need to know much more about how femmes perceived themselves and how they were seen by those who loved them. Certainly the erotic clarity that was for me and many other femmes at the heart of our style has never been clearly understood by sexologists or by feminists.

Since the butch-femme tradition is one of the oldest in lesbian culture, it came under investigation along with everything else when the sexologists began their study of sexual deviance. The feminine invert, as femmes were called then, was viewed as the imperfect deviant. The sexology literature from 1909 stated that the "pure female invert feels like a man."[6] A few years later, the femme is described as an "effeminate tribadist."[7] In the 1950s, our pathology was explained this way:

> The feminine type of Lesbian is one who seeks mother love, who enjoys being a recipient of much attention and affection. She is often preoccupied with personal beauty and is somewhat narcissistic ... She is the clinging vine type who is often thought and spoken of by her elders as a little fool without any realization of the warped sexuality which is prompting her actions.[8]

And then the doctor adds the final blow: "She is more apt to be bisexual and also apt to respond favorably to treatment." Here the femme lesbian is stripped of all power, made into a foolish woman who can easily be beckoned over into the right camp. Historically, we have been left disinherited, seen neither as true inverts nor as grown women.

An example from early twentieth-century lesbian literature also shows the complexity of the femme tradition. In *The Well of Loneliness*, published in 1928, two major femme characters embody some of the mythic characteristics of femmes.[9] One is an unhappy wife who seduces Stephen Gordon, the butch heroine, but then betrays her, choosing the security of a safe life. The other is Beth, the lover Stephen turns over to a future husband at the end of the novel so she may have a chance at a "normal" life, thus enabling the author to make a plea for greater understanding of the deviant's plight. The reality of the author's life, however, gives a different portrait of a femme woman. Lady Una Troubridge, the partner of Radclyffe Hall, who saw herself as Hall's wife, was a major force in getting *The Well of Loneliness* published, even though she knew it would open their lives to turmoil and worse.

> She [Radclyffe Hall] came to me, telling me that in her view the time was ripe, and that although the publication of such a book might mean the shipwreck of her whole career, she was fully prepared to make any sacrifice except — the sacrifice of my peace of mind.
>
> She pointed out that in view of our union and of all the years that we had shared a home, what affected her must also affect me and that I would be included in any condemnation. Therefore she placed the decision in my hands and would write or refrain as I should decide. I am glad to remember that my reply was made without so much as an instant's hesitation: I told her to write what was in her heart, that so far as any effect upon myself was concerned, I was sick to death of ambiguities, and only wished to be known for what I was and to dwell with her in the palace of truth.[10]

Why Radclyffe Hall with this steadfast femme woman by her side could not portray the same type of woman in her lesbian novel is a topic that needs further exploration. Troubridge's cry, "I am sick of ambiguities," could become a femme's motto.

What this very brief examination of examples from sexology and literature points out, I hope, is how much more we need to know, to question, to explore. Femmes have been seen as a problem through the decades both by those who never pretended to be our friends and now by those who say they are our comrades. The outcry over the inclusion of a discussion of butch-femme relationships in the Barnard sexuality conference was a shock to me; I had waited for over ten years for this part of my life to be taken seriously by a feminist gathering. I marched, demonstrated, conferenced, leafleted, CRed my way through the 1970s, carrying this past and the women who had lived it deep within me, believing that when we had some safe territory, we could begin to explore what our lives had really meant. Yet even raising the issue, even entertaining the possibility that we were not complete victims but had some sense of what we were doing, was enough to encourage a call for silence by feminists who feared our voices. Those of us who want to begin talking again are not the reactionary backlash against feminism, as some would call us. We are an outgrowth of the best of feminism in a new time, trying to ask questions about taboo territories, trying to understand how women in the past and now have had the strength and the courage to express desire and resistance. We ask these questions in the service of the belief that women's lives are our deepest text, even the life of a femme.

Notes

1. See Muriel Dimen, "Politically Correct? Politically Uncorrect?" in *Pleasure and Danger: Exploring Female Sexuality*, edited by Carole S. Vance (Boston: Routledge & Kegan Paul, 1984), pp. 138–148, for a discussion of the origin and development of standards of political correctness and incorrectness, particularly in regard to sexuality.

2. The work of Madeline Davis and Liz Kennedy documenting the Buffalo lesbian community pre-1970 will be a major breakthrough in ending this silence. See their article earlier in this volume.

3. Albert Memmi's *The Colonizer and the Colonized* (New York: Orion, 1968) is an especially helpful text in clarifying cultural struggle in a prerevolutionary period.

4. This is analogous to blacks not eating fried chicken (because that is what whites think all blacks do) when one loves eating it, both for the taste and the memories of home it evokes. One way of resisting this forced disinheritance is to make the cultural activity an in-house affair, where only members of the family share the pleasure. Many butch-femme individuals and communities have adopted this form of resistance. They exist on the edges of the women's and lesbian-feminist movement, or some members of the community cross over, helping to build organizations and feminist projects, but returning at night to butch-femme relationships.

5. I want to make clear that butch-femme style differed from community to community and over time. I have written elsewhere of butch-femme couples who appeared similar, both with short hair and in trousers; see *Heresies 12: Sex Issue*. Photographs of this style can be seen on many *Ladder* covers. The way straight people viewed these couples walking hand in hand in the 1950s was often hostile, with the added taunt of "Which one of you is the man?" for the less visibly defined couple. I think any of us from that time would be able to distinguish the butch from the femme by subtle differences in walk, how the shoulders were held, or how the heads bent during conversation.

6. Katherine Bement Davis, *Factors in the Sex Life of Twenty-Two Hundred Women*

(New York: Harper & Brothers, 1929). Davis here is citing August Forel, *The Sexual Question* (New York: Rebman, 1908).

7. Frank Caprio, *Female Homosexuality* (New York: Grove, 1954), p. 18.

8. Ibid., p. 19. Caprio supports his characterization with a quotation from Dr. Winifred Richmond, *The Adolescent Girl* (New York: Macmillan, 1925).

9. Radclyffe Hall, *The Well of Loneliness* (London: Jonathan Cape, 1928).

10. Lady Una Troubridge, *The Life and Death of Radclyffe Hall* (London: Hammond & Hammond, 1961), pp. 81–82.

Ina Rimpau & Carolyn Gammon

Cira and Yolanda:
An interview

The following interview took place in Montreal, January 12, 1991, in Spanish, French, and English.

Carolyn: We thought we'd start with a few details: your names, ages, where you were born ... Who wants to start?

Cira: Cira Domingues! I was born in Havana, Cuba, fifty-two years ago, in 1938. I've been gay, to my knowledge, about half of my life. I've been always in a relationship; they usually tend to last fourteen years, that's my average! Not a bad average ... I was born outside of Havana in La Vibora, Montilla. It was a very small town and there was some gay people and everybody thought they were lepers or something.

Ina: Men or women?

Cira: Men and women.

Carolyn: What did they call them?

Cira: Ah, *la tortillera* [dyke]! *El maricon* [fag]! Nobody was friends with them. My family always said that I was for the underdog, because I was friends with people of a shady nature. My mother said, "Oh, why do you have to be friends with them?" So I got a bad reputation. So I live up to it! That's the way it started.

In Cuba, I had a sort of relationship with a woman when I was fourteen years old and she was much older, American. That's what gave me a taste for it. I got married to get out of Cuba; it wasn't a "love affair," just a convenience marriage. Then when I came to Canada, in November 1957, I stayed three years with my husband. [Immigrants who obtain their Canadian citizenship by marrying Canadians have to remain married for a minimum of three years.] I broke up because I met a girl and I went to live with her ... for fourteen years. After that, I met another girl, a very good friend, and we started going together and we went out for ... fourteen years! And after that I met another girl [*gestures to Yolanda*] and we're good for another ten years.

Yolanda: I was born the sixteenth of January, 1944, in Santiago de Chile. From the age of five, I've been a lesbian! My mother found me with the neighbor's girl. [*Pretends to lift a girl's dress*] I was looking at *everything*! I was looking at her genitals. Five years old!

Cira: It's a good thing that she changed her strategy of finding girls.

Yolanda: That's why I started! When my mother found me, she scolded and spanked me. "You *pig*! What are you doing?!" But I was innocent, I didn't understand. I thought it was great. My mother really shocked me, because she made such a fuss ... and after that I thought it was even better!

Ina: But all children do that.

Cira: Yes, you're right. I played doctor all the time.

Yolanda: I never changed. I'm worse!

Cira: She had a relationship with *una tipa* [this gal], for how many years? Ten?

Yolanda: Ten years. My first relationship, in Chile. But we never lived together.

Carolyn: Were they called *tortillera* and *maricon* as in Cuba?

Yolanda: Oh yes, in Chile too. We also say *marimachos, mariconas machos* [macho fags], or *te gustan las patitas de chancho* [you like pigs' feet]. Only vulgar people said that. Before, it was really looked down on, but now, it's more normal. They ignore it.

Cira: If you ignore it, maybe it'll go away...

Yolanda: The family never understands. They're always ashamed to have a homosexual son or lesbian daughter.

Cira: In her family, there's lots of homosexuals.

Yolanda: Yes, my uncles, two uncles.

❖

Carolyn: Do you identify as butch and femme?

Cira: Yes, I think so.

Carolyn: You're...

Cira: What do you think? [*Laughter*] I think it's because in a relationship there's always one — I won't say stronger physically or mentally, but who has more initiative. I think I could be a butch, but I think I'd be a very

Yolanda Duque and Cira Domingues, with Attis, January 1991

mariconada butch; I'd be a very faggoty butch. I'm strong and I'm mentally strong.

Carolyn: What makes you a femme? Is it certain jobs you do? Roles you take? Ways you dress?

Cira: I think, actually, you have that feminism [*sic*] in you. Yolanda could dress in a dress and put lipstick on and she'd still be a butch. And me, I could dress in men's clothes and I'd still be very much of a femme. I'm much more feminine. I think it's something you're born with. And I always seem to have a propensity for butch-looking women more than other feminine women, though I admire them. I recognize beauty whenever I see it.

Carolyn: Yolanda, do you identify as butch?

Yolanda: Yes, because I'd feel ridiculous putting on earrings, painting my nails ... It's not my way. Also because I've always liked very feminine women. For this, I'd say I identify as butch. I don't go for other women like me.

Carolyn: For you, is it something you were born with? How do you live it? Through clothing? Attitude? Or by ... the bedroom?

Yolanda: I don't look at a woman and figure she's butch or she's femme.

149

What happens in bed is something between two women. But, as I said, I like soft women.

Carolyn: Even if they have muscles like Cira?

Yolanda: I discovered her muscles after! [*Laughter*]

Cira: Too late!

Yolanda: Yes, it was too late.

Cira: But I'm not always flexing my muscles.

Carolyn: Are there other words for *butch* and *femme* in Chile?

Yolanda: Couples in Chile say *Mi marido y mi mujer*. The femme says, "This is my husband," and the butch presents her *chica* as her wife.

Cira: Before, the butches here said it, too. Especially the French people.

Ina: What if both are femme or both butch?

Yolanda: *Mi amiga* [my girlfriend].

Carolyn: Are there still a lot of butch-femme couples in Chile?

Yolanda: Yes, still today. It's notorious. When you see a couple you immediately figure who's who. When there's a couple of feminine *muchachitas* [young girls], everybody laughs; they say, "What do they do in bed? Play with dolls?" And the relationships don't last. They're two rival femmes.

Cira: The problem is, it's usually the first relationship that they happen to have.

Carolyn: So couples that last are butch-femme couples?

Yolanda: Exactly.

Cira: Yes, because they complement each other.

Yolanda: Yes, you must have a complement.

Carolyn: But femme women, in the streets, are often taken as straight, whereas someone like Yolanda — you're much more obvious as a lesbian. How do you feel about being taken as a straight woman, Cira?

Cira: It doesn't bother me a bit, never has, because I know what I am. I never lead on to anybody about my sexual preference, it's my business.

Yolanda: Men don't bother me; they've never followed me in the street. I think they sense it. But with Cira, the landlord kisses her hand and all that, yechh. She attracts men.

Carolyn: Do you feel harassed sometimes because you look like a butch?

150

Yolanda: In Chile, yes. At work. There was this girl who came to meet me every day; it was really obvious. One of my colleagues started rumors that she was my woman and when I heard about it I went to talk to him. I said, "You're just jealous because I have a pretty woman, your woman looks like a witch!" After, we became good friends. Finally, the whole department knew; one would tell the other. But I had more respect after they knew I was lesbian than before. They shaped up.

Ina: Were there other lesbians at your work?

Yolanda: Not that I knew of. Because many butches disguise themselves at work, wear makeup, paint their nails ... But you can tell by their manner.

Cira: Men are so easily fooled!

Carolyn: They dressed as femmes to pass as straight?

Yolanda: Yes, that's what I'm talking about. Then in the evenings when they go to the bars, they put on their jeans...

Cira: That's what I find sad.

Yolanda: You have to keep up appearances; you can lose your job. Many people lose their jobs. In the ministries, anyone who works for the government, in public relations — and that's where you'll find lots of lesbians.

Carolyn: Yolanda, do you think your butch appearance had an effect on your encounters with Canadian immigration officials?

Yolanda: I think so, yes. The minister's representative always looked at me top to bottom, my clothes ... even my age, forty-six years old, not married ... such a sad thing. [*Laughs*] I never said I wanted to marry here and have kids like everyone else said. Yes, I think there's discrimination.

Carolyn: So it didn't help you.

Yolanda: No. But I'm not going to change. I wasn't about to put on lipstick. I wore sporty clothes.

Carolyn: Cira, have you ever been lovers with another femme?

Cira: Yes, I have. My very first affair in Cuba.

Ina: Were you a butch then?

Cira: No, it was the first relationship. She was older, twenty-eight. I was fourteen. She wanted to help me to study. That's the first time I came across the word *lesbian*, *tortillera*. My stepfather realized what relation we had; I didn't, just — I loved her. She was a stewardess.

Carolyn: What type of relationship did you have?

Cira: Friends. I think she saw more than other people, that I had potential,

I don't know. At first it was a very innocent relationship; then it turned into a very passionate relationship which lasted about six months. It was a very enjoyable first experience.

She wasn't a femme. She looked butchy. It's hard to explain, she was very butch, yet she was very feminine, because she wore lipstick and she wore beautiful perfume. I didn't know if she was a butch or femme...

Carolyn: Because you didn't think like that?

Cira: No. I just liked her.

Carolyn: Then you came to Canada and you're attracted to butch women — what made the change?

Cira: I don't know. I guess I always liked butch women. [*Laughs*]

Carolyn: Yolanda, were you ever attracted by other butches?

Yolanda: No. Not even at five years old! She had long hair, she was tiny.

Cira: I've seen a lot of changes over the years. Like when I came out — that was 1959, when I had my first experience here in Montreal — in those days the scene was very butch. We had a lot of run-ins with people and we had to run through laneways and hide under cars, because in that time, the men were really after the butches. They cut their pants off, cut the legs of the pants off in the middle of winter, with knives or scissors or whatever.

Carolyn: Do you remember what bars you went to?

Cira: Yes, the Zanzibar, which was a very nice club on Saint André Street — they had shows. And in those days it was the femme and the butch, and the femme dressed with dresses, with the crinoline and the big beehive, and the butch dressed ... like men. Men's shoes. I remember they used to look so ridiculous. Like, now they have beautiful shoes for men, but in those days it was ugly shoes they were wearing. But they wore that because they identified like that, and they wore a shirt and collar and tie.

Carolyn: Was there a lot of jealousy, say if another butch...

Cira: Oh yes! A lot of fights. Especially the French girls — they were very, very flirty.

Ina: Was it like femmes could talk to other femmes and butches could only talk to other butches?

Cira: Yes. That's right. We used to go to the club, a nice club — they had a room where people used to sit to talk, like a dressing room where people would leave their coats. They had seats, sometimes a couple would wait for another couple to come. The butch goes to get the car and the femme waits for the butch to come and get her. It's very, very nice; nothing wrong with that. It was very ... easy. Not that I prefer it, but it was fine with me.

152

Carolyn: It's changed now.

Cira: It's changed a lot. First of all, there's no nice clubs where you can really feel comfortable. Now they're very noisy. In those days they used to have a doorman come and seat you at a table. They had shows, nice shows ... It was more normal, I liked it better. And you were more safe also in the clubs than you are now.

The Zanzibar was for women. Then there was one on Sherbrooke Street, also for women, and the women were very well treated, much more than they were in the seventies. I think from the seventies on, things really changed; it wasn't as nice. First of all, you were not safe if you went to a club. The Pont de Paris when it first opened — the doorman there was a real son of a bitch. I broke his glasses and I was barred there for over a year. I broke his tuxedo.

Carolyn: You're the femme and you're doing this?

Cira: I didn't care. I was putting some music on the jukebox and he came behind me and he grabbed my ass, so I just broke his glasses. He was going to throw me down the stairs, but I held on tightly and said, "If you throw me, you go with me." My girlfriend was trying to pull on him too, but I was faster and I was much more mad!

I went to live in New York, and that was a nice experience. Ava Gardner went there, a lot of movie actors...

Ina: Went to the bars?

Cira: Yes. To the Eighth Wonder, like the wonders of the world. It was on Eighth Street and Sixth Avenue, in the Village. There you could see the difference — that was in '64 and already there was not this butch and femme; they all looked like butches. It was very hard to tell who was who and what was what.

After living there for three, four months, I was dying to meet gay people, but there was so many places, and coming from Montreal, you hear so many stories, so you were very careful. I used to go to that club in the afternoons and I met a lot of people, dancers. It was a nice kind of place, because the average dykes used to go there. And in the Village, the Night Owl used to be open at night; there used to be writers; I met a lot of beautiful writers ... Alexander King.

In Cuba too they had nice clubs. Not anymore. I was on my own for two or three years in Cuba and I frequented lesbian clubs. One was called Carmen's in Havana. Another was called Rancho Luna. The Rancho Luna was outside Havana. They had movies.

Carolyn: They were bars just for women?

Cira: No, mixed, boys and girls.

Carolyn: Were the couples mostly butch and femme?

Cira: There, yes.

Carolyn: And you went even though you weren't lesbian at the time?

Cira: I was looking. Because after I had that affair with that girl, Olympia — she looked just like Ava Gardner; she had green green eyes and black black hair ... She was a Cuban born in Florida; her family lived there and she was a stewardess, so she traveled back and forth. She had a place on the beach. She wouldn't take me to the clubs; I was too young. And I never saw her again, because my stepfather said if he ever found out about it, he'd make her lose her job, put her in jail.

Carolyn: Did he find you together?

Cira: I used to go to school on bicycle, in the summer, two o'clock in the afternoon, a hundred degrees. And my bicycle broke down — that's the way I met her. I was sitting by the side of the road and I didn't know what to do with my bicycle, and she stopped. She was with another — now, I realize, a gay boy. They were acting like they were a couple, but they weren't a couple; he was more femme than she was! But in Cuba at the time, the stewards and stewardesses didn't get married; they only hired the ones that were not married.

I started skipping school and going over to the beach house. My stepfather followed me. He found us coming back from the beach house and stopped her. He was very, very possessive of me. That's a long story.

Carolyn: Back to Chile. How old were you when you had your first relation; what bars did you go to?

Yolanda: I was part of a soccer team and met my first lover there. I was twenty and she was eighteen.

Carolyn: She was a femme and played soccer?

Yolanda: Yes, with her long hair.

Cira: There were two teams, the femmes and the butches.

Yolanda: *Las chicas malas y las chicas buenas* [the bad girls and the good girls]. The butches versus the femmes!

Ina: Who won?

Yolanda: The butches!

Cira: So she was on the other team?

Yolanda: Yes. We didn't go to bars then; there were groups that got together at one person's apartment or another. After that, four years later, 1969, there were many bars but always mixed ... El Clavel, La Casa de la Luna.

In Chile there are *many* butches; it's difficult to find a femme! When a

154

femme comes into a club, all the butches pounce on her. The femmes are lucky!

Carolyn: Why do you think there were more butches?

Yolanda: It's a phenomenon I just don't understand. Maybe the climate... [*Laughter*] But it's difficult to find a femme.

Cira: Maybe because it's a patriarchal country — the father is boss, very macho. I think that's why, because women find that only by imitating men they can have freedom. They see the way their mothers are treated and they don't want to identify with that.

Yolanda: My mother looked like a butch. Very dominant.

Cira: Yes. There are more butches over there because of the way most men beat their wives. Men are very *machista*. They work, they keep the money, they give their wives a couple of dollars, and they go out.

Yolanda: Yes. I don't like weak women — feminine, yes, but not weak or fragile. I don't like sad women — that's why I love Cira, because I am a bit melancholic, a bit sad. I need someone more lively, feminine and alive.

Carolyn: Comparing your experiences as a lesbian in Chile or Canada — was it easier to live as a lesbian there or here? And how about living as a butch here or there?

Yolanda: I don't find much difference. There's discrimination at the workplace everywhere.

Carolyn: And you lived in Argentina?

Yolanda: For fourteen years. There's lots of femmes in Argentina! All the Argentinian femmes wanted to know me, I was very popular when I arrived.

Cira: From what she's told me, the men in Argentina are weaker so that's why there's more feminine women.

Yolanda: But they appear like butches—

Cira: They have strong characters, most Argentinian women.

Yolanda: But they have a very feminine way about them.

Cira: That's what I was saying. In a country where the male is the head of the household—

Yolanda: Yes, the men say a lot but they're not very macho — *machomenos*.

Cira: You don't find Argentinian men beating up their women, because the women would kill them when they're sleeping.

Yolanda: There are many bisexual women, many, many, many.

155

THE PERSISTENT DESIRE

Carolyn: Why did you leave Chile?

Yolanda: There was a *coup d'état*, and my family was very involved politically, especially my brothers and father. They were members of the Communist party. They were persecuted by the military authorities. They had to leave Chile and they came to Canada. And I left for Argentina for the same reasons.

Carolyn: Why did you leave Argentina?

Yolanda: Because there, too, I had many political problems. It was the same situation with the military, a *coup d'état*. In Argentina I participated in many political groups — pacifist, not communist. But when you are in a country with a military regime, they just think of you as activists; no matter what kind, it's a reason to persecute you.

Carolyn: Were you ever persecuted as a lesbian?

Yolanda: Never. Not me.

Carolyn: Even though it was evident that you were butch?

Yolanda: Even so. I don't know why, but others, yes.

Cira: Because she always looked like a little old teacher.

Yolanda: Oh yes! In Argentina, Buenos Aires, I went to a bar called Tibos with a friend, a huge bar with a discotheque, very nice. There was a place for women and a place for men, but when the police arrived, everyone danced together to create the illusion...

When we arrived, there was no one. "What's going on?" we asked. The owner came and said that cops had come with two buses and took everyone, even without their ID and coats. I was afraid, but he said, "Never mind." ... Then, ten or fifteen minutes later, everyone started coming back and they all told what happened, how the police took their fingerprints, photos from all sides. The women were booked as prostitutes, because there's no law against being lesbian. And the guys were booked for sodomy.

That night nothing happened to me. I really liked the atmosphere and went back other times, and once, when everyone was dancing, the cops came, ten of them, yelling, "Against the wall!" All the women [went] to one side, men to the other, but the fags didn't know which wall to go to, and the butches didn't know which wall to go to. [*Laughter*] Everybody was running from one wall to the other. They lost their cool. My gay friend was trembling. I told him to get his ID, because that's what they'd ask for.

The cops asked for our papers. But one said to me, "Get out of here — you look like a country schoolteacher! Get off home." So I left and my friend stayed.

Carolyn: You left your girlfriend there?!

Yolanda: Noooo! I'd *never* do that; I was with a gay male friend. He was taken and charged with sodomy.

Then one time I was walking in the street and I hear a car horn. It was the same police sergeant; he just wanted to say hello!

❖

Carolyn: Okay, now some questions on the bedroom. Did you ever know any stone butches, a butch who didn't want to be touched?

Cira: Oh yes, I knew many like that. I never slept with any, but I knew couples, one where the woman was butch butch...

Yolanda: But that's mental; how can you not want to be touched?

Carolyn: Did she take her clothes off?

Cira: Not all. Carmen was very feminine, she looked like a little doll, and she told me about that. She got used to it; she just lay there and relaxed, enjoyed everything; she didn't have to do anything. She never had to make love to the other one. At first it was hard, but she got used to it.

Yolanda: But that's a butch who's repressed.

Cira: No, she doesn't find herself repressed; she enjoys a woman.

Ina: It didn't exist in Chile?

Yolanda: Yes, yes, it did. There are many who don't like to be touched. And there are women who confuse you for a man at a crucial moment. When you're making love, they confuse you for a man and want you to put it in. It only happened to me once.

Cira: What did you do?!

Yolanda: I slapped her and left.

Ina: She didn't mean put your fingers in...

Yolanda: No, she said, *"Meteme el coso* [Put it in me]."

Carolyn: She thought you were a man?

Yolanda: No.

Carolyn: She wanted you to use a dildo.

Cira: Perhaps.

Yolanda: If I'd had one, I would have put it in. [*Laughter*]

Carolyn: So have you ever had a lover use a dildo, Cira?

Cira: No, and I don't think Yolanda even knows what it is.

Yolanda: No, I don't.

Carolyn: We have some! We'll talk about it later.

Yolanda: Always things to discover...

Carolyn: But you know couples who use dildos?

Yolanda: Yes, I know there are some using it in Argentina; I've heard it spoken of. Not in Chile, though.

Carolyn: You don't know what they're called in Spanish?

Cira: No.

Yolanda: *Pene-vibrador?* Or in Argentina they say *consolador.* [*Laughter*]

Cira: Obviously, it was named by a man!
I think Yolanda misunderstands the point; she thinks if a woman wants to be penetrated, it's because she's not really gay. I think that's baloney.

Yolanda: No, I don't think that. I think that a woman who wants a man will go find herself one, not one of those electric things.
All this stuff — I've never used them, never thought of them, and nobody's suggested using them. How I make love or how others make love to me, I feel good. I don't know if I'll ever need this thing. Maybe?

Carolyn: For us, they're toys, like having toys in the bathtub, in the swimming pool ... or in the bedroom.
Do you find you have butch or femme roles in bed?

Cira: I think so.

Yolanda: With all lovers, always butch.

Cira: Her, *siempre arriba* [always on top]!

Yolanda: *Siempre arriba!* I'm happier that way.

Cira: Sometimes you can change positions; it doesn't mean that you're more butch. I'm very flexible. I'm more flexible than she is.

Yolanda: Okay, don't make advertisements for yourself! [*Laughter*]

Carolyn: So you can change roles, top or bottom; it doesn't bother you?

Yolanda: No, I always like to be on top.

Cira: I meant I am flexible, physically and mentally. I'm less rigid in my habits.

Yolanda: I concentrate. I don't think of anything else.

Carolyn: In romantic situations, like when you two met or with other lovers, is it you who makes the first move?

Yolanda: If I take the initiative? Never, never, the women always search me out! [*Laughter*] They pulled my ears...

Ina: But usually the butches go after the femmes, no?

Yolanda: Yes, but *they* seduce me.

Ina: What about you, Cira; do you make the first move?

Cira: I give them an ultimatum: Stop the bullshit and get around to it. I'm leaving now; you want to come? You don't want to come? You stay.

Ina: You could say that she takes the initiative!

Cira: I've only slept with three women and usually I had a relationship with them, not just a pickup. All my relationships have been long-lasting.

I never played around. And now that I'm getting older, I think I should have!

Carolyn: Can you tell if a woman is butch or femme by looking at her?

Cira: Most times.

Carolyn: Or a lesbian?

Cira: Yes.

Carolyn: How?

Cira: I don't know. Intuition, or certain traits that people do have. If you talk to a person and watch her, you can tell if she's butch or femme, or if she's gay.

Carolyn: Here in Canada, a lot of women deny that they're butch or femme; they say they're just women.

Yolanda: It's difficult here, because they all look alike. In Chile it's easier.

Cira: Butch is *butch.*

Carolyn: When you arrived here, Yolanda, you found it hard to find a lover; I remember you went to a dance at Concordia University and you said there were no beautiful women! I think you were saying that there were no femmes, only butches.

Yolanda: That's right, I thought, My god! I better change! [*Laughs*] No, no, not really. No, I was thinking, I'd better bring over a woman from Chile or Argentina, if I didn't want to remain alone. I didn't like the women here.

Carolyn: Do you find that you divide your housework according to butch and femme?

Cira: We don't do it intentionally, but it happens. I'm the cook...

Yolanda: She does the wash...

Cira: Yolanda shovels the snow, because I have asthma. But I like doing cooking. It's my profession, and I also like doing it.

Yolanda: She never lets me cook.

Cira: Yes! I let you.

Yolanda: No, she says, "You don't do it like that!" She's never tried my cooking.

Cira: She's the one who pays the bills, and I do the shopping.

Yolanda: I hate shopping.

Cira: But it doesn't mean I can't do it. I would do it. But we don't do it because you're the butch and so you have to do these jobs.

Yolanda: No, it's very natural. But in Chile, the femme does the domestic chores, and the butch does repair jobs, painting, because she's stronger, physically and mentally. In my first relationship, I worked, I paid for everything, and she was just pretty, she never worked.

Carolyn: How long were you with her?

Yolanda: Ten years. Maria lived with her mother and we were together on the weekends at my small apartment.

Ina: Didn't you mind her not working?

Yolanda: No, but she *was* demanding, and she cost me a lot.

Carolyn: What did she tell her family?

Yolanda: Her mother discovered everything. She yelled at me, "*Maricona! Leave my daughter alone!*"

Carolyn: She yelled that at you for ten years?

Yolanda: For ten years.

Cira: "My daughter's not a dyke! You are!"

Yolanda: *Her* daughter seduced *me!* We broke up and I left for Buenos Aires one year before the *coup d'état*, then I returned to Chile and we met on the street, in downtown Santiago, face to face, and started talking, and we started seeing each other again. I told her I was returning to Argentina because I was having problems, and she said, "I'll come with you." But in Argentina her behavior changed. She started to demand a lot, same as in Chile. I told her we both had to work, but she said she didn't want to, so I said, "Sorry, life's different now, Argentina's more expensive than Chile." So I took her to a hotel, which she didn't like, because there wasn't a phone in the room and no hot water. Ten days of this, and she bugged me the whole time. She was very jealous, because everyone knew me in Argentina. I hadn't had a girlfriend during the time we were apart — I'd missed her ... But when she started fighting with me all the time, I told her to go back to Chile. It was finished. When she saw my mind was made up, she got violent. She tried to strangle me...

Cira: She was real feminine [*laughs*], a big woman.

Yolanda: ...I screamed and somebody came and knocked on the door and she stopped.

Carolyn: Did she hurt you?

Yolanda: She left me all black here. [*Gestures to her neck*] Then she cried all night long. The next day I bought her ticket to Chile; we didn't speak to each other all day. The day after that, I took her to the train station, she boarded the train crying, she held on to my hand, the train started to move and she didn't let go of my hand! So she left and I took up my life.

Carolyn: You got her out of your system.

Yolanda: That's it. So when I got back to the hotel, she'd left me love notes all over the place, under the mattress, in all my pockets, saying she loved me and she'd never forget me. I threw them all in the garbage! It was over. But four, five years later, the receptionist at my *pension* told me, "You've had a visitor, from Chile!" I said, "Who?" and she described her, and I thought, Oh, god! My stomach started to ache. She'd found me. But she'd changed a lot, she looked like a butch, cut her hair; she'd put on a lot of weight, and she was so vulgar! When I saw her, I said, My god! I was in love with *that*! I must have been crazy! She wanted to get back with me, she told me she'd never forgotten me, that she'd been with a lot of women, women who resembled me, blah blah. But I'd completely forgotten her. I told her, "I'm sorry, but I don't love you." At the time I had an eighteen-year-old girlfriend, just for fun. I was thirty-three. It was no good for me; I don't like young women. It was just to have someone. And you know, I had to ask her parents' permission to go out with her!

Carolyn: And they gave it to you?

Yolanda: Yes! Her mother and father invited me to tea and asked me what I wanted with their daughter. I treated it like a game but they were serious! I said, "I'll treat her well; I'm an honest person." It lasted three months. I got tired!

Ina: So they regarded you as a good husband for their daughter?

Yolanda: Yes, because I had a job, they were very pleased.

Ina: Was she an only child?

Yolanda: No, they had several. She was the youngest.

THE PERSISTENT DESIRE

Carolyn: But they knew you were a lesbian?

Yolanda: Yes. I don't remember her name.

Ina: Yolanda! That's awful!

Cira: You see, she had a lot of relations, but none of them long-term.

Yolanda: I got bored with her.

Carolyn: Have you read about butches and femmes, and where?

Cira: Yes, magazine stories in the States. They were much more open than here — that is, ten or fifteen years ago.

Ina: Did you read *The Well of Loneliness*?

Cira: Yes, it was the first gay book I read. I always thought they should make a movie out of it. I see it in my eye's mind [*sic*].

Carolyn: But it didn't affect you?

Cira: Yes, I cried all the way through it. The first time I read it I was married, and we were driving through the States, to Cape Cod, and the descriptions were just like the countryside. I read it with a dictionary ... very difficult.

Carolyn: Who did you identify with, in the book?

Cira: I guess with Mary.

Carolyn: Didn't you find it scary, didn't it turn you off?

Cira: No.

Carolyn: Because Ina read it when she was fifteen and it turned her off becoming lesbian for ten years.

Ina: The thing is, the way she described it, you were a lesbian if you wanted to be a boy! I *never* wanted to be a boy; I thought my brothers were idiots!

Carolyn: But what about Mary?

Ina: She's such a stock character. The protagonist is Stephen, everything happens around her, you *have* to identify with her.

Cira: Well, I didn't. But I thought, My god, what a horrible life that is.

Carolyn: You knew better by that time, 'cause you'd had your fling in Cuba.

Cira: Sure, I knew. I didn't think that it had to be that way.

Carolyn: What did you read, Yolanda?

Yolanda: At twenty-seven, I read *La Batarde*, by Violette Leduc. By that time, I recognized my condition.

Cira: Her malady!

Carolyn: Have you ever seen it as a sickness?

Yolanda: When I was fourteen, yes. I was in high school and I fell in love with another schoolgirl.

Carolyn: A lesbian?

Yolanda: No! I fell in love for free! It was platonic, I mean. On my way home, I thought, Why aren't I a man? — for the conquest, to seduce her. She pulled all kinds of scenes with me, and bugged me for not being a man. Later, in another school, one of my classmates told me she loved me. I trembled like a leaf! Like I told you, the girls went after me. I got used to it. In the washroom, she grabbed my arms and said [*through gritted teeth*], "I love you!" We were fourteen, fifteen.

Carolyn: And later you stopped wishing you were a man.

Yolanda: Yes, I forgot about that. When I was working in Argentina, I was working as an accountant for Citroën. A big factory, with six hundred workers. Adriana was the secretary for the finance manager. She had to pass behind my desk every morning to get my boss's signature. And every time she passed behind me, she'd sing and flirt.

Carolyn: How?

Yolanda: She always wore see-through blouses. And she walked through my office like this. [*Flaps her wrists, wriggles her shoulders*] So I stared! She wasn't gay, but she'd discovered that I was. She was trying to seduce me. So Christmas came, and everybody was sending anonymous presents. I sent one to Adriana, and included a love poem that I'd copied, in printed letters. She didn't know at first who'd sent it, but she investigated. She came up to my desk, and read everything on it, which was typewritten, of course. But I had a magnifying glass, and had printed my name on it. She picked it up, looked at it, looked at me, and started to sing. "*Si, si, si, te quiero con el corazon...* [Yes, oh yes, I love you with all my heart...]." That's what she sang every time she walked by my desk. My friends were driving me crazy. But I didn't want to expose myself. I have a horror of making a fool of myself. So I said, She's not going to play with me! But she went to the limit! And she won me.

One Saturday, when we were working overtime, we all went out for lunch, and she sat beside me and rubbed her leg against mine. I tried to ignore her, but it wasn't easy. She ordered whiskeys at noon. I looked at her and thought, Waugh! I left work an hour early and phoned her. "When are we going to stop this?" I asked her. She said, "Whenever you want." But a telephone operator at the office had been listening in, and she told everyone. So everybody started to whisper: "*Las mariconas!*" But *she* wasn't.

163

THE PERSISTENT DESIRE

Cira: She was curious!

Yolanda: When I arrived at work the following Monday, everybody was staring at me. I thought, What's up? Another co-worker, a Chilean woman, was smoking frantically — she didn't smoke — and said, "Oh! Everybody says you're a dyke! I want *you* to tell me the truth!" She was scared. So I said, "Yes, I'm a lesbian; it's nothing to worry about." And she said, "Yes, but everybody says you and Adriana do it over the phone, and Adriana showed you her tits!" You see, everyone had been watching us, and we hadn't realized. The girl had been *waiting* for one of us to make that phone call. I went to the bathroom and people were going on about *las mariconas* and I just washed my hands.

So Adriana's boss, a woman, came to me and said she'd heard I had a problem, maybe she could help me. She said she knew a woman psychologist, and I asked her, "What's she like?" — I took it as a joke. I said, "I'm not sick! There are lots of lesbians — am I the first one you've met?" She said, "Oh yes! Excuse me! I thought you needed help!" I said, "No thanks."

Day after day, there was always somebody who wanted to talk to me. Even my boss. He was Chilean. [*Acts very macho*] "Yolanda, sit down. Coffee?" I said, "Sure." "Cigarette?" I said, "Thanks." He said, "Everybody says you're a lesbian." I said, "Really?" He said, "What do you say to that?" I said, "Yes, I'm a lesbian. You're going to fire me for that? I thought you were very pleased with my work." "No, I'm not going to fire you. I don't care what you do in bed. But you have rotten taste! This woman's crazy!" [*Laughter*] He said the director general had called him. He said he wouldn't fire me for being a lesbian. "She does her work well, doesn't cause any trouble, doesn't fuck on her desktop!" He said he didn't care!

Carolyn: So you went out with Adriana?

Yolanda: Well, much later, after this huge scandal. People were pointing us out as *las mariconas*...

Cira: She wasn't happy about that, was she?

Yolanda: No, she denied it many times. Finally, we made a date, in a café, and she invited me home. Her parents had a big appliance store; the house was in the back. She said to her father, "Look, I'm going in back with my friend, so no phone calls or anything, okay?" Her father said okay. We went to her room and she stretched out on her bed...

Cira: The seduction!

Yolanda: With two whiskeys...

Carolyn: How was she dressed?

Yolanda: She wasn't dressed. Know what she said to me? "So, show me what you can do." I didn't like that.

Cira: It was like: Here's the dessert!

Carolyn: After all that!

Yolanda: I didn't like it. I left.

Carolyn: Without making love?

Yolanda: No. She was very angry with me.

Ina: No kidding!

Yolanda: At work she became my enemy. She was a real pain. I didn't look at her, didn't speak to her. I was disappointed. I thought, I went through all that for nothing, for a woman who wanted to use me like a sacrificial rabbit!

Cira: Your boss was right!

Yolanda: Yes! I did have bad taste!
So I got a job with Peugeot, and before I left, my boss gave me a big dinner in a restaurant. He gave me a bunch of roses, and all the girls from my section were there and making jokes. So in the middle of the meal, Adriana appeared. Everybody fell silent. They hated Adriana, you see; everybody was on my side. "Here comes the beast!" "Here comes the madwoman!" She came up to me, kissed my cheek, wished me luck, and left.

❖

Carolyn: Do you two like to dress up for one another?

Cira: We like to make ourselves pretty for each other. We don't do it often...

Yolanda: I like dressing the way she likes it.

Cira: I dress for myself. I don't mind wearing dresses, dressing pretty, I like dressing in satin and so on. I feel comfortable in it.

Yolanda: I'd like to dress like a *pasha*, with a harem!

Carolyn: How do you like to dress up?

Yolanda: Comfortably, to my taste, sporty. I don't like too much elegance.

Carolyn: You don't like wearing skirts?

Yolanda: Never.

Carolyn: Not even for Canadian immigration?

Yolanda: Not even.

Carolyn: Do you ever switch roles?

Cira: Where and when? [*Everybody laughs*]

165

THE PERSISTENT DESIRE

Carolyn: In bed? On the street?

Cira: I am the way I am.

Ina: Have you ever done that for a costume party? Just as a gag, you dressed up butch and Yolanda dressed up femme?

Cira: No. But I've only been with Yolanda for two and a half years, so we haven't really experimented...

Carolyn: What turns you on about butches?

Cira: I've never put my finger on it!

Ina: I don't believe that! [*Laughter*]

Carolyn: You can't figure out what attracts you about butches?

Cira: Not really. I like the person. If they happen to be a butch, they happen to be a butch.

Carolyn: But still, you've mainly found butches. So there must be something...

Cira: ...about them, yes. But I don't know what it is.

Carolyn: Yolanda, what attracts you about femmes? Their clothes, hair?

Yolanda: The eyes, first and foremost. Then, the breasts...

Carolyn: The body shape?

Yolanda: Yes. I like nicely shaped women. Beautiful women ... But if her mind isn't beautiful, I don't like her, eh? One has to complement the other. I won't go out with a pretty girl who talks garbage. That's why it's hard to find a woman to my taste. I've spent a lot of time alone.

Carolyn: What attracted you to Cira?

Yolanda: The first thing? [*Cira motions*] Her bum! Because when I opened the door at Pat's house, she climbed the stairs, zzzoom, in front of me and I watched her and went, Oh, la la! After that, her eyes. Because through her eyes I got to know her personality. She was very nervous...

Cira: I was broken up ... I wasn't sleeping, I wasn't eating.

Yolanda: I got in her car and the way she drove! I thought, What have I gotten myself into?! And she wouldn't look at me directly...

Cira: I wasn't over my relationship. I felt like I was being unfaithful. I am a very faithful person. If I'd looked at her directly, I would have felt as if I was breaking down that barrier and the other relationship's over...

Yolanda: The night I met her I wrote a poem: "Let me get to know your soul, beautiful little girl with the sad eyes."

Carolyn: You gave it to her?

Yolanda: Yes. Her eyes were very sad. She laughed, ho ho ho, but her eyes were hiding something. I said, "What are you hiding behind your sad eyes?"

Cira: I wasn't very happy.

Yolanda: I wondered, What's wrong? After three days she told me her whole story. I figured, Well, you have to start over, there's always hope...

Cira: I didn't want to be in this relationship, because I wasn't finished with that relationship.

Yolanda: You took my hand.

Cira: Because I had my high heels. Remember that night? I was so foolish. I was dressed up, because I was going to go out to supper with my ex. And she left me hanging there; she never came; she never called me. And when Yolanda called me, I was crying; I was just going to take my clothes off and she called me and said, "There's this meeting at the Simone de Beauvoir Institute; why don't you come?"

Carolyn: I remember that night.

Cira: I was all dressed up, and I was the only girl there dressed up with a dress. I smelled so good.

Yolanda: I was very happy, because that's what I like!

Cira: I had my high heels; I was dressed to kill.

Carolyn: You looked lovely!

Cira: And after that there was a full moon; it was beautiful. We went to a special place where I used to go by myself when I wanted to think and get away from it all.

Yolanda: I found her very sensitive, very special.

Cira: Underneath the bridge, going to St. Helen's Island. So I took her there — I always went there by myself, I'd never been there with anybody else. You know, I was afraid at certain times to do myself in because it was so easy just to let go. At one point I was in my car and I was going there, just rolling, rolling, and I wasn't going to stop.

Carolyn: Did you get together that night?

Yolanda and Cira: Noooo.

Yolanda: Ten days later.

Cira: *She* would have...

THE PERSISTENT DESIRE

Yolanda: She told me, "No, no, no, no ... okay."

Carolyn: What attracted you to Yolanda, in the beginning?

Cira: She was very sweet, very happy. But she's changed. She was joking, she used to laugh a lot. We had a very good mind together, like we could talk about any little thing like this and exaggerate it and make a big thing out of it.

Yolanda: We've both changed.

❖

Yolanda Duque finally achieved refugee status after four years of battling racist, ageist, and lesbophobic Canadian and Quebec immigration policies. Cira and Yolanda run a restaurant, El Rincon Latino, in downtown Montreal, where Cira serves *guayaba*, a reddish oval fruit, split to look like a vulva, with a dollop of cream cheese spread along the center, to blushing customers!

Marion Paull

A letter from Australia

n 1961, about halfway through my second lesbian relationship, I learned a new word.

When I read, in English or American journals, about lesbian lives, I feel so unsophisticated. I was a lesbian then too. But I never thought of myself as a bull dyke or a bar dyke or a passing woman — because these words have only recently come to me. The word I learned back in 1961 was *lesbian*. The brother of the woman I was having a relationship with found out about us and called me a lot of interesting words, which on the whole I didn't understand, but I looked up *lesbian* in the dictionary. My next relationship taught me the next word: *butch*.

I was born and brought up in Melbourne, Australia. In the fifties, when I was a teenager, I hung around with the straight girls I had grown up with. We sang in the church choir together, went to the theatre together. I went to jazz dances with them wearing jeans, a roll-neck sweater, a duffle coat. I remember one girl was only allowed to go because I undertook to bring her home. It never surprised me that no one questioned what I wore or where I went. I just did what I did.

Passing woman was a term I didn't learn until the eighties. If by *passing woman* you mean a dyke who can (and does!) pass for a man in a straight world, then I became one of those too. But that was later.

I think for me the die was cast in childhood. My very earliest memory is from Brighton, a bayside suburb of Melbourne, in a house we left when I was eighteen months old. I remember my mother going away without me. To put this into context, I should say that it was 1940, my father had gone to war, my mother was not going far, and there must surely have been some other responsible adult in the house. Nevertheless, if I close my eyes, I can hear the gate squeak shut and I can see her feet, just her feet and ankles, through the bars of the little gate. I can see the striped canvas sandals she was wearing, and how they came up high around her fine ankles. I have not inherited her ankles.

THE PERSISTENT DESIRE

Throughout my childhood, whenever my behavior was not appropriate, she still did what she wanted and went where she wanted, and if I couldn't be relied on to behave myself, I was left behind. As a result, I was one of the best behaved children you would ever meet.

This, of course, is only my perception. She herself would tell you that I was naturally good and lovely and that she gave her whole life to caring for me and providing for me. All I know is that even today if you turn away from me I tremble.

Of course, it is hardly surprising that, coming from one who, in my perception, did exactly what she wanted without question, when the time came for me to leave home, I, too, did exactly what I wanted without question. Or politics or high ideals or anything else.

In the third grade we did a little play for the end of year called *The Princess and the Woodcutter*. The girl who was the princess was the only one in the class who had long blonde hair. I was the woodcutter, because I was the biggest and would be able to carry her off at the end. At least, that's how I remember it. I certainly remember the feeling of the role — the trousers and the boots, rescuing the maiden in distress, and living happily ever after in the forest. I think this gave me a taste of what was possible. I spent a lot of my adolescence being tall, dark, and handsome and looking for a princess.

As a teenager in the early fifties, I was somewhat introverted. I remember feeling depressed. I read a lot, ignored the real world, failed my academic exams, and generally mooned about. I never fell in love in the teenage kind of way, although I indulged in a lot of idealistic dreaming. I was active in the church, taught Sunday school, sang in the choir, and so on. I always walked my friend Phyllis home from choir practice (otherwise she wasn't allowed to be out so late — 9:30 p.m. — my god), and I would kiss her good night at the garden gate. I remember her father flinging up the window of their front room. "Phyllis, come in here!" he would roar. But no one ever questioned who I was or what I thought I was doing.

I left school at seventeen, without qualifying for university, but with a very broad education that included playing two musical instruments as well as singing, ballet, and several languages.

In the summer of 1956–1957, before I started work, I went away on holiday with my mother. We revisited the beach resort of my childhood, although we didn't stay with the same people and of course it had changed. But in 1957 it was still a small village with a milk bar, a store, two churches — one Anglican and one Catholic — and no pub. There never had been a pub. People who wanted to drink alcohol had to drive to Queenscliff. People like us didn't drink, and anyway, no lady would go to a hotel.

And here, in this little out-of-the-way beach resort, I met my first lesbian. I didn't know the word, but I knew I wanted to kiss her. My mother met her first. She was staying at the same guest house, and unlike us, she had a car. She was maybe ten years older than I was, very sophisticated and very discreet. In the beginning I think I was just a holiday amusement, but the relationship lasted some three years. It was with her that I spent my first night out all night. We sat on the sand dunes and talked, and watched the ships and talked some more. We sat comfortably on an old blanket from her car, and I never realized that time was passing at all. It was only when the sun rose again that I realized that I had been out all night. Mother didn't say anything except that I must be tired and should have a rest after breakfast. There would have been quite a fuss had I been late for breakfast.

During the course of that relationship we wrote to each other nearly every day, in French, and I stayed with her most weekends. One time she took some photographs of me with her horses — well, they were probably of her horses, really — and her mother thought I was some new stable hand. I wasn't trying to "pass" but I was.

Then I was working, of course. And studying at night. And learning how to paint scenery. And living away from home, although still in Melbourne, and having another affair, this time with a married woman. I was quite "out," never having had the sense to be "in." She didn't like that I was out; she felt it compromised her and made life difficult for her sons. Later on I heard that she remarried. I understood why, but I hoped she missed me.

A friend introduced me to a little coffee lounge in the city called Prompt Corner. It was run by two dykes, one of whom is still a TV actress. They used to have play readings on Sunday nights that I found great fun. The lesbians who frequented this coffee lounge were all considerably older than I was, and very closeted. In fact, I was quite unaware that many of them were lesbians — I just thought they were nice people. There were definitely no passing women there — unless you use that term to describe women who pass for straight women in a straight world! A lot of them were friendly with the gay boys, and they provided one another some degree of protection.

Melbourne in 1958 to 1962 was truly a Victorian town. People used to say that in Adelaide you were defined by the church you went to, in Sydney by how much money you had, but in Melbourne by what school you had gone to. It was a conservative place, and it was important to be in the right class, at the right schools. We had a Liberal government both in the state and federally. There was no open hostility to lesbians, although gay men were considered to be a bit much. Of course, no one actually knew a lesbian. I never encountered any opposition, even at work. But other dykes were fired from their jobs and given notice to quit their homes, and some went to great lengths to disguise themselves. No doubt part of the reason that I didn't suffer any discrimination was that I did have the right background and the right school and so on. Some of the very nice people I met at Prompt Corner had been to the same school. I also met my next lover there, and it was she who introduced me to the pub scene.

She didn't so much introduce me as show me off. And I was so fascinated at the idea of meeting all these others that I wasn't scared; in fact, I wasn't self-conscious at all. I remember wearing a white roll-neck jersey that had been my father's and a pair of jeans — nothing special. It was March 1962.

We walked into the beer garden that Saturday afternoon hand in hand. I was wide-eyed. One of her friends shrieked out over the hubbub, "Shit, she's gone straight!" but she hadn't; it was only me. And yet I don't have a masculine face or hands. It seems to be all in the bearing. I never called myself a passing woman. I just did what I did. When you're tall and fairly slim, it isn't hard. Some of the butches I knew strapped their breasts down with elastic bandages, but I just wore a singlet one size too small and a generous shirt. I'll tell you, it's easier to pass in winter than in the summer. It's also easier to pass when you're younger. Now that I've passed fifty, my face is too soft and flesh is accumulating in the most unmanly places.

In the sixties in Melbourne, there were no women's dances or women's bars or women's anything really, except ladies' lounges. A ladies' lounge is a side room or sometimes a small bar where a lady can go for a drink. A man, of course, drinks in the public bar. There are still some outback pubs where men refuse to allow women into the public bar.

There were one or two "leso pubs," in the sense that groups of lesbians tended to congregate there. Would you call them gay bars? I didn't like them, mostly because I didn't drink more than a beer or two. I didn't like some of the dykes there either, especially the ones who got drunk and got into fights. Not in the ladies' lounge, of course. We congregated in the "beer garden" — outdoors, a few seats and tables, and a long struggle back inside to get beer by the jugful. I went because that's where the scene was. From 1957, when I started work, until 1962, when my new lover took me to this pub (the George in Prahran, as I remember), I thought I was one of four lesbians in Oz — and I'd been lovers with the others!

Of course, it wasn't a bit like the scene in the United States. We had a rather quaint rule called six-o'clock closing — the pubs all closed at six p.m. We would gather during the afternoon — Saturday afternoon, of course, since at least some of us had to work for a living — and leave when we were thrown out, only to regroup in one another's homes to party on. I wouldn't say we were exactly welcome at these pubs, but our money was. Toilet arrangements were somewhat primitive. Straight women in these pubs usually objected to our using the toilets, and there was no way we were going to use the men's. One publican solved this dilemma by installing metal rubbish bins with wooden toilet seats on them in the shed off the beer garden where we used to congregate in summer. You can imagine the state these would be in by six o'clock. It was almost a relief to be thrown out, yet no one ever complained.

The toilet situation, as I said, came about because the straight women weren't prepared to let us use the normal toilets. The men also showed a great deal of animosity as the day wore on and it became obvious that we had all the girls with us. There were some beaut brawls. On one occasion, I remember, one little tough dyke had her head kicked by one of these guys. Their aggression usually brought all of us much closer than would otherwise have been the case.

Some of these dykes I met in the pub were in the military, although most military dykes were far too discreet to frequent a place like the George. But there were lots around, and many of them got caught up in the great purges of the sixties. Most of them kept to themselves; they had their own groups and didn't mix much outside, which I suppose they felt was safer and still seems to be the case today. There was a couple living in the same block of flats as we were at one time. This block was very popular with the gay boys too, because it had so many entrances that no one could ever be sure just which passageway or doorway you had gone into. Anyway, the girl in the army was under threat of being thrown out of the military, and so she deliberately got herself pregnant by one of the men she worked with — to "prove" she was straight. She left the military with an honorable discharge on medical grounds to have the baby, and she and her lover moved to the country to live, but it didn't work out and I lost touch with them.

And what were we wearing then? Casual stuff mostly. For going to straight dances (there weren't any other kind, remember — it was a straight dance or no dance) I would wear a suit, a narrow tie, and pointed, lace-up shoes, or sometimes a sport jacket and dark trousers, and she would wear maybe tight pants and sandals or a frock with a very full skirt. And maybe she would wear makeup. I don't recall ever going with someone who "had her hair done." I had my hair cut in a semicrew with a square neck at one time. It was reddish brown then; now it is black going on gray. It's easier to pass if your hair is light and your skin is not too clear.

By the end of 1962, my lover and I were both playing in the same orchestra, though, to be brutally frank, they only had me because they needed her. One night after the show — was it *South Pacific?* — we went to St. Kilda to find something to eat. There was a place that was open late and that served great pasta. This was Melbourne, remember, in the early sixties, where the pubs were just beginning to learn about staying open after six p.m. and the only people around after midnight were prostitutes, criminals, and pimps. So there we were, having a well-earned supper, albeit in a restaurant with a certain reputation, when the police arrived. I think there had been a brawl, but I don't really remember, because I was tired and I was there only for the food. Everyone in the place was marched outside onto the footpath, lined up a couple of feet apart, and questioned about why we were in such a disreputable place at such an ungodly hour of the night. I heard my friend give a false name, but I was too slow-witted for that. However, for some strange reason, I gave my mother's address. Then the cop asked me whom I lived with and I said, "My mother," and then he asked me why I "dressed like that" (I was wearing a tuxedo, of course — what else would a member of the orchestra wear?) and did my mother know, to which I replied, "Of course — she does my washing." And I got a fatherly lecture about nice girls like me not going to places like this — and that's all! I nearly wet myself afterwards.

It was during this relationship that I lived as a man. Well, we lived as a married couple actually. It seems to be much easier to be accepted as a man when you're with a girl. I worked as a man at this time too, which, I can assure you, taught me a lot about men. I had been brought up by my mother and gone to an all-girls school, and my total experience with men was with the Sunday school superintendent and the vicar. I was totally ignorant about men. They had no relevance to my life. In 1963 I learned a lot about men. I also learned to swear.

The flat we lived in was in fact the upstairs part of a terrace house. The landlady thought it was a bit odd that I did the ironing, but nice odd. She used to introduce us to her friends. I was working as a man then too. We had been in Tasmania for a few months and came back to Melbourne broke. I wasn't having any brave ideas about passing; I needed a job. I had been looking, but there was nothing about, so I put on a clean shirt and tie and went into the local Commonwealth Employment Service office. You had to go there to apply for the dole, but they were supposed to find you a job if they could, and in those days they quite often could. They got me a job, screen-printing in a sheet metal factory. I never intended to stay there, and I had no real plans for living as a man for the rest of my life. As usual, I was just doing what I was doing, no politics, no ideals, no long-term plans.

After some months, I started looking around for a more "suitable" job. It was fairly boring working in that factory, screen-printing "FIRE HYDRANT" on the fire hydrants and "FIRST AID" on the first aid boxes, so I started reading the ads in the papers and writing off a few applications. Merging back into the straight world was going to be quite a challenge in itself.

I had to let my hair grow long enough so that I didn't look too butch when I applied for the white-collar jobs as a woman, but at the same time I didn't want to look too poofter at work either. The other problem was changing clothes. Obviously, I couldn't leave our little love nest in a dress, nor could I be seen in the neighborhood like that, as many people knew us by sight at least. So I used to pack my skirt and shoes in a little bag and take the train to the other side of Melbourne. If the carriage was empty, I'd change on the train as quickly as possible and then get off. On a busy day, I'd have to stay on for quite a way, and when I got off the train, I'd change in the ladies' lavatory. It seems on reflection to be a matter of how I carried myself, but women never cared that I entered looking very masculine and left looking rather less so. I don't like to think about what might have happened had I been caught making the transition in the men's loo. I think it also helped that the transition wasn't too radical. I was simply exchanging the trousers for a skirt and the lace-up shoes for something more casual, adding perhaps a cardigan but never high heels or lipstick.

So you had to be big and strong. So you had to take responsibility. So you had to be the breadwinner. So you wouldn't be caught dead in a dress (except for the purposes of earning a living, of course, although some butches refused to work unless in trousers) or in the kitchen. Most of these things I had learned as a child, reared in a household by a mother who had no difficulty at all with the concept of having to earn our living. I remember we had a cleaning man, which I guess was somewhat unusual at the time. My mother said she wouldn't ask a woman to do all that heavy work, particularly as we had so many stairs. He was also the cleaner for a theatrical household who provided him with permanent seats at the theatre, and from about the age of five I went to every show, every change of program with him. This gave me a great love of the theatre, and gave my mother some time off, I've no doubt, although I've no idea what she did with that time. Perhaps it's only since the seventies that we've become more aware of what other people are doing. I was certainly raised to "do as you will, harming none."

In 1964, I had an English friend who underwent a total transformation when she came home from work. I have been sitting in her kitchen talking to her lover when she came home. With not so much as a "Hi, how are you," she would walk right past as though I weren't there. Then I would hear the shower, and soon she would come back into the kitchen. Gone would be the court shoes, skirt, and blouse. The hair would be brushed back and even her glasses changed, for goodness' sake. I don't know how she could handle making that change every day. Another friend worked for IBM. She was femme, so the dress thing wasn't important, but the strain of remembering to say "him" instead of "her" and never being too specific about where she had been weekends and so on eventually got to be too much and she killed herself.

Being butch, being a passing dyke or whatever other label you put on it now, was at that time not a political statement or a stand taken; it was just what I did. There were all sorts of rules about how to behave, but these seemed to apply to public behavior and were the sorts of things I did naturally, like opening doors for her, carrying the heavy stuff, paying the bills. Other things done at home didn't seem to matter much — boring things of everyday life like ironing and housework. All those years of fresh white surpluses for church and white shirts for school had taught me how to iron, and my skill was enhanced by a dear friend who had been sent to a convent for rehabilitation after her family threw her out of their home because she got pregnant. The convent took in washing to provide money. She taught me how to iron a perfect shirt in under four minutes, and I never met a girl that didn't prefer me to do the ironing.

I don't know about taboos in private, because there was one big taboo and that was that you never told what you had done in bed with someone else. I think I would have liked to have known what other dykes did around sex, because I do remember that it was *not* all right for a butch to be touched sexually and it is only recently that I've been able to be touched and I sometimes feel awkward about that. Do not assume that this has meant that my sex life has ever been anything but amazing and wonderful! I have always had a strong sex drive and I've shared that with some great women. And learning to be touched hasn't made sex "better," only different. However, I'm not so relaxed about it that I'm going to tell you about it.

I may have been butch and I may have passed, but I certainly hadn't found my spiritual home in that bar scene. Many of the girls were prostitutes, and many of the dykes were not working or were living off the girls. Sometimes you would meet a butch who worked as a prostitute to keep herself. Most drank too much; many were into drugs and petty crime.

Within our community there were great passions and great fights. I was threatened at gunpoint, I remember, over a little gold ring set with a blood coral that had been made specially for me and was a gift from a previous lover. One evening I took it off and put it on the end of the piano whilst I was playing, as was my habit. One of our visitors took it home and didn't want to return it. After the confrontation and the threats, I went away for six months, and it was then for the first time that I lived as a man. When I returned to Melbourne, I met this same dyke in the city. I remember wondering how I should greet her, if at all, when she approached me, wanting to know how much money I could give her toward some other dyke's bail. She didn't even get mad when I said I couldn't give her any because I was out of work and in fact was in town looking for a job. She just wished me luck and went on her way.

After I made the transition back into the straight world, at least as far as regular work was concerned, we bought a house in the suburbs and settled down, but the quiet suburban life was too much for the relationship and we had quite a bust-up. I went overseas, and she went back to her wilder friends. It was April 1964.

For a while I lived in Christchurch, New Zealand. Melbourne may have been conservative, but Christchurch was something else altogether. There was no scene in 1964. By chance, a straight friend asked a neighbor to mind her child in an emergency. That neighbor was a gay guy. He saw me coming to visit my straight friend and, immediately recognizing a dyke when he saw one, invited me to meet him and some friends at the weekend. No one had a car. No one in New Zealand had a car, it seemed. We all met at the station to travel to Littleton, which is a port town, and which had a pub, not a gay pub, but one where gay people sometimes went. Wow!

Over a period of five to six months I met maybe ten dykes, in couples. I also began a relationship with a straight woman artist that was to last for the next six years. Her reaction to becoming a lesbian was a new one for me. Instead of my wearing a skirt and being "just a friend" or wearing trousers and passing, she really liked me to collect her after work in a suit that had a skirt so no one could be in any doubt about whom she was going with. It wore off after a while, although by then everyone knew, of course.

Our relationship was still outwardly butch and femme, which was set off by the fact that I was tall and dark and she was small and blonde. Because she had been married and had five children, some of whom lived with us, most of the time she expected to cook and clean and wash and iron, and so anything I did was regarded as a blessing instead of an obligation. When we came back to Australia in 1965 and she was working too and there was only one sixteen-year-old living with us, of course I did my share, but I think we both made sure that our friends did not catch me doing this. Again, it was a question of public appearances rather than private behavior. And, of course, things were beginning to loosen up a little. Flower power and all that.

I moved to Canberra in 1970. As a newcomer, I was invited to a small party soon after I arrived. And there, to my amazement, I was greeted with some anger by a public servant who said that my being there as an out and obvious dyke threatened them all. I had never met so many lesbians keen to remain under cover. Even in 1991 the public service has lots of closet dykes. I am more upfront than ever now, and it is finally a political statement.

In 1970, I was dragged into the women's movement by a new lover, and again I found that the way I looked was a big problem. We were asked to go to our local WLM meeting to talk about living as lesbians in a straight society, and of course, they all looked at this six-footer with short dark hair and trousers, accompanied by her lover, who was five feet four with shoulder-length light brown hair, and they accused us of role-playing, imitating heterosexual couples. They expressed their disappointment in a very aggressive way, I recall. They never stopped to look at what we were *doing*. We hung in there for about a year before we went overseas. One child was born in England and another was conceived before we returned to Canberra, and our straight sisters weren't the only ones to be aggro about that.

It seems to be going beyond mere role-playing when a lesbian couple has children. We had them because she wanted her own children, I like children, we could afford it, and we were able to organize artificial insemination. We did not have children to make a political statement. Straight sisters in the movement said we were once again aping heterosexual behavior. Lesbians were heard to say it was disgusting and why couldn't we have dogs like everyone else. If we thought at all, it was only about enlarging our family and how happy we were to have children. (P.S. You can look us up in Gillian Hanscombe and Jackie Forster's book *Rocking the Cradle* [Alyson, 1982].)

I won't talk about the role of the lesbian nonmother, except to say that it is a difficult one. All along I've done things because I wanted to. I've never wanted to be in the closet, which is just as well, as I am too obvious to get away with it. I have always been a lesbian, and I have always gotten away with passing without really trying to and sometimes without even meaning to. Being a man is not something I aspire to. In fact, you could say that I don't have any time for men. A separatist is really what I am, but that, too, is more because I prefer to live without men and independent of them than for any deep and political reasons.

This account of being butch in the fifties and sixties may leave you feeling somewhat let down. I suspect that is because it isn't as straightforward as you would like to think. The fifties and sixties were challenging times. We survived as we saw fit. There were not the politics you find today. The lifestyles were based on what we all knew — the heterosexual lifestyle. We put on a public facade and invented the rest. In my opinion, there wasn't much butch-femme role-playing *within* relationships, but those of us who were serious about making our relationships work put in the same kind of effort any couple puts in to make sure that both parties get what they want out of it. The fifties and sixties were interesting times — there were no facilities or support networks for women or lesbians then. We did what we could with what was available. The literature was limited. Politics were nonexistent. We looked after one another, both within relationships and in the general community. We went out to dinner. We went to the theatre or to see a movie. If wearing drag made that easier, that's what we did. If there was no women's dance and you wanted to go dancing, you did. You went in a suit and a tie, you took the prettiest girl you knew, and you had a ball.

As the sixties grew up, I started to develop some political awareness, and in 1967 I was one of a small group of lesbians who came together to form the Australasian Lesbian Movement. We had a very grand title and some rather grand ideas. It was the time of gay liberation, although we did not want to have anything to do with the gay boys. We had a newssheet, got ourselves some press coverage, and tried to reach as many lesbians as possible. In 1970, I was dragged into the women's movement. From 1972 to 1975 in London, I was active in various lesbian groups. Back in Australia in 1975 and based in Canberra, I went back into the women's movement. Since then, more and more I find myself working only with lesbians. I still wear trousers and I haven't learned to cook. My previous partner and I were together for eight years, and we had two children through artificial insemination by donor (AID) when we were living in London. We haven't lived together for the last twelve years, but we still see lots of each other, even going away for holidays together as a family. We all have the same family name. The boys are pretty well grown up now and have always been fully aware of the whole situation. The younger one asks only that his mother not embarrass him in front of his friends — he's a bit self-conscious at fifteen. My ex and the woman who has been my lover ever since we split up are also good friends. The three of us went bush walking in the Snowy Mountains last weekend. We've had to get on because of the children, especially when they were small, but now we enjoy one another's company just for the sake of it. In August we'll be having a special celebration to mark twenty-one years of the three of us knowing one another.

I don't know how to end this. It hasn't been easy writing all this stuff down, although the memories are strong. All those women I used to know but haven't seen for twenty years and more — I wonder what they are doing now. Every so often news filters through — one died in a particularly horrible car smash; another killed herself with an empty syringe, an act that may or may not have been deliberate. At Christmas I got a card and a photo from one of my friends who had been discharged from the army in the purges of the early sixties. It's a great photo of a great dyke and on the back she's written, "Still a resemblance to James Dean, huh?" Some things never change.

Frankie Hucklenbroich

Excerpts from a crystal diary

In the midsixties, I spent several years as your basic, garden-variety junkie. My drug of choice was methamphetamine crystal, a pure and potent powder with a "rush" that turned my brain into a maze of neon tubing and my veins into liquid gold. (Or so, like any other speed freak, I thought.) I also thought my life was wild and exciting and creative, and constantly high and that constantly "tripping," I had it made. I knew a lot of people who were in the same shape and felt the same way; there has always been a gay and lesbian junkie subculture. Leaving it in 1967 was one of the hardest things I've ever done. How did I first join it? The same way anyone can: I joined it step by step.

This story is about two days I spent in a skid row hotel room in San Francisco shooting crystal into my arm and watching a police stakeout that didn't exist.

The cops are still watching me through their binoculars. They're perched on top of a smokestack a few blocks away, and from where they are they have a straight view right into this room. We live on the third floor. There isn't a windowshade.

If I hang a sheet up in the window now, they'll just get agitated. After all, we've been here for a couple of months without bothering to cover the window and it would look suspicious to suddenly go around hanging curtains. The last thing I want is for those cops up there to get more pissed off than they already are.

I wonder where they got the smokestack idea?

I haven't left this room for some time — at least a couple of days but maybe more. At first I just didn't have any reason to split. I was doing some writing, a long poem for Diane, and getting into my books. Then yesterday morning I spotted them up there on the smokestack, and now I'm scared to leave.

Last night I didn't turn any lights on. I just sat by the window all night in the dark watching the sidewalk in front of the hotel. I thought the cops might climb down the stack and then come sneaking up on me through the foggy streets.

But nothing happened except there was a nasty fight between two hookers outside the bar on the corner. One of the hookers sliced open the other one's face with a straight razor, and in the pink light from the neons, the blood that sprayed everywhere looked like wine. Only one prowl car showed up for the fight, and when its black-and-white snub nose came around the corner, the hookers and the crowd watching the fight all melted away like magic. The one with her face laid open ran up the street with her hands pinching her new lips together and blood pouring down her arms and dripping from her elbows, and then she dodged into an alley between two buildings. When I saw the prowl car, I held my breath, but the car just went on past the hotel and turned into the alley after the injured hooker, the fog turning and swirling in its headlights.

When the sun came up this morning my own cops were still in place. I wonder if they're plainclothes or just harness bulls?

❖

They're after Diane.

They're waiting for Diane to come home or for me to hit the bricks and eventually lead them to her. I'll never give them Diane. Never. Never. If they finally do crash the room, they can bust me, take me in, jack me around, whatever they want, but I won't give them Diane. In another day or two something will happen to make them lose interest. Or else they'll come in and roust me. One or the other. Unless she comes home, Diane will be safe either way.

She'll be so safe, she won't even know what I had to go through to keep her that way, until she has to send somebody to bail me out. Honor among thieves and all that shit.

Right now Diane is probably at Hank's place on Folsom Street dryfucking her brains out. That's how she gets her crystal. Our crystal. By fucking Hank. He's the biggest crystal dealer in town and Diane — with her butterscotch-colored hair and smoky voice and mad eyes — backfired on him. I could tell him that the voice is just from using so much crystal, but he probably already knows that, and if he's like me, his fingertips still tingle and his groin melts like wax when she talks to him. He loves her. He still uses her for a runner, but he actually loves her, which impresses me. Hank's hurt some people really bad, and the word on the street is that he's offed a couple of people as well, and you wouldn't expect someone like Hank to get all soft about a chick, any chick, even Diane. So we both love her. She has a power and she uses it.

She uses. Crystal. Hank. Me. Anybody anytime for anything. I've seen her operate, and she can knock you out with one slashing lift of an eyebrow. She has a power and she uses it. But it's okay.

There go the little sparks of sun off the ends of the binoculars again. There's a woman up there too. A lady cop. Probably gay. Probably butch. I can't see a femme climbing up there. Diane might. If she were a cop.

What a thought!

But there has to be a woman up there. I feel that. My scalp and the back of my neck have that electric feeling I used to get when a woman was watching me and I was pretending not to know it.

Diane left me two full tablespoons. Packed tight, not fluffed up. Even with my tolerance, two measured spoons should last me until she can come back. She has her faults, but she's never let me run dry yet, not since the first time she slid a needle into my vein and showed me the cosmic lights. And she never complains.

I know I'm expensive. It takes a lot of fucking for a lot of crystal for her to feed my arm. She takes care of things. Diane says I should look at Hank as nothing but a trick, and fucking a trick is just her job. But I hate Hank. As a matter of principle.

She says, That's silly, what about the hookers you've been with? Did you hate their tricks? I tell her, No, but they didn't mean anything to me and you do. Then she just laughs and says, You can't say I didn't warn you, baby.

And sometimes I even feel kind of sorry for Hank. He just won't believe Diane's really a lesbian. He thinks if he ignores me, I'll go away. He thinks if he *doesn't* ignore me, the idea of competition from a woman will make him less of a man.

I don't know what I think anymore.

❖

One of the first things Diane ever said to me was, Everybody uses everybody, Frankie. I still didn't believe that, even after my time on the streets. Another thing she said when I first knew her was, You're too butch for me, I like to control my situation. We're going to have to change your head around a little.

I didn't believe that either. I was going to change Diane.

I was going to save her. From Hank. From crystal. From the vultures that were always surrounding her with their hands out. From the head games. From herself. I had a blindness for Diane. She told me and I wouldn't listen.

I thought I was Sir Lancelot and she was my Guinevere. I just needed to convince her. Wonderful me was going to show her wonderful her. My hand to god, I looked at her and white picket fences were scribbled in my eyes. I looked at her and wanted to enter a little cottage after a hard day's work at some factory and holler, Honey, I'm home! I wanted us to buy a poodle and a Volkswagen. God help me, I wanted her to start wearing aprons in and high heels out. Diane would cook. I would take out the trash, mow the lawn, and change any flat tires on the car. Meanwhile, I'd be writing reams of excellent lesbian poetry in the evenings, each word a modest offering to her. I would then preen beneath her fulsome praise. And I'd bury my grateful face between her legs at least nightly. That's how it was going to be for us. I was beside myself. Besotted. She made me snort and whinny and paw the sand.

After we got together and I moved in with her almost without her knowing it and I started using out of curiosity and also to prove to her that crystal can be done for fun without changing your whole life and I promptly got hooked almost without my knowing it, I grew to understand her better. Or maybe less. Maybe they're both the same thing.

❖

Hank's street name is "Big Man," but not because of his size, as he is just a short, mean-eyed, middle-aged guy with skinny arms and legs. "Big Man" refers to the incredible amount of crystal he controls and to the people he bought the franchise from, who take care of him. Everyone on the streets except me and Diane is pretty much afraid of him, and I might be leery of him too if I didn't have Diane standing between us. Big Man truly dislikes me.

On the other hand, if it weren't for Diane, I wouldn't even know him, much less have spent so many afternoons sitting in the chair by the window watching him fuck her into the mattress while she smiled at me from under her arm if they were fucking doggy style or from whatever position they were busy licking, sucking, fucking, gulping, slapping, biting, mauling, and grunting, Unh! unh! unh! I'm no watch freak.

Being there was bad. Being somewhere else would have been worse.

There is a small rose with two delicate green leaves tattooed on her shoulder. The tracks on her arms are like ropes.

Don't get me wrong. I could have left them alone. Nobody asked me to stay. It was just that one minute we'd all be sitting around bagging crystal into nickel and dime and quarter bags and fifty-dollar spoons, fluffing it through a couple of flour sifters to make it go further and not talking much but concentrating on the count and the scales, taking care of business, and the next minute they'd be rolling around on the floor or the bed and pulling at each other's clothes, and it was *our* bed, *our* floor, *my* woman, and I couldn't just say, Oh, excuse me, I see that you're fucking; well, I think I'll just run down to the corner for a carton of milk. This was the way things were: he was our bread and butter and insurance that we'd never have to worry about where our next bag was coming from, but I wasn't about to let him drive me out of the pad.

It was home, after all.

So I stayed fried, kept my face nice and bland even when he'd turn his piggy eyes back to me and grin. I maintained my cool. He'd be pulling his clothes on, and I'd pop a couple of frosty longnecks and say, Ready for a beer? as I handed him one and passed the other to Diane.

One time when they were in the middle of fucking, he turned his head and looked at me and said, Come on, Frankie, you ride my pony for a change. And he pulled his big dick out of Diane and used his hand to wag it back and forth at me like the tail of a dog. Come on, Mr. Butch, he said. Come on over here, girl.

Instant paranoia.

What to do? What to do?

But Diane reached up real fast and grabbed his face in her fingers and turned him back to her and said, Let her alone, Daddy, maybe I don't want to share you, and Hank laughed and rolled her onto her stomach.

I thought, Thanks, baby.

They finished fucking, and Hank said he had some business and Diane should meet him later on that night. Coltrane was blowing at a club in North Beach and Hank wanted to go down and take him in. While Hank dressed, Diane ran around the room naked gathering up his watch and his hat and the briefcase he uses for a stash bag, and when he went out the door, he pecked her on the cheek just like some square headed for the office and said, Catch you later, honey, and I wanted to kill him. I wanted him dead real hard and messy, but then my very next thought was, But what about our habits? See, between the two of us, we hit up a good eighty, ninety bucks' worth a day. And it's rising.

Crystal is the Great Simplifier.

❖

The smokestack belongs to a brewery that's right near Mel's Drive-in on Van Ness, where I used to work as a carhop for a while when I first came to San Francisco. That was a couple of years ago, after Dawn and I broke up. I'm almost thirty now. Between Dawn and Diane I played the field. Cocktail waitresses. Strippers. Hookers. A belly dancer. A couple of "nice" women. Joe Studley, that was me.

I was with Dawn for four years. Before that I was with Kim for three years. Before that I also played the field, learning about women and gay life and how to be a butch. And before that I was with Lil, but that only lasted for six weeks before she dumped me. Lil was the first woman I ever went to bed with — brought me out and didn't even know it. I was ashamed to tell her. I was just this great galumphing girl from Missouri, on my own in Los Angeles and in love for the first time in my life. I knew what I wanted, but I had only the haziest idea of how to get there, so I tried and tried to fake it, and of course I failed dismally. But I thought she hung the moon.

Except for Diane, I don't know where any of them are now. I miss that.

The way I met Dawn was I walked into a place called the Cellar because it was below street level. You opened a door and had to go down a flight of concrete steps to get to the bar and some rinky-dink tables and a small dance floor. There she was, dancing with a stocky young dude with very white skin and dark hair. (Later I'd find out he was her high school sweetheart and they were engaged. Great for my ego.)

Anyway they were a pair of straights, or so my instinct told me, but as I reached the bottom of the steps he spun her and she wound up facing me. We were so close I could have touched her, and the butch in me and the bitch in her said, Well, hello there! and when the music stopped I walked by their table to see what they were drinking. Coors. I bought three bottles at the bar and went over and pulled up a chair.

They played it very sophisticated. Thanked me for the brews and we exchanged names and then I asked them, What are you doing in a gay joint?

Bob said they didn't know it was when they came in, and once they ordered, they figured they might as well stay and dance a few sets.

A little local color? I grinned.

Dawn laughed, but Bob just smiled at me over the rim of his glass. He was a very nice guy. Very mellow and laid back. Dawn and I kept looking at each other, but Bob didn't seem to notice or maybe he just felt secure. I thought about how Dawn moved like a young tiger on the dance floor.

We made chitchat. Dawn was going to Chouinard's School of Art. Bob was down for a visit. They were from Vegas. The Mormon part, Bob said, laughing. Finally he got up and headed for the john. I looked at Dawn and said, Come home with me. She stood up and picked up her purse and followed me outside, and we ran to the cabstand on the corner and I took her home for the next four years. The point of all this is that there are times and people — just a few — that happen to you without warning, leave you stunned, and change your whole life.

Even after they're gone, you're different because of what you became when you were with them.

❖

Every woman who's ever really mattered to me I met in some crazy, accidental way, and our connection was always immediate. Lil in the Marlin Inn. Kim in Coffee Dan's. Diane in Chukker's.

Chukker's is on Turk and Taylor in the middle of the Tenderloin District, and it was quiet that night, which is unusual even at four a.m. I'd split from a party over in North Beach, but I was feeling pretty good and not yet ready to wrap it up, so I swung by Chukker's to see what was shaking and it looked like nothing was. A couple of bull dykes were at one of the tables, a femme we used to call Lean Doreen because she was so skinny lay stretched out and snoring in a booth, a local junkie was nodding in a corner, and an old queen with a really bad red toupee sat at another table watching the door. That was it.

I took a table and the waiter swished over and I said, What's up, Candy? Looks like a morgue in here.

No booze! he said, *very* annoyed. Can't run an after-hours with no booze! Cops raided earlier. We were closed for three goddamn hours! *Some*body forgot to take *care* of somebody. Come back tomorrow. We'll be set by then. How 'bout a Coke for now?

I said, Okay, but when I got the Coke, it was lukewarm and I was sorry I ordered. I was just getting ready to leave when Diane walked in.

Hair falling in her eyes. Cheekbones like knives. But beautiful in sandals and bell-bottoms and a black velvet blouse that looked like a medieval tunic. She didn't look left. Didn't look right. As far as she was concerned, the place was empty. She climbed up on a bar stool and laid a big purse on the bar, taking things out and examining them with care and putting them back in the purse again.

Candy walked down the bar and spoke to her, and I saw her shake her head, no. When I caught his eye, I waved him over.

Who's that? I said.

Diane Ferrari, and she's bad news. Don't go looking to get burned, my friend.

Me? Get burned? Candy. Surely you jest.

He gave me a look. This one you should pass on, he said.

So how come I never saw her around before?

Sometimes she's here every night for a few hours. Then she'll disappear for a couple of weeks or months. I don't know where else she hangs out. She's a busy lady, he said.

Yeah? What's her story?

A speed freak. Real heavy-duty. Nice lady, but messed up bigtime. Smart too.

Whaddaya mean, smart?

Books, he said. She always carries three or four in that saddlebag of hers. Sometimes she'll sit by the jukebox, I mean right *by* it, so she can get enough light to read by. Whole place'll be jumping and there she sits reading away. I hear she's gay, but I never seen her with a woman. Just junkie fags or alone.

Smart, huh? Bring me another Coke, okay?

Candy shrugged. You're making a mistake, dear, he sang.

I just grinned at him from the top of my ego. I said, Better yet, I'll pick it up at the bar. A cold one this time, okay? I walked over with him and got my Coke, and then I moved down the bar next to her. She glanced at me and went back to digging through her purse.

I said, What are you reading tonight?

She turned to face me, and her look was definitely unfriendly. What do you want? she said.

Now I was not used to this kind of a reception. I didn't know whether to be annoyed or amused. So I settled for intrigued and decided to try direct with this one. I'll be honest with you, I answered. I asked Candy about you. Your name's Diane and you're bright as well as good-looking. You like to read. So do I. I don't know what I want yet, but when I do, I'll tell you. If we're on speaking terms. Are we?

She was glaring at me, so I tilted my head and smiled to show her how harmless I could be. Just a sheep in wolf's clothing.

You're being honest with me, huh?

That's right. I am.

Don't you know — and the mad lights I'd get to know so well were dancing in her eyes even in that dark place — that honesty is just another word for a certain subtle ignorance?

She actually said that. Who *is* this? I thought. Out loud, of course, I had to say, Let's go for breakfast. We'll talk about books. You can explain honesty to me.

We stared at each other. Then she said, I'm reading *Steppenwolf*. Also *The Duino Elegies*. Do you know who Rilke is?

I nodded and I saw her smile for the first time. The next thing she said was, Good. We can skip breakfast. What I'd really rather do is take a shower with you.

Right then I knew I was a goner.

❖

One year ago I cruised this town in spit-shined boots and suede-front sweaters. My shirts went out to the laundry and came back with heavy starch in the body and extra heavy in the collars and cuffs. I wore ascots with stickpins and I always wore black stretch pants with the straps under the insteps so I'd have a sharp line from the top of my boot to my waist. I was always clean. I wasn't disposed to have another "relationship."

Now I have Diane.

Our relationship is monogamous, according to her. According to her, Hank doesn't matter, because he just fucks her. She says fucking is business and eating pussy is emotional and nobody eats her pussy but me. It's funny, but I don't even do that much anymore. We're always so busy. Selling crystal. Scoring crystal. Shooting crystal. Tripping. It's like we're celebrating. Diane goes out only for business. Everything we really need is in this room. We can go on like this forever.

That's fine with me.

Judith Schwarz

Technicolor dykes

Spike the Dyke, known to our boss as Jan N——, where are you now? Have you heard anything from Margarita or Tall Terry over the last twenty years? Bobbie MacD——, known to your mother as proper, Bostonian-bred Barbara, known to many of us as the fastest tongue in the West: are you still giving delight in the night to some lucky woman?

Alice and Harriet, the last I heard you two were running a photo-finishing plant somewhere in Michigan. Still together? If so, you'll be celebrating your twenty-fifth anniversary right about now. Good for you! But I will always wonder what would have happened if I hadn't been hit by a car on the way to put the make on Harriet during the wee hours of night shift while, you, Alice, were off visiting your family.

Carol H——, I heard from mutual friends that your ex-lover Dorothy married a man. Her two grown children, whom you raised together, refused to attend the wedding if you weren't invited to the reception, or so the grapevine said. Did you go? Did you want to go? Does it even matter to you anymore what she does? And has anyone heard if Anita S—— went back to El Salvador with her savings as she always talked about doing? Remember how she saved half of her two-dollar-an-hour wages while her lover Carmen went to nursing school? Somehow, I hope that they are still in California, teaching *gringas* like me how to dance away the homesickness so many of us felt.

All you gorgeous, strong women who worked at Technicolor, Inc., in San Francisco during those wild years of the 1960s and early '70s — I need you more than ever now. I'm far away, a little lonely, and a lot older, wanting a good heart-to-heart with someone else who remembers it, too. I need to know if you're alive, to hear your stories once again of the military witch-hunts of the 1950s, of getting kicked out of a Seven Sisters college on simple suspicion of so-called deviancy, of the families that took you to doctors or tried to institutionalize you when they found lipstick on your collar that wasn't your shade or a batch of hot love letters from your ex-army buddy. I need to hear again how you found love when even

Daughters of Bilitis meetings were fearful to go to, long before women's centers and music festivals existed, when bars were few and far between (not to mention dangerous as hell), but you went anyway because you *had* to.

If your memory needs jogging, I was the nineteen-year-old who had just quit my job at Bear Photo Finishing when they moved from their ancient factory behind the San Francisco Opera House to the distant suburbs. I started at Technicolor as a negative cutter on night shift in May 1963. When I was a kid back home in Phoebus, Virginia, how could I have known that someday I'd be wearing a work smock with the famous Technicolor logo I'd seen so often on the Lee Theater screen? And though I knew when I took the job that the company had a great name in photography and film, how could I have known that I was walking into Lesbian Heaven, where lesbians made up nearly half the work force? And I sure didn't know you were all in the middle of a union fight to replace the no-account company union with an AFL-CIO real one, or that I got a ten-cent-an-hour raise to color print inspector after the first month over Gloria M—— simply because both the supervisor and I were WASPs and she was Chicana.

That is, I didn't know until one of you made damn sure to tell me, taking me aside in the dump of a restroom to let me know just what was what, and why I was getting such hateful glares up and down the work area. It was the belated beginning of my political education, after a total whitewash in the truest sense of the word by my Southern high school. Still, all the time I was growing more politically aware, I stayed heterosexually oblivious until I was lucky enough to make a switch to days. Just before I changed over, the night shift supervisor, Randy, warned me about the notorious day shift.

"Watch out for the queers, honey," Randy whispered to me. When I asked how to tell who was and who wasn't, she looked at me as if I hadn't two brain cells to knock together.

"Hell, baby, you can always tell a dyke! *Everyone* knows they all have chapped lips."

How we enjoyed repeating that legendary straightism once I discovered I Was One, Too. That took about a year and a half, but then, I always was a slow learner.

I miss you all, damn it. Did I make you up? Or just some of the stories? Do you remember it the way I do? The seductive hot looks along the conveyor belt; the so-called coffee breaks that for some of us were really femme makeup breaks; the butches taking long drags off their butts, leaning against the restroom doorway so we femmes would have to slide slowly, deliciously, past them, breast to breast, on the way out of the "ladies' lounge" (that cesspool). For all the joking about it, no one was so desperate for a make-out place that we ever went near that broken lump of a daybed unless we were truly ill.

THE PERSISTENT DESIRE

The *longing* I remember, the undercurrent of passion, the incredible things we did to get a little loving. Ike J—— (never to be confused with Spike, your mortal enemy on day shift), do you remember me still? Do you recall working as a pricer at the end of the moving inspection belt? One morning, as the dozens of photo packets came down the line, a few dropped off the end to the floor. You swiveled around on your stool to pick them up. Having just raced to clock in, I was now taking my time, sauntering to my place on the line, when I saw a packet fall near my left high heel. You were the toughest butch on day shift, and the first woman supervisor. You had *prestige*. Something devilish came over me as I leaned down and picked it up. Slowly handing you the packet, I looked into your eyes and whispered, "That wasn't so easy to do. I sure don't want the guys lookin' up my skirt today of all days. I forgot to put any panties on."

Your mouth fell open, and the packet slipped through your wet fingers back onto the floor as tiny drops of sweat broke out across your forehead under your DA haircut. Your foot hit the conveyor belt button, sending a cascade of packets down the belt, creating a logjam before you. I strolled to my work area laughing softly, hugging myself inside with the sweet thrill of femme power.

What a wonderful day that was, full of sexual highs! You didn't do a darn thing right all day. Your lover from the customer service department — now, what *was* her name? — kept throwing worried, then suspicious, looks at you. But even if you write and say, "Schwarz, you're full of it," telling me that one of my cherished erotic memories is a crock, I'll gladly give up my version of our mutual past for the present-day reality of your burly self.

Spike. Oh, *Spike!* Remember the party at 17 Mars Street when I went exhausted off to bed long before everyone had left? You were far gone, playing "Wedding Bell Blues" on the hi-fi over everyone else's howls of protest, smoking weed, and drinking God-knows-what, until someone finally smashed the 45-rpm record over her knee. Along about three a.m., you climbed out one of my housemate's windows, clung by your finger-tips as you inched along the slanted roof, and then climbed through my bedroom window. And do you remember how *mad* I was? "Damn it all, Spike, I'll never get your footprints off my pillowcase! A couple more inches and you'd have flattened my nose! You're drunk."

Christ, I was miffed! And you — you stood there swaying, smelling of booze and cigarettes, a half-hangdog, half-proud expression plastered all over your puss.

"Aw, Jud! I near friggin' kill myself to get to you and what kinda welcome is this? Shouldn'ta locked your door. Butch gotta climb all over hell and gone just to be a little friendly." Your short, plump fingers closed softly but demandingly over my breasts. "C'mon, baby. I'll buy you a dozen pillows. Be nice to me."

Memory reminds me that my nipples were hard whenever your hands came within five feet of them, whether at work or in lovemaking. As angry as I was, my body responded as I threw open the door and demanded you leave my room. I am wet with memory as I write this.

The spring of '66, Carol H——, you came to work as a truck driver, picking up undeveloped film from drugstores all over the city and delivering it to the plant late each afternoon. You said, "Just call me Bear. Everyone does." What a handsome butch you were (and probably still are), with the bit of gray just beginning to shine through your dark, curly hair. In the arrogance of my youth, I thought of you as the distinguished older woman (you were all of thirty-two), and it only added to your appeal that you "still" played softball at your advanced age. Somehow, I wangled an invitation to one of your games. Ah, the ecstasy of riding beside you to a San Mateo suburban ball park, entering through the players' gate with you, sitting up in the bleachers holding your jacket "in case you get chilly." Mmm ... And when I found out that you carried an extra set of clothes and your toothbrush in the trunk of your car "just in case," all ladylike restraints were gone. You never had a chance. I wonder if you still think that sex-filled night was all your idea? True, the code said that the butch always takes the lead and makes the first move, but we femmes knew that if we waited for some of you shy, more silent ones to get around to it, softball season would be long gone by the time we shared more than the first stammering conversation. I wanted you too much to let that happen. You were nicknamed "Bear" for your great bear hugs, but I learned that you gave much more than just good hugs to your women.

After a few years there, I learned to run one of the color photo printers. Montana Jean, whose last name I can't remember or never knew, came to work one summer on the last leg of her cross-country trek. Are you reading this, tall-in-the-saddle Jean? One of your jobs was picking up the finished rolls of paper from us printers to take to the developer. You'd come into the darkened printing room, your dark t-shirt contrasting sharply with your overall blondeness, and call out, "Anyone got a roll ready?"

You, too, were one of the quiet ones, but cocky and too self-assured for my taste. I was between lovers, and a little crazed that summer. It didn't take much to make me feel like doing something outrageous to pass the time. In mid-August, I'd had enough of your smirk as you leaned against the partition of my curtained cubbyhole, challenging me with "Are you ready yet, madam?" as you looked down at me seated at my printer.

"Damn right I am," I said, jumping up and closing the black curtains in your face. You waited outside, shooting the breeze with Bobbie across the aisle, as I shut off the dim lights, opened the printer doors, and expertly unloaded the exposed roll. Then I reloaded quickly with new paper and closed the machine before opening the curtains. Swiftly I went through the usual routine, not caring that I hadn't been close to finishing the roll.

Then, as you waited outside the curtains, I thrust my hand under the waistbands of my skirt and panties, rubbing two fingers over my clit just long enough to get wet. It didn't take long. The wetness had started as soon as I realized what I was going to do. I drew back the curtains to give you the exposed roll. You strolled over to take it from me, the smirk renewing. Handing it to you, I said, "Wait, Jean. There's something on your face." Reaching up to brush off an imaginary bit of lint, my still-damp fingers lingered under your nose as I touched your upper lip, then sat back down and turned on my printer. You stared at me dumbfounded for a split second, licked your lip, then dashed out of the darkroom, shocked to your core. But later — days? weeks? hours? — that same sensuous full mouth was sucking my clit deliciously into the gap between your two front teeth as the song on the radio moaned with me about your "driving me slowly out of my mind." You were the first lover to go down on me. Did you know that then? Would I have had the guts to let slip my pose as a worldly woman of vast experience enough to tell you the simple truth?

Truth wasn't my best stock in trade. Who was it that said, "If I weren't a writer, I'd be the biggest damn liar known on earth?" Well, I was the most constant liar I knew. Ask me the time of day and I'd say five minutes earlier or later than reality for no good reason. Ask me if it was raining, and I'd look out at the puddles forming and say, "Nope." No rhyme or reason, just a "pathological liar," as my first woman lover sneeringly called me. (She was an alcoholic, but I wasn't into name-calling.) I had lied for survival for too long as a teenager to stop even when I no longer had to. It was second nature. Those years had been unbearably horrible, and I still wasn't sure whether or not life was worth sticking around for.

Technicolor was a good place for me to heal. The repetitious work helped, the images constantly shifting in front of me as I flipped through and inspected thousands of photographs each night, slowing down now and then to daydream over an especially beautiful Hawaiian sunset or happy family Christmas scene. Somehow, it helped me begin to cope with the raw wounds I carried around that no one else could see. But once in a while, out of nowhere, I would feel myself start to sink. The painful memories of sexual assault by my mother's latest husband, the anguish of watching Mom being beaten after he'd dealt with me, all the hidden horrors my little sister endured would surface and nearly kill me with anger and shame. I was sure no one would believe me if I told the truth that twisted my guts into knots when I least expected it. Always around my menstrual periods, almost always at the sight of my mother's flowery handwriting or my sister's childish scrawl on an envelope postmarked Texas, as they reminded me that they were still living the nightmare. But I was no longer there to even try to protect them.

How you helped me, my co-workers and friends at Technicolor. Long before I heard the term *support network*, you were there for me, individually and collectively. Sometimes, in the middle of an otherwise commonplace shift, a photo would pass through my hands and trigger some foul memory. All hell would break loose inside me: headaches, stomach pains, bitter tears. I couldn't stop the night from descending, and it terrified me. In the midst of my sorrow and grief, I would completely lose my ability to see colors. Me, a color print expert. I would barely make it to the bathroom before the racking sobs would start.

Our supervisors seldom knew what was going on. Whoever could get away would come after me, standing in the next toilet stall and softly, soothingly, trying to calm me through my sobs. How much I loved you for caring! How close I was to the edge so many times, with only your concern and silly jokes keeping me going. Dear, straight, grandmotherly Helen M———, your big pillowy breasts comforted me many a time as you rocked me on the daybed, not giving a damn what anyone who dared to look twice at us thought. I haven't forgotten. Nor your truly awful jokes, Ike, when you were the one to come for me. You were so awkward, so scared in your own way, trying to deal with this temporary lunatic with the bloodshot eyes and the mascara running down her cheeks. But still you tried.

And when you came to my rented room later to check on me, Ike, you seemed to be the only one who knew that what I wanted most wasn't sex but to be held. When the need was heavy, I usually wasn't able to tell whether I ached with sexual desire or with the hunger for comforting words and caring talk. I was lucky enough to have a desirable young body and a personality that liked to please. So sex was what I got more often than friendly small talk. This is not a complaint, mind you — just an observation.

Ah, dear women, I want to know you now that we've got a couple of decades under our expanding belts. What became of you all when I went off to college after ten years of our wild and woolly ways? Somehow I foolishly thought I could always just go back, maybe work a summer shift or something, and pick up where we left off. So I mourned as much as if I were still there when I heard that the Sunday night shift had come to work one evening to find that the creeps who ran the joint had locked everyone out without warning. Since it was a union shop, they had closed it up, eventually opening up another, more automated plant thirty-one miles away. Scuttlebutt had it that if they had opened the new plant within thirty miles of the old, by union contract they would have had to rehire the old employees. What must it have been like for those of you who had never worked anywhere else in your whole life? So many Technicolor dykes took their jobs for the chance to work comfortably with other lesbians. Many of the women had never worn a skirt to work in their whole lives. Did they at least give pensions to the ones close to retirement? Not likely. And could that replace the warm comradery lost with the closing of the old plant?

I heard that Ike and her lover moved over to the new plant and were rehired because they had learned how to use the mainframe computer in the early 1970s. That gives me hope that maybe they are doing better financially now. Honey Lee C—— had left long before, and her fame as a photographer was growing. Word had it that Bear went to trade school with her severance pay, and was happily using her new skills. But most of my old co-workers lost contact with one another as they all went their separate ways.

Now, I still find myself drawn to looking at old photographs, and as I travel around doing slide shows about lesbian lives, always, always, I wonder how you are. At the Lesbian Herstory Archives, I often refer researchers to the same copies of *The Ladder* that I used to hide in a bag in the darkroom at Technicolor. The grapevine would always let it be known where to find the bag with the latest copy, and it would pass from woman to woman until the last lesbian had sifted through its tattered pages for the life-giving messages it gave us. But still, when I asked you all to come with me to a Daughters of Bilitis Gab 'n' Java, you always refused.

"Who wants to hang out with those stuffy dames?" Ike would say. "Hell, half the time they don't have enough beer at their dances."

DOB functions and the women who attended them were hardly stuffy, but there was a perception that DOB women were more middle-class than us "working dykes." For one thing, they never comfortably called themselves dykes, even in jest. I felt caught in the middle, wanting to go to college but not believing I could do it, knowing that the Daughters of Bilitis was pointing the way out of our narrow options as lesbians but not sure exactly how we were going to pull it off, and always wanting to know if any "average" lesbians (not just Gertrude and Alice and Natalie and Virginia and those movie stars we all gossiped about) lived full and happy lives before we came along.

Remember when we'd get lucky in the old days and the bar owner would lock the front door, put a lookout at the peephole, crank up the jukebox, and we'd fish to "I Want You, I Need You, I Gotta Have You" or some such thing? Well, the words still hold true. I refuse to grow up and grow old reclaiming only other lesbians' histories. I want to know about the women in *my* life — you. I want to find you, give you a bigger bear hug than even Bear will give back, and begin to build even more memories for the long nights and days ahead. Where did you go? Who are you now? How has life been treating you? I want to hear how you're doing, laugh with you, touch your wrinkles, and show off mine. I want to introduce you to my lover, who'd really like to hear another version of these old stories by now. Hell, I even want to meet Ike's partner and learn her name after all these years.

Where are you, San Francisco's wonderful warmhearted Technicolor Dykes?

Jul Bruno

The following is excerpted from an oral history tape recorded at the Lesbian Herstory Archives, New York, 1981. From the LHA collection.

This is Jul. This is Jul. I want to make it very clear. And this story is for Maria.

This is about the first time I used a dildo. Of course, the first time I was in the presence of one, I used one. This story happened when I was seventeen. It happened a long time ago and it has been completely removed from my consciousness for many years. I mean, I'm sure I remembered it in the four or five years following it, but I never realized how important it was — and then I removed it in the seventies, when it wasn't politically correct. I completely removed it from my mind and it's through having that talk that we had on another tape about dildos that I remember the first time. And it's important.

So there I was in a bar. Right. By myself. I was about seventeen years old. Phony proof — had to be in the bar. So, whatever you had to do to get into the bar, I did. So there I was and I was operating. I was on. I was going home with somebody tonight. Actually, I was going wherever we were going, so if it had to be the backseat of a car, who cares? I still lived home with my parents. I was in a club in Chelsea. I'm sorry, I don't remember if it was Kooky's or the Nautilus. It was one of those two clubs.

Of course, it took me three or four hours to get dressed. I made sure I didn't sit down, because the crease would get ruined in my pants and stuff like that. Every hair was in place. I guess it was Kooky's — a long bar and at the end of the bar was the dance floor; behind me were mirrors to my left; the bar was to my right. I always made it a point to stay at the front end of the bar where the door was so I could shoot a glance down the whole bar and see who came in and went out. Especially when I was there for what I was there for that evening.

There was a woman sitting at the bar who I thought was much, much older than I was. She was about twenty-four or twenty-five. But I thought, My God, this is a *woman* and I'm just a kid. But in terms of sexuality, when

I was seventeen, I hadn't used a dildo yet, but I had really been in and out of bed a lot. It sort of didn't fit with my age, you know. Anyway, there I was and I had my hand in my pocket and I was throwing poses as usual, every fifteen minutes changing the pose, smoking cigarette after cigarette. It's getting to feel like one o'clock in the morning already, you know — nothing was doing. People were getting frantic; couples were leaving.

The woman was sitting at the bar by herself. She was an Italian girl; she had long, black, flowing, curly hair. Every now and then she'd look over her right shoulder at me and I was — something else I used to do when I was in a bar, I would stay in one spot, because I wouldn't want to be mistaken about whether or not someone was cruising me. If they kept looking at that spot, they had to be looking at me. I made sure I was in the mirror and my correct side was showing.

So, there I am at the bar and she's got a drink in front of her and I'm standing next to her and she's sitting on the stool. But early, like at about one o'clock — the club closed at three or something — it was understood at about one o'clock that we were going to go and be alone together, me and her, and I was sweating. I was freaking! Can I handle this? Will you look at this woman! She got up to go to the bathroom — I took one look at her body and I said, "Your knees are getting weak from this one; would you take a closer look!"

When we were leaving — it was up to her. Hey, I didn't care if it was eight years or eighteen years. When she was ready, that's when we were going. I had my hand in my pocket and I'm throwing poses and shooting glances up and down the bar, and she's got her head turned and she's looking right into my eyes, and I am looking elsewhere trying to be very cool, very aloof, and I'm already plotting that I'm sleeping with her this night and what am I going to do with her anyway. And she says to me something about we were "going to have a really good time, you know." And I said, "Oh yeah. Oh yeah! Uh huh." Really good time, and she's "You really think so?" And I'm giving her reassurances like "Leave it to me; we'll have a wonderful time!"

"You wouldn't mind if I guaranteed that, would you?" she said. I said, "No. No. How would you guarantee it?" Like really I didn't know what she was talking about. And she said, "Well, we can bring a friend." So I'm trying to be very cool, and I'm gulping and the sweat is on my brow, I have my hand in my pocket, and I'm trying to be so cool. And I said, "Oh, yeah. What does she look like?" I'm thinking of somebody else in the bar, like, Oh, fuck, this is going to be a ménage! I'm seventeen years old. This one with the tits — with the ass — and she wants somebody else in the bed too! I didn't have enough hands, enough legs. This is going to be a ménage!

"What does she look like? Where is she?" And I'm trying to be like "Sure, I do this all the time." And she says, "She is not a *she*, she's an *it* — and it's in my bag!" She didn't know where she would end up that night and she wanted a dildo, right? Could you have seen me? Seventeen years old! Seventeen years old saying, "Oh, sure." Not knowing where the fuck I'm going to put it.

But I'm trying to be so cool, like I've seen it a million times before and, of course, I know exactly what to do with it, of course, of course. So I'm like "This is nothing at all." And then I start hoping I get hit by a car on the way out of here or something, because what am I going to do? To be in bed with this woman to begin with was making me nuts! And it was clearly defined that she was the femme and I was the butch. I knew what she wanted. She wanted me to make love to her. So there she was with the bag, and there I was knowing I wanted to do whatever she wanted me to do and not knowing if I knew for sure how to do it. All right. So it was three o'clock. We leave.

She didn't have a car; she lived with her grandmother in a two-bedroom apartment in Manhattan. I was just following along wherever she wanted to go. And I had my eye on the bag. The bag — the fucking bag! And I'm checking out the size of the bag and I'm thinking, Oh, how big can it be?

We're on the bus and I'm hoping that a million people will get on and off so it would keep stopping so I had time to think about it. Or maybe she would lose the fuckin' bag. We get off the bus; we get up to the apartment. It was in Upper Chelsea — it was not far. We get up to the apartment. She puts her hand on my face and says, "We can't wake up my grandmother. Just sit here. I'm going to go in the bathroom and get dressed." Or undressed, whatever she was doing. This was a fast operator. So what does she do? She leaves her bag on the table in the living room. And what do I say? "Let me check this out." Because I had already, in the past hour, decided that if I could only get a look at it, I think I could handle it — just 'cause I'm good with my hands — you know what I mean. I could figure out what to do with it or — it was actually not the dildo itself that gave me trouble, but the harness, or how do you wear it? How do you wear it in such a way that you have control of it? So I had this feeling that if I can see it, I'll be all right.

I'm sitting and I'm looking at the bag. And I'm looking at the bag and I'm saying, "But what do I have to lose here?" I had to be alone with it for a minute. And I'm thinking, All right, what if she's gonna come out of the bathroom very fast? I only need a minute. Let me go over there quickly and do it. But then I'm thinking, Anybody that operates in the bar could be a real fast dresser. So I decided to scratch it. There'll be another opportunity.

I didn't even know how it was going to get from the bag to my pelvic area. I knew it was ending up in my pelvic area. This I knew. This I knew. So, all right, she comes back to the living room, she takes me by the hand, right? The bag is on the table. She takes me to the bedroom; she's showing me pictures on her wall, this and that. We're talking very quiet, very low. She says, "I just have a few more things to do in the bathroom and then you can go in." She leaves the door open to the bathroom. I'm standing around, both hands in my pockets, fully dressed. I decide to go into the living room. This is my idea: I'm going to go into the living room. I'm going to get the bag. If I can have the bag on my person, I'm already close, all right? I'm gonna get the bag; I'm gonna walk into the bathroom. And this is what I do. I go into the bathroom and hand her her bag and I say, "Want your bag?" and she says, "Well, no." What do I do with it? I put it down next to the toilet bowl. Now the bag is in the bathroom, which is where I am going to be shortly, because I am going to say I have to go to the bathroom, all right? The bag is in the bathroom!

A bag — it's not an unusual thing for a person's pocketbook to be in their own bathroom. So she's gonna forget. This is what I was hoping — that she's gonna forget that it's there. And she did. Anyway, I'm standing by the door and I'm saying, "Listen, I'm gonna be a few minutes in the bathroom," and I knew I had an excuse to close the door, because I'm a butch. She's a femme and part of her enticing me was to get undressed or be doing her hair, this and that, with the door open. But I knew that I could easily have said to her I needed to have all my clothes on and it would have been acceptable.

She left, saying, " You can use it now." And she walked right out of the bathroom — the bag is on the floor. I go in and I close the door! I'm in there. I'm in there. I open the bag and there is this little satin-type pull-string pouch thing — oh, please! This is it. This is it. I see it, face to face. I see it face to face. I'm not going to leave you hanging — and I knew what to do with it. That's all. That's the story.

Then I came out of the bathroom and we were in bed. I don't know when she went to get the bag. We were in bed and I'm — I remember I'm really intent on pleasing her and I was on top of her. I was wondering how we get around to putting it on, you know. I didn't know, but I had enough self-confidence about using it and about putting it on that whatever it was going to be, it was gonna be.

And I was on top of her and she said something in my ear. "Um um um um um..." And I said, "What?" and felt stupid. "What?" Because I was supposed to know what I was doing. "Um um um um..." and I said, "Oh shit!" This must be it. I must have been supposed to have done it already, you know. And she said, "Put your hand under the pillow." And there it was. I don't know how it got there — when she got it there — but there it was.

Dear DOB Sisters

The following letter from the LHA collection is one of thousands that were written to Daughters of Bilitis chapters in San Francisco and New York; they give a vivid picture of what life was like for working-class butch-femme lesbians of this time. This one is reprinted from the Lesbian Herstory Archives Newsletter, *no. 8.*

December 1969

Dear DOB Sisters,
For some time now I have been receiving mail from you; I feel quite close to you through your newsletter. It is much like a letter from home each month. I would love to come to the meetings and functions, but my late working hours and our two small children at home make that quite impossible to do. My wife, Michelle ,and I feel we know all of you through your names and articles in the newsletter; you are truly a household word. Our neighborhood is not at all oriented to gay life, nor is there any gay socializing nearby. Most of our friends are straight, and though it's pleasant, it is not as rewarding as one letter from DOB each month. It is our only link to a chain too far away to get to. I thank you for that.

I have read so often of the heartaches and humiliations suffered in trying to make a world of people who don't understand just try to. I understand these problems very well. In this new year, we must remember all the struggles we have gone through for recognition as a wholesome, normal people. All the marches, debates, and still the terrible degradations some of us have had to endure. All of this is our reason for God's placing us here. If at one point in the year just one of the thousands of people we have encountered turns to a friend and says, "You know, I think I understand them," well, then we have made some progress, haven't we?

My wife, Michelle, and I have done this, and I thought you might like to know about it.

In the beginning of 1969, we found ourselves pretty much in hot water. I had left a job in New York to live in Jersey with Michelle. She wanted to move to New Jersey and so we did. Finding an apartment was pretty

199

rough, because I had not yet gotten settled in a job, but we did manage eventually to get into a housing project that was still nice for the kids and Michelle.

After all was settled, furniture and all, we set ourselves down to living normally again with all the chaos involved with moving — you know this is not an easy task ... but it was all done rather quickly. My wife is very capable, and with me taking the kids out for the afternoon, she really got the house together. When we returned, I found a home where I had left a barren apartment that echoed everything we said. Michelle had even managed to hang curtains.

We sent Lori, our oldest, out to play, and soon after she came home crying. A little girl she had been trying to play with told her that her mother said not to play with her. After much comforting, all settled down, and we shrugged it off, because often strangers moving into a building are not welcomed right away.

Time went on and soon we found out there had never been any lesbians in this project before, nor were there any "known" lesbians in this area. Michelle and I were almost totally ignored. Michelle did have one or two who would say hello to her, but me they wouldn't speak to. I am very pronounced in my appearance; there is not mistaking me for what I am: I am a butch and Michelle loves me that way. Everything I wear she picks out for me, and she gives me my haircuts. I am a product of her and we are content with it. Although the men and women in the building seemed to feel my appearance was a threat to them — getting on the elevator with me was out of the question — with Michelle they would hesitate and get on anyway.

I believe to this day the only thing that helped was Michelle's way with the house and the kids. She kept a spotless home, and she is an excellent mother. Slowly she would run into a woman in the laundromat who might comment on how well behaved the children were. Each time, Michelle would run home simply elated; nothing could have been better than someone really talking to her. It was such a small thing that meant so much to me. I thought I would ask her to move, but she said she is here and she will stay whether they liked it or not.

Then I decided I would take her out for a night, go into New York, be with other gay people for a while; she might feel better. Michelle asked one of the teenage girls in the building if she would sit for the children that night. The girl said no first, then said that her mother finally consented. All was fine until the day after we went out. I came home and found Michelle totally wrecked! It seems the girl went home after sitting for us and was asked by her mother if she was propositioned, molested, or asked to return when we were both home. Well, I think Michelle's heart was broken; she adores children, and teenagers to her are still babies. Michelle is from a professional family, so I believe her nice manner was inherited and would have been a lot nicer than my manner at that point. She went to talk to the mother that evening. I don't know what was said to this day, but the girl is still baby-sitting for us, no questions asked. Soon after, we were known as "pretty nice people, but don't be alone with them."

Michelle asked a woman one day if she wanted a ride to the store with her. The woman said all right as long as her husband did not know. Each month passed until summer finally came, when the usual habit of the women in this building is to sit outside with their chairs and talk. We passed this group of sunbathers quite often, and usually the air was pretty tense or the conversations would cease. It was very heartbreaking for Michelle. She had not wanted to be a part of any gossip or coffee cloth [coffee klatch], but the complete withdrawal from her was a bit too much. My heart went out to her then, as it does whenever she does something really great, which is pretty often.

But slowly people started giving credit where it belonged. Michelle and the kids won them over whether they liked it or not. First with the children, then with our home. One day the electricity went out, and our Lori walked a man all the way up to the twelfth floor, holding his hand, because he had a heart condition; she even saw him to his door.

Then the day came when Michelle and I were giving a birthday party for Lori. The children were to come at one p.m. and leave at three p.m. The party lasted until eight that night. Michelle even cooked dinner for all fourteen kids. They loved it; the kids just wouldn't go home.

The next day our phone rang constantly, mothers calling asking what we did, the children never stopped talking about how wonderful Michelle and I were, how they loved us. From the mouths of babes came the answer.

Now when Michelle and I go out the door, ten kids rush to kiss her hello, and couldn't they please come with us? Even the mothers are surprised at the affection they have for Michelle, a truly wholesome and normal affection too. Today in this community they know that lesbians are not stag-film replicas or degrading. Today when they need a good meat loaf recipe or their hair done, even an interior decorator or baby-sitter, they simply call on the two lesbians who moved up to the twelfth floor two years ago.

We all have our struggles. Isn't it just great when we make enough headway to walk into a restaurant and not have the waitresses huddle in a corner whispering, or walk down the theater aisle and everyone keeps watching the picture, or walk down a street unnoticed?

Love to all of you,
Joanne, Michelle, Lori, Danny

Rocky Gámez

From *The Gloria Stories*

Every child aspires to be something when she grows up. Sometimes these aspirations are totally ridiculous, but coming from the mind of a child, they are forgiven, and given enough time, they are forgotten. These are normal little dreams from which life draws its substance. Everyone has aspired to be something at one time or another; most of us have aspired to be *many* things. I remember wanting to be an acolyte so badly I would go around bobbing in front of every icon I came across whether they were in churches or private houses. When this aspiration was forgotten, I wanted to be a kamikaze pilot so I could nosedive into the church that never allowed girls to serve at the altar. After that I made a big transition. I wanted to be a nurse, then a doctor, then a burlesque dancer, and finally I chose to be a schoolteacher. Everything else was soon forgiven and forgotten.

❖

My friend Gloria, however, never went beyond aspiring to be one thing, and one thing only. She wanted to be a man. Long after I had left for college to learn the intricacies of being an educator, my youngest sister would write to me long frightening letters in which she would say that she had seen Gloria barreling down the street in an old Plymouth honking at all the girls walking down the street. One letter said that she had spotted her in the darkness of a theater making out with another girl. Another letter said that she had seen Gloria coming out of a cantina with her arms hooked around two whores. But the most disturbing one was when she said that she had seen Gloria at a 7-11 store, with a butch haircut and what appeared to be dark powder on the sides of her face to imitate a beard.

I quickly sat down and wrote her a letter expressing my concern and questioning her sanity. A week later I received a fat letter from her. It read:

Dear Rocky,

Here I am, taking my pencil in my hand to say hello and hoping that you are in the best of health, both physically and mentally. As for me, I am fine, thanks to Almighty God.

The weather in the Valley is the shits. As you have probably read or heard on the radio we had a hurricane named Camille, a real killer that left many people homeless. Our house is still standing, but the Valley looks like Venice without gondolas. As a result of the flooded streets, I can't go anywhere. My poor car is underwater. But that's all right. I think the good Lord sent us a killer storm so that I would sit home and think seriously about my life, which I have been doing for the last three days.

You are right, my most dearest friend, I am not getting any younger. It is time that I should start thinking about what to do with my life. Since you left for school, I have been seeing a girl named Rosita, and I have already asked her to marry me. It's not right to go around screwing without the Lord's blessings. As soon as I can drive my car, I'm going to see what I can do about this.

Your sister is right, I have been going around with some whores, but now that I have met Rosita, all that is going to change. I want to be a husband worthy of her respect, and when we have children, I don't want them to think that their father was a no-good drunk.

You may think I'm crazy for talking about being a father, but seriously, Rocky, I think I can. I never talked to you about anything so personal as what I'm going to say, but take it from me, it's true. Every time I do you-know-what, I come just like a man. I know you are laughing right now, but, Rocky, it is God's honest truth. If you don't believe me, I'll show you someday. Anyhow it won't be long until you come home for Christmas. I'll show you and I promise you will not laugh and call me an idiot like you always do.

In the meantime, since you are now close to the university library, you can go and check it out for yourself. A woman can become a father if nature has given her enough come to penetrate inside a woman. I bet you didn't know that. Which goes to prove that you don't have to go to college to learn everything.

That shadow on my face that your sister saw was not charcoal or anything that I rubbed on my face to make it look like beard. It is the real thing. Women can grow beards, too, if they shave their faces every day to encourage it. I really don't give a damn if you or your sister think it looks ridiculous. I like it, and so does Rosita. She thinks I'm beginning to look a lot like Sal Mineo, do you know who he is?

Well, Rocky, I think I'll close for now. Don't be too surprised to find Rosita pregnant when you come at Christmas. I'll have a whole case of Lone Star for me and a case of Pearl for you. Till then I remain your best friend in the world.

Love, Gloria

203

THE PERSISTENT DESIRE

I didn't go home that Christmas. A friend of mine and I were involved in a serious automobile accident a little before the holidays and I had to remain in the hospital. While I was in traction with almost every bone in my body shattered, one of the nurses brought me another letter from Gloria. I couldn't even open the envelope to read it, and since I thought I was on the brink of death, I didn't care at all when the nurse said she would read it to me. If this letter contained any information that would shock the nurse, it wouldn't matter anyway. Death is beautiful insofar as it brings absolution, and once you draw your last breath, every peccadillo is forgiven.

I nodded to the matronly nurse to read my letter.

The stern-looking woman found a comfortable spot at the foot of my bed and, adjusting her glasses over her enormous nose, began to read.

Dear Rocky,

Here I am taking my pencil in my hand to say hello, hoping you are in the best of health, both physically and mentally. As for me, I am fine thanks to Almighty God.

The nurse paused to look at me and smiled in a motherly way. "Oh, that sounds like a very sweet person!"

I nodded.

The weather in the Valley is the shits. It has been raining since Thanksgiving and here it is almost the end of December and it's still raining. Instead of growing a prick I think I'm going to grow a tail, like a tadpole. Ha, ha, ha!

The matronly nurse blushed a little and cleared her throat. "Graphic, isn't she?"

I nodded again.

Well, Rocky, not much news around this asshole of a town except that Rosita and I got married. Yes, you heard right, I got married. We were married in St. Margaret's Church, but it wasn't the type of wedding you are probably imagining. Rosita did not wear white, and I didn't wear a tuxedo like I would have wanted to.

The nurse's brow crinkled into two deep furrows. She picked up the envelope and turned it over to read the return address and then returned to the letter with the most confused look I have ever seen on anybody's face.

Let me explain. Since I wrote you last, I went to talk to the priest in my parish and confessed to him what I was. In the beginning he was very sympathetic and he said that no matter what I was, I was still a child of God. He encouraged me to come to mass every Sunday and even gave me a box of envelopes so that I could enclose my weekly tithe money. But then when I asked him if I could marry Rosita in his church, he practically threw me out.

The nurse shook her head slowly and pinched her face tightly. I wanted to tell her not to read anymore, but my jaws were wired so tight I couldn't emit a comprehensible sound. She mistook my effort for a moan and continued reading and getting redder and redder.

> *He told me that I was not only an abomination in the eyes of God, but a lunatic in the eyes of Man. Can you believe that? First I am a child of God, then when I want to do what the church commands in Her seventh sacrament, I'm an abomination. I tell you, Rocky, the older I get, the more confused I become.*
>
> *But anyway, let me go on. This did not discourage me in the least. I said to myself, Gloria, don't let anybody tell you that even if you're queer, you are not a child of God. You are! And you got enough right to get married in church and have your Holy Father sanctify whatever form of love you wish to choose.*

The nurse took out a small white hanky from her pocket and dabbed her forehead and upper lip.

> *So, as I walked home having been made to feel like a turd, or whatever it is abomination means, I came upon a brilliant idea. And here's what happened. A young man that works in the same slaughter-house that I do invited me to his wedding. Rosita and I went to the religious ceremony, which was held in your hometown, and we sat as close to the altar rail as we possibly could, close enough where we could hear the priest. We pretended that she and I were the bride and groom kneeling at the rail. When the time came to repeat the marriage vows, we both did, in our minds, of course, where nobody could hear us and be shocked. We did exactly as my friend and his bride did, except kiss, but I even slipped a ring on Rosita's finger and in my mind said, "With this ring, I wed thee."*
>
> *Everything was like the real thing, Rocky, except that we were not dressed for the occasion. But we both looked nice. Rosita wore a beautiful lavender dress made out of dotted swiss material. Cost me $5.98 at J.C. Penney. I didn't want to spend that much money on myself, because Lord knows how long it will be until I wear a dress again. I went over to one of your sisters' house, the fat one, and asked if I could borrow a skirt. She was so happy to know that I was going to go to church that she let me go through her closet and choose anything I wanted. I chose something simple to wear. It was a black skirt with a cute little poodle on the side. She went so far as to curl my hair and make it pretty. Next time you see me, you'll agree that I do look like Sal Mineo.*

The nurse folded the letter quietly and stuffed it back inside the envelope, and without a word disappeared from the room, leaving nothing behind but the echoing of her running footsteps.

After my release from the hospital, I went back to the Valley to further recuperate from my injuries. Gloria was very happy that I was not returning to the university for the second semester. Although I wasn't exactly in any condition to keep up with her active life, I could at least serve as a listening post in that brief period of happiness she had with Rosita.

I say brief because a few months after they got married, Rosita announced to Gloria that she was pregnant. Gloria took her to the doctor right away, and when the pregnancy was confirmed, they came barreling down the street in their brand-new car to let me be the first to know the good news.

Gloria honked the horn outside and I came limping out of the house. I had not met Rosita until that day. She was a sweet-looking little person with light brown hair who smiled a lot. A little dippy in her manner of conversing, but for Gloria, who wasn't exactly the epitome of brilliance, she was all right.

Gloria was all smiles that day. Her dark brown face was radiant with happiness. She was even smoking a cigar and holding it between her teeth at the corner of her mouth.

"Didn't I tell you in one of my letters that it could be done?" She smiled. "We're going to have a baby!"

"Oh, come on, Gloria, cut it out!" I laughed.

"You think I'm kidding?"

"I *know* you're kidding!"

She reached across Rosita, who was sitting in the passenger seat of the car, and grabbed my hand and laid it on Rosita's stomach. "There's the proof!"

"Oh, shit, Gloria, I don't believe you!"

Rosita turned and looked at me, but she wasn't smiling. "Why don't you believe her?" she wanted to know.

"Because it's biologically impossible. It's ... absurd."

"Are you trying to say that it's crazy for me to have a baby?"

I shook my head. "No, that's not what I meant."

Rosita got defensive. I moved away from the car and leaned on my crutches, not knowing how to respond to this woman, because I didn't even know her at all. She began trying to feed me all this garbage about a woman's vaginal secretions being as potent as the ejaculations of a male and being quite capable of producing a child. I backed off immediately, letting her talk all she wanted. When she finished talking, and she thought she had fully convinced me, Gloria smiled triumphantly and asked, "What do you got to say now, Rocky?"

I shook my head slowly. "I don't know. I just don't know. Your woman is either crazy or a damn good liar. In either case, she scares the hell out of me."

"Watch your language, Rocky," Gloria snapped. "You're talking to my wife."

I apologized and made an excuse to go back into the house. But somehow Gloria knew that I had limped away with something on my mind. She went and took Rosita home, and in less than an hour, she was back again, honking outside. She had a six-pack of beer with her.

"All right, Rocky, now that we're alone, tell me what's on your mind."

I shrugged my shoulders. "What can I tell you? You're already convinced that she's pregnant."

"She is!" Gloria explained. "Dr. Long told me so."

"Yes, but that's not what I'm trying to tell you."

"What are you trying to tell me?"

"Will you wait until I go inside the house and get my biology book? There's a section in it on human reproduction that I'd like to explain to you."

"Well, all right, but you better convince me or I'll knock you off your crutches. I didn't appreciate you calling Rosita a liar."

After I explained to Gloria why it was biologically impossible that she could have impregnated Rosita, she thought for a long silent moment and drank most of the beer she had brought. When I saw a long tear streaming down her face, I wanted to use one of my crutches to hit myself. But then, I said to myself, "What are friends for if not to tell us when we're being idiots?"

Gloria turned on the engine to her car. "Okay, Rocky, get outta my car! I should've known better than to come killing my ass to tell you something nice in my life. Ever since I met you, you've done nothing but screw up my life. Get out. The way I feel right now I could easily ram up one of them crutches up your skinny ass, but I'd rather go home and kill that fucking Rosa."

"Oh, Gloria, don't do that! You'll go to jail. Making babies is not the most important thing in the world. What's important is the trying. And just think how much fun that is as opposed to going to the electric chair."

"Get outta the car *now!*"

I did.

Rita Laporte

The butch-femme question

From The Ladder, *1971*

Whenever a group of lesbians gathers together over a period of time, this question invariably comes up, and for some of us, it has become probably the most boring question of all time. Nevertheless, the question is very much alive today, has in fact become more pertinent again in view of women's liberation. The answers given to the question range from "It is a pseudoquestion, a matter of aping heterosexual relationships," to the conviction that it is a delightful reality. Why is it that this question is still so much alive today and no nearer solution among lesbians themselves?

Lesbians are born into the heterosexual world of sex stereotypes just as are heterosexuals. As they mature and gradually surmount the first big hurdle, that of acknowledging and accepting their nature, they are, for the most part, quite without lesbian models on the one hand, while imbued with heterosexual stereotyping on the other. Some lesbians fall in with that stereotyping easily and thoughtlessly, imagining themselves to be essentially male; others toss it out completely, settling for an oversimplified female-to-female relationship. Most of us, however, have experienced a real meaning to that miserable, slang phrase *butch-femme*. But this is hardly the end of it. The anti-butch-femme contingent tries to make our lives miserable by making fun of what to them is a ridiculous copycat existence. Many young lesbians therefore find that their own kind can be as vicious as heterosexual society.

Among those lesbians who try to think sanely and without rancor about the problem, little progress has been made, because they uncritically accept heterosexual male psychologists' pronouncements. One strange theory is that masculine lesbians — i.e., butches — are really men born into a female body and that feminine lesbians — i.e., femmes — learn or are conditioned to fall in love with butches rather than heterosexual males. We have all been thoroughly conditioned to think the adjectives *male* and

208

masculine are interchangeable, as are *female* and *feminine*. This is a mental straightjacket under which not only lesbians but all of society suffers. Before going further into this matter, let us look more closely at the butch-femme phenomenon with a sociologist's eye. This is the eye of the heterosexual male, who sees himself as the center of humanity as once he saw the earth the center of the universe. (There may be other "centers" equally valid — e.g., women, lesbians, etc.)

Most lesbians live in great isolation, whether alone or married to a woman, but there are many small pockets of lesbians, usually gathered together around a big city gay or lesbian bar, that may be designated lesbian subcultures. The "bar scene" tends to have considerable consistency from city to city. Its habitués come for the most part from the lower socioeconomic stratum, and it is here that the butch-femme phenomenon is played out in its crudest form. It is here also that most of the "research" on lesbianism takes place, for the 90 percent or so of lesbians who do not care for this milieu are invisible to the researchers. It is here that one encounters a genuine copying of heterosexual sex roles. The butches are not simply more masculine women; they imitate males at their worst. No male has spoken more derogatorily of his "chicks" than some of these butches. And the femmes manage to outdo the sexiest of sex bunnies. An elaborate game is played where, if a strange butch happens to smile or say hello to another's chick, she is apt to get slugged in the best barroom brawl tradition. Chicks are strictly property. Being small of stature myself, I would prefer the relative safety of a waterfront sailor's bar to the toughest of lesbian bars. But fortunately most lesbian bars offer no such danger, but they do exhibit much of the less brutal male-female, dominance-submission behavior, exactly that kind of behavior feminists loathe.

Many, if not most, lesbians, including those belonging to the upper socioeconomic stratum, do at one time frequent these bars, knowing nowhere else to meet with their own kind, or what they hope will be their own kind. Many of these lesbians are appalled by what they see and sense the unnaturalness of it. In their revulsion they throw the baby out with the bath water, throw out the whole butch-femme phenomenon. What they are left with is: "We are all women, aren't we? Therefore we are all feminine and must not deny our femininity." Yet many lesbians know a middle ground, though it may have taken them many years to find it, to accept it, and to be thoroughly comfortable about it. This is the true butch-femme phenomenon.

I would like to digress here for a moment to point out a common error of sociology: to discover what should be, just find out what is. This sort of thinking is particularly misleading where lesbianism is concerned. We lesbians have a very difficult time of it, for we have no models other than the, for us, irrelevant heterosexual models. Even if heterosexual sex roles *were* right for all heterosexual women, they could hardly be right for lesbians. And this brings us back to the straightjackets of female equals feminine and male equals masculine. Since many lesbians, about 50 percent, are simply not "feminine" as interpreted by heterosexual society, that leaves them nothing to be except "masculine," which means "male."

As yet there is no reliable sociological study on the behavior of lesbians, let alone their inner life. A study that is based upon a true, statistical sampling does not exist, because most lesbians hide too well for such a study to be possible. But, even if such a study were possible, what would it prove? Such a study would include all those confused lesbians who were trying either to imitate heterosexual behavior patterns or to deny them altogether. It is quite probable that the reality of lesbianism is known only to a minority, and that minority consisting of lesbians over thirty. Truth is hardly a matter of a vote. The lesbian can arrive at her own truth, if she ever does, only by much soul searching and experience of life. It is not easy for any human being to achieve an authentic inner life. Women's liberation has taught many a heterosexual woman this, but one still finds studies that "prove" the female to be passive and all those other attributes that add up to a creature no one would care to be, least of all the lesbian.

How are we lesbians to escape or resolve the butch-femme controversy? Let us once and for all separate female from feminine and male from masculine. All lesbians are female, but most assuredly not all lesbians are feminine, no matter how one defines that elusive word. It might be wise to discard altogether the words *masculine* and *feminine*, for heterosexual men have so loaded them in their own favor. All sorts of desirable qualities such as courage, strength, ambition, leadership, aggressiveness, and mental brilliance are said to be masculine, which means attributes pertaining to the male only. The lesbian is living proof that these qualities can just as well belong to the female, that they are, in short, human qualities. And yet the persistence of the butch-femme controversy points to a residue of meaning to the words *feminine* and *masculine.* The words have a real, relational meaning. They refer to qualities that exert a mutual attraction, analogous to the attraction between the north and south poles of magnets, to use an inanimate example. Here we get down to the bedrock level of experience, the level not covered by sociological investigation. A butch, however "feminine" she may appear to the general public, feels something she is inclined to label "masculine" and that impels her toward a more feminine lesbian. She may form a strong *friendship* with another butch or a femme, for she is not confused between "falling in love" with a woman and forming a deep friendship with a woman. A femme will find herself attracted to the more masculine appearing woman (again, it may be a woman who "passes" as "feminine" to society at large, but whose masculinity is sensed by the femme).

A danger here is that the reader will think there are two and only two kinds of lesbians, the butch and the femme. This is merely a shorthand way of labeling. The qualities of femininity and masculinity are distributed in varying proportions in all lesbians (in all human beings, but we are here dealing only with lesbians). A butch is simply a lesbian who finds herself attracted to and complemented by a lesbian more feminine than she, whether this butch be very or only slightly more masculine than feminine. Fortunately for all of us, there are all kinds of us. Some femmes prefer a very masculine butch; many do not. No doubt, there are some women, confused and brainwashed by heterosexual sex roles, who think they want the butch chauvinist lesbian, the lesbian who outmales a male. I say, "No doubt," for every kind of human being exists, but in my experience femmes have soon turned away from such types.

Having hypothesized the four separate qualities or traits — female-ness, maleness, femininity, and masculinity — I am left with the problem of defining them. This is an almost impossible task, in view of centuries of cultural overlay and eons of wishful thinking on the part of men. I can define femaleness and maleness only as those aspects of personality that derive from the biology and physiology that distinguish the sexes. But what these aspects are is largely unknown, though I suspect they pertain to differences in the sexuality of female and male. My personal definition of maleness is a negative one — a quality that precludes any erotic feeling. Whatever may be learned eventually about these two qualities, it is not germane to this discussion, as all lesbians are female. And whatever femaleness is, it is a constant when considering lesbians.

A tougher problem is defining femininity and masculinity. It would indeed simplify matters if butch-femme were no more than the imitation of male-female. Then we could dispense with those two traits as nothing more than cultural convention. The scientific principle of parsimony, that the simplest theory is the best, will seldom work where human nature is concerned. Human nature is more complicated than we are able to con-ceive in theoretical terms. Since femmes and butches are meaningful categories, so are the adjectives *feminine* and *masculine*. This is so despite the fact that much if not most of what is today designated masculine or feminine is neither, is simply human. Take aggression, for example. The male loves to think that this is a virtue of his alone, and in its cruder aspects perhaps, such as war and street fighting, it is. But there is a wealth of aggressiveness in the female, else how would there be any women's liberation movement? Or take grief. Though the male is not supposed to cry, which is very similar to enforcing a taboo against laughing when something is funny, he can feel grief and should be permitted to cry, since this is a human expression of feeling.

Let me begin with my assumption that masculinity and femininity are essences of some sort that have ontological reality. But a mental essence cannot be seen; it is a concept, rather like the concept of an electron, that has an explanatory value. Masculinity can be felt or observed only as it expresses itself through the body, in behavior, however subtle. We posit something we call intelligence, but we can become aware of it only in a live, awake, and acting person. No one could determine the intelligence of someone in a catatonic state. Measuring intelligence is full of pitfalls, for it can be measured only in and through a particular culture. We have the same problem with femininity and masculinity. No one can express these qualities in a cultureless vacuum. A child of decided masculine nature, whether male or female makes no difference, will tend to express this nature by engaging in activities that the culture, however arbitrarily, has designated "masculine." The little tomboy, if her immediate cultural environment (parents and kindergarten) is not too restrictive, will play husband to another little girl's wife and mother role. These girls may or may not be lesbians, but the little butch is apt to persist longer than the little heterosexual tomboy, because her inner masculinity insists more strongly that she flaunt convention. We all have not only a generalized urge to live, but an urge to live as our inner nature directs. Too often cultural straightjackets distort us beyond recognition, as would be apparent if we could see into souls. We all know now that Helen Keller was a very intelligent woman, but the average person would not have thought so, seeing her as a young child. The means for her expressing her intelligence were blocked until her teacher opened up the way through touch. Few of us are blocked in this physical manner, but all women are blocked in cultural ways. But, just as Helen Keller found a way around her terrible physical handicaps, some women find ways to pierce through the heavy veil of cultural distortion. Butches and femmes who have found each other in love and marriage are such women, however much they hide their true selves from society.

Those lesbians who persist in denying any meaning to butch-femme are simply those who either have no experience of this attraction or who are denying it in their fear of being accused of copying heterosexuals. In either case their denials mean nothing, for those of us who know the delight in finding our true mate, one who is like us and yet different, stand witness to the reality of butch-femme. As for copying heterosexuals: as someone has said, there is no worse butch-femme relationship than the male-female one of the heterosexual world. But, though all heterosexual relationships are butch-femme, they vary tremendously. We cannot out of hand condemn all heterosexual relationships. What is so bad about most of them is not their butch-femme quality but their *in*equality. It is the dominance-submission or master-slave quality of the relationship that is outrageous. A lesbian marriage that tries to imitate this aspect of the heterosexual marriage is equally rotten. There is nothing inherently wrong with a division of labor in a marriage, so long as it is freely chosen and the labor of the wife is as worthy as the labor of the husband. While most heterosexuals are hopelessly caught up in a sliding scale of values imposed on the everyday activities of living — what the male does is important, what the female does amounts to little or nothing — we lesbians need pay no attention to this. Housework is a bore and nothing more. It is neither femme nor butch activity. What wrecks heterosexual marriages is not so much the kind of work the woman is expected to do, but the underlying implication that she must do it because she is the inferior. The butch-femme lesbian marriage that has no place for male or butch chauvinism, that in no way attempts to copy male-female relationships, that is a positive union of two authentic women, one more masculine and one more feminine, is a model of marital happiness that heterosexuals would do well to study.

❖

This is what lesbians should try to do in the difficult search for their own truth. They should neither copy heterosexual life nor react against it. They must find their own way, unconcerned about how much or how little it turns out to resemble aspects of heterosexual life. We cannot say out of hand that everything heterosexual is bad. We may find that some heterosexual pronouncements about life and love are happy ones. This should hardly be cause for surprise in view of the fact that heterosexuals are human too. We lesbians, unlike male homosexuals, know that the basic heterosexual distortion is the myth of male supremacy. In theory lesbians should be free of this and growing up lesbian should be easy. Perhaps it would be if lesbians grew up with each other in a lesbian world. But lesbians, unlike heterosexual women, grow up in total psychological isolation from each other. All we see is the heterosexual world and we must cope alone with our inner emotions as they gradually make their way into consciousness. Many of us fall by the wayside, some going through life in a completely heterosexual fashion, others finding only partial and unhappy solutions, and numbers of us finding fulfillment in a marriage of two persons who complete each other in equality *and* difference. What are some of the hazards awaiting the growing lesbian?

Let us begin with the "tomboy." She is not as damned as the "sissy" boy, destined to become a more feminine homosexual, for females are not so important, and, anyway, she will outgrow it. I was a tomboy and will never forget, when in my twenties and upon meeting a grownup who had known me as a child, being complimented upon turning into a fine — i.e., "feminine" — woman. I was at the time playing the heterosexual to the hilt, dressed in a skirt, wearing lipstick, and acting like a lady rather in the fashion of an accomplished drag queen. That "compliment" had the flavor of an insult, though it was meant well and it did at least compliment my acting ability. I cannot say that all tomboys are butch lesbians, but many are. There is a wide range of butchness to begin with, and the outward aspects of butchness are variably modified by upbringing. The more "privileged" tomboy is apt to be far more pressured into learning to "act like a lady" than her freer, less "privileged" sister. The story of a friend of mine illustrates how tomboys or butch lesbians are born, not made.

There are today a number of young women who, in the course of "consciousness-raising" sessions in women's liberation, have come to realize they are lesbians (have "come out," as the expression goes) or are wondering whether they might be. These are women who have, at least before joining women's liberation, experimented with heterosexual sex relations. In their newfound lesbianism they proclaim that butch-femme must go. They are hopelessly confusing the heterosexual relationship per se with its almost universal tendency to be a master-slave relationship and then to transfer this reprehensible aspect of heterosexuality over into lesbianism. This ignores the fact that there are heterosexual marriages wherein the male-female attraction does not entail any master-slave, dominance-submission, superior-inferior connotations (albeit such marriages are hard to find). For the real lesbian, however, even such a fine heterosexual relationship is out of the question. Her inner nature makes impossible the enjoyment of sexual relations with any man. It does not follow that a polarity of attraction, whether male-female or butch-femme, must go. What these women seem to be seeking is "friendship plus sex" or an eroticized friendship. This is a far cry from a true marriage between a feminine and a masculine lesbian.

The heterosexual, in her limited view of human relationships, imagines that it is biological sexual differentiation that determines the attraction of erotic love, that, if one woman is so attracted to another woman, it must be an attraction of same to same — hence the word *homo-* (Greek for *same*) *sexual*. But human beings are a good deal more complex, and blindness to the very real difference, which might be called a psychosexual one, between butch and femme cannot make it go away. The persistent need to do so proves only that many lesbians are still infected with heterosexual stereotyping, still confuse heterosexuality per se with female oppression. Let us now ignore the heterosexual world and its problems and try to look at the lesbian world as if it were the only one, or, like the sociologist, place the lesbian at the "center."

This woman, during her childhood, would have made me look like a sissy. In her late teens she fell into the error of thinking herself to be essentially male, having, like all of us, only the models of male and female sex roles to go by. She dressed like a man and held her own with the "malest" of them. This woman, unlike me, grew up virtually free of parental control and, while I went into a phase of trying desperately to be properly "feminine" — that is, typical female — she erred in the opposite direction. Then, around the age of seventeen, she came under the guidance of an older lesbian who pointed out to her the folly of her course. My friend tossed away her male costume and tried to be a woman. A few years later, dressed in a feminine suit, nylons and girdle, a frilly blouse, and a coquettish hat, she sat on a park bench waiting for a friend. Some minutes later a policeman tapped her on the shoulder and said, "Don't you know you can be arrested for impersonating a woman?" Amusing as this story is, it contains considerable truth. My friend *was* impersonating. When I met this woman she was in her thirties, she dressed comfortably, made no fuss one way or the other about being female, and was simply butch.

The essence of butchness is interior, psychological, emotional — a form of psychosexuality as fundamental as heterosexual male, heterosexual female, or femme. Some butches are easily recognizable by outward manner and gesture by even the most naive heterosexual, but most have picked up from the prevailing culture outward behavior that makes "passing" easy. Only the experienced eye of another lesbian can spot the little telltale gestures. A factor of consequence in this matter of behavior is the butch's own attitude toward herself. If early on she has fully accepted herself, she ceases to be concerned with every little gesture that might give her away. She presents a naturalness that offends no one despite her being thought of as a masculine woman. In contrast, the butch who fears herself, who is overly sensitive to the ridicule generally heaped upon the masculine woman, may suffer the torments of hell. Day in and day out she tries to disguise her inner masculinity; she may even manage to hide it from herself. To others she appears strange and unnatural. Though she has thoroughly accepted her lesbianism, she knows not what to do with this tender masculinity hidden within her. In some instances this leads to her taking the role of the femme. This is a curious inversion of her true self, one that points out the reciprocity or mirror-image aspect of butch-femme. For the qualities of butch and femme are not opaque to each other — the butch senses the nature of the femme by what it is she seeks in another, and vice versa. An analogy might be the right and left hands. These two hands, though the same in most ways, are also the exact reversals of each other.

An interesting sidelight in this connection is the masculine, apparently heterosexual, woman. There are some very masculine women who have never questioned their heterosexuality. And then something happens to such a woman that puts the fear of God into her — perhaps a lesbian, taking this woman's "lesbianism" for granted, assumes she is butch and says something to that effect. Overnight, such a threatened masculine woman may discard her masculine clothes, get her hair redone, and appear all frilly-feminine and unnatural looking. Many will insist that such a woman *is* heterosexual. No, this is an extreme case of denying one's self. So long as this woman was convinced of her heterosexuality, she was unaware of her masculinity. It is often easier to spot a lesbian who does not know she is one, for in this state of ignorance of herself she does not know how to hide the truth. The lesbian who knows herself also knows how to conceal it. This is sometimes carried to amusing extremes, as when lesbians go to meet their lesbian friends from out of town and mingle with heterosexual women who are also meeting their women friends. The women who kiss each other are heterosexual. We have covered three possible errors butches may fall into: imitating men, denying their masculinity, or playing femme. These are errors in addition to the basic one of

215

denying the reality of butch-femme altogether. What errors await the young femme?

She too is aware that there is supposed to be something unnatural about a masculine woman. If she is drawn to the masculine quality in a woman, that must mean she is *really* drawn to, or should be drawn to, a male, but she knows this cannot be. The least she can do, she thinks, is to try to feminize the butch of her choice. She is not denying her own masculinity, but her butch's masculinity. Another form this may take is that the femme denies and fears her femininity, since femininity in our culture is synonymous with inferiority. She early made up her mind, however unconsciously, that she would not be subjected to the feminine role (and rightly so as defined by heterosexuals) and now cannot accept herself as femme in the lesbian relationship. She has it too firmly rooted in her mind that feminine (heterosexual type) equals passive and inferior. "*Passive?*" Whether or not the words *passive* and *active* apply properly to heterosexuals, they do not describe the butch-femme lesbian relationship. That so-called passivity can be most active and that so-called activity becomes indistinguishable from passivity. One might say the butch is actively passive and the femme is passively active and make of that what you will.

More common than the butch who has accepted a femme role is the femme who fancies herself butch. This is not simply a denial of femininity. It is more often sheer confusion. If one is attracted to a woman, one must be masculine or manlike. And too, since femmes are indistinguishable from heterosexual women, the young lesbian is not aware of any difference and imagines that all women (except lesbians) want someone masculine or as malelike as possible. Like society in general, she has swallowed uncritically the notion that all lesbians are mannish. This leads some femmes into pathetic role-playing. It is written all over them that they are desperately acting a role, wearing a facade that is hopelessly out of place. And it happens that a loving lesbian couple may consist of a butch playing femme and a femme playing butch. Each is acting out in herself what she desires in the other. This is not necessarily as bad as it sounds for, if they truly love each other and their relationship is a truly equal one, that they have their "roles" upside down is not fatal. But it is hard on each one as a complete person.

I look back with amusement to my early days in the lesbian world when it seemed to me that there was a terrible excess of butches. How unfair that there should be only one femme for every five or more butches. In later years, again to my amusement, it began to look the other way around. So many butches were afraid to stand up and be counted that those of us who did ... well. But all is well — nature provides. There is a butch for every femme and a femme for every butch.

To summarize so far: put schematically, growing up lesbian means first to come to know and accept one's attraction for women; then to understand and to know experientially the butch-femme reality; and lastly to know whether one is butch or femme. I question whether one could know butch-femme if one grew up entirely alone. This knowledge grows out of one's relations to others, particularly in a love relation. What one comes to understand is that a butch is as real, as ontological, a being as a heterosexual male. And so is a femme as real a being as a heterosexual woman. Just as a woman is not some kind of inferior man, or male manqué, as Aristotle, St. Thomas Aquinas, and Freud would have it, so a butch is no imitation male nor is a femme a woman whose emotions have strayed in illness from their proper object, a male. We have, then, as fully equal and authentic types of human beings: femme, butch, heterosexual women, and heterosexual men.* When I finally arrived at this simple existential truth that I, as a butch, am as fully valid as anyone else, a tremendous load was lifted from me.

❖

We have shown that femmes and butches do indeed exist in their own right and not as distorted lesbians caught up in aping heterosexuals. I cannot say that all lesbians fall into these two categories, nor is the answer to this of much importance. Ultimately every individual must try to find her true inner self, however restrictive her society. But it helps to know what others have found to be their truth. It helps to know that the variety of authentic women is greater than heterosexual society would have us believe. I would like now to discuss more in detail the nature of the butch-femme relationships, as opposed to butches and femmes separately.

Since human beings are not disembodied spirits, they tend to express feelings growing out of their inner nature in outward behavior. Culture provides behavior molds, and without culture a specimen of homo sapiens would not be human. A cultureless human being is a contradiction in terms, for our humanness can develop only in some cultural context. On the other hand, culture is confining, and the more primitive the culture, the more confining it is. Ancient Greek culture was the most liberating culture for men that history has so far known, because it provided fully for homosexual as well as heterosexual relationships. But its terrible restrictiveness on women was its limitation and the cause of the death of Greek civilization. Our American culture today is providing a slightly better milieu for heterosexual women, but it lags behind Greek culture in its frantic heterosexuality. Our culture provides no place and no molds or patterns for lesbians. This is both a drawback, to put it mildly, and an advantage. Lesbians must work out their own patterns of behavior, a very difficult undertaking, but we can do this in total freedom once we have

---

* Also included are male homosexuals, but I do not care to go into their problems with butch and femme, itself an interesting morass of confusion with the culturally assumed inferiority of women.

set aside heterosexual models as irrelevant. It is a bit ironic that the total condemnation of lesbianism by a world that also proceeds as though we did not exist should, at the same time, provide us with total freedom, but so it is.

"The institution we call marriage can't hold two full human beings — it was only designed for one and a half." So says sociologist Andrew Hacker. He was, of course, referring to heterosexual marriage. The lesbian butch-femme marriage can and usually does hold two full human beings. And this is not because it is a friendship arrangement wherein each partner respects the other as a person and agrees to play at sex from time to time, where each goes her own way but provides warmth and affection for the other, where both carefully divide the chores so that neither one gets stuck doing more of the menial. There is nothing wrong with such friendships. Anyone who has achieved so fine a relationship is fortunate indeed. But such a relationship is not a marriage. Nor can one say that a marriage, based on love and entered into for life on a monogamous basis is for everyone. What is so terrible today, among lesbians and among women's liberationists, is the attempt to deny the beauty and authenticity of such lifelong, monogamous lesbian marriages. Those of us who seek such a love or who have found it are supposed to be uptight, ensnared in the Judeo-Christian mythology of the "sanctity" of marriage (perverted from the heterosexual reality), unliberated spirits afraid of our sexuality. It is good that many women today are thinking about and experimenting with new patterns of living and loving. It is very bad that they are assuming that all old patterns of living and loving are wrong. The mutual love of a butch and femme is a very old pattern, and for some of us, the happiest.

A "whole person" is yet not whole. Each of us seeks someone or some idea or God to complete us. The phrase "whole person" does not mean an individual who has need of nothing and no one. Each of us needs more than herself, though we do not all need or want the same thing. A butch needs and seeks a femme for her completion. A heterosexual woman needs and seeks a man, but, because of the oppression of women, finds that she must become that half person in the heterosexual marriage of one and a half. In her rage at so horrible a fate, she thinks that making her husband do the dishes while she tinkers with the car will somehow change things. Such solutions attack only the behavior, the symptoms, and not the basic disease. In a typical butch-femme relationship the butch will work on the car while the femme washes the dishes. Why does this in no way strain the relationship? Because neither the butch nor the femme has attached any inferior-superior significance to these activities. They are both chores necessary to the maintenance of the household. The butch does express her masculinity in car-mending activity, since that activity has a masculine connotation in our society and we all need to express ourselves in behavior. However, it may happen that the butch does not even drive, let alone know anything about a car. It may be the femme who has a knack with things mechanical. Sensible grownups will not quibble over who does what, for one's masculinity or femininity may be expressed in thousands of bits of behavior. Each lesbian couple is free to decide upon its division of labor. Behavior itself is of secondary importance. If the butch has delusions of superiority, no amount of activity juggling will change anything.

There is something immature about heterosexual marriages and those butch-femme marriages that imitate them. How can there be a fulfilling love between a master and a slave, however subtle these distinctions may be? I think all of us can understand the pleasure there is in lording it over someone else. We can all fall into this human (not male or female) foible. But it is a far smaller pleasure than the joy of love, and one cannot have both at the same time with the same person. But love, the kind I am speaking of here, is not easy and there is no reason why it should be right for everyone. Any time one embarks upon a particular course, one at the same time foregoes many other courses. The truly monogamous lesbian, butch or femme, is so not out of a morality picked up from the church or elsewhere, but out of a deep desire to dedicate herself to one particular other person. She simply does not enjoy promiscuity, or changing partners. Like the monotheist, who prefers one God to many, she prefers to be faithful to one person for life. And this in no way restricts her in friendship.

On the contrary, being happily married, her freedom to choose friends is unlimited. She can choose as friend someone she could not stand to be married to. She need not worry about whether she should proceed to a sexual liaison of temporary or more permanent character, for her whole sexual life revolves around the person she loves. She may or may not have made this decision consciously, but in either case it frees her. She is made whole by her love, her marriage, and this wholeness gives her the freedom to grow into the fullness of her humanity. The femme is made whole in union with the butch she loves as the butch is made whole by her femme, a wholeness no amount of friendship can give them. I do not know how to put into words the difference between this lesbian love and a friendship that includes sex. There is a kind of feeling between a butch and femme in love with each other that is neither purely erotic nor purely friendly, though these feelings are present too. There is a total and liberating kind of possession, each of the other and each by the other.

Chea Villanueva

Excerpts from
In the Shadows of Love

Six

I am six years old when I knock on your door. Your mother answers. "Can Dale come out to play?" I am breathless. My heart pounds through the white t-shirt covering my thin chest.

Your mother nods. "All right, but don't go too far."

I grab your hand without hesitation. You run with me knowingly. Knowing we will play The Game today. "Is your sister home? Is her boyfriend with her?" You squeeze my hand.

We climb the fence in the back of the house I share with my parents and older sister. The venetian blinds covering the window are slightly open. My sister is making out on the couch with her boyfriend, Tony.

Dale and I take turns peeking. "Shh," I say. I take her hand and pull her to the ground. "Let's play that I'm Tony and you're Sissy."

She pulls away. "But why can't *I* be Tony and *you* be Sissy? Why do I always have to be the girl?"

"Because I say so. I'm *never* gonna be a girl!" My feelings are hurt and I run. Dale chases me and I am happy. I stop running. "C'mon," I say, "let's go back and watch them kissin' and then I'll kiss you too."

We kiss all afternoon on the back steps in the yard. The afternoon sun is setting. My sister straightens her dress. Her boyfriend stands up reluctantly. My father will be home soon.

"Dale!" It is time for Dale to be going too.

"My mother's calling me."

I stand up and jam my hands in the pockets of my jeans reluctantly, mimicking Tony. "Well, I guess I'll see ya tomorrow and we can kiss again." I take a cigar band out of my pocket along with a penknife, lucky penny, baseball cards. "Here, Dale, let's pretend we're married." I slide the cigar band ring over her finger. "But don't forget, *I'm* gonna be the husband and *you're* gonna be the wife."

Chea Villanueva,
Philadelphia, 1990

"Dale!" Dale's mother is calling again.

"Okay, Tony, I'll see ya tomorrow." Dale smiles. A new game has started...

Ten

I am ten years old and my mother is dead. I am alone in the house that I share with my father. He's left for his night job at the factory and I am left alone. I dial your number. You answer.

"Did he leave?"

"Yeah. Can you sneak out?"

I make myself ready for Dale. I comb my hair back with water, put on a clean undershirt. Dale is here in a few minutes. I hear her whistle. Hear her coming in through the back door. She is crying. "They're fighting again! I hate when they fight!"

I ask her, "Dale, did you eat yet? My father left me some food." We eat with the venetian blinds turned down and the radio turned low. We know we have to hide what we have no name for. Dale washes the dishes. I watch her with a warm glow spreading up my thighs. "C'mon, Dale, let's lie on the couch." The couch is narrow. I lie on top of her. I unbutton her blouse. She pulls the shirt over my head. We lie still, chest to chest, lips to lips. "Dale, I want to do something different. Let's take our pants off this time." There is no hesitation and in moments two pairs of jeans are on the floor. "Now take off your underpants."

221

She hesitates with this new order. "But what if your father comes home?"

"Don't worry about it. I put the chain on the door."

She slides her underpants down. I am back on top of her. We are naked. Chest to chest, lips to lips, bare pubis to pubis. I grind into her. Force her to ride with me. This new thing feels good, but I wonder if there is something more...

Thirteen

Today I am thirteen. Dale is here. She is staying over again. Her parents fight more on the weekends. It is night. The room is dark except for the single glow from the television set. We are watching the TV with my father. He falls asleep in his chair. I slip my hands up Dale's blouse on the couch. Her breasts are so much bigger than mine. Mine are two small bumps, but Dale doesn't mind. I squeeze them with both hands. Feel her sweat running from her armpits. I pinch her nipples. She digs her nails into my hands. Pulls my hands from her breasts. "This feels good," she breathes. From the TV, Diana Ross and the Supremes are singing. "Whisper you love me, boy ... You know how to talk to me, baby..." I feel a familiar wetness between my legs and I tug at the elastic waistband of her shorts. Slide my hand down lower till I touch the fabric of her panties. My hand enters and I slip my finger into her groove. My wetness spreads. Deeper. I join hers. She joins mine. Deeper. My father stirs from his chair. We move apart fast. He reaches for the light. Faster. Dale pulls up her waistband. Smooths out her shorts. I wipe her wetness on my jeans.

Sixteen

We are sixteen. Dale and I are lying on my bed. My father is at work. Her parents are fighting again. On these nights she sleeps with me.

She is naked. Like Lady Godiva's, her long chestnut hair hides her breasts. I brush the hair away and begin the night's ritual. But tonight is different. I have never tasted a woman and so this night will be special. She bites my neck, my ears, and comes in my mouth.

I am dreaming I have a penis. I put it deep inside of her and make babies for days. She is crying, "It hurts," and I slip my fingers from her vagina. She takes my hand and places it on her naked belly. My fingers are bloody from probing too far. She has given me her virginity. I lick the blood from my fingers.

Seventeen

I am seventeen. A runaway from reform school. Short hair slicked back into a DA with a little help from Olivo, I am wearing King's Men after-shave, white shirt open at the collar, black V-neck bad-boy sweater, jeans, penny loafers.

I wait at the gate of St. Dominic's for Dale. I am sentimental. I hum, "Ain't no mountain high enough, ain't no valley low enough, ain't no river wide enough to keep me from you..." The bell rings, signaling the end of the school day, and pretty girls in navy uniforms step lively out the door. I lean against the wall of the schoolyard, hands in pockets, cigarette dangling from the corner of my lips. Pretty girls glance shyly at the pretty, delinquent boy and I look back boldly. The pretty girls blush.

Dale! She sees me. Waits till the yard is clear of prying eyes. No one must know. I see a nun who taught me in the sixth grade and I lower my face. A worldly black man saunters by: "Bulldagger! Ain't nothin' but a bulldagger!" The nun looks. My heart thumps, there's a lump in my throat, I remember the song, "Ain't no mountain high enough..." The nun walks on. All she sees is a young boy. Dale is coming toward me. One more step and she walks out the gate. Dale! I take her arm and we walk far from the school, far from the world, far from worldly black men. We enter an alley. We need no words. I lean her against a wall. I put my leg between hers, she drops her books, we kiss long and hard. A man enters the alley to pee. We break away. I look for a bottle to break over his head. Ready to protect my girl, ready to fight for my butchness. But all he sees in his wine stupor is a boy and a girl. The man zips up his pants, embarrassed. The man leaves. He was young once.

Dale cries, "I never thought I'd see you again." I cry with her. We both know this moment can't last. Too soon the cops will be looking for me, too soon we'll have no place to go. I don't want to make love in an alley. Don't want to limit our love to the street. "Baby," I say, "I just had to see you. I gotta go now, but promise you'll wait for me." Dale promises and whispers all her love forever with her mouth and tongue and hands...

Eighteen

I am eighteen years old. Home from reform school. I am fighting with my family. My sister wants me to look like a girl. My father wants me to get a job. My brother-in-law doesn't want me in his house. No one understands me. No one but Dale.

Funny, but I haven't seen much of Dale since the first night we spent together after my release from reform school. Everything seemed like old times then. Dale met me at the bus terminal. We bought popcorn and smoked cigarettes in the back of the bus that would take me home and back to the comfort of Dale's arms. She was still wearing the gold friendship ring I had given her at sixteen. But something had changed since the night we'd made love in my father's yard. We'd had a couple of beers that night and I wanted her badly. Badly enough to tear her blouse and reckless enough not to care who caught us. She wanted me too. Wanted me enough to spread her legs under the light of the moon. We were both naked from the waist down when my next-door neighbor caught us. There I was on top of Dale, and there was Dale moaning, "Do it harder, baby..." All at once a flash of light brought us back from the brink of another climax. Something changed when the talk started and my family started to pressure me to go out with boys.

Dale was never at home when I called, and she was suddenly too busy to come out and walk with me. I no longer heard the familiar whistle outside my bedroom window after my dad left for work. I slept for weeks in our love sheets smelling her scent, rubbing my face in it, listening to Carole King singing, "Tonight you're mine completely, you give your love so sweetly ... will you still love me tomorrow..."

I found out soon enough that she was seeing this guy Sammy. It broke my heart, but I still had to see her. She had to choose between us. It was going to be either Sammy or me. She could not have us both. I wanted her to choose me. If she wanted a man, I would be her man. I slicked my hair back, put the switchblade in the back pocket of my chinos, and donned my black leather jacket. I wanted her badly enough to put up a fight.

I found her and Sammy parked in a car near her house. They were in the front seat. He had his hand on her leg. She had her lips on his mouth. I was sick with jealousy and tried to break the rolled-up windows with my fist. My hands were bleeding when Sammy got out of the car.

"What's the matter, butch? You lose your girlfriend or somethin'?" Sammy laughed and came toward me swinging a baseball bat. "Look, bitch. I want you to stay away from my girlfriend or I'll mess you up bad. She doesn't want to see you anymore!" Sammy spit. "Everybody in this neighborhood knows you're a fuckin' dyke."

Dale came between us as I closed in on Sammy with my knife. I would kill the bastard! I wasn't afraid of him or his bat. Dale's scream tore through my heart, ripped out my guts, and left me lying on a cold street.

"Stop! Just stop! Leave him alone and leave me alone. I don't want you anymore! Things are different now." She cried and tried to hug me. I ran away. I didn't want them to see my tears.

Myrna Elana

Dancing with Dennie

Summer 1976

Fifteen, stepping to
under a mirror ball:
black heels &
beige lace dress
pink & blue scallops
over my breasts—
pure '40s, the way
the skirt twirled up
my thighs as I
followed her
on the black floor
of a Santa Cruz gay bar:
the Dragon Moon,
where I passed
for 21 & spun—
clung to her arms
suspended over
moves of her cowboy boots—
that tall dyke
who danced me
as our lovers watched,
then whispered
treaded close & whispered,
Are you bi or what?
making me think twice
for years
before wearing a dress
to dance

Sky Vanderlinde

Loving Blue

The first time I saw her was at my first lesbian event, the summer of
'78, at one of those conferences at P.S. 41 on Eleventh Street off Sixth
Avenue, remember those? Well, it was the first lesbian gathering I'd ever
gone to, and I was full of a million different emotions. I was afraid,
astonished, curious, amazed, and somewhere in there I was proud, fiercely
proud. It was a weekend event and I went every day, going home at night
thinking I was the only lesbian who had ever stepped foot on Staten Island,
let alone lived there.

I went to the opening folk dance event. I went to workshops on all sorts
of things including one on sexuality. I was very brave. I didn't talk to many
women, maybe to no one; I don't remember. I do remember feeling very
shy. The closing meeting took place on Sunday morning, and that's where
I remember seeing her — Doris. I think I'd seen her around during the
weekend videotaping various things, but I really looked at her now.
Everybody had gathered in the school's auditorium. As Doris was setting
up her equipment to film the session, an argument began about who
would and who wouldn't want to be filmed, and what were they going to
do with the film anyway? Suddenly this discussion/argument became the
event of the morning. There was Doris, on the stage, arguing passionately,
and obviously angry at the need to do so, about the importance of filming
this gathering and creating a record of ourselves. How crucial it was to get
it all on film, film that would be seen by other lesbians, maybe even be
sent around the country so that women who were isolated could see the
faces, hear the voices of dykes in the big city. So that those women who
figured that they were the only lesbians in Ohio, Kansas, Texas could look
at this big gathering of New York City dykes and see their options, know
more of the reality of lesbians in 1978, feel some pride. And all the more
urgent for us, a people with no history, a people whose history had been
consistently, almost methodically eradicated over and over again. Well, I
was more than convinced. I who was so in the closet that I was stifling
from lack of air said with my whole self, *Yes*, take my picture, do anything

226

you want, but get it all down on your videotape. I was with her one hundred percent.

During this political controversy, and in the minutes before and after it, while Doris was moving equipment, setting up, and directing her little crew, I stared at her. Safe in the anonymity of my seat among scores of women in this auditorium, I stared at her, fascinated by her air of authority, by the way she moved, that she seemed so in herself, so in control. I'd watched her all weekend, but this was a chance to watch her for a prolonged period while she worked. Watching people doing work they love, when they don't know they're being watched — it's a chance to see into their souls in a special way. Well, I watched, I saw, and I was fascinated. Of course, I couldn't help also noticing the woman who was her assistant: a pretty woman with dark, curly hair and a very sweet face, who was obviously more than just an assistant to Doris. I wanted to scratch her eyes out. I didn't have a clue as to what that meant. I really didn't have a glimmer as to why I was so fascinated by Doris, or why I thought her friend's face was too sweet, or why I was glad I thought her friend's legs weren't nearly as nice as mine. Hmm. To be so out of touch. But, yes, that's where I was at. I was twenty-five and had had only one lover, for seven years, and that relationship was in the process of ending, which I probably also didn't realize. So I absolutely feasted my eyes on this Doris. Short, graying hair combed off her face and styled around her ears and on her neck like a man's. Small, wiry body, dressed in the androgynous look of the seventies, but no doubt wearing clothes off the men's racks in the stores. She was obviously older than I was, but Pretty Face looked just about my age. I had never seen anybody like Doris, so obviously a dyke, so obviously strong, proud, happy. She was at home in her body and on the earth in a way I had previously associated only with men; it was compelling in a woman and I wanted it for myself. And there was her conviction, her persuasive, undeniable — at least to me — political arguments, and her anger at needing to convince these women of basics they should have been born knowing. I never forgot her, nor did I forget my insane desire to scratch out the eyes of her pretty friend.

The next two years brought a lot of change into my life. After my first lover and I broke up, I moved into Greenwich Village, had affairs with several women, and became politicized. My feminism finally became more than just a few vague ideas. I began to explore leftish politics, and I began to shed my homophobia like the deadweight that it was. I came all the way out of the closet, and it was glorious. I told my family and those friends who didn't already know. I became the radical dyke teacher at the university and began teaching women's studies and gay studies. I went to gay demonstrations, and I walked in the gay pride march each year. And, of course, at all those gay events, I saw Doris. Pretty Face was no longer with her, but she was always surrounded by women and usually at the center of some hub of activity. I watched her, still fascinated.

THE PERSISTENT DESIRE

August 10, 1980. It seemed like any other hot, sunny summer day in New York City. I met my friend David at Washington Square Park that morning, the gathering place for a demonstration that would march up Eighth Avenue. There was a good turnout, lots of people, lots of brightly colored banners. David introduced me to some of his friends, and then it was time to line up and start walking. Before we left the Village, I'd already spotted Doris. She looked terrific, as always. She had on those khaki pants from the army-navy surplus store that were so popular at the time, and a short-sleeved shirt with the sleeves rolled up. For most of the length of the march, David and I walked near her group, and again I had the chance to watch Doris at work. She was radiant. The depth and magnitude of her spirit shone through her. When she wasn't shouting the demonstration slogans, she was talking and laughing with her friends. Every time I turned to look at her, she either had her arm around some woman or was holding someone else's hand. She was always involved, always busy — talking, listening, chanting slogans.

David and I trudged along, doing our part, too. At times one or the other of us would wander off to talk with someone we'd spotted in the crowd. Sometimes I found myself walking behind Doris's group and I kept thinking, "What a fine-looking woman, what a great body" — about Doris, of course. Early in the day I'd pointed her out to David, who didn't find her nearly as interesting as I did, for obvious reasons.

By midafternoon we reached our gathering point and the rally started. I listened to some of the speakers but found myself getting hot, tired, and ready to go home. In the press of the crowd I'd lost track of David, and I hadn't seen Doris or her group in quite a while. Just as I was heading for the subway station, though, I ran into David, and while we were saying our good-byes, whom should I glimpse? I pointed her out to David again and then got the impulse to go up to her and say something. David encouraged me, gave me a push, and sent me on my way.

So I walked up to her, found myself looking directly into incredible blue eyes, and said — blushing hotly — "Hello, Doris, my name is Deirdre. I've seen you around for years and just thought I'd say hello."

"Hi! Well, you know, my name isn't Doris anymore. I've just changed it to Blue."

I don't know what I said next. I know my blush got a lot deeper and hotter, which hadn't seemed possible. My heart was pounding so hard, I thought it would burst from my chest, or at the very least that she and everyone else could see it banging about in there. I felt like an idiot for getting her name wrong, although there was no way on earth I could have known about her new name. Whatever I said in response, the next thing I became aware of was Blue telling me that she'd just become a grand-mother. She was thrilled with the whole thing and proud as could be of her daughter and her new grandson. I was stunned. I thought, "Oh my god! I'm picking up a grandmother and I've never even dated a mother!

How old *is* she?" Somehow it was clear to me, in this second or third minute of speaking with Blue, that rather than "saying hello," I was definitely at least trying to pick her up.

We chatted for a few minutes until it became apparent that the time for a simple "Hello, I'm glad to meet you" had passed. Neither of us wanted to turn away. So at Blue's suggestion, we found ourselves having a cool drink in a coffee shop, leaving the demonstration behind for a few minutes. Much later she told me that when that moment between a simple hello and something-else-altogether happened, she knew she didn't want to let me go — she felt good talking with me and didn't want to stop. Hooray!

We ambled back over to the demonstration, talking, as I remember it, about her name change, her grandson, the demonstration, my teaching, and how about walking downtown and having dinner together? We managed to disentangle ourselves from a few friends who wanted to join us, and we headed south, back through the streets we'd walked up earlier that day. I liked being with her. We were a little awkward with each other but didn't lack for interesting things to talk about. We paused once near some bushes when Blue spotted a butterfly and held her hand out toward it, as though inviting it to land on her. "Oh, do they come to you?" I asked, completely believing that wild creatures would come trustingly to her hand. She smiled enigmatically and we walked on.

We made our way to the Christopher Street pier, where we sat down to watch the sunset. In response to one of her questions, I told her about my need to leave my family's home when I was seventeen, about feeling stifled by my WASP, upper-middle-class environment. I had known there was more to life, different people with different problems, and I was desperate to leave my bland, two-dimensional world for something broader, more colorful, more sustaining. Months later she told me that this had been important to her, and was one of the things that had drawn her to me.

We ranged over many subjects as we sat in the evening sunlight. At one point we lay side by side on the hard cement of the pier, still talking, not touching. But the desire to touch was growing. I'd look into her blue eyes and feel the wanting grow in me. I liked the sound of her voice. Her face, not beautiful by society's standards, was marvelous — pronounced cheekbones, generous nose, a sensuous mouth with a full lower lip, and those eyes — blue, intelligent, vibrant — completely captivating. And I was completely captivated and weak in the knees over her.

After deciding to have dinner together, we walked over to my studio apartment on Tenth Street so that I could feed my cats. My tortoiseshell cat, Jenny, walked over to where Blue sat leaning against my bed and began studying her. Blue reached out to touch her and in seconds this shy, reserved cat was rolling on her back in complete, ecstatic abandon. I was embarrassed at my cat's revealing my feelings so freely, and I was also jealous. As if reading my thoughts, Blue said, "Maybe her mother would like a little petting," and she leaned toward me and kissed me. Ah, we had begun.

We had dinner at a Mexican restaurant in the neighborhood. I don't know what I ordered. I probably didn't eat much of it anyway. For some reason, keen sexual anticipation kills my appetite for food — always has. But we lingered over the food we weren't eating. And it was there, in that restaurant, that Blue began telling me her stories. I heard about her coming out in the French Quarter in New Orleans in 1952 when she was sixteen, about her being arrested repeatedly just for being gay. I learned she had worn men's clothes and dated women who wore dresses and high heels. She told only a few of her stories that night, but already Othello's description of his wooing of Desdemona was echoing in my head: "My story being done, / She gave me for my pains a world of sighs ... She loved me for the dangers I had passed."

I wanted this woman to touch me. I wanted to kiss her and to get lost in her. I went home with her. And was astonished again, at her apartment, which was bursting at the seams with life. One wall, floor to ceiling, was books. In the middle of the kitchen, which was in the middle of the apartment, was a tiny bathtub. There were an alcove with a loft bed, a tiny bedroom near the front door, and Blue's bedroom off the living room. And there were women everywhere. The living room was full of roommates and visitors. I was surprised, and a bit dismayed. I wasn't altogether certain I'd been invited to spend the night and I didn't know how we'd work out the logistics in such a crowd. But as though they sensed the delicacy of our situation, the women seemed to gradually melt away into the night, and then Blue made clear that she wanted me to stay.

When she came back from the bathroom, I was in her bed, naked. I didn't mean to be bold, but I hadn't known what else to do while I waited, and since we'd agreed we were going to bed, it seemed the obvious thing to do. Leaving the light on, she slipped in next to me and there was that delicious first moment of skin meeting equally soft skin from head to toe. Our mouths found each other and gradually our kisses grew more passionate. She was definitely the one orchestrating our lovemaking. My boldness had ended with taking off my clothes. I'd never been touched quite like this before. That air of being at home in her body and in her world, of being in control, that had fascinated me from the first moment I saw her was in her lovemaking, too. I surrendered completely.

As she turned us so that she was on top of me, she pulled back a little to look at me. I opened my eyes and saw her face, suffused with passion, poised over me, her eyes heavy with desire, her face drawn thinner, longer with that desire, and her full, rich lips reaching out to mine. I recognized this beloved face. My heart broke open with the profound, incontrovertible knowledge that I had known and loved this woman for centuries. Our lovemaking that night was for me a spiritual experience unlike any I'd ever had before. It was always to be that way with Blue for me.

We made love for hours, until the night gave way to the dawn. We couldn't get enough of each other. I loved how her fingers felt inside me, and as I'd come to the rhythm of those fingers, I'd try desperately to take them in all the way to my heart. More than once, in our passionate efforts to become one, she sat us up, one arm around me, one hand inside me. I was hers, body and soul.

In the following weeks and months, we made love at every opportunity. We also went to work, did our laundry, and spent time with friends, often quite tired. And Blue continued to woo me with the stories of her life. I had never met an "old-time butch" before, let alone fallen in love with one, so I had some learning and adjusting to do. The integrity with which she had lived her life and her unquestioning acceptance of herself — of the motherless child who had sought refuge in the reform school; of the young, ardent butch in love with a stripper; of the working-class young mother; of the many varied selves she had been, including the radical feminist dyke I had met — made opening my heart and mind simple. How else to respond to integrity but to answer it in kind? Unreasoned prejudices and judgments dropped from me, blinders serving only to keep me from things and people I knew nothing about.

I loved watching her comb her hair. She'd brush the sides back with the palm of one hand while combing the hair off her face with the other. I loved seeing the lift in her arms, her slightly masculine gestures as she patted her hair into place. The care she took with her appearance — she was quite fastidious — intrigued me. Her clothes were always neat, everything just so. She would change her shirt if she didn't like how the collar lay. This was all new to me. Previously I'd seen only "feminine" women spend this much time dressing. As for me, I just put my clothes on, ran a brush through my hair, and was done with it.

The first time we got dressed up was to go out for dinner and dancing. I don't remember what either of us wore, but I'll never forget the boots she put on. As I watched, she retrieved from the back of her closet a pair of black, leather, ankle-high boots that had a stretchy panel on the inside so they could be pulled on. I didn't show it, but I was surprised and dismayed. In my limited experience, no one wore boots like that, except maybe some men twenty years earlier. That was it. The boots were part of her "old-time butch" wardrobe, unlike the more "acceptable" androgynous clothes she wore now. She showed them to me with delight and pride. I admired them, hiding my feeling that once again I was in a foreign country.

Later, at the Cajun restaurant, I learned about eating crawfish and crabs, and heard more stories of her life in New Orleans. As we walked to Identity House, where the dance was being held, I felt everything shift inside me. I let go of the last vestige of my fear, my judgment of her difference. I understood that to love her was to love *all* of her completely, boots included. She was so fine, so extraordinary, that I couldn't not love her, and suddenly I saw those boots as the beautiful and hard-earned badge of pride that they truly were.

We had the dance floor nearly to ourselves that night. By some lucky quirk of fate, they were playing music from the fifties and sixties. We moved into each other's arms, exploring a new way of moving together. She led, of course, which was fine with me. I followed her precise movements, embracing all of her.

As we danced and later, as we bicycled home, I thought of the stories she had told me and lived each one again briefly. In her courtship of me, she had also shown me her photo album, filled with pictures of her at every age, as well as pictures of her family and loved ones. So as I relived the stories of her life, I could see her clearly in my mind's eye. The busy late-night streets of Greenwich Village faded away; I saw only Blue on the bike in front of me, and Blue as she used to be.

Many of those images remain with me clearly, but among the strongest is a photograph of Blue in her midtwenties. It's from a series of formal studio shots of her and her daughter, Linda. Blue is dressed very conservatively in a white blouse and dark skirt. Mother and daughter stare solemnly at the camera, posed in rigid politeness for eternity. In one photo, Blue is alone, sitting erect in the wing chair, her hands carefully folded in her lap. It's a shocking picture. The tension between the conventionality of the trappings — the setting and her clothing — and the woman herself — a personality larger than life, trying to contain itself; a lesbian; a butch in conflict with society and to some extent with herself; and a woman of obvious, profound sensuality — this tension screams out at the viewer, demanding response.

As we neared home, the visions faded, and everyday reality resumed its customary place. This, too, was such a familiar scene — walking or biking through the Village with Blue. On nearly every block someone would wave or say hello to her. We stopped frequently to talk with these friends and acquaintances, and I'd already learned to allow plenty of extra time when planning to go anywhere. Blue's friends fondly called her the "lesbian mayor of New York." We all laughed when we did, as she did each time she heard it, but there was some truth to it. She had been active in New York's gay community since before the Stonewall uprising and had been a founding member of numerous groups and organizations in the years since. She had opened her home to gay people in need for years. Through it all, she had held on to her self-respect and her past, even when admitting to ever having been a butch was "politically incorrect." I was awfully proud to walk hand in hand with the lesbian mayor of New York.

We locked our bicycles together to a parking sign and climbed the stairs to our home. As always, the apartment was filled with women, but this time there was no question about what would happen. We talked with our friends, took turns getting ready for bed, and eventually found ourselves in each other's arms again.

232

We always made love by the soft yellow light of the lamp on the dresser. The big window next to the bed was open, the curtain swaying slowly in the late summer breeze. Lying on our sides in each other's arms, we kissed slowly, gently, letting the passion build quietly. I slipped my hand under her t-shirt to touch the smooth, soft skin of her back. We looked into each other's eyes, smiling, as we moved in unison to lift the other's shirt over her head. Leaning over her, I lingered as my eyes caressed her now-so-familiar beauty: her face drawn with passion, eyes deeply blue, cheeks flushed a light pink, full lips a darker pink, and the delicate skin of her slender shoulders and upper chest sprinkled with freckles that drew my eyes to the rise of her small breasts, and my mouth to meet her nipple.

We gave ourselves simply and fully to each other as the warm summer night air slipped around and between us, adding its caresses to ours. We made love with our eyes, as well as with our hands and mouths, finding endless pleasure in our bodies as we moved through our dance of love: Her chest rising, her head thrown back as the heat of my mouth at her sweet, inner lips rose through her. The line of her shoulder and arm, the bend of her elbow as her hand inside me opened me, inflamed me. Through the night, we looked into each other's eyes again and again, seeking and sharing the tides of passion, seeking and sharing our deep, abiding love for each other. At one point, as I felt the fire climbing my legs, gathering in my center, claiming me, she whispered, "Open your eyes." I did, and as my life forces gathered under her demanding fingers, as the urgency built, as I lost all thought and became swirling, driving sensation, our eyes met and held one another. As I slipped over that threshold where all is suspended, hushed; as my body exploded into orgasm, a quasar pulsing from the center of my being; as I cried out, our eyes clung, our souls mingling, loving.

Much later, when we were ready to sleep, Blue moved into my arms. I lay on my back, one arm under her as she, on her side, snuggled her head into my shoulder and fitted her body to mine. I held her close, one hand in her fine hair, one hand on her back, my lips against her forehead. She murmured, "I feel like I've waited my whole life to be held like this." I, too, had waited my whole life to hold someone like this. We had found each other, and our love that had lasted through centuries had blossomed again. As we drifted off to sleep, the curtain swayed gently in the night air and the moonlight slipped over us.

Melinda Goodman

Lullabye for a butch

Saturday night November 1980
I am 23 driving a '68 Delta east on 4
to the George Washington Bridge
jockeying with other drivers
coming off routes 80 and 47
for a clear veer to the lane my lover
works, the 3-to-11 post-Thanksgiving shift

She grabs my hand as I fly
money green flags
in her direction
laughing over the moan of diesel brakes
her wool-gloved fingers pry then tangle
in my naked palm
Ignoring the blaring horns outside the booth,
our mutual radios pump the club
version of Grace's "Warm Leatherette"
as she steps out on exhausted concrete
to place an orange cone
between my bumper and the
bumper behind mine

I like her uniform:
fresh polyester dark blue
and bright white collar
topped with overcoat,
scarf and ski cap for the blizzard on the way.
If it snows the Port Authority
puts her up at a motel otherwise
she stays at my place but has to be back
by dawn or be counted AWOL

So she's up before five
folding her flowered pajamas
into the bottom drawer
of my colonial chest
with handles like rings
through a bull's snout
"You got my nose"
moaned the only teenaged woman
who ever loved me
and my tollbooth honey
reminds me of her
as I chain the door behind her
hearing steps down five flights
to the street, the bridge,
and the gunmetal morning

I always loved
gentlemanly attentive butches
even those who won't fuck
for the first five dates
'cause they "want to get to know you"
till you beg
and by that time
you're married
They want to make sure
all those free concerts
fish dinners
and stories about home
won't get thrown back
in their teeth
After all...
butches are vulnerable
It's the femmes that are fierce
with their long legs
and tight jeans
making you watch them
Butches are the sweet ones
with their clean shined shoes
and socks
and underwear
smelling of baby powder
and Camay
I loved
the way she wrote her name
in purple script

THE PERSISTENT DESIRE

all over the top sheet
of my coloring pad
when supper was done and the dishes stacked
I wish I could kiss her now
slide my tongue through her teeth
erase the years I fell
for women as distant as Queens
is from the Bronx
Just hold this butch in my arms
make her know

It's not the 2 condominiums
she bought with rare pennies
collected on her job
but *her*
her strong back
and big hips
and corny sparkling eyes
when she walks around
to open the door
on my side of the car
in front of the skinny eyes
of the fat boy dealers
strutting in and out
of their customized vans
and the heads rolling in
from Jersey
She doesn't even see
the tooth-sucking teens
as she walks back around
in her ten-gallon brim
to slide behind the wheel
Doesn't tell me where we're
going till we're parked and walking
out of the lot
up the block
arms linked
to see Patti Labelle
live at the Savoy
and I'm on my heels
all night screaming
through till the last song
running my fingers up the back of her neck
till the walls come down, tables break in half,
everybody's glass explodes

ice cubes hailing the city for miles
as Patti rains on
somewhere
over the rainbow
way up high
there's a
land that I dreamed of
once in a lulla-
bye.

From a letter from Mexico, 1981

From the LHA collection

I want to talk to you about Bustamante. The soil is so hot and the weather so cold in winter that you cannot grow as big a variety of fruit trees as you can in my mother's hometown, for instance. It lies very close to the most impressive mountain range I have ever seen; you have only to drive twenty to thirty minutes from Alicia's house and you will find yourself on the outskirts of the Sierra Madre in an area of mostly naked rock with only a few enormous pine trees. It is a good sight and a nice little town.

Bustamante is a rather unusual place in that it is something like a bastion of lesbianism in the northern part of Mexico. It is difficult to imagine a little village with a population of no more than a thousand people where this kind of life is possible. One out of three or four women there has had a lesbian experience, besides all the women from Monterrey, like Alicia herself, who built country houses there because of the atmosphere.

Anyway, there is a lady in Bustamante who lives across the street from Alicia's, whom you should really meet some day. She is so unusual that I'm sure somebody should write a book about her after she dies. She is in her seventies now. She dresses like a man — shoes, shirt and trousers, and hat — and started many years ago with no money at all growing vegetables in her backyard and then going around on a bicycle selling them, then bought a motorcycle and used that until she broke both her hips (on different occasions), and now drives an old big panel truck. Now she deals with cattle and the mandatory walnut plantations, buys and sells land, and has a lot of money in the bank but can hardly read or write.

The most extraordinary aspect of her life is that forty years ago she abducted an impressively beautiful girl (I saw photographs) from her house in Monterrey (from a middle-class, very conservative, good family) and took her on horseback to Bustamante to live there as her wife. You can imagine the hostility she had to face living that kind of life in a little village forty years ago in traditionalist Mexico. But now she is a *cacique* (tribal chief) and everybody comes to her for advice on everything you can imagine. She has a lot of political influence, and practices a simple kind of witchcraft very popular in the area, but more than anything, at seventy-something she runs after young girls all the time, to the extent that her "wife," who is older than she is, sometimes chases both her and the girls with a rifle. She lives at one end of town, to which she was ostracized many years ago, very near the mountain and a beautiful canyon with a river, but now Monterrey lesbians have grouped around her house and formed something like a *"colonia."*

Donna Allegra

Butch on the streets, 1981

Painkillers. I think I must have taken every pill short of the ones they use for birth control. I mean, like, I wouldn't know how to begin to get pregnant, but I could deal with modern technology coming up with a treatment to ease this one pain that won't let me rest in peace sometimes.

I may not be anybody's prize-winning puppy, but I'm all I've got and I like to take good care of the old girl. It took me a long time to understand the kid and get used to my evil ways, but I came around, I like being a butch. I like being with other butches with our nicknames and ball games — women with muscles and pretty faces. I don't believe in bisexuals and cannot for the life of me find a femme. I don't like men and I don't let them fuck me.

For me to live in this man's world, I need some kind of painkiller, something I can pull out at a moment's notice and put between me and the men on the street, because sometimes, I could really kill 'em. They're the foulest beasts walking on two feet and they're always in packs, just like dogs. It wouldn't be so bad if the women that like them so much would keep them on leashes, curb them, and shoot the strays, but the dudes be all over the place pissing and dropping their turds every which way. And even faggots piss on trees.

So, like, between the men and the dogs, I need some way to keep the weight off my head. I live in New York City, and we dykes may be everywhere like the t-shirts and buttons say, but there aren't that many of us running around loose and free. And I get tired of watching my back and front, and having to look sideways because these men are so damn crazy.

It's not like there's a neighborhood or a space that's all our own where we could have gone to, hung out at, and worked through our growing pains as baby butches. I guess a lot of us learned our ways alone and in secret and we still come out with all the different styles of butches. I really dig on how I can always tell another butch, even if she's in straight drag.

I know for me, I used to read a lot of books. They had this soft-core pornography in the sixties that I gobbled up as a young girl, with titles like *Strange Friends, Forbidden Love, The Twilight World,* and *The Lonely People.* On the covers there'd be these women looking very unhappy, like they were yearning for something they'd never be able to have. I could tell just by the titles which books were meant to be about me, and after a while, I knew that if the last page had a man and a woman talking together, it wasn't a happy ending.

It was hard buying the happy endings. I was in my early teens going to the counter with all the shame and fear that the man I'd have to pay would know what I was reading about, and by that, know what I was — something bad, a subject for pornography. I'd sneak the books into the house and wouldn't even want to share them with my brother, who'd been my first and best friend, and is one man I'd kill for still. I'd feel worse about myself, because he and I had always shared our various and assorted treasures like dirty books, but not these: I'd read them by myself under the covers with a flashlight and hide them under my mattress until Friday, when my mother would change the sheets, and on that day, I'd hide my secret life in the closet.

I used to buy the idea that I was "sick." The "sick" theory gave me some whys and wherefores about the way I had to take to bed to learn about what straight boys and girls are able to go find out with each other in alleyways, backyards, parks, and the movies. I didn't know then that what I was reading was truly the perverted version. That pornography was written for straight men — including all the psycho-socio-anthropological scientific bullshit studies on gay women written by Ph.D.s.

I look back now and see where those books and their ideas rotted my guts and crippled my moral structure. The real crouch and limp came from the drafting of my people — women-loving women — as the whipping girls so that straight society could feel high and holy.

Folks can see the most honorable and upright butch bopping the streets, minding her own business, and they can have a righteous fit over her. We don't have to do anything except be our natural selves and some of these people will think they have a perfect right to use us as toilet paper and then go home to plot us into their fantasies. Men always do this to women any which way: wiping all their mess on some woman who is by herself and they're in a bunch in front of their corner store. After they make their little comments and noises, they're all smiling and at ease and feeling good and cooled out with each other.

If you watch the woman, she looks embarrassed and angry. She feels stupid and she's usually trying to cover that up and pretend that none of it affects her. Now if she's the type of butch who won't calmly take the shit, the men will have to work harder to take it to another level if they want the satisfaction that comes from wiping a person away. They have to go and tell each other that she wants to be a man, or they can act as if they just can't understand "freaks" and how, "If she wants to be a man so bad, why doesn't she come out and fight like one?" Then that dude's brothers can go into their man act and have the pleasure of holding him back from supposedly going after her ass. They'll be soothing themselves while trying to pull this one and be saying, "Hey, man. You got to be cool, because that is a woman and when she meets the right fella, she'll straighten up and fly right." And he says, "Yeah, man, I just got all beside myself. Bulldaggers and faggots, jim. Hey: you know they both use toilet paper for padding," and they laugh and slap five and their eyes are shining. Their whole beings lighten up. They've jerked off and are relieved.

Okay, that's them. They get to feeling whole and healthy, but the butch-type woman who said, "Fuck y'all. You can keep your shit and kiss my ass behind it," is mad as hell and fit to be tied. She doesn't have anybody on hand that she can make sense to. There's no dog she can kick or make a nigger out of to transfer her shit to, so she's got to carry the load and steam with those juices, sweating it out alone. She probably takes it home and finds it in the mirror in frowns and frustration.

So you can see why I talk about a painkiller. I would like to have a pill that I could share with everybody fair and square. We'd all pop it and come the next day, the streets would be cleared of men, the straight women would loosen up, and the butches would be at ease with each other. That's what I would call medical attention for a serious disease that's getting epidemic. I think we should give the afflicted hope: let them know: homophobia can be cured.

Amber Hollibaugh & Cherríe Moraga

What we're rollin' around in bed with: Sexual silences in feminism

A conversation toward ending them

This article was derived from a series of conversations we entertained for many months. Through it, we wish to illuminate both our common and our different relationships to a feminist movement to which we are both committed.

The critique

In terms of sexual issues, it seems feminism has fallen short of its original intent. The whole notion of "the personal is political" which surfaced in the early part of the movement (and which many of us have used to an extreme) is suddenly and ironically dismissed when we begin to discuss sexuality. We have become a relatively sophisticated movement, so many women think they now have to have the theory before they expose the experience. It seems we simply did not take our feminism to heart enough. This most privatized aspect of ourselves, our sex lives, has dead-ended into silence within the feminist movement.

Feminism has never directly addressed women's sexuality except in its most oppressive aspects in relation to men (e.g., marriage, the nuclear family, wife battering, rape, etc.). Heterosexuality is both an actual sexual interaction *and* a system. No matter how we play ourselves out sexually, we are all affected by the system inasmuch as our sexual values are filtered through a society where heterosexuality is considered the norm. It is difficult to believe that there is anyone in the world who hasn't spent some time in great pain over the choices and limitations which that system has forced on all of us. We all suffer from heterosexism every single day (whether we're conscious of it or not). And as long as that's true, men and women, women and women, men and men — all different kinds of sexual combinations — must fight against this system, if we are ever going to perceive ourselves as sexually profitable and loving human beings.

By analyzing the institution of heterosexuality through feminism, we learned what's oppressive about it and why people cooperate with it or don't, but we didn't learn what's *sexual*. We don't really know, for instance, why men and women are still attracted to each other, even through all that oppression, which we know to be true. There is something genuine that happens between heterosexuals, but which gets perverted in a thousand different ways. There *is* heterosexuality outside of heterosexism.

What grew out of this kind of "nonsexual" theory was a "transcendent" definition of sexuality wherein lesbianism (since it exists outside the institution of heterosexuality) came to be seen as the practice of feminism. It set up a "perfect" vision of egalitarian sexuality, where we could magically leap over our heterosexist conditioning into mutually orgasmic, struggle-free, trouble-free sex. We feel this vision has become both misleading and damaging to many feminists, but in particular to lesbians. Who created this sexual model as a goal in the first place? Who can really live up to such an ideal? There is little language, little literature that reflects the actual sexual struggles of most lesbians, feminist or not.

The failure of feminism to answer all the questions regarding women, in particular women's sexuality, is the same failure the homosexual movement suffers from around gender. It's a confusing of those two things — that some of us are both female and homosexual — that may be the source of some of the tension between the two movements and of the inadequacies of each. When we walk down the street, we are both female and lesbian. We are working-class white and working-class Chicana. We are all these things rolled into one and there is no way to eliminate even one aspect of ourselves.

The conversation

CM: In trying to develop sexual theory, I think we should start by talking about what we're rollin' around in bed with. We both agree that the way feminism has dealt with sexuality has been entirely inadequate.

AH: Right. Sexual theory has traditionally been used to say, *People have been forced to be this thing; people could be that thing.* And you're left standing in the middle going, "Well, I am here, and I don't know how to get there." It hasn't been able to talk realistically about what people *are* sexually.

I think by focusing on roles in lesbian relationships, we can begin to unravel who we really are in bed. When you hide how profoundly roles can shape your sexuality, you can use that as an example of other things that get hidden. There's a lot of different things that shape the way that people respond — some not so easy to see, some more forbidden, as I perceive S/M to be. Like with S/M — when I think of it I'm frightened: why? Is it because I might be sexually fascinated with it and I don't know how to accept that? Who am I there? The point is, that when you deny that roles, S/M, fantasy, or any sexual differences exist in the first place, you can only come up with neutered sexuality, where everybody's got to be basically the same because anything different puts the element of power and deviation in there and threatens the whole picture.

CM: Exactly. Remember how I told you that growing up what turned me on sexually, at a very early age, had to do with the fantasy of capture, taking a woman, and my identification was with the man, taking? Well, something like that would be so frightening to bring up in a feminist context ... fearing people would put it in some sicko sexual box. And yet, the truth is, I do have some real gut-level misgivings about my sexual connection with capture. It might feel very sexy to imagine "taking" a woman, but it has sometimes occurred at the expense of my feeling, sexually, like I can surrender myself to a woman — that is, always needing to be the one in control, calling the shots. It's a very butch trip and I feel like this can keep me private and protected and can prevent me from fully being able to express myself.

AH: But it's not wrong, in and of itself, to have a capture fantasy. The real question is: Does it *actually* limit you? For instance, does it allow you to eroticize someone else, but never see yourself as erotic? Does it keep you always in control? Does the fantasy force you into a dimension of sexuality that feels very narrow to you? If it causes you to look at your lover in only one light, then you may want to check it out. But if you can't even dream about wanting a woman in this way in the first place, then you can't figure out what is narrow and heterosexist in it and what's just play. After all, it's only *one* fantasy.

CM: Well, what I think is very dangerous about keeping down such fantasies is that they are forced to stay unconscious. Then, next thing you know, in the actual sexual relationship, you become the capturer; that is, you try to have power over your lover, psychologically or whatever. If the desire for power is so hidden and unacknowledged, it *will* inevitably surface through manipulation or what-have-you. If you couldn't *play* capturer, you'd be it.

AH: Part of the problem in talking about sexuality is *it's so enormous* in our culture that people don't have any genuine sense of dimension. So that when you say "capture," every fantasy you have ever heard of from Robin Hood to colonialism comes racing into your mind and all you really maybe wanted to do was have your girlfriend lay you down.

But in feminism, we can't even explore these questions, because what they say is, in gender, there is a masculine oppressor and a female oppressee. So whether you might fantasize yourself in a role a man might perform or a woman in reaction to a man, this makes you sick, fucked-up, and you had better go and change it.

If you don't speak of fantasies, they become a kind of amorphous thing that envelops you and hangs over your relationship and you get terrified by the silence. If you have no way to describe what your desire is and what your fear is, you have no way to negotiate with your lover. And I guarantee you, six months or six years later, the relationship has paid. Things that are kept private and hidden become painful and deformed.

When you say that part of your sexuality has been hooked up with capture, I want to say that absolutely there's a heterosexist part of that, but what part of that is just plain dealing with power, sexually? I don't want to live outside of power in my sexuality, but I don't want to be trapped into a heterosexist concept of power either. But what I feel feminism asks of me is to throw the baby out with the bathwater.

For example, *I think the reason butch-femme stuff got hidden within lesbian-feminism is because people are profoundly afraid of questions of power in bed.* And though everybody doesn't play out power the way I do, the question of power affects who and how you eroticize your sexual need. And it is absolutely at the bottom of all sexual inquiry. I can't say to you, for instance, I am trying to work through being a femme, so I won't have to be one anymore.

CM: But what is femme to you? I told you once that what I thought of as femme was passive, unassertive, etc., and you didn't fit that image. And you said to me, "Well, change your definition of femme."

AH: My fantasy life is deeply involved in a butch-femme exchange. I never come together with a woman, sexually, outside of those roles. Femme is active, not passive. It's saying to my partner, "Love me enough to let me go where I need to go and take me there. Don't make me think it through. Give me a way to be so in my body that I don't have to think; that you can fantasize for the both of us. You map it out. You are in control."

It's hard to talk about things like giving up power without it sounding passive. I am willing to give myself over to a woman equal to her amount of wanting. I expose myself for her to appreciate. I open myself out for her to see what's possible for her to love in me that's female. I want her to respond to it. I may not be doing something active with my body, but more eroticizing her need that I feel in her hands as she touches me.

In the same way, as a butch, you want and conceive of a woman in a certain way. You dress a certain way to attract her and you put your sexual need within these certain boundaries to communicate that desire ... And yet, there's a part of me that feels maybe all this is not even a question of roles. Maybe it's much richer territory than that.

CM: Yes, I feel the way I want a woman can be a very profound experience. Remember I told you how when I looked up at my lover's face when I was making love to her (I was actually just kissing her breast at the moment), but when I looked up at her face, I could feel and see how deeply every part of her was present? That every pore in her body was entrusting me to handle her, to take care of her sexual desire. This look on her face is like nothing else. It fills me up. She entrusts me to determine where she'll go sexually. And I honestly feel a power inside me strong enough to heal the deepest wound.

AH: Well, I can't actually see what I look like, but I can feel it in my lover's hands when I look the way you described. When I open myself up more and more to her sensation of wanting a woman, when I eroticize that in her, I feel a kind of ache in my body, but it's not an ache to *do* something. I can feel a hurt spot and a need and it's there and it's just the tip of it, the tip of that desire, and that is what first gets played with, made erotic. It's light and playful. It doesn't commit you to exposing a deeper part of yourself sexually. Then I begin to pick up passion. And the passion isn't butch or femme. It's just passion.

But from this place, if it's working, I begin to imagine myself being *the woman that a woman always wanted*. That's when I begin to eroticize. That's what I begin to feel from my lover's hands. I begin to fantasize myself becoming more and more female in order to comprehend and meet what I feel happening in her body. I don't want her not to be female to me. Her need is female, but it's butch because I am asking her to expose her desire through the movement of her hands on my body and I'll respond. I want to give up power in response to her need. This can feel profoundly powerful and very unpassive.

A lot of times how I feel it in my body is I feel like I have this fantasy of pulling a woman's hips into my cunt. I can feel the need painfully in another woman's body. I can feel the impact and I begin to play and respond to that hunger and desire. And I begin to eroticize the fantasy that *she can't get enuf of me*. It makes me want to enflame my body. What it feels like is that I'm in my own veins and I'm sending heat up into my thighs. It's very hot.

CM: Oh, honey, she feels the heat, *too.*

AH: Yes, and I am making every part of my body accessible to that woman. I completely trust her. There's no place she cannot touch me. My body is literally open to any way she interprets her sexual need. My power is that I know how to read her inside of her own passion. I can hear her. It's like a sexual language; it's a rhythmic language that she uses her hands for. My body is completely in sync with a lover, but I'm not deciding where she's gonna touch me.

CM: But don't you ever fantasize yourself being on the opposite end of that experience?

AH: Well, not exactly in the same way, because with butches you can't insist on them giving up their sexual identity. You have to go through that identity to that other place. That's why roles are so significant and you can't throw them out. You have to find a way to use them, so you can eventually release your sexuality into other domains that you may feel the role traps you in. But you don't have to throw out the role to explore the sexuality. There are femme ways to orchestrate sexuality. I'm not asking a woman not to be butch. I am asking her to let me express the other part of my own character, where I am actively orchestrating what's happening. I never give up my right to say that I can insist on what happens sexually ... Quite often what will happen is I'll simply seduce her. Now, that's very active. The seduction can be very profound, but it's a seduction as a femme.

CM: What comes to my mind is something as simple as you coming over and sitting on her lap. Where a butch, well, she might just go for your throat if she wants you.

AH: Oh yes, different areas for different roles! What's essential is that your attitude doesn't threaten the other person's sexual identity, but plays with it. That's what good seduction is all about. I play a lot in that. It's not that I have to have spike heels on in order to fantasize who I am. Now that's just a lot of classist shit, conceiving of femme in such a narrow way.

CM: Well, I would venture to say that some of these dynamics that you're describing happen between most lesbians, only they may both be in the same drag of flannel shirts and jeans. My feeling, however, is ... and this is very hard for me ... what I described earlier about seeing my lover's face entrusting me like she did, well, *I want her to take me to that place, too.*

AH: Yes, but you don't want to have to deny your butchness to get there. Right?

CM: Well, that's what's hard. To be butch, to me, is not to be a woman. The classic extreme-butch stereotype is the woman who sexually refuses another woman to touch her. It goes something like this: She doesn't want to feel her femaleness because she thinks of you as the "real" woman and if she makes love to *you*, she doesn't have to feel her own body as the object of desire. She can be a kind of "bodiless lover." So when you turn over and want to make love to her and make her feel physically like a woman, then what she is up against is *queer*. You are a woman making love to her. She feels queerer than anything in that. Get it?

AH: Got it. Whew!

CM: I believe that probably from a very early age the way you conceived of yourself as female has been very different from me. We both have pain, but I think that there is a particular pain attached if you identified yourself as a butch queer from an early age as I did. I didn't really think of myself as female, or male. I thought of myself as this hybrid or something. I just kinda thought of myself as this free agent until I got tits. Then I thought, *Oh oh, some problem has occurred here...* For me, the way you conceive of yourself as a woman and the way I am attracted to women sexually reflect that butch-femme exchange — where a woman believes herself so woman that it really makes me want her.

But for me, I feel a lot of pain around the fact that it has been difficult for me to conceive of myself as thoroughly female in that sexual way. So retaining my "butchness" is not exactly my desired goal. Now that, in itself, is probably all heterosexist bullshit — about what a woman is supposed to be in the first place — but we are talking about the differences between the way you and I conceive of ourselves as sexual beings.

AH: I think it does make a difference. I would argue that a good femme does not play to the part of you that hates yourself for feeling like a man, but to the part of you that knows you're a woman. Because it's absolutely critical to understand that femmes are women to women and dykes to men in the straight world. *You and I are talking girl to girl.* We're not talking what I was in straight life.

I was ruthless with men, sexually, around what I felt. *It was only with women I couldn't avoid opening up my need to have something more than an orgasm.* With a woman, I can't refuse to know that the possibility is just there that she'll reach me some place very deeply each time we make love. That's part of my fear of being a lesbian. I can't refuse that possibility with a woman.

You see, I want you as a woman, not as a man; but I want you in the way *you* need to be, which may not be traditionally female, but which is the area that you express as *butch*. Here is where in the other world you have suffered the most damage. My feeling is, part of the reason I love to be with butches is because I feel I repair that damage. I make it right to want me that hard. Butches have not been allowed to feel their own desire because that part of butch can be perceived by the straight world as male. I feel I get back my femaleness and give a different definition of femaleness to a butch as a femme. That's what I mean about one of those unexplored territories that goes beyond roles, but goes through roles to get there.

CM: How I fantasize sex roles has been really different for me with different women. I do usually *enter* into an erotic encounter with a woman from the kind of butch place you described, but I have also felt very ripped off there, finding myself taking all the sexual responsibility. I am seriously attracted to butches sometimes. It's a different dynamic, where the sexuality may not seem as fluid or comprehensible, but I know there's a huge part of me that wants to be handled in the way I described I can handle another woman. I am very compelled toward that "lover" posture. I have never totally reckoned with being the "beloved" and, frankly, I don't know if it takes a butch or a femme or what to get me there. I know that it's a

249

struggle within me and it scares the shit out of me to look at it so directly. I've done this kind of searching emotionally, but to combine sex with it seems like very dangerous stuff.

AH: Well, I think everybody has aspects of roles in their relationships, but I feel pretty out there on the extreme end ... I think what feminism did, in its fear of heterosexual control of fantasy, was to say that there was almost no fantasy safe to have, where you weren't going to have to give up power or take it. There's no sexual fantasy I can think of that doesn't include some aspect of that. But I feel like I have been forced to give up some of my richest potential sexually in the way feminism has defined what is, and what's not, "politically correct" in the sexual sphere.

CM: Oh, of course, when most feminists talk about sexuality, including lesbianism, they're not talking about Desire. It is significant to me that I came out only when I met a good feminist, although I knew I was queer since eight or nine. That's only when I'd risk it because I wouldn't have to say it's because I want her. I didn't have to say that when she travels by me, my whole body starts throbbing.

AH: Yes, it's just *correct.*

CM: It was okay to be with her because we all knew men were really fuckers and there were a lot of "okay" women acknowledging that. Read: white and educated ... But that's not why I "came out." How could I say that I wanted women so bad, I was gonna die if I didn't get me one, soon! You know, I just felt the pull in the hips, right?

AH: Yes, really ... Well, the first discussion I ever heard of lesbianism among feminists was: "We've been sex objects to men and where did it get us? And here when we're just learning how to be friends with other women, you got to go and sexualize it." That's what they said! "Fuck you. Now I have to worry about you looking down my blouse." That's exactly what they meant. It horrified me. "No no no," I wanted to say, "That's not me. I promise I'll only look at the sky. *Please* let me come to a meeting. I'm really okay. I just go to the bars and fuck like a rabbit with women who want me. You know?"

Now from the onset, how come feminism was so invested in that? They would not examine sexual need with each other except as oppressor-oppressee. Whatever your experience was, you were always the victim. Even if you were the aggressor. So how do dykes fit into that? Dykes who wanted tits, you know?

Now a lot of women have been sexually terrorized and this makes sense, their needing not to have to deal with explicit sexuality, but they made men out of every sexual dyke. "Oh my god, *she* wants me, too!"

So it became this really repressive movement, where you didn't talk dirty and you didn't want dirty. It really became a bore. So after meetings, we *ran* to the bars. You couldn't talk about wanting a woman, except very loftily. You couldn't say it hurt at night wanting a woman to touch you ... I remember at one meeting breaking down after everybody was talking about being a lesbian very delicately. I began crying. I remember saying, "I can't help it. I just ... want her. I want to feel her." And everybody forgiving me. It was this atmosphere of me exorcising this *crude* sexual need for women.

CM: Shit, Amber ... I remember being fourteen years old and there was this girl, a few years older than me, who I had this crush on. And on the last day of school, I knew I wasn't going to see her for months! We had hugged good-bye and I went straight home. Going into my bedroom, I got into my unmade bed and I remember getting the sheets, winding them into a kind of rope, and pulling them up between my legs and just holding them there under my chin. I just sobbed and sobbed because I knew I couldn't have her, maybe never have a woman to touch. It's just pure need and it's whole. It's like using sexuality to describe how deeply you need/want intimacy, passion, love.

Most women are not immune from experiencing pain in relation to their sexuality, but certainly lesbians experience a particular pain and oppression. Let us not forget, although feminism would sometimes like us to, that lesbians are oppressed in this world. Possibly, there are some of us who came out through the movement who feel immune to "queer attack," but not the majority of us (no matter when we came out), particularly if you have no economic buffer in this society. If you have enough money and privilege, you can separate yourself from heterosexist oppression. You can be *sapphic* or something, but you don't have to be queer. It's easier to clean up your act and avoid feeling like a freak if you have a margin in this society because you've got bucks.

The point I am trying to make is that I believe most of us harbor plenty of demons and old hurts inside ourselves around sexuality. I know, for me, that each time I choose to touch another woman, to make love with her, I feel I risk opening up that secret, harbored, vulnerable place ... I think why feminism has been particularly attractive to many "queer" lesbians is that it kept us in a place where we wouldn't have to look at our pain around sexuality anymore. Our sisters would just sweep us up into a movement...

AH: Yes, we're not just accusing feminism of silence, but our own participation in that silence has stemmed from our absolute terror of facing that profound sexual need. Period.

There is no doubt in my mind that the feminist movement has radically changed, in an important way, everybody's concept of lesbianism. Everybody across the board. There's not a dyke in the world today (in or out of the bars) who can have the same conversation that she could have had ten years ago. It seeps through the water system or something, you know?

Lesbianism is certainly accepted in feminism, but more as a political or intellectual concept. It seems feminism is the last rock of conservatism. It will not be sexualized. It's *prudish* in that way...

Well, I won't give my sexuality up and I won't *not* be as feminist. So I'll build a different movement, but I won't live without either one.

Sometimes, I don't know how to handle how angry I feel about feminism. We may disagree on this. We have been treated in some similar ways, but our relationship to feminism has been different. Mine is a lot longer. I really have taken a lot more shit than you have, specifically around being femme. I have a personal fury. The more I got in touch with how I felt about women, what made me desire and desirable, the more I felt outside the feminist community, and that was just terrifying, because, on the one hand, it had given me so much. I loved it. And then, I couldn't be who I was. I felt that about class, too. I could describe my feelings about being a woman, but if I described it from my own class, using that language, my experience wasn't valid. I don't know what to do with my anger, particularly around sexuality.

CM: Well, you've gotta be angry ... I mean what you were gonna do is turn off the tape, so we'd have no record of your being mad. What comes out of anger ... if you, one woman, can say, *I have been a sister all these years and you have not helped me...*, that speaks more to the failure of all that theory and rhetoric than more theory and rhetoric.

AH: Yeah ... Remember that night you and me and M. was at the bar and we were talking about roles? She told you later that the reason she had checked out of the conversation was because she knew how much it was hurting me to talk about it. You know, I can't tell you what it meant to me for her to know that. The desperation we all felt at that table talking about sexuality was so great, wanting people to understand why we are the way we are.

CM: I know ... I remember how at that forum on S/M that happened last spring, how that Samois* woman came to the front of the room and spoke very plainly and clearly about feeling that through S/M she was really coping with power struggles in a tangible way with her lover. That this time, for once, she wasn't leaving the relationship. I can't write her off. I believed her. I believed she was a woman in struggle.

And as feminists, Amber, you and I are interested in struggle.

The challenge

We would like to suggest that, in terms of dealing with sexual issues both personally and politically, women go back to CR groups. We believe that women must create sexual theory in the same way we created feminist

---

* Samois is a lesbian-feminist S/M group in the San Francisco Bay Area.

theory. We need to simply get together in places where people agree to suspend their sexual values, so that all of us can feel free to say what we do sexually or want to do or have done to us. We do have fear of using feelings as theory. We do not mean to imply that feelings are everything. They can, however, be used as the beginning to form a movement which can *politically* deal with sexuality in a broad-based, cross-cultural way.

We believe our racial and class backgrounds have a huge effect in determining how we perceive ourselves sexually. Since we are not a movement that is working-class dominated or a movement that is Third World, we both hold serious reservations as to how this new CR will be conceived. In our involvement in a movement largely controlled by white middle-class women, we feel that the values of their cultures (which may be more closely tied to an American-assimilated puritanism) have been pushed down our throats. The questions arise then: *Whose* feelings and *whose* values will be considered normative in these CR groups? If there is no room for criticism in sexual discussion around race and class issues, we foresee ourselves being gut-checked from the beginning.

We also believe our class and racial backgrounds have a huge effect in determining how we involve ourselves politically. For instance, why is it that it is largely white middle-class women who form the visible leadership in the antiporn movement? This is particularly true in the Bay Area, where the focus is less on actual violence against women and more on sexist ideology and imagery in the media. Why are women of color not particularly visible in this sex-related single-issue movement? It's certainly not because we are not victims of pornography.

More working-class and Third World women can be seen actively engaged in sex-related issues that *directly* affect the life-and-death concerns of women (abortion, sterilization abuse, health care, welfare, etc.). It's not like we choose this kind of activism because it's an "ideologically correct" position, but because we are the ones pregnant at sixteen (straight *and* lesbian), whose daughters get pregnant at sixteen, who get left by men without child care, who are self-supporting lesbian mothers with no child care, and who sign forms to have our tubes tied because we can't read English. But these kinds of distinctions between classes and colors of women are seldom absorbed by the feminist movement as it stands to date.

Essentially, we are challenging other women and ourselves to look where we haven't (this includes through and beyond our class and color) in order to arrive at a synthesis of sexual thought that originates and develops from our varied backgrounds and experiences. We refuse to be debilitated one more time around sexuality, race, or class.

Madeline Davis, Amber Hollibaugh, & Joan Nestle

The femme tapes

April 24, 1982, marked the public start of what was to become known as the "sex wars" in the lesbian and feminist community. On that day several hundred women gathered to attend the Scholar and the Feminist IX Conference held at Barnard College in New York City. The title of the conference sounded innocent enough — "Towards a Politics of Sexuality" — but the night before, several members of Women against Pornography had called the college informing them of the unacceptability of several of the speakers. When I arrived at the campus that bright spring morning, I found a picket line walked by women wearing black t-shirts stating their position on certain sexual practices and handing out leaflets that named the unacceptable speakers and topics; butch-femme was included in the list. As a result of the repressive atmosphere surrounding the conference, a sexual speak-out was held in a performance space in Soho. There all of us who had been declared beyond the pale spoke our piece. Out of this turmoil came the femme tapes. Madeline Davis, Amber Hollibaugh, and myself met that weekend to talk as femmes. Even though we taped the five-hour talk for eventual use, we did not realize what silences we were breaking and therefore what follows is an edited version. *
—Joan Nestle*

Joan: I just feel so many things have come together and split apart this weekend.

---

* **Amber Hollibaugh notes:** In 1982, Joan, Madeline, and I spent an afternoon talking, crying, and describing our lives and histories to each other as well as revealing the state we now found ourselves in as old-gay femmes in the lesbian community. The talk was passionate and revealing. And for me, almost ten years later, it is still too raw to expose on the printed page. No matter that I have written openly about much of my sexual past as a sex worker or queer, there are still places too vulnerable to illuminate publicly — especially because the

254

Amber: More than anything else I just want us to talk. In a way that's never happened before. I never sat at a table before with two other femmes who knew they were femmes and talked about what that meant. I feel terrified and I need it. What I have been thinking about is this question. In all these conversations I have been having with butches, they always talk about their role confusion: Are they a man or not a man? Why did they want to fuck women? But it seems they always had an image of themselves; they could always look at the movies and see the boy kissing the girl, and they were the boy. Well, you know, it occurs to me that the reason it is so hard to figure out why you are a femme is that there are really no images in the other direction. When I thought about kissing a man, I could only imagine a woman kissing a man, because I couldn't imagine what a woman would look like in that place, but I also knew that I wanted to get kissed. It keeps coming up for me over and over: I don't have any images of femmes. I don't get it. I know I am one; it is not like gender dysfunction, where I think I am a man. I am not straight. What am I? I don't get as oppressed on the street in the same way, but it makes me confused in terms of gender. Am I a real woman? It just really blows me away. No wonder femmes don't know how to talk about it — there is no imagery.

J: A role model that I took in the very early fifties was Pat Ward, who was a well-known prostitute. She was part of the Mickey Jelke trial, which was then all over the papers and the radio. I used to come home from school — I was around ten or eleven, and play that I was Pat Ward on trial, because I knew she was sexual and so was I. I had already been masturbating and I had sexual feelings. I remember seeing pictures of her, wearing a white blouse with a Peter Pan collar. She looked very prim in the middle of all this sexual discussion about her, and she became the woman I wanted to be. I used to play-act that I was this prostitute who had a public sexual image but no one really knew her.

A: I had images of what sex star I wanted to be, but I didn't have my partner. The butches had their partners.

J: I was thinking about the right to sexuality, but it was tied up with being the "wrong woman" and yet maintaining a part of yourself. She became that symbol.

Madeline: I think I always felt that I was the "outrageous woman" in some

---

act of revelation, I have come to believe, must happen only when one is ready to deal with its possible impact or misinterpretation in a bigger world than that of friends and lovers. In that conversation with Joan and Madeline, there is still too much I continue to wrestle with or confront. Until I have resolved many of the stories I told there, I cannot publish it in its entirety. So, I have sadly and lovingly removed most of my sections from our talk that afternoon while being proud and grateful that Joan and Madeline are publishing their own sections of the dialogue. (1991)

way also, but I had partners that supported that image. Some of my partners were very feminine men. They were Sal Mineo when he was a pretty, big-eyed, soft-looking baby-butch type. So I was satisfied for a long time with them and wondered why my girlfriends were into muscle and macho, because I wanted men who were sweet. Even when I was coming out, I went back and forth some. I went with a couple of guys who were faggots and were quite effeminate.

J: The first adult person I loved and lusted after was a gay man.

M: I loved that combination of toughness and softness, that combination of masculinity and femininity. And then I began looking for it in women too — the toughness in women that still had womanness in it. I started going to gay bars when I was eighteen, but I thought I was straight. A friend took me there. They were wonderful and fascinating, but I still thought it was the men in those bars that I was going to fall in love with or be attracted to. The first butch woman I saw tending bar, at the Midtown in Buffalo, turned my knees to water. I knew it was a woman, but it was this combination that made my stomach flutter, made my hands sweat, so powerful, so scary. Was this a girl?

A: Was this a girl? Am I in trouble?

J: Am I in heaven?

M: Both. When I first started sleeping with women, I thought it was being experimental, so I allowed myself to do it and remain safely "progressive." I could have fucked, as Mabel said, poodles, if I maintained the excuse that I was "expanding my horizons."

A: I think we should give our ages.

J: I am forty-two. One of the reasons I am excited about us doing this tape is that I think that when we are working out how we came to our sexuality and what it means to us, we are really working out a lot of things about women's sexuality in a larger sense. The femme is a kind of puzzle from all perspectives. No matter who looks at us, we are a puzzle. Sometimes we are a puzzle to ourselves.

I was raised by a mother who was a very sexually active woman and Mabel Hampton, who was a lesbian. Mabel took care of me from age ten. I started masturbating when I was four. The whole life I lived felt sexual. I always knew my mother was out screwing around. I knew there was something different about her. Other mothers didn't speak to her because of her sexual activities. And then I had lots of sexual contacts with young girls who "did things" to me, like one young girl who masturbated me on the floor of a bathroom with my back against the bathtub when I was around six or seven. Another girl and I experimented with tinker toys. It was all exploration, and it was interesting. Penetration by women, which is important to me, goes back that far. Early on in the Bronx, I was discovered by my mother playing at sex with a cousin. She was on top of me, and I remember us both being hauled before these adult women and the guilty one was going to be the one whose pants were open. Then another element in the sexual soup was my brother's ordeal. He was molested by — I don't call him a homosexual; the society did, the police did, but I call him a sick man. I had to entrap him, and then my brother had to testify. The whole house was filled with sexual secrets. Something was wrong with my brother; something was wrong with this man.

I felt really early that I was a lesbian, even though I experimented very much with men. Many years later, in graduate school, I even had a man as a mistress. I never let him fuck me, but I jerked him off, I went down on him, I did everything to play with this thing called a penis. But this was different. It was exploring what I knew I was not going to have and what seemed to make men special. All the time I was doing it, I was sleeping with women and I started going to bars as soon as I could get in. I went to Pam Pam's on Sixth Avenue, a bleak but well-lit coffeehouse where all the below-age butches and femmes hung out. One of the assumptions that gets me angry when we are talked about by other people is the assumption that we are sexually naive, that roles were given us. I started making love to Roz, a best girlfriend, when I was ten. I would go to her house three or four times a week and make love to her. I went down on her almost every night. My own home life was falling apart, and I found comfort between Roz's legs; ironically, in her home with a real mother and father, I found safety between her legs; I thought I was now like everybody else. So when a person says to me, "How can you say you were a femme before you went to the bars?" I know we have a big difference in our backgrounds. I went to the bars with a sexuality, but some women never give me that autonomy, because they think, No, your sexuality didn't happen until you were twenty. I think class and protected backgrounds enter here.

A: Yes, the age of consent comes with the role.

M: I am forty-one. I have a sister who is three years younger and a brother who is eleven years younger. My father was a factory worker, my mother a homemaker — the Jewish version of Ozzie and Harriet! My parents were extremely loving. They would sit on the couch and neck. They were physical with each other in a truly affectionate way. We also allowed nudity in our house — back and forth from the bathroom and the bedroom; no one covered up. Even my father. I saw male and female genitals and breasts from before I can remember anyone said you weren't supposed to. We weren't physically demonstrative, but I knew that my parents had a loving relationship and were sexual with each other. Since that time, my mother has talked to me about her sex life with my father. They did it everywhere! And they let me know that sex was okay. Also, my mother had been to nursing school and we had lots of books around. I saw anatomy pictures and got to know what vaginas were and what anuses were and what clitorises and what elbows and what necks were, and they all had the same value. I was never told that genitalia were bad — or good. They were functional, like a liver or a pancreas. No one ever said there was anything to hide or be afraid of. I didn't experiment sexually in my younger years, except for masturbation. I told my mom at twelve that I had masturbated. All she said was, "Make sure your hands are clean!" It's pretty amazing to remember — that was 1952. The first time I even necked was with the thirteen-year-old boy down the street. I was twelve. He kissed me in the bathroom at my girlfriend's house — it was the only room with a lock on the door — and I looked in the mirror to see if my face had changed. We used to worry whether people could tell that we had been kissed! Sometime later he touched me ... on top ... over the white man's shirt I was wearing with rolled up jeans. Again I went to the mirror. Many years later, after the first time I had sex, I also checked my face. I don't really know what I expected to find. And all that checking — was it curiosity or guilt? I think it might have been more curiosity. I remember feeling very proud of these transitions into womanhood.

I was seventeen when I decided it was time for sex. It was really a well-considered decision. I had been going to beatnik coffeehouses and had met a man who was an artist and a writer. He was more than twenty years older. I told him, "You are going to be my first."

He said, "Your first what?"

"I am going to have sex for the first time with you."

He was amused. "You have got to be kidding; you're a virgin? You have never had sex before? Get out of here. I am not going to do this. I won't take that responsibility. Listen, I'll tell you what. Think about it for a year."

A: A year, not a week?

M: He was terrified. He was thirty-nine. I didn't think I needed that much time, but I talked about it with my girlfriends for months and I waited. A year later, almost to the day, I saw him again. We had gone to his apartment with a lot of people from the coffeehouse and were partying. When the others started leaving, I told him I would like to stay for a while, and when everybody left, I said, "Well, I am ready."

He said, "What are you talking about?"

"You told me to come back in a year if I really wanted to have sex with you."

He couldn't believe I had actually waited a whole year, but I told him I had picked the person I wanted to be the first. After we made love the first time, I told him how much I'd liked it and wanted to do it again. He said, "You must have done this before. You are too comfortable." I think guys always say that. You must have experience because you like it too much. Can't somebody just like it? Anyway, I was just into it. We had an affair that lasted — along with other affairs — for about four years, until he got married to someone else. I went on to lots of other men in my life, until I realized something important — I wasn't coming! In all that time there were only three men that I allowed, and taught, to make me come. I just sensed there was something alien and untrustworthy about them. Just before I got married, I started to go to gay bars a lot. I began really looking at the women. But even though I thought they were beautiful, and I even had a couple of "passions," I basically discounted the significance of those relationships. Instead, I spent my energies trying to be what I was supposed to be while still being irresistibly drawn to what I was.

❖

J: I found out only after my mother's death in 1978 that she had been gang-raped when she was fourteen by three young men in their twenties. I also understood then how much she struggled to keep any sexual desire intact after that and how closely related domesticated sex and respectability or safety is for women. In order to marry my father, who was working his way up in the furrier industry — this all has so much to do with the garment industry — she had to fake that she was a virgin, and she wrote about how she learned to put a rubber band inside herself so that there would be blood on the sheets, because that was the only way she could get married. Her message to me was that she hated the marriage, that she felt confined, restricted. My father died very young, five months before I was born. My mother gave me a legacy of difference. I felt different because I was the daughter of a woman who did not have a husband, who had lots of lovers, who was never protected, it seemed to me, except by her own fortitude.

At times I felt gender confusion, because I looked very boyish and since I was ten I had been having this affair with Roz, the daughter of a kosher butcher, that I have already mentioned. Roz was a very big woman, although she was my age. One day Roz and I had been out shopping and I was wearing a gray blazer and gray slacks and had very short hair. My mother got on the bus and walked right by me. I shouted, "Ma, it's me"; when she turned around, she looked like she was going to faint and she started screaming at me, "Don't you ever dress that way again, don't you ever dress that way again." I just knew that I looked like a pervert, the fifties word. I looked like a boy.

Another time my difference really hit me was at my junior high school prom. Roz and I were best friends, so if one wasn't there, the teachers would say, "Where is your better half?" I had been making love to Roz all these times, but I had never labeled it.

M: Did she make love to you?

J: I just met her again recently. I have no clear memory, but I knew we took turns. We had these games like Sultan and His Harem. I am sure she did, but I have no memory of it. I only remember my making love to her, but I do remember with great clarity when I labeled my difference. We were at the prom and she was wearing — we both were — a low-cut dress. She was sitting down and I was standing above her. I was thirteen or fourteen years old and I looked down and I saw the swell of breast and I said, I like that, I want to touch that, I am queer. That wasn't a particularly femme response. At that moment, I froze in recognition of what I was. I recognized desire as the most dangerous, most defining action, not the fact that I had touched her all those years. That was when I knew. At the same time I was dating this tough guy, Denny — we called them "hoods" — who was sent to reform school regularly for stealing hubcaps. Roz and I used to spend a lot of time talking about fucking. She was going out with the guy she was going to marry at seventeen. Denny felt me up in the movies and gave me huge hickeys on my neck. One night, after a movie date, he was kissing me good-bye at a bus stop, and I kissed him with my mouth closed. I remember him saying, "Open your mouth; you kiss like a schoolteacher." It was so clear to me that there was a way to be sexual and I had to find it. All of this has to do with how I came to my femmeness. I was confused about what kind of woman I was; about how to be a woman that didn't make me a victim. I didn't know what I was. The first time I slept with a man, he masturbated me and I came, because I had been doing it with women. I said, "Is that it?" and he said, "Well, you're supposed to touch me," but I really didn't want to. I was more attracted to men who were smooth operators. They excited me.

My first woman lover had been dating my brother. She was a very small woman who didn't look like a butch. I was eighteen and was terrified; she had never been with a woman before. My mother would go to work, and she would come to the house and join me in bed. One of the first things she did was put her hand under me so that she could feel the warmth of my pee. I couldn't put it all together, except that I was in a world where people did things that didn't follow formulas. The first time she said she was in love with me, we were down in the Village. I felt terror well in me, and I said, "I'm going to walk this out of you," and we walked from the Village to Central Park and back, which is many miles. I was at her house a week later. She gave me a glass of scotch. Then she put her hand inside of me and the whole thing started. When she did that, she touched in me what my whole life would be, but at that moment I was not looking forward with joy. I was terrified, too anxious to feel desire.

M: My first sexual experience with a woman was different from the way I expected it to be. I had already been fucking a lot of men, even loving a few of them. They were in a strange way — when you said you liked tough, hard men — the men I loved. Although they were pretty and sweet, they were outlaws, they were poets, they smoked dope, they sold dope. I used to help run abortions back and forth to Canada, but inside I was a good girl, a nice Jewish girl. And someplace inside of me, as rebellious as I have become, as crazy and as outlandish as that body harness I wore yesterday [at the speak-out on sex], there is a good girl in me that will probably be there staring wide-eyed until I die, and it is very hard for me to put these two people together. But the men I was with were also in their own way outlaws and outside the social order and also nice — but restless. When I met the first woman who would be my lover, Bobbi had taken me over to the home of this woman's friend. It was November 29, 1963, at 12:37 in the afternoon! It must have been important to remember that so clearly. We pushed her car out of the snow. Her name was Dawn, but she was Beebo Brinker.* She was tall and slim with dark, wavy, slicked-back hair and blue eyes. I had read the novels and I was looking for her and there she was. We went to this gay bar called the Senate on the west side of Buffalo, and we got just absolutely bombed, and I went home with her that night. Actually, we went to the home of Bobbi's current girlfriend, and Dawn and I slept on Karen's floor. Dawn made love to me, and it was one of the most boring sexual experiences. [*Roars of laughter*]

A: Old Beebo really didn't come through with it.

M: I thought, Jesus Christ, what is going on here! This is supposed to be the fantasy. I mean I am living the fantasy; what happened here? I am not even sure I came, but I realized the second time around a few days later that it was because I was so drunk and there wasn't anything that would have worked. I was anesthetized. Within the next few days, we slept together again, then I came, then the fantasy happened, and I fell in love with her. I was just out of my mind about that woman. I was in love with Beebo Brinker with a different name. I wanted that fantasy and I got her and I was going to make her that person, but as most fantasies do, it backfired. She looked real butch, but she wasn't so butchy, and I was quite surprised that there were other things to consider. I knew how to make love to men; I had learned well, took to it easily. But I didn't know how to make love to women at all. I thought they probably smelled funny, and I didn't think I could do it, so I never had oral sex with her, but I did touch her manually and made her climax and that was the way she came. It was quite a different experience from the next woman I got involved with about four months later, who really was a stone butch. She put her hand up inside of me and she came! And then I thought, "There was something else happening here." And this was a woman whom I was not in love with. She was cute, a short chunky version of Beebo Brinker; they were all dark with blue eyes then! You know it's been a type I have been after. I didn't

---

* The butch hero of a series of paperback novels written by Ann Bannon and available at most drugstores in the sixties; Beebo Brinker was the American working-class version of Stephen of *The Well of Loneliness*. The series is now available from Naiad Press.

find too many, but after a while my tastes expanded. They had to. But I still look down the street after a dark-haired, blue-eyed woman. Anyway, this was a woman who was obviously crazy about my body — the second woman — and I got a whole other feeling suddenly. I mean the men wanted to fuck me, they liked me, but this was a woman who *loved* my body. I never really loved my body. I was comfortable with it. I knew where all its parts were and that it was functional. But I was always somewhat overweight. I never thought I was pretty, and to this day, you know, eight hundred people can say you're gorgeous and you're never going to believe it. But here was a woman who, when she touched me, trembled, and god — the world opened up. But I still felt the social pressures, and soon after that I got married. Allen was living with me at the time I was seeing that woman — we were living together but not married. We both thought he was very liberal about the whole thing. We talked about it many years later, and he said that the reason he didn't mind my seeing her was that he felt it was inconsequential. Women didn't matter. But his consciousness has been raised tremendously since that time. He said, "I should have known, but it was not the time for me to know that women were terribly important to women, and I did not know that about you."

I said, "I didn't know it about me." Who knew? We were married in less than a year. Lots of reasons for the breakup — mostly he was too young and I think I was too ... too self-determined. I returned to Buffalo. After I got married and came home, I didn't see anybody for six months. Then I became fascinated with this gay guy whom I brought out heterosexually. Believe me, that was so strange. He did drag — beautifully. This was my first clear indication of an attraction to androgyny. Soon I moved into an apartment house that was managed by a woman who was a dyke. I knew all her friends. I had come back from this marriage very hurt. I think I had been in love with the mythology of marriage and felt like such a failure. My parents' marriage was a wonderful, successful marriage. Why couldn't I do it right? [*First side of tape ends*]

❖

M: [*In mid-discussion about making love to some butch women*] There is a real interesting dynamic to set up — a master-slave dynamic. When she makes love to you, she is fucking you senseless and being masterful over you, and when you make love to her, you are servicing her. That's how I see it. You almost treat the clitoris like the end of a penis. You lick it with an up-and-down motion rather than a circular one. Most of the time you don't enter her. Some butches are anal erotic and can tolerate external anal touching or slight penetration or even a lot of oral anal penetration. [This would not be a safe sex practice.] It's not as threatening; it's not vaginal. Sometimes if you set up the dynamic that you are servicing them, it works.

A: I think you must be right. I know I have done that, but most butches I have been with till now have been so blown away by even their right to be orgasmic in that context ... anything you did was more than they ever expected. They never expected a return on that desire. That was never part of the expectations, and their desire came from your ability to translate their messages, but I have never known butches who demanded their orgasms. That is a new thing that has happened. That is not to say they didn't come or want to — that wasn't going on, and in fact the dynamic that you described is exactly what had to happen. But I want to come and I want certain things to happen. I am real defined about how I want to be fucked. I have never known a butch who was equally defined about how she wanted to be fucked. They were real defined about what they wanted to do but not around being fucked.

J: It's two languages going on.

A: That's right. I have two sets of images: one image is of a butch and the other image is of a whore, but something that has the actual translation of my desire as a femme is a difficult image for me to figure out. Some butches feel that when they make love, that is the most important act, while I want the emotion behind it. They want our love behind the desire. Sometimes the emotions are so threatening, they want to do it all through the body. Sometimes the act of service frees up the ambivalence about the boundaries of a female body.

J: It's a kind of helpful objectification. When I adore a butch's body with my tongue, I am making love to her total womanness, but in a way she can live with.

A: When I am making love to a butch who has held back for a long time, I become frightened that I will not be able to do it right. I get frozen, and then we are both frozen. You can't make love like that, you have to have a flow that happens between two people — some dynamic that doesn't threaten them in a way that gets you both moving. I really feel it is the heart of the other side of butch-femme problems...

J: This can happen in all sexuality. Each sexuality has to work it out in its own language, and this is our language, but sex is always metaphor — about freedom and control.

❖

J: I have had butch lovers who took great pride in their ability to ejaculate.

M: I am on a research team about this in Buffalo. It is called the Graffenburg spot. You have to learn how to make love to a woman who can do this. The spot moves around; it moves forward. I have been working with the dean of the Nursing School on a research project on the Graffenburg spot — we're publishing an article in *Nurse-Practitioners*. The Buffalo research in the lesbian community is trying to figure out which women are orgasmic in that way and ejaculate in that way. That's how I found out: I am also an ejaculator.

J: Do you think all women can do it?

M: It's possible. The data so far shows that about 30 percent do. It's conceivable that all women might be, but the study isn't conclusive so far. The problem is figuring out how to achieve it. In heterosexual sex, you get the spot best from the back or with the woman on top, but it seems that women can do it much more easily together and that's why more lesbians are much more orgasmic in that way than straight women. That's because we can curve our fingers to get at the spot and a penis can't.

A: Where is it? I mean, when you have your hand up someone's cunt, where is it?

M: It's directly under the shaft of the urethra; it's before you get to the cervix, and it's a soft spot that swells as you stimulate it. It moves as you get closer to orgasm, and the orgasm that you have from pushing on the Graffenburg spot causes the space behind the cervix to widen out. You get a larger space that moves upwards from stimulation of the G spot. As you get closer to orgasm, the spot moves up to about here [*gesturing*], and you have to pull forward a little with your fingers curved. Most doctors don't know what it is. They think it's incontinence.

J: But it doesn't taste like urine. Carol, my dear early lover, was afraid to come because she gave off so much liquid.

M: A lot of women who are ejaculators like that do what is called retrograde ejaculation, which means that they are so frightened of it that they hold it back, and then right after sex, they immediately have to go right to the bathroom and they don't understand why. It is a buildup of amino acid — phosphatase. It's high in glucose. You can taste it. It's sweet.

J: Not only is it sweet, it's not sticky, so when you are trying to finger-fuck, you don't know what to do because the penetration is very hard because it is watery. What do you do?

M: You can use KY jelly, and that probably is a good idea.

A: So you are a female ejaculator?

M: Yes, I am, but not to the extent many other women are. It's not uncommon, but a lot of women are scared of it and think they are peeing, and then they hold it back and yell, "No." It's a matter of learning how to relax and realize that it's normal, natural for them.

❖

J: One of the issues that became clarified for me as a result of yesterday was that many of today's feminists see us as ahistorical, as if we are stuck in time and never change, as if we are that bad fifties thing. But I am always learning more about this way of loving. I have changed in the last twenty years. Now I want to incorporate into my femmeness my new layers of experience. I want to be the best of our desire without apologizing for it, and I want us to know our own history. Butch and femme can change and grow.

A: It has been the worst problem around butch-femme. I mean, that's the thing we have always been accused of, and someplace there was truth in it — someone wasn't getting pleasure someplace that they needed. I have always felt that way about butch-femme stuff. There was someplace I had to twist myself around in order to make it happen. I mean, that was the technique of the good femme, of finding a way against that incredible butch barrier to be the lover of a butch. That was some of the tease and some of the—

M: Right — physically, I had to learn how to do things like learn how to use my hipbone, but more emotionally, to submit and engage in the drama that creates a setting in which they can comfortably find their orgasm. There's something kind of theatrical about being femme. It is not at all phony, but it seems like we learn to heighten our differences and create settings. We are the ones who make the surroundings safe and appropriate. You know — it's hard work! But we will do almost anything for them, the women we love and need so much.

J: There is so much irony in this. Deb came out into feminism, but she is in her own way a natural butch. She isn't like any kind of butch I had known before. She likes to be made love to. Now I can give back part of the body that has been pleasured. I think I was very caught up in emotional gratitude to women that I made love with, that lived with me. I would have driven a stone butch crazy. I provided a home; butches always came to live with me. I would find a butch living in some dingy place, not taking care of herself. My desire was to take her home, feed her, love her, reward her for being the freak on the street. I was always moved by the contrast of flagrant courage and obvious need for tending. Now that I am forty-two years old — that's another thing: being a femme doesn't even stay physically the same. I am a different femme at forty than I was at twenty. I have to be. I feel differently about my body.

While we are making these tapes, I am thinking, What did I do wrong?

A: Yes, your sexuality changes, and so when you are into roles, it's real scary to figure out what that means.

J: Hopefully, they'll change with us.

A: But I think part of the thing that is so painful about being a femme is that it is also very tied up in image and very tied up in sexual flirtation and very tied up in your ability to seduce, and that is very threatened by age and illness — you name it, all that kind of stuff — so if you can not be a femme, which obviously for the three of us is not going to be an option, then you are really torn. I don't think it is the same for butches and for femmes. You're looking in the mirror a whole lot and saying, "Hey, wait, there is a serious problem here. What am I going to do — what does an old femme do?"

J: I hear myself asking for more reassurance, but also I am more active in bed now. When I was younger, I would lie back and enjoy being enjoyable. Now sometimes I use borrowed passions. When things are rough, I will sometimes use scenes, fetishes, public sex nights to work out some of the femme fantasies that I can't find in bed for a while. Deb has been very understanding about this. When I was having trouble coming, I fantasized servicing a roomful of butches on my knees. I then found an opportunity to live this desire out and it was wonderful. Butches are not men for me, ever.

I have never felt beautiful, but within the last few years before I got sick, I reached a point where I did; I really did. It lasted such a short time, and now because of the illness, I feel like damaged goods. I feel like I don't know how to hold together what little knowledge I had about being a woman. I am so grateful to this new leather community that has formed; since I have new horrors to face, I must have new ways to explore. But you are so right. We have to keep talking — what does a femme do when she is fifty?

M: It's not just age. Any negative self-image leaves you so vulnerable. I was knocked out yesterday when a few women came up to me in the end and some said, "I love what you wrote," but one woman said, "You are so fucking beautiful. When are you going to be back in town?" It was astounding, what those words meant to me. Sometimes I feel so needy for approval. The woman I just started seeing said to me over the phone, "I love your ass, I love your tits. I love your cunt. I would like to congratulate the architect." [Laughter] It made me feel so worthwhile, so precious. It was also tied to a recognition that my femmeness was appreciated.

J: That is something we have in common — the love for those butch hands and how they hold our deepest selves in them.

A: That's why we can't give it up. There has been no social validation for being a femme, and yet all of us — the three of us — have stayed femme in a movement that absolutely thinks it is the most despicable thing. I can't not be a femme, just as I can't not be a lesbian, because with butches I really do know what it is to be a woman.

J: Exactly, exactly.

A: I really do learn for at least that moment. I might get up out of that bed and say, "I am ugly, I am terrible, I am this, I am that—"

J: Yet, as I said at the conference, my femme style is what I have chosen to do with my womanness. I can taste it; I can feel my breasts and they aren't a burden. It isn't anything I am apologizing for. It isn't what makes me vulnerable on the streets; it's the thing that works. It is the thing someone wants. It becomes a gift rather than a cause for whole kinds of oppression, and that is why I love them so deeply.

M: Yes, absolutely. When they put their hands on you and that sound comes out, that *ahhh*...

A: You could die for that sound, for that look. There are textures I have never felt on my skin that they can create. It is a shocking thing to be unequivocally wanted for your femaleness in this culture. That's why femmes love their butches so much, but it is a real trick, because you are with a woman and what does it mean for her not to feel female? I mean, not that you are making her not that female, but what does it mean, how does that gender dysfunction of hers play into it, because she doesn't want to feel that intensely female? Or there is a real question about what that means, because she has had to perceive herself in masculinity [*sic*] in order to want you, so the heat isn't the same on her side. I mean that you may really be right, that it is a femme attitude of adoring a butch that is the weight of the other side.

M: Worship.

A: Complete worship.

J: I can spend hours looking at the side of Deb's face as she drives the car; there is adoration, there is a thank-you for making things safer. It's not my words, my way to say words like *gender dysfunction*. I feel that what they are trying to do is have power, and women do not have models for having power, and so they derived their own model. I am trying to say that as femmes we found a way to create a sexual space for ourselves that made us different from the traditional woman and yet let us honor our women selves. We exiled ourselves from one land but created another. I have a feeling that butches started with a certain clarity also, and that clarity — I can't speak for them, but I can hypothesize — was about how to be powerful in their bodies and their visions of themselves, the same way we wanted to be in our femme, giving selves. The language binds us. I am not sure it is masculinity, even if they say it is and it looks like it. They too chose exile from gender to be another kind of creation. I used to think that *butch-femme* was one word, one reality, and now I know that even if I were alone for the rest of my life, I would be a femme. I would miss my delights, however.

Madeline Davis

Roles? I don't know anyone who's "playing"

A letter to my femme sisters

April 1982

Dear Amber and Joan:
  Sisters — finally to sit with women I truly feel are sisters. What an experience making "the femme tapes!" Our mutual hysteria at finding someone else who recognized that hunger, that desperate need, that desire to be "fucked senseless" and to know that we have, do, and would put up with some incredible shit to get it. The tears we held back, covering our mouths and lowering our eyes at all the energy we have expended trying to fit in, break out, mold others, please them, please us ... god ... how often we have actually shed those angry, frustrated, sad, and often even fulfilled tears. Femmes we are — looking weird but somehow straight. We can pass, and it is so hard to explain that we can hate our ability to pass. It has been both our allure and our betrayal, because we are dykes — women who are absolutely crazed for women — and how scary we are to our butches and even to ourselves. What do we do with it all? Struggles within struggles within struggles.

We join a movement for support, and who understands us but each other? We celebrate "them," their butchiness, because they take the shit on the streets for us. And to them, who are we? Beautiful, soft, sensual witches they have somehow found in the night. And are we real? We have hardly been introduced.

More. I want more of you both. I need you. I have been so lonely for so long and have not known it until now. Perhaps this is something like Third World lesbians coming together or S/M dykes finding one another. Whatever it is, we are the root of something beautiful and powerful. I have such hope for us — to be able to allay the fears of the women we have loved and continue to love and desire so incredibly; to find our own special femme strength that is surely not "playing," but, as for our butches, is truly

268

who we are; to know somehow inside that we, too, are Amazon warriors fighting ancient battles — even the battle to love our flirtatious, seductive, calculating, knowing, innate femme power.

Had we the energy that day, the five hours we spent could have gone on for five days. We will have the energy. It is a special fight all our own. Learning trust is so hard. I think it was easier for me, because I could leave the scene of my/our exposure and return home to a city in which I have no real femme friends I trust, no femmes with whom to share ... not the passion but the passion for the passion. But I can't really ever leave you. If we can die who we are, we can also live it and explore it with bravery. We can tear ourselves apart so that we can make ourselves whole. We need one another too much to let it go.

I love you both,
Madeline

Madeline Davis

Epilogue, nine years later

Dear Joan and Amber:
I've just reread our conversation for the fifth time. Nine years ... it hardly seems possible. We were all in one kind of romantic or sexual mess or another. Even so, we were pretty damn clear about ourselves. I think what struck me most was the depth of our loneliness. Here we are, three women who look straight, walking down the street harboring "thoughts." I remember once, years ago, seeing a woman walk into the suburban library where I worked. She had on net stockings and a black miniskirt and lots of makeup. Something about her turned me on so intensely that I had to retreat to the back room. Know how I felt? I felt queer! That's what we are. Women who look and act like girls and who desire girls. We're just the queerest of the queers. It makes me laugh, but it also makes me feel so different. For butches, their masculinity makes them seem more "normal." We're kind of like those women in the "lesbian" porn movies — long hair, lipstick — except we're real. We desire everything about our butches — even their womanness. I think that's pretty queer.

In answer to the question "What does a femme do when she's fifty?" well, here we are! Doing anything different, ladies? No — me neither. Facing rough times. A little achier. A little more weary. But still all of who we are and evermore shall be. They told us femmes turn butch as they get older. Maybe more assertive, less able to put up with shit, more able to go for what we want or need. But it's all femme. It remains our task to make the world more beautiful for them and, in turn, for ourselves. And what is their task? To be nicer to us, I think. We're very special, a rare breed. And there aren't many of us around. We deserve some excellent treatment!

The more I think and write about this, the more I miss you. The Movement is a bit more "liberal" with us lately, but they still don't seem to get it. We're still so different. And it really makes me angry. Frankly, I don't understand not being role identified. Sure, I believe them when they say that they are not, but it all seems so "the same" to me and sort of boring. They're too busy holding hands and swaying and singing about "filling

270

up and spilling over" (or is that throwing up and falling over?). Well, there you have it. My reaction to being treated like a dinosaur by my "sisters." I'm fifty. I can afford to be mad!

So, where am I now with all of this? I've been very fortunate to find a lover who totally appreciates exactly who I am. What a wonder, not to have to change or adjust for someone. I still engage in the usual battles about butch-femme when I have the energy. Lately, a dear friend — an old-time butch — told me she still holds that femmes aren't real lesbians. I was driving the car when she said it, and she's lucky we didn't swerve into a plate glass window! Actually I do understand — I don't agree, but I understand. I still believe that we are the queerest of all, and although there's really no status in it, we're mighty proud of it.

And, Joan, thank you from the bottom of my frilly little heart for putting this book together. For lots of us, it will be a room of our own.

Love to both of you,
Madeline

Jeanne Cordova

Butches, lies, and feminism[1]

> First they came for the Communists,
> But I didn't speak because I wasn't a Communist.
> Next they came for the Jews,
> But I said nothing because I wasn't a Jew.
> Then they came for the Catholics,
> But I remained silent because I was a Protestant.
> Finally they came for me,
> But by that time there was no one left to speak.
>
> —Martin Niemoeller (Germany, 1944)

Someday they'll come for the butches. Who will speak for us? Passion keeps me alive. When I cease to live audaciously — that day I'll die. Being a butch has been the most troublesome and most delicious experience of my life. Being a butch — like being a woman, a lesbian, having a soul — is not something I can dismiss. I believe butches are born, not made. Since this is my birthright, I choose to glory in it. When I comb my hair back and strut out my front door, being butch is my hallelujah.

❖

As a butch I've walked a hundred alleys, seen a thousand stares. The question in those eyes is always the same: "Are you a man or a woman?" I've come to know that the hate I thought I saw in those stares is really fear. The cold, cruel eyebrows are really pleading, "What are you, if you are not male or female? I cannot know you as neither; I cannot understand you. I hate you because I don't know you."

Being a coconut butch (brown on the outside, white on the inside) from an upper-middle-class family, I was spared most of the direct hits my butch pals took on the blue-collar streets of East Los Angeles. In the late sixties, I worked in the prison system, where butches were vigorously stripsearched by male guards. Out on the streets, I would have many close calls and one near hit.

272

On the outskirts of feminism in '72, I stopped at a traffic signal next to a dyke bar in North Hollywood. The car in back of me repeatedly bumped my fender. Furious, I jumped out of my car, marched back, and leaned my flattop into the driver's window demanding, "You blind, drunk, or just stupid, Mister? How about staying off my fender?"

His beer-glazed eyes registered me. "Fuck you, bull dyke!" He jabbed a fist in my face.

"Don't you just wish..." I laughed.

Just then the light turned green and I rushed back to my car. Sweeping around the corner and into the parking lot of Joanie Presents, I parked. As I walked toward the bar, I gulped. Archie Bunker had followed me. He was coming at me with a crowbar.

The goddess was with me that night. The man thundered past me and smashed his crowbar into my car's rear window.

He was in a rage because this bull dyke was neither male nor female. I'd eclipsed his gender boundaries.

❖

Society demands that gender define existence. Humankind is agender-phobic. No one wants to answer the question "What is a butch?" because few languages in the world have words to define those who stand between the genders.

"To role or not to role?" has never been the question. This twenty-year lesbian debate is moot. There have always been butches and femmes. Sappho was a femme top.

Feminists don't want to define butch because any true definition of butch must include recognizing yang energy as positive. For two decades, all male energy has been damned as destructive, invasive — wrong. I believe yang energy is also implementive, manifestive, and, yes, necessary.

To me, a butch is a recombinant mixture of yin and yang energy. Like recombinant DNA, a butch is an elusive, ever-resynthesizing energy field, a lesbian laser that knits the universes of male and female. Some have said feminist butch *is an oxymoron. I say it's a paradox. A feminist butch is a dyke who has survived the Cuisinart blades of feminist rhetoric. To survive being butch you have to have been born with an ornery spirit.*

❖

The second of twelve children, I was four when my mother, Joan Francis McGuinness, passed by the back porch and saw me sitting on the grass, talking to myself. As she tells her favorite story, "Jeanne was holding one foot in her hand and she said, 'The devil tells me to take off my shoes. My mommy tells me not to take off my shoes. But I'm going to take them off anyway.'"

My parents failed to appreciate my ornery spirit, but I was always thankful that neither of them were slouch potatoes. My mother bore life long labor under Catholicism, her driven husband, and more than her share of the title "vice president" of every business my father dumped on her. My bootstrap West Point father made Catholicism look like a democracy. A medical discharge aborted his military career but did not save my siblings and me from having to rise from our bunk beds each morning to his reveille, "Sunrise in the swamps. Up and at 'em!" I was born with my mother's flair — "Dare to do it differently" — and my father's arrogance — "You can be anything in the world!"

Except a lesbian, except a butch.

❖

A playground dyke, I ignored my older sister, who floated rose petals down the storm drains and held court over "Miss America" pageants. I preferred romping through "Bamboo Land," building forts with my baby brother, Bill. He and I gathered the neighborhood boys in the 'burbs of Orange Grove fifties California and galloped away the years of childhood playing Lone Ranger, hardball, and King of the Mountain. I was Bill's Arthur, he my Lancelot, as we conquered West Covina.

Bra fever

The day I became a girl, my life was over.

"This is the stupidest thing I ever saw." I flung the bra out my bedroom window and screamed at my mother, "You can't expect me to wear that. It's meant for a horse."

Several years earlier, my mother had chased me through the streets demanding that I put on a shirt. It was sad enough not to be able to cavort topless in the summer's heat like Bill, but now, this bra outrage! I'd heard my sister and my girlfriends talking about "the day I'd get to wear a bra." They'd made it sound as if donning the new garment signaled a wondrous rite of passage. Clearly, I'd misunderstood. At first I thought my mother had simply bought me the wrong thing. When my mind finally accepted that *this* was a bra, I felt crazy. There was nothing wonderful about this harness. Were my sister and my girlfriends wrong, or was I wrong?

❖

I wasn't cut out to be a girl. This might sound contradictory, since I was obviously cast with two breasts and accessories for the part, but somewhere inside I always thought my body was lying to me. If I liked all the things that "only boys" got to do, then somehow I must be a boy. Before feminism came along and said, "Girls can be anything they want to be," I had no mental options save thinking I was a boy. Reality had set in with no explanation.

❖

All I knew then was that "the bra" was the beginning of the end. It portended strange things. Like changing your personality when boys came around. And acting stupid so that they would come around.

In high school I quickly discovered I could kill two birds with one stupid act by hanging around my girlfriends. While boys stumbled over themselves flocking to the dollhouse, I'd enjoy female company and appear to be heterosexually correct.

This thinking was partially successful. I acquired the friendship of the best-looking girl in my class. I would later learn that becoming the confidante of the prom queen is one of the few privileges doled out to teenaged baby butches. Prom queen types, themselves sick of boys, like to hide behind the creased shirt of a little dyke girlfriend. Then, too, we were no competition. We baby butches offered what they *really* wanted, adoration without pawing.

This stratagem worked. I spent the weekends with Miss Prom Queen and her entourage. But I gave myself away with other aberrant behavior. I spent my school week with Miss Cukras, my softball coach. I was obsessed with softball and Miss Cukras. In my junior year, when Miss Cukras left my school for another assignment, I became visibly depressed. Mother noticed. She also observed that I didn't wear my bra when playing softball and that I spaced my dates out to one per month and was home "so early!" from them.

❖

Years later, I would learn that my mother noticed a lot of "odd" things. But in my adolescent savoir faire I was sure she knew less than I. I was a Catholic and Catholics believed J.F.K. was the Second Coming. What did I know? As the cacophony of puberty clanged, I began to absorb a vague sense that something was very wrong.

❖

As I searched for an identity, my alienation deepened. Standing out at shortstop, ever vigilant for grounders, I tried to unscramble the plays in my inner diamond. Why didn't I really *belong* to any of the in-crowds? I was smart and funny, so the brains accepted me. The socialites had to let me come to their parties because Sharon, the prom queen, was my best friend. And I was a hero to the girls' varsity club because I pitched well. But the brains thought the girl jocks were weird. The girls' varsity never debated Socrates. And the boys couldn't even spell *debate*.

My mother invented butch oppression. She clouded my adolescence with Catholic confusions like "Don't play with boys" and "Why don't you have a boyfriend?" Her ultimate torture came in my junior year: "If you

275

expect to go to camp this summer, I want you to enter the Junior Miss Contest ... and win ... like your sister."

The cabaret stage lights slapped the platform runway and my tightly bound breasts. The green light signaled my turn as I hyperventilated in my corseted yellow formal. The runway looked longer than a Concorde escape path. I'd never make it. My mother's words replayed in my head: "Put one leg in front of the other; swing your hip all the way around each time." She called this "poise." I called it disabled. Gratefully, I suffer posttraumatic stress syndrome and cannot to this day remember how Jeanne Cordova ran the Junior Miss gauntlet and lived.

❖

Today I argue with my lover, "Are butches more oppressed than femmes, or vice versa?" But back then there was no debate. High school years are much harder on butches. Femmes passed as straight, even to themselves. Butches can't. We stick out like G.I. Joes in Barbie Land.

❖

The contest convinced me there was no place for me. I didn't fit. Except on the pitcher's mound or at shortstop, where I was alone.

I finished high school with Sharon, striding with her over to the boys' quad every day. None of them seemed interested in me, but I didn't care, because I got to comb Sharon's hair every recess in the girls' bathroom. I never brushed my own. I tried to explain to Sharon that constantly combing one's hair was vain. My mother was always reading to us from a book that clearly said, "Vanity, of vanities, all then is vanity, but to love God and serve him alone." Sharon said she'd never read *The Imitation of Christ*. When I offered my antivanity rationale as a defense for the state of my hair, my mother clarified, "Jeanne, you are confusing the secular and spiritual worlds."

Apparently, I remained confused. I entered the convent directly after high school.

Convent boot camp

If I hadn't been raised in the babbling cloister of my family's naivete I might have understood what Mother General meant when she said my induction test scores indicated that I had "a problem with authority." I might have realized then, instead of later, that I was an uppity dyke.

I arrived on Entrance Day wearing my James Dean wraparound sunglasses, sincerely believing that the warriorship of my patron saint (butch dyke Jeanne d' Arc) was spiritually motivated. I left the holy sisterhood one year later thoroughly edified by the carnal motivations and wraparound body of novice Sister Marie Immaculata. My boot camp in the sisterhood of the Immaculate Heart of Mary (detailed in my autobiographical novel, *Kicking the Habit) did* clarify my lesbianism. It did not further my butch identity. Once again, I was out in the secular world, but with no habit to shroud this unpenitent butch body.

Leaving the convent, I felt wondrously liberated. I was a lesbian! At long last, I knew who I was. Unfortunately, no one else did.

Somehow I landed at Cal State L.A. in a boy-girl-boy-girl student housing complex. (I later deduced that my mother had deliberately steered me into this coed purgatory.) I wandered this wasteland, subjecting myself to another year of trauma in the heterosexual zone.

Since the opportunity was at hand, I had decided to try heterosexuality. I reasoned that since I loved making love with a woman, and fully intended to pursue them for the rest of my life, perhaps I should test my decision with an empirical experiment — a man.

Paul was a flop in bed, but he was an excellent role model. An Italian New Yorker who had no interest in anything more sociological than the girls he lived next to, Paulo Bonaventura was an adorable rake. A jockey by night and a probation officer by day, Paul was exactly what Cordova — my budding butch persona — wanted to be when she grew up. I watched how Paul seduced women in Las Vegas and carefully researched quality men's shops for the latest in gentlemen's attire — for him, of course.

After six months, I remembered my original hypothesis, and I finally made it with my jockey. Peggy Lee sang "Is That All There Is?" as Paul answered the question for me. All I can say about sex with Paul is that I felt rather queer.

❖

Men want desperately to believe that lesbians either hate men or just haven't found the right one. Paul was everything a woman would want — sexy, gentle, caring. Still boring. I suppose it's too hard for men to admit the simple truth: for lesbians, sex with them is like peanut butter compared to caviar, like "The Donna Reed Show" competing with Gone with the Wind.

❖

I put Paul on a plane to Sicily, forgetting at the airport to ask, "Will you be back?" Returning to my silent, lonely apartment, I lay on my couch for weeks racking my brain. Where could I meet other homosexuals? In desperation I put an ad in the local *Los Angeles Free Press:* "Young, Lonely, Gay, Woman. Would like to meet similar for friendship. Please call."

One week later, "Similar" showed up on my doorstep with red, three-inch fingernails and platinum blonde hair covering an ass urgently in need of covering. But Toni took one look at me and said, "Baby Jail Bait, you're no kinda dyke," and was gone before I could even ask her if she were a real lesbian.

The following morning I called every Parks and Recreation listing in the Los Angeles phone book. Where would I find homosexual girls? On the softball field, of course! One month later, a few days past my twentieth birthday, I was at a dyke bar in Pico Rivera. I was in paradise.

❖

Unbeknownst to this would-be gay virgin, Pico Rivera was the home of the biggest, baddest dykes in East L.A. In Mexican-American culture, the dykes were butch, and the femmes weren't. But what did I, ex-nun, know of such things? I was a "gay girl." I thought the life was simple.

❖

It was the summer of '68 and my contemporaries were "on strike," marching down the Sunset Strip in bell-bottoms and beads screaming, "Out Now!"

I didn't want out. I'd just found my way in.

Judy had picked me up on the first day of softball practice. Standing five feet barefooted, Judy worked for the phone company and thought "abstract thinking" meant absentminded. But Judy was the cutest thing I ever saw. At twenty, cute is enough. Judy wore men's black stud-toed wing tips, a frosted ducktail, and low-waisted trousers. I thought this was the standard gay girl's uniform, and of course, I wanted one. And I wanted Judy.

Yet, one hot spring night six months later, as I sat with Judy's arm around me at Tullies, I absentmindedly discovered the truth behind Judy's uniform. Through the smoke, I observed the girls at the bar. The same three dykes always lit the cigarettes of their partners. Their partners sat on stools while the dykes stood. The tough-looking ones paid for the drinks and they slung their arms around the seated girls.

"That'll be $3.50 for the last round." The waitress stopped in front of us. Judy lifted her arm off my neck and reached for her wallet.

The next Saturday, Judy took me shopping with her to Sears. As she strode past the women's department, I was confused. When she began ruffling through the shirts in the men's section, I was hooked.

Ever since my bra days, I had hated shopping. Shopping with Mom meant more torture garments. Shopping with Mother Superior meant a new set of rosary beads. Shopping with Judy was a delight. My fingers brushed the flannel shirts and explored the sharp creases of zip-front trousers. The muted, solid colors spoke to my soul! Here were clothes a girl could wear. Judy flew into a rage as it became evident I was buying clothes for myself, not her. I quickly began to realize that Judy was the cigarette lighter, not the lightee. And so was I. Judy and I broke up the next day. She yelled at me, "You're no kinda femme." But I stuck through the day-long argument and obtained a frantic, but complete, education on "butch-femme."

❖

My relationship with Judy also showed me that my parents thought being butch was at once more acceptable and more reprehensible than being femme. That Christmas my father literally threw Judy out of his home. He wouldn't abide "that kind of woman." In the decades that followed, bringing my femme lovers home would be easier. My parents simply denied that my feminine girlfriends were lesbians. Me? I was harder to get rid of.

❖

"The gay life" was becoming more complicated. Judy was right. I was no kinda femme, but I didn't know much about being a butch either. Clearly, I had missed something critical. I would have to learn a new set of behaviors: how to treat a lady, how to get a date, how to take her to bed.

School had always come easily to me, but no course came as naturally as "Butch 101" (part of a curriculum that was available to any baby butch making the bar scene). Abruptly I switched bars, giving myself a tabula rasa for my new identity. I studied the clothes of the butches at Tommy's in the slums of Baldwin Park, and I frequented Sears and bought accordingly. I stood in front of my mirror practicing how to knot a tie. A week before the Halloween of 1969, I broke down in frustration and called Brother Bill.

"I've got a costume party." I explained my tie problem. Bill knew I was gay and "no kinda femme," but he didn't understand what a butch was.

❖

As a youngster, I'd been my father's substitute son until the illusion crumbled at puberty. Bill, my junior by two years, was right there to pick up the spoils. As "son," he got my father's business, my mother's love, the mantle of the family name. As "daughter," I became superfluous in the scheme of family power. I learned early that men had what I wanted: money, power, and women. And I could do it my way, by being a butch.

❖

Finally, in pinstripes and cholo boots, Cordova as Butch was ready to venture back into East L.A. I was primed for real practice. That's when Charlene, the only straight woman I've ever wooed, sashayed into my life. A former model, she was the most ravishing, silken-night hair-down-to-her-ass beauty I'd ever seen in Gayland. She later told me that she really wanted a man and that she had mistakenly wandered into Tullies that night having just broken up with her boyfriend. But Butch 101 also taught, "There's no such thing as a straight girl — only virgins looking for the right girl." "Being a dyke" was "being a man." Being tough, or at least convincingly *in control*, defined the choreography. Naturally, I didn't take Charlene's protestations seriously. I knew I was the "right girl" for her. I followed Butch 101 steps, convinced that Charlene and I were the perfect couple.

THE PERSISTENT DESIRE

Six months later, Charlene ran off with her male theater director. I advanced to Butch 201: "How to tell the difference between a femme and a straight girl. *Before.*" This lesson was more sophisticated. Charlene had treated me like a man. Butching out for her hadn't made me feel close to her.

❖

Much to my surprise, I didn't feel any more natural being treated like a man than I did being treated like a woman. I thought I hated being a woman, that I was really a man trapped in a woman's body, a transsexual. At the wizened age of twenty-one, I'd nearly fulfilled my ambition. In the eyes of my girlfriend and friends I'd almost become a man. But in this new role I remained foreign to myself. Worse yet, it didn't work. Charlene left.

❖

Butch 201 taught me that a real lesbian femme was a gay girl who wanted her butch to look masculine but *be* a woman. This gave me new pause for thought. How could I be a man and a woman at the same time, in one body? Was this possible?

The day I discovered that my Cal State Abnormal Psych text called me "gender dysfunctional," I brought my text home. In a furious burst of rare culinary endeavor, I flung butter in a frying pan and threw Abnormal Psych on the burner. Moments later, Judy came flying out of the bedroom, gasping, "What's that horrible smell?"

"I'm sending Abnormal Psych back to hell where it belongs," I answered calmly, spatula in hand. "I'm frying this heresy like a good Catholic."

❖

It would take gay liberation and feminism another several years to show me that "gender dysfunction" really didn't exist; that I was not wrong, they were. My parents and Catholicism had taught me to accept the gender dichotomy. The patriarchy had created this "disease" by rigidly classifying male and female behavior according to anatomy. By this definition, my little-girl-bodied, male-behaving self was "sick." Insisting that the world was flat, as millions once did, also led to equally unhealthy conclusions about the universe.

I would eventually become a political activist, because my ornery spirit knew, long before my mind could explain, that our gay place in the world had been fundamentally misdefined. If men and women weren't divided and gender were accepted as fluid, I wouldn't be perceived as deviating from a nonexistent norm. And neither would the other one or two billion queers like me. I wasn't a transsexual. I was simply individual, gender and psyche, a recombinant dyke.

As a baby butch revolutionary in the seventies, I would soon learn that society defined "normal" to codify how those in power wanted to their world to be. "Normal" had nothing to do with Catholicism, or even God, but everything to do with power and money.

Being a butch was not the world's idea of being powerful or successful. It was a wonder I survived long enough to find my own power.

Butch Code limitations

Feminism came to my rescue.

I enrolled at UCLA for my junior year, which meant moving across town, leaving Pico, and leaving my buddies who worked for Pacific Telephone by day and drank by night. But my wardrobe of ties was now complete and I'd managed, with some Ivy League suspenders and a host of L.L. Bean blazers, to set my own butch style. I was working full-time in Watts and was finally within sight of my degree in social work. My career plans were clear. Like Cesar Chavez, I was going to save the ghetto. All I needed was a new bar and a new girl.

I found the former quickly enough by joining the softball team at the 7th Circle, a seedy little dive that despite its reputation as a "reds" (we're not talking politics) bar became my weekend home. Home was completed the night I met Gayle there and took her to my one-bedroom in the Fairfax district (later to become West Hollywood).

Doing the swagger thing at the Circle, I protected Gayle from unwarranted advances, threw a few punches to establish my territory, and refined the codes of Butch 301: honor your dyke buddies, it instructed, don't make it with a buddy's girl and expect to keep her friendship. Don't flaunt your one-night stands in your girlfriend's face — make sure your friends don't either. Don't trust ki-kis (switch-hitters who flip-flopped from butch to femme depending on who they were trying to make). And *above all*, never let on if you find yourself sexually attracted to another butch.

The Butch Code was obviously a limited worldview. I grew bored. I didn't need a twelve-step program to see the ravages of alcohol on the faces of my sage butch mentors. I didn't then agree with my generation about marching in the streets against our country's war (I'd spent the sixties in the cloister and in Pico; I didn't even know where Vietnam was). I had no political consciousness, but I was frustrated and pissed off. I wanted being queer to mean more than spending my life in a bar.

❖

On October 3, 1970, I walked into my first "homosexual meeting." I hadn't heard about Stonewall, but I knew I was in the right place. A stone butch named Carole sat at the head table, and the whole room buzzed with talk about "religion and the homophile." Six months later, I succeeded Carole as president of the Los Angeles chapter of the Daughters of Bilitis and opened the first lesbian center in the city. History had surged forward. By that time we talked about "gay rights."

THE PERSISTENT DESIRE

One day I found a leaflet crammed in the mailbox of our DOB Center. It was from another organized group of gay girls, the Lesbian-Feminists. I'd heard about them through the dyke grapevine. No one knew what their name meant, they were reported to be "wierdos," and they were known to hang out at a center for women. This sounded ominous, but the leaflet gave an address and said, "All women welcome." I decided queer unity must prevail; I would visit their territory.

Feminism and the butch closet

It was not love at first sight. Listening to my "sisters" that first night was one of the most disorienting experiences of my life. These women *forbade* use of the word *girl*. No one flirted with anyone. No one even asked my name, much less noticed my new wing tips. The Lesbian-Feminists did nothing but talk for *five* solid hours. And they weren't even discussing an outing or anything tangible. They were spouting some convoluted religious politic. It had to be religious, because they were all intensely righteous. I thought I knew the religions of the world, but this was a new one. Apparently it was also very ancient, because one of them proclaimed their "matriarchy" was as "old as history itself."

By midnight I was convinced I'd received the wrong information. These girls weren't lesbians. There were no butches. Many of them looked vaguely feminine, in the hippie style of the day. A clunky sandal seemed to be their shoe of choice, but none of them wore makeup. I knew no bona fide femme would go out in public without makeup or heels.

Concluding that they were some kind of crackpot sect, I rose to leave. As I stomped across the wood floor, enjoying how the chains on my boots clanged through their meanderings, the one called "Radical Rita Right On" shouted at me, "What kind of lesbian are you?"

❖

I began to wonder.

Feminism healed the core contradictions of my life. Feminism said I was clearly a woman, but that I could be any kind of woman I wanted to be, and that in fact I was "an amazon," a kind of proud, free woman who refused to be defined by the rules of patriarchy. This sounded great. Certainly more enhancing — and more workable — than my former analysis of myself as an unrequited transsexual.

Feminism defined "the enemy" I had been looking for all my life. I knew "they" had it wrong about gender dysfunction. I knew "they" wanted me dead. But I also knew that the enemy wasn't the military-industrial complex. In these groups I recognized dear old Dad. I knew these folks only wanted money. Issues about gender were deeper and had to do with basic definitions of male and female. These issues, I suspected, had to do with power. My new philosophy explained why the enemy hated queers so much that they'd kill us in our own bars. Feminism explained "sexism" as the economics of world power through the control of women's sexuality. *Men* were the enemy — the political system called the patriarchy.

"The androgynous imperative"[2]

Almost against my will, the early seventies turned me into a "lesbian-feminist." Feminism tore apart my butch identity. A former Catholic, I could smell heresy before I heard it. Feminism was heretical to "the gay world." Feminism struck at the core. Feminism said, "A lesbian is the rage of all women condensed to the point of explosion." I had no idea what this meant, but I knew it wasn't Webster's. I came to embrace and love lesbian-feminism, because I knew these weirdos were right. Innately, I'd always felt lesbianism was more than sexual behavior. Lesbianism embodied a political rage, an ornery core.

The new blasphemy attacked my trappings as well as my core. Feminism eliminated dirty dancing: leading my partner was "heterosexist"; bumping and grinding was plain ol' "sexist." The Lesbian-Feminists said it was wrong for femmes to wear makeup, patriarchal to indulge in monogamy, and "male-identified" (a mortal sin) for butches to wear ties. In fact, the Lesbian-Feminists insisted there was no such thing as butch-femme. It was a "heterosexual cop-out." (By then I knew that *anything* heterosexual was anathema.) These frizzy-headed, unshaven interlopers decreed that "womyn" who acted like men (butches) or like girls (femmes) were not even lesbians! Feminism's only analysis of "butch" was as synonymous with "male" — which meant thoroughly politically incorrect. I didn't have a political analysis to explain my butch self, so I gave myself up to "the larger struggle."

❖

It wasn't too hard to adopt the new uniform of my faith. I already had hiking boots, 501s, and several denim jackets. (All I needed was a few political buttons on my chest.) This had not been my everyday outfit, but I had to admit, denim wore well for the decade. It was cheaper than replenishing my tie-and-suspender collection. So, on the outside, I became an instant androgyne.

❖

One might well ask: Why would a self-respecting, adamant butch dyke ever buy such crap? Wasn't I settled in my identity, clear about who was a lesbian and who was not, happy in my bed and in my head?

❖

Obviously not.

THE PERSISTENT DESIRE

When I returned to DOB and tried to explain feminism, my chapter thought I'd taken leave of my senses. I intuited that the secret plot to vote me out of office at the next election was born that evening in *their* rage at a president who obviously wanted to change their way of life.

A butch without metal

The dress code was hard on Gayle, whom the Lesbian-Feminists labeled a "female impersonator" because of her polished nails and make-up. Gayle said she wanted nothing to do with a women's "liberation" movement that bound her.

My own chains had become something of a problem. Doing reconnaissance on my favorite chain-link black leather boots, Radical Rita Right On had advised me, "You can't expect to retain a position of leadership with male-identified chain on your shoes." My dark night of butchdom came one evening as, with pliers, I pried off the gold chains slung around the ankles of my boots. Looking up at my bedroom wall, I read Judy Grahn's poster poem, "a common woman is as common as a common loaf of bread." Snapping the chain off my second boot, I almost cried and wondered if Grahn's persona, Edward the Dyke, would have liked my boots. I reached into the back of my closet, pulled a piece of black velvet out of my sex-toys box, and gently wrapped my chains in it.

Reshod, I stood in requiem in my boots. They were naked. I was stripped. I'd spent my life learning how to take my power through my feet. I'd drawn strength through the ground, through my boots. Felt the energy shoot out through my words, my hands. Now, a link in my butch power chain was severed. What did it mean to live as a butch without chains?

❖

Shortly thereafter, Gayle and I filed for divorce on the grounds of political incompatibility. Like thousands of others, she had been turned off by feminism's dogma before she heard its deeper truth. In the divorce, Gayle got our toy box. She said I wouldn't be needing it, because, "obviously, lesbian-feminists don't know how to fuck."

❖

But lesbian-feminists were adroit in fucking each other over. Robin Morgan was right: sisterhood was powerful.

On a drizzly Los Angeles night in February 1972, I sat with my lesbian-feminist self and dozens of similars. We were tête-à-tête with a large group of straight feminists for a "Straight-Gay Dialogue." I hadn't yet figured out why feminism was always misnaming the obvious. Radical Rita Right On said, "We are redefining our sexist language." I figured that, like me, everyone secretly knew that these "Straight-Gay Dialogues" were

284

Deborah on Eighth Street, NYC: Evolution of an image
1954—Totally acceptable
1964—Perfectly understandable
1974—Somewhat questionable
1984—Politically incorrect
1994—Role model

a euphemism for "bringing the straight ladies out," as my old Pico crowd would have put it. Language was such a problem in those days.

I was sitting there nervously slapping my hiking boots together, probably lost in a retrograde daze, when I heard a voice call out, "Are there any butches in the room?" Subconsciously, I shot my hand up.

A hush swept the room and brought me into the present. I panicked. There was only one other woman in the room with her hand raised. "Damn!" I swore to myself, recalling the leader's question as I felt my face turn as blue as my denim. I'd been nailed by the androgynous imperative!

"This meeting is for women-identified women *only*. All butches must leave," the leader decreed. Having come to accept that all discussions in the women's movement were collectively decided except when someone actually decided something, I stood and strode.

"This is politics. Don't take it personally." The older butch slammed the door in back of us as she put her arm around my shoulder. "They'll change their minds tomorrow anyway. Come home with me. I know just what you need."

I took Butch 401 from this older butch mentor, and became the first graduate of her school, "The Robin Tyler Academy for Butches." Robin showed me my first dildo (lab included), butch positions for three-ways,

285

and how to top a butch. This postgraduate work was especially valuable, if not politically consistent, because in the early seventies feminism taught that sleeping across roles was sexist. If you were butch, your "egalitarian," politically correct partner had to be another butch. The same held for femmes. This queer situation became the basis for the now infamous "short, meaningful relationship." I tried it. This one of the few butch lessons I flunked.

❖

My twenty-year friendship with Robin Tyler was born that day in the "wander underground" of a movement that didn't understand its own. As butches we organized marches for "choice," wondering when ours would come. Robin and I and a growing cadre of closet butches banded together to fight for our identities. Butch bonding was also powerful. No one understood a sexual outlaw like another sexual outlaw. If the personal really was political, my personal reality proved there had to be such a thing as a feminist butch.

The Jaded Butch League

No local feminist rag, including my own *Lesbian Tide*, would accept an ad for our political organization, the Jaded Butch League. So we organized secretly. At JBL meetings, we pondered (theoretically, of course) the political paradox of why so many lesbian-feminists hated us but wanted to sleep with us. Our *top* theoretician, Yolanda Retter (who publicly called herself "Yoli the Terrible" just to scare the white-girl feminists with her Latin anger), helped us safely discover our own sexism. With the added motivation of trying to be politically as well as sexually acceptable to our newfound lesbian-feminist lovers, we painfully peeled off some of the layers of our sexism. Objective reality was also changing. It was impossible to retain any sense of "femme as weak" when your lover was shouting at you nightly through a bullhorn on Hollywood Boulevard.

Nevertheless, lesbian-feminist debate over "role-playing" raged through the seventies, placing a strong third on feminism's politically incorrect Top Ten — just behind "sadomasochistic woman hating" and "monogamy." Feminism makes strange bedfellows.

Steel-magnolia femmes

Not all was bleak for me during the decade. There were pockets of feminists who accepted me as a butch. One such dominant entity was the Radical Feminist Therapy Collective, who ran the Westside Women's Center — collectively, of course. In the midseventies, the RFTC defined lesbian-feminism in Southern California. I was not a therapist, but I was publicly redistricting the human condition (*and* sleeping with one of its members), so I was admitted to this august body of all-*femme* "super-dykes." (Politically correct lesbian-feminists were "dykes" — not to be confused with the politically incorrect "butches.") During my stint with the RFTC, I came to believe that the Blessed Virgin must have been a lesbian-feminist femme. Mary, too, was gorgeous, paradoxical, didn't sleep with men, and gave up her male son.

Through the RFTC, with Gahan Kelly, Jane Herman, Judy Freespirit, and Gudrun Fonfa — leaders who birthed the concepts of fat liberation, feminist therapy, and looksism — I learned that not all feminists hated butches. The collective coined the term *post-power femme*, which meant a feminist, femme-identified lesbian who was so secure in her power that she didn't have to deny her femininity. These were the steel magnolias of lesbian-feminism, the true mothers of invention, before whom this butch was — just fine!

Raging butch publisher: The *Lesbian Tide*

Meanwhile, life on my own newspaper, the *Lesbian Tide*, was a study in lesbian contradiction and feminist paradox.

How did a raging butch get to be publisher of the nation's premiere lesbian-feminist paper of the seventies? Like much of the turbulent seventies, it was a dialectic accident. I snuck in the back door.

In 1971, when DOB abbreviated my "communist" (Women against the War) presidency, they offered me the booby prize of remaining on the Board of Officers by holding the lowest position — newsletter editor. I accepted. I'd been editor of my high school paper; I knew the power of the press. From here, as Marx would say, it was just a hop, skip, and a jump as this editor collided with herstory. I changed the name of my four-page mimeograph from the *DOB Newsletter* to the *Lesbian Tide*, because I could *feel* the tide of herstory changing. The whole world was.

Realizing its mistake, the DOB membership soon voted me and my communist tide out of the organization. Politically, I'd been gone for months already. But I was now free to invite my lesbian-feminist soul mates onto the staff.

The mates of the not-so-collective Tide Collective reflected the infra-chaos of our movement. In addition to my paradoxical self, there was an archetypal lesbian-come-lately (from heterosexuality) feminist femme, co-editor Sharon McDonald; our very own politically correct Vassar white girl, Shirl Buss (who later processed her own organization, White Women against White Women against White Women against Racism, to death); an old-gay femme, Barbara Gehrke, a former navy woman who thought women's liberation meant changing laws to make women free (poor dear!); and a bisexual, Cheri Lesh, who also must have crept in some window simply because she was a great writer. Lesh taught me that there were indeed a small percentage of human beings who did not find gender a factor in sexual attraction.

My ten-year indenture, 1970 to 1980, to the *Tide* and this outrageous family of women helped me survive lesbian-feminism. With our Vassar analysis editor, Buss, I completed my studies in lesbian-feminist language: *androgynous* was a synonym for *butch*; cheating on your lover was called "having a nonmonogamous relationship"; and "role-playing" was "consciousness raising." Learning all these new things was called "networking" or "skill building" depending on the environment you were studying. And, of course, fighting for your identity, even unsuccessfully, was called "processing."

As the undercover butch publisher of the *Lesbian Tide*, I edited major features such as "Are Roles Really Dead?" and quoted myself as the anonymous "Mariane" (pretty femme, pretty clever) — defender of the now ancient heritage of butchdom. I survived through coups and controversy, not the least of which was whether the *Lesbian Tide* was a "lesbian-feminist" publication, or a "feminist lesbian" publication.

❖

Lesbians of the nineties might rightly wonder why their foremothers spent three years in this ridiculous semantic debate when they could have been proclaiming "Queer Power" on the "Donahue Show." What can I say? It seemed important at the time. I was a dyke long before I learned to spell feminism, so I was adamant that no Jennie-Come-Lately politic was going to give my lesbianism second billing as a descriptive adjective. I was not just a feminist who happened to be a lesbian. That would be as silly as calling myself a butch feminist. Somewhere in my gut I knew feminism had both saved me and shoved me back into the closet. Feminism rescued women, but it subverted lesbianism.

Butch wars with NOW

I wish I could say that gliding into the eighties, our feminist foremothers finally copped to their mistaken interpretation of lesbianism as a solely political position. Perhaps Betty Friedan and Gloria Steinem never found themselves in a real lesbian "position" — so it's not their fault. Being a dyke is a you-had-to-be-there fundamental. Perhaps we lesbians had no business allowing straight men *or* straight women to define us.

My butch's war with feminism finally culminated in 1983, when the president of the California National Organization for Women (NOW) was arrested for murder. The infamous story of the State of Louisiana's attempt to use Ginny Foat's ex-husband to discredit the women's movement is well chronicled in Foat's book, *Never Guilty, Never Free*. What is not revealed in that or any other book is the story of the butch oppression that occurred during this "victory."

On the miserable morning of January 11, my more-butch-than-thou roommate, Jean O'Leary, and I were disarranged on my living room floor discussing politics and women as usual when our also-closeted butch bud, Ivy Bottini, telephoned to report, "The FBI picked up Ginny. We've got to fight back!"

Ivy, known as L.A.'s "grandmother" of lesbianism, stomped over in her black denims a half an hour later. By dinner, "The National Ginny Foat Defense Fund" was fully phoned and had raised $10,000 toward Ginny's bail. For four grueling months, the three of us worked twelve-hour days responding to press calls from around the country, speaking, and organizing the political and financial effort to get Ginny, our post-power lesbian femme sister and personal friend, out of the slammer. As if the task at hand wasn't impossible enough, answering the *Chicago Tribune*'s phone request to speak to "Mrs. Cordova" made the work almost schizophrenic. But we were committed. Our personal lives ground to a halt. This was a matter, perhaps, of life and death.

Ginny's organization, NOW, as usual came *later* to their daughter's defense. While they "discussed" the controversial hot potato of how a murder charge would play to housewives in South Dakota, NOW leaders sent secret "Right on, sisters!" notes of thanks that we dykes were actually doing something.

Finally NOW made up its mind, just weeks after my living room carpet got worn through with the dozens of dyke feet using my house as defense headquarters. Jean, Ivy, and I got the word from National NOW Board member and lesbian-feminist Jean Conger: "We need you to step aside."

"Why?" we screamed at Conger. "We've done a great job!"

"We ... ah, NOW ... the lawyers have decided that Ginny's lesbianism can't become a factor in the Louisiana courtroom," she explained. "It's too dangerous."

"We never expected NOW to out Ginny in court." I swallowed. "What's Ginny's lesbianism got to do with us remaining chairs of the defense fund?"

"The press wants personal interviews with the directors of the defense fund. I'm supposed to take over, now." Conger paused and looked at Ivy, Jean, and I in our 501s, our legs thrown up on chairs, our cropped hair by now standing on end. She was addressing the three most "obviously butch" dyke leaders in Southern California.

"Butches are good enough to raise money," I muttered to my buds, "but not 'appropriate' for the *L.A. Times*. It's called, it's time to 'pass.'"

NOW, fronted by lesbian femmes and earring butches, passed. For once, NOW didn't even try to make excuses. There was nothing to say.

The next night I threw logs into the fireplace of my empty living room. As the fire crackled, I wondered what sound would issue from the mouths of the dyke crew coming the next day expecting to continue work. I counted the exhausting years since my twenty-first birthday. Thirteen years of having to prove my butch self to a sisterhood that would never understand, much less champion, the kind of woman I was. I recounted the times when, despite my leadership in the California movements, I'd not been invited to appear on TV talk shows. I wasn't an acceptable lesbian role model. Never mind that drag queens and bull dykes led the Stonewall riots. By the mideighties, the right wing of gay liberation and the women's movement was in full control of our "revolution."

Like most radical philosophies, feminism had separated itself from its own radical vision: freedom from gender. It had widened the patriarchy's definition of a "real woman" but left me out. I could be anything I wanted to be, except a butch.

The flames from the fireplace turned my olive green poster of Jill Johnston's *Lesbian Nation* into a sickly purple. Johnston had called lesbianism "the feminist solution." This butch still had no solution. I wept.

The femme within

I went on to find my own solution.

Shirley MacLaine's voice reverberated through the ballroom speakers as some six hundred of us — gay, straight, male and female — lay in meditation on the carpet of the Holiday Inn. We were living experiments in MacLaine's 1987 workshop, "Channeling Your Higher Self."

I punched my black leather purse into a tighter pillow underneath my head. My purse, whom I lovingly called "my yin chromosome," had been with me through nearly two decades of the lesbian civil wars. She'd been the butt of much harassment by lesbian-feminists and stone butches who didn't understand the difference between a butch purse and a femme purse. A butch purse is an only child. Femmes have as many purses as shoes.

Shirley MacLaine, as far as I knew, didn't understand the difference between a butch and a femme, but she was about to reconcile both identities in me. As our meditation deepened into its second hour, the New Age guru led us: "I want to take you back to your primordial selves," she whispered. "Back to the moment you were whole, back before the great separation. I want you to meet your real 'other half.'

"If you are filled with yang energy, this person is your yin double. If you are a nurturer, this person is your evidencing soul mate. This man-woman is your twin flame, your complete balance, your perfect lover, your intimate friend. I want you to imagine that you really see her-him; you see beyond his himness, her herness. You see perfection. You introduce yourself ... shake hands ... sit and wonder at this wonder. They are everything you've always searched for. Imagine touching. Imagine making love. This person is you."

In this altered, holy instant, I met my femme self. I knew immediately who she was: my mother, my lover, my daughter — my lost yin self. She was "the right girl" for me. And I was her butch. As our moment of ecstatic orgasm came, I felt my spirit move over. Her presence filled my cells.

There was a rush, then a calm ... a fire, then a peace. Yin met yang, *raw balance*. I'd never known what it felt like to be a woman in quite the same way as this spirit felt inside me. That afternoon my perfect lover was within me and all mine. The world was safe. This butch would never be alone again.

❖

Being butch, femme, straight, bi, transsexual is our gender identity, our gender destiny. It is not our job to redefine who we are; it is merely our job to discover who we are — and make a safe-land for our reality. This is why, in the early nineties, as I watch the dawn of "queerism" redefining the parameters of gender, I know that someday we'll understand that sexuality is more outrageously free than even we radical feminists dared believed.

Epilogue

> And today,
> against corduroy, a gray
> tie, pinpricked with red.
> ...Narrow swatch
> of knotted cloth, its stitches
> close and even — how does it
> elicit such a strange rush,
>
> magnetic
> paths of wanting?   —Christine Cassidy, 1990

Last night I sat talking to my lover and some new friends in a straight lounge in a heterosexual San Francisco hotel. I wore my tie, the gray-and-burgundy paisley one, and my Humphrey Bogart gray fedora. Feminism had tried to airbrush butches out of lesbianism. But "the sexually non-conforming"[3] had not been tamed. Now a middle-aged butch, I was finally dressed again.

I'd spent the weekend at the Outwrite '91 Gay and Lesbian Writers' Conference, flirting with straight waitresses, sitting in the very fine company of five outrageous feminist lesbian femmes — all of them activists, all, like Jo Ann Loulan, pushy power femmes who are once again raiding the borders of the lesbian nation. We'd spent most of the three days in the hotel's restaurant and dubbed our table "The Erotic Table Gang." We fugitives had dissected and reclaimed butch-femme — the ultimate lesbian archetype, the secret of our power. Perhaps, I thought, the reality of butch-femme was our witch potion, the solution too powerful, the goddess name even we cannot speak, the core of a woman who transcends gender, the ornery spirit self that refuses definition.

I'd lived these hours as my real self. I'd felt again the pride and passion of being a pariah in a movement of lip-synch radicals. Looking across my future, I knew my last forty years in this lifetime might undergo many more radical definitions. But being a butch would always be my "erotic dance,"[4] my waltz with myself, a solo if necessary. I had returned to who I was.

It was late in the fogbound bay night and I realized my lover and I would spend most of the night in the cold airport, trying to find a flight home to L.A. But I also knew anything was worth having spent two days in the company of women who knew who I was. Now a butch for twenty-three years, I've met only a handful of "self-avowed" femmes. Half of them had sat at my table that weekend; the other half have been my lovers. So to Jo Ann, to Adrienne and Robbi, to Christine and my own lover, Lynn, to the power femmes of the lesbian nineties ... and to my femme self ... I say, "Thank you. You make this butch safe in the world."

Notes

1. My warmest thanks to editors Christine Cassidy and Lynn Harris Ballen. For further details, see *Sexism: It's a Nasty Affair!* (New York: Free Press, 1976) and *Kicking the Habit: A Lesbian Nun Story* (Los Angeles: Multiple Dimensions, 1990), by Jeanne Cordova. Related material is also published in the *Lesbian Tide* (1970–1980), and in Jill Johnston's *Lesbian Nation* (New York: Simon & Schuster, 1973).

2. Jo Ann Loulan, *The Lesbian Erotic Dance; Butch, Femme, Androgyny and Other Rhythms* (San Francisco: Spinsters, 1990).

3. Camille Paglia, *Sexual Persona* (New Haven, Conn.: Yale University Press, 1991).

4. Loulan, *The Lesbian Erotic Dance.*

Judy Lederer

Another letter

March 30, 1991

Dear Joan:
On with the story...

It is the winter of 1987. I have gone to Boston for an Alix Dobkin concert, for which my friend Linda had gotten tickets. Linda is in her early forties and has just "come out" (another story). I am fifty-three and, as you know, an old-school butch.

It is raining as we walk from her car to the theater. I have learned to accept that it is okay for her to drive me, okay for me not to open the car and other doors for her, though instinct and habit tell me it is somehow "wrong" not to do so and old habits die hard, so ... I move from the inside of the sidewalk to the curbside. She asks, in curiosity, not in protest, "Why did you do that?"

"It's in my contract."

"Your what?"

"My contract. My butch contract. I could lose my butch badge if I didn't protect you from being splashed by passing whatevers."

"You are funny!" she said.

"You think I'm kidding?" I said.

"Hell, yes," she said, and then looked at me and said, "You mean people really did play 'butch-femme'?"

"It wasn't a game. It was how it was. It was respect, it was deference, it was important."

"My God, you're serious!"

Indeed, I was.

As I left for home the next day, she said, "I'll be out next weekend, and you can show me that contract and the badge."

"Okay," I said, "if I can find them. I'm pretty sure someone walked off with the badge..."

I didn't think much about it until she arrived the following Saturday morning. "I have something for you," she said, "but first I have to tell you how I got it. I stopped at a tag sale, and there was a guy there making up badges, to order. So I picked up a blank purple one and said, 'Please put "Butch" on this.'

"'For your husband?' he questioned.

"'No.'

"'Butchy?' he said.

"'No, just "Butch."' He gave me the funniest look, then got out two stars and added them to the badge, one over the word and one under, and he smiled.

"'The top star isn't straight,' he said, and indeed, it was a little out of line.

"'That's right!' I said emphatically. Then I paid him and ran, and here it is!"

I was touched. I still am. It remains one of my most prized possessions. And now, I'm told I may even wear it, because "butch is back."

Hell, honey, butch never left ... and butch has always been a little out of line.

Hope this story cheers you. I always smile when I think about it. Linda is still of the true and only faith and I am proud to have had a hand in it, so to speak.

With much love to you, as always,
Judy

Marivic R. Desquitado

A letter from the Philippines

Dear Joan:

Greetings from the Philippines!

Let me take the opportunity to surprise you with a letter from a country they label Third World.

Before I go any further, let me first introduce myself. My name is Marivic R. Desquitado; I am forty-nine years old, and I have been a tomboy since I was born. I was born in Manila, which is in Luzon, but I grew up here in Davao City, one of the major cities on Mindanao. We are one hour and forty-five minutes from Manila by jet plane and three days away if one takes the bus.

Where did I get your name and address? I was working with the Women's Studies and Resource Center. This agency caters to women and their problems because of discrimination by society. I met Diane J. Allen when she came over as one of the "exchange visitors" of GABRIELA (a cause-oriented women's organization). We were introduced and we talked about lesbianism. When she left, she promised to send me some reading materials about lesbians abroad. She kept her promise. Among the materials she sent was your essay "Butch-Fem Relationships: Sexual Courage in the 1950s."

It is only now that I got to seriously read the materials Diane sent me. I have resigned from the women's agency I was working with. Part of my work there was to talk to groups of women that we were organizing. Subjects like human rights, U.S. imperialism, poverty, and women's oppression were discussed. Sometimes I would be invited to speak to a heterosexual group about why we have become an impoverished country and the need to organize.

I am writing this letter hoping to form a link with the lesbian world in your country. I was wondering why there is so much fuss about the words *lesbianism* and *feminism*, about role-playing?

THE PERSISTENT DESIRE

In the Philippines we are better known as tomboys, T-birds, *babaeng bakla* (woman faggot), or *pars*, which is a Tagalog word for *pare*, meaning the men who stood as sponsors in ceremonies such as weddings and baptisms. Lesbians are those women who fall in love with tomboys/T-birds/*pars*. The terms *butch* and *dyke* are never used here and are understood by only a few. Many tomboys here claim that they are not lesbians. When introducing our women lovers to intimate friends, we say, "Meet my girlfriend," or, "She's my wife," but not "woman lover." Here, if a tomboy gets involved with both men and women, we simply call her "bi," which is short for bisexual. But in the Philippines, a tomboy is a tomboy in spite of her preferences.

Prejudice against us is still very strong here. We do not have bars, restaurants, clubs, stores, hotels, or presses that cater exclusively to lesbians. However, just recently, a club opened in Manila that caters to lesbians. It was recently constructed and caters to moneyed lesbians, for I have heard it is a very expensive place to go. If ever a news article about lesbians appears in a newspaper, it always reads like this: "Tomboy Stabs Girl," or "Woman Killed by Tomboy." And if ever lesbianism is used in the films, it is always in a distorted way.

Because I never hide my real identity as a tomboy, I still feel animosity directed at me every time I go on dates with a woman. I don't wear skirts and don't use makeup, but I dress respectably. I do wear pants and polos or men's shirts but not men's undergarments, because I believe that no matter how many millions of men's jockeys I might wear, I am still a woman. However, I have felt and thought like a "man" for as long as I can remember. My parents, four brothers, and a sister did not even try to make me act more feminine. They were unlike some other parents I know who did physical harm to their children who turned out to be gay or a tomboy.

As a child, I never played with dolls. It was always toy guns and wooden swords and boys as playmates. I was nine years old when I experienced that funny feeling that I now know as getting turned on, toward an older girl. I wanted to kiss her and go to bed with her, but I couldn't tell her, because I didn't know what to do. Schoolmates, neighbors, and playmates called me a tomboy. Although I did not hide my personality as a tomboy, men would still court me. I do not hate men. I prefer women, because it is a woman who excites me. I have gone out with men to picnics, dances, drinking sprees, but I have never had sex with a man, unlike some other tomboys who did before they became lovers of women.

Courting a woman is the concern of all tomboys. From my personal experiences, the courting stage is similar to what any man does — love letters or notes, flowers and chocolates, invitations to movies and gatherings, and visits to the girl's family. During the courtship stage, the problem arises not with the girl but with her friends and family. These are the people that cause us headaches, sleepless nights, and heartaches. Rarely do we have girlfriends whose families and friends vote for us. They always

Marivic Desquitado,
tomboy, 1990

disapprove, because they claim it is immoral for two women to fall in love. These are the people who are very much a part of our society, which scorns and ridicules us as if we are pariahs. These are the people, and many of them are very religious, who believe white is white and black is black, who talk a lot about ethics and morality, and who think they are now somebody because they are not like us. These people treat us like intruders. They are the same people who called you deviant, the kind who appears to be so pious, so moralistic that they appear not to have sinned at all. They are the kind who teaches their children to scorn and ridicule us.

Throughout the years I have suffered insults and derision. I have been treated with disgust by these people. I have grown callous to their insults behind my back; they dare not say them to my face, because I will always challenge them to a fistfight. I remember years back when my girlfriend and I were walking hand in hand in a downtown area and we passed by a group of men who were just standing there ogling people. One of them made an obscene remark, calling my girl "the whore of a tomboy." I saw an empty soft drink bottle, picked it up, broke it, and turned back to where the group was sitting. I swung the broken bottle at one of them. My girlfriend was so frightened, she dragged me away from that place, but not before telling them to fuck themselves.

There are still lots of things to be said about lesbian life here in the Philippines. We're lucky here, because we don't get beaten up just because we wear men's clothing. But a tomboy who dresses like a man rarely finds a job that pays well. It is always the low-income positions that await them — security guards, janitors, cooks, messengers, carpenters, vendors.

Because of the patriarchal system that permeates our Philippine society, the majority of tomboys that I know practice the same family relationships, especially those who live together. If possible, the tomboy is the family provider and the other woman stays at home doing the cooking, washing, cleaning. But because of the economic hardships that we are now facing, many of these women find work outside the house.

Despite the sneers and insults, I am proud to say I have fought back in my own quiet way by not hiding in a closet, by being myself. Even if I do not shout to the world that I am a tomboy, my personality exudes a man in a woman's body. I let everyone see that the woman I am with is my woman. We go to public discotheques and dance together. We go to any public restaurant or bar and hold hands. We go home together, sleep together, eat together, and plan things together. But you know, in spite of the happy feeling my girl and I share, there are still many hecklers in the neighborhood who shout insults in the night, taunting me to come out and daring me to fight. Only my girlfriend keeps me from going berserk. These men are jealous of our life together.

Because the Philippine system is a copycat of the American capitalistic system, there exists a wide gap between the rich T-birds and the poor. The rich tomboys tend to group among themselves, while the poorer tomboys stay with one another. If only all the lesbians would unite, we would be a very strong force to be reckoned with.

About two years ago, I tried to organize a group of tomboys at the encouragement of Dwayne, an Australian woman. This was when I was still working with the Women's Studies and Resource Center. Dwayne was then a visitor who had come to the Philippines in one of our exchange visitor programs. She was the first foreign visitor in this program to discuss lesbianism openly with me. I worked for three years in this agency that had women for its clientele, and yet lesbianism was never discussed. I do believe in the women's movement, in the emancipation movement, but lesbianism was not a part of the women's movement here. The priority was educating the people that imperialism, capitalism, and fascism must not be allowed any longer on Philippine soil. I tried to organize the tomboys. I contacted some of my friends in the lower-income bracket, the tomboys who dressed as men. I wanted to explain to them the importance of communicating with lesbians abroad. I got discouraged, because they wanted the lesbians abroad to help them find work there. You know, I can't blame them. They want to go abroad, earn dollars so they would be free of the poverty that has held them chained for so many decades. Yes, it is wrong and it is right. Politics is always tied to whatever we do. But will we lesbians be held in bondage by a society that looks upon us as abnormal freaks just because they consider it immoral to love the same sex?

I hope this will be the start of a series of communications between us. If ever you're planning to visit the Philippine lesbian scene, just let me know. I would like to know more about what is going on in your country.

Sincerely,
Marivic R. Desquitado

Lyndall MacCowan

Re-collecting history, renaming lives: Femme stigma and the feminist seventies and eighties[1]

Listen, my answers may be different than yours, but don't run from the question.
—Rita Mae Brown[2]

Several years ago, I asked the students in a women's studies class on lesbian history and biography to name themselves, for the duration of the class period and on whatever basis they liked, either a butch lesbian or a femme lesbian. Butch-femme identity was the scheduled topic, and I intended to have the students choose "sides," then divide into groups — one butch, one femme — each of which would define its own characteristics as well as those of the other. If your group was butch, what was it that made you butch? What attributes made the members of the other group femme? How would someone else know which you were? If you were looking for a date at the local lesbian hangout, how would you go about approaching someone? My plan was to use the groups' definitions to elicit a discussion of butch-femme identity, behavior, and sexuality; I wanted the students to brainstorm, to produce their own parameters of butch and femme instead of relying on well-worn stereotypes. In asking them to pick an identity, I stressed that their choice was arbitrary, and that it was make-believe. In no way did it have to reflect the way they saw themselves. If they felt butch, they could choose to be femme; if they related to neither concept, they could mentally flip a coin. The choice they made didn't matter: this was only an exercise.

Prior to class, students had been asked to read Margaret Nichols's "Lesbian Sexuality: Issues and Developing Theory," from *Lesbian Psychologies*, as well as two of the classic articles on butch-femme, Joan Nestle's "Butch-Fem Relationships: Sexual Courage in the 1950s," and Amber

Hollibaugh and Cherríe Moraga's "What We're Rollin' around in Bed With: Sexual Silences in Feminism."[3] I made three assumptions in preparing for the class: First, I assumed that most students would have done the readings, and so would have gained some insight into how it felt to identify as either butch or femme, as well as some knowledge of the controversy that surrounded those identities during the height of 1970s lesbian-feminism. Second, I assumed that every lesbian carries an internal mental and emotional picture of "butch" and "femme," however inaccurate or unarticulated. Third, I assumed that these particular students would hold few of the rigid political views about the "oppressiveness" of butch-femme that so characterized the preceding generation of lesbians — my generation. The women in the class were, on average, twenty-two years old, and many had only recently come into their lesbianism. Further, this was 1988, not 1976. There was much evidence that butch-femme was enjoying a revival in the surrounding lesbian community of San Francisco; indeed, it seemed that "roles" were being treated as so much changeable costuming, approached with an ease unknown to a 1960s lesbian. Therefore, I assumed that the students would approach the topic with a reasonable amount of objectivity and curiosity, that they would be able to play with lesbian sexual identities without fear of judgment. I imagined we would have a lively session in which we would create our own definitions of butch and femme.

Alas, the best-laid plans sometimes go madly awry. Only my first two assumptions were valid: the students had done the readings, and did, indeed, have definite notions about butch and femme. My instructions given, all but one or two reluctantly chose an identity and, with a great deal of chair scraping, joking, muttering, and laughter, began moving to sit on the appropriate side of the room. Once settled, however, their voices rose in a cacophonous chorus of protest. They didn't want to be forced to choose a role. Roles were artificial. Roles were oppressive. Roles were heterosexual. Individuals asserted loudly that they "didn't fit the stereotype," or were "in the middle," or "didn't want to be labeled," or were "both." Their competition to be heard over one another made clear that they didn't think butch-femme was a suitable topic for experimentation. As far as they were concerned, I had unjustly pigeonholed them in asking them to choose; worse, I had made them pigeonhole themselves, and they would have none of it.

As the noise level lowered somewhat, I tried to turn their objections into a basis for discussion. I accepted their refusal to even temporarily choose a "role"; could they tell me why? What meaning did butch-femme have for us as lesbians that it brought forth such strong feelings? What limitations would have been imposed had they been willing to accept being in one or the other category? Their response was to repeat that roles were artificial, limiting, and the basis of sexism. They were unable to grasp that their reactions were significant. Choreographing a political analysis of their group rejection of the exercise or a self-examination of their personal revulsions to sexual "roles" seemed no more possible than having them choose one. Asking them to stop, to step back and observe what had just happened, to think about what their reactions might mean was like shouting into the wind. Only when I took the focus completely away from them, making myself into both subject and object by talking about what it meant to me to identify as a femme, did any kind of dialogue become possible. Then, they were curious; they *were* interested in butch-femme as a lesbian issue — as long as the butch or the femme was someone else. They wanted to know about my relationships with butch women, about what coming out had been like, about why I needed to call myself "femme," about what, exactly, a femme was, anyway. Our conversation reminded me of the well-intentioned straight audiences with whom I talked about lesbianism during the early 1970s: I supposed I should be grateful they weren't refusing to listen. By the end of class, the students were happy to affirm that the discussion had been "interesting." I, on the other hand, although relieved to have salvaged something from the lesson, felt like a failure as a teacher. As a femme, I felt like an outsider and a freak.

❖

April 1991
Dear Joan,
   I don't know why I wasn't better prepared for the students' reaction; that experience in the women's studies class wasn't the first time identifying as a femme has left me feeling like a freak. I suppose I keep hoping time has mellowed the need for lesbian conformity, but even when I'm prepared for the hostility butch-femme can draw, a part of me is still surprised by it. I was again reminded, with the publication of Jo Ann Loulan's The Lesbian Erotic Dance,[4] *that ten years' discussion about butch-femme hasn't created more receptivity. The book has prompted another outcry that butch-femme is imitative, oppressive, and reactionary, even though it reads mainly as an argument for naming lesbian sexual diversity. I would have thought, given her popularity as an author, speaker, and therapist, that if anyone could get a hearing on butch-femme, Jo Ann Loulan could.*
   How wrong can I continue to be? I had only to look in a lesbian and gay newspaper at the letters about The Lesbian Erotic Dance *to know that the lesbian-feminist attitude toward butch-femme is firmly entrenched. The sarcastic and vitriolic tone employed by the writer of one letter in particular[5]; her repetition of twenty-years-stale stereotypes about butch-femme sexuality; the ease with which she offered a description, as though from personal knowledge, of what "the pre-feminist lesbian bar scene was like" when she, in fact, had no experience of it; and her appellation "heterosexual imitation" were all tiresomely familiar. The continued vehemence with which butch-femme is denigrated, the callous denial of our experiences, and the general suspension of rational thought that occurs at the suggestion that we might*

exist beyond the stereotypes should tell us by now that more is being discussed here than the acceptability of sexual variation.

The continued negative reaction to butch-femme has led me to want, for six years now, to write an academic article on butch-femme that could find its way into the women's studies literature. I know it's a large topic, but I had in mind to trace butch-femme back to the women who married women while passing as men (and contrast them to the "Boston marriages" of the same period), present examples of butch and femme women from lesbian fiction, discuss the connection between butch-femme and issues of class and race, address the concept of "passing" (either as male or as heterosexual), along-side the nineteenth-century creation of the notion that "real lesbian equals butch," and finish with an analysis of why butch-femme identities and sexualities were the first things to be sacrificed by lesbian-feminism in the 1970s. In the process, I intended to define what butch and femme are, but mostly I wanted to write something "objective" and "scholarly" that couldn't be dismissed as mere "personal testimony."

This endeavor was not, I thought, as impossibly ambitious as it might sound. The documentation is there, and my premise is a simple one: the real issue underlying butch-femme is one of lesbian identity, and of differing definitions of "lesbian." It is this, coupled with the theory (which I think is wrong) that gender is one of the primary causes of women's oppression, that accounts for our continued rejection by lesbian-feminists. However, this "scholarly, intellectual" treatise has done nothing but sit in my computer in a dozen incomplete pieces. For six years, off and on, I have ripped it up and started over, edited and rewritten, ripped that up and started over again, changed voice and approach — all to no avail, and finally, a week ago, I admitted I can't do it. In the admission, I realized why: I'm too angry. I've been trying to write impersonally about a subject that's too close to the bone, and while weighted down with a rage I've not wanted to acknowledge.

I feel like such a coward. I'm not usually afraid of anger. But this is not a clean, sharp rage, the kind let go of through naming injustice and being heard. It's muddied by self-doubt, and a lack of language, and fear. Nor am I sure how much of the rage stems from injustices I can personally claim, and how much is in the name of others with whom I stand but who might speak more clearly for themselves than I. Indeed, I'm not sure I've the right to be angry, though I am anyway. And what I'm angry at is feminism, specifically lesbian-feminism, despite its being a movement whose benefits I can name and touch, and whose philosophy has shaped my entire adult life and the history of my generation. I am angry because its message has been plain these past two decades: as a lesbian who is femme, I'm not considered worthy of liberation.

Some of my problem in admitting anger has to do with the hesitation with which I name myself femme. Oh, I know that's what I am, have known ever since the Heresies 12: Sex Issue *came out in 1981. But although I've affirmed the validity of butch-femme in every lecture on lesbianism I've* given during the past five years, and say publicly I'm femme, I still feel insecure with the word. I'm not sure, "objectively," what it means. There's a constant whisper that I don't measure up. Or that who I am doesn't have to be called that. How much comes from lesbian-feminism's stereotypes or its relegation of "femme" to a past I didn't live, I can't tell. I know of no present-day definition of femme that's positive or that encompasses the different decades in which you and I came out. Lesbian-feminism tries to prevent my connecting the name with my life, our collective lives; some days, it succeeds.

Too, anger seems useless. The "dialogue" on butch-femme has been one-sided: who we are is dismissed; we speak from an unequal position; we speak in their terms. You know about this. Lesbian-feminism's very language defines us as outside the pale. As an example, a student in another women's studies class once asked, "When we are trying to get away from inequality and male-female stereotypes, why do some lesbians go into femme-butch roles?" She was nineteen years old, newly out, and sincere. But her words predefined and prejudged butch-femme as an imitation of heterosexual gender stereotypes. Where did she come by those preconceptions, twenty years after "The Woman-Identified-Woman" [6] was written? Rhetorically, I wonder how a broadside that should have been no more than a call for solidarity against media dyke baiting became a full-blown political theory. And I find myself tempted to dismiss the worst reactions to butch-femme, at least those from lesbians whose generation wrote "The Woman-Identified-Woman," as the fanaticism of a minority whose attachment to "political correctness" will eventually die with them. Very few, after all, still adhere in a pure form to the lesbian-feminist political philosophy constructed in the 1970s; I have come to think of those few as members of a religious cult for whom belief is the ground for salvation.[7] "The Woman-Identified-Woman" has little meaning for 1990s lesbians; if they have read it at all, it's often no more than as an interesting historical document. Yet the assumptions lesbian-feminism made about butch-femme twenty years ago, based on the equation of women's oppression, sex roles, gender, and sexual orientation, have come to hold an unquestioned, unanalyzed hegemony. One need only label butch and femme "roles" to have judged them negative, unequal, heterosexual, and false. What good is being angry if I must prove that femme is none of those things before I will be heard?

Yet, I am angry. This movement claimed respectability and thus moved forward by enforcing a silence about the reality of many of our lives. I find myself weighing losses, imagining what might have been if what was meant to liberate us had not become yet another source of oppression. I know "what if" can't be answered. Lesbian-feminism has irrevocably changed the shape of our worlds, and in all fairness, given where we came from, I don't know if it could have happened otherwise. Still, I do regret. I feel cheated of other options, left to go on armed with only a severed past and negative definitions. I feel crippled. I have too much fury over that to be able to write an objective *piece defending butch-femme. What I can say is subjective, and not likely to be heard by those who insist that butch-femme lives perpetuate women's oppression.*

❖

I am sixteen. It is the summer of 1972 and I have been out for barely a month. I am sitting in Scott's, part of the exodus of Daughters of Bilitis members who come to the bars after Wednesday night meetings. Scott's is owned and run by an older butch lesbian named, predictably, Scotty, and has something of a mixed clientele. About a third of the women are regular "butch bar dykes" in their forties and fifties. The rest are unremarkable neighborhood women or DOB activists who don't think of themselves as frequenting bars. Scott's is one of my favorite places, only in part because they rarely bother with ID checks. In a quiet residential neighborhood, it lacks the predatory straight men of La Cave, the sleazy feeling endemic to Kelly's, and the tough role-playing rumored to be required in a bar I haven't been to called Leonarda's.

There is nothing unusual about the evening or the group, just a bunch of DOBers having a beer in a lesbian setting. As I am five years under the legal drinking age and need to remain inconspicuous, I don't leave the table, and only half listen to the conversation without contributing much. This allows me to watch the butch women clustered around the pool table across the room. Part of my staring is simple curiosity: butch women don't often wander into DOB. Part — most — is motivated by a depth of lust that surprises me. The women I am watching are fascinatingly attractive. Their faces have been lived in; their body language conveys self-assurance and the toughness born of surviving pain. One, in particular, moves with the grace of controlled power, but I'd gladly go home with any of this group sporting ironed shirts and DA haircuts, who have strong hands, "men's" biceps, and female contours semidisguised in men's pants. My barely controlled desire is, of course, invisible to the women across the room. It's evidently obvious, however, to someone at our table. As individuals begin well-I-have-to-go-to-work-tomorrow farewells, a new DOB member, whose name I'm not sure of and with whom I've had maybe five minutes' superficial conversation, asks me home with her. Out of pure shock — among other things, she is so thoroughly feminine-looking that I wonder how she came here — and lack of practice in saying no gracefully, I accept.

The night turns into a week. But as she's even less experienced than I am, it is a week of frustrating attempts at sex that keep us up until two or three a.m. I can't decide which of us is the failure. I seem to want an unknown signal or behavior that is missing, nor can I seem to please her. When we're not engaged in fumbling bedroom attempts, we carry on a desultory, half-joking, tentatively serious conversation about Which One Of Us Is The Butch. Neither of us is sure just what "butch" really is; we know no one who claims that term, nor has anyone said one of us ought to. Still, the concept seems important; each of us wants the other to fill the niche. We reach no

304

conclusions until one evening when she comes home with a bouquet of daisies and a $1.99 riding crop from a five-and-dime store. She hands me both saying, "I've decided you're the butch." Embarrassed, I laugh and accept, momentarily glad to have something settled. She is, after all, relatively more feminine than I am. But I can't find in myself the butch persona I felt in the women at Scott's, whose presence evoked from me a heat that is lacking in this encounter. Is the criterion one of appearance? I have hair that reaches past my waist and am fond of three-inch earrings. Or does it have to do with aggression? I'm the one who was picked up. I am confused. She is not. Indeed, having decided I'm butch seems key to another decision: our "one-week stand" is now, sans discussion, a relationship.

Later that night, I awake in a state of terror and panic. I feel so trapped that the walls appear to be moving toward me. How did I come to be here with a stranger who has dubbed me butch and decided we are now married? With fear and confusion outweighing guilt, I dress quietly and collect my things. I don't know how to untangle my ignorance about why the sex doesn't work, about why one of us must be butch, about why I can't become butch. "Lesbian" seems incomplete; I know only, vaguely, what I am not. I don't know how to explain or apologize, so I let her sleep, and leave without even writing a note. I take the riding crop with me, a memento of having, for a moment, fit a clear category.

Two years later, I run into her — in the waiting room of the therapist we both see, no less! — and finally apologize for my lack of kindness and grace in disappearing in the middle of the night. I still don't know how to explain why I was not what she wanted.

A decade later, after I've learned to name myself femme, I come across the riding crop in a box of keepsakes. Only then do I realize that "femme" was not in our vocabulary of options in 1972. And I begin to wonder: how is it that butch remained named, but femme became invisible?

❖

> *By conflating lesbianism (a sexual experience) with feminism (a political philosophy), the ability to justify lesbianism on grounds other than feminism dropped out of the discourse.* —Gayle Rubin[8]

Much of the discussion of butch-femme has taken place within the arena of sexuality, as part of the larger "sex wars" that have divided lesbians during the last decade or so. I don't think this is wholly inappropriate. Certainly, butch-femme is about sex, and so is loaded with all the cultural and political baggage that comes with any feminist discussion of sexuality and its power to be both oppressing and liberating. Butch and femme *are* forms of lesbian sexual expression. However, I think it simplistic to view the hostility butch-femme generates as merely another thematic variation on the debates about sadomasochism, lesbian "pornography," or bisexual behavior. Nor is the reaction to butch-femme wholly based on a fear of the visibility it gives to sex between women. Denial of lesbian sexuality was part of an unspoken compromise lesbian-feminists thought it necessary to make with heterosexual feminism,[9] but I don't think the disavowal of butch-femme can be attributed to just a refutation of heterosexual myths or a need for feminist acceptance.

To approach butch-femme as *only* about sex is to doom dialogue to its current stalemated (and stale) exchange of cries of "politically incorrect" and "antisex." Sex, in this instance, also signifies the *meaning* of lesbian: the lesbian-feminist rejection of "controversial" sexualities is as often a rejection of "lesbian" as a *sexual* identity as of what other women do in bed. As Gayle Rubin implies in the quote above, the making of lesbianism into a *political* identity denied its validity as a sexuality. This is especially important to the question of butch-femme, because butch and femme are gender constructions that arise from a sexual definition of lesbianism. Lesbian-feminists misunderstand butch-femme because each side is working from a different definition of "lesbian." Butch-femme has been made invisible because lesbian sexuality has been made invisible.

Yet our challenge to the idea of lesbianism as a political, rather than a sexual, identity needs to incorporate more than the right to sex per se. It is time to explicitly say that the lesbian-feminist analysis linking women's oppression with gender, sex roles, sexuality, and sexual orientation is both simplistic and inaccurate, and has long outlived its ability to fuel a movement for women's — let alone lesbians' — liberation. Not only has it failed to liberate lesbianism as a sexual identity, it has failed to liberate gender. I think it necessary to expand Rubin's statement: *In the equating of women's oppression with the existence of gender, and the conflating of sex roles with sexual behavior and sexual orientation, the need to expand gender, define sexual identity, and construct gender to reflect sexuality dropped from the agenda of liberation.*

The way in which lesbians were renamed "normal women" resulted in the removal of lesbianism's meaning as a sexual category, a removal that has served to perpetuate, in a new guise, and from political lesbianism rather than patriarchy, the same old oppression of lesbians on the basis of our sexuality. In making gender the primary culprit of women's and lesbians' oppression, especially in making the rejection of butch-femme "roles" one of the linchpins on which lesbian liberation turned, lesbian-feminism truncated a historically lesbian effort to reformulate women's gender roles. Under lesbian-feminist analysis, butch-femme came to symbolize, simultaneously, the "old" (sexual) construction of lesbianism, and the oppressive (genderized) heterosexuality that "new" lesbianism was supposed to cure.

❖

It is early in 1973 and I have found my first permanent — and legitimate — job at a San Francisco law office, through a listing at the Women's Switch-

board. It's only part-time with not much money, but it's enough to pay the rent, and they don't mind that I'm gay. It's also enough to buy a car: a funky 1959 Volkswagen Bug that cost $75 because most of the passenger's side is caved in. It has a distinct personality. It also has an engine that needs rebuilding. This I am undertaking at a gas station across the bay, which is managed by a lesbian named Jo. Every day at noon I hop on a bus to go spend the rest of my day poring over John Muir's Idiot's Guide to Volks-wagens, soaking filthy engine parts in gasoline, swearing at stubborn bolts, and trying to keep the grease out of my hair.

Learning how to take apart an engine and put it back together again from scratch is marvelous fun. My dream of a working car, however, is based on more than wanting increased mobility or a need to feel competent. A car is a kind of security. I figure if I end up homeless again, I can sleep in the VW, instead of in a doorway or an unheated warehouse. Going to the gas station has an added attraction. I have a definite case of the hots for Jo. Jo is butch. Not only is she butch, she passes. Ninety percent of the customers for whom she pumps gas, repairs carburetors, or fixes brakes assume she's a man. This amazes me. How can anyone not see she is a woman? We joke about pulling a fast one, concluding that straights sure are dumb.

I want Jo to notice me. We talk a lot, and she tells me stories. About growing up in a tough, working-class neighborhood in a city back east. About how she always loved cars and knew how to fix them. About how she joined the roller derby in order to come to California, and about the lesbian relationships in it. About wearing a tux to take her girlfriend to the prom ten years ago. This impresses me, and I want to know how she got away with it. She shrugs and says she learned how to fight early, so no one messed with her. She's not particularly analytical about being gay or butch; she's always been this way; that's how it is. The driving need in her life is to be able to do as she wants, to be able to take care of her own. The gas station is part of that goal. I'm entranced. I wouldn't care if she were a circus performer. I just want her to take me to bed. She is sinuous, powerfully graceful. Trim and compact; solid muscle. Looking at the strength in her hands makes me dizzy.

At a loss, I begin flirting with her, teasing her about sex. An axiom around the gas station is that women are better car mechanics than men because of our smaller hands. I say her hands are likely good for other things, too. I go through all sorts of contortions to get her to make the first move, and am shocked at myself. I'm afraid I'm too obvious; I've not done this before.

At first, she is leery. Don't I have a lover? I do, sort of. She worries about how old I might be. I do not tell her I'm seventeen. At last, one night near closing time, she pounces on me. Locking up seems to take forever, and we stumble, finally, toward the cot in the tool room. Making love with her outdoes my fantasies. She is soft and hard in just the right combination; I imagine her a panther, a sleek, hypnotic darkness. She tells me I move like the ocean, and indeed, I am being held in motion by tides I hadn't known

about. *She knows exactly what she is doing. For once, I can surrender,
without fumbling or having to orchestrate anything.*

*Outside of sex, we're more equivocal. We talk vaguely about a "rela-
tionship," but neither of us can really imagine it. The gap between our
backgrounds is too great, and if the pictures of her former lovers, all
big-breasted super-blondes, are any indication, I'm not what she wants. She
wants a family life, a "wife," a woman with children. I want to be free, to
have an education, to not be poor, to live in San Francisco. Even for the sake
of sex, I can't see myself in a stucco apartment with straight, conventional
neighbors. She doesn't ask; I don't offer. When I finish my car, I drive across
the bridge for the first time and do not see her again.*

❖

What does it mean to be a lesbian?

What does it mean to be a woman who loves women? In the early
1970s, the emerging lesbian-feminist movement took that question to
mean "What does it mean to be a woman-who-loves-women in a society
that hates women?" and answered by saying it meant rejecting the female
role and society's woman hatred. It answered that to be a lesbian was to
engage in "self-love that expresses itself in love of other women and thus
in rebellion against a woman-hating society ... [I]n a society so steeped in
woman-hatred, for a woman to love another woman — for a woman to
love herself — is a miracle indeed."[10] Lesbian-feminism defined lesbians
as the only healthy women in a sick society and lesbianism as an act of
resistance to male domination. According to "The Woman-Identified-
Woman":

> A lesbian is the rage of all women condensed to the point of explosion.
> She is the woman who, often beginning at an extremely early age, acts in
> accordance with her inner compulsion to be a more complete and freer
> human being than her society cares to allow her ... [O]n some level she
> has not been able to accept the limitation and oppression laid on her by
> the most basic role of her society — the female role.

It further said lesbianism was

> a category of behavior possible only in a sexist society characterized by
> rigid sex roles and dominated by male supremacy ... In a society in which
> men do not oppress women, and sexual expression is allowed to follow
> feelings, the categories of homosexuality and heterosexuality would dis-
> appear.[11]

Lesbian-feminism argued that "heterosexual" and "homosexual," like
"masculine" and "feminine," were artificial categories created solely to
reinforce those sex roles — presumably, people were bisexual. Since sex
roles oppressed women, and since heterosexuality *was* woman's sex role,
feminism argued that women's oppression could be overcome by rejecting

feminine heterosexuality and redefining one's self through other women. It dismissed sexual orientation per se as false, named lesbians "the vanguard of the revolution," equated lesbianism with liberation, and declared that all women could, and should, become lesbians.

❖

Dear Joan,

I've always been reluctant to tell people that I came out in 1972, after women's liberation and the Stonewall riots. In the popular history of lesbianism, that year attributes a meaning to my identity that holds no truth for me. I remember, some six months after I came out, hearing that there were two "kinds" of lesbians: "old-gay" lesbians, who had come out before 1969 and saw lesbianism in sexual terms; and "political lesbians," who came out after 1969 and understood the political meaning of love for women. Since the line of demarcation was 1969, I was ipso facto a political lesbian. But in fact, my experience encompassed only DOB and the bars, and as it happened, I didn't have much contact with lesbian-feminism, or read "The Woman-Identified-Woman," until 1974. The world of DOB and the bars was fast disappearing under the onslaught of lesbian-feminism. I was confused by the implication that "lesbian," as I was experiencing it, no longer existed, and I remember feeling shocked and betrayed the first time I heard the concept "political lesbian."[12] The imposition of historical categories thus placed me, as early as 1972, in a kind of limbo. Since this was the 1970s, my lesbianism had to do with the issues of women's oppression, even if I didn't know it.

It would've been heretical then, as it still is now, to be a lesbian and assert that feminism has little meaning for me — imagine trying to be an atheist in fourteenth-century Europe. Yet such a statement is true, and it's important I say it, because feminism has come to overshadow lesbianism's meaning. It's not that I don't believe women are oppressed, but I've never been able to identify myself with that all-encompassing group "woman." I've never been anywhere near being as oppressed as a woman as I am as a lesbian. Some of that, I know, is the result of a historical privilege. I came to adulthood after women's liberation had begun to change the way women are viewed, and there's no doubt my life was easier. Another part of that is a fluke, a perverse kind of luck: I didn't grow up in a household with sex roles or where labor was divided into "men's work" and "women's work." I also didn't grow up thinking of myself as a girl.[13] I didn't think of myself as a boy, either. As Joanna Russ says, "There are men, women, and intellectuals."[14] I was raised an intellectual, my body a kind of neutered vessel for my brain, with the expectation that I would go to college and get a job. As such, I was exempted from the rules and indoctrination meant for girls.

I felt barred from girls' things for another reason: I started falling in love with women when I was seven, and girls — women — were heterosexual by definition. My wanting women rather than men, therefore, simply ham-

mered home the belief that I was neither male nor female. I looked like a girl, but I was an alien. Then when I came out, I didn't have to worry anymore about not being a woman: I was a lesbian. Although I thought of women's oppression as a problem of straight women, it never occurred to me to view lesbianism as a route to liberation. I knew women's oppression wasn't why I was gay. At sixteen, however, I wasn't about to be caught out as wrong, either. I kept my mouth shut and listened.

If 1972 was the wrong year to come into lesbianism as a sexual, rather than a political, identity, it was also the wrong time to be femme — so much so that I was denied even a history I could regret having missed. In retrospect, I'm amazed at how thoroughly "femme" disappeared from the lesbian terrain. I remember hearing the words butch and femme used in only two ways. One was in Del Martin and Phyllis Lyon's Lesbian/Woman, published not long after I came out. In it I read about butch-femme as the silly stereotype of us that straights had; Del and Phyl said they weren't butch and femme because they hadn't found the usual heterosexual division of household labor or social skills of any use.[15] And I heard "butch" used in reference to specific women who were masculine-looking. It wasn't meant as a pejorative, just as a description. What I never heard was any lesbian called "femme." I don't think butch-femme, as a hyphenation referring to real lesbians, was supposed to exist. There was no word that named my response to butch women, just as there was no term to describe the dynamic of the longest lasting lesbian relationship any of us knew about, the balanced combination of Del's reserve and Phyllis's charm, Del's strength and Phyllis's open sexuality. We engaged in unconscious double-think: butch-femme didn't really exist, so if we met a butch-femme couple, only the butch partner, at best, was named.

❖

I often think lesbian-feminism's one great contribution was the naming of lesbians as women. By pointing out that the exclusion of "lesbian" from "woman" was a means of sexist social control, it in one stroke removed the weight of a portrait in which we were untouchable, pathological, deviants. I'm grateful for that gift. I also feel it came at a high price, for the redefinition of "woman" to include "lesbian" ultimately narrowed the boundaries of the latter more than it stretched those of the first. In looking back, my "preliberation" image of "lesbian" as something distinct from "woman" was not just a product of internalized oppression. It also named the real way in which my experiences as a lesbian differed from those of heterosexual, or formerly heterosexual, women. Lesbian-feminism, though it named us women, never asked the question "What does it mean to be a woman-who-loves-women in a society that hates queers?"

It's not that I didn't try to understand women's oppression. When I joined a lesbian-feminist collective, I waited a long time to hear my experience named, but I never did. Everyone spoke so confidently about "all women's experience" that I concluded that all the ways in which mine differed were the result either of luck or of oppressions insignificant beside the larger ones of women as a group.

It was at the same time that I heard of butch-femme as a negative thing of our unliberated past, mostly through the books I, and everyone else, was reading. Everyone hailed *Rubyfruit Jungle* as "the first lesbian novel" (*The Well of Loneliness* didn't count). In it the protagonist defines butch-femme as "male-female" and proclaims it "the craziest, dumbass thing I ever heard tell of." She asks, "What's the point of being a lesbian if a woman is going to look and act like an imitation man?" and answers, "Hell, if I want a man, I'll get the real thing ... [T]he whole point of being gay is because you love women."[16] *Sappho Was a Right-On Woman*, long the only lesbian history book available, said much the same thing, but in greater detail, naming butch-femme a bygone style. Butch-femme "roles" were inhibiting to personal growth, it said, a product of false socialization, proof of identity confusion, sexually limiting, artificial, and most likely to be found among "lower-class [*sic*]" lesbians in bars.[17]

Outside the books, I don't think anyone talked about butch and femme. Instead, butch-looking women were simply called "apolitical," and any woman who looked feminine was treated as straight. One result of this was that, although I rented rooms in a house owned by a butch-femme couple, I never asked them about what their lives were like, because I couldn't approach them without using words, *butch* and *femme*, that might give offense.

❖

What does it mean to be a lesbian?

To be a lesbian means to be queer. It means to fall in love each year with at least one girl in my classroom, as well as with the bus driver, the baby-sitter, the camp counselor, and my fourth-grade teacher. It means to spend the night, at the age of nine or ten, at another girl's house and to touch her anywhere I can get away with. It means knowing I'm a freak. It means, at thirteen, spending all my time at a teacher's home and, when my mother decides this woman is a cover for a boy, being thrown out of the house. It means knowing that I am not a woman. It means pushing away a friend who's crying because someone has called her a lesbian. It means knowing I am alone. It means falling in love with girls and, at the same time, despising their femininity, their obsession with makeup and boys, their lack of strength or brains. It means knowing that both the kind of woman I want and the kind of woman I am don't exist, do not have names.

To be a lesbian means to come out in high school and be greeted with silence. It means to go to San Francisco and wind up living on the streets. It means to go hungry and to sleep in doorways, or at the DOB office, or on the concrete floor of a warehouse, or to walk all night through the city.

It means being in the emergency room of S.F. General one late night and seeing a woman rolled in who's been knifed for being a lesbian, and may not live. It means knowing other lesbians who one day put a gun to their heads and pull the trigger. It means claiming lesbianism as a sexual desire that is an unescapable sledgehammer pounding in my blood. It means running to the nearest gay bar, the military, the convent, the gay rights movement, or the closet. It means acknowledging that being a lesbian, if it does not someday make me kill myself, is something that can get me killed.

To be a lesbian means to be sexual, even though women aren't supposed to be sexual, and to experience that sexualness with other women.

❖

It's popular now to portray the 1970s as "antisex" or "sexless," but while I think that an evocative metaphor, it too easily rewrites history. My memory is that there was just as much bed hopping and sexual intrigue going on in our collectives as ever there was in Natalie Barney's 1920s Paris salon, perhaps more, since we were also muddling our way toward the ethical parameters of nonmonogamy. Indeed, the strength of nonmonogamy as an ideal created a sexual milieu a friend once described saying, "Everyone's *real* relationship is with their therapist."[18] Rather than the decade being "antisex," I think in the early seventies the "old" concept of lesbians (beings driven primarily by sex) came together with its newly formulated antithesis (affectionate compatriots) and created the belief that, as lesbians, we all could be, and should seek to be, sexually successful with every dyke we met.

During my three years in the collective, I went to bed with a number of women, less out of genuine attraction or sexual need than because I was eighteen, nineteen, or twenty, and that's what everyone around me appeared to be doing. About half the time, the evening ended up in fumblings and frustrations that were quickly glossed over. When I looked back later, I noticed the "failures" were almost always with women who, like me, had always been lesbians, and whom I now know to call femme. The "successes" were more likely to be with "movement lesbians," but though that sex was pleasant, it lacked the passion and power I really wanted. In retrospect, knowing whom to go to bed with would've been easier had "roles" not disappeared. But the point's not that I couldn't ask, "Are you butch or femme?" rather, that what should have been a normal period of sexual experimentation through which I came, via trial and error, to know what I wanted resulted instead, in the context of lesbian-feminism, in a sense of failed lesbian identity. Feminism told me that what I did in bed was political. And the assumption was that any two women armed with feminist theory and *Loving Women*[19] ought to be able to make *something* work in bed. Women who failed but could attribute their problems to nonmonogamy at least had an openly debated theoretical premise to challenge. Those of us whose failure was felt on the level of sexual competence, stemming from a need for identities we couldn't name or that didn't exist, had no such theory to re-examine. Lesbian-feminism's confusion of sexuality with politics, and its merging of "lesbian" with "woman," meant that by 1977, at age twenty-two, I'd concluded I wasn't much of a lesbian and neither, once again, could I possibly be a real woman. I had survived coming out in high school, and living on the streets, but I couldn't handle the lesbian-feminist movement.

❖

It is the fall of 1975. I am working at a straight, part-time job in a bank, and devoting my every spare moment to volunteering in a women's bookstore. I have cut my hair to dyke regulation shortness, forsworn jewelry and mascara, and dress only in jeans, corduroys, and boys' shirts. I've stopped going to bars. My evenings are taken up by the bookstore. It's a place that matters tremendously to me, beyond all the exciting "firsts" it provides. Lesbian books are being published by the hundreds, and we stock them; lesbian art hangs on the walls; we sell lesbian records and host lesbian performers. I am helping to make lesbians visible, to provide information about who we are. I want only one thing: for no more lesbians to go through, as I did, the pain of being an isolated, unnamed freak simply for desiring women. I squelch the discomforts that come with working here and count on my enormous defenses, plus the ability to keep the bookstore's inventory in my head, to keep me from too much critical scrutiny.

One day a new woman and her soon-to-be-ex lover of ten years join the collective. Anais stands out. She has long copper red hair, creamy freckled skin, and an ultrafeminine body I once would have sold my soul to have. What makes her most visible is her long skirts. Only two other women have ever worn skirts here: both the only straight women, both harassed into leaving. After a time I begin to notice, during the collective meetings I try to tune out, that Anais is the target of an increasing amount of criticism, none of it terribly specific. When I listen, I hear her whispered about. No one knows her from other circles. She looks straight. Her lover's appearance is more butch than anyone else's. Her lover uses a man's name — not something unisex like "Pat" or "Jo" but "Mike" — and its incongruity jars.

Anais and I draw together, saying the things we dare not speak too loudly, even to ourselves. Talking about the constant criticism and judgments and restrictions. About the self-confidence of the others, which we don't have. About the racism. About the dismissal of people's real lives and the obliteration of differences. About the cost and pain of being lesbian and the need to make that be different, and how no one here seems to feel that. About her struggle to stay sane in the face of bad love affairs, rape, abortion, efforts to be straight, poverty, drug overdoses, suicide attempts, her essentially over relationship, her need to write. She resonates to a part of me denied in the bookstore. She is working-class, of mixed race and light enough to pass, old gay, and, though I'm not sure of the term, femme. She makes sense to me. Most of the collective thinks her a little crazy, too overtly sexual, and trashes her constantly.

Before long, our empathy spills into physical attraction, but we don't go to bed. She wants to; I won't. She wants a relationship but won't leave Mike unless I promise to move in with her. She courts me, sending me letters full of sex, passion, romance, and pain, writing me beautiful poetry, bringing me cards and flowers. She won't take no for an answer. It is flattering and I bask in it, but I refuse to give in. I say again that I still hurt from a recent breakup; I'm emotionally exhausted; I don't want another relationship now. That this feels too complicated and we're both on the rebound. That I'm leery of a relationship based on lust and empathy. But between us we create enough steam to fuel the entire industrial revolution. We make out wildly in between my nos. We kiss in the back room of the bookstore until neither of us can stand upright. We drive to the park and, wrapped in a quilt and the smell of grass, lie in each other's arms beneath cherry blossoms and sunlight. She is soft, and hot, and unafraid of sexual need. She kisses like no one else, ever. My blood has been replaced with molten gold infused with the smell of spring. Still, we do not go to bed. Finally, she returns to Mike for a last try. I fall back into an old on-again-off-again relationship. We avoid each other.

Some six months later, Anais and I run into each other at a performance of Susan Griffin's Voices and come back to my place afterward to catch up. She has left Mike and is living alone for the first time. She is in a writing group, and in therapy, and has decided to be celibate. I've been obsessively reading lesbian novels written before the advent of lesbian-feminism, and becoming enraged at the ease with which preseventies lesbian history and lesbian diversity have been denied. The hint of a larger lesbian world is part of the growing problems I am having — we both are having — with the bookstore. She has begun to identify openly as a woman of color, yet the otherwise all-white collective ignores her while they spend hours wondering Where The Women Of Color Are. Class issues have also arisen, amidst much denial, in addition to the usual acrimony, the lack of business experience, and the unending effort to arrive at political purity — at the cost of tasks necessary to staying open. The collective is headed for another major split or purge, and neither of us knows if she can take it again or where else to go.

The evening draws past midnight. Our efforts to re-establish connection lead to our talking ourselves, despite reservations, into bed together. It is a mistake. No old passion sparks, and when she begins making love to me in a way I have made love only to a butch lover, I freeze into rigidity. This is not the first time sex has failed to work for me, but this is different, emotionally devastating as well as sexually frustrating. She blames, accuses, and wants to be taken home. I blame in return, and say it shouldn't matter. I drive her home through the blinking traffic lights and San Francisco fog, trying not to notice how much I hurt.

Two days later, she sends me a vicious, and beautifully written, poem about my frigidity. She does not speak to me again. A month later I find that she and a friend with whom I've also slept, successfully only the first time, are comparing notes. I worry about the kind of reputation I must be getting. I always thought sex was the one thing I was good at, but experience is beginning to tell me otherwise.

A year later, in 1977, I leave all my movement commitments to live with a woman who has been in the closet since 1967. She has never had anything to do with feminism. We're not very compatible in bed and so sex is infrequent, but she is willing to commit to me, and she has no connection to a past I want to forget. Anais, in particular, comes to symbolize what I want to forget. It's more than sexual passion inexplicably vanished. Losing her is losing an emotional connection between just-becoming-articulated selves, a common place to stand against a feminism that denies who we are, a bond somehow bound to our sexual needs. I feel I have betrayed part of myself.

Sometime in 1978, the bookstore goes under. I do not go to the closing party.

❖

The denial of erotic categories, coupled with the mythology that we could all get into bed together, served to foster profound doubts in many of us about our ability to be sexual at all. Further, when the internal conflicts got too great and, in an attempt to salvage a vestige of self-esteem, we removed ourselves from the arena of "political correctness," what we managed to rediscover was so truncated, caricatured, and pejorative that claiming it involved yet another struggle for self-worth. I might wish for a butch lover like Beebo Brinker,[20] but butch in the seventies was a cartoon. Mighty Mo from *Rubyfruit Jungle* is a "diesel dyke" whose approach is to "barrel down ... slam on her brakes ... and bellow."[21] By the 1980s, femmes were named "sellouts" who reclaimed heterosexual privilege and used it to oppress butch lesbians.[22]

Finding the lived reality of butch-femme beneath the stereotypes is difficult. The predominance of lesbian-feminist preconceptions, and their remarkable similarity to the heterosexual myths, means everyone "knows" how to tell who's butch and who's femme. Who can fix a car? Who does the dishes? Who makes the first move in bed? Who looks more believable in a skirt? Whose hair is shortest? Butch-femme is simultaneously both a straight image we apply to ourselves as a joke and a visible part of the lives of historical lesbians (Gertrude and Alice) whose fame we use to justify our existence. As such, it is easy to assume that "real" butch-femme always exists elsewhere. From Rusty Millington, in *Word Is Out*, who is clearly butch but denies it by comparing herself to someone else who is *really* butch,[23] to everyone who told me I *couldn't* be a *real* femme because I was "too tall/too intellectual/too small breasted/too rarely seen in a skirt," the message is that one might get away with being "into roles" as long as one doesn't call them that. I am reminded, ironically, of Joanna Russ's litany of the requirements for "real lesbians," and her conclusion: "There *are* no real lesbians; *real* lesbians have horns."[24] The speed with which women who reclaimed the words *lesbian* and *dyke* say they "can't relate to labels" never fails to amaze me.

In the past, butch-femme appears to have been an admixture of heterosexual expectations and genuine challenges to the traditional construction of female gender; the shape it takes in the 1990s, one hopes, might break free of the former if lesbian-feminists would stop naming us an imitation. What is most difficult in claiming butch-femme in a "postliberation" era, however, is untangling both the homophobia that defined "real lesbian" as butch and butch-femme's association, like that Del and Phyl make, with only a heterosexual portrait. Sally Gearhart remembers:

> I think the pressure was from society, which made me feel that, if I was not a woman in the sense that the society said a woman should be, then I must be butch. I don't think I understood that there could be femme lesbians. I didn't want to do the things ordinary women did, so therefore I must be like a man, and therefore, I think I dressed and acted more butch than I probably was.[25]

Under this equation, femme is not quite a "real lesbian." Pat Bond recalls:

> There was a lot of pressure to look butch if you were [butch]. And, of course, you wanted to, 'cause you wanted to be identified as a dyke. I was never too good at it. I looked really funny trying to look like a man. Men's pants look funny because I'm very short waisted and big busted. Trying to wear the short haircut with sideburns shaved over the ears, I looked like the missing link.[26]

The standards of lesbian-feminist androgyny are equally intolerant. I've heard from more than one younger lesbian a reluctance to claim the name "lesbian" because the movement conveys "it means having to give up being a girl."[27] For a long time, I thought I couldn't be femme because I had never been straight. Lesbian-feminism seems determined to portray butch-femme as rigid, even though butch and femme characteristics can be interchangeable, subtle, and allow for more variation than do heterosexual sex roles. Degrees of butchness and femmeness — stone butch, butchy femme, femmy butch, ki-ki — are named points on a spectrum that is shortchanged when portrayed as masculine-feminine extremes. It is difficult to imagine heterosexual patriarchy allowing women to experiment with and choose sexual roles or no role at all. Yet, it is from feminists that I still hear that I can't wear a skirt, whereas my butch lover Jo never thought knowing how to rebuild an engine made me less femme.

As an issue, butch-femme is fraught with ambivalence and denial. When Jo Ann Loulan asked lesbian audiences around the United States if they had ever rated themselves or been rated by others on a butch-femme scale, 95 percent acknowledged that they had. Yet the same percentage also affirmed that they "did not consider butch-femme to be an important concept in their lives." Loulan points out that this is a statistical anomaly; rarely does a group insist that a universal experience is universally unimportant.[28] In a separate but related survey, Loulan found that one-third of her respondents identified themselves as either butch or femme, but that fully three-quarters of those who did so claimed *not* to demonstrate that identity in obvious ways within the lesbian community. If Loulan's data is valid, a substantial proportion of one-third of the community is "in the closet" about a butch-femme identity.[29]

❖

Fall 1986. In a women's studies class for which I am a T.A. we are having a discussion about feminine appearance and liberation. Does what one wears reflect one's feminist consciousness? Sexual orientation? One of the lesbian students, a woman with short hair, dressed in faded jeans, a flannel shirt, quartz-crystal jewelry, and buttons that proclaim both her politics and her sexuality, says that she dresses as she does so that she'll be visible to other lesbians. She looks for sisters based on what they wear, and says it's important that she be able to recognize other lesbians, and be recognized as a lesbian herself, when walking across campus. I agree with her sentiment about visibility; I also know that she would not recognize me, with my nail polish, heels, and curled and colored hair, as a "sister lesbian."

Two hours later, I meet my lover in downtown San Francisco for lunch. Together we are markedly visible as queers, not because we are holding hands, but because she is butch enough to be assumed male at first glance, and by corporate standards, I am female, but not very feminine. We are stared at by nearly everyone, several swiveling their heads to keep us in view while their bodies walk past us. At lunch, the group of men at the next table spend more time glancing furtively at us, whispering to one another, than they do eating. Their looks are a combination of hostility, curiosity, and disgust. Were this another setting or a different time of day, I would worry about overt harassment. But this sort of thing happens all the time, and so far we've been safe. As I ask the waitress for more coffee, I think of the lesbian student in the morning class and wonder, "How visible is visible? To whom?"

❖

It's time we acknowledge that a basic assumption of lesbian-feminist theory is irrevocably flawed. Its construction of both "woman" and "lesbian" is based on a white, middle-class, *heterosexual* experience of woman's oppression; the political analysis and the liberating behaviors that arise from it have meaning only for those who have lived (or attempted to live) that lifestyle. Though such a lifestyle is indeed the norm to which all other groups are expected to conform, to proclaim the resistance appropriate to that particular experience as also appropriate to others is to continue the same eradication or punishment of difference practiced by the dominant culture. There *is* a construction and experience of "lesbian" apart from that which arose from feminism's second wave, and as with class and race, it is not a variation on a more central theme of "all women's experience." In particular, not all our experiences of "gender" are the same, and gender roles are not the root cause of either sexism or heterosexuality.

Gender systems are a cultural universal. Every society organizes its members into two or more genders. Gender expresses and signals two things: what tasks an individual performs (division of labor) and with whom (what other gender) one has sex. However, the degree of distinction between genders, the rigidity with which they are applied, the particular characteristics given to each, and the number of genders that are recognized vary enormously. It's generally true that where women are oppressed, homosexuality, especially lesbianism, is also repressed as a gender or identity, though it may be accepted as a behavior.[30] What is not true is that a gender system always implies sexism or homophobia.

There's no question that sex-role conditioning in our male-dominated society is one of the primary means by which women's oppression is perpetrated. Gender systems (which sex roles express), however, are not intrinsically oppressive. What is oppressive in our society is the linking of biological sex (female or male) to gender identity (woman or man), gender or sex role (feminine or masculine), sexual object choice (opposite), and sexual identity (heterosexual). Barbara Ponse calls these correlations "the principle of consistency."[31] It is this system, *and the denial of any other construction of gender*, on which sexism is founded. The problem is the correlations, not the specific components.

What's oppressive about gender, defined sex roles, in our society is that they are limited to two, rigidly correlated with biological sex, and obsolete, in a complex industrial society, as an expression of who does what work. The sex-role oppression that feminism means to criticize is rooted in the social restriction, the male=aggressive=breadwinner and female=passive=housewife model of heterosexuality; traditional heterosexual sex roles are but symptoms of that restriction. Gender per se is not the problem, and I think it impossible, as well as pointless, to try to rid ourselves of it. Certainly, lesbian-feminism has not been able to: its "androgynous" norm is itself a gender, serving precisely to signal that one is a woman who sleeps with women. Butch and femme are also genders, reflecting a complementarity of personas within a woman-to-woman relationship.

The (heterosexual) definition of a lesbian, prior to lesbian-feminism, was twofold. First, a lesbian was defined by her sexual behavior; second, in keeping with the principle of consistency, a lesbian was defined as any woman who didn't follow normal female role behavior. In challenging heterosexual feminists' fear of lesbians by arguing that loving women was just another step along a continuum that rejected role limitations, lesbian-feminism incorporated exactly the principle of male dominance it meant to refute, complete with all its conflated meanings. Lesbian-feminism's construction of lesbian is simply the second heterosexual definition writ large. Though the movement began by questioning the link male dominance made between gender role (feminine) and gender identity (woman), it never went any further. Heterosexuality is not a sex role. Neither is lesbianism.[32] Lesbian-feminism mistook the *function* lesbians serve in a heterosexist society — that of an outcast group into which women could fall if they stepped out of line — for lesbianism's *meaning*.[33]

One of the consequences of using lesbianism's assumed challenge to sex roles to justify lesbian sexuality is that this left lesbians to a large extent desexualized and in an identity limbo. In defining as a lesbian any woman who stepped outside the boundaries of accepted femininity, lesbian-feminism encompassed a whole range of behaviors not necessarily linked to loving women. And legitimizing lesbian sex through its political potential created a circular argument: if one had properly rejected sex roles — that is, if one was a valid lesbian — one would choose only sexual activity that was roleless; if one did not choose such a sexuality, one was, by definition, not properly political; and if one was not political, one's lesbian sexuality couldn't be accepted. Where lesbian-feminism was "antisex" was in its justification of lesbianism.[34] Lesbian-feminism became a form of permission much like marriage: it was okay to have sex within it, but anything outside those bounds was taboo.[35]

By proclaiming lesbianism something all women could and should choose, lesbian-feminism defined lesbianism as a learned process, a mere matter of beginning to see women as whole people worthy of love. Such a definition enabled previously heterosexual women, women who had never before considered sex with a woman, to become lesbians. Similarly, women who had previously discovered lesbianism but had made themselves conform to a heterosexual (married) life found in the movement social approval for claiming lesbian lives. However, by rejecting "heterosexual" and "homosexual" as false categories, lesbian-feminism denied the experiences and needs of women, like me, who had always been homosexual.[36] I don't mean to imply that women who came out through the movement are somehow less than "real" lesbians; if nothing else, the events of the past twenty years have taught us how complex the construction of sexual behavior and identity is. Most lesbians can't be categorized as simply *either* "sexual" *or* "political." But I do think that coming to a lesbian identity via "Gee, what a great idea, that never occurred to me before" differs enormously from coming to it via "How am I going to live with this difference?" What's important is that one path not overshadow another as we seek ways to resist a society that would rather we didn't exist.

❖

Dear Joan,

    It's primarily with butch women that the conflicting identities of "lesbian" and "woman" come together for me. Certainly, it is butch women who have given me back my body, with whom sex silences the constant yammering of the intellectual tape recorder and the old message that my only value is my brain. It is butch women who made wanting sex okay, who never said I wanted it "too much" or thought I got too wet. With so many other women I was either "an ironing board," or "a slut"; it was butch women who taught me about multiple orgasms and the incredible high of fisting, who made it okay to want to be made love to until I was too spent to move. It was butch women who made it right to give by responding rather than reciprocating, to make love by moving beneath them instead of using my tongue or hands. It was butch women who gave me permission to not be in control at all times, and butch women who didn't think it vain that I wanted to be pretty, who, indeed, made me feel beautiful.

    I don't suppose anyone is to blame for the fact that fitting into the feminist androgynous norm reinforced a childhood vision of myself as neutered, or that in short hair and thrift store boys' clothes I felt like the skinny street kid I'd too recently been. If I looked in the mirror dressed as a feminist, I saw street trash or an older echo of poor white trash,[37] yet I knew if I dressed the way I wanted, I'd be treated as a different kind of trash — and for that I do blame. The history that made the abjuring of gender and overt sexuality important for so many women simply wasn't mine. Not that it had to be, but no room was made for other realities. Women's fear of rape was an issue, but lesbians' fear of the street violence that came with visibility was never mentioned. Women's problems with self-esteem were examined endlessly, but no one seemed to think about the lesbian legacy of suicide. I heard so much about women's pain around sexuality (and only rarely of the joy), but I don't think anyone ever talked about the kind of lesbian pain that butch-femme sexuality answers.

    I hesitate to say we take a different pain, unrelated to rape, incest, or insensitive heterosexuality, to bed with us, for fear someone will say, "See, I knew roles were damaging." Or worse, that "it's our own fault" because it comes from something we're not supposed to have: active sexual desire. Though time has dimmed my visual recall, I don't think I will ever forget the woman who was knifed for holding hands with her lover. Some days she comes to bed with me, and then I need someone who wants me enough to make the loving worth the risk. I want to answer a lover not with gentleness but with a strength that conveys, "You don't have to blow your brains out for desiring me." It may be too general a statement, but I think women's sexual pain comes when sex is used as punishment for being female. Lesbian's sexual pain comes from being sexual, and butch-femme is one way of healing that. I don't believe one pain to be more real than another, but ours is never spoken of, and that needs to change.

❖

The main justification for invalidating butch-femme is that it's an imitation of heterosexual roles and, therefore, not a genuine lesbian model. One is tempted to react by saying, "So what?" but the charge encompasses more than betrayal of an assumed fixed and "true" lesbian culture. Implicit in the accusation is the denial of cultural agency to lesbians, of the ability to shape and reshape symbols into new meanings of identification. Plagiarism, as the adage goes, is basic to all culture.

In the realm of cultural identity, that some of the markers of a minority culture's boundaries originate in an oppressing culture is neither unusual nor particularly significant. For instance, in the United States certain kinds of bead- and ribbon work are immediately recognizable as specific to Native American cultures, wherein they serve artistic and ceremonial functions. Yet beads, trinkets, ribbons, and even certain "Indian" blanket patterns were brought by Europeans, who traded them as cheap goods for land. No one argues that Indians ought to give up beadwork or blanket weaving, thus ridding themselves of the oppressors' symbols, because those things took on radically different cultural meanings in the hands of Native Americans. Or consider Yiddish, one of the Jewish languages. Although Yiddish is written in Hebrew characters and has its own idioms and nuances, its vocabulary is predominantly German. Those who speak German can understand Yiddish. Genocidal Germanic anti-Semitism dates back to at least the eleventh century. Yet East European Jews spoke "the oppressor's language," developing in it a distinctive literary and theatrical tradition. Why is it so inconceivable that lesbians could take elements of heterosexual sex roles and remake them?

❖

It is June 1987, and I am sitting in a workshop on "Lesbians and Gender Roles" at the annual National Women's Studies Conference. It is one of surprisingly few workshops on lesbian issues, particularly since, at a plenary session two mornings later, two-thirds of the conference attendees will stand up as lesbians. Meanwhile, in this workshop the first speaker is spending half an hour on what she calls "Feminism 101," a description of heterosexual sex roles. Her point in doing this, she says, is to remind us of the origin of roles, "which are called butch and femme when lesbians engage in them." She tells us the purpose of her talk will be to prove, from her own experience, that "these roles are not fulfilling" for lesbians. She tells us that the second speaker will use lesbian novels from the 1950s to demonstrate the same thesis. And, indeed, the second speaker has a small stack of 1950s "pulp paperbacks" with her, many of them the titles that, when I discovered them in the mid-1970s, resonated for me in a way that the feminist books published by Daughters and Diana Press did not.

I consider for several minutes. I'm well versed in lesbian literature, particularly in the fifties novels, and don't doubt my ability to adequately argue an opposing view with the second presenter. I am curious to see if she will use the publisher-imposed "unhappy ending" to prove that roles make for misery. I also decide I'm willing to offer my own experience to challenge the first presenter's conclusions — though I'd much rather sit with her over coffee and talk. She is in her midforties and, although she claims to have renounced it, still looks butch. Even if she speaks of roles negatively, she has been there and I want to hear her story. Then I look around me. Everyone is under thirty. There are a few vaguely butch-looking women present who'd very likely consider themselves to be as androgynous as everyone else, and not a single, even remotely femme-looking woman besides myself. I recall Alice Walker's advice to "never be the only one in the room." Quietly, I get up and walk out. I go to no other lesbian presentations at the conference.

❖

Butch and femme are lesbian-specific genders, two of potentially many ways to be both a lesbian and a woman. They are unliberated only in the sense that they need liberating from the assumption, made by heterosexuals and lesbian-feminists alike, that they are an imitation of heterosexuality, a clinging to vestiges of heterosexual femininity or an attempt to masquerade as a man. As Judy Grahn has said about being butch:

> Our point was not to be men; our point was to be butch and get away with it. We always kept something back: a high-pitched voice, a slant of the head, or a limpness of hand gestures, something that was clearly labeled female. I believe our statement was "Here is another way of being a woman," not "Here is a woman trying to be taken for a man."[38]

The butch-femme legacy of the 1950s that lesbian-feminism so quickly decries does appear at times to have had its own oppressions and sexist attitudes (particularly directed toward femmes), but these should not be an excuse for obscuring its fundamental legacy of resistance to heterosexual norms. Butch-femme lesbians claimed the right to play with gender and sex roles long before 1970s feminism began to critique sex and gender. Such an exploration has had to proceed despite heterosexual oppression and the oppressive restrictions of lesbian-feminist androgyny. It will be a long day before heterosexuality is no longer compulsory, one made no shorter while one group of women centralizes their experience as "universal" and interprets everyone else's for them.

Lesbianism and feminism contain the potential to liberate gender roles from their identification with biological sex, and to create a multiplicity of genders that more accurately signal sexual desire, posture, and temperament. This needs to proceed, however, not from the imposition of a lot of hastily codified rules but from explorations that allow individuals to name what fits, to use labels to clarify, not to restrict. Masculine and feminine become oppressive if they are the only options available, as do butch and femme if every lesbian must be one or the other; so, too, for the mandate for androgyny within the feminist movement. Not every lesbian, including those who have always been lesbians, is, or should try to become, either butch or femme; women who spent years in unhappy conformity to heterosexual restrictions before becoming lesbians should not have to apologize for viewing lipstick or ties as anathema. Likewise, we need not create a "butch-femme continuum." The "butch-femme scale" developed by Loulan[39] may be a useful research tool for measuring lesbian attitudes, but it also perpetuates the portrait of butch-femme as masculine-feminine, belittling and appropriating identities that are not based on hair length. Finally, we need to be aware of the nuances that arise from different classes and cultures. What is butch to a Jewish lesbian is not necessarily butch to a lesbian from Philadelphia's mainline, a lesbian from Harlem, or a lesbian from Thailand.[40]

The lesbian-feminist movement, in the enthusiasm of its power, came too quickly to answers about the causes of oppression, and the means to liberation, answers that have turned out to be incomplete. Too much of lesbian life, especially butch-femme life, was denied in the process, and it needs to be said plainly that a movement that claims to speak for all women but cannot now listen is not going to liberate anyone. We need to take back "lesbian" as a sexual definition disburdened of any political justification.

In particular, it's time we reclaim the right to fuck around with gender.

Notes

1. No endeavor is ever accomplished in isolation; no writing is solely the product of one person's ideas. In particular, I am indebted to the thoughts of, and conversations with, Keri Baum, Sarah Brooks, Linci Z. Comy, Deva DeFusco, Lois Flynne, Sally Gearhart, Nina Kaiser, Ruth Mahaney, Kellan McCracken, Jane Robinson, Angie Romanogli, Jaen Treesinger, and Corky Wick. Each has contributed substantially to my understanding of either butch-femme or its opposition among feminists. I am grateful to Priscilla Alexander for insisting that I could and should write what I thought, who fought with me (and won, more or less) about voice and style, and who edited stoically while in the background I muttered, "Whaddya mean, it isn't perfect?" I also want to acknowledge the courage of Joan Nestle, Cherríe Moraga, and Amber Hollibaugh, whose willingness in 1981 to publish a part of their lives broke the feminist-imposed silence surrounding butch-femme. I would not be here without their voices. Finally, I wish to thank Eve Myers for asking her question, and Ruth Mahaney for waiting faithfully six years for me to write something on this subject.

2. Rita Mae Brown, "Dedicated to All Women Who Haven't Loved a Woman,"

THE PERSISTENT DESIRE

in *Songs to a Handsome Woman* (Baltimore, Md.: Diana Press, 1971), p. 11.

3. Margaret Nichols, "Lesbian Sexuality: Issues and Developing Theory," in *Lesbian Psychologies: Explorations and Challenges*, edited by the Boston Lesbian Psychologies Collective (Chicago: University of Illinois Press, 1987), pp. 97–125; Joan Nestle, "Butch-Fem Relationships: Sexual Courage in the 1950s," *Heresies 12: Sex Issue*, vol. 3, no. 4 (1981): 21–24, reprinted in Joan Nestle, *The Restricted Country* (Ithaca, N.Y.: Firebrand Books, 1987), pp. 100–109; Amber Hollibaugh and Cherríe Moraga, "What We're Rollin' around in Bed With: Sexual Silences in Feminism: A Conversation toward Ending Them," *Heresies 12: Sex Issue*, vol. 3, no. 4 (1981): 58–62, reprinted in this volume.

4. Jo Ann Loulan, *The Lesbian Erotic Dance: Butch, Femme, Androgyny and Other Rhythms* (San Francisco: Spinsters, 1990).

5. I think the letter, from the *San Francisco Bay Times* (vol. 12, no. 3, p. 18), is worth quoting in near entirety:

> ...Nor does she have a clue in the lesbian feminist herstory department. But no problem — there are plenty of stereotypes of the anti-sexual feminist on which she can call to validate her fantasy that "our [lesbian] sexual identities" really have to do with a dynamic of attraction copied from heterosexuality.
>
> ...We dumped butch/femme precisely because it was artificial and because it repressed our sexuality. In the prefeminist lesbian bar scene, women had to pick one role and stick up to it, or be shunned as untrustworthy. Butch/femme was the basis of a pitiful plea for tolerance on grounds that we must be somewhat normal, because we, too, had a husband-type partner and a wife-type partner. Women were overjoyed to have an alternative community for which they could abandon this system.
>
> So, Joanne [*sic*], women in the '70s told you it was "imperative to identify as androgynous." And you *believed* them? Maybe *you* were "so programmed to be androgynous" that *you* "couldn't think of how else to be or how else to dress." But whether as a '70s hippie or an '80s lipstick lesbian, I've always had hair at least to my shoulder and lots and lots of wonderful women lovers. Country hippies, professional women, suburban matrons and softball dykes — all of them feminists, all of them utterly delighted to have lesbian sex ... Had anyone been silly enough to tell us there were proper and improper ways to make love, we would have laughed in their faces.
>
> It seems to me that many of the women now building up the mythology of the "Sexless Seventies" are in denial about how easily they gave in and went along with ideas they now say were rigid and repressive. Having bought into the heteropatriarchy's stereotype of feminists as uptight and anti-sexual, they now feel compelled to outbimbo each other ... All Joanne Loulan [*sic*] has proven is that lesbians are living and loving however they choose — without PC or butch/femme. This is what lesbian feminism has always been about and what the spineless weenies of any decade will never understand.

One small irony about this letter is that its author is a male-to-female transsexual whose right to call herself a lesbian was the subject of a very heated national debate in the early 1970s. Not only has she apparently forgotten what it feels like to be judged and dismissed, she also seems to be "in denial" that she was still physically male during much of the "lesbian sex" with "lots and lots of wonderful woman lovers" she boasts of, perhaps because it's hardly a credible position from which to dismiss butch-femme as a heterosexual imitation.

6. Radicalesbians, "The Woman-Identified-Woman," in *Out of the Closets: Voices of Gay Liberation,* edited by Karla Jay and Allen Young (New York: Douglas Books, 1972), p. 172. "The Woman-Identified-Woman" was first distributed in mimeograph form at the second Congress to Unite Women, held in New York City, in 1970.

7. Clarification of some of the ideas in this article came while I was reading "Whose Country Is This, Anyway?," chapter 12 in Thomas Friedman's excellent book on the Middle East, *From Beirut to Jerusalem* (New York: Farrar Straus Giroux, 1989). Chapter 12 is about the complexity of Jewish identity. What is relevant here is the story of secular, and ultra-Orthodox, Israeli parents who, a generation ago, each took their children to visit the others' neighborhood and witness a lifestyle that would surely soon die out. Of course, neither has, and by all accounts, those divisions are today among the deepest in Israel.

8. Gayle Rubin, in Deirdre English, Amber Hollibaugh, and Gayle Rubin, "Talking Sex: A Conversation on Sexuality and Feminism," *Socialist Review* 11, no. 4 (July–August 1981): 43–62.

9. See Loulan, *The Lesbian Erotic Dance,* p. 27. The assertion that butch-femme realities were bargained away in return for heterosexual acceptance is not new; compare Nestle's "Butch-Fem Relationships." Nestle also states, in this same article, that "the butch-fem couple embarrassed other Lesbians (and still does) because they made Lesbians culturally visible — a terrifying act for the 1950s." I don't disagree, but with the advent of lesbian-feminism, I think the embarrassment has become more complicated.

10. Sally Gearhart, "The Miracle of Lesbianism," in Sally Gearhart and William R. Johnson, *Loving Women, Loving Men* (San Francisco: New Glide Publications, 1974), p. 128.

11. Radicalesbians, "The Woman-Identified-Woman," pp. 172, 174.

12. The term *political lesbian* has had different meanings at different times. In this instance, it was explained to me as meaning a woman who consciously gave up relationships with men to become a lesbian until sexism and women's oppression ended; the woman who explained it to me defined her lesbianism that way. I remember actually feeling nauseated, and wanting to walk away from her confidence as quickly as possible. I thought, but didn't say, "Great. After liberation you can go back to men, but I'll still be queer, so where does all this leave me?"

13. I don't think femmes very often say this. The conventional wisdom is that femmes grow up with a normal feminine (and heterosexual) identity, and it's the butch women who talk about having been tomboys, who say, "I was hoping I could become a boy — and then I got tits."

14. Joanna Russ has the rare ability to express entire concepts in one short, oftentimes funny, sentence, and many of her one-liners remain with me for years after I read them in a book. This particular one is likely from *How to Suppress Women's Writing* (Austin: University of Texas Press, 1983) or possibly *On Strike against God* (New York: Out & Out Books, 1980).

15. Del Martin and Phyllis Lyon, *Lesbian/Woman* (San Francisco: Glide Publications, 1972), pp. 6–7.

16. Rita Mae Brown, *Rubyfruit Jungle* (Plainfield, Vt.: Daughters, 1973), p. 130.

17. Sidney Abbot and Barbara Love, *Sappho Was a Right-On Woman* (New York: Stein & Day, 1972), *passim,* although most of the analysis of butch-femme is concentrated on pp. 92–98.

18. Thank you, V.C.

19. Nomadic Sisters, *Loving Women* (Mountain View, Calif.: Nomadic Sisters, 1976).

20. Beebo Brinker is a Greenwich Village butch in a series of novels by Ann Bannon: *Women in the Shadows* (1959), *Journey to a Woman* (1960), and *Beebo Brinker* (1962). They were originally published in New York by Fawcett Gold Medal, and have since been reprinted by Naiad Press.

21. Brown, *Rubyfruit Jungle,* p. 129.

22. See Linda Strega's "The Big Sell-Out: Lesbian Femininity," *Lesbian Ethics* 1, no. 3 (Fall 1985): 73–84; and Ruston, Bev Jo, and Linda Strega, "Heterosexism Causes Lesbophobia Causes Butch-Phobia," *Lesbian Ethics* 2, no. 2 (Fall 1986): 22–41.

23. *Word Is Out,* Adair Films, 1977, and Nancy Adair and Casey Adair, eds., *Word Is Out: Stories of Some of Our Lives* (San Francisco: New Glide Publications, 1978). The book and movie versions are somewhat different. In the movie, Rusty Millington's interview is edited in a way that implies she disavows being butch. The text of her interview in the book (which does not include all the text of the movie), however, reads as a strong affirmation of her and Pam's relationship as one that is butch-femme (pp. 47–48).

24. Joanna Russ, "Not for Years But for Decades," in *Magic Mommas, Trembling Sisters, Puritans and Perverts* (Trumansburg, N.Y.: Crossing Press, 1985), p. 29.

25. Interview with Sally Gearhart, June 28, 1988.

26. Pat Bond, quoted in Adair and Adair, *Word Is Out,* p. 58.

27. Thank you, R.J.

28. Loulan, *The Lesbian Erotic Dance,* pp. 42–43. In the statistics of social science, 95 percent is considered a "universal experience."

29. Ibid., pp. 260, 266. Loulan's sample size is small, and admittedly skewed toward lesbians willing to be out in lesbian and feminist settings. I can't help but wonder how much higher a percentage of *all* lesbians (especially among those who avoid feminism) identify as butch or femme.

30. The subject of gender is very complex. The only point I wish to make here is that gender systems, though universal, are not the monolith of modern sexist sex roles we tend to believe them. For examples of societies with three or more genders, see Walter Williams, *The Spirit and the Flesh* (Boston: Beacon Press, 1986), and David F. Greenberg's *The Construction of Homosexuality* (Chicago: University of Chicago Press, 1989), though the latter is difficult to wade through. For a discussion of correlations between the oppression of women and the repression of lesbian genders, see Evelyn Blackwood, "Sexuality and Gender in Certain Native American Tribes: The Case of Cross-Gender Females," *Signs: Journal of Women in Culture and Society* 10, no. 1 (Autumn 1984): 27–42.

31. Barbara Ponse, *Identities in the Lesbian World* (Westport, Conn.: Greenwood Press, 1978), pp. 24–30.

32. To the extent that male domination tries to enforce heterosexual as part of feminine behavior, lesbians do depart from "the feminine role." But it's not the departure that makes us lesbians, and straying from femininity in other ways does not a lesbian make. The relationship between gender and sexual orientation is similar to the relationship between race and class. Most people of color in the United States are also either working-class or poor, and there is no doubt that racism plays a major part in keeping them within that class status. However, one does not have to be a person of color to be poor, nor are, for instance, middle-class African-Americans no longer black. Lesbian-feminism, however, said that all women who challenged sex roles were lesbians, and in turn insisted that lesbians abrogate all vestiges of "roles."

33. For an analogy, see any collection of James Baldwin's essays. He (and others of his generation) pointed out that blacks, in a white society, function as "a bottom to which no white person could ever fall," and thus as a means of obscuring the hierarchy of class that also operates among whites. Yet no one ever suggested that being on the bottom was what defined African-American identity — or, for that matter, that everyone who was working-class or poor was somehow "black" because of a common class status.

34. There is a strand of lesbian-feminism that believes *all* sex to be oppressive, destructive, and so forth, but fortunately, it's not a popular one.

35. Indeed, because it is a gender system, butch-femme has come to occupy the position of "whore" relative to lesbian-feminist "marriage," not only in a literal sense, where the whore is the woman with whom sex is illegitimate and unspoken, but in a more symbolic one, wherein butch-femme, particularly because of its class and race associations, has become another manifestation of the "whore stigma": that portrait of uncontrolled sexualness given groups deemed "other" by a dominant culture, whether "other" is "lower class," Jewish, black, Asian, "primitive people" — or lesbian. For a discussion of class and race intersections with butch-femme, compare Hollibaugh and Moraga's "What We're Rollin' around in Bed With," Nestle's "Butch-Fem Relationships," and Amber Hollibaugh's "Desire for the Future: Radical Hope in Passion and Pleasure," in *Pleasure and Danger: Exploring Female Sexuality*, edited by Carole S. Vance (Boston: Routledge & Kegan Paul, 1984), pp. 401–410. For the whole stigma, compare Gail Pheterson, "The Social Consequences of Unchastity," in

Sex Work: Writings by Women in the Sex Industry, edited by Frederique Delacost and Priscilla Alexander (San Francisco: Cleis Press, 1987), pp. 215–230, or *The Whore Stigma: Female Dishonor and Male Unworthiness* (Amsterdam: Dutch Ministry of Social Affairs, 1985), by the same author.

36. Not to mention the agony that heterosexual women have gone through to be viewed as sincere and committed feminists.

37. Although I was raised in the suburban middle class of California, I'm one generation away from the back hills of East Kentucky. Appalachians are derided through comics like "Barney Google and Snuffy Smith" and TV programs like "The Beverly Hillbillies," or romanticized in movies like *Coal Miner's Daughter.* "Hillbillies," "hicks," "briars," and "moonshiners" are more common epithets than "poor white trash," but the fear of being labeled with *that* particular phrase was a terror of my childhood, one not at all helped by the fact that I look like the ethnic type.

38. Judy Grahn, *Another Mother Tongue* (Boston: Beacon Press, 1984), p. 31.

39. Loulan, *The Lesbian Erotic Dance.*

40. I am thinking, particularly, of the fact that what is Jewish butch may more likely arise from a tradition of Talmudic scholarship than from James Dean movies, with thanks to Gayle Rubin and Priscilla Alexander for conversations about this. For more on this topic, see Gayle Rubin's article in this volume. "Butch" does appear to be international; in Thailand, "butch" is a more or less socially accepted gender role (Unchana Suwannanond, personal communication).

2. Desire

"I can dress as feminine and sexy as I want. I do it for my butch and for myself."
—Salena Billie Barone

"For me, butch is not only an outward appearance and style, but the way in which I view some women, in and out of bed. I'm proud of that view and the behavior it evokes. I know it's different from most lesbians today."—J.C. Barone

Madeline Davis

Old femme

I know what I am
>   when I look at old pictures
>   long, wavy hair, eyeliner, mascara
>   demure and mysterious.
I know what I am
>   when I wander on my lunch hour
>   to sample new fragrances
>   and linger near lace lingerie.
I know what I am
>   when I paw through these letters
>   still warm with old passions
>   held firmly in wide rubber bands.
I know what I am
>   when the sight of white t-shirts
>   and the smell of Old Spice
>   can still make me shiver and smile.
I know what I am
>   in the dark when you fill me
>   your hands and your mouth
>   in the heat of the heart of my center
I know what I am.

Pam A. Parker

Der Rosenkavalier

Travesty, we call it, when a woman
plays a man, I mean, his part,
it could only be play, a part
in breeches — stand and part the rose
and gold curtain, stride booted,
spurred into the *Marschallin*'s boudoir,
embrace her, take hold the way
a woman who fucks women does,
lay both hands on her swelling
rib cage, expanded to power her voice,
slide both hands to her waist,
pull her up close, full front, turn,
the divan at the back of her knees;
kneeling over her, drag
both hands down, centerward,
thumbs together surmount
her mound, capture her clit;
fingers flat on her belly, curve
down to part her lips, two thumbs
back to back slide in, out and in,
if she cares for that, though the lover's part
is to give what she likes best
what she takes best, makes herself blessed—
those two thumbs baptizing themselves
are a part I don't need breeches
to play, only the lover's art.

Christine Cassidy

When she wears a tie for me

The first time,
she wanted kudos for style—
her silk the color of wine,
bordeaux, matched my enameled
nails. I knew she was all mine

that night we
dressed up for each other, she
and I shy as teens, itchy
for kisses snuck between songs.
I longed for her to take me—

no problem
if the traffic hadn't been
so thick on Broadway. Brazen
behavior she rather likes—
uppity dykes unbuttoned

(or unlaced,
to be precise) from the waist,
ready for her tongue to taste,
her hand to give. Brown satin
the second time: my pulse raced

as I touched
it to my breasts. Narrow swatch
of knotted cloth, its stitches
close and even — how does it
elicit such a strange rush,

THE PERSISTENT DESIRE

magnetic
paths of wanting? It's phallic,
she says. Innate, totemic
strength. I concede, though other
signs rouse power — concentric

circles, swirls
etched in soft stone; the loose curls
of fronds I see in carved, burled
oak; the wheatfields in her eyes;
an oyster's ivory pearl.

And today,
against corduroy, a gray
tie, pinpricked with red. Waiters
hovered like bees while she teased
and tried to tempt me to stray

from the cool
demeanor, professional,
I proffered over lunch. All
my defenses rapidly
fell. Over coffee, I failed

to keep my
composure, wanting her tie
in my mouth, down my throat. I
would squeeze then twist the flared base,
the familiar mystified,

resistant
yet yielding to persistent
fingers clenching her. On bent
knees I'd slowly lick its tip,
torture it, desire extant

in her grip,
my head pulled down to worship.
My reply, red nails I slip
to the knot, along her seam.
I smell her need as her hips

press to my
face, the silk damp where I wind
it over my hand, her tie
a spent piece of herself, used
as I wished, for the first time.

Yvette and Maggie, butch-femme couple, 1991

Christine Cassidy

Dear Billie

Dear Billie,
I'd offer apologies
for flirting at the party
but I know what you'd say — it's
not all that necessary—

and besides,
I'm enticed, your cool minx eyes
assessing me the way I've
come to enjoy. Why didn't
you, at the end, kiss me? I'd

have given
you skirt, but had determined,
while dressing, not to flirt. Then
I saw you, whispered in your
nappy hair, smiled a lot, and

had to touch.
Why is it you're the one butch
—my new lover won't say much—
who feeds me information
from the hand, and won't begrudge

my hunger
for knowing somewhat better
whom I've been lusting after
—granted I'm a little late,
a shy date — these last few years?

Fourteen now,
since I've been comfortably out.
Longer, if you count Girl Scouts,
the woman whose flint-lit fires
kindled mine. I stayed closemouthed

about sex,
watched the playground mavericks
pick out sides while I grew breasts,
lip-synched to Janis Joplin,
and fantasized what came next.

That same thrill,
chasing after boyish girls
—rough girls with flaccid pigtails—
who swaggered off fields and courts,
has gotten me in trouble

more than once.
When I wore a cocktail dress
(another time, only lace)
to seduce the dykes in suits
at Seven Sisters dances,

I wish you
had been there with your etudes
of history, tales accrued
not from books. Sea Colony
stories circa '62

my favorite:
at twenty you learned the gait
and gaze that femmes would covet.
You stroked my knee, reminisced.
I thought, does femme etiquette

permit one
bite into your neck, or none?
You laugh at my abstention
and my burn to know just what
you butches want, how and when.

THE PERSISTENT DESIRE

You say I
couldn't take what's on your mind.
What's on mine might terrify
you more. Or is this a coax
you expect, or will you try

to please me
when I visit? If you feed
me raisin scones and stories,
I'll reply in kind — naive
but willing, my dear Billie.

Gwendolyn Bikis

Cleo's gone

'm just getting ready to wash my white school blouse when the phone rings.

"Baby sister. What's shakin'?" It's Marla, calling from Charlotte. From the Girls' Club, no doubt, she's talking so streetlike.

"Nothin' doin'," I reply. "You coming home this weekend?"

"I just might. But that sure isn't the reason I'm calling. I just got a call, long distance. From Cleo."

I feel my breath leave me. Already I'm certain this isn't going to be real good.

"She asked me to send her some math books." A pause. "Tammy? She called me from the Wake County Jail. She's 'up against a li'l charge' is all she'll tell me. And she's not sounding too proud of whatever it is she's been charged with *this* time."

I can see the loose little shrug that Cleo'd give, acting cool and shucking, all the way into ... Into prison, this time. Soon as I think it, I know it, know it from the trembling in my voice: "Aah, Maarla—"

Cleo's gone, gone for sure now. Gone for good.

❖

Cleo was Marla's Little Sister, adopted as soon as I went off to college (as soon as I "deserted the mother bosom for the devil white world," as Marla insisted on putting it). I think that I was supposed to be jealous, now that Marla had a substitute, but I was the one who ended up getting that laugh. And Marla was the one who insisted on my meeting Cleo, a fact that I have many times reminded her of.

"I'm working on getting her off the street," Marla had explained to me, on our way over to the Morningside projects across the way from the Girls' Club. "If I can keep her eye on the basketball, I'll be able to get her back into a school, and get her learning how to read and write, so she'll have something to fall back on besides her shady-side companions."

We were walking along the littered sidewalk between two buildings as bare and plain as the brick box my sister Ruthanna stays in, up in Baltimore. Baltimore or Charlotte, it didn't make one difference: both projects seemed alike: ugly, dirty, and way too noisy.

We'd come up on a fence around a weedy asphalt courtyard where bunches of people were smoking and drinking, with a radio playing outside a window:

Hey, some people are made of plastic—
You know, some people are made of wood...

"Cleo's pretty tough," Marla whispered, "so don't be scared, now." She cupped her hands around her mouth and called toward the courtyard: "Cleo Timmons."

"Yo, sistah." Was Cleo playing, or was that the way she really talked? (Would she be angry to know that was my first thought on her "style"?)

From the radio, the song played on:

But, baby, I'm for real—
I'm as real as real can be...

Cleo, as you first looked to me — leaning back on that fence, your elbows hooked behind the metal posts, looking long and tall and untouchable, in shades and leather jacket and tight black jeans, with black suede tennis shoes on. Your hair grease sparkled in the sun, your hair trailing down below your turned-up jacket collar. You looked tough, all right — although I wasn't scared.

If what you're looking for is good loving,
Then whatchya see is whatchya get...

Marla had taken me by the hand. "I want you to meet my baby sister. Tammy."

Cleo leaned back even farther and lifted her shades. What was it? I'd never before *felt* any woman's eyes move over my body the way that Cleo's were. Then she smiled, so wide and free I saw right away the little gap between her two front teeth. "Yo, baby sistah. I'm Marla's Little Sister." She smiled wider, then dropped her shades back down as though she weren't yet ready for me to see her.

I got to say it again:
Whatchya see, baby, is what you get...

But I hadn't really *met* Cleo till I saw her play, saw her legs and arms as long as licorice sticks, licorice so whiplike she nipped the ball out of the other players' fingers, snapped and plucked the rebounds before they hit the backboard, jumped so quick it seemed there were springs in her knees. Cleo was just a bit darker than me, and built wiry, all tight and smooth at once. If I were to sculpt her, I'd do it all in wire, but no sculpture I could create would ever do her justice. Because Cleo *moved* like silk sliding through water.

Man, oh man, when I think of how gone I was over that girl ... from the early spring of those months I stayed with Marla, managing her team, until the July day she made me leave, I had one hopeless schoolgirl crush. I'd sit on the sidelines making like my own Girls' Club cheerleading squad, until everybody started to see who I was really cheering for. And the thing about it was, Cleo didn't need more cheering.

"F that 'everybody's a star' stuff. I'm the only star on this team." And she'd thump her ball a couple of times off the locker room bench, as if to punch the point home. After she was given her Most Valuable Player trophy, every kid on the block wanted Cleo's autograph. I remember her smiling in a mob of kids, her face still shining with sweat, her royal red jacket snapped closed over her shoulders, signing scrap after scrap of paper. "Good luck. Signed C.L."; "Happy baskets, signed C.L." Even though she couldn't write very well (the ink pen looked funny, bobbling loosely in her fingers), she grinned through every minute of it. "That might be the only time you'll see Cleo happy to be holding a pen," Marla grumbled. Sometimes she'd get so discouraged with her other Little Sister.

Like anyone with an awkward name, Cleo always had plenty of nicknames — C.L., Likorish, Lik-Stick Timmons — all of them hiding the name of — Cleotha. Cleo hated Cleotha, hated it with a red-eyed passion, hated it like she hated being stepped on. Cleotha reminded her of a "dumpty country girl with glasses," a girl who'd be afraid of someone like Cleo, so afraid that she'd give up all her lunch money, let herself be kissed, then offer over her sandwich.

"I beat plenty of kids up for food when I was a child," Cleo bragged. "I just had to, they was being so greedy. It ain't *polite* to eat in front of folks who just ain't got. It ain't right, so I had to start on them." Cleo rubbed her fist in the palm of her hand and shook her head in sadness that at least looked real.

"I would have given you some," I recall my saying.

"You would have given me *all*, baby." She smiled then, showing off the squareness of her chin.

Cleo is an Aries, like me: sometimes we're so selfish, we don't even know we're being it. Or so Marla says. (I suppose I should have *offered* Cleo all of my sandwich. Marla would have.) Even so, I do believe that Cleo's a whole lot more selfish than me. *I* would think twice about kissing someone, especially some other girl — even more, some other girl who, most likely, would not want it — but Cleo claimed that she only picked the girls who'd want it. After she picked me, and after she kissed me, she told me, "I knew you'd like it, once I did it, so I just went ahead and did." And that smile again: flashing, then closing, like the quick white glint of a pocketknife.

THE PERSISTENT DESIRE

Cleo thought she was smooth, but she sure had one quick attitude. Let someone step on her toes wrong (in a basketball game, for goodness' sake!) and Cleo'd go off. I remember seeing tears in her eyes one time, she was so hurt that someone had made her so red-hot mad. I can still see the way she got, cutting her eyes and snarling about "someone." That time, I think, "someone" had draped Cleo's jacket over their own "stinkin', sweatin' shoulders." By mistake, but you sure couldn't tell Cleo that, just like you couldn't tell her that this wasn't the training school, where everyone just naturally stole from her, the youngest and the skinniest of all.

That's how I knew, the game she let me wear her jacket for a whole entire two quarters, that Cleo really thought of me as "her girl."

After that game, after everyone was gone, with the showers dripping and me innocently picking up the dirty towels, Cleo backed me up against the lockers, and her mouth was spicy with the taste of Good 'n' Plenty. I knew, after that day, that it was only a matter of time before I'd be back on the bus toward Alma.

❖

Cleo ... your sleek legs flying, your lanky muscles stretching tight the stripes around your socks, around the hems of your red silk, real tight basketball shorts...

Her jump shots were so smooth she could have been diving up through water, and watching her make them put me in the shivers, as though she were sliding, silkenly, all along the most secret of my places. She'd bounce and flick that ball around a helpless tangle of legs and arms that hopelessly tried to stop her. One time, she dribbled the ball right out of "some chick's" fingers, then, darting and springing around her, bounced the ball — I swear — right through the girl's outspread legs, catching it off the bounce before the poor girl even had the chance to think of turning around. "Smooth black is hard to attack" was Cleo's motto for her playing style, but it applied as well to all her other ways, on all her other days, in all the other places.

"Cleo's Back," said the front of her favorite black sweatshirt, in bright pink letters. "Cleo's Gone," said the other side. "Slick" was the word she'd use to describe herself, because like every true Player, Cleo had two sides: street side and court side. On the court, Cleo most liked to wear her lucky black canvas hightops, but coming in off the street, she always wore new suede or leather tennis shoes, and she cussed if someone so much as scuffed them, and fussed when someone (like Marla) merely asked her where she'd gotten them from.

"Because she knew I was actually asking her where did she get the wherewithal to get them from."

Everybody knew that Cleo had absolutely no visible means, other than hanging around the littered, rotten-smelling courtyard of the M.C. Morningside Homes, hanging out supposedly empty-handed.

"But you never can tell what-all I got in my socks or my secret pockets," she bragged.

I'd gone over to the Morningside to look for her, that last morning I spent with her ("You have exactly twenty minutes to go and say good-bye to her," Marla said, and tapped her wristwatch, and I knew she thought she was being fair to give me that), but I didn't have to look far. Cleo was waiting for me in the stairwell of her building, on a step with her ball in her hand.

"Hi, baby sis." She stood and flicked her leg muscles. And she smiled, her tongue pressed teasingly to the gap between her teeth.

"Hey, Likorish," I said, in a voice thick with all my misery.

"Ah, don't be taking it that way." She reached for my hand and pulled me toward her. Her ball had dribbled away into a corner. "Just 'cause big sis don't want you hanging out with big old bad-ass me no more."

"I couldn't give a care *what* Marla wants," I decided out loud. Now, what did I do that for, I remember thinking, because what Cleo did then was press her bare lanky leg into my — you know. My breath froze: what was she doing to me? I fell helplessly into a shiver.

Her tongue was on my lips, and she was pressing me closer and moving her kissing to my cheek, my chin, all down my neck. All I could do was close my eyes and try very hard not to make a noise. Where in the world was Marla when I needed her?

"You have such a long, long neck," she was crooning, and what did I do but smile and stretch it longer for more kisses? Both her hands were holding tight to my behind, so I couldn't get away. I reached for her own round, high-riding ... "Hey, girl!" And she pulled back from me, so suddenlike she scared me, and slapped my wrists away.

"What, Cleo?" I almost felt like crying.

"Let's go upstairs," she whispered, hotly, in my ear, with her hands holding mine behind me.

Feeling shamed and tough and sneaky, I crept up the four flights right behind her. "Sssh." Cleo put her finger to her mouth as she quietly opened her apartment's door. "Auntie-dear is sleeping." We slipped inside, past a darkened living room-kitchenette, on into Cleo's bedroom, where she latched the door. I looked around, a little desperately, because there certainly wasn't much in that little bedroom to offer any distraction, or even conversation: just a very neat bureau with her trophy on it, a poster of a long tall player with his arm arched ready to sink a basket, and a made-up bed with her tennis shoes — all eight pairs — neatly lined up under it. Cleo grinned, noticing, of course, where I was looking. "I'll be your good girl if you'll put your shoes underneath my bed," she sang. She was leading me right to it, sliding her hand along her pillow. "I want to rub your tummy till your cherry turns bright red." By now her hand was all up under my blouse, her fingers gently pinching the sweetmeat of my belly, creeping down toward my zipper.

343

Next I knew, I was on my back, barefooted, with my skirt off and Cleo's fingers inching up my thigh, close to my...

"M-a-arla," I wanted to yell. Why didn't I?

She began massaging me down there, with the strong commanding palm of her hand, the whole while singing in my ear: "Won't your sister be disgusted, when she see your cherry busted?" I might've tried to reply, or wanted to wiggle away, but I couldn't hardly, because she was holding me down and covering my mouth with her lips, her kiss, and one of her long, sleek legs was sliding up between mine, so that my belly had begun to shake. Escape was even harder when she slipped her fingers under my panties. "Take yo' drawers off, sugar babe?"

Well, what could I do? I let her take my panties off. "Ride me, baby," she begged me, her breath hot, almost sobbing. "Wrap 'em all around me." Then she was sliding and gliding all over me, until I caught her rhythm deep down inside my middle, all through my shivering secret places.

"Oooh." My eyes popped open when she put her fingers there, pumping them in and out as I felt myself foam like clabber and tighten around her. And she pulled me up tight, churning in and out until my hips rocked the bed so hard, so steady, that its springs begin to sing. Cleo was laughing as I thrashed and bit the pillow; she was laughing and kissing me rashly around my face. "You really like that, huh, baby, huh?" I was swooning, seeing nothing but velvet wings brushing their black tips across the midnight sky. I couldn't even moan, she had my mouth so covered, my lips and tongue so tightly wrapped and pressed in hers.

"Oh, Tammy, that's some sweet—" and she used that *p* word, that nasty, sticky-sweet word. Evil, coming from a street curb, but here just soft and tender, the way I'd never heard it. I groaned and pushed myself up tighter.

"*Cleo!*" Cleo's auntie's voice, just the other side of the door. Cleo's hand came away from me so fast I collapsed back onto the bed.

"Ma'am?"

"It's someone here to see you."

She stood up, wiped her fingers on her bedspread. "We'd best get you redressed, baby sis. It's probably big sis now."

Just like Marla, always right on time but never coming right when I wanted her. Marla had her hand propped up on her hip, and her foot tapped impatiently while I asked the aunt for an ink pen and paper so that I could at least get Cleo's address.

"I'll write," I promised Cleo's laughing eyes, and hugged her oh-so-stiffly. "Time to go, Tammy" was all that Marla said, and I could tell by the tightness of her lips and the way she wouldn't even look at Cleo, or my very wrinkled blouse, that she knew.

Outside, I felt obliged to explain: "We was just—"

"Tamara, you know, I ain't even gon' ask." I could tell how upset she was by her grammatical slip.

344

"It wasn't anything, Marla."

"I am sure it wasn't. I am sure she just led you up there, like Mary had a little innocent lamb."

And you know, to this day that is probably what Marla is telling herself.

I throbbed the whole ride home, wriggling restlessly in my bus seat just at the thought of Cleo's fingers there inside me. Damn Marla, damn, I swore, squirming hooked through the middle on a stiff velvet rope. I would have sworn even harder if I'd known that would be the last time I'd ever see Cleo. A couple of months after Marla sent me away, Cleo disappeared anyway, and nobody that Marla asked was telling where to.

Myrna Elana

Photograph

I think of you
all the way away
beyond green slats of fence,
the amber reflection in oil
of bergamot — I still
smell you on my fingers—
I told you I like
butch older women

In bed with you—
all the secrets
and folds of
your more than sixty years
deciphered, clear
radiating more than
decades of possibilities
under my palms, my lips
the curled strength,
and need, of my fingers

We touch hands,
then snap away
as if bundled together
by invisible bands,
that catapult us out
against an indigo drop of stars
a green picket fence
extending out of the frame
around the corner

Laurie Hoskin

Billie

stone for all those years
and the touching came easy,
easier even than breathing.
stone for all her life
and cool like marble, rough
edged and veined and off limits
to fingers wanting to dance
across her surface. the pleasure
was in giving, in lying
above a woman and
hearing that woman call
her name, loud and long.
the pleasure was in taking
care and taking time
and exploring soft, wet places
at the end of a long
day. the pleasure was
in being stone, tight
and solid and sure
of her place in the world.
so stone, so handsome,
that even all these
years later I keep
the memory of her mouth
against me, taking care.

Joan Nestle

My woman poppa

You work at a job that makes your back rock-hard strong; you work with men in a cavernous warehouse loading trucks while others sleep. Sometimes when you come to me while I work at home, you fall asleep in my bed on your stomach, the sheet wrapped around your waist, the flaming unicorn on your right shoulder catching the afternoon sun.

I just stand and look at you, at your sleeping face and kind hands, my desire growing for you, for my woman poppa who plays the drums and knows all the words to "Lady in Red," who calls me sassafras mama, even when I am sometimes too far from the earth, who is not frightened off by my years or my illness.

My woman poppa who knows how to take me in her arms and lay me down, knows how to spread my thighs and then my lips, who knows how to catch the wetness and use it and then knows how to enter me so women waves rock us both.

My woman poppa who is not afraid of my moans or my nails but takes me and takes me until she reaches far beyond the place of entry into the core of tears. Then as I come to her strength and woman fullness, she kisses away my legacy of pain. My cunt and heart and head are healed.

My woman poppa who does not want to be a man, but who does travel in "unwomanly" places and who does "unwomanly" work. Late into the New Jersey night, she maneuvers the forklift to load the thousands of pounds of aluminum into the hungry trucks that stand waiting for her. Dressed in the shiny tiredness of warehouse blue, with her company's name white-stitched across her pocket, she endures the bitter humor of her fellow workers, who are men. They laugh at Jews, at women, and, when the black workers are not present, at blacks. All the angers of their lives, all their dreams gone dead, bounce off the warehouse walls. My woman grits her teeth, and says when the rape jokes come: "Don't talk that shit around me."

When she comes home to me, I must caress the parts of her that have been worn thin, trying to do her work in a man's world. She likes her work, likes the challenge of the machines and the quietness of the night, likes her body moving into power. When we go to women's parties, I watch amused at the stares she gets when she answers the traditional question "What do you do?" with her nontraditional answer "I load trucks in a warehouse." When the teachers and social workers no longer address their comments to her, I want to shout at them, Where is your curiosity about women's lives, where is your wonder at boundaries broken?

My woman poppa is thirteen years younger than I, but she is wise in her woman-loving ways. Breasts and ass get her hot, that wonderful hot which is a heard and spoken desire. I make her hot and I like that. I like her sweat and her tattoos, I like her courtliness and her disdain of the boys, I mother her and wife her and slut her, and together we are learning to be comrades.

She likes me to wear a black slip to bed, to wear dangling earrings and black stockings with sling-back heels when we play. She likes my perfume and lipstick and nail polish. I enjoy these slashes of color, the sweetened place in my neck when she will bury her head when she is moving on me. I sometimes sit on her, my cunt open on her round belly, my breasts hanging over her, my nipples grazing her lips. I forbid her to touch me and continue to rock on her, my wetness smearing her belly. She begins to moan and curves her body upwards, straining at the restrictions.

"Please, baby, please," my woman poppa begs. "Please let me fuck you." Then suddenly, when she has had enough, she smiles, opens her eyes, says, "You have played enough," and using the power she has had all along, throws me from my throne.

Sometimes she lies in bed wearing her cock under the covers. I can see its outline under the pink spread. I just stand in my slip watching her, her eyes getting heavy. Then I sit alongside her, on the edge of the bed, telling her what a wonderful cock she has, as I run my hand down her belly until I reach her lavender hardness. I suck her nipple and slowly stroke her, tugging at the cock so she can feel it through the leather triangle that holds it in place.

"Let me suck you," I say, my face close to hers, my breasts spilling out on hers. "Let me take your cock in my mouth and show you what I can do." She nods, almost as if her head is too heavy to move.

Oh, my darling, this play is real. I do long to suck you, to take your courage into my mouth, both cunt, your flesh, and cock, your dream, deep into my mouth, and I do. I throw back the covers and bend over her carefully so she can see my red lips and red-tipped fingers massaging her cock. I take one of her hands and wrap it around the base so she can feel my lips as I move on her. I give her the best I can, licking the lavender cock its whole length and slowly tonguing the tip, circling it with my tongue. Then I take her fully into my mouth, into my throat. She moans, moves, tries to watch, and cannot as the image overpowers her. When I have done all that I can, I bend the wet cock up on her belly and sit on her so I can feel it pressing against my cunt. I rock on her until she is ready, and then she reaches down and slips the cock into me. Her eyes are open now, wonderfully clear and sharp, and she slips her arms down low around my waist so I am held tight against her. Very slowly, she starts to move her hips upward in short strong thrusts. I am held on my pleasure by her powerful arms; I can do nothing but move and take and feel. When she knows I have settled in, she moves quicker and quicker, her breath coming in short hard gasps. But I hear the words, "Oh, baby, you are so good to fuck."

I forget everything but her movements. I fall over her, my head on the pillow above her. I hear sounds, moans, shouted words, know my fists are pounding the bed, but I am unaware of forming words or lifting my arms. I ride and ride harder and faster, encircled by her arms, by her gift.

"Give it all to me, let it all go," I know she is saying. I hear a voice answering, "You you you you," and I am pounding the bed, her arms, anything I can reach. How dare you do this to me, how dare you push me beyond my daily voice, my daily body, my daily fears. I am changing: we are dancing. We have broken through.

Then, it is over. We return and gently she lifts me off her belly. I slide down her body, rest, and then release her from the leather. We sleep.

Yes, my woman poppa knows how to move me, but she knows many other things as well. She knows she will not be shamed; she knows her body carries complicated messages. My woman poppa, my dusty sparrow, I know how special you are. Your strength, both of loving and of need, is not mistaken for betrayal of your womanness.

Dress shirt

A gold watch,
A leather wristband,
Your hands,
Perfect under starched white cuffs.
Under crisp cotton, your skin
    Golden, smooth over muscles
        Harder, rougher underneath.
        Gold and black,
I get to help with the links and studs,
    And feel your shirt on my cheek.

Your hands fascinate me,
    Watch flashing gold under cuffs—
Watching you touch
    This, grasp
        That, manipulate...
I wonder about your hands
    Smoothing my body,
        Rougher inside...

Under you I am
    Soothed, yielding...
You push me harder: I
Struggle, wanting
    All of your hands.
I think I will make you sweat
    Till you take your shirt
        Off

Scarlet Woman

Roll me over
and make me a rose

This morning you amazed me
    in my sleeping you
        moved into my dream
           with fast hands
Sure hands on my sleepy ass
    on my clit
        in my cunt
Engorging
Under fast hands alarmed
    into instant arousal I
Gasp
    sliding under covers
You grasping me I could be unsure
    of my turn-on
        before arising
But riding your command I am
    carried away

You move in faster than
    I can decide
        to trust you
I hang on to you
    galloping me over waves
        pounding scarlet
My brain is asleep and my
Cunt is a rose
    riding your hand

Roll me over in the morning
    lover
    and make me a rose

Audrey Grifel

Sweet suit suite

When I was eleven or twelve years old, I used to shop in the boys' department at Bloomingdale's, just as the other prepubescent private school girls did. That was where you could purchase polo shirts, Shetland sweaters, and all the other socially acceptable androgynous clothing for our age group and gender. They fit and suited me just fine, but what would have suited me even better was nothing other than an actual suit: the three-piece variety made of thin-wale, beige corduroy with brown, simulated leather buttons.

I knew exactly where they hung in the boys' department, and I paid them a visit each time I was in the vicinity. It's funny, but though I can't remember at the time ever seeing a girl or woman in one of these suits, that did not hinder my imagination of what that would look like. Neither did the shortage of real-life models ever lead to any questions about why exactly there was one. Somehow I had simply gotten it into my head that such a sight would be wonderful. And, though once again I felt no need to ponder precisely how I knew this, clearly, the most appropriate person to wear such a suit would be me.

Picturing myself in the suit, I was suddenly a lot taller and older and stunningly sophisticated. The suit seemed to have the almost magical power to make me strong, wise, just. This vision of myself naturally included physical as well as mental capabilities well beyond those of an eleven- or twelve-year-old, but who was I to disbelieve the suit's mystique?

I never tried one on. Although the desire to own one felt perfectly natural to me, it had been met with a mixture of mocking laughter and horror by my mother. Something about her response definitely said, "No," and, "Tell no one." So the suits, like forbidden fruit, remained there untouched by me for years, moved at times from one corner of the department to another, but always just out of reach of my young body's many secret yearnings.

Roughly fourteen years later, as I was walking in the rain, I suddenly realized I was a butch. Everything made sense. My butchness came as much more of a surprise to me than my lesbianism, which, despite some years of procrastination on my part as to actually adopting it as a daily lifestyle, I always knew and comfortably accepted.

The way I ever so swaggered and stomped my clunky boots when I walked, and felt sort of proud of it, now made sense. The way I firmly held the umbrella over the woman I love and protected her from the rain as I guided her down that Brooklyn street took on new clarity. The freedom and invincibleness I feel after a close haircut I better understood. The pleasure and vanity I indulge in when I stretch my muscles to lift something that looks heavier than I can manage all at once held new meaning. The childlike glee I feel every time I discover something needing to be fixed in the house and the puffed-up self-importance that fills me each time I fix it had new significance for me. Even my tremendous need for control could now be explained. And my assertive overtures of passion in the dark where I gently but firmly demand submission most of all seemed to fit.

I gripped the handle of the umbrella tighter and walked along with, I'm sure, the stupidest grin on my face, flashing the woman I love periodic glances of affection as she continued to talk happily, oblivious to the volcano that had just erupted beside her. There, in the rain, as a flood of feelings and enlightenment washed my insides, I had one final glimmer of insight. I at last understood that without ever actually buying that three-piece suit made of thin-wale, beige corduroy with the brown, simulated leather buttons, I had been wearing one all along.

Sally Bellerose

Redheads

'm a sucker for a flashy redhead. Cherry has bucket seats, four on the floor, dual exhaust, and moves when you ask her to. She's getting old, driven just about every day for over twenty years. I know how she feels, so I pamper her.

Charlene's a pretty redhead too. The red hair is recent but the rest of her — painted lips, big breasts, big hands — they've been the same since I've known her. Charlene works hard. She moves when she's damn good and ready. Sometimes she lets me pamper her. Sometimes she pampers me.

We're lying on the bed with the moss green sheets in the Jungle Room of the Pines Motel. The desk clerk didn't blink when we checked in. Two women spending the night together doesn't interest him as much as a rerun of "McHale's Navy." There are life-sized cheetahs on the wallpaper, chasing one another around the room. Charlene has been calling me Tarzan all night. When I remember, I call her Jane, but that's my mother's name, life is confusing enough, so I forget.

Charlene hasn't decided if she's my girlfriend or not yet. She's got a lot on her mind. She works as a waitress three nights a week and goes to community college days. She hasn't declared a major yet. Charlene's almost forty. She's at an undecided stage of her life. Not that she's a wishy-washy type of person. She just makes her own decisions in her own time.

We're rolling around in bed and I say, "Charlene, whose girl are you?" Like you might say in the ear of the woman you are lying on top of, while she's got a handful of you. Most women would say, "Yours, baby," if not from passion at least from habit or politeness.

Not Charlene. She says, "I don't know, honey, it's too soon to tell." She goes right on moving her hips and groaning. I try to be cool, but it hurts my feelings. I've got to wonder what all this fucking is about. I've been around the block a few times and there's been more than one woman I've been undecided about myself, but we've been doing this every Tuesday and Friday night for months now. It's not too soon for me to tell. Charlene wants a better life; she's just not sure I'm going to be in it. I suppose I should be happy that she's being honest with me, but I feel like this is some kind of test drive. What can I do? I'm crazy about her. She's got the wheel.

There's another problem with this arrangement. I'm getting tired of this motel. It's exciting at first, but it gets old. We've been in the Jungle Room nine times. There's a trapeze in here, a trampoline too. You only need a two-foot bounce, straight up, to reach the trapeze, then it's a pretty limp swing. It's like sex: sometimes the idea of it is more exciting than the actual ride. Charlene's got plenty of extras. We don't have to be wasting our hard-earned money on all this equipment.

We're here because I live with my mother. My mother is old. Shit, I'm old. My mother would like Charlene. Charlene is a lady, respectful, unless she's mad. My mother would like Charlene, but I guess I better find out if Charlene's my girlfriend before I bring her home. It doesn't break my mother's heart that I'm this way anymore, but she wants to see me in a steady relationship before she dies. I'm trying.

We can't go to Charlene's place because her husband is there. That's how we met, through her husband. I'd say *husband* is the wrong word. That's what Charlene calls him. They lived together for a few years, like husband and wife. Now they just live together.

His name is Dave. I ran into him one day when he was waiting for Charlene outside of K-Mart. I pulled into the parking space next to him. Cherry was shining red, still wet from the car wash.

"Nice car," he says.

"Thanks," I say.

"'69?" he asks.

I nodded yes, got out, and locked Cherry up before heading toward K-Mart. He tried to start up his car, planned to have a quick one at the bar across the street. His engine wouldn't turn over. It was July, getting hot. Dave thought it was overheated, but I could tell, it was the battery.

"Want a jump?" I asked, unlocking Cherry's trunk and grabbing the cables. Before he gets his jump, we start talking cars. He loves Mustangs. Cherry's a Mustang. He couldn't get over her paint job or her interior. Wanted to buy her. I could see by the way he took care of his Impala he wouldn't maintain her. Besides, I wouldn't sell Cherry.

We decided we needed a beer more than the Impala needed a jump. We walked over to the bar. He left a note for Charlene. It was a small note written on the back of a book of matches. It said, "Next door," with an arrow pointing across the street. He stuck it under the windshield wiper.

The note was too short and the beer was too long. About an hour later Charlene walked through the side door of the bar pissed off and pushing a shopping cart full of K-Mart. She pushed the cart right over to our table and started unloading.

356

"Your shirts," she said and plunked six flannels in front of Dave, "three for twenty dollars."

"Your toilet paper." She plunked down thirty rolls one at a time. "Ten bucks."

Then she piled a few cans of mixed nuts, some cleaning stuff, and a *TV Guide* next to him on the bench, pricing as she went. She slid into the booth on my side and hoisted the real prize onto the table. "And one battery, $39.77 on sale," she said. "For one shithead."

Then she turned to me and said, "At least my husband chose a good-looking woman to leave me alone for, with a ton of his stuff, in the boiling sun."

She was stretching her points. It was hot but not boiling. Nobody has ever called me a good-looking woman, and like I say, to my mind, Dave is not really her husband. She was right to be pissed though. We should have waited for her.

So it's six months later and here I am lying next to Charlene in the Jungle Room again. She sits up in bed and says, "Baby, I've made up my mind."

I say, "Huh, what are you talking about?" My voice wasn't what you'd call gentle. It was five o'clock in the morning. We had a nice night, but we didn't get here till midnight, and when you're in a sixty-dollar room with a trampoline you tend to bounce around on it whether it's still a kick or not. So I was tired.

She says, "We belong together."

I say, "Yeah, we do," and roll over, hoping she'll do the same.

She shakes my shoulder, says, "Come on, wake up, honey. I want to go to confession."

I figure she means this literally, since we're not in the room with the altar and candles. I have mixed feelings. The "Baby, we belong together" part feels good. The confession part feels like trouble.

"What do you need to confess?" I ask.

"Us," she says.

I'm surprised to hear this, since, the very first time we met in that bar, Charlene explained to me that the Bible doesn't have a thing to say about women sleeping together. At first I thought it was just her way of flirting and pissing Dave off. I suppose it was all of that, but she also meant it sincerely, as a point of faith. I'm not religious myself, but I've got an aunt on my father's side that's a stone butch and she's a nun in good standing. Like Charlene says, the Church doesn't care as long as you don't go around bragging about it.

I say, "Honey, go to sleep. There's no sin in sex. Jesus loves you. I love you."

She says, "Don't be conceited. It's not just you. I've got a husband."

This husband stuff again. Charlene is honest, but she's prone to dramatics. It gets on my nerves. I say, "Come off it, Charlene. You didn't have a church ceremony and you've got no license, so you don't have a husband."

She says, "God knows we were married."

I say, "For Christ's sake." Which wasn't nice, because she really is upset and wants to do right religiously. I roll over. Charlene listens to all my problems, takes a real interest. I should do the same. I just wish she would wait until nine o'clock like usual. I sit up in bed meaning to apologize, but that kind of thing comes to me slow. Before I say a thing, she's hooking her bra around her waist and hoisting it up over her breasts, in a huff, and before I can pull up my pants she's out the door. I trip over the trampoline and peek through the mauve curtains. Charlene's leaning on Cherry and searching through my jacket pocket, which she grabbed on her way out. She finds Cherry's keys and off they go, together, my car for sure and my girlfriend, maybe.

These old cars have big gas tanks and Cherry's is full. They could be gone a long time. They won't find a priest awake at five o'clock in the morning. The saints in heaven are still asleep. For the next couple of hours I join them.

Now I'm waiting and waiting. It's after ten o'clock. I'm getting nervous. After eleven you have to pay for a full extra night. Cherry's got my wallet. It's under her front seat. I hope Charlene doesn't know it. I nod off in the chair by the bed, and thank you, Jesus, Charlene and Cherry screech in.

I meet her at the door and say, "You okay, baby?" Which is the right thing to say.

She says, "Like you care." But I can tell she's softened up. I glance beyond her, see Cherry safe, parked in her spot. Charlene sits on the bed and takes off her flats. She rubs her feet.

"Where have you been?"

"You bought me breakfast," she says and hands me my wallet. "Then I talked to Father John."

"Confession doesn't start till twelve o'clock," I say.

"That's why I went to the rectory, my dear."

I move a little closer, since she said, "My dear." "He heard confession in his living room?" I ask. I don't think that's kosher.

"No, at the breakfast table. He had to. I told him I was having a crisis of faith. It's his job, after all."

"So are you absolved?"

"Well, I told him about my husband, and he said the same as you: no church, no sacrament, no husband. He said my sin was having sex with a man I wasn't married to, but not as big a sin as if we were married and I were having sex with a different man or if I weren't having sex at all but did get married in the church and got divorced."

"Shit. What did he think when you told him about us?"

"Who cares what he thinks? None of it's any of his business. I just wanted this thing with Dave ended formally. God likes things to be ended formally. It's Father John's job to get messages through to Him."

Charlene looked incredible; her face was glowing, like she'd slept ten hours and really had talked to God.

"So did your message get through?"

"Well, sure, I've been gone five hours. Of course, I spent a couple hours of that at Denny's and the K-Mart."

"What did you get at K-Mart?" I didn't see a K-Mart bag, but I noticed she was wearing something different under her coat.

She took the coat off and smiled. Leopard-skin leotards, some new perfume I can't name. They sell all kinds of things at K-Mart. We're going to end up paying for an extra night. It's okay, we've never been alone in the daytime.

I say, "Charlene, now that you don't have a husband, maybe we can get a place of our own."

Sima Rabinowitz

To dance a w(h)ile

Steal down the dusky avenue
slip your key into the lock
climb over her swamp of a bed on the floor in the corner
slink like the Abyssinian she gave away
under the sheets as they stream across your back
in an unbroken loop
midnight, midweek, while she sleeps
and will wake woozy to the hairs on your wrist
standing smooth and separate.

Sidle up to dinner wearing only a black and lacy
shadow of fabric
eat with your fingers
draw the middle one between your tongue and upper lip
lick lightly
offer her chocolate or garlic
and the other hand.

Speak to her in foreign tongues or your own patois
embrasse-moi in her right ear, *bésame* now in her left
je t'aime, querida
or don't speak at all
not even when meaning gathers in your throat
her fingers gather between your thighs
talk like the slut she's made of you
every act an utterance.

Anna Romes

Paula Austin

Femme-inism

I saw Rhon across the grass, below the hill where I sat writing. We were at a conference somewhere upstate. I had seen her earlier getting out of a red sports car. She was stocky and dark skinned, with short hair and thick shoulders. She wore black, shirt and jeans and shoes. This time I yelled out to her and asked if she had gone into town. She smiled shyly and nodded. We sat together later that day in the big room where they were holding the workshop, me trying to create sexual tension.

When I was seeing Rhon, I was convinced she had hidden somewhere in the recesses of her clothing a penis. She was hard, the hardest dyke I had ever been with, not having been with many. Rhon was the first butch of color I had been with. She and I argued so much about gender roles that I became convinced that I with my long, curly hair and heels was not femme.

"We buy into those roles because they are the only models we have," I preached. "They limit us as women!" Rhon wore men's pants, men's shoes, men's shirts, boxer shorts, men's cologne. She didn't have my fears of rape and sexism. She talked about women as if she were not one of us. Ultimately, underneath all my moral superiority and anger and indignation, I was bewildered, because I was, after all, terribly attracted to her.

❖

It is 1991 and almost two years since I came out to my family and closest friends. Rhon was a year ago, when I was twenty-two. I don't know if I ever consciously chose to be femme. I was just who I was, a brown-skinned woman with large breasts and curly hair, who liked what she liked. All I knew of my new lesbianism was, vaguely, the type of woman I was attracted to. My first lover, when I was seventeen (although in our youth and homophobia we would never have dared call each other *that*) had long brown hair, broad shoulders, strong muscular legs, and thin beautiful pink lips. We went bike riding together every weekend. When I think of her now, or happen upon a picture of her smiling face, I realize what a "male" look she had begun to cultivate. Was that what had drawn us together as "friends"?

❖

Buddy wears loose black jeans, a sweatshirt, and a bomber jacket. She pulls a black, red, and white Harley-Davidson cap over her short brown hair. We sit in the car. She is driving.

"Here's my favorite hill." She zooms down, but it isn't fast enough, so she backs up to do it again. The streets are empty because it is very early morning. My hand rubs her sleek, muscular thigh. I feel the muscles contract. Tonight, with her hair unblown, wavy and close to her head, her "stomper" Dr. Marten shoes, and her cap, she looks the way I love for her to look. Like a boy. We ride down the hill. She doesn't like the car much. "Too small," she says. "I like big cars ... and big women." She looks at my breasts.

When we make love, she pumps me. Lying on her side, her body pressed up against me, her right leg parting mine, she moves her hand down between my legs. She plays in my wetness briefly. Then her fingers slide into me, one, sometimes two or three. Moving slowly, then rapidly, in and out, every motion deeper, stronger, harder. She says sometimes, amid all my moaning and wanting and passion for her, that she wishes she had a dick "to pump me hard." Often, I ask her to speak to me in Spanish, her native language, to hear her deep, sultry voice rolling her *r*'s.

I love the hardness, the hint of power and violence, the strength, the inkling of being owned. The way she lays her head on my full breasts she loves so much. How her hand fits around my waist, or how her long fingers move deep inside of me. Her deep, breathless sighs and moans as I move my tongue along her wet, hardening, pulsating clitoris. How she pulls me up when we have rested, lays me on top of her, then rolls me onto my back or stomach to play with me with her large, strong hands.

Even when Buddy goes to work in her corporate-bank-office regalia, she still looks hard to me. Her hair blown and fluffy, her suit and pumps, her trench coat. We sit on the train. These are the only times when people can't tell who's who or mistake me for the butch. I'm wearing my jeans and cowboy silver-tipped shoes and a black jacket. Across from us, a homeboy-type young man sits, looking from me to her. I've seen him watching, mouth watering at our touching of each other's hands and thighs. Suddenly, he catches my eye and says, "I don't mean no disrespect but...," then he addresses her, "I like your tattoo." He points at the tattoo of a blue-and-red unicorn on the side of her lower thigh. She says, "Thank you," and he looks at me, to make sure I am not angry. I nod slowly to him, my face stern. After all, it isn't every day that I get to be the butch. (And I take my role seriously.)

❖

I am not yet comfortable with my own femme-ininity. It is so looked down on — especially in a political community like the one in which I came out, of which I want to continue to be a part. *Femme* often carries the stigma of the word *feminine*, and being feminine has traditionally meant powerlessness, passivity, everything that being a woman has traditionally meant. When I first came out, I wanted to be butch. I wanted to outwardly defy patriarchy in general, and men in particular. I wanted them to see me on the subway as I rode to and from school and not feel they could stare and salivate and comment and harass as they pleased. I wanted them to look at me and know in some way I was as tough as they, maybe tougher, that I didn't like or want them sexually, especially sexually, and was in some way in "competition" with them. I wanted to laugh in their faces, saying, "Fuck you!"

❖

I am sitting in a pizza place one night with a friend of mine. Neither of us is very butch-looking. Nearby is a table filled with loud, white college boys having what may be their sixth pitcher of beer. I feel their eyes follow me as I go from the counter to my table with my food. I watch as their eyes follow my friend's ass as she heads toward our table or to the jukebox. Their talk and laughter get louder. We pay little attention to them initially, except to acknowledge our feeling that they may be a problem later in the night. We talk and laugh as well, as loudly as we please, feeling good about ourselves and our lesbianism.

Of course, they think we want them. "Checking us out, huh, girls?" one of them yells over to us. Anger. My choice puts me at risk. I am mistaken for a heterosexual woman. Michael, a man at my office, has asked me for a date. I say no many times, then finally say to him, "Michael, I am a lesbian, and while I am willing to be your friend, we could never be lovers. I am just not interested." His shock is not shock at all but rather a grin that says only that he could "get into that." He has not stopped asking me for a date.

I am constantly confronted by the prospect of rape. Men see me as theirs, and most dykes I pass on the street do not give me a second look. I am not recognized by those whose gaze helps make me a lesbian unless I am in a club or other social space with other lesbians, or am out with my butch lover.

❖

I am a black self-identified femme. My hair hangs in loose curls a little below my shoulders. I often wear makeup, and I like high heels, although I seldom wear them. My femme-ininity does not make me victimized. I have a choice in what I look like and who fucks me. The fear, of course, lies in questioning whether what I say and feel and believe about myself is politically correct or not. I still don't know.

In my angst over my femme-ininity, I question my own language. "What constitutes 'hard'? Does it refer to those who look most like men, and if so, what does that mean? If the women I like are 'hard,' and if 'hard' means looking like a man, then mustn't women inherently be 'soft,' at least in my mind?" Where is my thinking? Am I complicitly accepting the stereotypes created to limit women's, and men's, roles? This concerns me. So to whom should I be attracted to be a politically correct lesbian-feminist of color? And more importantly, what should I look like to be a politically correct lesbian-feminist of color?

I waver constantly. Who should I be, where, how? Why can't I look the way I look and be a feminist, smiling when my lover calls me "her woman"? And what does this all mean to me as a black woman? I want to claim my femme-ininity, recreate "femme," recreate womanhood to make it my own.

As a woman of color, I have spent most of my life wanting to be someone else. I learned to hate myself hearing, "You are too black, too short, too fat." Neither my hair nor my nose was ever straight enough. When I came out, much became clear. I found a true and passionate, powerful at times, inner voice that helped me to speak out and write. When I added homophobia to my already substantial list of battles, my life was still filled with the same intense struggle and pain. But there is a freedom in knowing the full extent of me, my ethnicity and culture, my sexuality, my womanness.

Being femme for me means wearing a short, tight skirt, garters, and three-inch heels when I'm going out. It means standing in front of the mirror putting on mascara and reddish brown lipstick. It means shopping for a low-cut blouse to reveal a hint of cleavage some nights. It means smiling, or sometimes pouting, when my woman puts her arm around my waist and, with her other hand, turns my face up to kiss hers. It means whispering, "I'm yours, own me," when she makes love to me. It means feeling sexy.

Being femme for me means risking the violence and sexism to be who I am. It means being mistaken for a straight woman and saying I'm not. It means fighting for the right for myself and my butch lover to dress the way we please and play the way we like. Yes, our roles can oppress us; they have in the past; they reflect the dominant culture as it now exists. But they do not have to. I take my life, my decisions and actions, into my hands, as they were meant to be. I constantly deconstruct my education, my language, my culture, my desires.

❖

It is 10:30 at night. I ride the D train to the Bronx. I feel exceptionally beautiful and strong. My hair is fluffed, my dress short, my stockings patterned and colorful, my shoes high and black and patent leather. I am on my way to a party. My lover will be there, but she does not know I am coming. I am excited about surprising her. I am excited about my low-cut, sleek black dress, my exposed legs, my hair. At least two men try to talk to me on the train, one who sits next to me, one across from me; they eye my legs. But tonight I am ready. "No," I say, "*please*, don't talk to me. Don't!" Eventually, one by one, they leave me alone.

When I arrive at the party, I stand at the top of the stairs watching Buddy from across the room. She is quiet by the window and someone shouts her name and she turns around. She glances at me and slowly walks toward me with that swaggering, macho walk I love so much. She climbs the stairs to me and puts her arms around me, burying her face in my neck. Warmth. She takes my bag from me. She takes my coat off and hangs it in the closet behind me, then returns to me. Stands in front of me, kisses me, her hand on my waist. Holds me out in front of her, looks me up and down, smiles at the heels, my legs, my bubbling cleavage. Her smile widening, she says, "You look like a girl," her hands in my hair. I smile, too, wanting to seem sophisticated but starting to giggle. "I am a girl!"

I feel independent, confident. I sit with her on the couch directly across from the big mirror on the wall. She wears a black cropped-neck men's shirt and baggy blue slacks. I watch us in the mirror, her arm around my shoulder, fingers brushing my bosom, my hand moving slowly on her thigh. I am who I want to be. It feels good.

Vivienne Maricevic

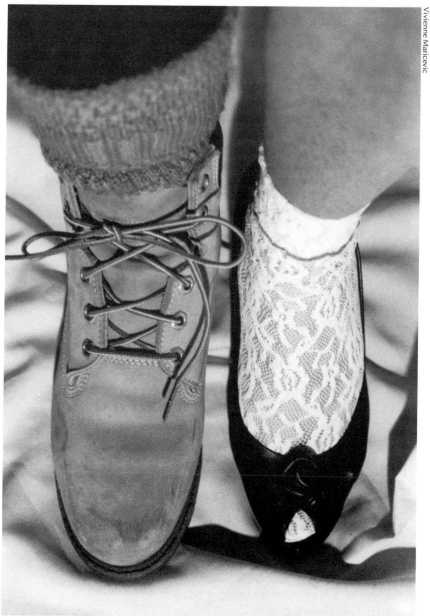

Butch-femme comparison, 1990

Pam A. Parker

The long view

The truly feminist solution would make me,
female that I am, good enough.
as good as any man, even that crucial male
the son my mother would love
and further, would make my mother,
who taught me first what's wrong
with being female, good enough.

I'm sure there is such a feminist solution,
floating in the future, maybe in my future.
And further, I'm sure there's a feminist future
where nobody needs this true solution,
because nobody has the problem.
I believe in these things.

It might be too late for me:
maybe only girls growing up now
will be able to act in ways we call butch
without having to know what we know.
Maybe their brothers won't know to hate them for it.

Adorno writes, I don't remember where, that we can't
imagine the truly new, the truly different.
In the worlds I now inhabit I feel, variously,
transgressive, damaged, reactionary.
I hope to feel at least differently
estranged in the new world I cannot imagine.

Sometimes I think the claim that butches
are damaged women who hate themselves
for being female is true, about me.

Other times I can't bear to accord
that much power to convention.

I won't hate my parents, who let me
grow up butch, and were pleased with me.
If they were horrified by my being female,
they only had to do what they did—
have another kid, a male.

On the other hand, being butch is not
only a shelter against a hard place.
It's got its pleasures and I take them.
Salesmen call me "sir."
Streetwalkers say, "What you doin' tonight, honey?"
My girlfriend dresses up for me,
    lets me undress her, lets me fuck her;
        doesn't ask what I can't give.

I won't lie: this is important to me.
And it's not truly feminist.
After years of disputing the correct line,
I admit it.
Though I remember all the women
who condemned me for being what I am,
and wanted me anyway.

Renay Sanders

The butch-femme balance

The goal

Yin — feminine energy. **Yang** — masculine energy. Yin and yang are not identities. They are both parts of the whole. Woman is not passive. Man is not assertive. When there is balance, wholeness, we are both receiving and giving. Patient and forceful. Gentle and strong. Yang (male) energy, brings knowledge. Yin (female) energy brings wisdom. One longs for the other. When we make that connection and utilize both energies at will, we will be on the path to wholeness. —*from the teachings of Taoism*

The journey

I considered my life to be planned, ordered, relatively content, until I was shown there was more to my plan than I had realized. As a married heterosexual woman, it had never occurred to me that the goals I had accomplished so far were actually processes on a path toward growth, expansion, and self-realization that I could not have fathomed as little as one year ago. The above reflects my lover's perception of her life at our "chance meeting" almost exactly, except that she was a stone butch and I was straight. She'd always felt that straight women were deadly to lesbians, meant only for fools bent on self-destruction, and she had seen enough to know that she would never get involved with one.

There were some other things that she did not do. As a stone butch, she did not identify comfortably with her female body, although her sex life was active and satisfying. She did not allow reciprocation from her lovers and, amazingly, received little argument. She was an expert lover who truly enjoyed satisfying women. She experienced such a high degree of arousal that orgasm was not difficult for her to achieve when moving on top of her lovers, but it never distracted her attention from pleasuring them. Socially and politically, she had to be in touch with and balance her energies to be a tough, militant activist — male energy — and a compassionate, sensitive friend — female energy. But in her stone-butch sexuality, she had to deny her female body, to avoid having it acknowledged by the touch of feminine hands. And, of course, giving oneself to another requires some degree of trust. She would not take the risk. On some level she knew that sexual vulnerability could leave her emotionally vulnerable. There was, too, the problem of looking in the face of her strong yang identity, so unlike the soft openness of her lovers.

You can imagine my fascination with her story. We had come from such different lifestyles, each involved in our own type of sexuality and relationships for a good eighteen years or so before we met.

I began sleeping with boys at a young age. My body took on curves at the age of twelve, the older boys noticed, and childhood abruptly ended. I was a sensitive girl with a desire for romance and love — concepts that are difficult for many lustful teenage boys, and many men, to comprehend. Often, boys would try to convince me that they really liked who I was as a person, but all they were doing was tricking the naive little girl into bed. They were showing me what they perceived my true value to be, and I suppose I bought it somewhere along the line. I perfected the art of pleasing men in every way, including bringing their fantasies to life. So, inevitably, group sex situations would arise over the years, and in these situations, of course, some women would make advances. But I had no lust for women. Male genitals were definitely the only type that stirred my interest.

I eventually married a man who couldn't have been more thrilled with my range of experience, but I had difficulty keeping up with his requests, and my perceived assets began to feel like liabilities after a time. Then we moved in next door to two women. I could tell they were a couple, and I assumed it was supposed to be a secret. But my husband began speaking with them and found they were a very nice couple, and the four of us soon became friends, enjoying barbecues, football games, and a variety of social events together. They became our favorite couple. Their relationship was not a secret to anyone they knew. My husband would play video games with one of the women, and they would entertain each other for hours with "boy-jock" activities, while the other woman and I talked and got to know each other well. We hit every subject that was meaningful to us. We shared our feelings, respected each other's opinions, and became good friends. For me, to find someone with whom I shared so much in common, and someone who was so bright and aware, was extremely rare. I admired her greatly and always looked forward to seeing her. I didn't find out until much later that she felt the same way. Being from such different worlds made it difficult to acknowledge how alike we were. How could she think just like a straight femme? How could I be so much like this hard-core butch? But deep below the surface we met, and shared, and the exterior stuff — well, I guess we just didn't look at it too hard.

When she told me they had decided to move out of state to start their own agency, I was hit hard by the news. But we were determined not to lose touch with this couple, so we visited and had regular phone contact and solidified the friendship.

Then, because of a number of unexpected circumstances, the couple broke up. This was an unbelievable shock to us all, and I spoke to my devastated friend daily by phone, trying to help her deal with the loss. As soon as I could break away, I flew out to see her. She had not yet had any contact with the lesbian community in her new town, so we decided that she had to go out and see what this new place had to offer. Off we went to the local women's bar in hopes that she might meet some new people and begin to put the loss of her four-year relationship behind her.

When we walked into the bar, I suddenly felt very self-conscious. Many people were watching me, as my long blonde hair, makeup, and high heels didn't quite blend with the surroundings. Ninety percent of the women in there were androgynous. The other ten percent appeared to be more role identified, and my friend clearly fell into this latter category. So we settled in for the evening, and after a drink and a dance or two, she began to look quite comfortable. I was really enjoying myself too. It was pleasant to be in a bar where there were no men taking turns trying to pick me up.

After a while, a slow song came on and she asked me to dance. As we headed to the dance floor, I wondered how I would do this. I had never danced slow with a woman before, and I expected to feel rather silly. But when we touched and began to move together, her energy felt very ... familiar. It felt nice. I moved in closer to synchronize our rhythm on the dance floor. She moved sensuously — just the way I like. I looked up at her and her smile was very shy, her eye contact brief, and her face slightly flushed. At first curious and intrigued, I then became aware of another feeling. I felt very full, very soft breasts pressing against my body as we danced, and I was struck by how much this softness moved me. She saw me delighting in the feel of her, and although normally this would have exceeded her level of comfort, having a little femme on her arm, this first night out, helped to soothe the bruises left by her ex-lover. That I was straight didn't matter; it still helped. So throughout the evening, every time a slow song began we found ourselves magnetically drawn to the dance floor. She held me as a man would, yet her body was definitely all woman, and that sweet shyness was something in between. Amazing contrasts, and quite a strong combination.

Afterward, we sat on the couch at her apartment discussing the bar and the different people we had observed. She had mentioned earlier, when she picked me up at the airport, that I could have the bed and she would take the couch, but since it was a king-sized bed and we knew each other so well, I didn't feel the formality of separate rooms was necessary.

I suppose I was a little naive, because as I lay in bed that night, I felt a hand come to rest on the back of my thigh. I looked up at her. I was very surprised that she would actually touch me this way, but I had to admire her courage. In the dark I said, "Talk to me." She didn't know how to respond. She had reacted to a feeling, a natural desire when being so close to someone you are attracted to, but now she was apprehensive. We had an important friendship, and I was a straight married woman. By her own rule, I was off limits. She began to feel she had made a serious mistake, one that would be awkward to fix. But the tense moment for her was brief. I responded to her touch and eased her concerns. I moved closer and began kissing her lips very softly. Instantly, she was on top of me, her thigh between my legs, moving so slowly at first, so sensually, that I knew in the world of women this was an experienced lover. Her movements became more lustful with each thrust, and her breath quickened with her pace as she pressed her body against mine. I felt her large breasts moving back and forth against my torso through the fabric of her button-down men's shirt. The clothing added a delicious combination of mystery and sin that was so extremely sexual to me that I had to reach my hand between her legs, right inside the thin fabric that separated us. It was the first time I had ever placed my hand on an aroused woman, and as I slid into her warmth, her sweetness soaked me completely, and I could not resist the complete eroticism touching her evoked.

She shuddered and moaned and the spasms began right in my hand, and I knew in that instant that I had to have more of her. Much more. I laid her down and covered her with kisses and loving caresses, and as the hours turned into days, she fully abandoned herself to my passion for her as I explored all the wonders of this unbelievably responsive lover. And then I held her and kissed her tears away. Tears that I as a woman could fully understand. Tears of bittersweet longing, finally fulfilled. Her soul had been opened and her emotions flowed as she spoke to me about who she had been before she and I began. She said she had never given herself to anyone before, and never felt so desired. She felt like a woman in my protective arms, and it frightened her. She would try to withdraw to a safer, more familiar place, but somewhere in my eyes, she saw a safer place than she had ever been before. I had never held anyone so close — so close that we felt like one being. I had never felt such sweetness in lovemaking. The term *lovemaking* finally made sense to me. She had found her beautiful womanhood in my caresses. I found my strength as a woman, my virile passion, as she looked up at me with her soft, loving eyes. We broke through boundaries we never knew existed, and we found the other side of ourselves.

The balanced energies — the yin and the yang — had come together within us to make us more, to open our minds, to enlarge our inner worlds and increase our capacity to feel more and do more in the world outside. Through the opening of the stone butch, a fuller woman was found inside, and as I watched her bud and bloom within my love, I felt blessed with the honor of assisting in her awakening. As I held the beautiful new being gently in my arms, I found myself unable to let her go. Not completely. Not ever.

In the world, my lover and I are butch and femme. (Yes, she is still very butch.) You can spot us a mile away. I am the petite feminine blonde with the soft clingy dress and the little spiked heels in whose presence the men and the butches feel their yang drives stir. She is the butch with the button-down shirt and the loose tie, tight black jeans, men's shoes. With her hot sexy smile and her confident swagger, you know she is butch right down to her soul. Femmes, even straight women, respond to all that yang energy — batting their eyes and smiling sweetly — without even thinking about it. She'd even flipped a butch or two on their backs in her day, just because she could. But this traditional butch enjoys treating her femme like a lady. She opens my doors; she buys my drinks; she likes to give me jewelry, lingerie, flowers. She even likes to lay me down and make love to me like a "proper butch" should, because she always considered it the butch's job to please her lover in every way and completely spoil them. But if she wants to spoil this femme, she has to let me place my hands on either side of her tie and touch the voluptuous softness, the sight of which teases me unmercifully, pushing against that cotton shirt. Her response is immediate, and she completely forgets about what a "proper butch" should do.

For her, there is no time to experience a full-blown identity crisis as a butch, and no reason to. The expansion and self-discovery happened too fast and were too important to expend a lot of energy hanging onto the past. And the expectations of our individual cultures just cannot be allowed to minimize the growth and awakening that have occurred, and continue to occur, for both of us. We believe that the earth is no more than a large schoolroom, and we are here to learn as much as we can about the things that really matter. We believe all people are awakening, little by little. A glimpse at a time. And if we can all learn to embrace change by realizing that change is always on the path toward growth, then we will not be afraid to look at ourselves and look at our lives and see what changes would facilitate our journey toward balance, knowledge, wisdom, and wholeness.

Is it any wonder, then, that butches and femmes seek each other out? Not when you realize that yin and yang long for each other, and an important part of wholeness depends on finding that connection. Identify as you choose, if there is joy in it. Be honest and loving, require the same from others, and enjoy your journey.

Sonja Franeta

Bridge poem

Black cat lady of night
immense, moist, teeth gleaming
covers us in her tender chill.
Desire lopes in my heart
only my own echo knows
saxophone low notes follow
I alone approach the bridge
where my girl waits.
The bridge shakes with every
car and truck, lights miss her,
water glitters beyond steel rails.
The bridge where our pain will
turn to pleasure. I promise.

As a child I'd hear bitch/
shit/ cunt/ slaps/ threats/ cries
and I discovered how to rub
the hurt away on myself
never touching directly, maneuvering
my stuffed dog, the blanket.
Times I'd meditate on
Jesus Christ and his crown of thorns,
the sufferings of saintly martyrs,
and had nunly orgasms.
My shiny wolf-buckle belt,
my jeans and boots and leather
jacket now, my knife at my side.
I see her. Jacket and leather
skirt pick up some shine.
Should be painted—
interrupted grace.

375

THE PERSISTENT DESIRE

The bridge shakes randomly.
I'm wet, I'm sure she is too.
Werewolves used to fascinate me,
but I was a quiet child, quiet and shy;
I got quieter with every hit
from Mommy and Daddy. It would all pile up
and I'd suddenly tell them off. I'd just
get it again. I only wanted tenderness,
to be held, to be allowed to choose,
to be held and rubbed.

She's taking off her clothes without a word.
I listen for sounds, nothing,
only the bridge giving
as she holds the rail
and bends her round
trusting ass toward me.
We meet once a month
at a different place,
our ritual to ease life.
I know tonight she must
have my hand, her pussy's mouth
is hungry. I will be slow and
patient. I'll stay with her.
I promise.

There was crying. Consulting
with my brother and sister
I crept down the stairs.
Daddy held Mommy in a corner
gently slapping her face.
It was red, she was crying,
the intimacy between them,
his suppressed yelling,
he above her as they stood
close like lovers.
I didn't know what to do.
She told us, "Go away."
He seemed lost, mesmerized.

She's beautiful and wild—
my girl — and opens like a pro,
hugs my hand like the world
is about to end, comes

like a night full of stars.
I love to fuck her, I want to be
under her, I'm tough with her.
Then she lies on the bridge grating.
I slurp her wet, lick her sweat.
My cunt presses against the grateful
bridge. I fuckin' come, I bring my cool
belt buckle to the top of her hot cunt,
I bite her breasts, I lick her tears.

> Once upon a time a little girl was lost
> in the forest, I whisper in her ear. She ran
> fast as she could — she swore she heard
> snapping wolves, panthers, a bear
> thump behind her.
> She was scared and no one was there
> to take care of her. She got
> so tired she had to stop.
> Hiding behind a great rock,
> trying to breathe quietly,
> shivering with dread, she waited.
> After a time, one by one,
> out from behind bushes
> and trees — deer, rabbits,
> a curious badger came to her,
> they sniffed then licked
> her hands, tickled her tearful face.

The night lady begins to ride us,
she presses hard against my covered
ass, she's all over my back,
I love it, don't want nothin' else,
then she bites my neck and
leads her rough tongue
in a straight line
through my short dark hair

Arlene Istar

Femme-dyke

She was talking about her eight-year-old niece. "I think she's a dyke." I smiled. "What makes you think that?"

"Well," she said, "she's really into sports, and she never wears dresses, and she has short hair ... You know, she has all the signs."

I smile and begin to agree, and suddenly something freezes up inside. I look at my butch lover and realize, "You're not describing dykes, you're describing butches!"

In the lesbian community though, butches *are* our image of dykes. Butchness is the hub of our lesbian universe. Lesbians are never described as women who wear dresses and high heels, or have long nails or hair, or as women who dislike sports. Oh, we all know there are lesbians like that, but somehow they are different, not like "us," somehow not authentic. I was a baby femme-dyke. I played with dolls and loved dressing up. I wore makeup and perfume. I envied girls who had nice clothes that I couldn't afford to buy. I hated sports, and I never worked on cars.

And I loved women. I seduced almost all the girls I was friends with in junior high and high school and into college. And although I also slept with men until college, I never denied my love for my girlfriends or denied that I made love to them (although perhaps I would have minimized the importance of it).

Although the role models for all of us growing up as lesbians leave much to be desired, I couldn't find any role models as a femme. The only girls I could recognize as dykes were butches — girls who appeared to avoid other girls as much as they avoided boys. Being a hippie, I was never drawn to superstraight girl drag, such as shaving my legs, which made me somehow as different from my straight friends as I was from the dykes (read: butches).

Butch dykes seem to have had a deep sense of themselves as different from a young age. Butches I've loved or known as friends presented a presence in the world when they were adolescents, and often even as toddlers, that signaled their differentness from most of the other girls. This differentness was obvious in the way they chose to dress or how they stood, and in their interest in "boys'" things. Mostly it was a rejection of femininity and the social expectations that went with it. What has always been interesting to me is that this did not necessarily translate into sexual exploration with other girls. Sometimes they were not even aware of their sexual feelings for girls. Certainly, if they did identify their differentness as sexual, they were very leery of acting on it. The price they were paying for being different was already too high.

Perhaps all people *feel* different in a world that denies difference, but the experience of knowing oneself to be lesbian in a homophobic world is to feel the stigma of difference as perversion, the ultimate in otherness. As a femme, though, my difference was not obvious. It wasn't so much that I could pass; it was simply that I liked being a girl. I fit in among other girls and was very much one of them, except, of course, for this secret perversion I carried with me. And, indeed, that is how it felt. I looked acceptable on the outside, but inside was this desire, this craving that made my easy access to girls' locker rooms and slumber parties an anxious, exciting, confusing, and guilty experience. Do you understand? I desired my girlfriends. And to my horror, they began to suspect it!

Let me tell you how it all began. I was eleven years old and my mother was at work. My best friend, Linda, was at my house and we decided to play a game. Actually, it was her suggestion. This was the game: she would be a boy, and I would be a girl, and we would pretend we were on a date. (It was not uncommon for girls to "practice" kissing one another at this age, so this didn't seem strange to me.) We pretended we went out to dinner, and then after dinner she took me home, which happened to be to the door of my mother's bedroom. And she kissed me. I mean she *kissed* me. And then she threw me down on my mother's bed and kissed and groped and squeezed my just-budding breasts. I can remember the wetness between my thighs, and the newness and exhilaration of it. We remained lovers for about two years, although we never would've called it that. We never touched under our underwear, because we wanted to be virgins when we got married. (But you can't imagine how wet underwear can get.) We knew what we were doing was "lesbian" and made lesbian jokes. Her nickname was Charlie and mine was Arny. And although we didn't have words for it, I always knew that she was the butch and I was the femme. I can still see Linda slouching in her peacoat, dragging on a cigarette held in the corner of her mouth, hands pushed into the pockets of her jeans, nudging me into an alleyway or the corner of the schoolyard so that we could make out before we went home for dinner. And none of this had anything to do with the fact that that we were both "boy-crazy," and often had boyfriends, and spent much of our time together talking and fantasizing about boys. I can't quite remember what happened to change this relationship, or how much its ending had to do with her sister discovering us making love one day. I have kept in touch with a few people from this time in my life but lost touch with Linda a long time ago. I do hope that Linda found her way to the lesbian community (and to this day I look for her there) and is able to celebrate her butch self. But somehow my gut tells me she's busy seducing all the "straight" femme girls in Canarsie.

Although Linda was my first, she'd been around the block a few times. I soon followed her lead. Another ten years would pass before I had sex with another butch, however. For the next decade, I had "relationships" with men and seduced all my close girlfriends.

A friend's mother warned her about me. "I think Arlene is a lesbian," she said. Goddess, that word sounded so perverted and cruel. I became indignant with denial. But being cute and pretty and one of the girls, I suffered no repercussions from these accusations.

All of the girls and women I had sex with identified as straight, at least at the time. But then again, so did I. After all, the only lesbians I knew were butches, so my only choices were to butch it up, or play it straight, and I tried both. I do think, though, that I was able to be sexual with so many girls because I was femme, because I fit in. It was my girlness that enabled me to be invited to sleep over their houses and my girlness that allowed them to let me touch them without fear.

Growing up as a femme-dyke was in some ways like growing up Jewish: there was this sense of invisibility, of knowing you were not like the others, the majority, even if you looked like them. You see I didn't really *know* I was a lesbian, any more than I really knew I was a Jew. In my Jewish neighborhood everyone was Jewish; only in the outside world did my Jewishness become differentness, and there, I felt the difference even when others couldn't recognize it. As a femme-dyke, I fit into a socially pre-scribed role as a girl with which I was mostly comfortable, except for this one little thing — I wanted to fuck my girlfriends. This difference only became obvious when it became painful. As my straight girlfriends grew up, they wanted to get on to the "real thing," as did I, but we had different things in mind.

Then along came the women's movement, or, rather, along I came into the women's movement. Now, this was more like it. For the first time, there were women more like me. But what I soon discovered was that the women who looked like me were all straight. All the dykes still looked like butches. But I must admit, androgyny being what it is, the poles seemed less far apart and I was able to fit in as a hippie bisexual feminist type.

In my attempts to attract some of the dykes, I tried to be less femme. I really did. I cut off all my long pretty hair. I wore flannel shirts, hiking boots, and white cotton underwear. And I did meet and fuck more women, and, yes, dykes, but somehow the sex left something to be desired. It was better than sleeping with straight women and better than sleeping with hippie men, and it was warm and soft and home, but, well, it wasn't hot.

Interestingly, only after coming out did I have the freedom to experiment with my femminess in a way I'd never experienced before. Even though I was always "one of the girls," I was also a street kid and, later, a hippie. I never allowed myself to dress too sexily; after all, I was a feminist. In my fantasies, though, I had always worn lace undies and low-cut shirts that showed my cleavage.

Over the next few years, I began to meet women who liked and encouraged my fantasies. Yes, they were butches. They were butches who liked my femminess, and celebrated it. I began to explore these fantasies that spoke to this deep part of my identity, first at home in bed, and now, still haltingly, in public.

Butch women exhibit such strong sexual energy that it has taken me many years of loving them to understand that the bravado is often a cover for their own sexual concerns. Butches and femmes expect butch women to take the lead, to have vast sexual experience and no performance anxiety. My experience, however, is that femmes have far more sexual experience and less performance anxiety, and are usually the ones to take the sexual lead. Butches are good at standing around looking ready, but femmes are more often the ones to reach out for what they want. There are more butches in the streets than there are in the sheets.

I find myself feeling frustrated while writing, thinking you, the reader, must picture me as far more femme than I am. Although I enjoy wearing skirts, I often wear pants. I rarely wear makeup (although I do have a fetish for nail polish), and I proudly wear my facial hair. I neither love nor hate to cook or clean house and have healed (finally) my codependent need to be eternally present for my partner. By nobody's standards am I "delicate, docile, deferential, ladylike, refined, and genteel," as femininity is traditionally defined, although some might argue that I am "soft, tender, and submissive" — but only under the right circumstances. One friend, trying to reconcile my very assertive presence with my femme drag, called me a transvestite butch! I do not fit anyone's stereotype of a feminine woman, any more than I fit anyone's stereotype of a dyke.

A few years ago, I bought a pair of warm winter boots. I worked in an agency where all the women wore heavy femme drag, and even if I hadn't been out, my differentness was apparent. I wasn't sure if the agency would even let me wear boots to work. I walked into my office, and two male co-workers immediately began playfully whistling. "Ooh, new boots — how butch," they teased me. Later that evening, I met my lover and another friend, both butch identified. They too teased: "Ooh, new boots — how femmy," they said. And I suppose that's what being a femme-dyke means. The boys think I'm butch, and the girls think I'm femme.

It seems to me the real message of butch-femme identities is an acknowledgment of the full range of female, and lesbian, sexuality — actually the full range of human sexuality, because the truth is that regardless of their sexual identity, both women and men can experience either or both ends of this continuum — which is why transvestites and transsexuals make so many of us uncomfortable. Butch-femme is the tip of the iceberg of issues that call into question matters of sexual and gender identity.

Although I know my identity to be femme, I am not saying that all lesbians are either butches or femmes, nor am I saying that they should be. Many lesbians seem to be perfectly comfortable being androgynous, being femmes with femmes or butches with butches, or just being "themselves." I am not trying to fit all of the lesbian nation into my paradigm; what I am trying to do is to broaden the lesbian paradigm so that women like me not only fit but are celebrated in our own right, and not derided for not being real lesbians.

I am also aware that some lesbians change their identities depending on their lovers or the time of their lives. These roles are not static, nor should they be. I know a handful of butches who have gone femme and a few femmes who have gone butch, and I say *mazel tov*. I also know quite a few butches who, in the privacy of their own homes, like frilly teddies and makeup (butches in drag, or transvestite femmes?). And many, many femmes who are carpenters and softball players and who like butches on their backs in bed.

I also need to say that it is not only butches who attract me. All kinds of women attract me, and for that matter, femme women have a particular attraction for me, because they validate me by being role models who teach me that femininity is not weakness.

We have limited our options by desexualizing our community. The rhetoric says that we develop our politics from our personal experiences, except, of course, when our personal experience is too sexy. In our effort to examine the sexual exploitation of women, we have denied our lesbian heritage, as well as our current options.

Discerning what is femme and what is butch is very difficult, since most of us who use these terms use them to define who we feel we are, and do not mold our behavior to fit existing stereotypic roles. I call myself femme because it describes who I feel I am, once I figured out it wasn't a bad word. It does not mean that I love to cook, or that I never wear pants, or that I can't paint a house or seduce a woman. It does mean that I love the feel of my femininity, that I experience my essential self, sexually and socially, as female.

I love to dress up pretty for my lover. I love the feel of lace on my body against the feel of strong woman hands. I love to curl up in my lover's arms. I love our oppositeness — her starched white shirts against my silky ones, her sneakers and loafers in the closet next to my girly shoes, her short, neatly trimmed nails against my longer, polished nails. I love the power of my femmeness, the traditional feminine power to seduce and overpower her with a gentle touch.

It is not, however, a lack of strength, this femmeness, as any butch can tell you. A friend of mine who truly loves femmes describes femmes as soft, pretty women who will break a bottle over your head if you cross them.

Femme identity is exactly that — an identity. I can no more explain it than I can my lesbianism. And they *are* connected. I often wonder if I were straight, if I could afford to be as femme.

I suppose some people think passing as straight is a blessing, but I'm not one of them. I like people to know I'm a lesbian. It's not always easy for them to read the signs when the signs they associate with lesbians are butch signs. I think that straight people know that there is something different about me, but I'm not always sure they know what it is.

Sometimes dykes fear that femmes are not real lesbians. Some years ago, a femme friend of mine began dating a rather butch woman. There was no denial of this dynamic in the relationship, and although the butch clearly loved the femme for all of her femmeness, every time my friend went shopping and bought a dress, or had her hair done (read: did something femmy), her lover would become terribly insecure and wonder if her lover were going straight.

This just highlights the reality that we have no way to perceive traditional feminine traits as being lesbian. Perhaps so many lesbians like to seduce straight women because they are really attracted to femmes and once most women come out they are molded into typical (butch) lesbians.

Certainly, for me, claiming my identity as a femme has been as empowering as claiming all the identities "I was taught to despise": being woman, dyke, Jew, working class, disabled, and so on. I love being a girl. And I love that there are so many ways to be a girl. But I do have one question: when talking about butch-femme relationships, why does butch always have to come first?

Kate Berne Miller

I, in the bow of the ferry

I, in the bow of the ferry,
in my black leather jacket,
face into the cold wind.
You, warm behind me,
your hands in my pockets
pulling me close.

You at the bar
in your heels and satin dress.
You dancing — lithe as any cat,
my hands on your hips.
Your green eyes with that dark look,
smoke before flame.

I with my legs spread
on the table — waiting.
You in your black slip
with your hands in me.
Your tongue of fire
between my thighs—
amazing to burn so
in such a wet place.

You on the beach,
your taste in my mouth,
your smell in my dreams.
You — moving under me,
you crying out, your salt tears,
my hunger for you.

Kitty Tsui

Who says we don't talk about sex?

*Portions of the following article, which has been greatly con-
densed for this publication, were presented in a keynote speech
at the Horizons Lesbian Conference in Chicago, Illinois, in
April 1990.*

I was born thirty-eight years ago and raised to be a nice Chinese girl. But
nice Chinese girls don't grow up to be dykes or rebels. And I turned
out to be both.

I grew up in silence. Though I was part of a large extended family, we
ate in silence. There was no conversation or laughter, just the sound of
soup spoons and chopsticks against the rice bowls. I was not encouraged
to talk, express emotions, or ask questions. I grew up with a heritage of
silence.

I was a girl child, the first born in a traditional Chinese family, raised
to be seen but not heard, raised to excel in school but not to be curious,
raised to be someone's wife but not to be a person of my own. When I was
growing up in England, Hong Kong, and San Francisco, I read everything
I could get my hands on, but none of the books spoke of my own
experience. I started writing when I was eleven years old to fill the silence
and to turn the years of rejection into affirmation.

You're probably wondering what the hell any of this has to do with
lesbian sex. The answer is — plenty. What I write is shaped by my history
and experiences both as a Chinese woman and as a lesbian.

Chinese is my first language. But I was fluent only in the words my
parents deemed it necessary for me to know. I was certainly not taught the
words for breast, cunt, ass, or orgasm. There were no words for sex;
therefore, sex did not exist.

I came out as a lesbian when I was twenty-one, but I didn't start writing
about sex until almost a decade later. Sure, I wrote love poems, but I never

385

Kitty Tsui, 1988

wrote about sex. I was, after all, a nice Chinese girl and we didn't talk about things like that.

❖

I have always loved women passionately. I love the way a femme moves across a dance floor, knowing all eyes are focused on her. I love the hard eye-to-eye look from another butch as she sizes me up as competition — or her next conquest. I love the fluid seduction in a femme's eyes. I love the long line of her neck, her delicate earlobes and soft lips, painted some shade of red or unpainted but deeply flushed from having been kissed long and hard. Many times. I love the curve of her breast, the hardness of her nipples, the softness of her stomach, the fullness of her ass, her legs with a faint covering of hair or long and sleek in black silk stockings. I love the strength in her thighs, the firmness of her biceps, the feel of her forearms as she takes me. I love the smell of her heat and the place of pleasure between her legs. I love her ankles and her delicate toes and her soft instep where I run my tongue until my teeth are gripping her Achilles tendon. I love the smell of her, the taste of her, the feel of her, the sight of her. I love women passionately.

❖

Some women do not attend my theater or literary events for fear of supporting my sexual politics. I have been accused of recruiting. Never mind that I have a long history of writing, community organizing, and activism. Now I am judged solely for my leather sexuality. It's never been easy being different, but I have always survived. I will continue to speak out, write truths, and make waves. My countryman Mao Zedong wrote, "Dare to struggle, dare to win." I say, dare to write. Dare to be different. And who says nice Chinese girls don't talk about sex?

Mary Frances Platt

Reclaiming femme... again

Yes, it's true: I was the type of young femme who managed the girls' basketball team in high school, just to be able to take in the sight of all those butches parading their muscles up and down the court. I found Girl Scout camp to be femme heaven and reveled in being able to explore my athletic self and still maintain my femmeness. And, to my horror, I have to admit pushing Tina away from my breasts in the back seat of a Buick while attending Mount Saint Mary Seminary.

And then there was feminism ... Although I came out as a "gay" woman _before_ reading _The Feminine Mystique_, the seventies brand of white feminism had me trimming my nails and cutting off my hair. Soon I was outfitted in farmer jeans and high tops. And still I was told by my "sisters" that I didn't "look like a dyke" (read: I didn't look butch).

I began to lead two lives — one as an outrageous, skirted, lipsticked femme while I worked in and traveled with carnivals, and another as an imitation butch back home in the women's community. Eventually, I pulled the pieces of my being back together and proclaimed boldly, "I am a working-class lesbian femme."

So, I had maybe six years of reveling in unleashing my seductive femme self when, as lives go, mine changed: slowly at first and then more dramatically.

Recurring back pain and limited range of motion were finally diagnosed. Soon after came decreased mobility. No more mountain climbing. No long mall walks in search of the perfect piece of sleaze. No more standing against kitchen walls while being gloriously fucked by some handsome butch. I stopped using alcohol and drugs, became ill with what is now known as CFIDS (Chronic Fatigue Immune Dysfunction Syndrome), and began to use a three-wheeled power chair.

The more disabled I became, the more I mourned the ways my sexual femme self had manifested through the nondisabled me: cruising at the local lezzie bar, picking a dyke whose eyes refused to stray from mine, dancing seductively, moving *all* of me for all of her. Cooking: love and suggestion neatly tucked into the folds of a broccoli quiche. Serving my date in varying, sleazy clothing, removing layers as the meal and our passion progressed. And making love ... feeling only pleasure as my hips rose and fell under the weight of her. Accomplishment and pride smirked across my face as her wrists finally submitted to the pressure of strong, persistent hands. These are the ways I knew to be femme, to be the essence of me.

It's been five years now since I began using a wheelchair. I am just awakening to a new reclamation of femme. Yes. I still grieve the way I was, am still often unsure how this femme with disabilities will act out her seduction scenes. I still marvel when women find passion amidst the chrome and rubber that is now a part of me.

There have been numerous dates, lovers, relationships, sexual partners, and flirtations along the way. Cindy, Jenny, Ellie, Emma, Diane, Dorothy, Gail, June, Clove, Lenny, Cherry, Diana, Sarah I, and Sarah II. You have all reminded me in your own subtle or overt, quiet or wild ways that I am desirable, passionate, exciting, wanted.

Yes, I am an incredibly sexual being. An outrageous, loud-mouthed femme who's learning to dress, dance, cook, *and* seduce on wheels; finding new ways to be gloriously fucked by handsome butches *and* aggressive femmes. I hang out more with the sexual outlaws now — you know, the motorcycle lesbians who see wheels and chrome between your legs as something exciting, the leather women whose vision of passion and sexuality doesn't exclude fat, disabled me.

Ableism tells us that lesbians with disabilities are asexual. (When was the last time you dated a dyke who uses a wheelchair?) Fat oppression insists that thin is in and round is repulsive. At times, these voices became very loud, and my femme, she hid quietly amidst the lies.

Now my femme is rising again. The time of doubt, fear, and retreat has passed. I have found my way out of the lies and the oppression and moved into a space of loving and honoring the new femme who has emerged. This lesbian femme with disabilities is wise, wild, wet, and wanting. Watch out.

Sima Rabinowitz

Lullaby

The last time you played a team sport it was kickball. You would sooner drink the coffee black than go to the store for milk without at least a little eyeliner. Given a choice, you would rather have been the Helen Shaver character than that actress with the French name who went all over talking about her husband in interviews so that everyone would know she wasn't really a dyke. You read poetry on your lunch hour. You have not let anyone, in the last decade anyway, trim your hair so much as a centimeter above your shoulder blades. In short, you are a femme. Femme enough to giggle when your girlfriend calls you a slut. Femme enough to know when to call her the same.

She can make a basket one-handed from anywhere on the court. She hasn't worn a pair of nylons since she waited tables as a teenager at the HoJo's in Saginaw. Once she wanted to be Spider-Man, but now she would probably choose Janet Flanner. You think it's pretty obvious. She's a butch. Butch enough to pick you up and carry you across the room. Butch enough to put you down when you say you've had enough.

So at first you think she's joking when she teases that your sperm count is too low and makes up silly names combining yours and hers. At first you think she is trying to figure out if you have some secret fantasy when she stops to look at the miniature snowsuits on your weekly shopping spree to Target for cigarettes and toilet paper. At first you think she is being playful when she weighs the pros and cons — turkey basters or a clinically tested approach.

But, no, she is serious. She is purposeful. She is expectant. Your butch wants to have a baby.

You don't know what she must be feeling, because you have never imagined a baby in your belly, have never picked out names, made cooing noises, never shopped for bassinets, never expected to compare diapers or choose a preschool. You never dream baby sounds or baby smells. But she has. For as long as she can remember, she says.

She wants to feel a baby growing in her womb. She wants to hold a baby to her breast. She wants to watch a baby learn to crawl, to walk, to run, to shoot hoops. She wants to teach a baby to love women, to love the world. You are not sure that you want to have to love a baby. But you are sure that you love her.

Christine Cassidy

Walt Whitman:
A model femme

A journal entry

Still haven't decided whether or not to go to the femme group's discussion on role models tonight ... There's the question of talking about Walt Whitman. What would I say? That he wasn't afraid of touching the feminine in his books or life? That his strength lay in receptivity? I think that's the essence of Whitman. He also didn't do one damn thing he didn't want to — rejected his brother's offer to move in with them when they left Camden, rejected money-making offers in favor of servicing his art.

But why him and not, say, Dickinson? Dickinson was self-cloistered, rarefied, and Whitman was a flamboyant egalitarian, self-published and extremely ambitious, as if he knew his work would never find its audience without his persistence. Dickinson believed no one would understand her even after she was dead and buried. And of course she was right. Whitman spelled it all out in *Leaves of Grass.* He was firmly lodged in his body — Dickinson the antithesis: ethereal, completely of the mind. What makes Whitman a model femme, for me, was his passionate belief in the power of the body — "Not an inch nor a particle of an inch is vile" and

I believe in the flesh and the appetites
Seeing, hearing, feeling, are miracles, and each part and tag of me
    is a miracle.

Divine am I inside and out, and I make holy whatever I touch
    or am touch'd from.

Any good role model gives to the student faith in herself, in her abilities. I have always chosen my role models for their strength, for their seeming fearlessness. I am learning to dive through fear, confront it and plough through it, trusting myself and my lover's hands that I'll come out the other side. Whole. Stronger. I think of Linda Gregg's poem "Whole and

Without Blessing." I am the only one who can bless my life, shape it, form it, give it breath. And here is Whitman:

> One world is aware and by far the largest to me, and that is myself,
> And whether I come to my own to-day or in ten thousand or ten million years,
> I can cheerfully take it now, or with equal cheerfulness I can wait.

"And if the body were not the soul, what is the soul?"
I've had butches say to me, "I can break you." But I am unbreakable. Whitman says, "When I give I give myself." It is all about choice and respect and trust: sex, loving, strength, receptivity. She is everything and nothing without me, as I am everything and nothing without her. Choosing her — not once, but each time — is the gift I give her. I give her my body and all its idiosyncrasies, its details, its curves and aromas, its soft and bony landscape, its reachable and unreachable places.

What I accept in being femme is not passivity. It is active receptivity — passionate curiosity, that hunger insatiable — for knowledge, for touch, for power received and transformed. Whitman again:

> I know I am solid and sound,
> To me the converging objects of the universe perpetually flow,
> All are written to me, and I must get what the writing means.

For me to really understand anything, I have to take it into my body. I have to become it, live it, and charge it with my own imagination. There are things I will never comprehend — childbirth, death (Virginia Woolf: "The one experience I shall never describe") — but I also know that in being open, receptive, I begin to understand the world, my life, my lovers. I begin to get what the writing means.

Cathy Cade

Femme on bike, 1990s

Mykel Johnson

Butchy femme

The radical lesbian-feminist community in which I came out did not "believe" in butch-femme. It was the eighties; I was in my thirties. I learned that butch-femme was role-playing, just a mimicry of heterosexual roles, and we had come beyond that now. We were women-identified women. And, yet, there was a contradiction. My first summer at the peace camp, newly out, I remember talking with my friend, deciding who was butch and who was femme, femmy butch and butchy femme. It was intimate and playful, this talking, interspersed with talk of whom we thought attractive and in what ways.

I asked my first lover if she thought I was butch or femme. She avoided an answer, knowing that I wanted her to say butch but believing just the opposite. Definitely, butch was better in my mind, somehow more lesbian, more dyke. It took me a while to identify as femme, and to articulate what butch-femme means in my life. I am still sorting it out. I'm not sure if what it means for me is the same as what it means for others in our culture. Maybe we are sorting it out again as a community.

My first experiences as a lesbian did not give me a way to understand what being a femme lesbian might look like. When I was still a "straight" feminist, I had begun to question the rules and roles society laid out for women. I stopped shaving my legs, wore pants, didn't wear makeup, got comfortable with my body. I learned a new way of perceiving beauty, particularly through going to women's music festivals. I started being attracted to lesbians, especially to very "dykey" lesbians. I wasn't attracted to straight women. "Dyke" seemed to symbolize the radical woman, the one who challenged the standards for feminine behavior and dress.

My strongest experience of first being lesbian was of being able to initiate sex with and make love to women I was attracted to. I was thirty-one before I made love to a woman for the first time. I had been made love to (by men) in many ways. But I had never made love to a woman. I was thrilled that I could feel her breasts, kiss the softness of her cheeks, reach my fingers into her cunt, taste her juices, pleasure her clitoris with my tongue until she dissolved in delight. The new wonder of it all accentuated the sides of myself that felt more butch, and yet it was butch women I was attracted to.

My growing awareness of butch and femme came out of my relationship to lovers who identified as butch. Even though I came out as a feminist-identified lesbian, once I was out I became more and more queer identified. This happened for me in the context of growing into an erotic self-understanding, more than a gender or political understanding. I came to identify as femme, because of my profound attraction and response to butch women.

For the butch women I have loved, the experience of being butch went back to childhood, to not fitting into gender expectations for girls. She may not have had words to name it, perhaps just feelings of isolation or a sense of failure, perhaps rejection by other girls or boys at puberty. The toughness in her stance was a way of holding herself strong against the harassment she encountered on city streets, in women's restrooms, from parents and siblings trying to mold her into a shape she did not fit. It was from my butch lovers and friends that I learned what it means to be queer. Being femme for me is linked to my treasuring of butch women, to my deep erotic need and hunger for the very qualities that have banished her. To be femme is to give honor where there has been shame.

Likewise, a butch woman brought honor to my shame, a shame that lay in my capacity or failure to let go into sex and pleasure. I remember feeling that sex was difficult for me, that I took too long to come, that I had some problem. A butch lover responded by being delighted that we could make love for hours, letting me know that her pleasure in giving to me need not be shortened by too quick an orgasm. What had been a liability was transformed in her eyes into an asset. Something about butch, then, meant that she loved to make love to me. She would get really turned on by making love to me; sometimes my orgasm would be enough for her to come without any other stimulation. This experience was profoundly freeing to me. I could let go and receive, not afraid that I was taking too much time or energy or attention. Her hunger and skill dissolved the fear in my wounded self of receiving sexual caresses. In the wealth of such generosity, I was freed to linger, freed to give back, released from a timid scarcity of enjoyment.

My femme eroticism was not passivity but receptivity. Being good in bed as a femme meant communicating my responses. Moaning, talking, breathing, shifting, letting her know the effect her lovemaking had on me, letting her know what I wanted. To be femme with her meant to be vulnerable, to open to her the thoughts and feelings of my imagination, to let her know the inner recesses of my mind as well as my body.

Loving a butch woman also meant learning the places she held back, recognizing her hesitations with regard to receiving my caresses. Old wounds taught her to withhold vulnerability and prefer self-sufficiency.

As she kindled a fire in me, she warmed herself to the possibility of melting when my hands sought her barriers. More often than not when we made love, a butch woman first made love to me, and then I would make love to her. Full of relief, she would open to me her own secret passages, her face shining. Here was someone who could take her, too, give what she loved to give.

Whereas for my lovers the experience of butch was first about not fitting into female gender norms, for me the erotic interplay was focal. My sexual desire was my teacher. In my own erotic vocabulary, butch and femme were linked first to the distinction between "making love to" and "being made love to," but then, more deeply, to an inner rhythm of desire that correlated with which of those activities was the doorway into sexual feeling. For me, being femme means that my desire gets sparked most readily by feeling someone desiring me, yielding to her pleasure in making love to me. I need to be able to trust her giving, not as something that will indebt me to her, but as something that thrills her. This releases in me the hunger to reciprocate, to feel in my hands the magic that can fill her longing.

One very butch lover told me she thought of me as butch too, and that she was attracted to butch women. So then I had to think about this again. Is it butch to be "tough," to have an attitude? We got off playing with the energy of "attitude." Meeting each other in power. I liked to fuck her. With her I experienced the pleasure of my whole hand in the cunt of a woman. That feels like a very butch pleasure. But then, when we wrestled, I wanted her to win. I wanted her to pin me down and take me. Is this femme?

All this leads me to say "butchy femme." Sometimes we say "butch-over-easy" and "femme-over-easy." I think that with a butch woman I am freed up to be as butch as I want to be. I learn to walk the street with a don't-mess-with-me attitude. I can revel in the pleasure of taking a woman, the power of taking this woman who only gives herself when she chooses. Her strength frees me to be strong, to stretch to all of my power and to meet her in her power.

And yet I can also say that it is with a butch woman that I am freed up to be most femme. Sorting out what a "public" femme dykeness is for me has been harder. It seems to me that femme dykes, as well as butch dykes, fuck with gender. We are not passing as straight women. Lesbian femme is not the same as "feminine" — especially not the same as the "Feminine-looking lesbian seeks same for discreet relationship (no dykes)" found lately in personal ads. A femme dyke is not trying to be discreet.

There is something in femme, in fact, that is about creating a display. A femme dyke displays the erotic power of her beauty. She is bold enough to claim that power in a culture that has maintained a tyranny of "beauty norms" that may or may not include her. Even if she is "beautiful" by these male standards, a femme dyke may do something to disrupt the image, intentionally break the rules. And she breaks the cardinal rule: her audience is female, not male. She flashes her eyes and smiles in a lesbian direction. A femme dyke is not domesticated but wild. Some toughness somewhere frames the letting go. We are "bad girls." We all need to be taken. In the intricate dance between butch and femme, who is taking whom?

Even as I am writing this, I remember someone referring to me as butch, and how many times I have been called "sir" in the last few weeks. A femme dyke may need to walk down the street just like a butch dyke, alert to the dangers around her. When I am single, I need the butch power of emotional self-sufficiency. What I display to the public world is likely to be a challenge, as I protect myself with a hard strength. Yet femme does not mean weak or incompetent. Being in the gaze of a butch lesbian gives me the courage to risk the femme power of erotic display. I am conscious of where and when I can create this magic. Sometimes, I can only do so in the privacy of our sexual intimacy.

I do not call this changeability androgyny. My lovers and I might be fluid about who is in a butch mode or a femme mode at any given moment, but we still play with this particular erotic polarity. I want both butch and femme, not something homogenized in between. This is not a value judgment on the erotic patterns of other women. This is an attempt to find words for the patterns in me. When I speak of these intimate things, I am drawing from my memories threads of similarity and variation. Butch women differ, and I differ with different women, but patterns emerge that make this language intelligible to me, resonate in me.

Between us we create a circle of something like worship, a ritual of mutual incarnation. With a butch dyke as priestess, I come to the goddess within me who is female, I come to beauty within me, ecstasy within me. I am femme priestess to her, discovering in her a female power that is the very power rejected by the society around her, everything a woman is never supposed to be. Even as she teaches me with tongue and touch and trembling to love my woman body, so I in turn enfold her in a circle of my treasuring, where her stories, her wounds, and her power can be revealed.

Sandia

A bright daylight anthem

In the country of the young
we didn't write about sex:
it was always at the door,
in my bed, on the kitchen floor,
with my lover or yours
or any woman who had to spend the night
in our small mountain community.
Because the snowy roads were impassable at night,
because we wanted to wake up with four breasts
forming a mountain range under the blankets.
We took pictures the drive-up Fotomat wouldn't develop:
my tongue was in places they couldn't color-screen.
Once, as we slowly wound our way up Jemez Peak,
crawling 25 miles per hour in your baby blue Volkswagen van,
your hand reached for the hole in my sweats.
A finger wormed its way inside my cunt,
stroking me in one   long   sinuous   line.
I knelt in the space between the seats
and spread my legs for you,
biting your nipple harder at each hairpin turn.
When the circular motions of your finger
had traveled a few more curves and miles
I closed my eyes to the sides of the mountain
that the van kept missing
and exploded while you tried to downshift.
When I came back and my head had cleared
you said: "Touch me. Quick."
The van was headed down the south side of the pass.
"You're not serious."
I took a handful of wet from my cunt
to give you a momentary thrill.

THE PERSISTENT DESIRE

When I reached through your unzipped jeans,
you were already sopping in your own juices,
and my hand came out steaming in the frozen air.
"Keep touching me."
Your voice was imperative.
"How will you keep your eyes on the road?" I yelled.
"Touch me."
When you screamed, I grabbed the wheel with my free hand.
You opened your eyes and waved at the semis passing us
in the light snow that had begun to fall.

In the country of the old
do they imagine passion
sliding in a side door
and straddling them?

I who do not belong to either of those two countries,
know California is a civilized country with no snow.
There is no custom for staying overnight
and mostly it is the butches who are still visible.
I found you at a poetry reading.
Were you drawn by the nape of my neck?
Did you know I was ripe?
Did it show in my eyes the next afternoon
when you asked me to walk along the beach?
While my toes curled around hot sand
you sized me up to see if I had entered
the numb valley of middle age:
                Do you go to work with these chin whiskers?
Your voice was husky in my ear,
as if you were speaking through a conch.
The ocean waves lapped in the background.
                I can't be bothered worrying about it.
                I don't think anyone looks at me that way,
                anymore.
You turned me around to face you.
                They don't notice this long white hair?
You pulled on the cherished whisker.
I looked at you, only a thin film of a mask remaining,
my mouth opening and closing wordlessly.
                Say what you're thinking — don't censor.
Your forefinger was in front of my lower lip.
                I was fantasizing.
                We could do the usual ritual:

Date for a while.
Trade recent sexual histories.
Your finger paused before meeting the skin:
Only the young have time for that.
I was with a woman monogamously for five
years. There's been no one since she left.
I don't remember when we knew to head for my car.
We went the long way, you stroking my thigh.
I like making love on the move,
I closed the front door and turned to you,
but not on the floor anymore.
Your open mouth came down on me.
Our tongues met in a line of lightning
unleashed deep in my cunt.
I hooked my finger in your belt loop,
our mouths still connected, and led you into my room.

This is where I want to make love to you.
I see in your face a promise
that never lost its spunk,
in your attitude—what some call butch
and I call a bright daylight anthem.
—that's what's making me wet.
This is the face I want to see
in the sacred dark.

We poured out of our clothes as if our skin had gotten us here.
We rolled over and over, our legs curled around each other.
I pressed my need against your thigh for ballast,
dizzy headed from not breathing.
Your finger slid down between my thighs, between the hair,
and I thought you'd enter me,
but you rolled your finger lengthwise in my juices,
moving sideways between the lips.
I whispered, "Slow."   You stopped time.
Your tongue made circles in my mouth,
your fingers danced to the rhythm.
I cupped your ass, sliding into you from behind,
and you roared up and down on my finger,
rising, falling into the arms of gravity.
I'm throbbing past relief, past the need for only orgasm.
The mystery is wider.   It has a mind of its own.
My tongue roams down your body
past the folds of the continental shelf,

THE PERSISTENT DESIRE

falling into the rings of fire that I lick,
sliding along the whorls of skin and hair,
meeting the face of promise
waiting in the dark wrinkled crevices.
This is a big place.   You climb in with me.
We get lost among the secrets.
Your hot tongue opens the country of no time
and we ride the hot tail of the mystery home.

Lee Lynch

Jacky and the femme

One night in the middle of that cold, cold winter, Jacky was eating a Gardenburger and drinking steaming Red Zinger tea at the Devon Avenue Neo-Diner. The public radio station was warming its listeners with Sousa marches from last summer's band concerts. Out of the corner of her eye, Jacky saw the cook burst from the kitchen and quickstep to her table with a wide, eager smile.

"How've you been, babe?" she asked Camille.

Startled, Jacky watched as Camille threw her arms around this stranger.

The cook looked like a man, a little man with badly cut hair and chino slacks that bagged around her bony haunches.

"Sorry," the cook said to Jacky. "You mind me giving your lady a squeeze? I'm Donny."

So this person _thought_ like a man too. "Why would I mind?"

Camille took Donny's hand between her own, and patted it in time to the Sousa march as they laughed at some shared memory. Jacky had never seen Camille act coquettish before.

The stranger returned to the kitchen. Jacky said, "What a sexist thing to ask, like I own you."

Camille lowered her eyes as if to hide her smile. "When I first came out, I was as femme as they come."

"With _her_?"

Donny stood at the kitchen door with a fat woman, pointing.

When the woman approached them, there was something sultry in her walk, graceful in the sweep of her arms, come hither in the smile she flashed.

"You caught yourself a strong, handsome one this time, didn't you?" Chick said to Camille.

Jacky felt like a prized pig. Or husband. The women beamed at her.

"What kind of games are you playing, Camille?" she asked between gritted teeth.

Chick's laugh was a gurgle from somewhere within that expanse of bosom. "A hot-blooded Latin if you ask me."

Jacky had never seen such alluring eyes. With glossy red fingernails, Chick drummed the Sousa march on Jacky's flannel sleeve.

"If this little lady ever gives you the blues, you come and see Chickie, you hear?"

Jacky stuttered, wanted to smile, scowled, pulled her arm away, and immediately was aware of the heat those gentle fiery fingers had left behind.

Beguiled, she watched as Chick sashayed through the tables, long flowered dress swaying from her hips. Jacky had just about caught her breath when she noticed Camille's fingernails. Not painted, but nicely manicured.

"You know," she said, "we've been together almost two years and I've never even noticed your walk."

Camille hid her face behind her tea mug, but Jacky caught the sparkle in her eyes. "You're too scared it'll turn you on."

Would it be so wrong to enjoy what these old-timey dykes had loved in each other all along?

"Oh, Goddess," she said, horrified. "What if it's not being sexist I'm afraid of at all?" she asked Camille. "What if I'm just plain afraid of being a real queer?"

Lee Lynch

Stone butch

Who is more womanly
than the stone butch?
who knows better
how to deny her own
feelings, how to feel
good only when
she's made another to

Who was better taught,
learned more thoroughly?
Who practiced giving
with more ardor?
To kill her own need
she'd stop breathing
before her body felt

They said she denied
her womanhood, when she *was*
their ultimate woman,
knowing only giving,
giving only good,
only good when giving:
womanly: stone butch.

Dorothy Allison

Her thighs

I was thinking about Bobby, remembering her sitting, smoking, squint-eyed, and me looking down at the way her thighs shaped in her jeans. I have always loved women in blue jeans, worn jeans, worn particularly in that way that makes the inseam fray, and Bobby's seams had that fine white sheen that only comes after long restless evenings spent juggling one's thighs one against the other, the other against the bar stool.

After a year as my sometimes lover, Bobby's nerves were wearing as thin as her seams. She always seemed to be looking to the other women in the bar, checking out their eyes to see if in fact they thought her as pussy-whipped as she thought herself, for the way she could not seem to finally settle me down to playing the wife I was supposed to be. Bobby was a wild-eyed woman, proud of her fame for running women ragged — all the women who had fallen in love with her and followed her around long after she had lost all interest in them. Hanging out at softball games on lazy spring afternoons, Bobby would look over at me tossing my head and talking to some other woman and grind her thighs together in impatience. The woman was as profoundly uncomfortable with my sexual desire as with my determined independence. But nothing so disturbed her as the idea other people could see both my lust and my independence in the way I tossed my hair, swung my hips, and would not always come when she called. Bobby believed lust was a trashy lower-class impulse, and she wanted so to be nothing like that. It meant the one tool she could have used to control me was the very one she could not let herself use.

Oh, Bobby loved to fuck me. Bobby loved to beat my ass, but it bothered her that we both enjoyed it so much. Early on in our relationship, she established a pattern of having me over for the evening and strictly enforcing a rule against sex outside the bedroom. Bobby wanted dinner — preferably Greek or Chinese takeout — and at least two hours of tele-vision. Then there had to be a bath, bath powder, and toothbrushing, though she knew I preferred her unbathed and gritty, tasting the tequila she sipped through dinner. I was not supposed to touch her until we

406

J.C., 1991

entered the sanctuary of her bedroom, that bedroom lit only by the arc lamp in the alley outside. Only in that darkness could I bite and scratch and call her name. Only in that darkness would Bobby let herself open to passion.

Let me set the scene for you, me in my hunger for her great strong hands and perfect thighs, and her in her deliberate disregard. When feeling particularly cruel, Bobby would even insist on doing her full twenty-minute workout while I lay on the bed tearing at the sheets with my nails. I was young, unsure of myself, and so I put up with it, sometimes even enjoyed it, though what I truly wanted was her in a rage, under spotlights in a stadium, fucking to the cadence of a lesbian rock-and-roll band.

But it was two years ago, and if I were too aggressive she wouldn't let me touch her. So I waited, and watched her, and calculated. I'd start my efforts on the couch, finding excuses to play with her thighs. Rolling joints and reaching over to drop a few shreds on her lap, I scrambled for every leaf on her jeans.

"Don't want to waste any," I told her and licked my fingers to catch the fine grains that caught in her seams. I progressed to stroking her crotch. "For the grass," I said, going on to her inseam, her knees, the backs of her thighs.

"Perhaps some slipped under here, honey. Let me see."

I got her used to the feel of my hands legitimately wandering, while her eyes never left the TV screen. I got her used to the heat of my palms,

407

the slight scent of the sweat on my upper lip, the firm pressure of my wrists sliding past her hips. I was as calculated as any woman who knows what she wants, but I cannot tell you what magic I used to finally get her to sit still for me going down on my knees and licking that denim.

It wasn't through begging. Bobby recognized begging as a sexual practice, therefore to be discouraged outside the darkened bedroom. I didn't wrestle her for it. That, too, was allowed only in the bedroom. Bobby was the perfect withholding butch, I tell you, so I played the perfect compromising femme. I think what finally got to her was the tears.

Keeping my hands on her, I stared at her thighs intently until she started that sawing motion — crossing and recrossing her legs. My impudence made her want to grab and shake me, but that, too, might have been sex, so she couldn't. Bobby shifted and cleared her throat and watched me while I kept my mouth open slightly and stared intently at the exact spot where I wanted to put my tongue. My eyes were full of moisture. I imagined touching the denim above her labia with my lips. I saw it so clearly, her taste and texture were full in my mouth. I got wet and wetter. Bobby kept shifting on the couch. I felt my cheeks dampen and heard myself making soft moaning noises — like a child in great hunger. That strong, dark musk odor rose between us, the smell that comes up from my cunt when I am swollen and wet from my clit to my asshole.

Bobby smelled it. She looked at my face, and her cheeks turned the brightest pink. I felt momentarily like a snake who has finally trapped a rabbit. Caught like that, on the living room couch, all her rules were momentarily suspended. Bobby held herself perfectly still, except for one moment when she put her blunt fingers on my left cheek. I leaned over and licked delicately at the seam on first the left and then the right inner thigh. Her couch was one of those swollen chintz monsters, and my nose would bump the fabric each time I moved from right to left. I kept bumping it, moving steadily, persistently, not touching her with any other part of my body except my tongue. Under her jeans, her muscles rippled and strained as if she were holding off a great response or reaching for one. I felt an extraordinary power. I had her. I knew absolutely that I was in control.

Oh, but it was control at a cost, of course, or I would be there still. I could hold her only by calculation, indirection, distraction. It was dear, that cost, and too dangerous. I had to keep a distance in my head, an icy control on my desire to lose control. I wanted to lay the whole length of my tongue on her, to dribble over my chin, to flatten my cheeks to that fabric and shake my head on her seams like a dog on a fine white bone. But that would have been too real, too raw. Bobby would never have sat still for that. I held her by the unreality of my hunger, my slow nibbling civilized tongue.

Oh, Bobby loved that part of it, like she loved her chintz sofa, the antique armoire with the fold-down shelf she used for a desk, the carefully balanced display of appropriate liquors she never touched — unlike the bottles on the kitchen shelves she emptied and replaced weekly. Bobby loved the aura of acceptability, the possibility of finally being bourgeois, civilized, and respectable.

I was the uncivilized thing in Bobby's life, reminding her of the taste of hunger, the remembered stink of her mother's sweat, her own desire. I became sex for her. I held it in me, in the pulse of my thighs against hers when she finally grabbed me and dragged me off into the citadel of her bedroom. I held myself up, back and off her. I did what I had to do to get her, to get myself what we both wanted. But what a price we paid for what I did.

What I did.
What I was.
What I do.
What I am.

I paid a high price to become who I am. Her contempt, her terror, was the least of it. My contempt, my terror, took over my life, became the first thing I felt when I looked at myself, until I became unable to see my true self at all. "You're an animal," she used to say to me, in the dark with her teeth against my thigh, and I believed her, growled back at her, and swallowed all the poison she could pour into my soul.

Now I sit and think about Bobby's thighs, her legs opening in the dark where no one could see, certainly not herself. My own legs opening. That was so long ago and far away, but not so far as she finally ran when she could not stand it anymore, when the lust I made her feel got too wild, too uncivilized, too dangerous. Now I think about what I did.

What I did.
What I was.
What I do.
What I am.

"Sex," I told her. "I will be sex for you."
Never asked, "You. What will you be for me?"
Now I make sure to ask. I keep Bobby in mind when I stare at women's thighs. I finger my seams, flash my teeth, and put it right out there.
"You. What will you let yourself be for me?"

Jan Brown

Sex, lies, and penetration: A butch finally 'fesses up

When I was seventeen, I worked the street. I used to tell tricks that I would stay all night for $100, that I would swallow for $40, that I never came with anyone else but with them it was different.

I lied back then for survival. It was just good business. I got paid more.

The person I was back then has been dead for half a lifetime, but lately I've been thinking about more-current lies. The lies about fucking and about sex that the person I became, and those like me, have told, have believed, got you to believe, and that all of us have needed for so long.

We've had our asses on the line for a long time. We're the dykes on the sexual edge, the radical fringe of lesbian. We started the dialogues on fucking, butch-femme, S/M, dominance and submission — the how, the why, and what it all meant. We spoke at workshops and conferences, did hours of counseling over beers or coffees, and started the support groups. Some of us wrote the books and made the videos. We all got shit on from great heights. We argued, explained, fought, consoled, and recruited.

We also lied a lot.

It's those lies that I've been thinking about lately. The lies we needed to tell and the lies we all needed to hear.

My first two girlfriends wouldn't let me fuck them. Penetration was not what lesbians did, I was told. With the exception of a menstrual sponge, entering a vagina with anything, even a finger, was what men did to us. Penetration represented the kind of inherently oppressive sex we were trying to leave behind. Well-read girls knew that fucking was a vestige of the hetero-patriarchal power structure. Women, we all knew, came by clitoral not vaginal stimulation.

The quicker thinking and cleverer among us pointed out that hets did cunnilingus too, but it still remained a relatively guilt-free mainstay of the correct lesbian.

We said that penetration which occurred between two women of inherent equality wasn't a metaphor for power imbalance. Because of their shared history as women, there was no difference between who was doing the fucking and who was getting fucked. The fuck was an equal exchange.

This explanation, originally viewed with suspicion, eventually relieved almost everybody.

The reality, for me and my kind, whatever we told you and whatever you believed, is that fucking between equals is passionless. Penetration without context is meaningless. Sex that is gentle, passive, egalitarian, and bloodless does not move us. Lesbians were right to be so suspicious about penetration back then. There really is, in fact, no equality in penetration.

When we fuck, we possess. When we are fucked, we become the possession. For some, the only time in our lives we can give up control or achieve total control is as we are taken or as we take.

❖

Remember when we all agonized over our fantasies? For many years we struggled with the guilt about what we saw behind our closed eyelids. We would talk about our rape fantasies, our fascination with being overpowered. We'd talk with our hands over our eyes about our jerk-off routines. The image that took us by force was often male. We knew that in those guilt-ridden fantasies, the responsibility was no longer ours and there was no consent involved.

Many of us felt like traitors in the grip of, and betrayed by, nonlesbian, unfeminist, and self-destructive sexual fantasies.

The party line, via Andrea Dworkin and, later, Sheila Jeffreys, was that lesbians raised in a hetero-patriarchal society could not help but internalize oppression and turn it into self-hate. Every lesbian was advised to examine and analyze her fantasies, recognize them for the damage they represented, and work to change them. Later (Jeffreys again), the still aroused but guilt-ridden were directed to cease fantasizing at all. Apparently, divesting oneself of the taint of misogyny was impossible. The only answer was no fantasy at all.

We at our side of the fringe, who looked like we were having a good time in spite of it all, were approached by lesbians who couldn't seem to abide by the no-fantasy party line edict. We explained to them that even though many of us might jerk off to gang rape, torture, daddy in our beds, and other undeniably incorrect imagery, it was really nothing to lose sleep over.

We emphasized the simple difference between fantasy and reality. We explained the control we had over our fantasies that we didn't have in the real situations. We did not lust after real rape, real incest, or real torture. The pull was in our ability to finally direct what happened to us. The eroticism, we soothed, was in the power we had for the first time to control the uncontrollable.

Well, we lied. The power is not in the ability to control the violent image. It is in the lust we have to see how close we can get to the edge. It is in the lust to be overpowered, forced, hurt, used, objectified. We jerk off to the rapist, to the Hell's Angel, to daddy, to the Nazi, to the cop, and to all the other images that have nothing to do with the kind of lesbian sex that entails murmurs of endearment, stroking of breasts, and long slow tongue work. And, yes, we also dream of the taking. We dream of someone's blood on our hands, of laughing at cries for mercy. We wear the uniform and the gun; we haul our cocks out of our pants to drive into a struggling body. Sometimes, we want to give up to the strangler's hands. Sometimes, we need to have a dick as hard as truth between our legs, to have the freedom to ignore "no" or to have our own "no" ignored.

Many of us graduated from the university of self-destruct. Some of us are street survivors, incest survivors. We lived with abusive boyfriends or drifted through years of substance use. We carry many kinds of scars. All of us see ourselves as the "other," as the "alien queer." We each have our own history, but what links us is what we lust after. Those images, that sex, keeps us alive — out of prisons and locked wards, abusive relationships, and bad-odds fights in bars.

We don't need to be judged, pitied, or analyzed. We practice the kind of sex in which cruelty has value, where mercy does not. We arrive at places where adrenaline inspires us. What keeps those of us who refused to abandon our "unacceptable" fantasies sane is the knowledge that there are others like us who would not leave because we scream, "Kill me," at the moment we orgasm.

We lied to you about controlling the fantasy. It is the lack of control that makes us come, that has the only power to move us.

Soon after the great vaginal penetration question was settled and the antifantasy faction was dealt with came the issue of the lavender silicone cucumber-shaped dildo.

Even though dykes had been using all kinds of dildos for years, no one talked about it. It was seen as bar dyke and regressive, certainly not lesbian-feminist.

Few lesbians would admit to owning one. I can remember a screaming fight I had with someone at a pro-and-con porn workshop who was denouncing the use of dildos as, yet again, "What men do to us — not what lesbians do."

I'd been told she kept hers in a shoe box under the bed.

Our answer was to explain that dildos were absolutely lesbian. They were our heritage and history, a link with those who had bravely gone before. Dildos did not represent the penis. Couldn't we take ours off and put it in the drawer? It was a removable object purely for pleasure and did not endow its wearer with any innate ability to keep its recipient barefoot, in the kitchen, or oppressed.

Then we threw away the lavender silicone cucumbers. They were embarrassing and they broke. We bought bigger dildos; we wore them under our jeans (or our skirts). We bought the kind with simulated veins and balls from porn shops. We walked differently when we wore them to the bar. Girls bought us drinks, we used the men's john. I named my collection of graduating sizes "The Tools of the Patriarchy." We looked people in the eye when we had that bulge in our crotches. Some of us perfected our long-forgotten skills of rolling on a condom.

A very butch friend asked me for help in figuring out why she liked her femme girlfriend to fuck her with a dildo. "Nerve endings," I told her. It meant she had the right anatomy to come from vaginal stimulation. And we were both happy with that lie. The reality is what we both knew, that we all want to be fucked senseless, as Sharon Olds points out in "The Solution." More than that, some of us need to be also taken sexually in a way possible only by being entered and used by a cock and what that represents. Because we are dykes, we want a dyke on the other end of that cock.

We lied to you and I lied to my friend. Plastic dicks represent much more than sex toys for pleasuring nerve endings in vaginas. When we strap one on, it becomes ours.

We found it difficult to lie to anybody about blow jobs, though. Nobody would have believed us anyway. The imagery has no equality. A woman is on her knees, her throat is full, her lips are at the base of another woman's cock. It is about the urge to dominate, take, and degrade. It is about the fierce need to submit. To serve somebody. The hit is in the very lack of the traditionally erogenous. The throat has no nerve endings. The dick is, after all, man-made. The neurons firing in the mind make up for their lack. The heat is in the history. Context.

Remember when the whisper campaign about fist-fucking started? Fist-fucking, we were told, was violent and dangerous. Unsafe, unnatural, misogynistic, and dangerous. Not true, we countered, and after all, it was at least queer (except for one friend I know who was introduced to it by imaginative bikers). Faggots fist-fucked each other in the ass — we fisted cunts and the occasional asshole. Fisting was natural, lesbian, and safe, we reassured. Couldn't babies' heads come through that passage safely?

We developed technique. Small hands were prized. We became lubricant connoisseurs. Big hands became more prized — knuckles up, knuckles down, the ninety-degree twist. Fisting made a lie of the myth of the vaginal orgasm.

But, okay (you were right), fisting is dangerous after all. Yes, we lied, but the danger is not in the potential for soft tissue damage. The danger lies in the transformation from a body with an intellect to a body with a need. We realize we really are corporeal as well as intellectual and sometimes need overrides. Fisting is out-of-control sex. To be fisted is to be taken back to the animal — to what we were told we didn't ever want to become.

Then there is the ongoing and contentious great butch debate, or what I call the "Is my butch my boyfriend?" argument.

We always told you that, although we were butch, we really didn't want to be men. Butch was not synonymous with male, we promised. Butches might look very masculine, but in reality we were butch women. There was, in fact, nothing male about us.

Guess what? Right again. We lied. There is little "woman" left in us.

Even though many of my butch buddies "pass" on the street, most of us, me included, couldn't hang out safely with the boys at the pool hall without breast reduction and a handgun. Still, we do not think of ourselves as women. Or, in fact, as lesbians.

Now I'm not talking about middle-of-the-road androgynous, butchy types here. I'm talking "other" again. When we hook up with another butch sexually, we are faggots. When we have a girlfriend, we become her man.

We become male, but under our own terms, our own rules. We define the maleness. We invent the men we become.

So now I guess it's time to get around to that most cherished and well-loved old lie about butches, the one I and most of the rest of us out here on the edge told ourselves for so long we almost believed it. The lie that destroyed a few of us along the way. The one that says butches don't need to get fucked.

Like faggots who only cruise "straight" men, we are accused of being the homophobes in our community. We are told we are the dykes who hate women, who deny our own sexual feelings because they are women's feelings, who therefore must always be the active, never the passive, in the fuck.

The glorious and sacred myth of the stone butch. Lesbian herstory and all that. It's the lie we tell that says butches don't hunger too for someone who would know what we needed instead of believing what we told them we wanted. And who could take us down.

The truth, for many stone butches, is that we failed as women early on. Butch is who we are, but also who we had to become. The existence of an individual sexual need in us is incongruous to the women we almost invariably choose as partners — the successful-as-female lesbians.

We have a horror of the pity-fuck. We cannot face the charity of the mercy orgasm or the thought of the contempt in our partners' eyes when we have allowed them to convince us that they really do want to touch us, to take us, that they really do want to reach behind our dick and into the cunt we both wish did not exist.

The myth of the stone butch says that we don't need, that the sexual gratification we get is from doing the fucking.

Girls, we lied to you for years. We knew you wouldn't want it any other way. The price a butch pays for getting fucked, real or imaginary, has been more than many of us can bring ourselves to pay. Living the lie makes us harder than stone.

So, there it is. You suspected us all along anyway, didn't you? We did lie — but we told you what you wanted to hear and sometimes what we needed to hear, too.

Those of us out here on the edge were the ones who talked about sex when nobody else did, wrote about it, put ourselves on the line and tried to figure out what it all might mean. You ridiculed us, you laughed at us, you lied about us, you copied our clothes, you protested against us, but you jerked off over us. Ultimately, some of you joined us.

And why tell all of this and why now? Not that any of us feels guilty, you understand. It's just that some of us were believing our own mythology. Losing ourselves in our own lies, losing ourselves in our yearning to cease being the "other."

I like the smell of the truth, and maybe we need a whiff of it. Once in a while.

Pat Califia

The femme poem

I have this very bad habit of
Falling in love with the women
I'm sexually attracted to.
If I could just rid myself
Of this vice,
I'm sure happiness would be
Just around the corner.

All of you
Are so damned expensive—
Oh, not in terms of money.
I don't mind the money.
If I minded it,
I'd have some.

But you cost me time.
The kind of time spent in tears
By the telephone,
Knowing if you don't call
I'm worth nothing.
That's something I never did
In high school, for chris'sake.

I'm a sucker for all of you:

Little boys who need their mother
(A sinister, seductive, strict older woman).
Tough street fighters who need somebody
To keep them from getting their noses broken again
(I hang onto your belt, saying fiercely,
"Don't you dare, it's not worth your spit!").

Cocksmen with dicks too big
For most women to take
(And I can, and I love it).
Broad-shouldered women who need somebody
To lean on them
(So take care of me).
And women who can never have what they want
Because the world will not allow them
To be complete human beings — that is, men.
(So shout at me, frighten me, blame me, humiliate me.
I'll shout back, but I won't break you.
The next day, you can wear me on your arm
And every man who makes more money than you do
Will see me and be jealous of you.)

Being a successful femme
Means making a butch desire you
And then enduring when that lust
Turns into suspicion.
"If you want me," she sneers,
"You must really want a man."
Nobody knows how much it hurts
When you go out on the street
And straight men tell you
The same damned thing.

But what I want is you, a woman.
All of you.
The muscles in your forearms and thighs
When you hold yourself over me,
Between my legs,
Filling me.
The accurate and vulgar terms
With which you dissect and label me.
The smell of your cologne,
Your suits in my closet,
Your leather,
Your boots and ties and hats and uniforms
And men's handkerchiefs and men's underwear.
Your dangerous jobs and all that endless,
Bitter shop-talk.

And the way you buck under my mouth
Or around my hand
Or inside my ropes

417

THE PERSISTENT DESIRE

When I make love to you.
I want that too.
I know how to make love to
Your woman's body
Without taking your masculinity away.
It's just our secret.
Nobody else needs to know
How it's done
Or even that I do it at all.

The lipstick, the perfume, the garter belts,
The high heels, the dresses, the long hair.
The sidelong looks, the requests for a chair,
A light,
What do *you* think I should do?
Why don't you order, dear?
Honey, would you drive?
Zip me up, please.
Unzip me now, now, hurry,
What I really need is a good, hard fuck
And a strong shoulder to sleep on—
All that's for you.
Not for my father or my husband or my boss.
Because you know what it means
On your good days,
When you don't hate yourself or me
And you aren't out of work or sick or drunk.

Because with you it's finally safe
To be a woman.
The feminine qualities
That win me the world's contempt
Put a light in your eyes,
Make you feel like you're finally
Getting a little of what you deserve.

That's why I keep coming back
To all of you, dammit,
No matter how many times you try to
Take my fights away from me
And take my power tools away from me
And take my job away from me
And take my Levis and boots away from me
And even take my cock away from me.

Because in your arms,
I am valuable.
You aren't sorry I wasn't born a boy.
I'm your gift, your prize, your treasure,
Not a disappointment,
A simpleton,
A voracious black hole in lesbian space.

Because I know what you want
Without even thinking,
And I'll give it to you
Even when I'm mad at you
Just to deny some aid and comfort
To the man.

So treat me like a lady
A whore
Your lover
Your lover
The woman who loves you
Who could not love you
If you were not a woman,
Who could not love you
If you weren't virile.

Tell me it will be different this time.
No broken windows, no black eyes,
No jealous rages, no dirty dishes.
You don't even have to make it be different.
Just tell me it will be
And I'll stay
As long as your kisses
Can make me hope.

Pat Califia

I love butches

I love butches.
The muscles, the short hair,
The refusal to pick up
Where their mothers left off.

I especially love
The angle of a knee
Wearing its way out of a faded pair
Of 501s,
Scraping the dirty floor of a dark alley,
Kneeling in the dark,
Sucking cunt.
My cunt.

My fingers can always find
A hold in that short hair—
Even a crew cut.
I just twine right down to the roots
So I can grab that head
And turn it to look at me,
Cunt juice smeared and shining
Across that James Dean jawline.

I'm a connoisseur of the practiced sneer
That says, "Look out, I'm tough."
A butch who has her pose down makes me smile.
"Darlin'," I say, sliding through
The shadows at her back,
"How fine you are."
I flex my claws, apply them gently

To her neck, pick up the fabric
Over a nipple, and slice it open so
The teacup-sized tit peeks through.
I lick the fear off her neck and purr,
"I really don't care
Who's butch and who's not
As long as I get to fuck you."

I love butches
Because I'm the woman
Who takes up where their mothers
Were afraid to go.

I can't resist the call of that
Deep, smoldering anger,
The girlboy who can never forgive herself
Until Mama relents and says
(Standing in a dark doorway,
Spraying herself with a perfume atomizer),
"Forget the old man.
Come to my bed tonight."

Butches need my hands,
My mouth, my eyes
Because I see, I handle, I bestow
The hard-on, the female phallus,
The sweet prick of the androgyne
Forever erect at the service of women.

Understand me—
My tricks are butches.
Not men, not boys,
Butches.

Even if they seem like boys
With female parts to you,
I know they are women.
And I am there for the part of them
That needs to be taken out of control—
Not with contempt,
Not as competition,
But as reassurance, a reminder
Of the body's truth
Inside the fantasy,

THE PERSISTENT DESIRE

The body that makes
All fantasies possible.

I am, after all, a lesbian.
I lust after beautiful women,
And butches are the most beautiful women
In the world.

Pat Califia

Gender fuck gender

You make me wish I had a cock.

Between your long colt's legs
I press and press,
Imagining the swell and rigid length
Shoved into you,
Your juices welling up around it,
Pumping them out of you,
Fucking you until I come,
Staying in you until I get hard again
And fucking you again,
My cock coming out smeared with
Your thin and my thick fluids,
The shaft tangled in a net of
Your clear strings
Knotted with my milky white ones.

On your belly,
You make me hurt to have a cock,
To wrap my arms around
Your boy-slender waist,
Bite into the cords of muscle
That bind your broad shoulders,
Cover your ass
(The cheeks small, taut as a boy's
But round, not squared-off above the thigh)
With my broader hips
And take you
Up the ass,
Cockhead against the tight sphincter
Until my words in your ear,

THE PERSISTENT DESIRE

Whispered but sharp as spears,
Open it up
To the shove and thrust and hump.

House me
In your body.
Give me
Your open holes—
Mouth, cunt, ass,
Cupped hands—
Your nipples to bite
While I drill you,
Have you,
Use you,
Fuck you until the
Rapidly closing and opening,
Fluttering and swallowing
Circle of your weeping satin sheath
Coming
Milks me and I come, too,

Come in you.

Maybe then I could have enough of you,
Fuck you, hear you groan, seize your thrashing hips,
Stare into your open mouth
While I hurt and fill and punch into you,
Fuck you and be satisfied,
Feel that I have finally had
Enough of you.

Or would I just fuck you
Until my cock was as raw
As your cunt gets
Every time I dabble my fingers
In your oil
And my biceps swell
And my forearm gets hard
With the need to drive into you,
Pull you back onto me,
Make you ride me like a locomotive piston
To that crazy destination
That has no name and no hotels.
It's only a whistle-stop.
You can never stay there.

Pissing takes longer.
But oh the ride to get there,
Oh to arrive and wait
For long mindless seconds
Until you are snatched away.
Oh to leave it and get just a little ways away
And be grabbed by the back of the neck
And put on the train again,
To be driven back
To hang in air
Over it
Again again again—

Fingernails in my back,
My name ringing in my ear,
Blood in my mouth,
Biting myself so I will not rend you.

What I want from you
Is more than a cock could give me.
Getting a hard-on, blasting my load into you
Would only make me come myself,
And get stupid and sleepy afterward,
Forget the ache the itch the craze to
Have you again
On your back, your belly, your side,
Fuck you onto the floor and
Back up onto the bed,
Against the wall and
Through the mattress—

God, oh God.
Stop me.
You will have to stop me.
I cannot stop myself.

Barbara Smith

The dance of masks

Tonight I feel hot. I don't just mean that I feel randy, horny, whatever your euphemism is. I mean, I feel more than sexual; I feel powerful; my whole body is sizzling with something that feels outside and beyond me and yet at the same time has its beginnings in me.

Like when my neighbor phones me and says, "Okay, what's her name?" and I act all innocent and coy and say, "I'm sure I don't know what you mean." And she says, "Come on now, who's the new woman?" and I prolong the innocence and protest, "What makes you think I'm seeing someone?" And she replies, "Because you're walking differently. Because your head is up, your shoulders are back, your stride has a purpose, and, my god, your chest is puffed out like a strutting pigeon, so don't fucking lie to me, girl!" That's how I feel tonight, except the feeling comes from me.

Or other times, when one of the women at work makes some comment about my new haircut, such as when it's really short they know I'm feeling bad about something. But they're straight — well, that's another story — and they don't understand the message. Short hair means business, means no more messing, means I'm getting serious, getting back to myself. Short hair means tidying up my act, getting down to it, being a dyke, being butch. Short hair is me, and over the years I might have fucked around with perms and mohicans and crimping and trying to grow a tail and all the rest of that butchy-femme nonsense, but it's like masturbating with your own image. In the end you want the real thing.

So tonight I feel hot. In my cunt I can feel something's going to happen. Tonight I am hot to trot, as they say. Had a good night's sleep. Woke up feeling alive. The sun was streaming through the shades, and for once the cat hadn't shat under the bed. Checked the post. Not only no bills, but that check I'd been waiting for for ages had finally turned up and it was hundreds of pounds more than I'd expected. So, first step, bank it, pay the bills — oh, nothing nicer than seeing all those red forms being stamped one after another by the bank clerk — and then work out how much is left. What can I buy?

426

New clothes, of course, and a haircut, because I'm going out tonight and I want to look so sharp and cleaned up that I'll cut someone. Feel like an overgrown field, like watching my dad getting ready for some big dinner or something, watching him lather his stubbly face and shave off the deadwood, stroke after stroke with the razor. He always wet-shaved when I was a little girl. I'd watch him clear away the facial debris, slick back his hair with Brylcreme, everything smoothed down, everything in its place and no superfluities. Just enough and no more.

My dad is wiry, spare face, prides himself on being the same weight now as he was in the air force during the war. A very dapper man, my dad, looks good in a suit, a three-piece suit since he always wears the waistjackets too, shirt pressed just right, suit just back from the cleaners, small knot in his tie, hankie in his breast pocket, and no sideburns, so you can see all his face. Never hides under sideburns, moustache, or beard. And his face shines, his cheekbones standing out and gleaming white in the reflection of the bathroom light as if he had warpaint on. I always thought my dad was David Niven, minus the moustache, and I wished that I could shave my face too.

Shaving for men is not the same as makeup for women, you know, even though they are similar rituals on the face of it, so to speak. Shaving is a revelation, a paring off of layers of dirt, dead skin, and unwanted bristle. It lays bare the man, and he can't hide from himself. But makeup is a pasting over of the cracks, a concealment — not a conceit, because makeup can only work with what you've got in the first place. It's a guessing game, but one that intrigues me. I love women in makeup. I want to know what's underneath but without removing the pancake, mascara, lipstick. No, they're not dolls. They are actors in an ancient theatre, real people playing fantasies, actors playing characters wearing comic or tragic masks. I am as fascinated by the mask as I am curious to remove it.

So I stroll up to that unisex hairdresser someone recommended. I want a short back and sides like my dad; I want it really short, so short that no one will be able to resist running her hands over my hair, against the direction of growth, to feel it bristle busily under her palms. No one, thank god, can resist that bristle. Yeah, I want to cut and bristle; I want clean straight lines.

Then up the West End. Oxford Street, New Bond Street, Knightsbridge? Yeah, let's go to the posh places, get good clothes with a good cut, dole out a bit more dosh because it's going to be worth the extra. I want to cut a clean straight line. I want a suit, a nice tailored sharp man's suit, and a smooth pair of boots that I can see my face in. I want a crisp shirt that feels like it crackles when I move. Listen to me: sharp, cut, bristle, crisp, crackle; like breakfast cereal, I'll make so much noise that they'll hear me coming before I arrive. I want to cut a clean straight line. I want to cut a broad swath through the fallow field. It's not only femmes who can make an entrance.

427

Butch on the streets, femme in the sheets maybe, but I've been fucking around with the femme in me for too long now. No wonder no one knows how to read me anymore, no wonder I don't know how to act anymore. I don't know who I am, and if I don't know who I am, how can I know what I want? And if I don't know what I want, how the fuck are they supposed to know? No, knock it on the head. Playing around with contradictions is fine if you know what you're doing, but if you don't, forget it. Go back to basics and start again. The minute you lose it, this playing around, knock it on the head and buy a suit. So be cool. Dress for yourself. I like me butch, I know me butch, I know how to act butch. Be butch and dress for sex.

Well, that's what you want, isn't it, sex? You want a good fuck, don't you? Of course, I do, but I want an interesting chase. Don't want a pushover, don't like it too easy. I like a little challenge on the way to foregone conclusion: fancied you the minute you walked in thought you'd never come over blah blah. I want to be obvious, obviously butch, obviously on the make, obviously want a fuck, obviously want to connect with someone. Steaming with passion, I want to smell of it, I want to ooze it, I want it sweating out of every pore, written in and between every line with no room for ambiguity, hidden behind every gesture and always on the surface, manifest in every easy joke that always gets a laugh, so far into me that it's almost in the background, my hungry cunt standing behind me like a predatory shadow. Watch out, here comes Barb with her cunt on a lead again. Yeah, but which one's the cunt? And does it bite?

So I'm going to stand at that bar, real cool, and hunt. Stand where I get a clear view of the door. Watch them all come in, eyeing them up and trying them on for size. I want to play that frightening, dangerous game with myself — how long can I act the cool butch? How long can I stand there looking mean and moody or bored or uninterested when my heart is racing with anticipation? How long can I pretend to them that it doesn't matter, easy come, easy go? How long can I keep it going before I run out of steam and they realize I'm lonely and shy and embarrassed?

You can see through me if you want, but be gentle with what's underneath. In these situations I have only a patina of power, lying along the surface of my skin. I want to want and be wanted so badly that the merest finger touch, the slightest lifting of a femme's eyebrow when she evaluates me, feels like a knife slipping under my skin. But sometimes I can balance on that knife edge; sometimes it doesn't cut my skin. Sometimes I'm so on the spot, so well measured, so poised with my posing, that I can breakdance on the point of a needle.

Tonight all the jokes will be funny. I will be the entertaining, laugh-a-minute, woman-of-the-world butch. I will be the writer with the funny anecdotes, the witty comments. I will be barbed and bristling, busy, busy with my butch performance. I will stand at that bar and select my femme, who picked me out moments beforehand anyway, and I will dance my butch's dance for her. I will be dapper and aching to please this woman who spied the shark and reeled her in with a hand line. I will stand there with my strong, clean, straight, sharp lines and wait for her to lay a gentle hand on me that will barely touch me, that will stroke me like a feather, that will soften the hard edges but not take away their power to cut. And she will slip her femme's dagger beneath my chain mail and expose the soft flesh underneath. And later, when she strips for me, when she dances her femme's dance for me as both reward and punishment, when she reveals the lace and satin and silk underneath, she will show me that vulnerability has its own power.

There was a woman once for whom I danced my butch's dance. And she danced her femme's dance for me and showed me what was underneath the mask. She was soft and curvy and as hard as flint, and she showed me that the mask was not a lie, not hers of apparent soft femininity nor mine of seeming steel and bluster. She taught me the excitement, the meaning of contradiction — not a flat negation of mutually exclusive opposites but the energizing of molecules oscillating constantly from one extreme to the other, always in flux.

And she initiated me, as surely as any high priestess, into the wonders of women's power. She would lay her soft, curvy, naked woman's body on the bed, place her hands behind her head, and unconsciously flex a brace of muscled biceps, and I'd think: where the fuck did they come from? Hidden strength, deceptive power, always beneath the tranquil surface, a mask of apparent vulnerability and powerlessness. But with one swift movement women's power lashes out of the soft curves and slaps you in the face with startling muscularity, a punishment for simplistically and impudently believing that the looked-at have no power.

Nothing is as it seems. Women are strong. Women can open doors for themselves, carry their own suitcases, change a tire, repair a fuse — if they want to. It all comes down to choice. If men want to set us up as being both Madonna and Whore simultaneously, then they have to accept that we might contrarily choose to be both. Our strongest choice, the one they didn't allow for, is to choose not to choose.

This is what I love about women, what I love about femmes, what I love about myself. I danced my blatant butch's dance for such a femme once, who thought I was powerful in that angular way, but who could take me in the palm of one hand like a precious talisman and excite me to power simply by touching me. She could hold me like that in a doorway, in midsentence, neither in nor out, neither touching nor untouching. She could suspend my movement and move me to the core of my being. She could stop my breath, my heart, and in that instant of timelessness I would die a thousand deaths, held in suspended animation, in the thrall of her femme's powerful contradiction, and my cunt would ooze its admiration.

And on occasion, I have danced the femme's dance too, for myself and for another. I have danced it on the street and in the privacy of my home. I have danced it in the real world out there, and in the context of my imagination. In my fantasy, I can do anything and everything. I danced the femme's dance and I danced it well. Took off my butch's mask, maneuvered myself to the edge of the cliff, and drove myself to distraction. I stood in front of the mirror that usually reflected my cock, and dressed myself in a lacy camisole, garter belt, and nylons. I put makeup on my face, where normally I dreamed of shaving straight lines. I put femmy earrings in my ears. I put on the femme's mask and danced the femme's dance and watched myself in the mirror. And when I danced this femme's dance, I danced the butch's dance too, somewhere in my head. I became a whore for myself and wanted to straddle my own thighs, lower myself onto my own cock, and fall in love with myself.

A dildo is not a penis, but it is a mask. Cunt can also be a mask. Why can't I be anything and everything I please just because I want it and it pleases me? I can wear my cock and admire it in the mirror, like the satyr and the mask and the mirror of revelation. I can fuck my lover with my cock mask, I can take it off and fuck myself with it, or she can fuck me with it. Or I can put it away and forget about it. Tell me, how many men can castrate themselves, bugger themselves with their own cocks, fellate their own cocks attached to someone else's body, take their cocks off, put them in a drawer and forget them — all that and not bleed to death? I can do anything that a "man" can. I can do anything that a woman can — if I so desire. And if I do not so desire, I can choose not to choose.

Arlene Stein

All dressed up, but no place to go? Style wars and the new lesbianism

When boyish girls make their way onto the pages of *Glamour*, Madonna blurts out to a bemused David Letterman that she and actress friend Sandra Bernhard frequent a certain lesbian bar in New York, and five cute dykes go on "Donahue" to proudly proclaim their sexuality, something is going on. Suddenly, almost imperceptibly, lesbianism is becoming a more visible part of our cultural landscape.

It is a very different public face than that which came before. The man-hating, bra-burning, rabble-rousing dyke — the butt of Fellini's satire in *City of Women* and the object of ridicule for many others — long coexisted with an image of lesbian sensuality that was the stuff of pornographic fantasy. When they do appear, those images increasingly are replaced by real-life symbols of androgynous strength (Martina Navratilova) or quirky artiness (Sandra Bernhard or k.d. lang) — which isn't to say they appear very often. And those few times that they do, the "*l*-word" is almost always conspicuous by its absence.

These trends probably don't signify a generalized thawing of homophobia or sexism as much as they represent the commercialization and popularization of feminist culture and the avant-garde art world — which many lesbians populate in discrete and not-so-discrete ways. Every day millions of us still fight internal and external battles just to claim the freedom of sexual choice. But in a few particularly tolerant areas of the nation, and increasingly among the young, hip, and artsy, it's almost (but not quite) cool to be queer. It is in these pockets, and to a lesser extent in other areas of the nation, that the new lesbian fashion is incubating.

The lesbian look has never been monolithic; it's always reflected a rich combination of cultural forms and styles — local and national, underground and commercial, multicolored and polyethnic. But generally speaking, the "new lesbian" face peeking through today's mass culture is young, white, and alluring, fiercely independent, and nearly free of the anger that typed her predecessors as shrill and humorless. To tell whether she is *really* one of us, your radar must be finely tuned. For better or for worse, this is the public face that many younger women who have come out in the eighties are seeing and taking as their models.

What is the meaning of style for contemporary lesbian identity and politics? Are today's lesbian style wars skin-deep, or do they reflect a changed conception of what it means to be a dyke? If a new lesbian has in fact emerged, is she all flash and no substance, or is she at work busily carving out new lesbian politics that strike at the heart of dominant notions of gender and sexuality?

The elements of lesbian style

> *They loved it! People weren't used to seeing women look the way they looked — dressed up. After that they wouldn't go to a club unless it had a dress code ... Before it was really sad. We really had no place to go.* —Caroline Clone, owner of a San Francisco club for "lipstick lesbians"[1]

In the 1970s, lesbian-feminists fashioned themselves as antifashion, flying in the face of reigning standards of femininity, beauty, and respectability. Wearing a flannel shirt and baggy pants was an affront to the dominant culture that liked to keep its women glossy and available, as well as a way for dykes to identify one another. In a world where feminist energies were channeled into the creation of battered women's shelters, antipornography campaigns, or women's music festivals, primping and fussing over your hair was strictly taboo.

Lesbian-feminist antistyle was an emblem of refusal, an attempt to strike a blow against the twin evils of capitalism and patriarchy, the fashion industry and the female objectification that fueled it. The flannel-and-denim look was not so much a style as it was antistyle — an attempt to replace the artifice of fashion with a supposed naturalness, free of gender roles and commercialized pretense.

Situated in this framework, today's self-conscious embracing of high heels, short skirts, and other utterly feminine trappings — along with a general revival of interest in fashion and appearance among many lesbians — has been interpreted by some as a plainly regressive set of developments. When lesbian-feminists see young femmes strutting around in makeup and panty hose, they may see women intent on fitting in, assimilating into the straight world, shedding their anger, and forgetting their roots. It's somewhat like the clash between dark- and light-skinned blacks described by poet Langston Hughes in the 1920s: "The younger blacks were obsessed by money and position, fur coats

Morgan Gwenwald

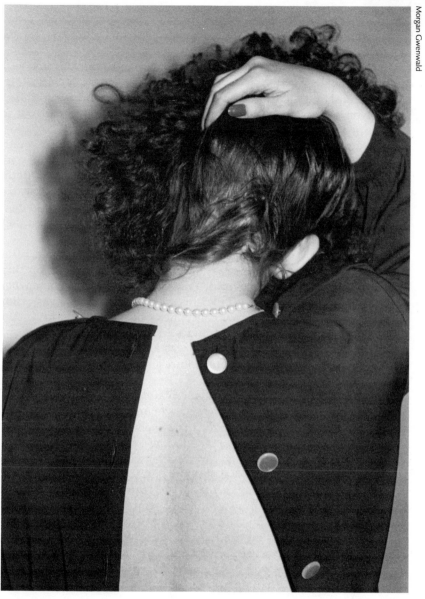

Femme, 1989

and flashy cars; their ideals seemed most Nordic and un-Negro." Replace Nordic with "straight," Negro with "lesbian," and you get the picture.

Many lesbians also associate the resurgence of gendered fashion with a return to butch-femme roles and forbidden love in smoky bars. Roles were a central and highly valued feature of lesbian culture — until they were given a bad rep by feminists and consequently stamped out as vestiges of a patriarchal past.

Today, roles *are* enjoying a renaissance among younger dykes, women who never fully parted with their butch and femme identities, and feminists who are finally recognizing the error of their ways. Many women have found that roles are an erotic charge, a way of understanding sexual preferences and of identifying and attracting potential lovers and friends. But it's clear that roles mean something very different today than they once did.

Joan Nestle, cofounder of the Lesbian Herstory Archives, has written that butch-femme in the fifties was "a conspicuous flag of rebellion" in a highly stigmatized, secretive world, a means of survival in an age when gender rules were heavy as lead weights. Being a butch was an assertion of strength against very narrow conceptions of what it meant to be a woman. Wearing a leather jacket and slicking back short hair wasn't simply an experiment with style — it was an embracing of one's "true nature" in the face of the dominant culture's notions of what it meant to be a woman: feminine and coy.[2]

Butch-femme roles, at least in their prefeminist incarnation, linked sexuality, appearance, and, frequently, economic position in a highly ritualized way. Dress was a reflection of sexual style, a signal to potential sexual and nonsexual partners, a clue to one's sensibility on a range of related issues, and a pretty good indicator of whether you worked as a secretary or an elevator operator.

Implicit within that old notion of roles was a great deal of permanence and consistency. One's identity as butch or femme was an essential part of one's being. Once a femme, always a femme. The same for butches. By imposing rules and placing limits on self-expression, roles eroticized difference, providing security and regularity in a tenuous, secretive world. They were often proud statements of lesbian resistance, but they were also the expression of an oppressed minority faced with a paucity of alternatives.

Today's embracing of roles, though, is not a throwback to the 1950s. For many women, adopting a role is more a matter of play than of necessity; roles are more ambiguous and less naturalized. Many dykes still identify more strongly with one role than the other, but now there is a greater possibility of choice. Eighties butch-femme — if it can accurately be termed such — is a self-conscious aesthetic that plays with style and power, rather than an embracing of one's "true" nature against the constraints of straight society. Gone is the tightly constructed relationship between personal style, erotic preference, and economic position — the hallmark of roles during the prefeminist era.

There is no longer a clear one-to-one correspondence between fashion and identity. For many, clothes are transient, interchangeable; you can dress as a femme one day and a butch the next. You can wear a crew cut along with a skirt. Wearing high heels during the day does not mean you're a femme at night, passive in bed, or closeted on the job. "Different communities have their own styles," commented Joan Nestle recently, "but on a good bar night the variety of self-representation runs the whole gamut from lesbian-separatist drag, to full femme regalia, to leather and chains."

The new lesbianism is defining itself against the memory of the old by rejecting the antistyle of the past. As the owner of a new lesbian nightclub in San Francisco implies when she praises the fact that women are "finally dressing up," lesbians are feeling good about themselves today (implying that they didn't in the past). Even the *Wall Street Journal* reports that "lipstick" lesbians are clashing with flannel-shirted "crunchies" in the hallowed halls of Yale. Lesbian-feminism is on the wane, and lifestyle lesbianism — particularly among younger, urban dykes, is on the rise.

Lifestyle versus politics

Popularized by advertising and marketing experts, *lifestyle* has become one of the buzzwords of the 1980s; it is used to refer to yuppies, gay men, and others thought to possess greater-than-average amounts of disposable income, or those who are at least willing to part with what they have to create the illusion that they do. Implicit in the use of this terminology is the belief that *lifestyle* is opposed to *politics:* you are either self-absorbed and obsessed with Things and Style, *or* you are ascetic and devoted to Higher Ends.

The American Dream, that manifestly apolitical vision, is predicated on buying a home, filling it with consumer durables, and insulating it as best as you can from outside intrusions. Laboring in dull jobs during the day, we should live for the weekend, for freedom, for shiny objects. The market and its plastic pretensions have pervaded all corners of our lives, distorting our needs and shaping our desires.

Lesbian-feminism, born of the counterculture, was partially conceived as a challenge to this crass materialism. Throughout the 1970s, while some gay men were busily carving out commercial niches in urban centers, many lesbians scoffed at such activities, and chose instead to build a nonsexist, antimaterialistic world. The asceticism and political correctness that frequently accompanied these pursuits may have been the unintended consequence of a defensive separatism. But politicizing every aspect of personhood, many later discovered, was just too tall an order to live with.

In 1970, the Radicalesbians declared, "A lesbian is the rage of all women condensed to the point of explosion." Today, we've lightened up. Witness the new lesbian comedians and novelists who convey a sense of lesbian life, warts and all, by constructing characters driven by anger, jealousy, and revenge — as well as love and community. The sex debates of the early 1980s, coupled with the increasing acknowledgment of racial, ethnic, and other forms of difference, have broken down the idea of a seamless, transhistorical lesbian identity that we all share.

Though lesbian communities are perhaps less politically organized, less cohesive, and less homogeneous in thought and action than they were ten years ago, activism hasn't completely vanished. The recent emergence of the Lesbian Agenda for Action, a citywide political organization in San Francisco, is a testament to this, as is the recent National Lesbian Rights Conference sponsored by NOW or even the large number of dykes who staff numerous AIDS-related organizations. But it is a lot more difficult to pack an auditorium with women committed to any one issue than it was in the 1970s. There is a seeming multiplication of diverse subcultural pockets and cliques — corporate dykes, arty dykes, dykes of color, clean and sober dykes — of which political lesbians are but one among many.

What does it mean that often the most visible players in our communities today are lipstick lesbians, given that lesbian communities are more fragmented, that it's harder to scrounge for a living, and that — for many women — political involvements fail to provide the sort of personal sustenance they once did? The rise of the femme and the new ambiguity of lesbian style could be interpreted as a sign of retrenchment. It could be argued that lifestyle lesbianism promotes assimilation over separation, and style over substance, and is a sign of our growing conservatism.

Yet many lesbians today don't see it that way. Instead, they experience this new attention to lifestyle as a freedom, a testament to the fact that their identity is now a matter of personal choice rather than political compulsion. As a once-fervent activist remarked recently, "After years of holding myself back and dressing to hide myself, shopping, I've found out, can be a real joy."

Calling the new lesbianism a retrenchment and embracing it as a freedom both appear to reflect popular sentiments. Is there a way to reconcile them without lapsing into a simplistic plea to smash style, or a lamentation that politics is oh-so-boring so why not shop till we drop? Can we transcend the puritanism (shared by the left and the right in this country) that one has to suffer to be noble, without depoliticizing lesbian identity?

Politics in a new lesbian world

> *You can analyze me to death, but it's just that I grew up as a tom-*
> *boy and I prefer my hair being short and I love Nudie suits. Yeah,*
> *sure, the boys can be attracted to me, the girls can be attracted to*
> *me, your mother ... your uncle, sure. It doesn't really matter to me.*
> —Country-western singer k.d. lang[3]

My friends and I are all rabid fans of k.d. lang, a Canadian who sings traditional torch ballads tongue-in-cheek; appears regularly on Johnny Carson sporting a butch haircut, cowgirl skirt, and no makeup; and defies every prescription of what a woman in country music — and indeed pop music — should be. To most of her straight fans, k.d. lang is simply a quirky, tomboyish character, a performer whose powerful voice and compelling originality compensate for her lack of fit in a musical genre where it's usually easy to tell the boys from the girls. But to her legions of dyke devotees, she is divine. When a newly formed k.d. lang fan club sponsored a video night at one of the oldest dyke bars in San Francisco recently, the place was packed tighter than I ever can remember having seen it — testimony, perhaps, to how starved we are for media images of lesbianism, and to how attractive her image is to many of us.

She is one of a new breed of performers, all in their twenties, who came of age when women's music was *au courant*, but who've rejected that genre in favor of mainstream exposure. Without identifying themselves as dykes, they experiment with style and self-presentation, pushing up against the boundaries of what is acceptable for women. I've spent hours with friends discussing the pros and cons of whether k.d. and the others should come out, whether or not it really matters since, after all, *we* all know. Or is it all a big sellout? When she calls herself a tomboy and says that she doesn't care whether men or women are attracted to her, is it simply a ploy to maintain her cover?

This dilemma lies at the heart of the new lesbianism.

On the one hand, the new lesbianism deconstructs the old, perhaps overly politicized or prescriptive notion of lesbianism by refusing ghettoization, acknowledging internal group differences, and affirming the value of individual choice when it comes to style and political and sexual expression. On the other hand, it comes perilously close to depoliticizing lesbian identity and perpetuating our invisibility by failing, frequently, to name itself to others.

Some might argue that if we define politics broadly as a series of contests between competing cultural images — of what it means to be a woman or a lesbian, for example — then the new lesbian style can be seen as a political act, a public assertion of lesbian identity. Yet this new political strategy of cultural visibility, if it can be called that, is paradoxical, because it emerges at a point in our history when lesbian identity is in the process of reformulation.

If lesbianism ceases to be the defining aspect of identity for many women and becomes simply an image, and if notions of what a lesbian looks like break down as fashion codes change and recombine, will we lose sight of what it means to be a lesbian in a largely heterosexual world? As cultural critic Stuart Ewen argues, when power is at stake, a politics of images is no substitute for a "politics of substance." Images are too easily manipulated, their meanings complex and evanescent.

By skirting the issue of power (no pun intended), the new lifestyle lesbianism comes perilously close to giving credence to the liberal belief that today, any sexual choice is possible. While the fragmentation of lesbian identity and decoding of lesbian style may be a justifiable response to an overpoliticization of the personal, they run the risk of erasing the political dimension of lesbian communities. It may be easier to be a dyke today than even a decade ago, but the sobering truth remains that, in a heterosexist, male-dominated society, lesbianism is still not freely chosen. As Margaret Cerullo observed recently, the "hundred lifestyles" strategy, a strategy that calls for a pluralism of sexual choice, "doesn't represent an adequate response to the one lifestyle that has all the power" — heterosexuality.[4]

A little history lesson could go a long way. In the trenches of the style wars, it's easy to forget that political lesbianism paved the way for lifestyle lesbianism. Lacking a sense of history, the new lesbian defines herself against those who came before her, unaware of the fact that greater choice is possible today because lesbians (as well as many straight feminists) fought long and hard for it. By struggling to destigmatize lesbianism, and by forging institutional spaces within which it could flourish, lesbian-feminism was largely responsible for creating the conditions under which a new, more mainstream and less radical lesbianism would eventually take root. That many women experience the new lesbianism as freedom is perhaps testimony to the success, rather than the failure, of the old.

Recognizing this doesn't mean the old political models don't need revising. If the emergence of lifestyle lesbianism tells us anything, it is that we need a political language that acknowledges our diversity as well as our commonality, that embodies playfulness along with rage, and that faces outward as well as inward. Lesbian style may be one of the central battlegrounds for the reformulation of lesbian identity today, but style itself is an insufficient basis for a lesbian politic.

That doesn't mean we should all discard our newly purchased dresses and cowboy boots and begin to boycott the hair salon once again. Rather, it suggests we should embrace style — along with anger — to forge a lesbianism that can take on the new, more complex realities of the 1980s and 1990s.

Notes

1. Karen Everett, "Lipstick Lesbians Love the Night Life," *San Francisco Sentinel,* 28 October 1988.

2. Joan Nestle, "Butch-Fem Relationships: Sexual Courage in the 1950s," *Heresies 12: Sex Issue,* vol. 3, no. 4 (1981): 21–24, reprinted in Joan Nestle, *The Restricted Country* (Ithaca, N.Y.: Firebrand Books, 1987), pp. 100–109. See also Pat Califia, "GenderBending," *Advocate,* 15 September 1983.

3. Burt Kearns, "Canadian Cowpie," *Spin Magazine,* September 1988.

4. Margaret Cerullo, "Night Visions: Toward a Lesbian/Gay Politics for the Present," *Radical America* 21 (March–April 1987).

Myrna Elana

Define "community": This is a test

If my lover had a man's name
and I had to explain that
    to everyone

If my lover had a penis
   of her own
      and I had to explain

If my lover had a penis
   from birth and a woman's name
      and I had to explain
         that
         to everyone

If my lover had a cunt
   yet passed as a man
      and I had to
         explain

If my lover wore a dress
   but shaved and pissed standing up
      and I had
         to explain that
            to everyone

If my lover
   had a cloven hoof
      and a cunt and a penis

and we went along
the horizon line
shouting about it

only the people who mattered
would be left
anywhere near us

Joan Parkin & Amanda Prosser

An academic affair: The politics of butch-femme pleasures

W hat does butch-femme have to do with the academy? Until very recently, we, Amanda and Joan, had lived academically closeted within our respective butch-femme roles without supposing that sexual practice and textual theorizing could ever form bed partners. After all, why fuck up good sex with analysis? But one must take chances, and given the ostensible erotic aridity of the classroom, we thought it worth the risk to lubricate those tight passages of learning with our sexual desire.

As every "good" academic schooled in the white patriarchal tradition learns, the body is "bad" and should be kept a secret.[1] Since the seventeenth century, academic discourse has predicated bodily existence on thought (I think, therefore I am): any vestige of corporeal origins is shamefully closeted within disciplinary divisions that find their material expression in the desks and tables that tuck more than half of our bodies neatly away, safe from potential erotic contact with other bodies. Despite the obvious influences of the Cartesian model on the operations of the academy, within cutting-edge theoretical discourses the body is all the rage, springing onto the pedagogical scene under the auspices of post-modernist wannabe courses with titles such as "Conceiving the Body," "Writing the Body," "Reading the Body," and so forth, courses that claim to tackle head-on the problem of the elision of the sexual in modern thought. All of these "bodies" appear to burst out of the Cartesian strait-jacket in a jubilatory expression of the sexual in a setting that has until recently been the sealed site of the body's most shameful enigma.

Without doubt, the discourse of sexuality has become a legitimate, and indeed hip, object of study, and this is precisely where the problems lie, especially for those most sensitive to bodily elision. For as we, a butch-femme couple whose bodies clearly signify our desires, cannot help but recognize, the current topicality of sexuality in the academy is an institutionalization of sexuality, a further example of what Foucault has called "the deployment of sexuality," a term covering the production of sexuality by institutions, their will to "know" (observe, classify) the pleasures and pains of the body in order to contain its subversive potential.[2] Although sex has so artfully penetrated the academy, it is safely screened through institutionalized discourses such as law, pedagogical theory, and gender politics.[3] The disembodiment of desire entailed in this institutionalization of sexuality makes speaking from our desire an arduous task. The sexualized knowledge-power superstructure de-emphasizes and desexualizes our sex, sanitizing sexual practices while transforming them into discourse. Sexuality has ascended to an incorporeal sphere where it is subject to processes of metaphorization: the sexual body is repeatedly made to represent something other than itself. At work is a project that involves constructing sexual subjects as discursive objects (clearly an objectifying gesture) and inserting sexuality into theory (a move that sets apart our sexual practices from the theorizing going on so insistently around them).

Ironically, Foucault's discussion of "scientia sexualis" (the conjunction of power and knowledge that works to produce scientific "truths" of sexuality) functions as yet another element in this "deployment of sexuality." For his project of locating and describing the different moments in the history of sexuality requires translating these moments into a discourse that by its very nature constructs sexual subjects as discursive objects. Yet how can one talk about sex in theory without displacing the sexual subjects, veiling acts and eliding real pleasures through textuality? And what are we doing at present if not deferring our own desire to the "necessity" of a stoic theoretical language? Indeed, how can we, employing Foucauldian analysis, avoid producing text about sex in which pleasure falls through the holes of discursivity, of our will-to-knowledge as academics?

Where, then, should our project differ from Foucault's? Interestingly enough, Foucault, in providing warning signs that mark the limits of his usefulness to our work, unwittingly maps a way to answering some of the above questions. Not only has Foucault been noted for his blindness to a female sexuality,[4] but, as we have already suggested, his problematizing of agency — that is, of the individual act — makes any kind of personal subject position invalid. Our application of the Foucauldian model to butch-femme should be understood then as a refiguration of the outcome that not only a female but a lesbian sexuality (conceptually inclusive of both genders) might have on power structures when operating from a *personal* subject position.[5] What we are stressing is that sexuality, once institutionalized, is not in itself politically subversive. Inserting the signature into the sacrosanct practice of discursive objectification, however, creates possibilities for a radical restructuring of the academy, since the potential for subversion comes out of the locus of resistance offered by a particular subject position: a place determined not just by academic training but by ethnic, class, gender, and sexual identities. Only when sex can speak for itself (so to speak) rather than being spoken about, when the full range of a student's sociosexual experience is introduced, not as object of analysis but as method of critique, can real change occur in the academy. Until then no matter how hot the topic of sex, its potential for radically altering the academy will be forever neutralized, contained within objectifying practices that function like a decompression area for politically loaded and thus marginalized radical subject positions.

This neutralized zone is the closet in which we had been working. But let's not kid ourselves into thinking that here we are rid of the tightening embrace of those four walls, for our language, weighed down with the "necessity" of describing the current state of sexuality in the academy, is constantly slipping back into the cold style that silences the moan of desire. Language itself becomes the closet. We, as extreme sexual subjects, must moderate our queer style to be understood by those who would interpret and judge our work. Our very means of communication thus depends on our willingness to abandon the rhetorical arsenal of our personal territory (stockpiled mostly within the closet). If we do not, we cease to exist as speaking subjects within the academic world. Eliding our personal desires from theoretical language has thus become a matter of survival.

Let's face it: heads talk, bodies shock, and to come out is to say that we come, and while this is a pleasure shared by many, it is still considered an extracurricular diversion from more-serious academic work. It is no accident, however, that what is being marginalized is the explicitly sexual subject position that has the potential to disturb, if not erase, the current division between objective analysis and the personal that elitist institutional practices now so reverently keep intact. Keeping the present educational system in place is clearly within the interests of those in power, for it legitimates the central subject position of the professor, constructing it as the source of objectivity, while delegitimizing diverse and perverse subject positions that resist appropriation. For what is being lost in this moment of neglect? How does the homogenizing gaze of academia image butch-femme relationships? Perceived through a straight lens, isn't butch-femme too often seen as a distorted version of the heterosexual norm? How are we, Amanda and Joan, seen by the academy as we strip off layer upon layer of ill-fitting discourse within this space in which desire is expected to be veiled?

Act 1. Femme

Scene i. Graduate seminar, "The Subjects of Autobiography: Gender/Writing/Theory," City University of New York (CUNY), Fall 1990.

As I walk into my first feminist class of the season, dressed in my usual femme attire (tight skirt, slight pumps, red lipstick, black leather jacket, my hair tossed into that recently fucked style), it is business as usual. Notebooks and pens are at ease and students are freely chatting away during that informal space before the professor's entrance will formalize the discussion. I take the opportunity to check out the sexual makeup of the class (or cruise, as it were). There are a couple of straight men, two gay men, a majority of straight women (perhaps some femmes in there, too), and two lesbians with some definite butch potential (one becomes quite expert at sifting out what is essential to one's desire). The real butch of the two (as I will soon find out) looks at me with a still, casual glance, and I quickly turn my head so that she won't see the delight in my eyes that her cool look causes. And as the professor enters we check our desires so that we can interpret the role of gender in Frederick Douglass's *Narrative*.

Scene ii. Same. I stand in direct line with Amanda's cool gaze. The class watches and waits for our "performance" to begin: today is our day to introduce our personal narratives into the class. When I hear Amanda saying, "I am sick of seashores and shells, crystal, coral, conches, moonshine, and Georgia bloody O'Keeffe..." I respond: "I enter your attending discourse. A delicious shudder rips through me as I advance backward, my ass bared for you. At this moment there is a greater impetus toward succulent death than toward resistance, if death be the price that our pleasure requires. Your text — complete power — demands that I deconstruct the wall: I am at my limit. There is no release without gentle submission. For these are moments when I receive you fully — your strength, your hard butch self, is nurtured by my tenderness, and now your pleasure steals like an insatiable child the love that I give to you. I cry in a frenzy of desire as I advance toward your waiting mouth, toward the cutting edge, and the wall cracks — it's up to you. And just when I would give you my all, you uncuff the semantic shackles. I am unbound, I am ready to receive your language (dildo). The attending discourse penetrates me fully. I am released: I love you, Amanda, my beautiful butch lover, my woman." These words fall hard into the silence of the class.

Act 2. Butch

Scene i. Graduate Seminar, "The Subjects of Autobiography: Gender/ Writing/Theory," CUNY, Fall 1990. Reading for that week: Gertrude Stein, *The Autobiography of Alice B. Toklas.* Comment from a heterosexual, female, self-proclaimed feminist student in the context of a discussion of Stein's relationship with women as evidenced by the text: "Gertrude Stein just wanted to be a man."

Scene ii. Bathroom at Queens College, CUNY, five minutes prior to the class I teach. Washing my hands, I see reflected in the mirror a student opening the door to the women's room and hesitating as she catches sight of my reflection; her eyes travel from me to the women's sign on the door (a silhouette distinguishable from the male signifier only by a skirt) and back to me again. She repeats this movement, her gaze coming to rest on my dyke body, taking note of my butch attire, contrasting my men's pants and jacket with the sole mark of female gender affixed to the door: the skirt. Evidently deciding that she has come to the "wrong" bathroom, she leaves.

In the safe places outside the supervisory gaze of the academy, in the arms of my butch lover, Amanda, there is a place where different desires thrive and where no original model owns the sexual play between my feminine desire and her butch desire. Our sexual exchange is not based on imitation, for within the four walls of Amanda's room, the childhood, heterosexual memory constructions (Mommy, Daddy, big dick, little cunt) intersect with two female bodies, whose touch (never imagined in our early selves) disturbs the plastic coating of Daddy's and Mommy's erect and supple forms and transforms the Oedipal moment at the precise moment of its seeming reinstatement. Mommy's lipstick, Daddy's cock are smeared between our female bodies. For butch-femme desire, born from the conflict between the violation of a taboo (lesbianism) and the recalling of our memories (Mommy, Daddy) is a metamorphosis of unchosen sexual desire into the delicious gendered power play that my lover and I so deliberately recreate.

In other spaces, less safe places, hostile to the disruption of disciplinary walls, thick concretized conceptual divisions establish a binary opposition between a seemingly objective academic space and the personal erotics that butch-femme brings to the academy. The apparent truth of the normative heterosexual model and the charge that butch-femme distorts that model mirror the myth that the original historical reality wields more influence, more productive power on the world than the transformative identities proceeding from it. When there is always the possibility of the copy exceeding the original, of the dildo outsizing the dick, is it relevant to valorize authenticity?[6] Examining how the copy brings to the original a certain self-consciousness and how the copy that exceeds the original may contain the potential to radically alter its originary moment would be more productive. As with butch-femme and heterosexuality, the line between personal desires and the sexually "neutral" space of the academy is nonnegotiable. It defines, as it were, their separate existences — though the personal may transform this "neutral" space as much as butch-femme does heterosexual desire. The existence of the personal and butch-femme in the academy facilitates the dismantling of any pretense of objective truth concerning heterosexuality and displaces the originary moment from its once-privileged site of existence.

In other places, deceptive spaces, seemingly beyond the encompassing gaze of the penis, lies an apparent haven for those of us whose personal is not in alignment with originary objective truth. As feminists, we expect to feel at home when speaking of subjective desires in a domain that claims to take care of the personal. We do not expect discontinuity between our words and the language of feminism. Yet what we often encounter in feminist sites where we choose to think through our bodies, to speak as lovers, as butch-femme, is the silence of disapproval and of fear. What we discover in these moments of coming out as women who take sexual pleasure seriously is that, for most feminisms, sexual desire is still in the closet.[7] We need to make clear that we are not berating here the feminist movement's lesbophobia of twenty years ago, when lesbians within its ranks were too often perceived as the "lavender menace." For today, feminism in general proclaims that a lesbian agenda is no longer inimical to its projects; on the contrary, feminism seems to have sought to maximize the visibility of its queer contingent, has unlocked the closets it stood guard over in the seventies and dragged lesbians onto center stage. For although academic representations of sexuality are overwhelmingly heterosexual,[8] in some feminist scenes lesbians are clearly standing in the spotlight, and here lies the problem: we get to be actors in this theoretical theater only if we allow our sexuality to be (re)dressed by feminism, if we agree to clothe our desires in costumes provided by the directors.

Carole Vance's discussion in *Pleasure and Danger* of feminism's "rehabilitation" of lesbianism indicates how certain sectors of feminism have sought to co-opt lesbian sexuality as the most clearly marked exit from the phallocracy:

> Within feminism, lesbianism has been rehabilitated, undergoing a transition from the realm of bad sex to the realm of good sex, and within some sectors of the movement, given a privileged position as the most egalitarian and feminist sexual identity. With this exception, new feminist punishments are still meted out to the denizens of the same old sexual lower orders.[9]

The effects of this rehabilitation of lesbianism, this reclothing of exposed desires, have been severe; indeed, it is difficult to see lesbianism, as Vance seems to, as having escaped feminist moral birching, for with the privileges of having one's sexuality placed on a continuum of woman-identification,[10] of having lesbian identity made the site of a feminist nirvana beyond the phallus, comes the imposition of a whole set of norms and standards on our sexual practices. Where is room for me, the butch dyke with my strap-on, in this new order purified of masculinity? What happens to my femme's desire once I have been castrated by feminists-against-the-phallus, and what role is she left to play stripped of her feminine "bondage"? Where do S/M lesbians fit into this utopia of equal exchange? Can we still hit each other's G spots (can we still fuck?) now that the clitoris has been established as simultaneously the position to combat the phallus and the politically correct place to get turned on? Now that being lesbian in theory has become de rigeur, what are the effects on our sexual practices? What happens to the possibilities for sexual pleasure when we've been set up as "good" feminists precisely because we're not supposed to be concerned with the excesses of sexual pleasure?

Institutionalized feminism is all too frequently getting to "draw the line" of sexual permissibility. Beyond the line lurks the "excessive," which seems to reside in those instants when gender is subject to sexual play (butch-femme), in visual displays of the cohesion of desire and violence, of the points at which pleasure and danger intersect, of the moments when sex and rage are undifferentiated. This territory has been so thoroughly masculinized by some feminisms that explorations into it are frequently dismissed as antiwomen and antifeminist.[11] Certainly, in some feminist personal criticism, sex is okay but only in those forms that keep their distance from the excessive: what is privileged in the figuration of sexuality in current personal criticism is the understated, those sexual postures that are euphemized.[12] This new academic style resists those spectacles of sexuality that veer from this neutralizing dynamic, that take visible pleasure in explicitly sexual performances, that get off on role-playing. From the viewpoint of feminist personal criticism, these moments of speaking and enacting sex without the veil of euphemism exceed the personal.[13] The feminist project of valorizing the personal has not included sexual desires such as ours that refuse to participate in their own coy partial effacement.

These moments of writing are marked purely by love, love signified here as an academic affair. My femme, my love, my sweet: understand why I include these moments of exposure, why I make these revelations. It's vital that, through them, what is recognized is how our love affair — and these moments of telling it — collapsed and collapses the walls (never demolished as promised by feminism, only relocated) between the personal and the political, between the private and the public, between sexual desire and the academic discourse it props up. Understand why I need to tell of how we came together and continued in the place of excess, how we met in the verges of that class: you, the tragic lesbian, the masochist taking exquisite pleasure in your exclusion; I, the voyeuristic sadist, focusing my gaze from my position on the outskirts onto the field of activity within the classroom. Understand how our sexual pleasures have from the beginning refused to remain hidden behind the bedroom door, how they have always been inscribed in a public (academic) space, how our definitive feature of exceeding privatization can be read as a valid political gesture. Our pleasure cannot be reduced to individualistic hedonism, to the "mere personal," precisely because of the academic context in which it has been shaped and which it has reshaped. For the excess and violence of personal pleasure we have produced in the institution can operate and has operated for us as a public place from which to question, to exceed and violate academic standards, as a critical and political site of resistance.

Notes

1. In *Thinking through the Body* (New York: Columbia University Press, 1985), Jane Gallop explains how this "male European philosophical tradition" has failed to think through the body: "Rather than treat the body as a site of knowledge, a medium for thought, the more classic philosophical project has tried to render it transparent and get beyond it, to dominate it by reducing it to the mind's idealizing categories" (pp. 3–4).

2. Michel Foucault, *The History of Sexuality: An Introduction*, vol. 1 (New York: Vintage, 1990).

3. A representative sample of texts in which sexual pleasure, specifically women's sexual pleasure, is sublimated into the academically legitimated discourses of law, pedagogical theory, and gender politics might read respectively as follows: Ruthann Robson, "Lifting Belly: Privacy, Sexuality and Lesbianism," *Women's Rights Law Reporter* 12, no. 3 (Fall 1990): 401–427; Nancy K. Miller, "Mastery, Identity and the Politics of Work: A Feminist Teacher in the Graduate Classroom," in *Gendered Subjects,* edited by Margo Culley and Catherine Portugos (Boston: Routledge & Kegan Paul, 1985), pp. 195–199; Catherine A. MacKinnon, "Legal Perspectives on Sexual Difference," in *Theoretical Perspectives on Sexual Difference,* edited by Deborah Rhode (New Haven, Conn.: Yale University Press, 1990), pp. 213–225.

4. The volume *Feminism and Foucault: Reflections on Resistance,* edited by Irene Diamond and Lee Quinby (Boston: Northeastern University Press, 1988), contains essays that offer this critical perspective.

5. We speak of the "personal" here not in terms of the ideology of liberal individualism but to denote different sociocultural experiences.

6. We are indebted to Liz Dalton for her brilliant discussion of the possibility of copies exceeding originals in her "Dildo Manifesto," a short section of a paper given at the "Rage" Conference, May 15, 1991, City University of New York Graduate Center.

7. "Ironically, the whole notion of 'the personal is political,' which surfaced in the early part of the women's liberation movement (and which many of us have used to an extreme), is suddenly dismissed when we begin to discuss sexuality … It seems we simply did not take our feminism to heart enough. This most privatized aspect of ourselves, our sex lives, has dead-ended into silence within the feminist movement." Amber Hollibaugh and Cherríe Moraga, "What We're Rollin' around in Bed With: Sexual Silences in Feminism: A Conversation toward Ending Them," *Heresies 12: Sex Issue,* vol. 3, no.4 (1981): 58–62, reprinted in this volume.

8. What comes to mind at this point are the recent dialogues on feminist theory edited by Linda Kauffman (*Gender and Theory: Dialogues on Feminist Criticism* [New York: Basil Blackwell, 1989]), which, with their boy-girl, boy-girl layout, are regimentally framed by heterosexuality.

9. Carole S. Vance, ed., *Pleasure and Danger: Exploring Female Sexuality* (Boston: Routledge & Kegan Paul, 1984), p. 22.

THE PERSISTENT DESIRE

10. The reference is to the lesbian continuum laid out by Adrienne Rich in "Compulsory Heterosexuality and Lesbian Existence" in the volume *Powers of Desire: The Politics of Sexuality*, edited by Ann Snitow, Christine Stansell, and Sharon Thompson (New York: Monthly Review Press, 1983) pp. 177–205.

11. Antipornography and anti-S/M feminists have been particularly obsessive in carrying out this project: at the vanguard appear such names as Andrea Dworkin, Catherine MacKinnon, Susan Griffin, Julia Penelope, Diana Russell.

12. One such euphemistic moment appears in Jane Tompkins's "Me and My Shadow," in *Gender and Theory*, edited by Linda Kauffman, pp. 121–139. The author reveals her desire to go to the bathroom, a metonymical desire, as she does not, after all, say what she wants to go to the bathroom *for*. The central point, however, is that she never actually goes within the text. Of most interest to me here is her design of letting us know more than once of her not going ("not yet"), of her self-control, of the restraints her writing enables her to impose on her desire. My bathroom scene stands, by way of contrast, as a tableau of deliberate and exquisite self-exposure: inside the bathroom, you are encouraged, as was my student, to see my butchness in its entirety. What my student ultimately misrecognizes I've made explicit for you: the markings of my sexual desire (perhaps, by the way, never more outstanding than in the public bathroom).

13. We speak here, as throughout this text, from personal experience. Papers we have submitted that work around sexual tropes have invariably met with a response that seeks to delegitimize the claim we make through our sexual identities to the feminist personal, and even on occasion to any feminist, position.

Barbara Ruth

Playing roles

Butch and femme?
Yeah, I think it matters.
It slides around
In how we are together
    Makes a difference
In who does what for whom
And how we feel about it.

But so do lots of things.
When my friends and I hang out
We play roles
The most common ones are
Crip and AB
And who gets which role
Depends on what
Needs to be done
Who's most able
At that particular moment.
And yes, it makes a difference
In who does what for whom
And how we feel about it.

And then there's race
And skin color, within race,
And religion, ethnicity,
And the way that none of these
Are quite the same.

Whether or not you can speak fluent English
And whose English you speak.
Where you come from

THE PERSISTENT DESIRE

If you're illegal
Whether or not you have need to know
What *la migra* is
When there's a knock on the door.

And class
How much money you have now
How much you grew up with
Whether or not you have resources
To fall back on
Should you fall.
All of these make a difference
In who does what for whom
And how we feel about it.

I don't think it's wrong
To ask which one's the butch
In a dyke relationship.
It's just not enough.
Ask as well
Who's been locked up
And for how long.
Who was raped by her father
And for how long.
Whose children have been stolen?
Who's been sterilized?
Who's in recovery
From what?
Who's a suicide survivor?
Who can pass on the street?
All of these make a difference
In how we are together.

So many categories
We don't yet know the words for.
Twenty years ago
If you remembered your incest
You thought you were the only one.

We come to one another
Wounded
And with power.
We come seeking
Speaking
Wisdom

We come close.

Because we're lesbians
We postulate
A universe.
The names we make ourselves
Will have to be
As delicious as our flesh
As unremitting as our rage
As complex and as simple
As our loves.

And if you choose to call
Some piece of that
Femme and butch
I won't object
So long as you don't think
We've said it all.

A celebration of butch-femme identities in the lesbian community

The following is a heavily edited transcript of a panel discussion held at the New York Lesbian and Gay Community Services Center, December 6, 1990. The panelists included Sue Hyde, Amber Hollibaugh, Deanna Alida, Lisa Winters, Val Tavai, Jewelle Gomez, Jill Harris, and Joan Nestle, with Stephanie Grant moderating. The full transcript is on file at the Lesbian Herstory Archives, P.O. Box 1258, New York, NY 10116.

Stephanie Grant, moderator: Our first panelist this evening is Sue Hyde. Sue has spent her last four years on the staff of the National Gay and Lesbian Task Force.

Sue Hyde: I've been a butch my whole conscious life. It took me about twenty years to come fully into lesbianism, but I was a baby butch at the age of five. I remember clearly the summer between kindergarten and first grade, my mother arranged for me to get a haircut. My long, sausage curls piled up on the floor around my chair at the beauty parlor. I climbed out of the chair, a new butchling in the world. Jeans and t-shirts and sneakers became my earliest, and have proven to be my most enduring, uniform of choice. But the uniform was just a symbol for the freedom of my butch childhood, during which I immersed myself in everything that a very small, midwestern river town could offer.

What does it mean to be butch? It's not about what I wear, although I am always clearly and firmly crossed in my dressing. It's not about my not using makeup or other accoutrements of womanhood, although I never do. And it's not about the length of my hair. And it's not about being tough. My girlfriend, who grew up at 92nd and Lexington Avenue, is much tougher than I. Being butch for me is totally about sex. I am butch because

I express desire for a woman in terms of how I can make her feel. I need —
and it's with no small amount of need — to be my lover's best lover. I need
to know from her that the failure I experienced at adolescence, that
moment of horror when I realized I could never be a man and in this
culture I would never quite be a woman either, can be transformed and
transcended through her profound pleasure and my pleasure at hers.

Evenings like this are very important, not because the fate of the world
rests on what we say but because lesbians need to know what lesbianism
is. We who are constantly under attack must invent and dream ourselves
in the face of vicious and vile hatred.

Moderator: Amber Hollibaugh is a writer, activist, filmmaker. She works
for the NYC Human Rights Commission in the AIDS Discrimination Unit.

Amber Hollibaugh: The politics of the sexuality of butch-femme is about
desire. I don't think we know very much about what the erotic engine is
that makes us move.

All of us have worked very hard to be queer, to be lesbian, to be out —
in spite of all the cultural stop signs. But there's a whole other dialogue
missing in our lives because of the pressure from outside and the censure
that comes from the way that we're judged just for being different.

The descriptions that I want to know, that I hunger for, are why we
want other women and how. The ways that we've constructed our ideas
of sexuality are very tiny. It's critical that we be able to say to each other
that this is not about style, not about roles as though we put them on
because we bought them in a store. It's about loving each other. It's about
caring passionately about each other's existence. It's about feeling each
other's mouths on each other's bodies. That isn't small.

The only time that I ever tried to kill myself was when I tried to figure
out how I could live with my politics and the fact that I was femme. That
didn't come from just a political community that I felt would judge me,
because then it was early on and I was old gay; it was a kind of a joke. It
wasn't like people were saying to me, "You can't be part of the movement."
I said to me, I can't be a part of my own political agenda if the way I want
women to make love to me is as a butch to a femme. It meant that I thought
I had to choose between my political vision and my sexual desire. I'd
already faced that to be a lesbian. I'd already walked that razor blade. So
to choose against the women I wanted to be with to have the political ideals
that I absolutely founded my life on seemed to be an intolerable contradiction, and it seemed to me that there was no choice, because I couldn't live
without either one.

That's why I think butch-femme is important to describe to each other,
to play with — not because most of us are butch-femme (I don't know
whether that identity actually means an enormous amount to the majority
of lesbians), but because where we draw our erotic lines, wherever we
match up against another woman, is the place we are willing to die for to

be queer. We've got to tell each other the degree of our commitment to each other. The desire between us is the engine that moves us.

Moderator: Our next panelist, Deanna Alida, is an opera singer. She teaches voice and theory and sings in voice recitals.

Deanna Alida: Until five years ago, I never realized the political magnitude of being a butch in this world. Recently, people have asked, "Why are you going to be on a butch-femme panel?" At first I was furious at them for daring to ask. Then I searched myself for the answer: "Because it's wonderful! Because I want to do it and because it has to be done!"

Being an opera singer all my life and being a teacher of singing, I felt alienated from the lesbian world at large. Being a butch alienated me from other lesbians. Being a butch lesbian alienated me within the operatic world. I was very lonely, as both worlds seemed to be exclusive, conservative, and elitist — though, oddly enough, I was never lonely in love, as there was a world of femmes just waiting for a good butch. The thrilling excitement of connecting with the right femme was an enormous source of energy and creative inspiration for an artist.

I cannot presume to speak for anyone but myself. For me, being a butch is about a primal attraction, an animal attraction to the femme: an irresistible attraction that unearths the depths of my being. It affects my deepest existence as a human being. Being a butch has been a lifetime of exploring and celebrating an animal lust and a deliciously uncontrollable urge toward another human being who shares the intensity of my passion and sexuality, primarily, unconditionally, in mutual acknowledgment of its power — and in surrender to its magic. Being a butch kept me alive. Femmes have given me years of the nurturing affirmation and appreciation I needed so much to love *myself* as a woman. Being a butch is living with a strong defense and with a deep, deep vulnerability — to be shared with and exposed only to those whom we trust implicitly. It is not an exclusive relationship; it is a perspective on life.

Moderator: Our next panelist, Lisa Winters, lives and works in the Bronx. She founded the New York Femmes, a support group for lesbian femmes. She is also the founder and cochair of Bronx Lesbians United in Sisterhood, and a producer for the Gay and Lesbian Independent Broadcasters.

Lisa Winters: I have always been a femme. Growing up, my mother encouraged me to be feminine, bold, strong, seductive, yielding, and able. She also encouraged me to climb trees, build things, and play sports.

I had a wonderful coming-out experience with a butch woman in upstate New York. I remember her telling me, "Lisa, the way you look and the way you act is beautiful and wonderful; it's so exciting to me. There are women who love you and who love who you are." This wasn't what I was told in the lesbian community at that time, because anything but androgyny was not politically correct.

The New York Femmes, 1991

The New York Femmes got its start about three years ago. I was feeling very isolated in the lesbian community, even though I was very active in three political organizations and satisfied with my work in these groups. Yet, there was a visible lack of femmes in these groups — no one with whom I shared a sense of homogeneity, even though I was with other lesbians.

After placing an ad in *Womanews*, NYC's feminist paper, I received thirty calls the first week alone. The first meeting was wonderful. The women were thrilled to find such an organization. Would it be funny if I told you that we tried to outdress each other at the first meeting, too? [*Laughter*] We told each other the femme version of our coming-out experiences. We planned and organized future topics, such as sex, isolation, butch-femme, femme-femme, supporting each other, dating, and group outings.

We went from meeting at members' homes to renting out space at the Lesbian and Gay Community Center. Thirty phone calls have translated to a mailing list of over one hundred. During the course of our growing stages, various issues had to be dealt with: women coming to meetings who were not lesbians, women who wanted to know what femmes were, butches who wanted to pick up femmes, and so on. We decided on two requirements to join: one, members had to be lesbian, and two, they had to be self-identified femmes. Being a self-identified femme meant that a woman identified in some way with the word *femme*.

Our bond as femmes goes beyond age, race, and class. Our femmes range from upper middle class to working-class, and our racial mix encompasses Afro-American, Latino, and women of European descent. Some of our femmes are in their forties and have been self-described as long as they have been lesbians; others, in their twenties, are new to the femme identification process.

The femme group evolved from an idea to an actual movement within the lesbian community. Not only do femmes have a space to support and nurture each other, but there has been a re-emergence of the butch-femme movement. This is seen by the start of the Butch-Femme Society, almost a year ago, and a larger contingency of women identifying with butch-femme issues.

Moderator: Our next panelist is Val Tavai. Val is a 27-year-old school-teacher who is currently working on a series of short stories about Polynesian butch-femme-identified lesbians. Born and raised in Hawaii, Val and her lover will be returning there to settle down and raise their own children, which Val looks forward to, since she has always wanted to be a daddy.

Val Tavai: I am the "baby butch" of the group. Being a self-identified butch under thirty, I've always been awed by the butch-femme mystique of the 1930s, '40s, and '50s. What helped with this admiration was that I was raised with a butch aunt who was always out. I think I share a respect common among younger butches for generations past, who believe that it's important to continue that which has always made butches unique — the ability to resist an oppressive heterosexual society by being who we are and defining what we desire in women.

Our subculture evolved between the sixties and nineties and allowed a new generation of butches to re-emerge in a broader, more radical style. The spectrum has changed for women who identify as butch. We can make self-identified statements of what we desire and what we can explore. A butch can be a bottom; a butch can desire other butches.

I am of Philippine-Samoan extraction; butch-femme is very much a cultural and class issue. Feminists of color always argue that white middle-class feminists have thrown all feminists into one group. If you understand the dynamics of cultural difference, that is impossible. There is a big cultural difference between butches of color and white middle-class butches.

As a new-generation butch, I still face the same kind of homophobia as did "old-culture" butches. Comments still fly on the street. Women distance themselves from me on the train. Men have a tendency to test their machismo by staring at me and trying to intimidate me. Yet there is a difference in generations. What I've inherited are the years lesbians have fought for visibility. In a sense, they made it easier for me to be out. They gave me the courage.

Morgan Gwenwald

Val Tavai at the butch-femme celebration,
New York Lesbian and Gay Community Services Center, 1990

Moderator: Our next panelist, Jewelle Gomez, is the new director of the literature program at the New York State Council on the Arts. Her novel *The Gilda Stories* was just published by Firebrand Books.

Jewelle Gomez: I'm going to talk from some notes from a panel I was on with Amber and Joan in Toronto a couple of years ago when the fury around butch-femme and other identities, such as S/M, was so high that some people here were under attack in their homes and on their jobs. If we seem at some points defensive when we are supposed to be so cool, it's because of that attack. Until that attack, I hadn't thought much about the femme identity one way or the other. I knew I usually went with butches, but as an identity, as a part of personality, it hadn't been an issue until those who were against me made it one. And I think they've rued the day.

As a writer who's also black, who's also a lesbian, a good part of my early life was spent examining mythology and stereotypes that were damaging to me. In order for me to write characters and create situations that I thought were true to the spirit of people I wanted to represent, I had to confront many stereotypes. During the sixties, there were some activists who built their careers on telling Afro-Americans what was correct and incorrect as betrayals of who we were. For a while, tap dancing became such an embarrassment that black people couldn't even say the words when we were by ourselves, much less when we were with white people.

Thirty years later, that art form has been reclaimed, and its roots in African rhythms and its usefulness in the survival of Africans in slavery in this country and the sheer genius of it as a dance form are all coming back to us. With butch-femme identity, something similar has happened. Embarrassment over butch-femme is an indication of belief in that simplemindedness, and it is very dangerous political thinking to accept a symbol as the thing itself.

The assumption that the male-female dyad is at the root of all human interaction is misleading and false. Rather than marriage as a root relationship or institution or primary relationship, I could say that the mother-child relationship is the primary dyad against which we could examine all other relationships, or I could say that the teacher-student relationship is the primary dyad. In that sense, heterosexual marriage would be considered an aberration of the mother-child or teacher-student relationship. The old folks have many sayings they use to express our perceptions of the polarity on which all the world is based. They say what goes around comes around, they say opposites attract, they say up ain't up unless down is down. Even scientists say for every action there is an equal and opposite reaction. But that principle was really lost when we began to analyze our relationships to each other.

Class and self-presentation in butch-femme relationships have been incredibly important in our lives. I know as a black woman who grew up in the underclass in Boston, butch-femme was the only identifiable expression of lesbianism in my community. Yet that expression, and the concept of butch-femme, has stirred many feminists to anger.

For me, historically the value of butch-femme has been twofold: one, the femme as subversive infiltrator, the one who sneaks into the heterosexual world unobtrusively and again gives the lie to what heterosexuals say lesbians are. And the butch to me has been the hero of open expression, the only woman who could openly say she was a lesbian in a very clear, concrete way.

Moderator: Our next panelist, Jill Harris, is a lawyer who works as a public defender for the Legal Aid Society of Brooklyn. She is thirty-two years old and a member of ACT UP. When she was four years old, she insisted on being known as Timmy.

Jill Harris: I'm butch and I'm proud of it and I'm out about it, so nothing that I say needs to be construed as anything other than that. But one of the things that I struggle with is an internalized misogyny that I'd like to talk about, and the hard time I have identifying myself as a woman or identifying with women. I remember one time in law school, I was in a workshop on racism and the facilitator started out by asking us to list the groups that we identify ourselves as members of and different ways we identify ourselves. I said I'm a lesbian, I ride a motorcycle — you, know, this and that. The facilitator said, "Well, you're a woman, right; you identify as a woman?" And I said, "Well, that's not really a category I would list." You can look at this culture and see examples of why you wouldn't want to identify as a woman. Women, lesbians, ask me, "How can you be a member of ACT UP — there are all those men, and, god, how can you deal with it?" Frankly, it's *because* of the men that it's comfortable for me.

Growing up, I had the same kind of experience that Sue described of this incredible freedom to be anything until puberty came and my body betrayed me and everybody started telling me that I had to start doing things differently. I felt that being a woman was about limitations and loss. The experience I had of my parents' relationship was that my mother was really into my father, really hot for him, and he humiliated her. He left her when she was pregnant and she was very vulnerable. I imagined my father as this dashing, sexy, powerful figure, and I wanted to be him, not her.

So I experience femaleness as vulnerability and, in some ways, humiliation. A part of what butchness has been for me has been avoiding vulnerability, and not being in touch with feelings. In some ways, it works. When you walk down the street looking the way I look, you just don't get as much shit. So there are ways that feeling invulnerable gets borne out. On the other hand, it's a trap, because as women we're vulnerable, right? And I can be taken for a faggot and get the shit beaten out of me; I can be taken for a dyke and get the shit beaten out of me; I am still vulnerable. So this sense of invulnerability that I sometimes project I feel is an illusion, and it's something that troubles me. In this butch-femme dynamic, where a femme is attracted to me for that projection, there's a trap built into it. When your vulnerability is made apparent, you're "found out" — and it can be a problem.

Recently, I was in a butch-butch relationship for quite some time. One thing I did in that relationship that I had a hard time doing in relationships with femmes was that I was able to be more in touch with those feelings of vulnerability and "being a girl."

What I'm afraid of is a rigidity that I see in myself and that I also see in other butches, a tenseness, a tightness that as we age gets more and more solid. I'm afraid of that. So I've been trying to loosen myself up a little, to be a little more fluid.

Moderator: We have as our last panelist Joan Nestle, teacher, author of *A Restricted Country*, co-editor of *Women on Women*, and cofounder of the Lesbian Herstory Archives.

Joan Nestle: They can't ever scare us out of the way we live. They can't judge us out of the way we love. They can't ridicule us out of it, because it is not a masquerade. It is our breasts and our — thighs. (I was going to say ass.)

My life as a femme has given me, both before the seventies and now, many reasons to say thank you. Saying thank you is a very high human art, and the touch of women has made me profoundly grateful. I brought a card with me that I received in the mail, because it's these kinds of words that keep me going. This is for all of us in this room. The woman who sent the card was thanking me for writing a butch-femme article: "My lover and I lived in the Village during this period, the fifties; neither of us have ever been in the closet. We walked the walk you described so vividly. I loved my Les dearly and she was all the things you say. I was her femme. I want to thank you so much for validating our existence."

When I talked about sex, it was often assumed that I didn't know about sexual abuse, that I didn't know about violence against women, and that because I chose to celebrate a passion or to describe a passion, I was immune from the anguish of being a woman in this society. I learned to listen every time I spoke; I learned to listen, and I could sort out authentic pain from rhetorical attack and learned that I had to address that pain. My whole life's work in some sense has been saying — along with others — that we cannot only have an anatomy of victimization. We are more than that. We must have an anatomy of desire, of celebration. We must not assume that because a woman speaks about passion she doesn't know pain. I'm also learning that if a woman speaks about pain, it doesn't mean that she doesn't know passion.

Audience member: I'm a femme under thirty, and my lover is a passing woman, a drag butch over forty, and we have a wonderful, fulfilling relationship that I celebrate daily, constantly. I want to thank everyone.

Audience member: I'm a woman, and if you think that I look like a man, then I'm a passing woman. I'm one of those flannel-shirt, work-boot, working-class lesbians who came out more than twenty-five years ago. I want to make a point about what we consider to be normal or natural in our self-expression.

Within the last two hundred years on this continent, women who looked like myself were treated with dignity and respect by their nations — in particular, Bar-chee-am-pe, the Crow woman chief. When 160 lodges took their places around the fire, she sat third. And there were the women named Sahaykwisa and Co'pak and Kauxuma Nupika, whose lives indicate that they had undergone the rituals for what would today be considered women transvestites. They were not only loved by the women who married them, they were respected and held in dignity by their entire communities. And I don't raise this to teach about native history, because native people can speak eloquently for themselves about that past, but because that is the history common to all our earliest ancestry, in every indigenous matrilineal society from the Arctic Circle all the way down to South America.

Women like myself, and men, who today are beaten on the streets for being transvestites, were held with respect and esteem, and that form of human self-expression is not only ancient, we need to remind ourselves, it predates patriarchy and it predates women's oppression. It's a natural form of self-expression. It's been declared its opposite by the same people who have used the divide-and-conquer tactics that people in this room have experienced with so much diversity.

What has changed now for women like me is that we can no longer walk down the streets and say we are women; we have to pass. We have to pass on our jobs, on the subways at night. It's like being banished. When the women's and the lesbian and gay communities became closed to us and the factory doors closed, we were literally exiled. We were exiled to a shore which will never be our home, and it's been a long and lonely journey for many of us. We were not part of the women's movement and we were not part of the CR groups. But imagine what we've learned in this time. And imagine the stories that we have to tell. If you open the door to us again, we can tell those stories.

Jewelle L. Gomez

Flamingoes and bears: A parable

Flamingoes and bears
meet secretly
on odd street corners.

Horses and chickens,
elephants and geese
look shocked and appalled.

Ostriches don't look at all.

Bear and flamingo
ignore greedy gazes
from disgruntled parents
and frightened sly weasels
who hiss
as the couple
strolls by.

Chance brought them here
from forest and sea,
but science won't agree
where
bears and flamingoes
learned how simple
building a nest
in a den can be.

Now flamingo and bear
sleep forever entwined
in all sorts of climes

464

be it rainy or snowy or sunny,
happy to know
there's room in this world
for a bear who likes palm trees

and a bird who loves honey.

Gayle Rubin

Of catamites and kings: Reflections on butch, gender, and boundaries[1]

What is butch?
Conceptions and misconceptions of lesbian gender

Attempting to define terms such as *butch* and *femme* is one of the surest ways to incite volatile discussion among lesbians. "Butch" and "femme" are important categories within lesbian experience, and as such they have accumulated multiple layers of significance. Most lesbians would probably agree with a definition from *The Queen's Vernacular*, that a butch is a "lesbian with masculine characteristics."[2] But many corollaries attending that initial premise oversimplify and misrepresent butch experience. In this essay, I approach "butch" from the perspective of gender in order to discuss, clarify, and challenge some prevalent lesbian cultural assumptions about what is butch.

Many commentators have noted that the categories "butch" and "femme" have historically served numerous functions in the lesbian world. Describing the lesbian community in Buffalo from the 1930s through the 1950s, Elizabeth Kennedy and Madeline Davis comment that

> these roles had two dimensions: First, they constituted a code of personal behavior, particularly in the areas of image and sexuality. Butches affected a masculine style, while fems appeared characteristically female. Butch and fem also complemented one another in an erotic system in which the butch was expected to be both the doer and the giver; the fem's passion was the butch's fulfillment. Second, butch-fem roles were what we call a social imperative. They were the organizing principle for this community's relation to the outside world and for its members' relationships to one another.[3]

While I do not wish to deny or underestimate the complexity of its functions, I will argue that the simplest definition of butch is the most helpful one. Butch is most usefully understood as a category of lesbian gender that is constituted through the deployment and manipulation of masculine gender codes and symbols.

Butch and femme are ways of coding identities and behaviors that are both connected to and distinct from standard societal roles for men and women.[4] Among lesbian and bisexual women, as in the general population, there are individuals who strongly identify as masculine or feminine as well as individuals whose gender preferences are more flexible or fluid. "Femmes" identify predominantly as feminine or prefer behaviors and signals defined as feminine within the larger culture; "butches" identify primarily as masculine or prefer masculine signals, personal appearance, and styles. There are also many lesbians (and bisexual women) with intermediate or unmarked gender styles. In the old days, terms such as *ki-ki* indicated such intermediate or indeterminate gender styles or identities. We appear to have no contemporary equivalent, although at times, *lesbian* and *dyke* are used to indicate women whose gender messages are not markedly butch or femme.[5]

Butch is the lesbian vernacular term for women who are more comfortable with masculine gender codes, styles, or identities than with feminine ones. The term encompasses individuals with a broad range of investments in "masculinity." It includes, for example, women who are not at all interested in male gender identities, but who use traits associated with masculinity to signal their lesbianism or to communicate their desire to engage in the kinds of active or initiatory sexual behaviors that in this society are allowed or expected from men. It includes women who adopt "male" fashions and mannerisms as a way to claim privileges or deference usually reserved for men. It may include women who find men's clothing better made, and those who consider women's usual wear too confining or uncomfortable or who feel it leaves them vulnerable or exposed.[6]

Butch is also the indigenous lesbian category for women who are gender "dysphoric." *Gender dysphoria* is a technical term for individuals who are dissatisfied with the gender to which they were assigned (usually at birth) on the basis of their anatomical sex. Within the psychological and medical communities, gender dysphoria is considered a disorder, as were lesbianism and male homosexuality before the American Psychiatric Association removed them from its official list of mental diseases in 1973.[7] I am not using *gender dysphoria* in the clinical sense, with its connotations of neurosis or psychological impairment. I am using it as a purely descriptive term for persons who have gender feelings and identities that are at odds with their assigned gender status or their physical bodies. Individuals who have very powerful gender dysphoria, particularly those with strong drives to alter their bodies to conform to their preferred gender identities, are called transsexuals.[8]

The lesbian community is organized along an axis of sexual orientation and comprises women who have sexual, affectional, erotic, and intimate

467

relations with other women. It nevertheless harbors a great deal of gender dysphoria.[9] Drag, cross-dressing, passing, transvestism, and transsexualism are all common in lesbian populations, particularly those not attempting to meet constricted standards of political virtue.[10]

In spite of their prevalence, issues of gender variance are strangely out of focus in lesbian thought, analysis, and terminology. The intricacies of lesbian gender are inadequately and infrequently addressed. *Butch* is one of the few terms currently available with which to express or indicate masculine gender preferences among lesbians, and it carries a heavy, undifferentiated load.[11] The category of butch encompasses a wide range of gender variation within lesbian cultures.

Within the group of women labeled butch, there are many individuals who are gender dysphoric to varying degrees. Many butches have partially male gender identities. Others border on being, and some are, female-to-male transsexuals (FTMs), although many lesbians *and* FTMs find the areas of overlap between butchness and transsexualism disturbing.[12] Saying that many butches identify as masculine to some degree does not mean that all, even most, butches "want to be men," although some undoubtedly do. Most butches enjoy combining expressions of masculinity with a female body. The coexistence of masculine traits with a female anatomy is a fundamental characteristic of "butch" and is a highly charged, eroticized, and consequential lesbian signal.[13]

By saying that many lesbians identify partially or substantially as masculine, I am also not saying that such individuals are "male identified" in the political sense. When the term *male identified* was originally used in early seventies feminism, it denoted nothing about gender identity. It described a political attitude in which members of a category of generally oppressed persons (women) failed to identify with their self-interest as women, and instead identified with goals, policies, and attitudes beneficial to a group of generally privileged oppressors (men). Though such women were sometimes butch or masculine in style, they might as easily be femme or feminine. One typical manifestation of male identification in this sense consisted of very feminine heterosexual women who supported traditional male privilege. On a more contemporary note, some of the feminine right-wing women whose political aims include strengthening male authority in conventional family arrangements could also be called male identified.

There are many problems with the notion of male identified, not the least of which are questions of who defines what "women's interests" are in a given situation and the assumption of a unitary category of "women" whose interests are always the same. But the point here is not a political critique of the concept of male identification. It is simply to register that a similarity in terminology has often led to a conflation of political positions with gender identities. A strongly masculine butch will not necessarily identify politically with men. In fact, it is sometimes the most masculine women who confront male privilege most directly and painfully, and are the most enraged by it.[14]

Varieties of butch

The iconography in many contemporary lesbian periodicals leaves a strong impression that a butch always has very short hair, wears a leather jacket, rides a Harley, and works construction. This butch paragon speaks mostly in monosyllables, is tough yet sensitive, is irresistible to women, and is semiotically related to a long line of images of young, rebellious, sexy, white, working-class masculinity that stretches from Marlon Brando in *The Wild One* (1954) to the character of James Hurley on "Twin Peaks" (1990). She is usually accompanied by a half-dressed, ultrafeminine creature who is artfully draped on her boots, her bike, or one of her muscular, tattooed forearms.[15]

These images originate in the motorcycle and street gangs of the early fifties. They have been powerful erotic icons ever since, and lesbians are not the only group to find them engaging and sexy. Among gay men, the figure of the outlaw leather biker (usually with a heart of gold) has symbolically anchored an entire subculture. During the late seventies, similar imagery dominated even mainstream male homosexual style and fashion. There are many rock-and-roll variants, from classic biker (early Bruce Springsteen) to futuristic road warrior (Judas Priest, Billy Idol) to postmodern punk (Sex Pistols). The contemporary ACT UP and Queer Nation styles so popular among young gay men and women are lineal descendants of those of the punk rockers, whose torn jackets and safety pins fractured and utilized the same leather aesthetic.

Within the lesbian community, the most commonly recognized butch styles are those based on these models of white, working-class, youthful masculinity. But in spite of the enduring glamour and undeniable charm of these figures of rebellious individualism, they do not encompass the actual range of lesbian masculinity. Butches vary in their styles of masculinity, their preferred modes of sexual expression, and their choices of partners.

There are many different ways to be masculine. Men get to express masculinity with numerous and diverse cultural codes, and there is no reason to assume that women are limited to a narrower choice of idioms. There are at least as many ways to be butch as there are ways for men to be masculine; actually, there are more ways to be butch, because when women appropriate masculine styles the element of travesty produces new significance and meaning. Butches adopt and transmute the many available codes of masculinity.[16]

Sometimes lesbians use the term *butch* to indicate only the most manly women.[17] But the equation of butch with hypermasculine women indulges a stereotype. Butches vary widely in how masculine they feel and, consequently, in how they present themselves. Some butches are only faintly masculine, some are partly masculine, some "dag" butches are very manly, and some "drag kings" pass as men.

Butches vary in how they relate to their female bodies. Some butches are comfortable being pregnant and having kids, while for others the thought of undergoing the female component of mammalian reproduction is utterly repugnant. Some enjoy their breasts while others despise them. Some butches hide their genitals and some refuse penetration. There are butches who abhor tampons, because of their resonance with intercourse; other butches love getting fucked. Some butches are perfectly content in their female bodies, while others may border on or become transsexuals.

Forms of masculinity are molded by the experiences and expectations of class, race, ethnicity, religion, occupation, age, subculture, and individual personality. National, racial, and ethnic groups differ widely in what constitutes masculinity, and each has its own system for communicating and conferring "manhood." In some cultures, physical strength and aggression are the privileged signals of masculinity. In other cultures, manliness is expressed by literacy and the ability to manipulate numbers or text. The travails of Barbra Streisand's character in *Yentl* occurred because scholarship was considered the exclusive domain of men among traditional Orthodox Jews of Eastern Europe. Myopia and stooped shoulders from a lifetime of reading were prized traits of masculinity. Some butches play rugby; some debate political theory; some do both.

Manliness also varies according to class origin, income level, and occupation. Masculinity can be expressed by educational level, career achievement, emotional detachment, musical or artistic talent, sexual conquest, intellectual style, or disposable income. The poor, the working classes, the middle classes, and the rich all provide different sets of skills and expectations that butches as well as men use to certify their masculinity.[18]

The styles of masculinity executive and professional men favor differ sharply from those of truckers and carpenters. The self-presentations of marginally employed intellectuals differ from those of prosperous lawyers. Classical musicians differ from jazz musicians, who are distinguishable from rock-and-roll musicians. Short hair, shaved heads, and Mohawks did not make eighties punk rockers more studly than today's long-haired heavy-metal headbangers. All of these are recognizably male styles, and there are butches who express their masculinity within each symbolic assemblage.

Butches come in all the shapes and varieties and idioms of masculinity. There are butches who are tough street dudes, butches who are jocks, butches who are scholars, butches who are artists, rock-and-roll butches, butches who have motorcycles, and butches who have money. There are butches whose male models are effeminate men, sissies, drag queens, and many different types of male homosexuals. There are butch nerds, butches with soft bodies and hard minds.

Butch sexualities

Thinking of butch as a category of gender expression may help to account for what appear to be butch sexual anomalies. Do butches who prefer to let their partners run the sex become "femme in the sheets"? Are butches who go out with other butches instead of femmes "homosexuals"? Does that make femmes who date femmes "lesbians"?

Butchness often signals a sexual interest in femmes and a desire or willingness to orchestrate sexual encounters. However, the ideas that butches partner exclusively with femmes or that butches always "top" (that is, "run the sex") are stereotypes that mask substantial variation in butch erotic experience.[19]

Historically, butches were expected to seduce, arouse, and sexually satisfy their partners, who were expected to be femmes. During similar eras, men were expected to inaugurate and manage sexual relations with their female partners. Both sets of expectations were located within a system in which gender role, sexual orientation, and erotic behavior were presumed to exist only in certain fixed relationships to one another. Variations existed and were recognized but were considered aberrant.

Though we still live in a culture that privileges heterosexuality and gender conformity, many of the old links have been broken, bent, strained, and twisted into new formations. Perhaps more importantly, configurations of gender role and sexual practice that were once rare have become much more widespread. In contemporary lesbian populations there are many combinations of gender and desire.

Many butches like to seduce women and control sexual encounters. Some butches become aroused only when they are managing a sexual situation. But there are femmes who like to stay in control, and there are butches who prefer their partners to determine the direction and rhythms of lovemaking. Such butches may seek out sexually dominant femmes or sexually aggressive butches. Every conceivable combination of butch, femme, intermediate, top, bottom, and switch exists, even though some are rarely acknowledged. There are butch tops and butch bottoms, femme tops and femme bottoms. There are butch-femme couples, femme-femme partners, and butch-butch pairs.

Butches are often identified in relation to femmes. Within this framework, butch and femme are considered an indissoluble unity, each defined with reference to the other; butches are invariably the partners of femmes. Defining "butch" as the object of femme desire, or "femme" as the object of butch desire presupposes that butches do not desire or partner with other butches, and that femmes do not desire or go with other femmes.

Butch-butch eroticism is much less documented than butch-femme sexuality, and lesbians do not always recognize or understand it. Although it is not uncommon, lesbian culture contains few models for it. Many

Radclyffe Hall, 1936

butches who lust after other butches have looked to gay male literature and behavior as sources of imagery and language. The erotic dynamics of butch-butch sex sometimes resemble those of gay men, who have developed many patterns for sexual relations between different kinds of men. Gay men also have role models for men who are passive or subordinate in sexual encounters yet retain their masculinity. Many butch-butch couples think of themselves as women doing male homosexual sex with one another. There are "catamites" who are the submissive or passive partners of active "sodomites." There are "daddies" and "daddy's boys." There are bodybuilders who worship one another's musculature and lick each other's sweat. There are leather dudes who cruise together for "victims" to pleasure.[20]

Frontier fears: Butches, transsexuals, and terror

No system of classification can successfully catalogue or explain the infinite vagaries of human diversity. To paraphrase Foucault, no system of thought can ever "tame the wild profusion of existing things."[21] Anomalies will always occur, challenging customary modes of thought without representing any actual threat to health, safety, or community survival. However, human beings are easily upset by exactly those "existing things" that escape classification, treating such phenomena as dangerous, polluting, and requiring eradication.[22] Female-to-male transsexuals present just such a challenge to lesbian gender categories.

Although important discontinuities separate lesbian butch experience and female-to-male transsexual experience, there are also significant points of connection. Some butches are psychologically indistinguishable from female-to-male transsexuals, except for the identities they choose and the extent to which they are willing or able to alter their bodies. Many FTMs live as butches before adopting transsexual or male identities. Some individuals explore each identity before choosing one that is more meaningful for them, and others use both categories to interpret and organize their experience. The boundaries between the categories of butch and transsexual are permeable.[23]

Many of the passing women and diesel butches so venerated as lesbian ancestors are also claimed in the historical lineages of female-to-male transsexuals. There is a deep-rooted appreciation in lesbian culture for the beauty and heroism of manly women. Accounts of butch exploits form a substantial part of lesbian fiction and history; images of butches and passing women are among our most striking ancestral portraits. These include the photographs of Radclyffe Hall as a dashing young gent, the Berenice Abbott photo of Jane Heap wearing a suit and fixing an intimidating glare at the camera, and Brassaï's pictures of the nameless but exquisitely cross-dressed and manicured butches who patronized Le Monocle in 1930s Paris.

THE PERSISTENT DESIRE

Some of these women were likely also transsexuals. For example, several years ago the San Francisco Lesbian and Gay History Project produced a slide show on passing women in North America.[24] One of those women was Babe Bean, also known as Jack Bee Garland. Bean/Garland later became the subject of a biography by Louis Sullivan, a leader and scholar in the FTM community until his recent death from AIDS. Sullivan's study highlighted Garland's sex change in addition to his relations with women.[25] It is interesting to ponder what other venerable lesbian forebears might be considered transsexuals; if testosterone had been available, some would undoubtedly have seized the opportunity to take it.

In spite of the overlap and kinship between some areas of lesbian and transsexual experience, many lesbians are antagonistic toward transsexuals, treating male-to-female transsexuals as menacing intruders and female-to-male transsexuals as treasonous deserters. Transsexuals of both genders are commonly perceived and described in contemptuous stereotypes: unhealthy, deluded, self-hating, enslaved to patriarchal gender roles, sick, antifeminist, antiwoman, and self-mutilating.

Despite theoretically embracing diversity, contemporary lesbian culture has a deep streak of xenophobia. When confronted with phenomena that do not neatly fit our categories, lesbians have been known to respond with hysteria, bigotry, and a desire to stamp out the offending messy realities. A "country club syndrome" sometimes prevails in which the lesbian community is treated as an exclusive enclave from which the riffraff must be systematically expunged. Everyone has a right to emotional responses. But it is imperative to distinguish between emotions and principles. Just as "hard cases make bad law," intense emotions make bad policy. Over the years, lesbian groups have gone through periodic attempts to purge male-to-female transsexuals, sadomasochists, butch-femme lesbians, bisexuals, and even lesbians who are not separatists. FTMs are another witch-hunt waiting to happen.[26]

For many years, male-to-female transsexuals (MTFs) have vastly outnumbered female-to-male individuals. A small percentage of MTFs are sexually involved with women and define themselves as lesbian. Until recently, lesbian discomfort was triggered primarily by those male-to-female lesbians, who have been the focus of controversy and who have often been driven out of lesbian groups and businesses. Discrimination against MTFs is no longer monolithic, and many lesbian organizations have made a point of admitting male-to-female lesbians.

However, such discrimination has not disappeared. It surfaced in 1991 at the National Lesbian Conference, which banned "nongenetic women."[27] Transsexual women became the *cause célèbre* of the 1991 Michigan Womyn's Music Festival. Festival organizers expelled a transsexual woman, then retroactively articulated a policy banning all but "womyn-born-womyn" from future events.[28] After decades of feminist insistence that

474

women are "made, not born," after fighting to establish that "anatomy is not destiny," it is astounding that ostensibly progressive events can get away with discriminatory policies based so blatantly on recycled biological determinism.

The next debate over inclusion and exclusion will focus on female-to-male transsexuals. Transsexual demographics are changing. FTMs still comprise only a fraction of the transsexual population, but their numbers are growing and awareness of their presence is increasing. Female-to-male transsexuals who are in, or in the process of leaving, lesbian communities are becoming the objects of controversy and posing new challenges to the ways in which lesbian communities handle diversity. A woman who has been respected, admired, and loved as a butch may suddenly be despised, rejected, and hounded when she starts a sex change.[29]

Sex changes are often stressful, not only for the person undergoing change but also for the network in which that person is embedded. Individuals and local groups cope with such stress well or badly, depending on their level of knowledge about gender diversity, their relationships with the person involved, their willingness to face difficult emotions, their ability to think beyond immediate emotional responses, and the unique details of local history and personality. As a community goes through the process of handling a sex change by one of its members, it evolves techniques and sets precedents for doing so.

Though some lesbians are not disturbed by FTMs, and some find them uniquely attractive, many lesbians are upset by them. When a woman's body begins to change into a male body, the transposition of male and female signals that constitutes "butch" begins to disintegrate. A cross-dressing, dildo-packing, bodybuilding butch may use a male name and masculine pronouns, yet still have soft skin, no facial hair, the visible swell of breasts or hips under male clothing, small hands and feet, or some other detectable sign of femaleness. If the same person grows a mustache, develops a lower voice, binds his breasts, or begins to bald, his body offers no evidence to contravene his social signals. When he begins to read like a man, many lesbians no longer find him attractive and some want to banish him from their social universe. If the FTM has lesbian partners (and many do), they also risk ostracism.

Instead of another destructive round of border patrols, surveillance, and expulsion, I would suggest a different strategy. Lesbians should instead relax, wait, and support the individuals involved as they sort out their own identities and decide where they fit socially.

A sex change is a transition. A woman does not immediately become a man as soon as she begins to take hormones. During the initial states of changing sex, many FTMs will not be ready to leave the world of women. There is no good reason to harass them through a transitional period during which they will not quite fit as women or men. Most FTMs who undergo sex reassignment identify as men and are anxious to live as men as soon as possible. They will leave lesbian contexts on their own, when they can, when they are ready, and when those environments are no longer comfortable. It is not necessary for gender vigilantes to drive them out. Some FTMs will experiment with sex change and elect to abandon the effort. They should not be deprived of their lesbian credentials for having explored the option.

The partners of FTMs do not necessarily or suddenly become bisexual or heterosexual because a lover decides on a sex change, although some do eventually renegotiate their own identities. An attraction to people of intermediate sex does not automatically displace or negate an attraction to other women. Dealing with their sex-changing partners is difficult and confusing enough for the lovers of transsexuals without having to worry about being thrown out of their social universe. Friends and lovers of FTMs often have intense feelings of loss, grief, and abandonment. They need support for handling such feelings, and should not be terrorized into keeping them secret.

In the past, most FTMs were committed to a fairly complete change, a commitment that was required for an individual to gain access to sex-change technologies controlled by the therapeutic and medical establishments. To obtain hormones or surgery, transsexuals (of both directions) had to be able to persuade a number of professionals that they were determined to be completely "normal" members of the target sex (that is, feminine heterosexual women and masculine heterosexual men). Gay transsexuals had to hide their homosexuality to get sex-change treatment. This has begun to change, and transsexuals now have more freedom to be gay and less traditionally gender stereotyped after the change.

More transsexuals also now exist who do not pursue a complete change. Increasing numbers of individuals utilize some but not all of the available sex-change technology, resulting in "intermediate" bodies, somewhere between female and male. Some FTMs may be part women, part men — genetic females with male body shapes, female genitals, and intermediate gender identities. Some of these may not want to leave their lesbian communities, and they should not be forced to do so. They may cause confusion, repelling some lesbians and attracting others. But if community membership were based on universal desirability, no one would qualify. Our desires can be as selective, exclusive, and imperious as we like; our society should be as inclusive, humane, and tolerant as we can make it.

Let a thousand flowers bloom

In writing this essay, I have wanted to diversify conceptions of butchness, to promote a more nuanced conceptualization of gender variation among lesbian and bisexual women, and to forestall prejudice against individuals who use other modes of managing gender. I also have an underlying agenda to support the tendencies among lesbians to enjoy and celebrate our differences. Lesbian communities and individuals have suffered enough from the assumption that we should all be the same, or that every difference must be justified by a claim of political or moral superiority.

We should not attempt to decide whether butch-femme or transsexualism are acceptable for anyone or preferable for everyone. Individuals should be allowed to navigate their own trails through the possibilities, complexities, and difficulties of life in postmodern times. Each strategy and each set of categories has its capabilities, accomplishments, and drawbacks. None is perfect, and none works for everyone all the time.

Early lesbian-feminism rejected butch-femme roles out of ignorance of their historical context and because their limitations had become readily obvious. Butch and femme were brilliantly adapted for building a minority sexual culture out of the tools, materials, and debris of a dominant sexual system. Their costs included obligations for each lesbian to choose a role, the ways such roles sometimes reinforced subservient status for femmes, and the sexual frustrations often experienced by butches.

The rejection of butch-femme was equally a product of its time. Feminism has often simply announced changes already in progress for which it has taken credit and for which it has been held responsible. The denunciation of butch-femme occurred in part because some of its premises were outdated and because lesbian populations had other tools with which to create viable social worlds. Yet wholesale condemnation of butch-femme impoverished our understandings of, experiences of, and models for lesbian gender. It subjected many women to gratuitous denigration and harassment, and left a legacy of confusion, lost pleasures, and cultural deprivation. As we reclaim butch-femme, I hope we do not invent yet another form of politically correct behavior or morality.

Feminism and lesbian-feminism developed in opposition to a system that imposed rigid roles, limited individual potential, exploited women as physical and emotional resources, and persecuted sexual and gender diversity. Feminism and lesbian-feminism should not be used to impose new but equally rigid limitations, or as an excuse to create new vulnerable and exploitable populations. Lesbian communities were built by sex and gender refugees; the lesbian world should not create new rationales for sex and gender persecution.

Our categories are important. We cannot organize a social life, a political movement, or our individual identities and desires without them. The fact that categories invariably leak and can never contain all the relevant "existing things" does not render them useless, only limited. Categories like "woman," "butch," "lesbian," or "transsexual" are all imperfect, historical, temporary, and arbitrary. We use them, and they use us. We use them to construct meaningful lives, and they mold us into historically specific forms of personhood. Instead of fighting for immaculate classifications and impenetrable boundaries, let us strive to maintain a community that understands diversity as a gift, sees anomalies as precious, and treats all basic principles with a hefty dose of skepticism.

Notes

1. I am indebted to Jay Marston for the conversations and encouragement that led me to write this essay, and to Jay Marston, Nilos Nevertheless, Allan Berube, Jeffrey Escoffier, Jeanne Bergman, Carole Vance, and Lynn Eden for reading the drafts and making innumerable helpful suggestions. Kath Weston kindly shared some of her work in progress. Thanks to Lynne Fletcher for ruthless editing (my favorite kind). I am, of course, responsible for any errors or misconceptions. I am out on this particular limb all by myself, but I am grateful to them all for helping me get here.

2. "**Butch.** 1. lesbian with masculine characteristics, see **dyke.** 2. non-homosexual man whose virile appearance both draws and repels the [male] homosexual. Syn: all man; butch number ... stud. 3. [gay male who is] manly in speech, in fashions and in bed; submission impossible. **Butch it up.** warning [to gay man] to act manly in the presence of friends who 'don't know' or the police who do. **Butch queen.** homosexual man whose virile activities and responsibilities make him hard to detect." Bruce Rodgers, *The Queen's Vernacular: A Gay Lexicon* (Straight Arrow Books, 1972), p. 39; see also **dyke,** pp. 70–71.

3. Elizabeth Lapovsky Kennedy and Madeline Davis, "The Reproduction of Butch-Fem Roles: A Social Constructionist Approach," in *Passion and Power: Sexuality in History,* edited by Kathy Peiss and Christina Simmons, with Robert A. Padgug (Philadelphia: Temple University Press, 1989), p. 244.

4. In this essay, I am taking for granted a number of things that I will not directly address. I am assuming two decades' worth of sustained critique of categories of sex and gender, including the argument that gendered identities, roles, and behaviors are social constructs rather than properties intrinsic to or emanating from physical bodies. Gender categories and identities are, nevertheless, deeply implicated in the ways in which individuals experience and present themselves. I also am aware of the many critiques that make straightforward use of terms like *identities* difficult. In this article, however, I am less interested in a rigorous use of terminology or theory than I am in exploring lesbian folk beliefs regarding gender, and aspects of gender experience among lesbian and bisexual women. I do not intend to exclude bisexual women by speaking mostly of lesbians. Many bisexuals have similar issues and experiences.

In addition, I am not interested in engaging the argument that butch-femme roles are a noxious residue of patriarchal oppression or the claim that butch-femme roles are uniquely situated "outside ideology" and embody an inherent critique of gender. For a statement of the first position, see Sheila Jeffreys, "Butch and Femme: Now and Then," *Gossip* 5 (London: Onlywomen Press, 1987), pp. 65–95; for the latter, see Sue-Ellen Case, "Towards a Butch-Femme Aesthetic," *Discourse* 11 (Winter 1988–1989): 55–73. Oddly, Jeffreys and Case pursue similar agendas. Each argues that lesbianism in some form is a road to philosophical or political salvation. For Jeffreys, this can be accomplished only by the lesbian couple who "make love without roles" (p. 90) while for Case it is the butch-femme couple that lends "agency and self-determination to the historically passive [female] subject" (p. 65).

Case's approach is far preferable to that of Jeffreys. However, both analyses are overblown and place an undue burden of moral gravity on lesbian behavior. Like lesbianism itself, butch and femme are structured within dominant gender systems. Like lesbianism, butch and femme can be vehicles for resisting and transforming those systems. Like lesbianism, butch and femme can function to uphold those systems. And nothing — not "mutual, equalitarian lesbianism" and not butch-femme — escapes those systems completely. Butch and femme need no justification other than their presence among lesbians; they should not be judged, justified, evaluated, held accountable, or rejected on the basis of such attributions of significance.

5. *Androgynous* is also sometimes used to indicate women somewhere between butch and femme. Androgynous used to mean someone who was intermediate between male and female, and many traditional and classic butches were androgynous in the sense that they combined highly masculine signals with detectably female bodies. Those who cross-dressed enough to successfully pass as men were not androgynous. This older meaning of *androgynous* is lost when the term is used to refer to individuals whose self-presentation falls somewhere between butch and femme.

6. I should make it clear that I do not consider any behavior, trait, or mannerism to be inherently "male" or "female," and that my operating assumption is that cultures assign behaviors to one or another gender category and then attribute gendered significance to various behaviors. Individuals can then express gender conformity, gender deviance, gender rebellion, and many other messages by manipulating gender meanings and taxonomies.

7. Ronald Beyer, *Homosexuality and American Psychiatry: The Politics of Diagnosis* (New York, Basic Books, 1981). There was opposition to classifying homosexuality as a disease before the 1973 decision and there are still some therapists who consider homosexuality a pathology and would like to see the 1973 decision revoked. Nevertheless, the removal of homosexuality from the *Diagnostic and Statistical Manual III* remains a watershed.

8. For an overview of gender issues, including some aspects of transsexuality, see Suzanne J. Kessler and Wendy McKenna, *Gender: An Ethnomethodological Approach* (Chicago: University of Chicago Press, 1978). For female-to-male transsexuals, see Lou Sullivan, *Information for the Female to Male Cross Dresser and Transsexual*, 3rd edition, (Seattle: Ingersoll Gender Center, 1990); and Marcy Scheiner, "Some Girls Will Be Boys," *On Our Backs* 7, no. 4 (March–April 1991): 20–22, 38–43.

9. Not all lesbians are gender dysphoric, and not all gender dysphoric women are lesbian or bisexual. For example, there are manly heterosexual women who sometimes attract (and confuse) lesbians. There are female-to-male transsexuals who are erotically drawn to women and identify as heterosexual men (even

when they have women's bodies), and there are female-to-male transsexuals who are attracted to men and consider themselves male homosexuals.

10. For a discussion of "mannish lesbians" in the historical context of the early twentieth century, see Esther Newton, "The Mythic Mannish Lesbian: Radclyffe Hall and the New Woman," in Hidden from History: Reclaiming the Gay and Lesbian Past, edited by Martin Bauml Duberman, Martha Vicinus, and George Chauncey, Jr. (New York, New American Library, 1989).

11. Older lesbian culture had many terms in addition to butch. Bull, bull dyke, bulldagger, dagger, dag, diesel dyke, drag butch, and drag king are among the expressive terms that were once more commonly in circulation. See Rodgers, The Queen's Vernacular, pp. 70–71.

12. For discomfort with the association of female-to-male transsexuals (FTMs) with butch lesbians, see a fascinating exchange that appeared in several issues of FTM, a newsletter for female-to-male transsexuals and cross-dressers. It began with an article in issue 12, June 1990, p. 5, and continued in the letters columns in issues 13, September 1990, p. 3, and 14, December 1990, p. 2. A related exchange appeared in issue 15, April 1991, pp. 2–3.

13. See Judith Butler, Gender Trouble (New York: Routledge, 1990), especially p. 23. For a study of butch-femme that contains a critique of Butler, although not on this point, see Kath Weston, "Do Clothes Make the Woman? Gender, Performance Theory, and Lesbian Eroticism," unpublished manuscript, 1992.

14. The concept "woman identified" explicitly links sexual orientation and certain kinds of "political" behavior (Radicalesbians, "The Woman Identified Woman," in Radical Feminism, edited by Anne Koedt, Ellen Levine, and Anita Rapone [New York, Quadrangle, 1973]). The concept of the woman-identified-woman presents problems beyond the scope of this discussion. But while it equated feminism with lesbianism, "woman identified" did not at that time mean femininity or female gender identity. In contrast to "male identified," it is rarely taken as a synonym for "femme," although it has often been used as a synonym or euphemism for lesbianism. Although the apparent relationships between feminism and lesbianism were exciting and trailblazing when this essay first appeared in 1970, much of what has gone awry within feminist politics of sex can be traced to a failure to recognize the differences between sexual orientations, gender identities, and political positions. Sexual preference, gender role, and political stance cannot be equated, and do not directly determine or reflect one another.

15. See, for example, On Our Backs, 1984–1991; Outrageous Women, 1984–1988; and Bad Attitude, 1984–1991. For a look at the evolution of lesbian styles in the eighties, see Arlene Stein, "All Dressed Up, But No Place to Go? Style Wars and the New Lesbianism," Out/Look 1, no. 4 (Winter 1989): 34–42, reprinted in this volume.

16. See Butler, Gender Trouble, p. 31. In addition, not only butches play with symbols of masculinity. Lesbian femmes can play with male attire, as do heterosexual women, for a variety of reasons. A suit and tie do not necessarily "make the butch."

17. This is similar to gay male usage. Gay men use *butch* to refer to especially masculine men (Rodgers, *The Queen's Vernacular*). For a humorous send-up of gay male notions of butch, see Clark Henley, *The Butch Manual* (New York: Sea Horse Press, 1982).

18. Several well-known butches of classic lesbian fiction exhibit some of the class spectrum of butch masculinity. Beebo Brinker is exemplary of white, working-class butchness (Ann Bannon, *I Am a Woman* [Greenwich, Conn.: Fawcett Gold Medal, 1959]; *Women in the Shadows* [1959]; *Journey to a Woman* [1960]; and *Beebo Brinker* [1962]). Randy Salem's Christopher "Chris" Hamilton is an educated, middle-class, white butch (Randy Salem, *Chris* [New York: Softcover Library, 1959]). Two of the upper-class, aristocratic cross-dressers are Jesse Cannon (Randy Salem, *The Unfortunate Flesh* [New York: Midwood Tower, 1960]) and, of course, Stephen Gordon from *The Well of Loneliness* (Radclyffe Hall, *The Well of Loneliness* [New York: Permabooks, 1959]). And butch takes many more forms than these few examples can express.

19. For a discussion of the differences between erotic roles such as "top" and "bottom," and gender roles such as butch and femme, see Esther Newton and Shirley Walton, "The Misunderstanding: Toward a More Precise Sexual Vocabulary," in *Pleasure and Danger: Exploring Female Sexuality*, edited by Carole S. Vance (Boston: Routledge & Kegan Paul, 1984).

20. Lesbians, in turn, provide models for other permutations of gender, sex, and role. I know a technically heterosexual couple that consists of a lesbian-identified woman whose primary partner is an effeminate, female-identified mostly gay man. The woman once told me she has "lesbian sex" with the "girl" in him.

21. Michel Foucault, *The Order of Things* (New York, Pantheon, 1970).

22. Mary Douglas, *Purity and Danger: An Analysis of the Concepts of Pollution and Taboo* (Boston: Routledge & Kegan Paul, 1966).

23. Transgender organizations directly address issues of variant gender and how to live with it, understand it, and customize it. Some lesbian and bisexual women gravitate to such groups to sort out their gender questions in a context that provides a more sophisticated awareness of the subtleties of gender diversity than is currently available within most lesbian communities.

24. San Francisco Lesbian and Gay History Project, "'She Even Chewed Tabacco': A Pictorial Narrative of Passing Women in America," in *Hidden from History: Reclaiming the Gay and Lesbian Past*, edited by Martin Bauml Duberman, Martha Vicinus, and George Chauncey, Jr. (New York, New American Library, 1989).

25. Louis Sullivan, *From Female to Male: The Life of Jack Bee Garland* (Boston: Alyson, 1990). In addition to the Garland biography, Sullivan wrote prolifically on transsexual issues and edited the *FTM* newsletter from 1987 to 1990.

26. It is interesting to speculate about how gay men will deal with FTMs who are gay male identified. Traditionally, gay male communities have dealt relatively well with male-to-female transvestites and transsexuals, while lesbian communities have not. But gay men are now faced with women becoming men, who may or may not have male genitals whose origins are undetectable. I hope

gay men meet the challenge of accepting gay FTMs with balance and good grace.

27. "Genetic Lesbians," *Gay Community News*, May 19–25, 1991, p. 4.

28. "Festival Womyn Speak Out," *Gay Community News*, November 17–23, 1991, p. 4. It is interesting to note that S/M was not a big issue at Michigan in 1991, nor was there controversy over S/M at the National Lesbian Conference. It saddens me that lesbians, from whom I expect better, appear so prone to need a target for horizontal hostility.

29. And if a woman who was disliked starts a sex change, the sex change becomes a convenient pretext to get rid of her/him. Obnoxious behavior that would be tolerated in a butch will often be considered intolerable in an FTM. Like other groups of stigmatized individuals, transsexuals are often subjected to particularly stringent standards of conduct.

Pat Califia

Diagnostic tests

You can tell she's a butch because
She lies on top of her woman
And puts her thigh up against
Her mount—
Holding her own cunt inches away
From skin and bone—
And rubs, pushes, watches
For the turning head,
The mouth opening as the eyes shut,
The tendons in the neck that stand out
As the clitoris retreats,
Heralding the femme's orgasm.

You can tell she's a femme because
She slips her leg up
Between her butch's thighs,
Spreads her knees wide
And groans, "Oh, that's good, stay right there."
(Thus beguiling her woman into
Allowing her own cunt to be
Rubbed gently as the femme responds
To each thrust
As if some pleasure were being forced
Inside of her,
Crying out for her lover,
Timing her own orgasm sounds
To coincide with the butch's
Real, badly needed, but silent
Come.)

THE PERSISTENT DESIRE

You can tell she's a butch
Because she makes you cry
When she's angry at things or people
Too big to slug it out with.

And you can tell she's a femme
Because she makes you cry
When you can't give her everything
You imagine she wants
That a man could give her.

You can tell she's a butch
Because her hair is close-cropped
As she carries her briefcase
Into the workaday world,
Dressed in a sensible linen
Businesswoman's skirt and jacket
To earn money to bring home to
Her female lover
Even if secretarial work
Is the only thing she can get.

You can tell she's a femme
Because she has long hair and wears
Greasy overalls when she has to change
The oil in the car,
And she's always afraid she might not
Remember how to do it,
But those assholes at the gas station
Charge too much money for it
And treat you rude besides.
Who needs it?

You can tell she's a femme because
She brings her lover
Breakfast in bed
And you can tell she's a butch because
She does the dishes and makes dinner,
Keeping an eye on the evening news,
Figuring it's the least she can do,
Keep the house from falling apart,
Since her girlfriend is supporting both of them
Until she gets her job at the plant back.

And then she makes love to her
Even though she's tired and
Needs to get up early
Because what else can she give her
To say, "Thank you.
I'm sorry other people
Try to make us feel like we're freaks.
I'm sorry for the world you've lost
Because you love me."

And the femme lets her
Just like she lets her
Paint the bathroom
And hang the pictures.
How else can you give your loved one
A little dignity and pride
In a world that has no use for
Women's strength or women's intelligence?

You can tell she's a butch
Because she's one of the boys
(And fucks one of them occasionally
To prove it).

You can tell she's a femme
Because no man will ever
Lay a hand on her again
Now that she's with another woman.

Look behind the shaded window.
There's a woman
Eating cunt
In the dark.
Study her hard.
Now that you've read this poem
Surely you can tell me
If she's a butch or a femme.

Joan Nestle

Our gift of touch

My life has taught me that touch is never to be taken for granted, that a woman reaching for my breasts or parting my legs is never a common thing, that her fingers finding me and her tongue taking me are not mysterious acts to be hidden away, but all of it, the embraces, the holdings on, the moans, the words of want, are acts of sunlight. I still watch with amazement your head between my legs, seeing the length of you, all the years of you, reaching for my pleasure. How in such a world as this, where guns and governments crush tenderness every day, can you find your way to that small, hidden woman's place? But you do, intent and knowing: you make the huge need come.

How can I ever grow accustomed to the beauty of your cheek against my breast or the protective strength with which you turn me over? How can I ever think it ordinary, your desire to caress the tighter places, to take the time to calm me and then to help me want what I cannot see? Or how you reach for me after I have pleasured you, pulling me up along your body, your fingers gently cleaning my lips that glisten with your taste? Or how you make a pillow of your shoulder, to comfort me after the coming?

Never will I take for granted in this world your generosity of exploration, how you have listened to my body and found what you could do, and the way you surprise me with it when I come to bed and reach for you and feel the leather straps around your waist. You never announce: you simply smile and do.

Never will I take for granted the miracle of your desire to comfort me, the trips you have taken to reach me, late at night, appearing at my door in your jeans and t-shirt, coming like the morning. Or when you stand before me, bare breasted, clothed only in your leather jacket and white socks, your small belly pushing forward, your eyes glinting with the depth of my response. How all stands still at that moment, and all the losses of time and all the fears of night fall at your feet. Or the flowers that arrive in the hands of a blushing stranger because you asked her to surprise me with your caring. Or the times you have held me against your heart, telling me it was all right to cry for everything.

My life has taught me that touch is never to be taken for granted, that a woman reaching for my breast or parting my legs is never a common thing.

Resources

The Butch Support Group of New York City

In the early 1980s, spurred by the increasing openness and ferocity of the sex debates, a group of self-identified butch women began meeting regularly to discuss common concerns. Initially, we came together hesitantly and tentatively, for on some level we had all bought the myth that butch women, strong, silent women with a hard veneer, wouldn't really be able to open up and talk to one another about feelings and ideas.

Now it is the 1990s, and the core of the group has remained constant, with only minimal changes as a few women came and went. We continue to meet regularly, at different women's houses, as we always have, each month focusing on a topic decided the month before. The going hasn't always been easy, and it still often isn't, but no successful group finds it so.

It did take a while for us to work together and trust one another enough to get past the initial hesitancies and stereotypes. Much of the first few years was spent trying to find common themes and feelings about butchness among a divergent group of women, all of whom were united only in our self-identified sense of being butch. To this day, I am not sure any one of us could define what *butch* means, but we do know we have shared many similar personal feelings and issues even if we have played them out differently externally. Over the years, we have found that when there are lulls in the group process, it has helped to read an article to start a new wave of discussion; since ideas lead to feelings and vice versa, we usually can move forward.

As a group, we have had very few rules, but those that we have had, I do believe, have helped hold us together. Since the first few meetings, called by friends talking to friends, we have been a closed group and limited in size. New women have joined only at times when several women have left because of changes in circumstance, and we felt we needed new energy so the group wouldn't become too small or die out. We don't advertise, and we don't charge fees. Most importantly, from the start we agreed that everything we talked about was to be considered confidential; this helped to establish a foundation on which to develop trust.

I write this to let other butch women know not only that we can talk to one another but that a shared voice within a larger community is both empowering and comforting. I invite you to form new groups.

For more information, call or write the Lesbian Herstory Archives, P.O. Box 1258, New York, NY 10116, 212-874-7232.   —Deborah Edel

Butch-Femme Network
8721 Santa Monica Blvd. #419
West Hollywood, CA 90069
213-650-9734

From Newsletter no. 3, February 1990:

"...The Butch/Femme Club has now passed its six-month mark. With over 75 members on the mailing list and numerous signs of growing interest, the Club has tapped into a ground swell of enthusiasm. The resurgence of roles, started at some point in the '80s, which some would argue never waned from popularity from the '40s and '50s and even prior, despite popular pressures, augurs well for the '90s. The death knell of 'politically correct androgyny' has been sounded; we can all breathe a sigh of relief in this climate of increasing tolerance and even celebration..."

—Joi, femme cofounder
Bronwen, butch cofounder

Butch-Femme Society
P.O. Box 281, Station A
Flushing, NY 11358
718-961-6236

The New York Femmes
212-829-9817

Lisa Winters, the founding force behind this group, tells of its history in "A Celebration of Butch-Femme Identities" in this volume.

For more information
Please remember that your area's lesbian and gay archives are excellent sources for more historical information on this subject.

The Lesbian Herstory Archives
P.O. Box 1258
New York, NY 10116
212-874-7232

The June Mazer Collection
626 N. Robertson Blvd.
West Hollywood, CA 90069
310-659-2478

About the contributors

Deanna Alida, a singer who was born and raised in New York City, developed her art applying highly disciplined classical vocal techniques over a span of twenty-five years. She regularly performed solo recitals in intimate concert halls, singing art songs and arias in five languages, and she sought to combine her vocal artistry with lesbian artistry. She taught singing and vocal projection from a philosophy based on "finding one's own voice." She died in a traffic accident in December 1991.

Donna Allegra is a denim dyke who works as a construction electrician and rides a ten-speed bike all over New York City. As a cultural journalist she has published reviews in *Majority Report* and *Womanews*, and she produced programming on feminist and lesbian issues for WBAI radio from 1976 to 1981. Her poetry, fiction, and essays have appeared in *Azalea, Heresies, Conditions, Common Lives/Lesbian Lives, Sinister Wisdom*, and *Lesbian Ethics*, as well as in such anthologies as *Lesbian Poetry, The Original Coming Out Stories, Out the Other Side, Home Girls, Finding the Lesbians*, and *Lesbian Love Stories* 2.

Dorothy Allison is a lesbian writer and activist who was born in Greenville, South Carolina, and now lives in San Francisco, where she works as an editor with *Out/Look*, a national lesbian and gay quarterly. *Trash*, a collection of short stories that reflect her upbringing in the South, was published by Firebrand Books in 1989; her poetry collection, *The Women Who Hate Me*, first published by Long Haul Press in 1983, is also available from Firebrand. *Bastard out of Carolina*, her first novel, has just been released by Dutton.

Margaret Anderson (1877–1973) was a flamboyant woman who was not afraid to take on the social norms of her day — or ours. Famed as a publisher of the avant garde, she cofounded, with her lover Jane Heap, the brave *Little Review* in the 1930s and later authored a three-volume autobiography chronicling her remarkable life.

Paula Austin, now twenty-three, says: "Though I am sure I have been a lesbian since I was very young, I've been out for only a few years. I came out in a circle of very out, supportive, political people, so being out and proud and ready to fight was natural and the only right thing to do. I internalized a great deal of negative stuff about being black and overweight, and I am still working on overcoming my education. I was always very ashamed of my size, particularly of my breasts. I suffered a lot of sexual abuse and harassment, for which I often felt shame and guilt. I am in the process of moving, writing, loving, working, recovering."

Bonni Barringer was born in Sacramento, California, in 1954, and raised somewhere on the road between Alaska and Florida. Considering herself a native of North America, she currently resides in Tampa, Florida, where she performs one of her ultimate butch roles — driving limousines. "When Butches Cry" comes out of her personal experience: raised quite butch by both parents, she has always found crying a difficult experience.

Sally Bellerose is a forty-year-old, willing-to-please, ready-to-dance, strong, loud writer, nurse, and mother. Her writing has appeared in *Sojourner*, *Common Lives/Lesbian Lives*, *Bay Windows*, and the short-story anthology *Word of Mouth*.

Gwendolyn Bikis resides in Oakland, California, where she is a member of the Oakland Black Writers' Guild. She holds a bachelor's and a master's degree in sociology from Northeastern University and is currently at work on an MFA at Goddard College. "Cleo's Gone" is an excerpt from her novel-in-progress, *Soldiers*. Other excerpts have appeared in *Conditions 15*, *Common Lives/Lesbian Lives*, *Catalyst*, the *Guilford Review*, and *The Goddard College Prison Anthology*. She wants to learn to play a saxophone and would like to have a motorcycle.

Jan Brown is thirty-six years old and lives in Vancouver, Canada. She's not enough of a cynic to give up wearing leather.

Jul Bruno was born in 1948 in Brooklyn, New York. With the help of 7 New York City Marathons, 3 weight-lifting competitions, 3 twelve-step programs, 5 ultramarathons, 1 female higher power, 1 gym teacher, 1 family-of-origin sister, 2 ex-lovers, 3 chosen-family members, and 1 therapist (to whom she has paid thousands of dollars), she has been able to survive 4 major broken hearts and 18 years of working for the City of New York. She now lives happily with her very cute and very butch lover, Sandy, in Staten Island, New York.

William Cullen Bryant (1794–1878) was an American poet and news editor, an abolitionist, a supporter of free trade, and an avid observer of American wildlife.

Elly Bulkin is a middle-class, middle-aged Jewish dyke who was a founding editor (1976–1984) of *Conditions*; editor of *Lesbian Fiction* and co-editor (with Joan Larkin) of *Lesbian Poetry*, two 1981 anthologies; coauthor (with Minnie Bruce Pratt and Barbara Smith) of *Yours in Struggle: Three Feminist Perspectives on Anti-Semitism and Racism* (1984); and author of *Enter Password: Recovery* (1990), a book about surviving child sexual abuse, the breakup of a long-term relationship, and the women's movement. She is currently an editor of *Bridges: A Journal for Jewish Feminists and Our Friends*. A longtime political activist and the mother of a grown daughter, she lives in Boston, where she writes grant proposals for a living and plays on a dyke softball team.

Pat Califia is a lesbian sex educator and activist whose fiction and nonfiction work about sexuality has been widely published in the gay and lesbian press.

Christine Cassidy was educated at Sarah Lawrence College and Columbia University. She works at Poets and Writers, Inc., and as a free-lance editor for Naiad Press. In 1988, she received a New Jersey State Council on the Arts grant in poetry. Her work has appeared in the *Beloit Poetry Journal, Mudfish, On Our Backs,* and other magazines. She lives in New York City.

Cheryl Clarke is a black lesbian, feminist, and poet. Since 1983, she has published three books of poetry: *Narratives: Poems in the Tradition of Black Women* (Kitchen Table: Women of Color Press, 1983), *Living as a Lesbian* (Firebrand, 1986), and *Humid Pitch* (Firebrand, 1989). Her poems, essays, and book reviews have appeared in numerous publications, among them *Home Girls: A Black Feminist Anthology, This Bridge Called My Back: Writings by Radical Women of Color, Belles Lettres, Sojourner, The Advocate, Callaloo,* and *Bridges.* She has been a member of the *Conditions* editorial collective since 1981. Now at work on a new manuscript of poems, tentatively titled *Experimental Love,* she lives and writes in New Brunswick, New Jersey. Ms. Clarke enjoys all her lesbian traditions, the femme, the butch, and the androgynous.

Jeanne Cordova lives, writes, and draws prickly inspiration from her cactus hillside garden at her home beneath the Hollywood sign. She is the author of *Kicking the Habit: A Lesbian Nun Story* and the founder and former editor of the *Lesbian Tide.* The Ma Bell of gay Southern California, she currently publishes *The Community Yellow Pages.* She is at work on her second auto-biographical novel, *Anicha,* a metaphysical lesbian love story.

Lisa E. Davis met her first openly gay people in 1959 in Macon, Georgia, and has lived happily ever after since — in New York City and its environs since 1966, and in Greenwich Village since 1974. With a Ph.D. in comparative literature, she taught for years at SUNY and CUNY, while publishing and lecturing widely on subjects related to Latin American culture. She quit in 1983 to take up word processing and to write fiction. She has published several translations from Spanish, including a volume by the Cuban poet Nancy Morejon, *Grenada Notebook* [*Cuaderno de Granada*], and is presently writing a novel entitled *Plenty More Where That Came From,* about Greenwich Village in the Roaring Forties.

Madeline Davis is chief conservator for the Buffalo and Erie County Public Library system and a cofounder of the Buffalo Women's Oral History Project. Active in the gay liberation movement since 1970, she is a singer and song-writer and in 1983 produced a recording, *Daughter of All Women,* a collection of original lesbian songs. A writer of poetry and essays and a coauthor of articles on lesbian history, she is currently finishing a monograph with Liz Kennedy, *Boots of Leather, Slippers of Gold: The History of a Lesbian Community,* to be published by Routledge in 1992.

THE PERSISTENT DESIRE

Marivic Desquitado is a Capricorn born in the Year of the Snake to a lawyer father and a housewife mother. Born and raised in the Philippines, she worked as a radio announcer after receiving her B.A. in mass communications. After then working with the Commission of Population for five years, she joined the women's movement, working with a nongovernment organization, the Women's Studies and Resource Center. At present she works as a scriptwriter for an AIDS drama project for TALIKALA, Inc., a grass-roots organization that works for hospitality women in Davao. She is currently finishing a book depicting the lives of ten prostitutes she interviewed.

Myrna Elana, born in Santa Cruz, California, in 1960, is a graduate student in creative writing at San Francisco State University. Her work has appeared in *Outrageous Women*, *Common Lives/Lesbian Lives*, *Ink*, and the *Santa Clara Review*. She sometimes wears high heels when she's feeling mean.

Leslie Feinberg came out as a baby butch in 1963 at the age of fourteen in Niagara Falls, New York, and came of age as a lesbian in the factory life of Buffalo. She writes from the unique vantage point of a woman who entered a female-to-male transsexual program in the early 1970s, and has written and spoken widely about her experiences as a passing woman. A political activist who has been a part of the lesbian and gay struggle since before the Stonewall Rebellion, a member of the Workers World Party for twenty years, and a contributing editor to *Workers World*, she has committed her life to fighting to bring into being a better world, free of all forms of bigotry.

Sonja Franeta is a poet and translator and earns her living as a machinist. A political activist who believes in using creativity for her own personal healing, she is choosing to concentrate on writing at this time. She's a femme who wants to be butch.

Rocky Gámez has published fiction in *Cuentos*, *Politics of the Heart*, *Intricacies*, *Wicked Girls and Wayward Women*, *Common Bond*, and *Women on Women*. She was born and raised in the lower Rio Grande Valley of Texas.

Carolyn Gammon is a butchy femme Anne-of-Green-Gables look-alike. She has plans to become a pan-cunnilinguist.

Jewelle L. Gomez is the author of two collections of poetry, *The Lipstick Papers* and *Flamingoes and Bears*, and a novel, *The Gilda Stories* (Firebrand, 1991). She is originally from Boston, where she was raised by her butch great-grandmother, Grace, and her femme grandmother, Lydia. She lives with her high femme cat, Buster, in Brooklyn, New York, where she is working on a collection of her essays.

Melinda Goodman is a lesbian poet who teaches adult basic education at Bronx Community College and poetry and literature at Hunter College. Her collection of poems, *Middle Sister*, is available from Inland Book Company. She is a former editor of *Conditions*, and her work has appeared in numerous lesbian and gay literary magazines and anthologies.

Audrey Grifel lives in Brooklyn, New York, and works in the field of deafness rehabilitation. She hopes one day to transplant herself to a small organic farm in rural America. Other than some articles in a few local lesbian newspapers and newsletters, this is her first publication.

Marguerite Radclyffe Hall (1880–1943) wrote five books of poetry, seven novels, and a collection of short stories. *The Well of Loneliness,* published in 1928, was her most explicit work on the subject of lesbianism, but all of her work can be read as comments on gender challenges. Hall shared her life with Lady Una Troubridge, who left her husband to live with John, her private name for Radclyffe Hall.

Mabel Hampton (1902–1989) was born in Winston-Salem, North Carolina, but spent most of her life in New Jersey and New York. Throughout the twenties and thirties, she performed with an all-women dance group, danced at the Garden of Joy nightclub in Harlem, and was a member of the chorus in several all-black productions at the Lafayette Theater in New York. During the Harlem Renaissance, she attended parties at the home of A'Lelia Walker, daughter of Madame Walker. Later in life, she was a domestic worker and a cleaning woman at Jacobi Hospital in New York. She lived with her lifelong partner, Lillian Foster, for more than thirty years on 169th Street in the Bronx. During the last ten years of her life, she became an active part of the New York lesbian and gay rights movement, appearing in the films *Before Stonewall* and *Silent Pioneers* as well as in a television special called *Lesbian Voices*. She was one of the founding spirits of the Lesbian Herstory Archives in New York.

Jill Harris works as a public defender in New York City. She is a member of ACT UP/NY and was one of the lawyers who represented the eight members of ACT UP's needle exchange program who were acquitted of criminal charges in June 1991. She grew up in Oregon and now lives in Brooklyn.

Amber Hollibaugh is a filmmaker and AIDS educator in the AIDS Discrimination Division of the New York City Commission on Human Rights. She has been a labor organizer and community activist since joining the civil rights movement during the freedom summer of 1964. She is high femme, a lover of stone butch women, and has been a lesbian sex radical and writer for twenty-six years. She is currently producing a documentary on women and AIDS called *Women and Children Last*.

Laurie Hoskin is a 31-year-old sober dyke who holds an MFA in creative writing and teaches composition at the University of Michigan–Flint. Her work has appeared in *Sinister Wisdom, Common Lives/Lesbian Lives,* and *Moving Out*.

Frankie Hucklenbroich was born in St. Louis, Missouri, a second-generation American of Polish, Irish, German, and Indian background. She left school at sixteen, at the start of her junior year, and left home at eighteen, rather than agree to live a "straight" life. She has worked in occupations as diverse as waitress, carhop, dog groomer, carnie barker, pub owner, and middle-management exec, spending as much time in illegal as in legal occupations.

With the encouragement and aid of a very dear friend, she went back to school in 1974 and graduated cum laude in 1976 with a bachelor's degree from California State University at Fresno. Currently moving in circles of respectability, she may change her mind tomorrow, and is still an outlaw at heart.

Sue Hyde constructs a butch life and dabbles in queer politics in Cambridge, Massachusetts.

Arlene S. Istar is a 33-year-old Jewish feminist therapist and educator who lives and works in Albany, New York, with her butch partner, one dog, four cats, and many fish. At heart an avid bibliophile, political letter writer, and spiritual seeker, she reclaims and recovers all of her selves while gardening.

Ira L. Jeffries, a journalist and playwright, graduated from the City College of New York with a B.A. in communications. She has seven plays to her credit, as well as several short stories and monologues. In 1985 she received an AUDELCO award for her play *Odessa*. As a journalist she has written for the *Amsterdam News, Sappho's Isle, B&G Magazine, Womanews*, and the *Innovative Women's Calendar of Connections Newsletter*. She is news editor for *Neighborhood News*, a Bronx publication, and serves as a volunteer in the Mayor's Office for the Lesbian and Gay Community under the directorship of Dr. Marjorie J. Hill.

Mykel Johnson is a working-class, white-skinned métis of European and Native (Montagnais) ancestry who lives in Boston. A diehard radical activist and city witch, she is trying to change the world, scrape together a living, and still find time to play. She just finished a doctoral degree in feminist theology and a book manuscript, *All of the Magic in Our Hands: A Lesbian Theology of Liberation*.

Elizabeth Lapovsky Kennedy is an associate professor of American studies and women's studies at the State University of New York at Buffalo and a cofounder of the Buffalo Women's Oral History Project. She is coauthor (with Ellen Dubois and others) of *Feminist Scholarship: Kindling the Groves of Academe* (University of Illinois Press, 1985). She has written several articles on lesbian history and is currently finishing a monograph with Madeline Davis, *Boots of Leather, Slippers of Gold: The History of a Lesbian Community*, to be published by Routledge in 1992.

Sandy Kern says: "I reached my present status of 'old' butch having survived the Brownsville, Brooklyn, ghetto into which I was born during the 'depressive' late twenties. I've worked at the same job in a well-known medical center on the East Coast for nearly four decades. In my fantasy life, I've been a pianist-conductor-composer, and I've managed to create, in real life, a small opera company as a sideline. I've had several long-term, live-in relationships, maintaining the responsibility of 'garbage removal technician' throughout. I'm currently without a mate and missing the companionship, but remain forever hopeful."

Rita Laporte "was educated at the Brearley School in New York City [and] the International School in Geneva, [and] received her B.A. from Swarthmore College and, later, a law degree from Boalt Hall, University of California. She served in the WAC during World War II, remaining in the enlisted ranks, after which she held a variety of menial jobs, the only employment available to female college graduates at the close of the war" (from *The Ladder*, 1971).

Judy Lederer was born in 1934 and has been "in the life" since 1948. She has lived in Essex County, New Jersey; in Greenwich Village; at Western College in Oxford, Ohio, and in the Dayton-Cincinnati area; in San Jose and Salinas, California; and in western Massachusetts. Her lovers have included Kitten, Willie, Ginnie, Carol Anne, Barb (no, *not* Bonnie), LuAnn, Jane, Muriel, Mary Ellen, Kelly, Leslie, Anne, Jan, Barb, Linda, and names forgotten — "my pleasure to have known you," she says.

Audre Lorde, teacher, the founder of Kitchen Table: Women of Color Press, and the author of ten collections of poetry and seven books of prose, including *The Cancer Journals*, was recently awarded the New York State Walt Whitman Citation of Merit, making her the State Poet. At the ceremony, she said she accepted the award on the behalf of "poets who are oppressed, silenced, disenfranchised, who write on scraps of paper in homeless shelters, in mental wards, in prison and squalid reservations." Lorde is a "black lesbian feminist warrior mother" who has given life to us all.

Lee Lynch came out in 1960. She and her lover, in their midteens, trailed women around Greenwich Village learning the ways of the lesbian people. Lee has been writing about lesbians ever since. She's published eight books with Naiad Press, the latest of which is a novel, *That Old Studebaker*. Her column "The Amazon Trail" appears in newspapers across the country. She lives in rural Oregon with her femme lover.

Lyndall MacCowan is a San Francisco femme who has spent most of the last two years in exile in Geneva, Switzerland. Her academic background is in women's studies and anthropology, and she taught the first lesbian literature course at San Francisco State University. She dislikes sleeping alone, bites her nails when writing, and is partial to passing women. She is currently working on a book and contemplating a (temporary) move to New York City. She is "domestically partnered" with Priscilla Alexander.

Marguerite McDonald (1931–1986) was born in Columbus, Ohio, and moved to Syracuse, New York, where she became the first woman underwriter in the Syracuse area. Her close friend and companion, Carol, describes her this way: "Marge lived in a big Victorian house in Syracuse. She was a collector — of about 8,000 books and 7,000 records. She built her own speaker system, had thousands of buttons, collected antiques, made candles, was a remarkable cook — anything she turned her mind to she could do. She also named Syracuse's lesbian bar, the Laurel Tree, which, oddly, went out of business the same month she died."

Kate Berne Miller is a 37-year-old, mixed-blood Cherokee-Irish rollover butch who lives in a low-income housing collective in Seattle with her husky,

Eclipse. She works at Red & Black Books, a collective also, and has a fondness for domineering femmes.

Cherríe Moraga is a poet, editor, and playwright. She is the co-editor of *This Bridge Called My Back: Writings by Radical Women of Color* and the author of *Loving in the War Years*. Her play *Shadow of a Man* won the Fund for New American Plays Award in 1990, and her most recent work, *Heroes and Saints*, will open in San Francisco in 1992, produced by BRAVA! For Women in the Arts. Ms. Moraga teaches writing and theatre in the Chicano Studies Program at the University of California, Berkeley.

Merril Mushroom was a bar dyke in the fifties. She is still the butch.

Joan Nestle had to do this book. She is a 51-year-old Jewish femme from the Bronx who owes all her travels in life to her lesbian community. Thank you, Jerri, Sandy, Jul, and, above all, Mabel.

Pam A. Parker's work has appeared in *Conditions, Semiotext(e) USA, Penthouse Forum,* and *Kenyon Review*. From 1986 to 1989, Ms. Parker served as an editor for *Conditions*.

Joan Parkin was conceived by two practicing heterosexuals in the last year of the "fabulous fifties." Her loving parents raised her in the long tradition of white "feminine" women, and so at the age of sixteen, she was well prepared to respond to the advances of butch women, much to the dismay of her parents. Since those earliest subversive moments, she has continued to re-examine her self, so artfully constructed by a predominantly homophobic, racist, and sexist culture. She has recently shifted her central operating place for radical and disruptive action to the academy, completing her doctoral work in comparative literature at the City University of New York.

Marion Paull lives near and works in Canberra in the Australian Capital Territory, teaches information science at the University of Canberra, and, with her lover of twelve years, produces *Wimminews*, the A.C.T.'s monthly feminist newsletter. Proud to be the kind of dyke who will never pass as straight, she loves reading, traveling for a reason, living in the country, and learning to write.

Mary Frances Platt, who has a master's in education, is an earth-changes worker and anti-ableism educator and activist. She is looking for butches to fulfill her growing list of "rising-again femme" fantasies.

Amanda Prosser, a butch Fulbright scholar from London, is currently teaching at Queens College, City University of New York, and working on a Ph.D. in English at CUNY. Her work, situated firmly within a feminist context, concentrates on lesbian sexuality/textuality: she likes to play with contemporary theory and is always looking for moments to lesbianize Foucault, Derrida, and the rest of the boys. Her agenda consists in taking excessive erotic and intellectual pleasure in the academy.

Sima Rabinowitz lives in Minneapolis, where she works as an academic advisor at the University of Minnesota. Her fiction and poetry have appeared in *Common Lives/Lesbian Lives*, the *Evergreen Chronicles, Hurricane Alice, Poetpourri*, and the anthology *Word of Mouth* 2. She has been an editor for the *Evergreen Chronicles* since fall 1990.

Ina Rimpau has just completed a Spinster of Arts degree in women's studies at Concordia University in Montreal. She has plans to become a pan-lingual librarian.

Gayle Rubin is a member of the San Francisco Lesbian and Gay History Project. She taught the first course on lesbian history for the Women's Studies Program at the University of Michigan in 1974. In 1976 she wrote a biographical essay on Renée Vivien, Natalie Barney, and some of the other prominent lesbians of early twentieth-century Paris. Her recent research has been on gay men. She is interested in the process of sexual community formation and is working on a book on the development of the gay male leather community in the United States after World War II. She lives with one cat and nine hungry filing cabinets.

Barbara Ruth began publicly identifying as a femme after reading Joan Nestle's writing on the subject in the early eighties. ("My friends didn't find the news surprising," she notes.) She defines herself as a lesbian-separatist who rejects femininity and is dyke identified, which means trying, when possible, to correct anyone's assumptions that she is heterosexual. "I also try to be an ally to butches, who endure more lesbophobia than I do, and reject any privilege I have for looking 'straighter' than butches. Being fat, brown skinned, and visibly disabled, I don't get a lot of lookist privileges. Being poor and bureaucratically impaired, I'm as 'out' as I can manage. And for all of that, I maintain that poor, fat, disabled butches of color have it rougher."

Renay Sanders, who is thirty-four, was born and raised in Southern California. She has worked as a hair stylist professionally for seventeen years and now owns a salon. This is her first nonfiction writing and her first publication.

Sandia is a fifty-year-old Jewish lesbian whose writings include *At the Sweet Hour of Hand in Hand*, a translation of Renée Vivien (Naiad, 1979); *Children of the Second Birth* (1980) and *Turtle Island* (1981), both collections of poetry from Fire Bear Press; and two unpublished novels, *The Return Crossing* and *Lodestar*. She is currently at work on a third novel, a fictionalization and reworking of the story of Sarah, set in the Florida Keys. Her poems and articles have appeared in *Sinister Wisdom, Matrix,* and the *Lesbian Unraveler.*

Scarlet Woman has been active in San Francisco's S/M community for seventeen years and was previously published in *Coming to Power*. She is a therapist, a mother, a leather crafter, and a notorious flaming femme.

Judith Schwarz has always loved "unruly and individualistic" women with "warm, friendly and staunch spirits" (originally said of the *Radical Feminists of Heterodoxy: Greenwich Village, 1912–1940*), from her mother and her family, to Joan, Deb, and her sister coordinators at the Lesbian Herstory Archives.

"This description fits my life partner, Janet, as clearly as one of our rock-the-roof bedtime laughs," she adds. "Lucky me, to share this life with so many fine women."

Barbara Smith is a British writer whose work has appeared in print since 1984, in various lesbian and gay publications on both sides of the Pond. Her most recent publications were in *Serious Pleasure* and *More Serious Pleasure*, both published by Sheba. Her first nonfiction work is an essay on women and ancient Greek mythology for the forthcoming Pandora anthology *A Feminist Companion to International Mythology.*

Arlene Stein has written about politics and sexuality for *The Nation, On Our Backs,* and the *San Francisco Sentinel* (where portions of her article first appeared). "All Dressed up, But No Place to Go?" is part of a longer project on the transformation of political identities in the 1980s.

Val Tavai is a 28-year-old butch of Samoan-Filipino ancestry who believes the voices of Polynesian lesbians have yet to be heard in a world filled with South Pacific stereotypes. She is currently working on a series of short stories about Polynesian lesbians who are butch-femme identified — none of which include throwing lesbian virgins into volcanoes. Val and her lover, Dale, live in Hawaii with their three dogs, Kaipo, Alika, and Mikela.

Alice B. Toklas (1877–1966) was the author of *The Alice B. Toklas Cookbook* (1954), *Staying on Alone* (1973), *What Is Remembered* (1963); "Some Memories of Henri Matisse" (*Yale Literary Review*, 1955), "They Came to Paris to Write" (*New York Times Book Review*, 1950), and "Sylvia and Her Friends" (*New Republic*, 1955). She also witnessed the San Francisco fire and earthquake of 1906, the two world wars, and the birth of modern art. In short, she was more than Gertrude Stein's secretary.

Violet Trefusis (1894–1972), the daughter of Mrs. George Keppel, who was mistress to King Edward VII, wrote novels in both English and French while she pursued her own passionate love affairs with women such as Vita Sackville-West.

Una Vincenzo Troubridge (1887–1963) was Colette's first translator and a talented singer and sculptor in her own right. She met her husband John (Radclyffe Hall) at a tea party on August 1, 1915. Together they faced the obscenity trials provoked by *The Well of Loneliness,* as well as everything else life brought them in their many years together.

Kitty Tsui is a 100 percent butch when she is in full leather and packing or in a t-shirt and 501s. In full makeup, an evening dress, and heels, or in black lingerie, she's 100 percent femme fatale. Recently divorced after a brief Chicago mistake, she is once again in recovery and in love ... with life.

Sky Vanderlinde is a white, middle-aged, middle-class, recovering w.a.s.p. who came out twenty years ago and is now very proud of her "old-time" dyke status. She's a writer, a musician, a grower of plants, a traveler, and a political activist who supports herself working as a nurse. She returned to

New York City from Sugarloaf Key, Florida, several years ago and currently lives with a great group of cats. The path she is on is one of following her heart and learning to love herself and others with increasing depth, gentleness, reverence, and delight.

Chea Villanueva is half Filipino and half Irish and believes this combination of strong cultures has helped make her what she is today. Much of her writing is based on people, places, and situations she has encountered in her own life. She lives in California with her lover, Theresa.

Lisa Winters is a proud founding member of the New York Femmes, a support group for self-identified lesbian femmes who are primarily attracted to butches. She is a resident of the Bronx, the cochair of Bronx Lesbians United in Sisterhood (BLUS), and a part-time psychotherapist and social worker in a south Bronx hospital. "Being a lesbian femme," she says, "although not a popular image in the contemporary lesbian community, has never been a contradiction for me or for the women who love me."

Permissions

"The Butch-Femme Question," by Rita Laporte, is reprinted from *The Ladder*, 15 (June–July 1971): 4–11. Permission given by Barbara Grier.

"Butch on the Streets," by Donna Allegra, is reprinted from *Fight Back! Feminist Resistance to Male Violence*, edited by Frederique Delacoste and Felice Newman. Minneapolis: Cleis Press, 1981. It first appeared in *Lesbians Rising*, the lesbian newspaper of Hunter College, City University of New York, Spring 1980.

"The Dance of Masks," by Barbara Smith, is reprinted from *Out/Look: A National Lesbian and Gay Quarterly*, Summer 1990. Permission granted by the author.

"Dear DOB Sisters" is reprinted from the *Lesbian Herstory Archives Newsletter*, no. 8 (Winter 1984). Permission granted by the archives.

"The Femme Question," by Joan Nestle, is reprinted from *Pleasure and Danger*, edited by Carole S. Vance. Boston: Routledge & Kegan Paul, 1984.

"Flamingos and Bears," by Jewelle Gomez, 1983. Permission granted by the author.

"From the Diary of Marge McDonald" is reprinted from the *Lesbian Herstory Archives Newsletter*, no. 10 (January 1988), and from the Marge McDonald Special Collection of the LHA. Permission granted by the archives.

"Her Thighs," by Dorothy Allison, is reprinted from *Trash*, by Dorothy Allison. Ithaca, N.Y.: Firebrand Books, 1990. Permission granted by the author and the publisher.

"Lesbian Style Wars," by Arlene Stein, is reprinted from *Out/Look: A National Lesbian and Gay Quarterly*, Winter 1989. Permission granted by the author.

"Miss Ogilvy Finds Herself," by Radclyffe Hall, is reprinted from *Miss Ogilvy Finds Herself*, by Radclyffe Hall. London: Hammond & Hammond, 1959. Permission granted by A.M. Heath and Co., Ltd.

"My Woman Poppa," by Joan Nestle, is reprinted from *Lesbian Love Stories*, edited by Irene Zahava. Freedom, Calif.: Crossing Press, 1989.

"Of Althea and Flaxie," by Cheryl Clarke, is reprinted from *Narratives: Poems in the Tradition of Black Women*, by Cheryl Clarke. Latham, N.Y.: Kitchen Table Women of Color Press, 1982. Permission granted by the author.

WHAT I LOVE ABOUT LESBIAN POLITICS IS ARGUING WITH PEOPLE I AGREE WITH, by Kris Kovick, $8.00. The truth is funnier than fiction. Here's an inside look at the wry and occasionally warped mind of Kris Kovick, featuring some 140 of her cartoons, plus essays on religion and therapy ("I try to keep them separate, but it's hard"), lesbians and gay men, politics, sexuality, parenting, and American culture.
• "Kovick's first sweetly subversive collection includes a handful of autobiographical essays whose words — sassy, combative, revealing, mind-tickling — flesh out the art of a self-proclaimed "weird dyke" who is also funny, smart, and wise in her take on lesbian and gay culture." — *The Advocate*

MACHO SLUTS, by Pat Califia, $10.00. Pat Califia, the prolific lesbian author, has put together a stunning collection of her best erotic short fiction. She explores sexual fantasy and adventure in previously taboo territory — incest, sex with a thirteen-year-old girl, a lesbian's encounter with two cops, a gay man who loves to dominate dominant men, as well as various S/M and "vanilla" scenes.
• "*Macho Sluts* is a walk on the wild side. Like a hustler who has been lying in wait, author Pat Califia saunters up to us, asks us if we're looking for a good time, and provides it. *Macho Sluts* does not flirt or dabble with sadomasochism — it is sadomasochism at its best. It is a springboard into dizzying sexual taboos. If you don't like it — or the culprits — tough shit. They probably wouldn't care for you either. And perhaps you will concur with one luscious tormentor that *Macho Sluts* could be 'your worst fear and your best fantasy.'" — *Gay Community News*

CHOICES, by Nancy Toder, $9.00. Lesbian love can bring joy and passion; it can also bring conflicts. In this straightforward, sensitive novel, Nancy Toder conveys the fear and confusion of a woman coming to terms with her sexual and emotional attraction to other women.
• "*Choices* really is a classic lesbian love story. It has everything required for a good read: plot, characters, action, erotica. I suspect that it may be the most popular novel since *Rubyfruit Jungle*." — *Off Our Backs*

LEAVE A LIGHT ON FOR ME, by Jean Swallow, $10.00. Morgan is a computer instructor who doesn't understand what exactly has happened to her long-term relationship with Georgia, nor what exactly is happening to the rest of her when she stands near Elizabeth. Georgia, forced into exile from the South she loves and from the alcoholic family she both loves and hates, doesn't understand why, after six years of recovery, she still hasn't found her way home. And Elizabeth, the rich and beautiful doctor, doesn't understand why she can't keep a girlfriend. But Bernice, who watches and waits, understands a lot by just being herself. Together, they move from a difficult past into a passionate and hopeful future.

• "This is not only an excellent and highly original first novel, it is also a good lesbian novel, which is a rarity. An engaging story of interesting, complex women who are lesbians dealing with universal issues of love, infidelity, friendship, and family pain." — *San Francisco Chronicle*

BI ANY OTHER NAME, edited by Loraine Hutchins and Lani Kaahumanu, $12.00. Hear the voices of over seventy women and men from all walks of life describe their lives as bisexuals. They tell their stories — personal, political, spiritual, historical — in prose, poetry, art, and essays. These are individuals who have fought prejudice from both the gay and straight communities and who have begun only recently to share their experiences. This ground-breaking anthology is an important step in the process of forming a community of their own.
• "*Bi Any Other Name* will change and/or validate more lives than any other volume published this year by a feminist or gay or lesbian small press." — *Bay Area Reporter*

DYKESCAPES, edited by Tina Portillo, $9.00. This anthology of lesbian short stories includes works by both new and established writers. Seventeen storytellers explore such diverse themes as racism, death, lesbian parenting, prison relationships, and interracial love and sex. They don't flinch from controversy: their stories also deal with role-playing, fat-positivity, and intergenerational affairs.
• "Controversy conscious and socially responsive, Portillo brings together a fine collection of writers." — *Lambda Book Report*

TRAVELS WITH DIANA HUNTER, by Regine Sands, $8.00. When 18-year-old Diana Hunter runs away from her hometown of Lubbock, Texas, she begins an unparalleled odyssey of love, lust, and humor that spans almost twenty years. Diana makes the most of her journey on her own — but she is rarely alone. The array of women drawn to Diana's wit and body is only overshadowed by Diana's own versatile capacity for meeting their amorous needs.
• "From the first innocent nuzzle at the "neck of nirvana" to the final orgasmic fulfillment, Regine Sands stirs us with her verbal foreplay, tongue-in-cheek humor, and tongue-in-many-other-places eroticism. There is little Regine Sands cannot imagine and no one Diana Hunter can't do." — Jewelle Gomez

ALARMING HEAT, by Regine Sands, $8.00. The author of the popular *Travels with Diana Hunter* is back with more tales of lesbian erotic adventure: sex under the stars in a very public planetarium; a wrong number that turns into an adventure; fun behind the driver's seat; and a peek at the lustful world of leather. *Alarming Heat* has something for every lesbian who's ready to look behind the curtain of propriety.

• "*Alarming Heat* is an orgasm pill in book form." — *Bay Area Reporter*

CRUSH, by Jane Futcher, $8.00. It wasn't easy fitting in at an exclusive girls' school like Huntington Hill. But in her senior year, Jinx finally felt as if she belonged. Lexie — beautiful, popular Lexie — wanted her for a friend. Jinx knew she had a big crush on Lexie, and she knew she had to do something to make it go away. But Lexie had other plans. And Lexie always got her way.
• "The characterization is outstanding: the hurt, bewildered Jinx; her loyal roommate; and the smooth, calculating headmaster. Lexie is a superb portrait of a fascinating but unreliable and dangerous personality." — *The Horn Book Magazine*

THE ALYSON ALMANAC, by Alyson Publications, $9.00. How did your representatives in Congress vote on gay issues? What are the best gay and lesbian books, movies, and plays? When was the first gay and lesbian march on Washington? With what king did Julius Caesar have a sexual relationship? You'll find all this, and more, in this unique and entertaining reference work.
• "A delightful collection of facts, lists, and trivia." — *The Weekly News* (Miami)

GAYS IN UNIFORM, edited by Kate Dyer, $7.00. Why doesn't the Pentagon want you to read this book? When two studies by a research arm of the Pentagon concluded that there was no justification for keeping gay people out of the military, the generals deep-sixed the reports. Those reports are now available, in book form, to the public at large. Find out for yourself what the Pentagon doesn't want you to know about gays in the military.
• "The PERSEREC Report rocked the Pentagon, blasting truth through the fog of official lies about lesbians and gay men in the armed forces." — Urvashi Vaid, executive director of the National Gay & Lesbian Task Force

LAVENDER LISTS, by Lynne Y. Fletcher and Adrien Saks, $9.00. This all-new collection of lists captures many entertaining, informative, and little-known aspects of gay and lesbian lore: 5 planned gay communities that never happened, 10 lesbian nuns, 15 cases of censorship where no sex was involved, 10 out-of-the-closet law enforcement officers, and much more.
• "An eclectic, wildly imaginative array of subjects. Be sure to buy *Lists* for the fun of it." — *New Directions for Women*

LESBIAN LISTS, by Dell Richards, $9.00. Lesbian holy days is just one of the hundreds of lists of clever and enlightening lesbian trivia compiled by columnist Dell Richards. Fun facts like uppity women who were called lesbians (but probably weren't), banned lesbian books, lesbians who've passed as men, herbal aphrodisiacs, black lesbian entertainers, and switch-hitters are sure to amuse and make *Lesbian Lists* a great gift.

• "This partly tongue-in-cheek, partly serious look at lesbian and woman-identified women's history covers enough information to be useful to the serious student. The power of the material comes from the skillful way the author makes the statistics come alive with revealing anecdotes." — *The Bloomsbury Review*

ONE TEENAGER IN TEN, edited by Ann Heron, $5.00. One teenager in ten is gay. Here, 26 young people from around the country discuss their experiences: coming out to themselves, to parents, and friends; trying to pass as straight; running away; incest; trouble with the law; making initial contacts with the gay community; religious concerns; and more. Their words will provide encouragement for other teenagers facing similar experiences.

• "Illuminating and moving, the collection is recommended reading for all teens and adults." — *New Directions for Women*

LEATHERFOLK, edited by Mark Thompson, cloth, $20.00. There's a new leather community in America today. It's politically aware and socially active. This ground-breaking anthology is the first nonfiction, co-gender work to focus on this large and often controversial subculture. The diverse contributors look at the history of the leather and S/M movement, how radical sex practice relates to their spirituality, and what S/M means to them personally.

• "*Leatherfolk* issues a bracing challenge to all of us — to begin to see where the carnal meets the soul. From so many fine writers one might have expected the exuberance and the wit gathered here, voices fresh and vital for being so uncompromised. But the rarer achievement is the tribal longing they evoke, full of fire and the power of transformation. In a world of hypocrites and false prophets, it's the outlaws who know where the spirit resides. Fasten your seatbelts and prepare for a shock to the system. If you want vanilla, read something else." — Paul Monette

• "The essays here are written so well that the spiritual, sexual, and political questions raised are not easily dismissed. Whoever peers into the cauldron of radical sex and spirituality that Thompson has compiled will be amazed and perhaps even enthralled by the reflections they see." — *Lambda Book Report*

FROM FEMALE TO MALE, by Louis Graydon Sullivan, $9.00. On Monday, September 21, 1936, the San Francisco *Chronicle* announced the shocking news on its front page: "'Jack Bee' Was Woman." And so ended the forty-year secret of "Jack Bee," who was born Virginia Mugarrieta in San Francisco in 1869. This well-researched book chronicles the life of a popular journalist who spent most of her life posing as a man. *From Female to Male* covers Garland's impoverished childhood in San Francisco, her well-publicized life in Stockton, California, and her travels to the Philippines during the Spanish-American War.

• "A dramatic retelling of the life of Jack Bee Garland. Sullivan's interpretation of Garland's life is his most original contribution to our history." — *Out!* (New Mexico)

THE LESBIAN S/M SAFETY MANUAL, edited by Pat Califia, $8.00. This handy guide is an essential item for leather dykes who want to learn how to play safe and stay healthy. Edited by best-selling writer Pat Califia, *The Lesbian S/M Safety Manual* deals with issues such as sexually transmitted diseases, emotional and physical safety, and the importance of communication in S/M relationships. There is more information in this slim volume than you can shake a whip at.

• "Good S/M educational material is hard to find, and material for women who play with other women is probably the rarest of all. *The Lesbian S/M Safety Manual* is an exception, providing well-written, informed advice on how to get started." — Womanlink

UNBROKEN TIES, by Carol S. Becker, $8.00. Through a series of nearly one hundred personal accounts and interviews, Dr. Carol Becker, a practicing psychotherapist, charts the various stages of lesbian breakups and examines the ways in which women maintain ties with their former lovers. Becker shows how the end of a relationship can be a time of personal growth and how former lovers can form the core of an alternative family network.

• "*Unbroken Ties* has the nitty-gritty feel of real life. There's a lot more craziness here, more raw pain, intense emotion, and a wide swathe of human behavior. These stories and Becker's way of categorizing them feel like lesbian life as I have lived and observed it." — *Bay Windows*

LIFETIME GUARANTEE, by Alice Bloch, $7.00. In this personal journal of a woman faced with the impending death of her sister from cancer, Alice Bloch goes beyond her specific experiences to a moving exploration of the themes of survival, support, and affirmation of life.

• "The tremendous power, beauty, and eloquence of *Lifetime Guarantee* comes from Alice Bloch's courage to look, to see, to think, to write. As a writer, from personal experience I know how difficult it is: one is called Cassandra when one speaks the truth; one feels like a liar when one does not." — Susanna J. Sturgis, in *Off Our Backs*

BEHIND THE MASK, by Kim Larabee, $7.00. Maddie Elverton is a fashionable member of English society in the early nineteenth century — a society which limits her aspirations to the confines of the bedroom and the drawing room. But Maddie leads a double life, a life of high adventure as a highway robber. Maddie's carefully balanced world becomes threatened when she falls in love with Allie Sifton, and must compete for the affection of her beloved with the hot-blooded law officer who pursues them both.

• "If you have a romantic bent, and if you have a yen for vicarious adventure, low-key intrigue, and some nicely done erotica, *Behind the Mask* is just the sort of spritely romp you're looking for. It's wonderful exercise for the imagination." — Lee Lynch

BETWEEN FRIENDS, by Gillian E. Hanscombe, $8.00. The four women in this book represent radically different political outlooks and sexualities, yet they are tied together by the bonds of friendship. Through their experiences, recorded in a series of letters, Hanscombe deftly portrays the close relationship between political beliefs and everyday lives.

• "A thoughtful and wide-ranging summary of where feminism has been and where it can take us." — *Sojourner*

A MISTRESS MODERATELY FAIR, by Katherine Sturtevant, $9.00. Restoration England provides the setting for this vivid story of two women — one a playwright, the other an actress — who fall in love. Margaret Featherstone and Amy Dudley romp through a London peopled by nameless thousands and the titled few in a historical romance that is the most entertaining and best researched you'll ever read.

• "Delightful, compelling, well-crafted tale which, when the reader is finished, makes her wish that the story never ends. Sturtevant's research of life and theatre in seventeenth-century London is thorough, making her work the more complex, and thus a bit more satisfying to read. She excels at evoking a time of extreme contrasts — life in the streets and on the stage, the busy sophistication of London versus the country's pastoral quiet, the different treatment accorded to women by virtue of their class and race, and the punishments for crimes considered to be 'unnatural' behaviour. Sturtevant blends history with adventure, erotica, and charm to create a lesbian romance that both entertains and sparks the imagination." — *Bay Area Reporter*

ALYSON WONDERLAND
Books about kids with lesbian and gay parents

HEATHER HAS TWO MOMMIES, by Lesléa Newman, illustrated by Diana Souza, $8.00. As the daughter of a lesbian couple, three-year-old Heather sees nothing unusual in having two mommies. When she joins a playgroup and discovers that other children have "daddies" her confusion is dispelled by an adult instructor and the other children who describe their own different families. Warmly illustrated by Diana Souza, *Heather Has Two Mommies* realistically approaches issues central to lesbian parenting: artificial insemination, the birthing process, and the needs of a lesbian household. Ages 3 to 8.

• "Every preschool and kindergarten, every church sunday school room, every doctor's office waiting room, every summer camp should have this book, if only to show children that differences are natural. Here's to a much needed genre — may its titles increase!" — *Off Our Backs*

GLORIA GOES TO GAY PRIDE, by Lesléa Newman; illustrated by Russell Crocker, $8.00. Gay Pride Day is fun for Gloria, and for her two mothers. Here, the author of *Heather Has Two Mommies* describes, from the viewpoint of a young girl, just what makes up this special day. Ages 3 to 7.

• "Leslea Newman has continued the pioneering work she began in 1989 with *Heather Has Two Mommies*. This book rings very true. Russell Crocker's illustrations are simple yet eloquent pencil drawings which contain much sensitivity and scope." — *Off Our Backs*

BELINDA'S BOUQUET, by Lesléa Newman; illustrated by Michael Willhoite, $7.00. Upon hearing a cruel comment about her weight, young Belinda decides she wants to go on a diet. But then her friend Daniel's lesbian mom tells her, "Your body belongs to you," and that just as every flower has its own special kind of beauty, so does every person. Belinda quickly realizes she's fine just the way she is. Ages 4 to 8.

• "God, where was this book when I was a fat little kid? This story eloquently gives a child perspectives on diversity, understanding, tolerance and self-acceptance." — *The Midtown Times*

HOW WOULD YOU FEEL IF YOUR DAD WAS GAY?, by Ann Heron and Meredith Maran; illustrated by Kris Kovick, cloth, $10.00. Jasmine, Michael, and Noah are all regular kids except for one thing: Jasmine and Michael have two gay fathers. Their classmate Noah has a gay mother. They have some unique concerns that they've never seen discussed by anyone else. This book, written by two lesbian mothers with help from their sons, will be a lifeline for other young people who face the same issues. It will also help their classmates, teachers, and parents to better understand just how varied today's families can be. Ages 6 to 12.

• "Kris Kovick's black-and-white line drawings are as interesting and complex as this story is. This is a solid book. You will find it a great teaching tool." — *Off Our Backs*

THE DUKE WHO OUTLAWED JELLY BEANS AND OTHER STORIES, by Johnny Valentine; illustrations by Lynette Schmidt, cloth, $13.00. After he outlawed jelly beans, the duke issued another proclamation: "I had

exactly one mother and one father, and I turned out so well, I think all
children should have exactly one mother and one father. Any that don't ...
why, we'll throw 'em in the dungeon." But the kids of the kingdom found
a way to stop him. Their story is one of five original and enchanting fairy
tales that make up this collection. Beautifully illustrated with paintings
and drawings throughout. Ages 5 to 10.

• "One of the outstanding children's books of the season." — Robert Hale,
in *The Horn Book Magazine*

SUPPORT YOUR LOCAL BOOKSTORE

Most of the books described above are available at your nearest gay or
feminist bookstore, and many of them will be available at other bookstores.
If you can't get these books locally, order by mail using this form.

Enclosed is $_____ for the following books. (Add $1.00 postage when
ordering just one book. If you order two or more, we'll pay the postage.)

1. _____

2. _____

3. _____

name: _____

address: _____

city: _____ state: _____ zip: _____

ALYSON PUBLICATIONS
Dept. H-90, 40 Plympton St., Boston, MA 02118

After December 31, 1993, please write for current catalog.